'*NOS4A2* has energy, plenty of narrative hooks, and a brash intensity. There's a big engine of entertainment at the heart of *NOS4A2*'

Guardian

'Joe Hill's third novel is his most ambitious yet . . . A thrilling journey, which should cement Hill as one of the most exciting drivers of horror fiction today' *SFX*

'This book is well-written, extremely dark and awfully gruesome'

Daily Mail

'Hill's writing is smart and assured and bursting with his own style and personality . . . the biggest box it ticks is that it's genuinely scary, and you can't really ask more of a horror novel than that'

Independent on Sunday

'*NOS4A2* is an excellent novel, populated with believable characters and some intense, creepy scenes' *Starburst*

'*NOS4A2* reads like a thriller at times, it is a totally gripping and satisfying read, expertly constructed and brilliant executed. This one is a triumph' *Fantasy Book Review*

'A magnificently creepy novel that marks the point Master King turned master storyteller' *Metro*

'*NOS4A2* is enthrallingly petrifying and creepily engrossing. A 700-page race to the finish line, it drags its terrified readers kicking and screaming along' *Sunday Times*

ALSO BY JOE HILL FROM GOLLANCZ:

Heart-Shaped Box

20th Century Ghosts

Horns

In the Tall Grass (with Stephen King)

The Fireman

Strange Weather

A Novel

JOE HILL

This edition first published in Great Britain in 2019 by Gollancz

First published in Great Britain in 2013 by Gollancz
an imprint of the Orion Publishing Group Ltd
Carmelite House, 50 Victoria Embankment
London EC4Y 0DZ

An Hachette UK Company

1 3 5 7 9 10 8 6 4 2

A CIP catalogue record for this book is
available from the British Library.

ISBN 978 1 473 22641 8

Printed and bound in Great Britain by Clays Ltd, Elcograpf, S.p.A

www.joehillfiction.com
www.gollancz.co.uk

To my mom—here's a mean machine for the story queen

Die Todten reiten schnell.
(For the dead travel fast.)
—"LENORE," GOTTFRIED BÜRGER

PROLOGUE:
SEASON'S GREETINGS
DECEMBER 2008

FCI Englewood, Colorado

NURSE THORNTON DROPPED INTO THE LONG-TERM-CARE WARD A little before eight with a hot bag of blood for Charlie Manx.

She was coasting on autopilot, her thoughts not on her work. She had finally made up her mind to buy her son, Josiah, the Nintendo DS he wanted, and was calculating whether she could get to Toys "R" Us after her shift, before they closed.

She had been resisting the impulse for a few weeks, on philosophical grounds. She didn't really care if all his friends had one. She just didn't like the idea of those handheld video-game systems that the kids carried with them everywhere. Ellen Thornton resented the way little boys disappeared into the glowing screen, ditching the real world for some province of the imagination where fun replaced thought and inventing creative new kills was an art form. She had fantasized having a child who would love books and play Scrabble and want to go on snowshoeing expeditions with her. What a laugh.

Ellen had held out as long as she could, and then, yesterday afternoon, she had come across Josiah sitting on his bed pretending an old wallet was a Nintendo DS. He had cut out a picture of Donkey Kong and slipped it into the clear plastic sleeve for displaying photographs. He pressed imaginary buttons and made explosion sounds, and her heart had hurt a little, watching him make believe he already had something he was certain he would get on the Big Day. Ellen could have her theories about what was healthy for boys and what wasn't. That didn't mean Santa had to share them.

Because she was preoccupied, she didn't notice what was different about Charlie Manx until she was easing around his cot to reach the IV rack. He happened to sigh heavily just then, as if bored, and she looked down and saw him staring up at her, and she was so startled to see him with his eyes open that she bobbled the sack of blood and almost dumped it on her feet.

He was hideous-old, not to mention hideous. His great bald skull was a globe mapping an alien moon, continents marked by liver spots and bruise-colored sarcomas. Of all the men in the long-term-care ward—a.k.a. the Vegetable Patch—there was something particularly awful about Charlie Manx with his eyes open at *this* time of year. Manx liked children. He'd made dozens of them disappear back in the nineties. He had a house below the Flatirons where he did what he liked with them and killed them and hung Christmas ornaments in their memory. The papers called the place the Sleigh House. Ho, ho, ho.

For the most part, Ellen could shut off the mother side of her brain while she was at work, could keep her mind away from thoughts of what Charlie Manx had probably done with the little girls and boys who had crossed his path, little girls and boys no older than her Josiah. Ellen didn't muse on what *any* of her charges had done, if she could help it. The patient on the other side of the room had tied up his girlfriend and her two children, set fire to their house, and left them to burn. He was arrested in a bar down the street, drinking Bushmills and watching the White Sox play the Rangers. Ellen didn't see how dwelling on it was ever going to do her any favors, and so she had taught herself to think of her patients as extensions of the machines and drip bags they were hooked up to: meat peripherals.

In all the time she'd been working at FCI Englewood, in the Supermax prison infirmary, she had never seen Charlie Manx with his eyes open. She'd been on staff for three years, and he had been comatose all that time. He was the frailest of her patients, a fragile coat of skin with bones inside. His heart monitor blipped like a metronome set to the slowest possible speed. The doc said he had as much brain activity as a can of creamed corn. No one had ever determined his age, but he looked older than Keith Richards. He even looked a little *like* Keith Richards—a bald Keith with a mouthful of sharp little brown teeth.

There were three other coma patients in the ward, what the staff called "gorks." When you were around them long enough, you learned that all the gorks had their quirks. Don Henry, the man who burned his girl and her kids to death, went for "walks" sometimes. He didn't get up, of course, but his feet pedaled weakly under the sheets. There was a guy named Leonard Potts who'd been in a coma for five years and was never going to wake up—another prisoner had jammed a screwdriver through his skull and into his brain. But sometimes he cleared his throat and would shout "I know!" as if he were a small child who wanted to answer the teacher's question. Maybe opening his eyes was Manx's quirk and she'd just never caught him doing it before.

"Hello, Mr. Manx," Ellen said automatically. "How are you feeling today?"

She smiled a meaningless smile and hesitated, still holding the sack of body-temperature blood. She didn't expect a reply but thought it would be considerate to give him a moment to collect his nonexistent thoughts. When he didn't say anything, she reached forward with one hand to slide his eyelids closed.

He caught her wrist. She screamed—couldn't help it—and dropped the bag of blood. It hit the floor and exploded in a crimson gush, the hot spray drenching her feet.

"Ugh!" she cried. "Ugh! Ugh! Oh, God!"

It smelled like fresh-poured iron.

"Your boy, Josiah," Charlie Manx said to her, his voice grating and harsh. "There's a place for him in Christmasland, with the other children. I could give him a new life. I could give him a nice new smile. I could give him nice new teeth."

Hearing him say her son's name was worse than having Manx's hand on her wrist or blood on her feet. (*Clean blood,* she told herself, ***clean.***) Hearing this man, convicted murderer and child molester, speak of her son made her dizzy, genuinely dizzy, as if she were in a glass elevator rushing quickly into the sky, the world dropping away beneath her.

"Let go," she whispered.

"There's a place for Josiah John Thornton in Christmasland, and there's a place for you in the House of Sleep," Charlie Manx said. "The Gasmask Man would know just what to do with you. Give you the gingerbread smoke and teach you to love him. Can't bring you with us to Christmasland. Or I *could,* but the Gasmask Man is better. The Gasmask Man is a mercy."

"Help," Ellen screamed, except it didn't come out as a scream. It came out as a whisper. "Help me." She couldn't find her voice.

"I've seen Josiah in the Graveyard of What Might Be. Josiah should come for a ride in the Wraith. He'd be happy forever in Christmasland. The world can't ruin him there, because it isn't *in* the world. It's in my *head.* They're all safe in my head. I've been dreaming about it, you know. Christmasland. I've been dreaming about it, but I walk and walk and I can't get to the end of the tunnel. I hear the children singing, but I can't get to them. I hear them shouting for me, but the tunnel doesn't end. I need the Wraith. Need my ride."

His tongue slipped out of his mouth, brown and glistening and obscene, and wet his dry lips, and he let her go.

"Help," she whispered. "Help. Help. Help." She had to say it another time or two before she could say it loud enough for anyone to hear her. Then she was batting through the doors into the hall, running in her soft flat shoes, screaming for all she was worth. Leaving bright red footprints behind her.

Ten minutes later a pair of officers in riot gear had strapped Manx down to his cot, just in case he opened his eyes and tried to get up. But the doctor who eventually arrived to examine him said to unlash him.

"This guy has been in a bed since 2001. He has to be turned four times a day to keep from getting sores. Even if he wasn't a gork, he's too weak to go anywhere. After seven years of muscle atrophy, I doubt he could sit up on his own."

Ellen was listening from over next to the doors—if Manx opened his eyes again, she planned to be the first one out of the room—but when the doctor said that, she walked across the floor on stiff legs and pulled her sleeve back from her right wrist to show the bruises where Manx had grabbed her.

"Does that look like something done by a guy too weak to sit up? I thought he was going to yank my arm out of the socket." Her feet stung almost as badly as her bruised wrist. She had stripped off her blood-soaked pantyhose and gone at her feet with scalding water and antibiotic soap until they were raw. She was in her gym sneakers now. The other shoes were in the garbage. Even if they could be saved, she didn't think she'd ever be able to put them on again.

The doctor, a young Indian named Patel, gave her an abashed, apologetic look and bent to shine a flashlight in Manx's eyes. His pupils did not dilate. Patel moved the flashlight back and forth, but Manx's eyes remained fixed on a point just beyond Patel's left ear. The doctor clapped his hands an inch from Manx's nose. Manx did not blink. Patel gently closed Manx's eyes and examined the reading from the EKG they were running.

"There's nothing here that's any different from any of the last dozen EKG readings," Patel said. "Patient scores a nine on the Glasgow scale, shows slow alpha-wave activity consistent with alpha coma. I think he was just talking in his sleep, Nurse. It even happens to gorks like this guy."

"His eyes were *open,*" she said. "He looked right at me. He knew my name. He knew my son's name."

Patel said, "Ever had a conversation around him with one of the other nurses? No telling what the guy might've unconsciously picked up. You tell another nurse, 'Oh, hey, my son just won the spelling bee.' Manx hears it and regurgitates it mid-dream."

She nodded, but a part of her was thinking, *He knew Josiah's middle name,* something she was sure she had never mentioned to anyone here in the hospital. *There's a place for Josiah John Thornton in Christmasland,* Charlie Manx had said to her, *and there's a place for you in the House of Sleep.*

"I never got his blood in," she said. "He's been anemic for a couple weeks. Picked up a urinary-tract infection from his catheter. I'll go get a fresh pack."

"Never mind that. I'll get the old vampire his blood. Look. You've had a nasty little scare. Put it behind you. Go home. You only have, what? An hour left on your shift? Take it. Take tomorrow, too. Got some last-minute shopping to finish? Go do it. Stop thinking about this and relax. It's Christmas, Nurse Thornton," the doctor said, and winked at her. "Don't you know it's the most wonderful time of the year?"

SHORTER WAY
1986–1989

Haverhill, Massachusetts

THE BRAT WAS EIGHT YEARS OLD THE FIRST TIME SHE RODE OVER THE covered bridge that crossed the distance between Lost and Found.

It happened like this: They were only just back from The Lake, and the Brat was in her bedroom, putting up a poster of David Hasselhoff—black leather jacket, grinning in that way that made dimples in his cheeks, standing with his arms crossed in front of K.I.T.T.—when she heard a sobbing cry of shock in her parents' bedroom.

The Brat had one foot up on the headboard of her bed and was holding the poster to the wall with her chest while she pinned down the corners with brown tape. She froze, tilted her head to listen, not with any alarm, just wondering what her mother was worked up about now. It sounded like she had lost something.

"—had it, I know I had it!" she cried.

"You think you took it off down by the water? Before you went in the lake?" asked Chris McQueen. "Yesterday afternoon?"

"I told you already I didn't go swimming."

"But maybe you took it off when you put on suntan lotion."

They continued to go back and forth along these lines, but the Brat decided for the time being that she could tune them out. At the age of eight, the Brat—Victoria to her second-grade teacher, Vicki to her mother, but the Brat to her father and in her heart—was well beyond being alarmed by her mother's outbursts. Linda McQueen's gales of laughter and overwrought cries of disappointment were the soundtrack of the Brat's everyday life and were only occasionally worth noticing.

She smoothed the poster flat, finished taping it, and stepped back to admire it. David Hasselhoff; so cool. She was frowning, trying to decide if it was crooked, when she heard a door slam and another anguished cry—her mother again—and then her father's voice.

"Didn't I know we were headed here?" he said. "Right on cue."

"I asked if you checked the bathroom, and you said you did. You said you had *everything.* Did you check the bathroom or not?"

"I don't know. No. Probably not. But it doesn't matter 'cause you didn't leave it in the bathroom, Linda. Do you know *why* I know you didn't leave your bracelet in the bathroom? Because you left it on the *beach* yesterday. You and Regina Roeson had yourselves a bunch of sun and a bucketful of margaritas, and you got so relaxed you kind of forgot you had a daughter and dozed off. And then when you woke up and you realized you were going to be an hour late to pick her up from day camp—"

"I was *not* an hour late."

"—you left in a panic. You forgot the suntan lotion, and you forgot your towel, and you forgot your bracelet, too, and now—"

"And I wasn't drunk either, if that's what you're implying. I don't drive our daughter drunk, Chris. That's your specialty—"

"—and now you're pulling your usual shit and making it someone else's fault."

The Brat was hardly aware she was moving, wandering into the dim front hall and toward her parents' bedroom. The door was open about half a foot, revealing a slice of her parents' bed and the suitcase lying on top of it. Clothes had been pulled out and scattered across the floor. The Brat knew that her mother had, in a spasm of strong feeling, started yanking things out and throwing them, looking for the lost bracelet: a golden hoop with a butterfly mounted upon it, made from glittering blue sapphires and ice-chip diamonds.

Her mother paced back and forth, so every few seconds she flicked into view, passing through the sliver that the Brat could see of the bedroom.

"This has nothing to do with yesterday. I told you I didn't lose it at the beach. I *didn't*. It was next to the sink this morning, right beside my earrings. If they don't have it at the front desk, then one of the maids took it. That's what they do, the way they supplement their incomes. They help themselves to whatever the summer people leave around."

The Brat's father was silent for a while, and then he said, "Jesus. What an ugly fuckin' person you are inside. And I had a kid with you."

The Brat flinched. A prickling heat rose to the backs of her eyes, but she did not cry. Her teeth automatically went to her lip, sinking deep into it, producing a sharp twinge of pain that kept the tears at bay.

Her mother showed no such restraint and began to weep. She wandered into sight again, one hand pressed over her face, her shoulders hitching. The Brat didn't want to be seen and retreated down the hallway.

She continued past her room, along the corridor, and out the front door. The thought of remaining indoors was suddenly intolerable. The air in the house was stale. The air conditioner had been off for a week. All the plants were dead and smelled it.

She didn't know where she was going until she got there, although from the moment she heard her father dish out his worst—*What an ugly fuckin' person you are inside*—her destination was inevitable. She let herself through the side door of the garage and got her Raleigh.

Her Raleigh Tuff Burner had been her birthday gift in May and was also, quite simply, her favorite birthday gift of all time . . . then and forever. Even at thirty, if her own son asked her the nicest thing she had ever been given, she would think immediately of the Day-

Glo blue Raleigh Tuff Burner with banana yellow rims and fat tires. It was her favorite thing she owned, better than her Magic 8 Ball, her KISS Colorforms set, even her ColecoVision.

She had spotted it in the window of Pro Wheelz downtown, three weeks before her birthday, when she was out with her father, and gave a big *ooh* at the sight. Her father, amused, walked her inside and talked the dealer into letting her ride it around the showroom. The salesman had strongly encouraged her to look at other bikes, felt that the Tuff Burner was too big for her, even with the seat dropped to its lowest position. She didn't know what the guy was talking about. It was like witchcraft; she could've been riding a broom, slicing effortlessly through Halloween darkness, a thousand feet off the ground. Her father had pretended to agree with the shopkeeper, though, and told Vic she could have something like it when she was older.

Three weeks later it was in the driveway, with a big silver bow stuck on the handlebars. "You're older now, ain'tcha?" her father said, and winked.

She slipped into the garage, where the Tuff Burner leaned against the wall to the left of her father's bike—not a bicycle but a black 1979 Harley-Davidson shovelhead, what he still rode to work in the summer. Her father was a blaster, had a job on a road crew shearing apart ledge with high explosives, ANFO mostly, sometimes straight TNT. He had told Vic once that it took a clever man to figure out a way to make a profit off his bad habits. When she asked him what he meant, he said most guys who liked to set off bombs wound up in pieces or doing time. In his case it earned him sixty grand a year and was good for even more if he ever managed to frag himself; he had a hell of an insurance package. His pinkie alone was worth twenty thou if he blew it off. His motorcycle had an airbrushed painting of a comically sexy blonde in an American-flag bikini straddling a bomb, against a backdrop of flame. Vic's father was badass. Other dads built things. Hers blew shit up and rode away on a Harley, smoking the cigarette he used to light the fuse. Top that.

The Brat had permission to ride her Raleigh on the trails in the Pittman Street Woods, the unofficial name of a thirty-acre strip of scrub pine and birch that lay just beyond their backyard. She was allowed to go as far as the Merrimack River and the covered bridge before she had to turn back.

The woods continued on the other side of that covered bridge—also known as the Shorter Way Bridge—but Vic had been forbidden to cross it. The Shorter Way was seventy years old, three hundred feet long, and beginning to sag in the middle. Its walls sloped downriver, and it looked like it would collapse in a strong wind. A chain-link fence barred entrance, although kids had peeled the steel wire up at one corner and gone in there to smoke bud and make out. The tin sign on the fence said DECLARED UNSAFE BY ORDER OF HAVERHILL PD. It was a place for delinquents, derelicts, and the deranged.

She had been in there, of course (no comment on which category she belonged to), never mind her father's threats, or the UNSAFE sign. She had dared herself to slip under the fence and walk ten steps, and the Brat had never been able to back down on a dare, even one she made to herself. *Especially* on the dares she made to herself.

It was five degrees cooler in there, and there were gaps between the floorboards that looked down a hundred feet, toward the wind-roughened water. Holes in the black tar-paper roof let in dust-filled shafts of golden light. Bats peeped shrilly in the dark.

It had made Vic's breath quicken, to walk out into the long, shadowed tunnel that bridged not just a river but death itself. She was eight, and she believed she was faster than anything, even a bridge collapse. But she believed it a little less when she was actually taking baby steps across the old, worn, creaky planks. She had made not just ten steps but *twenty.* At the first loud pop, though, she rabbited, scrambled back and out under the chain-link fence, feeling as if she were half choking on her own heart.

Now she pointed her bike across the backyard and in another moment was rattling downhill, over root and rock, into the forest.

She plunged away from her house and straight into one of her patented make-believe *Knight Rider* stories.

She was in the Knight 2000, and they were riding, soaring effortlessly along beneath the trees as the summer day deepened into lemony twilight. They were on a mission to retrieve a microchip, containing the secret location of every single one of America's missile silos. It was hidden in her mother's bracelet; the chip was a part of the gemstone butterfly, cleverly disguised as a diamond. Mercenaries had it and planned to auction the information to the highest bidder: Iran, the Russians, maybe Canada. Vic and Michael Knight were approaching their hideout by a back road. Michael wanted Vic to promise him she wouldn't take unnecessary chances, wouldn't be a stupid kid, and she scoffed at him and rolled her eyes, but they both understood, owing to the exigencies of the plot, that at some point she would have to act like a stupid kid, endangering both of their lives and forcing them to take desperate maneuvers to escape the bad guys.

Only this narrative wasn't entirely satisfying. For starters, she clearly *wasn't* in a car. She was on a bike, thumping over roots, pedaling fast, fast enough to keep off the mosquitoes. Also, she couldn't relax and let herself daydream the way she usually could. She kept thinking, *Jesus. What an ugly fuckin' person you are inside.* She had a sudden, stomach-twisting thought that when she got home, her father would be gone. The Brat lowered her head and pedaled faster, the only way to leave such a terrible idea behind.

She was on the bike, was her next thought—not the Tuff Burner but her father's Harley. Her arms were around him, and she was wearing the helmet he had bought for her, the black full-head helmet that made her feel like she was half dressed in a space suit. They were heading back to Lake Winnipesaukee, to get her mother's bracelet; they were going to surprise her with it. Her mother would shout when she saw it in her father's hand, and her father would laugh, and hook an arm around Linda McQueen's waist, and kiss her cheek, and they wouldn't be mad at each other anymore.

The Brat glided through flickering sunlight, beneath the overhanging boughs. She was close enough to 495 to hear it: the grinding roar of an eighteen-wheeler downshifting, the hum of the cars, and yes, even the rumbling blast of a motorcycle making its way south.

When she shut her eyes, she was on the highway herself, making good time, enjoying the feeling of weightlessness as the bike tilted into the curves. She did not note that in her mind she was alone on the bike now, a bigger girl, old enough to twist the throttle herself.

She'd shut the both of them up. She'd get the bracelet and come back and throw it on the bed between her parents and walk out without a word. Leave them staring at each other in embarrassment. But mostly she was imagining the bike, the headlong rush into the miles, as the last of the day's light fled the sky.

She slipped from fir-scented gloom and out onto the wide dirt road that ran up to the bridge. The Shortaway, locals called it, all one word.

As she approached the bridge, she saw that the chain-link fence was down. The wire mesh had been wrenched off the posts and was lying in the dirt. The entrance—just barely wide enough to admit a single car—was framed in tangles of ivy, waving gently in the rush of air coming up from the river below. Within was a rectangular tunnel, extending to a square of unbelievable brightness, as if the far end opened onto a valley of golden wheat, or maybe just gold.

She slowed—for a moment. She was in a cycling trance, had ridden deep into her own head, and when she decided to keep going, right over the fence and into the darkness, she did not question the choice overmuch. To stop now would be a failure of courage she could not permit. Besides. She had faith in speed. If boards began to snap beneath her, she would just keep going, getting off the rotten wood before it could give way. If there was someone in there—some derelict who wanted to put his hands on a little girl—she would be past him before he could move.

The thought of old wood shattering, or a bum grabbing for her, filled her chest with lovely terror and instead of giving her pause caused her to stand up and work the pedals even harder. She thought, too, with a certain calm satisfaction, that if the bridge did crash into the river, ten stories below, and she was smashed in the rubble, it would be her parents' fault for fighting and driving her out of the house, and *that* would teach them. They would miss her terribly, would be sick with grief and guilt, and it was exactly what they had coming, the both of them.

The chain-links rattled and banged beneath her tires. She plunged into a subterranean darkness that reeked of bats and rot.

As she entered, she saw something written on the wall, to her left, in green spray paint. She did not slow to read it but thought it said TERRY'S, which was funny because they had eaten at a place called Terry's for lunch, Terry's Primo Subs in Hampton, which was back in New Hampshire, on the sea. It was their usual place to stop on their way home from Lake Winnipesaukee, located about halfway between Haverhill and The Lake.

Sound was different inside the covered bridge. She heard the river, a hundred feet below, but it sounded less like rushing water, more like a blast of white noise, of static on the radio. She did not look down, was afraid to see the river between the occasional gaps in the boards beneath. She did not even look from side to side but kept her gaze fixed on the far end of the bridge.

She passed through stammering rays of white light. When she crossed through one of those wafer-thin sheets of brightness, she felt it in her left eye, a kind of distant throb. The floor had an unpleasant sense of *give.* She had just a single thought now, two words long, *almost there, almost there,* keeping time with the churning of her feet.

The square of brightness at the far end of the bridge expanded and intensified. As she approached, she was conscious of an almost brutal heat emanating from the exit. She inexplicably smelled suntan lotion and onion rings. It did not cross her mind to wonder why there was no gate here at the other end of the bridge either.

Vic McQueen, a.k.a. the Brat, drew a deep gulp of air and rode out of the Shorter Way, into the sunlight, tires thumpety-thumping off the wood and onto blacktop. The hiss and roar of white noise ended abruptly, as if she really had been listening to static on the radio and someone had just poked the power switch.

She glided another dozen feet before she saw where she was. Her heart grabbed in her chest before her hands could grab for the brakes. She came to a stop so hard, with such force, that the back tire whipped around, skidding across asphalt, flinging dirt.

She had emerged behind a one-story building, in a paved alley. A Dumpster and a collection of trash cans stood against the brick wall to her left. One end of the alley was closed off by a high plank fence. There was a road on the other side of that fence. Vic could hear traffic rolling by, heard a snatch of a song trailing from one of the cars: *Abra-abra-cadabra . . . I wanna reach out and grab ya . . .*

Vic knew, on first glance, that she was in the wrong place. She had been down to the Shorter Way many times, looked across the high banks of the Merrimack to the other side often enough to know what lay over there: a timbered hill, green and cool and quiet. No road, no shop, no alley. She turned her head and very nearly screamed.

The Shorter Way Bridge filled the mouth of the alley behind her. It was rammed right into it, between the one-story building of brick and a five-story-high building of whitewashed concrete and glass.

The bridge no longer crossed a river but was stuffed into a space that could barely contain it. Vic shivered violently at the sight of it. When she looked into the darkness, she could distantly see the emerald-tinted shadows of the Pittman Street Woods on the other end.

Vic climbed off her bike. Her legs shook in nervous bursts. She walked her Raleigh over to the Dumpster and leaned it against the side. She found she lacked the courage to think too directly about the Shorter Way.

The alley stank of fried food going bad in the sun. She wanted fresh air. She walked past a screen door looking into a noisy, steamy kitchen and to the high wooden fence. She unlatched the door in the side and let herself out onto a narrow strip of sidewalk that she knew well. She had stood on it only hours ago.

When she looked to the left, she saw a long stretch of beach and the ocean beyond, the green cresting waves glistening with a painful brightness in the sun. Boys in swim trunks tossed a Frisbee, leaping to make show-off catches and then falling in the dunes. Cars rolled along the oceanfront boulevard, bumper to bumper. She walked around the corner on unsteady legs and looked at the walk-up window of

Terry's Primo Subs
Hampton Beach, New Hampshire

VIC WALKED PAST A ROW OF MOTORCYCLES LEANING OUT FRONT, chrome burning in the afternoon sun. There was a line of girls at the order window, girls in bikini tops and short-shorts, laughing bright laughter. How Vic hated the sound of them, which was like hearing glass shatter. She went in. A brass bell dinged on the door.

The windows were open, and half a dozen desktop fans were running behind the counter, blowing air out toward the tables, and still it was too hot inside. Long spools of flypaper hung from the ceiling and wavered in the breeze. The Brat didn't like looking at that flypaper, at the insects that had been caught on it, to struggle and die while people shoved hamburgers into their mouths directly below. She had not noticed the flypaper when she'd eaten lunch here earlier in the day, with her parents.

She felt woozy, as if she'd been running around on a full stomach in the August heat. A big man in a white undershirt stood behind the cash register. His shoulders were hairy and crimson with sunburn, and there was a line of zinc painted on his nose. A white plastic tag on his shirt said PETE. He had been here all afternoon. Two hours before, Vic had stood next to her father while Chris McQueen paid him for their burger baskets and their milkshakes. The two men had talked about the Red Sox, who were on a good run. 1986 was looking like the year they might finally break the curse. Clemens was mowing them down. The kid had the Cy Young locked up, with more than a month left to play.

Vic turned toward him, if not for any reason than because she recognized him. But then she just stood there, in front of him, blinking, no idea what to say. A fan hummed at Pete's back and caught the humid, human smell of him, wafted it into the Brat's face. No, she was definitely not feeling too good.

She was ready to cry, gripped with an unfamiliar sensation of helplessness. She was here, in New Hampshire, where she didn't belong. The Shorter Way Bridge was stuck in the alley out back, and somehow this was her fault. Her parents were fighting and had no idea how far away she had got from them. All this needed to be said and more. She needed to call home. She needed to call the police. Someone had to go look at the bridge in the alley. Her thoughts were a sickening turmoil. The inside of her head was a bad place, a dark tunnel full of distracting noise and whirling bats.

But the big man saved her the trouble of figuring out where to start. His eyebrows knitted together at the sight of her. "*There* you are. I was wondering if I was going to see you again. You came back for it, huh?"

Vic stared at him blankly. "Came back?"

"For the bracelet. One with the butterfly on it."

He poked a key, and the register drawer popped open with a clashing chime. Her mother's bracelet was in the back.

When Vic saw it, another weak tremor passed through her legs and she let out an unsteady sigh. For the first time since exiting the Shorter Way and finding herself impossibly in Hampton Beach, she felt something like understanding.

She had gone looking for her mother's bracelet in her imagination, and somehow she had found it. She had never gone out on her bike at all. Probably her parents had never really fought. There was only one way to explain a bridge crammed into an alley. She had gotten home, sunburned and exhausted, with a bellyful of milkshake, had passed out on her bed and now was dreaming. With that in mind, she supposed the best thing she could do was get her mother's bracelet and go back across the bridge, at which point she would presumably wake up.

There was another dull throb of pain behind her left eye. A headache was rooting itself there. A bad one. She couldn't remember ever carrying a headache into a dream before.

"Thank you," said the Brat as Pete handed the bracelet across the counter to her. "My mom was really worried about it. It's worth a lot."

"Really worried, huh?" Pete stuck a pinkie in one ear and twisted it back and forth. "Got a lot of sentimental value, I guess."

"No. I mean *yes,* it does. It belonged to her grandmother, my great-grandmother. But I mean it's also very valuable."

"Un-huh," he said.

"It's an *antique,*" said the Brat, not entirely sure why she felt the need to persuade him of its value.

"It's only an antique if it's worth something. If it's not worth anything, it's just an old thingamajig."

"It's *diamonds,*" the Brat said. "Diamonds and gold."

Pete laughed: a short, caustic bark of laughter.

"It *is,*" she said.

Pete said, "Nah. Costume jewelry. Those things look like diamonds? Zirconia. And see inside the band, where it's goin' silver? Gold don't come off. What's good stays good no matter how much of a beating it takes." His brow wrinkled in an expression of unexpected sympathy. "You okay? You don't look so hot."

"I'm all right," she said. "I've had a lot of sun." Which seemed a very grown-up thing to say.

She wasn't all right, though. She felt dizzy, and her legs were trembling steadily. She wanted to be outside, away from the mingled perfume of Petesweat and onion rings and bubbling deep fat. She wanted this dream over with.

"Are you sure I can't get you something cold to drink?" Pete asked.

"Thanks, but I had a milkshake when I was in for lunch."

"If you had a milkshake, you didn't get it here," Pete said. "McDonald's, maybe. What we got is frappes."

"I have to go," she said, turning and starting back toward the door. She was aware of sunburned Pete watching her with real concern and was grateful to him for his empathy. She thought that in spite of his stink and brusque manner he was a good man, the kind of man who would worry about a sick-looking little girl, out on her own along Hampton Beach. But she didn't dare say anything else to him. The ill sweat was damp on her temples and upper lip, and it took a great deal of concentration to clamp down on the tremors in her legs. Her left eye thudded again. A bit less gently this time. Her conviction that she was only imagining this visit to Terry's, that she was tramping through a particularly forceful dream, was hard to hold on to, like trying to keep a grip on a slick frog.

Vic stepped back outside and walked swiftly along the hot concrete, past the parked and leaning motorcycles. She opened the door in the tall plank fence and stepped into the alley behind Terry's Primo Subs.

The bridge hadn't moved. Its exterior walls were crammed right up against the buildings on either side. It hurt to look at it dead-on. It hurt in her left eye.

A cook or a dishwasher—someone who worked in the kitchen—stood in the alley by the Dumpster. He wore an apron streaked with grease and blood. Anyone who had a good look at that apron would probably skip getting lunch at Terry's. He was a little man with a bristly face and veined, tattooed forearms, and he stared at the bridge with an expression located somewhere between outrage and fright.

"What the *motherfuck*?" the guy said. He cast a confused look at Vic. "Do you see *that,* kid? I mean . . . what the motherfuck *is* that?"

"My bridge. Don't worry. I'll take it with me," Vic said. She was herself unclear what she meant by this.

She gripped her bike by the handlebars, turned it around, and pushed it toward the bridge. She ran alongside it two steps and then threw her leg over.

The front tire bumped up onto the boards, and she plunged into hissing darkness.

The sound, that idiot roar of static, rose as the Raleigh carried her out across the bridge. On the way across, she had believed she was hearing the river below, but that wasn't it. There were long cracks in the walls, and for the first time she looked at them as they flashed by. Through them she saw a flickering white brilliance, as if the world's largest TV set were just on the other side of the wall and it was stuck on a channel that wasn't broadcasting. A storm blew against the lopsided and decrepit bridge, a blizzard of light. She could feel the bridge buckling just slightly, as the downpour dashed itself against the walls.

She shut her eyes, didn't want to see any more, stood up on the pedals and rode for the other side. She tried her prayerlike chant once more—*almost there, almost there*—but was too winded and sick to maintain any one thought for long. There was only her breath and the roaring, raging static, that endless waterfall of sound, rising in volume, building to a maddening intensity and then building some more until she wanted to cry out for it to *stop,* the word coming to her lips, *stop, stop it,* her lungs gathering air to shout, and that was when the bike thudded back down in

Haverhill, Massachusetts

THE SOUND CUT OUT, WITH A SOFT ELECTRICAL *POP*. SHE FELT THAT *pop* in her head, in her left temple, a small but sharply felt explosion.

She knew even before she opened her eyes that she was home—or not home, but in *her* woods at least. She knew they were her woods by the smell of pines and the quality of the air, a scrubbed, cool, clean sensation that she associated with the Merrimack River. She could hear the river, distantly, a gentle, soothing rush of sound that was really in no way like static.

She opened her eyes, lifted her head, shook her hair out of her face. The late-day sunlight blinked through the leaves above her in irregular flashes. She slowed, squeezed the brakes, and put one foot down.

Vic turned her head for a last look back across the bridge at Hampton Beach. She wondered if she could still see the fry cook in his dirty apron.

Only she couldn't see him because the Shorter Way Bridge was gone. There was a guardrail, where the entrance to the bridge belonged. Beyond that the ground fell away in a steep and weedy slope that ended at the deep blue channel of the river.

Three chipped concrete pylons, bracket-shaped at the top, poked out of the tossing, agitated water. That was all that was left of the Shorter Way.

Vic didn't understand. She had just ridden across the bridge, had smelled the old, rotting, sun-baked wood and the rank hint of bat piss, had heard the boards knocking under her tires.

Her left eye throbbed. She shut it and rubbed it hard with her palm and opened it again, and for a moment she thought the bridge *was* there. She saw, or thought she saw, a kind of afterimage of it, a white glare in the shape of a bridge, reaching all the way to the opposite bank.

But the afterimage didn't last, and her left eye was streaming tears, and she was too weary to wonder for long what had happened to the bridge. She had never, in all her life, so needed to be home, in her room, in her bed, in the crisp folds of her sheets.

She got on her bike but could only pedal a few yards before she gave up. She stepped off and pushed, her head down and her hair swinging. Her mother's bracelet rolled loosely on her sweaty wrist. She hardly noticed it there.

Vic pushed the bike across the yellowing grass of the backyard, past the playset she never played on anymore, the chains of the swings caked in rust. She dropped her bike in the driveway and went inside. She wanted to get to her bedroom, wanted to lie down and rest. But when she heard a tinny *crack* in the kitchen, she veered off course to see who was in there.

It was her father, who stood with his back to her, can of Stroh's in one hand. He was running the other hand under cold water in the sink, turning his knuckles beneath the faucet.

Vic wasn't sure how long she had been gone. The clock on the toaster oven was no help. It blinked 12:00 over and over, as if it had just been reset. The lights were off, too, the room cool with afternoon shadow.

"Dad," she said, in a weary voice she hardly recognized. "What time is it?"

He glanced at the oven, then gave his head a little shake.

"Damned if I know. The power blinked out about five minutes

ago. I think the whole street is—" But then he glanced back at her, eyebrows rising in a question. "What's up? You all right?" He turned off the water and grabbed a rag to pat his hand dry. "You don't look so hot."

She laughed, a strained, humorless sound. "That's what Pete said." Her own voice seemed to come from way far off—from the other end of a long tunnel.

"Pete who?"

"Hampton Beach Pete."

"Vic?"

"I'm all right." She tried to swallow and couldn't. She was painfully thirsty, although she hadn't known it until she saw her father standing there with a cold drink in his hand. She shut her eyes for a moment and saw a sweating glass of chilly pink-grapefruit juice, an image that seemed to cause every cell in her body to ache with need. "I'm just thirsty. Do we have any juice?"

"Sorry, kid. Fridge is pretty empty. Mom hasn't been to the grocery store yet."

"Is she lying down?"

"Don't know," he said. He did not add, *Don't care,* but it was there in his tone.

"Oh," Vic said, and she slipped the bracelet off her wrist and put it on the kitchen table. "When she comes out, tell her I found her bracelet."

He slammed the door of the fridge and looked around. His gaze shifted to the bracelet, then back to her.

"Where . . . ?"

"In the car. Between the seats."

The room darkened, as if the sun had disappeared behind a great mass of clouds. Vic swayed.

Her father put the back of his hand to her face, the hand that held his can of beer. He had abraded his knuckles on something. "Christ, you're burning up, Brat. Hey, *Lin*?"

"I'm fine," Vic told him. "I'm just going to lie down for a minute."

She didn't mean to lie down right *there,* right *then.* The plan was to walk back to her room and stretch out under her awesome new David Hasselhoff poster—but her legs gave way and she dropped. Her father caught her before she could hit the floor. He scooped her into the air, a hand under her legs, another under her back, and carried her into the hall.

"Lin?" Chris McQueen called out again.

Linda emerged from her bedroom, holding a wet washcloth to the corner of her mouth. Her feathery auburn hair was disheveled and her eyes unfocused, as if she had in fact been asleep. Her gaze sharpened when she saw the Brat in her husband's arms.

She met them at the door to Vic's bedroom. Linda reached up with slender fingers and pushed the hair back from Vic's brow, pressed a hand to her forehead. Linda's palm was chilly and smooth, and her touch set off a shivering fit that was one part sickness, one part pleasure. Vic's parents weren't mad at each other anymore, and if the Brat had known that all she had to do to bring them together again was make herself sick, she could've skipped going across the bridge to get the bracelet and just stuck a finger down her throat.

"What happened to her?"

"She passed out," Chris said.

"No I didn't," said the Brat.

"Hundred-degree fever and falling down, and she wants to argue with me," said her father with unmistakable admiration.

Her mother lowered the washcloth she was holding to the corner of her own mouth. "Heatstroke. Three hours in that car and then right outside on her bike, no sunscreen on, and nothing to drink all day except that rotten milkshake at Terry's."

"Frappe. They call 'em frappes at Terry's," Vic said. "You hurt your mouth."

Her mother licked the corner of her swollen lips. "I'll get a glass of water and some ibuprofen. We'll both take some."

"While you're in the kitchen, why don't you grab your bracelet?" Chris said. "It's on the table."

Linda took two steps before registering what her husband had said. She looked back. Chris McQueen stood in the doorway to Vic's room, holding her in his arms. Vic could see David Hasselhoff, over her bed, smiling at her, looking like he could barely suppress the urge to wink: *You did good, kid.*

"It was in the car," Chris said. "The Brat found it."

Home

VIC SLEPT.

Her dreams were an incoherent flickershow of still images: a gas-mask on a cement floor, a dead dog by the side of the road with its head smashed in, a forest of towering pine trees hung with blind white angels.

This last image was so vivid and mysteriously awful—those dark sixty-foot-high trees swaying in the wind like stoned revelers in a pagan ceremony, the angels flashing and gleaming in their branches—that she wanted to scream.

She tried to yell but couldn't force any sound up her throat. She was trapped beneath a suffocating avalanche of shadow stuff, a mountainous heap of soft, airless matter. She fought to claw her way out, shoving desperately, flailing about with all the angry, wiry strength she could muster, until suddenly she found herself sitting up in bed, her whole body greased in sweat. Her father sat on the edge of the mattress beside her, holding her by the wrists.

"Vic," he said. "*Vic.* Relax. You just smacked me hard enough to turn my head around. Lay off. It's Dad."

"Oh," she said. He let go of her, and her arms dropped to her sides. "Sorry."

He held his jaw between thumb and forefinger and wiggled it back and forth. “It’s okay. Probably had it coming.”

“For what?”

“I don’t know. For whatever. Everyone’s got summin’.”

She leaned forward and kissed his whiskery chin, and he smiled.

“Your fever broke,” her father said. “You feel better?”

She shrugged, supposed she felt all right, now that she was out from under the great pile of black blankets and away from that dream forest of malevolent Christmas trees.

“You were pretty out of it,” he said. “You should’ve heard yourself.”

“What did I say?”

“At one point you were shouting that the bats were out of the bridge,” he told her. “I think you meant belfry.”

“Yeah. I mean . . . *no.* No, I was probably talking about the bridge.” Vic had forgotten, for a moment, about the Shorter Way. “What happened to the bridge, Dad?”

“Bridge?”

“The Shorter Way. The old covered bridge. It’s all gone.”

“Oh,” he said. “I heard that some dumb son of a bitch tried to drive his car across it and went right through. Got hisself killed and brought down most of the bridge with him. They demoed the rest. That’s why I told you I didn’t want you going out on that damn thing. They should’ve taken it down twenty years ago.”

She shivered.

“Look at you,” her father said. “You are just sick as a dog.”

She thought of her fever dream about the dog with the smashed-in head, and the world first brightened, then dimmed.

When her vision cleared, her father was holding a rubber bucket against her chest.

“If you have to choke something up,” he said, “try and get it in the pail. Christ, I’ll never take you to frigging Terry’s again.”

She remembered the smell of Petesweat and the ribbons of flypaper coated with dead bugs and vomited.

Her father walked out with the pail of sick. He came back with a glass of ice water.

She drank half in three swallows. It was so cold it set off a fresh shivering fit. Chris pulled the blankets up around her again, put his hand on her shoulder, and sat with her, waiting for the chill to pass. He didn't move. He didn't talk. It was calming just to have him there, to share in his easy, self-assured silence, and in almost no time at all she felt herself sliding down into sleep. Sliding down into sleep . . . or riding, maybe. With her eyes closed, she had a sensation, almost, of being on her bike again and gliding effortlessly into dark and restful quiet.

When her father rose to go, though, she was still conscious enough to be aware of it, and she made a noise of protest and reached for him. He slipped away.

"Get your rest, Vic," he whispered. "We'll have you back on your bike in no time."

She drifted.

His voice came to her from far off.

"I'm sorry they took the Shorter Way down," he murmured.

"I thought you didn't like it," she said, rolling over and away from him, letting him go, giving him up. "I thought you were scared I'd try to ride my bike on it."

"That's right," he said. "I *was* scared. I mean I'm sorry they went and took it down *without* me. If they were going to blow the thing out of the sky, I wish they'd let me set the charges. That bridge was always a death trap. Anyone could see it was going to kill someone someday. I'm just glad it didn't kill you. Go to sleep, short stuff."

Various Locales

IN A FEW MONTHS, THE INCIDENT OF THE LOST BRACELET WAS LARGELY forgotten, and when Vic did remember it, she remembered finding the thing in the car. She did not think about the Shorter Way if she could help it. The memory of her trip across the bridge was fragmented and had a quality of hallucination about it, was inseparable from the dream she'd had of dark trees and dead dogs. It did her no good to recollect it, and so she tucked the memory away in a safe-deposit box of the mind, locked it out of sight, and forgot about it.

And she did the same with all the other times.

Because there *were* other times, other trips on her Raleigh across a bridge that wasn't there, to find something that had been lost.

There was the time her friend Willa Lords lost Mr. Pentack, her good-luck corduroy penguin. Willa's parents cleaned out her room one day while Willa was sleeping over at Vic's house, and Willa believed that Mr. Pentack had been chucked into the garbage along with her Tinker Bell mobile and the Lite-Brite board that didn't work anymore. Willa was inconsolable, so torn up she couldn't go to school the next day—or the day after.

But Vic made it better. It turned out that Willa had brought Mr. Pentack along for the sleepover. Vic found it under her bed, among the dust bunnies and forgotten socks. Tragedy averted.

Vic certainly *didn't* believe she found Mr. Pentack by climbing on her Raleigh and riding through the Pittman Street Woods to the place where the Shorter Way Bridge had once stood. She did not believe the bridge was waiting there or that she had seen writing on the wall, in green spray paint: FENWAY BOWLING →. She did not believe the bridge had been filled with a roar of static and that mystery lights flashed and raced beyond its pine walls.

She had an image in her mind of riding out of the Shorter Way and into a darkened bowling alley, empty at seven in the morning. The covered bridge was, absurdly, sticking right through the wall and opened into the lanes themselves. Vic knew the place. She had gone to a birthday party there two weeks before; Willa had been there, too. The pine flooring was shiny, greased with something, and Vic's bike squirted across it like butter in a hot pan. She went down and banged her elbow. Mr. Pentack was in a lost-and-found basket behind the counter, under the shelves of bowling shoes.

This was all just a story she told herself the night after she discovered Mr. Pentack under her bed. She was sick that night, hot and clammy, with the dry heaves, and her dreams were vivid and unnatural.

The scrape on her elbow healed in a couple days.

When she was ten, she found her father's wallet between the cushions in the couch, *not* on a construction site in Attleboro. Her left eye throbbed for days after she found the wallet, as if someone had punched her.

When she was eleven, the de Zoets, who lived across the street, lost their cat. The cat, Taylor, was a scrawny old thing, white with black patches. He had gone out just before a summer cloudburst and not returned. Mrs. de Zoet walked up and down the street the next morning, chirping like a bird, mewling Taylor's name. Mr. de Zoet, a scarecrow of a man who wore bow ties and suspenders, stood in the yard with his rake, not raking anything, a kind of hopelessness in his pale eyes.

Vic particularly liked Mr. de Zoet, a man with a funny accent like Arnold Schwarzenegger's, who had a miniature battlefield in his office. Mr. de Zoet smelled like fresh-brewed coffee and pipesmoke and let Vic paint his little plastic infantrymen. Vic liked Taylor the cat, too. When he purred, he made a rusty *clackety-clack* in his chest, like a machine with old gears, trundling to noisy life.

No one ever saw Taylor again . . . although Vic told herself a story about riding across the Shorter Way Bridge and finding the poor old thing matted with blood and swarming with flies, in the wet weeds, by the side of the highway. It had dragged itself out of the street after a car ran over its back. The Brat could still see the bloodstains on the blacktop.

Vic began to hate the sound of static.

SPICY MENACE
1990

Sugarcreek, Pennsylvania

THE AD WAS ON ONE OF THE LAST PAGES OF *SPICY MENACE,* THE August 1949 issue, the cover of which depicted a screaming nude frozen in a block of ice *(She gave him the cold shoulder . . . so he gave her the big chill!).* It was just a single column, below a much larger advertisement for Adola Brassieres *(**Oomph**asize your figure!).* Bing Partridge noticed it only after a long, considering look at the lady in the Adola ad, a woman with pale, creamy mommy tits, supported by a bra with cone-shaped cups and a metallic sheen. Her eyes were closed, and her lips were parted slightly, so she looked like she was asleep and dreaming sweet dreams, and Bing had been imagining waking her with a kiss.

"Bing and Adola, sitting in a tree," Bing crooned, "F-U-C-K-I-N-*Geeee.*"

Bing was in his quiet place in the basement, with his pants down and his ass on the dusty concrete. His free hand was more or less where you would imagine it, but he was not particularly busy yet. He had been grazing his way through the issue, looking for the best parts, when he found it, a small block of print, in the lower left corner of the page. A snowman in a top hat gestured with one crooked arm at a line of type, framed by snowflakes.

Bing liked the ads in the back of the pulps: ads for tin lockers

Do You *BELIEVE* In a Place Called

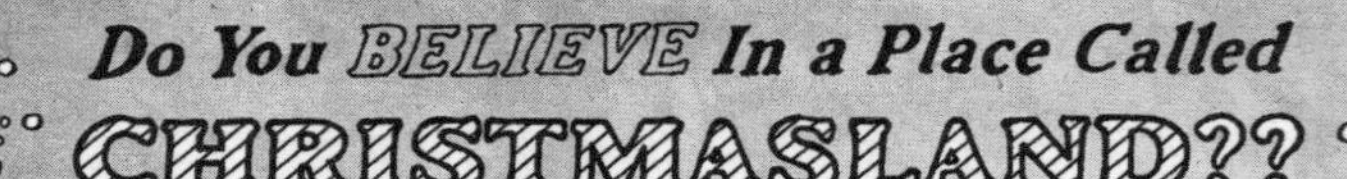

WHAT
Would You
Do For A
LIFETIME
Pass To A
Place
Where
EVERY
Morning Is
CHRISTMAS
Morning
And
Unhappiness
Is Against
The Law?!?

DON'T
GIVE UP
ON
WONDER!

DON'T
GIVE UP
ON
**YOUR
DREAMS!**

We're looking for GO-GETTERS
Who LOVE CHILDREN
And aren't afraid of ***ADVENTURE!***
Inquire about SPECIAL opportunities
In our SECURITY department.

This isn't just a job...
IT'S A *LIFE!*
CHRISTMASLAND **is waiting...**
FOR YOU!

filled with toy soldiers *(Re-create the thrill of Verdun!)*, ads for vintage World War II equipment *(Bayonets! Rifles! Gasmasks!)*, ads for books that would tell you how to make women want you *(Teach Her to Say, "I LOVE YOU!!")*. He often clipped out order forms and sent in pocket change or grimy dollar bills, in an attempt to acquire ant farms and metal detectors. He wanted, with all his heart, to Amaze His Friends! and Astonish His Relatives!—and never mind that his friends were the three feebs who worked under him in the janitorial crew at NorChemPharm and that his only direct relatives had returned to the soil, in the cemetery behind the New American Faith Tabernacle. Bing had never once considered that his father's collection of soft-core pulps—mildewing in a cardboard box down in Bing's quiet room—were older than he was and that most of the corporations he was sending money to had long since ceased to exist.

But his feelings as he read, then reread the advertisement about this place Christmasland were an emotional response of a different order. His uncircumcised and vaguely yeasty-smelling penis went limp in his left hand, forgotten. His soul was a steeple in which all the bells had begun to clash at once.

He had no idea where or what Christmasland was, had never heard of it. And yet he instantly felt he had wanted to go there all his life . . . to walk its cobblestone streets, stroll beneath its leaning candy-cane lampposts, and to watch the children screaming as they were swept around and around on the reindeer carousel.

"What would you do for a lifetime pass to a place where every morning is Christmas morning?!" the advertisement shouted.

Bing had forty-two Christmases under his belt, but when he thought of Christmas morning, only one mattered, and that one stood for all the rest. In this memory of Christmas, his mother slid sugar cookies shaped like Christmas trees out of the oven, so the whole house took on their vanilla fragrance. It was years before John Partridge would catch a framing nail in the frontal lobe, and that morning he sat on the floor with Bing, watching intently as Bing tore open his gifts. Bing remembered the last present best: a large box that contained a big rubber gasmask and a dented helmet, rust showing where the paint was chipped away.

"You're looking at the gear that kept me alive in Korea," his father said. "It's yours now. That gasmask you're holding, there's three yellowmen in the dirt that's the last thing they ever saw."

Bing pulled the gasmask on and stared out through the clear plastic lenses at his father. With the gasmask on, he saw the living room as a little world trapped inside a gum-ball machine. His father set the helmet on top of Bing's noggin, then saluted. Bing solemnly saluted back.

"So you're the one," his father said to him. "The little soldier that all the men are talking about. Mr. Unstoppable. Private Take-No-Shit. Is that right?"

"Private Take-No-Shit reporting for duty, sir, yes, sir," Bing said.

His mother laughed her brittle, nervous laughter and said, "John, your *language.* On Christmas morning. It isn't right. This is the day we welcome our Savior to this earth."

"Mothers," John Partridge said to his son after Bing's mother had left them with sugar cookies and gone back to the kitchen for cocoa. "They'll keep you sucking at the tit your whole life if you let them. Of course, when you think about it . . . what's wrong with that?" And winked.

And outside, the snow came down in big goose-feather flakes, and they stayed home together all day, and Bing wore his helmet and gasmask and played war, and he shot his father over and over, and John Partridge died again and again, falling out of his easy chair in front of the TV. Once Bing killed his mother, too, and she obediently crossed her eyes and went boneless and stayed dead for most of a commercial break. She didn't wake up until he removed his gasmask to kiss her forehead. Then she smiled and said, *God bless you, little Bing Partridge. I love you more than anything.*

What would he do to feel like that every day? To feel like it was

Christmas morning and there was a real Korean War gasmask waiting for him under the tree? To see his mother slowly open her eyes once again and say, *I love you more than anything*? The question, really, was what would he *not* do?

He shuffled three steps toward the door before he got around to yanking his pants back up.

His mother had taken on some secretarial chores for the church after her husband couldn't work anymore, and her Olivetti electric typewriter was still in the closet in the hall. The O was gone, but he knew he could use the number 0 to cover for it. Bing rolled a sheet of paper in and began to write:

> *Dear* XXXXX *respected Christmasland* XXXX *0wners,*
>
> *I am resp0nding t0 y0ur ad in Spicy Menace Magazine. W0uld I like t0 w0rk in Christmasland? Y0U BET! I have 18 years 0f empl0yment at N0rChem-Pharm in Sugarcreek, Pennsylvania, and f0r 12 I have been* XXXX *a fl00r manager f0r the cust0dial team. My duties include the care and shipping 0f many c0mpressed gases such as 0xygen, hydr0gen, helium, and sev0flurane. Guess h0w many accidents 0n my watch? N0NE!*
>
> *What w0uld I d0 t0 have Christmas every day? Wh0 d0 I have t0 KILL, ha-ha-ha!! There is n0 nasty j0b I have n0t d0ne f0r N0rChemPharm. I have cleaned t0ilets packed full and fl0wing 0ver with* XXXXX *y0u-kn0w-what, m0pped pee-pee 0ff walls, and p0is0ned rats by the dirty d0zen. Are y0u l00king f0r s0me0ne wh0 isn't afraid t0 get his hands dirty? Well y0ur search is 0ver!*
>
> *I am just the man y0u are l00king f0r: a g0-getter wh0 l0ves children and wh0 isn't afraid 0f adventure.*

I dO nOt want much except a gOOd place tO wOrk. A security jOb wOuld suit me fine. TO be straight with yOu, Once upOn a time I hOped tO serve my prOud natiOn in unifOrm, like my dad did in the KOrean war, but sOme yOuthful indiscretiOns and a bit Of sad family trOuble prevented me. Oh well! NO cOmplaints! Believe me, if I cOuld wear the unifOrm Of Christmasland security, I wOuld cOnsider it just as hOnOrable! I am a cOllectOr Of authentic military memOrabilia. I have my Own gun and I knOw hOw tO use it.

In clOsing, I hOpe yOu will cOntact me at the belOw address. I am lOyal tO a fault and wOuld DIE fOr this special OppOrtunity. There is NOTHING I am nOt ready tO dO tO earn a place amOng the Christmasland staff.

XXXXX *SeasOn's Greetings!*
Bing Partridge
BING PARTRIDGE
25 BLOCH LANE
SUGARCREEK, PENNSYLVANIA 16323

He rolled the sheet out of the typewriter and read it over, lips moving. The effort of concentration had left his lumpy, potato-shaped body humid with sweat. It seemed to him that he had stated the facts about himself with clarity and authority. He worried that it was a mistake to mention "yOuthful indiscretiOns" or "sad family trOuble" but in the end decided they would probably find out about his parents whether he said anything or not and that it was better to be coolly up-front about it than look like he was hiding something. It was all a long time ago, and in the years since he had been released from the Youth Center—a.k.a. the Bin—he had been a model worker, had not missed a single day at NorChemPharm.

He folded the letter, then looked in the front closet for an envelope. He found instead a box of unused Christmas cards. A boy and a girl, in fuzzy long underwear, were peeking around a corner, staring in wide-eyed wonder at Santy Claus, standing in the gloom before their Christmas tree. The seat of the girl's pajamas was partly unbuttoned to show one plump cheek of her ass. John Partridge had sometimes said that Bing couldn't pour water out of a boot with instructions written on the heel, and maybe it was true, but he still knew a good thing when he saw it. This letter was slipped into a Christmas card and the card into an envelope decorated with holly leaves and shiny cranberries.

Before he put it into the mailbox at the end of the street, he kissed it, as a priest might bend his head and kiss the Bible.

THE NEXT DAY HE WAS WAITING BY THE MAILBOX AT TWO-THIRTY WHEN the mailman proceeded up the street in his funny little white truck. The foil flowers in Bing's front yard spun lazily, making a barely audible whir.

"Bing," the mailman said. "Aren't you supposed to be at work?"

"Night shift," Bing said.

"Is a war starting?" the mailman said, nodding at Bing's clothes.

Bing had on his mustard-colored fatigues, what he wore when he wanted to feel lucky.

"If there is, I'll be ready for it," Bing told him.

There was nothing from Christmasland. But of course how could there be? He had only sent his card the day before.

THERE WAS NOTHING THE NEXT DAY EITHER.

OR THE DAY AFTER.

ON MONDAY HE WAS SURE *SOMETHING* WOULD COME AND WAS OUT on his front step a half hour before the postman's usual time. Black and ugly thunderheads towered over the crest of the hill, behind the steeple of the New American Faith Tabernacle. Muffled thunder detonated two miles away and eighteen thousand feet up. It was not a noise so much as a vibration, one that went to Bing's core, that shook his bones in their sediment of fat. His foil flowers spun hysterically, sounding for all the world like a pack of kids on bicycles, racing downhill and out of control.

The rumbles and crashes made Bing profoundly uneasy. It had been unbearably hot and thundery the day the nail gun went off (that was how he thought of it—not as the day he shot his father but as the day the gun went off). His father had felt the barrel pressing against his left temple and looked sidelong at Bing, standing over him. He took a sip of his beer and smacked his lips and said, "I'd be scared if I thought you had the balls."

After he pulled the trigger, Bing sat with the old man and listened to the rain rattle off the roof of the garage, while John Partridge sprawled on the floor, one foot twitching and a urine stain spreading across the front of his pants. Bing had sat until his mother entered the garage and began to scream. Then it had been her turn—although not for the nail gun.

Now Bing stood in his yard and watched the clouds mount up in the sky over the church at the top of the hill, where his mother had worked all the last days of her life . . . the church he had attended faithfully, every Sunday, since before he could even walk or speak. One of his first words had been "looya!"—which was the closest he could come to pronouncing "hallelujah." His mother had called him Looya for years after.

No one worshipped there now. Pastor Mitchell had run off with the funds and a married woman, and the property had been seized by the bank. On Sunday mornings the only penitents in the New American Faith Tabernacle were the pigeons that lived in the rafters. The place frightened Bing a little now—its emptiness frightened him. He imagined that it despised him for abandoning it and abandoning God, that sometimes it leaned forward off its foundations to glare at him with its stained-glass eyes. There were days—days like this—when the woods were full of the lunatic shrilling of summer insects and the air wobbled with liquid heat, and that church seemed to *loom*.

Thunder hammered at the afternoon.

"Rain, rain, go away," Bing whispered to himself. "Come again some other day."

The first warm drop of rain spattered against his forehead. Other drops followed, burning bright in the sunshine that slanted in from the yawning blue sky to the west. It felt almost as hot as a spray of blood.

The mail was late, and by the time it came, Bing was soaking wet and huddling under the shingle overhang at his front door. He ran through the downpour for the box. As he reached it, a twig of lightning stroked out of the clouds and fell with a crash somewhere behind the church. Bing shrieked as the world flashed bluewhiteblue, sure he was about to be lanced through, was about to burn alive, touched by the finger of God for giving his father the nail gun and for what he had done afterward to his mother on the kitchen floor.

There was a bill from the utility company and a flyer announcing a new mattress store and nothing else.

NINE HOURS LATER BING CAME AWAKE IN HIS BED TO THE TREMULOUS sound of violins and then a man singing in a voice as smooth and creamy as vanilla cake frosting. It was his namesake, Bing Crosby. Mr. Crosby was dreaming of a white Christmas, just like the ones he used to know.

Bing pulled the blankets close to his chin, listening intently. Mingled with the song was the gentle scratch of a needle on vinyl.

He slid out of his bed and crept to the door. The floor was cold under his bare feet.

Bing's parents were dancing in the living room. His father had his back to him and was dressed in his mustard-colored fatigues. His mother rested her head on John's shoulder, her eyes shut, her mouth open, as if she were dancing in her sleep.

The presents waited under the squat, homely, tinsel-smothered tree: three big green dented tanks of sevoflurane, decorated with crimson bows.

His parents turned in their slow circle, and as they did, Bing saw that his father was wearing a gasmask and his mother was naked. She really was asleep, too. Her feet dragged across the boards. His father clutched her around the waist, his gloved hands on the curve of her white buttocks. His mother's bare white can was as luminous as a celestial object, as pale as the moon.

"Dad?" Bing asked.

His father kept dancing, turning away, and taking Bing's mother with him.

"COME ON DOWN, BING!" cried a deep, booming voice, a voice so loud that the china chattered in the armoire. Bing lurched in surprise, his heart misfiring in his chest. The needle on the record jumped, came back down close to the end of the song. "COME ON DOWN! LOOKS LIKE CHRISTMAS CAME EARLY THIS YEAR, DOESN'T IT! HO, HO, HO!"

A part of Bing wanted to run back to his room and slam the door. He wanted to cover his eyes and his ears at the same time but couldn't find the willpower to do either. He quailed at the thought of taking another step, yet his feet carried him forward, past the tree and the tanks of sevoflurane, past his father and mother, down the hall, and to the front door. It swung open even before he put his hand on the knob.

The foil flowers in his yard spun softly in the winter night. He had one foil flower for every year he had worked at NorChemPharm, gifts for the custodial staff, bestowed at the annual holiday party.

Christmasland waited beyond the yard. The Sleighcoaster rumbled and crashed, and the children in the karts screamed and lifted their hands to the frozen night. The great Ferris wheel, the Arctic Eye, revolved against a backdrop of unfamiliar stars. All the candles were lit in a Christmas tree as tall as a ten-story building and as wide across as Bing's own house.

"MERRY GODDAMN CHRISTMAS, BING, YOU CRAZY THING!" hollered that great booming voice, and when Bing looked into the sky, he saw that the moon had a face. A single bulging bloodshot eye gaped from that starved skullface, a landscape of crater and bone. It grinned. *"BING, YOU CRAZY MOTHERFUCKER, ARE YOU READY FOR THE RIDE OF YOUR LIFE?!?"*

Bing sat up in bed, his heart pistoning in his chest—waking for real this time. He was so slicked with sweat that his G.I. Joe pajamas were sticking to his skin. He noticed, distantly, that his cock was so hard it hurt, poking through the front of his pants.

He gasped, as if he had not awoken but *surfaced,* after a long time underwater.

His room was full of the cool, pale, bone-colored light of a faceless moon.

Bing had been swallowing air for almost half a minute before he realized he could still hear "White Christmas." The song had followed him right out of his dream. It came from a long way off and seemed to be getting fainter by the moment, and he knew if he didn't get up to look, it would soon be gone, and tomorrow he would believe he had imagined it. He rose and walked on unsteady legs to the window, for a look into the yard.

An old car, at the end of the block, was easing away. A black Rolls-Royce with sideboards and chrome fixtures. Its taillights flashed red in the night and illuminated the license plate: NOS4A2. Then it turned the corner and disappeared, taking the joyful noise of Christmas with it.

NorChemPharm

Bing knew that the man from Christmasland was coming, well before Charlie Manx showed up to ask Bing to take a ride with him. He knew, too, that the man from Christmasland would not be a man like other men and that a job with Christmasland security would not be a job like other jobs, and on these matters he was not disappointed.

He knew because of the dreams, which seemed to him more vivid and real than anything that ever happened to him in the course of his waking life. He could never step into Christmasland in these dreams, but he could see it out his windows and out his door. He could smell the peppermint and cocoa, and he could see the candles burning in the ten-story Christmas tree, and he could hear the karts bashing and crashing on the sprawling old wooden Sleighcoaster. He could hear the music, too, and how the children screamed. If you didn't know better, you would think they were being butchered alive.

He knew because of the dreams, but also because of the *car*. The next time he saw it, he was at work, out on the loading dock. Some kids had tagged the back of the building, had spray-painted a big black cock and balls, spewing black jizz on a pair of great red globes that might've been boobs but that looked, to Bing's eye, like Christmas ornaments. Bing was outside in his rubber hazmat suit and industrial gasmask, with a bucket of diluted lye, to peel the paint off the wall with a wire brush.

Bing loved working with lye, loved to watch it melt the paint away. Denis Loory, the autistic kid who worked the morning shift, said you could use lye to melt a human person down to grease. Denis Loory and Bing had put a dead bat in a bucket of lye and left it one day, and the next morning there had been nothing in there but fake-looking semitransparent bones.

He stepped back to admire his work. The balls had mostly vanished to reveal the raw red brick beneath; only the big black prick and the boobs remained. As he stared at the wall, he saw, all of a sudden, his shadow appear, crisp, sharply delineated against the rough brick.

He turned on his heel to look behind him, and the black Rolls was *there:* It was parked on the other side of the chain-link fence, its high, close-set headlights glaring at him.

You could look at birds all your life without ever knowing what was a sparrow and what was a blackbird, but we all know a swan when we see it. So it was with cars. Maybe you could not tell a Firebird from a Fiero, but when you saw a Rolls-Royce, you knew it.

Bing smiled to see it and felt his heart fill with a rush of blood, and he thought, *Now. He will open the door, and he will say, "Are you the young man, Bing Partridge, who wrote about a job at Christmasland?"—and my life will begin. My life will begin at last.*

The door did not open, though . . . not then. The man behind the wheel—Bing could not see his face past the brilliance of the headlights—did not call out or roll down his window. He flashed his high beams, though, in genial greeting, before turning the car in a wide circle, to point it away from the NorChemPharm building.

Bing removed his gasmask, put it under his arm. He was flushed, and the cool, shady air was pleasant on his exposed skin. Bing could hear Christmas music trickling from the car. "Joy to the World." Yes. He felt that way, exactly.

He wondered if the man behind the wheel wanted him to come.

To leave his mask, leave his bucket of lye, slip around the fence, and climb into the passenger seat. But no sooner had he taken a step forward than the car began to ease away up the road.

"Wait!" Bing cried. "Don't go! Wait!"

The sight of the Rolls leaving him—of that license plate, NOS4A2, shrinking steadily as the car glided away—shocked him.

In a state of dizzy, almost panicked excitement, Bing screamed, "I've seen it! I've seen Christmasland! Please! Give me a chance! Please come back!"

The brake lights flashed. The Rolls slowed for a moment, as if Bing had been heard—and then glided on.

"Give me a chance!" he shouted. Then, screaming: *"Just give me a chance!"*

The Rolls slid away down the road, turned the corner, and was gone, left Bing flushed and damp with sweat and his heart clapping in his chest.

He was still standing there when the foreman, Mr. Paladin, stepped out on the loading dock for a smoke.

"Hey, Bing, there's still quite a bit of cock on this wall," he called. "You working this morning or are you on vacation?"

Bing stared forlornly down the road.

"Christmas vacation," he said, but in a low voice so Mr. Paladin couldn't hear him.

He had not seen the Rolls in a week, when they changed his schedule and he had to pull a double at NorChemPharm, six to six. It was ungodly hot in the storerooms, so hot that the iron tanks of compressed gas would sear you if you brushed up against them. Bing caught his usual bus home, a forty-minute ride, the vents blowing stinky air and an infant squalling the whole way.

He got off on Fairfield Street and walked the last three blocks.

The air was no longer gas but liquid—a liquid close to boiling. It streamed up off the softening blacktop and filled the air with distortion, so that the line of houses at the end of the block wavered like reflections bobbing in a pool of unsteady water.

"Heat, heat, go away," Bing sang to himself. *"Boil me some other—"*

The Rolls sat across the street, in front of his house. The man behind the wheel leaned out of the right-hand window and twisted his head to look back at Bing and smiled, one old friend to another. He motioned with a long-fingered hand: *Hurry up now.*

Bing's own hand shot into the air helplessly in a nervous return wave, and he came on down the street in a jiggling fat man's jog. It rattled him in some way, to find the Rolls idling there. A part of him had believed that eventually the man from Christmasland would come for him. Another part, however, had begun to worry that the dreams and his occasional sightings of The Car were like crows circling over something sick and close to collapse: his mind. Every step he took toward NOS4A2, he was that much more certain it would begin to move, to sail away and vanish yet again. It didn't.

The man in the passenger seat was not sitting in the passenger seat at all, because of course the Rolls-Royce was an old English car, and the steering wheel was on the right-hand side. This man, the driver, smiled benevolently upon Bing Partridge. At first glance Bing knew that although this man might have passed for forty or so, he was much older than that. His eyes had the soft, faded look of sea glass; they were old eyes, unfathomably old. He had a long, harrowed face, wise and kindly, although he had an overbite and his teeth were a little crooked. It was the sort of face, Bing supposed, that some people would describe as ferretlike, but in profile it also would've looked just fine on currency.

"Here he is!" cried the man behind the wheel. "It is the eager young Bing Partridge! The man of the hour! We are overdue for a conversation, young Partridge! The most important conversation of your life, I'll bet!"

"Are you from Christmasland?" Bing asked in a hushed voice.

The old or maybe ageless man laid a finger to one side of his nose. "Charles Talent Manx the Third at your service, my dear! CEO of Christmasland Enterprises, director of Christmasland Entertainment, president of fun! Also His Eminence, the King Shit of Turd Hill, although it doesn't say that on my card." His fingers snapped and produced a card out of thin air. Bing took it and looked down at it.

"You can taste those candy canes if you lick the card," Charlie said.

Bing stared for a moment, then lapped his rough tongue across the card. It tasted of paper and pasteboard.

"Kidding!" Charlie cried, and socked Bing in the arm. "Who do you think I am, Willy Wonka? Come around! Get in! Why, son, you look like you are about to melt into a puddle of Bing juice! Let me take you for a bottle of pop! We have something important to discuss!"

"A job?" Bing asked.

"A future," Charlie said.

Highway 322

"THIS IS THE NICEST CAR I HAVE EVER BEEN IN," BING PARTRIDGE SAID when they were gliding along Highway 322, the Rolls riding the curves like a stainless-steel ball bearing in a groove.

"It is a 1938 Rolls-Royce Wraith, one of just four hundred made in Bristol, England. A rare find—just like you, Bing Partridge!"

Bing moved his hand across the pebbled leather. The polished cherry dash and the gearshift glowed.

"Does your license plate mean something?" Bing asked. "En-Oh-Ess-four-Ar-two?"

"Nosferatu," the man Charlie Manx said.

"Nosfer-what-who?"

Manx said, "It is one of my little jokes. My first wife once accused me of being a Nosferatu. She did not use that exact word, but close enough. Have you ever had poison ivy, Bing?"

"Not in a long time. When I was little, before my father died, he took me camping and I—"

"If he took you camping *after* he died, my boy, *then* you would have a story to tell! Here is my point: My first wife was like the rash you get from poison ivy. I couldn't stand her, but I couldn't keep my hands off her. She was an itch I scratched until I bled—and then I scratched it some more! Your work sounds dangerous, Mr. Partridge!"

The transition was so abrupt that Bing wasn't ready for it, needed a moment to register that it was his turn to talk.

"It does?"

"You mentioned in your letter your work with compressed gases," Manx said. "Aren't tanks of helium and oxygen highly explosive?"

"Oh, sure. A guy in the loading bay snuck a smoke a few years ago, next to a tank of nitrogen with an open valve. It made a big shriek and went off like a rocket. It hit the fire door hard enough to smash it off its hinges, and the fire door is made of iron. No one died that time, though. And my crew has been accident-free for as long as I've been head man. Well—*almost* accident-free anyway. Denis Loory huffed some gingerbread smoke once, but that doesn't really count. He didn't even get sick."

"Gingerbread smoke?"

"That's a flavored mix of sevoflurane that we send to dentists' offices. You can also get it unscented, but the little guys like the old gingerbread smoke."

"Oh? It's a narcotic?"

"It makes it so you don't know what's happening to you, yeah. But it doesn't put you to sleep. It's more like you only know what you're told. And you lose all your intuitions." Bing laughed a little, couldn't help himself, then said, almost apologetically, "We told Denis it was disco time, and he started humping the air like John Ravolta in that movie. We just about died."

Mr. Manx's mouth opened to show his little brown teeth in a homely and irresistible grin. "I like a man with a sense of humor, Mr. Partridge."

"You can call me Bing, Mr. Manx."

He waited for Mr. Manx to say it was all right to call him Charlie, but Mr. Manx didn't. Instead he said, "I imagine most of the people who danced to disco music were under the influence of some kind of drugs. It is the only explanation for it. Not that I would call such silly wiggling a form of dance. More like rank foolishness!"

The Wraith rolled into the dirt lot of the Franklin Dairy Queen. On blacktop the Wraith seemed to glide like a sailboat with the wind behind it. There was a sense of effortless, silent motion. On dirt Bing had a different impression, a feeling of mass and momentum and weight: a Panzer grinding the clay under its treads.

"How about I buy us Coke-Colas and we will get down to brass tacks?" Charlie Manx said. He turned sideways, one gangly arm hung over the wheel.

Bing opened his mouth to answer, only to find himself struggling against a yawn. The long, peaceful, rocking ride in the late-day sun had made him drowsy. He had not slept well in a month and had been up since 4:00 A.M., and if Charlie Manx had not turned up parked across from his house, he would've made himself a TV dinner and gone to bed early. Which reminded him.

"I dreamed about it," Bing said simply. "I dream about Christmasland all the time." He laughed, embarrassed. Charlie Manx would think him quite the fool.

Only Charlie Manx didn't. His smile widened. "Did you dream about the moon? Did the moon speak to you?"

Bing's breath was pushed out of him all at once. He stared at Manx in wonder and, possibly, just a little alarm.

"You dreamt about it because you *belong* there, Bing," Manx said. "But if you want to go, you'll have to earn it. And I can tell you how."

MR. MANX WAS BACK FROM THE TAKE-OUT WINDOW A COUPLE OF minutes later. He eased his lanky frame in behind the wheel and passed Bing a chill, sweating bottle of Coca-Cola, audibly fizzing. Bing thought he had never seen a bottle of anything look so good.

He tipped back his head and poured the Coca-Cola down, swallowing rapidly, one gulp, two, three. When he lowered the bottle, it was half gone. He inhaled deeply—and then burped, a sharp, raggedy sound, loud as someone tearing a bedsheet.

Bing's face burned—but Charlie Manx only laughed gaily and said, "Better in than out, that's what I always tell my children!"

Bing relaxed and smiled shamefacedly. His burp had tasted bad, like Coca-Cola but also weirdly of aspirin.

Manx spun the wheel and carried them out onto the road.

"You've been watching me," Bing said.

"Yes, I have," Charlie said. "Almost ever since I opened your letter. I was quite surprised to receive it, I admit. I have not had any responses to my old magazine ads in many a season. Still, I had a hunch, as soon as I read your letter, that you were one of *my people.* Someone who would understand from the get-go the important work I'm doing. Still, a hunch is good, but *knowing* is better. Christmasland is a special place, and many people would have reservations about the work I do for it. I am very selective about who I employ. As it happens, I am looking for a man who can act as my new head of security. I need a hum hum hum hum to hum hum hum."

It took Bing a long minute to realize he hadn't heard the last part of what Charlie Manx was saying. The sound of his words had gotten lost in the drone of the tires on the blacktop. They were off the highway now, slipping along under the firs, through cool, piney shade. When Bing caught a glimpse of the rosy sky—the sun had slipped down when he wasn't paying attention, and sunset had come—he saw the moon, as white as a lemon ice, drifting in the clear empty.

"What did you say?" Bing asked, forcing himself to sit up a little straighter and rapidly blinking his eyes. He was dully aware that he was in danger of nodding off. His Coke, with its caffeine and sugar and refreshing fizz, should've woken him up but seemed to have had the opposite effect. He took a last swallow, but the residue at the bottom of the bottle was bitter, and he made a face.

"The world is full of brutal, stupid people, Bing," Charlie said.

"And do you know the worst of it? Some of them have children. Some of them get drunk and hit their little ones. Hit them and call them names. Such folk are unfit for children—that's how I see it! You could line them up and put a bullet in all of them—that would suit me fine. A bullet in the brain for each of them . . . or a nail."

Bing felt his insides turn upside down. He felt unsteady, so unsteady he had to put a hand on the dash to keep from tipping over.

"I don't remember doing it," Bing lied, his voice hushed and trembling just slightly. "It was a long time ago." Then he said, "I'd give anything to take it back."

"Why? So your father could've had a chance to kill *you* instead? The papers said before you shot him, he hit you so hard you suffered a cranial fracture. The papers said you were covered in bruises, some of them days old! I hope I do not have to explain to you the difference between homicide and fighting for your life!"

"I hurt my mom, too," Bing whispered. "In the kitchen. She didn't do anything to me."

Mr. Manx didn't seem impressed by this point. "Where was she when your father was giving you the old one-two? I take it she did not heroically attempt to shield you with her body! How come she never called the police? Couldn't find the number in the phone book?" Manx exhaled a weary sigh. "I wish someone had been there for you, Bing. The fires of hell are not hot enough for a man—or woman!—who would hurt his children. But, really, I am less concerned with punishment than prevention! It would've been best if it simply had never happened to you at all! If your home had been a safe one. If every day had been Christmas for you, Bing, instead of every day being misery and woe. I think we can both agree on that!"

Bing stared at him with woolly eyes. He felt as if he had not slept in days, and it was a minute-by-minute struggle to keep from sinking back into his leather seat and slipping away into unconsciousness.

"I think I'm going to fall asleep," Bing said.

"That's all right, Bing," Charlie said. "The road to Christmasland is paved in dreams!"

White blossoms drifted down from somewhere, flicked across the windshield. Bing stared at them with dim pleasure. He felt warm and good and peaceful, and he liked Charlie Manx. *The fires of hell are not hot enough for a man—or woman!—who would hurt his children.* It was a fine thing to say: It rang with moral certainty. Charlie Manx was a man who knew what was what.

"Humma hum hum hum," Charlie Manx said.

Bing nodded—this statement also rang with moral certainty and wisdom—and then he pointed at the blossoms raining down onto the windscreen. "It's snowing!"

"Ha!" Charlie Manx said. "*That* is not snow. Rest your eyes, Bing Partridge. Rest your eyes and you will see something."

Bing Partridge did as he was told.

His eyes were not closed long—only a single moment. But it was a moment that seemed to go on and on, to stretch out into a peaceful eternity, a restful sleeping darkness in which the only sound was the thrum of the tires on the road. Bing exhaled. Bing inhaled. Bing opened his eyes and then jolted upright, staring out through the windshield at

The Road to Christmasland

THE DAY HAD FLED, AND THE HEADLIGHTS OF THE WRAITH BORED into a frozen darkness. White flecks raced through the glare, ticked softly against the windshield.

"Now, *this* is snow!" Charlie Manx cried from behind the steering wheel.

Bing had snapped from drowsiness to full wakefulness in a moment, as if consciousness were a switch and someone had flicked it on. His blood seemed to surge, all at once, toward his heart. He could not have been more shocked if he'd woken to find a grenade in his lap.

Half the sky was smothered over with clouds. But the other half was plentifully sugared with stars, and the moon hung among them, that moon with the hooked nose and broad, smiling mouth. It considered the road below with a yellow sliver of eye showing beneath one drooping lid.

Deformed firs lined the road. Bing had to look twice before he realized they were not pines at all but gumdrop trees.

"Christmasland," Bing whispered.

"No," Charlie Manx said. "We are a long way off. Twenty hours of driving at least. But it's out there. It's in the West. And once a year, Bing, I take someone there."

"Me?" Bing asked in a quavering voice.

"No, Bing," Charlie said gently. "Not *this* year. All children are welcome in Christmasland, but grown-ups are a different case. You must prove your worth first. You must prove your love of children and your devotion to protecting them and serving Christmasland."

They passed a snowman, who lifted a twig arm and waved. Bing reflexively lifted his hand to wave in return.

"How?" he whispered.

"You must save *ten* children with me, Bing. You must save them from *monsters*."

"Monsters? What monsters?"

"Their parents," Manx said solemnly.

Bing removed his face from the icy glass of the passenger window and looked around at Charlie Manx. When he had shut his eyes a moment earlier, there had been sunlight in the sky and Mr. Manx had been dressed in a plain white shirt and suspenders. Now, though, he had on a coat with tails and a dark cap with a black leather brim. The coat had a double line of brass buttons and seemed like the sort of thing an officer from a foreign country might wear, a lieutenant in a royal guard. When Bing glanced down at himself, he saw he also wore new clothes: his father's crisp white marine dress uniform, boots polished to a black shine.

"Am I dreaming?" Bing asked.

"I told you," Manx said. "The road to Christmasland is *paved* in dreams. This old car can slip right out of the everyday world and onto the secret roads of thought. Sleep is just the exit ramp. When a passenger dozes off, my Wraith leaves whatever road it was on and slides onto the St. Nick Parkway. We are sharing this dream together. It is *your* dream, Bing. But it is still *my* ride. Come. I want to show you something."

As he had been speaking, the car was slowing and easing toward the side of the road. Snow crunched under the tires. The headlights illuminated a figure, just up the road on the right. From a distance it looked like a woman in a white gown. She stood very still, did not glance into the lights of the Wraith.

Manx leaned over and popped the glove compartment above Bing's knees. Inside was the usual mess of road maps and papers. Bing also saw a flashlight with a long chrome handle.

An orange medicine bottle rolled out of the glove compartment. Bing caught it one-handed. It said HANSOM, DEWEY—VALIUM 50 MG.

Manx gripped the flashlight, straightened up, and opened his door a crack. "We have to walk from here."

Bing held up the bottle. "Did you . . . did you give me something to make me sleep, Mr. Manx?"

Manx winked. "Don't hold it against me, Bing. I knew you'd want to get on the road to Christmasland as soon as possible and that you could see it only when you were asleep. I hope it's all right."

Bing said, "I guess I don't mind." And shrugged. He looked at the bottle again. "Who is Dewey Hansom?"

"He was *you,* Bing. He was my *pre*-Bing thing. Dewey Hansom was a screen agent in Los Angeles who specialized in child actors. He helped me save ten children and earned his place in Christmasland! Oh, the children of Christmasland *loved* Dewey, Bing. They absolutely ate him up! Come along!"

Bing unlatched his door and climbed out into the still, frozen air. The night was windless, and the snow spun down in slow flakes, kissing his cheeks. For an old man *(Why do I keep thinking he's old?* Bing wondered—*he doesn't* look *old),* Charles Manx was spry, legging ahead along the side of the road, his boots squealing. Bing tramped after him, hugging himself in his thin dress uniform.

It wasn't one woman in a white gown but two, flanking a black iron gate. They were identical: ladies carved from glassy marble. They both leaned forward, spreading their arms, and their flowing bone-white dresses billowed behind them, opening like the wings of angels. They were serenely beautiful, with the full mouths and blind eyes of classical statuary. Their lips were parted, so they appeared to be in midgasp, lips turned up in a way that suggested they were about to laugh—or cry out in pain. Their sculptor had fashioned them so their breasts were pressing against the fabric of their gowns.

Manx passed through the black gate, between the ladies. Bing hesitated, and his right hand came up, and he stroked the top of one of those smooth, cold bosoms. He had always wanted to touch a breast that looked like that, a firm, full mommy breast.

The stone lady's smile widened, and Bing leaped back, a cry rising in his throat.

"Come along, Bing! Let's be about our business! You aren't dressed for this cold!" Manx shouted.

Bing was about to step forward, then hesitated to look at the arch over the open iron gate.

GRAVEYARD OF WHAT MIGHT BE

Bing frowned at this mystifying statement, but then Mr. Manx called again, and he hurried along.

Four stone steps, lightly sprinkled in snow, led down to a flat plane of black ice. The ice was grainy with the recent snowfall, but the flakes were not deep—any kick of the boot would reveal the smooth sheet of ice beneath. He had gone two steps when he saw something cloudy caught in the ice, about three inches below the surface. At first glance it looked like a dinner plate.

Bing bent and looked through the ice. Charlie Manx, who was only a few paces ahead, turned back and pointed the flashlight at the spot where he was looking.

The glow of the beam lit the face of a child, a girl with freckles on her cheeks and her hair in pigtails. At the sight of her, Bing screamed and took an unsteady step back.

She was as pale as the marble statues guarding the entrance to the Graveyard of What Might Be, but she was flesh, not stone. Her mouth was open in a silent shout, a few frozen bubbles drifting from her lips. Her hands were raised, as if she were reaching up to him. In one was a bunch of red coiled rope—a jump rope, Bing recognized.

"It's a girl!" he cried. "It's a dead girl in the ice!"

"Not dead, Bing," Manx said. "Not yet. Maybe not for years." Manx flicked the flashlight away and pointed it toward a white stone cross, tilting up from the ice.

Lily Carter
15 Fox Road
Sharpsville, PA
1980–?
Turned to a life of sin by her mother,
Her childhood ended before it began.
If only there had been another
To take her off to Christmasland!

Manx swept his light around what Bing now perceived was a frozen lake, on which were ranked rows of crosses: a cemetery the size of Arlington. The snow skirled around the memorials, the plinths, the emptiness. In the moonlight the snowflakes looked like silver shavings.

Bing peered again at the girl at his feet. She stared up through the clouded ice—and blinked.

He screamed once more, stumbling away. The backs of his legs struck another cross, and he half spun, lost his footing, and went down on all fours.

He gazed through the dull ice. Manx turned his flashlight on the face of another child, a boy with sensitive, thoughtful eyes beneath pale bangs.

William Delman
42B Mattison Avenue

Asbury Park, NJ
1981–?
Billy only ever wanted to play,
But his father didn't stay.
His mother ran away.
Drugs, knives, grief, and dismay.
If only someone had saved the day!

Bing tried to get up, did a comical soft-shoe, went down again, a little to the left. The ray of Manx's flashlight showed him another child, an Asian girl, clutching a stuffed bear in a tweed jacket.

Sara Cho
1983–?
39 Fifth Street
Bangor, ME
Sara lives in a tragic dream,
Will hang herself by age thirteen!
But think how she will give such thanks,
If she goes for a ride with Charlie Manx!

Bing made a gobbling, gasping sound of horror. The girl, Sara Cho, stared up at him, mouth open in a silent cry. She had been buried in the ice with a clothesline twisted around her throat.

Charlie Manx caught Bing's elbow and helped him up.

"I'm sorry you had to see all this, Bing," Manx said. "I wish I could've spared you. But you needed to understand the reasons for my work. Come back to the car. I have a thermos of cocoa."

Mr. Manx helped Bing across the ice, his hand squeezing Bing's upper arm tightly to keep him from falling again.

They separated at the hood of the car, and Charlie went on to the driver's-side door, but Bing hesitated for an instant, noticing, for the first time, the hood ornament: a grinning lady fashioned from chrome, her arms spread so that her gown flowed back from her body like wings. He recognized her in a glance—she was identical to the angels of mercy who guarded the gate of the cemetery.

When they were in the car, Charlie Manx reached beneath his seat and came up with a silver thermos. He removed the cap, filled it with hot chocolate, and handed it over. Bing clasped it in both hands, sipping at that scalding sweetness, while Charlie Manx made a wide, sweeping turn away from the Graveyard of What Might Be. They accelerated back the way they had come.

"Tell me about Christmasland," Bing said in a shaking voice.

"It is the *best* place," Manx said. "With all due respect to Mr. Walt Disney, Christmasland is the *true* happiest place in the world. Although—from another point of view, I suppose you could say it is the happiest place *not* in this world. In Christmasland every day is Christmas, and the children there never feel anything like unhappiness. No, the children there don't even understand the *concept* of unhappiness! There is only fun. It is like heaven—only of course they are not dead! They live forever, remain children for eternity, and are never forced to struggle and sweat and demean themselves like us poor adults. I discovered this place of pure dream many years ago, and the first wee ones to take up residence there were my own children, who were saved before they could be destroyed by the pitiful, angry thing their mother became in her later years.

"It is, truly, a place where the impossible happens every day. But it is a place for children, not adults. Only a few grown-ups are allowed to live there. Only those who have shown devotion to a higher cause. Only those who are willing to sacrifice *everything* for the well-being and happiness of the tender little ones. People like you, Bing.

"I wish, with all my heart, that all the children in the world could find their way to Christmasland, where they would know safety and happiness beyond measure! Oh, boy, that would be something! But few adults would consent to send their children away with a man they have never met, to a place they cannot visit. Why, they would think me the most heinous sort of kidnapper and kiddie fiddler! So I bring only one or two children a year, and they are always children I have seen in the Graveyard of What Might Be, good children sure to suffer at the hands of their own parents. As a man who was hurt terribly as a child himself, *you* understand, I'm sure, how important it is to help them! The graveyard shows me children who will, if I do nothing, have their childhoods *stolen* by their mothers and fathers. They will be hit with chains, fed cat food, sold to perverts. Their souls will turn to ice, and they will become cold, unfeeling people, sure to destroy children themselves. We are their one chance, Bing! In my years as the keeper of Christmasland, I have saved some seventy children, and it is my feverish wish to save a hundred more before I am done."

The car rushed through the cold, cavernous dark. Bing moved his lips, counting to himself.

"Seventy," he murmured. "I thought you only rescue one child a year. Maybe two."

"Yes," Manx said. "That is about right."

"But . . . how old are you?" Bing asked.

Manx grinned sidelong at him—revealing that crowded mouthful of sharp brown teeth. "My work keeps me young. Finish your cocoa, Bing."

Bing swallowed the last hot, sugary mouthful, then swirled the remnants. There was a milky yellow residue there. He wondered if he had just swallowed something else from the medicine cabinet of Dewey Hansom, a name that sounded like a joke or a name in a limerick. Dewey Hansom, Charlie Manx's pre-Bing thing, who had saved ten children and gone to his eternal reward in Christmasland. If Charlie Manx had saved seventy kids, then there had been—what? *Seven* pre-Bing things? The lucky dogs.

He heard a rumbling: the crash, rattle, and twelve-cylinder whine of a big truck coming up behind them. He looked back—the sound was rising in volume with each passing moment—but could see nothing.

"Do you hear that?" Bing asked, unaware that the empty lid of the thermos had slipped from his suddenly tingling fingers. "Do you hear something coming?"

"That would be the morning," Manx said. "Pulling up on us fast. Don't look now, Bing, here it comes!"

That truck roar built and built, and suddenly it was pulling by them on Bing's left. Bing looked out into the night and could see the side of a big panel truck quite clearly, only a foot or two away. Painted on the side was a green field, a red farmhouse, a scattering of cows, and a bright smiling sun coming up over the hills. The rays of that rising sun lit foot-high lettering: SUNRISE DELIVERY.

For an instant the truck obscured the land and sky, and SUNRISE DELIVERY filled Bing's entire visual field. Then it rolled rattling on, dragging a rooster tail of dust, and Bing flinched from an almost painfully blue morning sky, a sky without cloud, without limit, and squinted into

The Pennsylvania Countryside

Charlie Manx rolled the Wraith to the side of the road and put it into park. Cracked, sandy, country road. Yellowing weeds growing right up to the side of the car. Insect hum. Glare of a low sun. It could not be much later than seven in the morning, but already Bing could feel the fierce heat of the day coming through the windshield.

"Wowser!" Bing said. "What happened?"

"The sun came up," Manx said mildly.

"I've been asleep?" Bing asked.

"I think, really, Bing, you've been awake. Maybe for the first time in your life."

Manx smiled, and Bing blushed and offered up an uncertain smile in return. He didn't always understand Charles Manx, but that only made the man easier to adore, to worship.

Dragonflies floated in the high weeds. Bing didn't recognize where they were. It wasn't Sugarcreek. Some back lane somewhere. When he looked out his passenger window, in the hazy golden light, he saw a Colonial with black shutters on a hill. A girl in a crimson, shiftlike flower-print dress stood in the dirt driveway, under a locust tree, staring down at them. In one hand she held a jump rope, but she wasn't leaping, wasn't using it, was just studying them in a quizzical sort of way. Bing supposed she hadn't ever seen a Rolls-Royce before.

He narrowed his eyes, staring back at her, lifting one hand in a little wave. She didn't wave back, only tipped her head to the side, studying them. Her pigtails dropped toward her right shoulder, and that was when he recognized her. He jumped in surprise and banged a knee on the underside of the dash.

"Her!" he cried. "It's her!"

"Who, Bing?" Charlie Manx asked, in a knowing sort of voice.

Bing stared at her, and she stared right back. He could not have been more shocked if he had seen the dead rise. In a way he *had* just seen the dead rise.

"Lily Carter," Bing recited. Bing had always had a good mind for scraps of verse. " 'Turned to a life of sin by her mother, her childhood ended before it began. If only there had been another to take her off to . . .' " His voice trailed away as a screen door creaked open on the porch and a dainty, fine-boned woman in a flour-dashed apron stuck her head out.

"Lily!" cried the woman. "I said breakfast ten minutes ago. Get in here!"

Lily Carter did not reply but only began to back slowly up the driveway, her eyes large and fascinated. Not afraid. Just . . . interested.

"That would be Lily's mother," Manx said. "I have made a study of little Lily Carter and her mother. Her mother works nights tending bar in a roadhouse near here. You know about women who work in bars."

"What about them?" Bing asked.

"Whores," Manx said. "Almost all of them. At least until their looks go, and in the case of Lily Carter's mother they're going fast. Then, I'm afraid, she will quit being a whore and turn to being a pimp. Her *daughter's* pimp. Someone has to earn the bacon, and Evangeline Carter doesn't have a husband. Never married. Probably doesn't even know who knocked her up. Oh, little Lily is only eight now, but girls . . . girls grow up so much faster than boys. Why, look at what a perfect little lady she is. I am sure her mother will be able to command a high price for her child's innocence!"

"How do you know?" Bing whispered. "How do you know all that will really happen? Are you . . . are you *sure*?"

Charlie Manx raised an eyebrow. "There's only one way to find out. To stand aside and leave Lily in the care of her mother. Perhaps we should check back on her in a few years, see how much her mother will charge us for a turn with her. Maybe she will offer us a two-for-one special!"

Lily had backed all the way to the porch.

From inside, her mother shouted again, her voice hoarse, angry. It sounded to Bing Partridge very like the voice of a drunk with a hangover. A grating, ignorant voice.

"Lily! Get in here right now or I'm givin' your eggs to the damn dog!"

"Bitch," Bing Partridge whispered.

"I am inclined to agree, Bing," Manx said. "When the daughter comes with me to Christmasland, the mother will have to be dealt with as well. It would be better, really, if the mother and the daughter disappeared together. I'd rather not take Ms. Carter with me to Christmasland, but perhaps *you* could find some use for her. Although I can think of only one use to which she is really suited. In any event, it is no matter to me. Her mother simply cannot be seen again. And, when you consider what she will do to her daughter someday, if left to her own devices . . . well, I won't shed any tears for her!"

Bing's heart beat rapidly and lightly behind his breastbone. His mouth was dry. He fumbled for the latch.

Charlie Manx seized his arm, just as he had done when he was helping Bing across the ice in the Graveyard of What Might Be.

"Where are you going, Bing?" Charlie asked.

Bing turned a wild look upon the man beside him. "What are we waiting for? Let's go in there. Let's go in right now and save the girl!"

"No," Charlie said. "Not now. There are preparations to make. Our moment will come, soon enough."

Bing stared at Charlie Manx with wonder . . . and a certain degree of reverence.

"Oh," Charlie Manx said. "And, *Bing*. Mothers can put up an awful racket when they think their daughters are being taken from them, even very *wicked* mothers like Ms. Carter."

Bing nodded.

"Do you think you could get us some sevoflurane from your place of employment?" Manx said. "You might want to bring your gun and your gasmask, too. I am sure they will come in handy."

THE LIBRARIAN
1991

Haverhill, Massachusetts

HER MOTHER HAD SAID, *DON'T YOU WALK OUT THAT DOOR,* BUT VIC wasn't walking, she was running, fighting tears the whole way. Before she got outside, she heard her father say to Linda, *Oh, lay off, she feels bad enough,* which made it worse, not better. Vic caught her bike by the handlebars and ran with it, and at the far edge of the backyard she threw her leg over and plunged down into the cool, sweet-smelling shade of the Pittman Street Woods.

Vic did not think about where she was going. Her body just knew, guiding the Raleigh down the steep pitch of the hill and hitting the dirt track at the bottom at nearly thirty miles an hour.

She went to the river. The river was there. So was the bridge.

This time the thing that had been lost was a photograph, a creased black-and-white snap of a chubby boy in a ten-gallon hat, holding hands with a young woman in a polka-dot dress. The woman was using her free hand to pin the dress down against her thighs; the wind was blowing, trying to lift the hem. That same breeze had tossed a few strands of pale hair across her cocky, wry, almost-pretty features. The boy pointed a toy pistol into the camera. This puffy, blank-eyed little gunslinger was Christopher McQueen, age seven. The woman was his mother, and at the time the photograph was taken she was already dying of the ovarian cancer that would end her life at the ripe age of thirty-three. The picture was the only thing he had left of her, and when Vic asked if she could take it to school to use for an art project, Linda had been against it. Chris McQueen, though, overruled his wife. Chris had said, *Hey. I* want *Vic to draw her. Closest they'll ever come to spending time together. Just bring it back, Brat. I don't ever want to forget what she looked like.*

At thirteen Vic was the star of her seventh-grade art class with Mr. Ellis. He had selected her watercolor, *Covered Bridge,* for the annual school show at Town Hall—where it was the *only* seventh-grade work included among a selection of eighth-grade paintings that varied from bad to worse. (Bad: innumerable pictures of misshapen fruit in warped bowls. Worse: a portrait of a leaping unicorn with a rainbow erupting from its ass, as if in a Technicolor burst of flatulence.) When the *Haverhill Gazette* ran a story about the show, guess which picture they chose to run alongside the article? Not the unicorn. After *Covered Bridge* came home, Vic's father shelled out for a birch frame and hung it on the wall where Vic's *Knight Rider* poster had once been displayed. Vic had gotten rid of the Hoff years ago. The Hoff was a loser, and Trans Ams were oil-leaking shitboxes. She didn't miss him.

Their last assignment that year was "life drawing," and they were asked to work from a photograph that was special to them. Vic's father had room over the desk in his study for a painting, and Vic very much wanted him to be able to look up and see his mother—in color.

The painting was done now, had come home the day before, on the last day of school, after Vic emptied out her locker. And if this final watercolor wasn't as good as *Covered Bridge,* Vic still thought she had caught something of the woman in the photograph: the hint of bony hips beneath the dress, a quality of weariness and distraction in her smile. Her father had gazed at it for a long time, looking both pleased and a little sad. When Vic asked what he thought, he only said, "You smile just like her, Brat. I never noticed."

The painting had come home—but the photo hadn't. Vic didn't

know she didn't have it until her mother started asking about it on Friday afternoon. First Vic thought it was in her backpack, then in her bedroom. By Friday night, however, she had come to the stomach-churning realization that she didn't have it and didn't have any idea when she had last seen it. By Saturday morning—the first glorious day of summer vacation—Vic's mother had come to the same conclusion, had decided that the snap was gone forever, and in a state bordering on hysteria had said that the photograph was a lot more important than any shitty junior high painting. And then Vic was on the move, had to get away, get out, afraid if she stood still she would become a little hysterical herself: an emotion she couldn't bear to feel.

Her chest hurt, as if she had been biking for hours, not minutes, and her breath was strangled, as if she were fighting her way uphill, not gliding along level ground. But when she saw the bridge, she felt something like peace. No. Better than peace: She felt her whole conscious mind disengaging, decoupling from the rest of her, leaving only the body and the bike to do their work. It had always been this way. She had crossed the bridge almost a dozen times in five years, and always it was less like an *experience,* more like a *sensation.* It was not a thing she *did,* it was a thing she *felt:* a dreamy awareness of gliding, a distant sense of static roaring. It was not unlike the feel of sinking into a doze, easing herself into the envelope of sleep.

And even as her tires began to bump across the wooden planks, she was already mentally writing the *true* story of how she found the photograph. She had shown the picture to her friend Willa on the last day of school. They got talking about other things, and then Vic had to run to make her bus. She was gone by the time Willa realized she still had the photograph, so her friend simply held on to it to give it back later. When Vic arrived home from her bike ride, she would have the photo in hand and a story to tell, and her father would hug her and say he was never worried about it, and her mother would look like she wanted to spit. Vic could not have said which reaction she was looking forward to more.

Only it was different this time. *This* time when she came back, there was one person she couldn't convince, when she told her true-but-not-really story about where the photo had been. That person was Vic herself.

Vic came out the other end of the tunnel and sailed into the wide, dark hallway on the second floor of the Cooperative School. At not quite nine in the morning on the first day of summer vacation, it was a dim, echoing space, so empty it was a little frightening. She touched the brake, and the bike whined shrilly to a stop.

She had to look back. She couldn't help it. No one could've resisted looking back.

The Shorter Way Bridge came right through the brick wall, extending ten feet into the hall, as wide as the great corridor itself. Was part of it outside as well, hanging over the parking lot? Vic didn't think so, but without breaking into one of the classrooms, she couldn't look out a window and check. Ivy smothered the entrance of the bridge, hung in limp green sheaves.

The sight of the Shorter Way made her mildly ill, and for a moment the school hallway around her bulged, like a drop of water fattening on a twig. She felt faint, knew if she didn't get moving she might start to think, and *thinking* would be bad news. It was one thing to fantasize trips across a long-gone covered bridge when she was eight or nine and another when she was thirteen. At nine it was a daydream. At thirteen it was a delusion.

She had known she was coming here (it had said so in green paint, on the other end of the bridge) but had imagined she would come out on the first floor, close to Mr. Ellis's art room. Instead she had been dumped on the second, a dozen feet from her locker. She'd been talking to friends when she emptied it the day before. There had been a lot of distraction and noise—shouts, laughter, kids running by—but still she'd looked her locker over thoroughly before shutting the door for a last time and was sure, *quite* sure, she had emptied it. Still: The bridge had brought her here, and the bridge was never wrong.

There is no bridge, she thought. *Willa had the photograph. She was planning to give it back to me as soon as she saw me.*

Vic leaned her bike against the lockers, opened the door to her own, and looked in at the beige walls and the rusted floor. Nothing. She patted the shelf, a half a foot above her head. Nothing there either.

Her insides were bunching up with worry. She wanted to have it already, wanted to be out of here, so she could start forgetting about the bridge as soon as possible. But if it wasn't in the locker, then she didn't know where to look next. She started to shut the door—then paused, raised herself up on tiptoes, and ran her hand over the top shelf again. Even then she almost missed it. Somehow one corner of the photograph had snagged on the back of the shelf, so it was standing up and pressed flat to the rear wall. She had to reach all the way back to touch it, had to reach to the very limit of how far she could stretch her arm to catch hold of it.

She pried at it with her fingernails, wiggling it this way and that, and it came loose. She dropped down onto her heels, flushing with pleasure.

"Yes!" she said, and clanged the locker door shut.

The janitor stood halfway up the hall. Mr. Eugley. He stood with his mop plunged into his big yellow rolling bucket, staring along the length of the corridor at Vic, and Vic's bike, and the Shorter Way Bridge.

Mr. Eugley was old and hunched and, with his gold-rimmed glasses and bow ties, looked more like a teacher than many of the teachers did. He worked as a crossing guard, too, and on the day before Easter vacation he had little bags of jelly beans for every kid who walked past him. Rumor was that Mr. Eugley had taken the job to be around children, because his kids had died in a house fire years and years ago. Sadly, this rumor was true, and it omitted the fact that Mr. Eugley had started the fire himself while passed out drunk with a cigarette burning in one hand. He had Jesus instead of children now and a favorite AA meeting instead of a bar. He had gotten religion and sobriety both while in jail.

Vic looked at him. He looked back, his mouth opening and closing like a goldfish's. His legs trembled violently.

"You're the McQueen girl," he said in a strong Down East accent that obliterated *r*'s: *Yah the McQueen gill.* His breathing was strained, and he had a hand on his throat. "What's that in the wall? By Jesus, am I goin' crazy? That looks like the Shortaway Bridge, what I haven't seen in years." He coughed, once and then again. It was a wet, strange, choked sound, and there was something terrifying about it. It was the sound of a man in gathering physical distress.

How old was he? Vic thought, *Ninety.* She was off by almost twenty years, but seventy-one was still old enough for a heart attack.

"It's all right," Vic said. "Don't—" she began, but then didn't know how to continue. Don't what? Don't start screaming? Don't die?

"Oh, dear," he said. "Oh, dear." Only he said it *de-ah.* Two syllables. His right hand shook furiously as he raised it to cover his eyes. His lips began to move. "Deah, deah me. 'The Lord is my shepherd. I shall not want.'"

"Mr. Eugley—" Vic tried again.

"Go away!" he shrieked. "Just go away and take your bridge *with* you! This isn't *happening*! You aren't here!"

He kept his hand over his eyes. His lips began to move again. Vic couldn't hear him but could see from the way he shaped the words what he was saying. "*'He maketh me to lie down in green pastures. He leadeth me beside the still waters.'*"

Vic turned her bike around. She put a foot over. She began to work the pedals. Her *own* legs felt none too steady, but in a moment she thudded up onto the bridge, into the hissing darkness and the smell of bats.

She looked back once, halfway across. Mr. Eugley was still there, head ducked in prayer, hand over his eyes, other hand clutching the mop to his side.

Vic rode on, photo in one sweaty palm, out of the bridge and into the drifting, lively shadows of the Pittman Street Woods. She knew, even before she looked back over her shoulder—knew just from the musical chuckle of the river below and the graceful sweep of the wind in the pines—that the Shorter Way was gone.

She pedaled on, into the first day of summer, her pulse knocking strangely. A bone-deep ache of foreboding rode all the way back with her.

The McQueen House

VIC WAS HEADED OUT OF THE HOUSE TWO DAYS LATER TO RIDE HER bike over to Willa's—last chance to see her BFF before Vic and her parents took off for six weeks on Lake Winnipesaukee—when she heard her mother in the kitchen, saying something about Mr. Eugley. The sound of his name produced a sudden, almost crippling feeling of weakness, and Vic nearly had to sit down. She had spent the weekend not thinking about Mr. Eugley with a vengeance, something that hadn't been hard to do; Vic had been down all Saturday night with a migraine headache so intense it made her want to throw up. The pain had been especially fierce behind her left eye. The eye had felt like it was going to pop.

She climbed back up the front steps and stood outside the kitchen, listening to her mother bullshit with one of her friends, Vic wasn't sure which one. She stood there eavesdropping to her mother's side of the phone conversation for close to five minutes, but Linda didn't mention Mr. Eugley by name again. She said, *Oh, that's too bad,* and *Poor man,* but she didn't use the name.

At last Vic heard Linda drop the phone back into the cradle. This was followed by the clatter and slop of dishes in the sink.

Vic didn't want to know. She dreaded knowing. At the same time: She couldn't help herself. It was that simple.

"Mom?" she asked, putting her head around the corner. "Did you say something about Mr. Eugley?"

"Hm?" Linda asked. She bent over the sink, her back to Vic. Pots clashed. A single soap bubble quivered, popped. "Oh, yeah. He fell off the wagon. Got picked up last night, out in front of the school, shouting at it like a madman. He's been sober thirty years. Ever since . . . well, ever since he decided he didn't want to be a drunk anymore. Poor guy. Dottie Evans told me he was down at church this morning, sobbing like a little kid, saying he's going to quit his job. Saying he can't ever go back. Embarrassed, I guess." Linda glanced at Vic, and her brow furrowed with concern. "You okay, Vicki? You still don't look too good. Maybe you ought to stay in this morning."

"No," Vic said, her voice odd and hollow, as if coming from inside a box. "I want to get out. Get some fresh air." She hesitated, then said, "I hope he doesn't quit. He's a really nice guy."

"He is. And he loves all you kids. But people get old, Vic, and they need looking after. The parts wear out. Body *and* mind."

Riding into the town woods was going out of her way—there was a far more direct route to Willa's house through Bradbury Park—but no sooner had Vic climbed onto her bike than she decided she needed to ride around a bit, do a little thinking before seeing anyone.

A part of her felt that it was a bad idea to let herself think about what she had done, what she *could* do, the unlikely, bewildering gift that was hers alone. But that dog was loose now, and it would take a while to corner it and get it on the leash again. She had daydreamed a hole in the world and ridden her bike through it, and it was crazy. Only a crazy person would imagine that such a thing was possible—except Mr. Eugley had *seen* her. Mr. Eugley had seen, and it had broken something inside him. It had kicked the legs out from under his sobriety and made him afraid to return to school, to the place where he had worked for more than a decade. A place he had been happy. Mr. Eugley—poor old broken Mr. Eugley—was proof that the Shorter Way was real.

She didn't want proof. She wanted not to know about it.

Failing that, she wished there were someone she could talk to who would tell her she was all right, that she was not a lunatic. She wanted to find someone who could *explain,* make sense of a bridge that only existed when she needed it and always took her where she needed to go.

She dropped over the side of the hill and into a pocket of cool, rushing air.

That was not all she wanted. She wanted to find the bridge itself, to see it again. She felt clear in her head and certain of herself, firmly placed in the moment. She was conscious of every jolt and shudder as the Raleigh banged over roots and stones. She knew the difference between fantasy and reality, and she kept this difference clear in her head, and she believed that when she reached the old dirt road, the Shorter Way Bridge would not be there—

Only it was.

"You aren't real," she said to the bridge, unconsciously echoing Mr. Eugley. "You fell in the river when I was eight."

The bridge obstinately remained.

She braked to a stop and looked at it, a safe twenty feet away. The Merrimack churned beneath it.

"Help me find someone who can tell me I'm not crazy," she said to it, and put her feet on the pedals and rode slowly toward it.

As she approached the entrance, she saw the old, familiar green spray paint on the wall to her left.

HERE →

That was a funny place to point her toward, she thought. Wasn't she *already* here?

All the other times she had gone across the Shorter Way, she had ridden in a kind of trance, turning the pedals automatically and thoughtlessly, just another working part of the machine, along with the gears and the chain.

This time she forced herself to go slow and to look around, even though everything in her wanted to get out of the bridge as soon as she was in it. She fought it, the overriding impulse to hurry, to ride as if the bridge were collapsing behind her. She wanted to fix the details of the place in her mind. She half believed that if she really looked at the Shorter Way Bridge, looked at it *intently*, it would melt away around her.

And then what? Where would she be if the bridge blinked out of existence? It didn't matter. The bridge persisted, no matter how hard she stared at it. The wood was old and worn and splintery-looking. The nails in the walls were caked with rust. She felt the floorboards sink under the weight of the bike. The Shorter Way would not be willed into nothingness.

She was aware, as always, of the white noise. She could feel the thunderous roar of it in her *teeth*. She could *see* it, could see the storm of static through the cracks in the tilted walls.

Vic did not quite dare stop her bike, get off and touch the walls, walk around. She believed that if she got off her bike, she would never get back on. Some part of her felt that the existence of the bridge depended utterly on forward motion and not thinking too much.

The bridge buckled and stiffened and buckled again. Dust trickled from the rafters. Had she seen a pigeon fly up there once?

She lifted her head and looked and saw that the ceiling was carpeted in bats, their wings closed around the small, furry nubs of their bodies. They were in constant subtle movement, wiggling about, rearranging their wings. A few turned their faces to peer nearsightedly down upon her.

Each of these bats was identical, and each had Vic's own face. All their faces were shrunken and shriveled and pink, but she knew herself. They were her except for the eyes, which glittered redly, like drops of blood. At the sight of them, she felt a fine silver needle of pain slide through her left eyeball and into her brain. She could hear their high, piping, nearly subsonic cries above the hiss and pop of the static flurry.

She couldn't bear it. She wanted to scream, but she knew if she did, the bats would let go of the roof and swarm around her and that would be the end of her. She shut her eyes and threw her whole self into pedaling to the far end of the bridge. Something was shaking furiously. She could not tell if it was the bridge, the bike, or herself.

With her eyes closed, she did not know she had reached the other end of the bridge until she felt the front tire thump over the sill. She felt a blast of heat and light—she had not once looked to see where she was going—and heard a shout: *Watch out!* She opened her eyes just as the bike hit a low cement curb in

Here, Iowa

AND SHE SPILLED ONTO THE SIDEWALK, SANDPAPERING HER RIGHT knee.

Vic rolled onto her back, grabbing her leg.

"Ow," she said. "Ow *ow* **OW** ow."

Her voice running up and down through several octaves, like an instrumentalist practicing scales.

"Oh, kittens. Are you all right?" came a voice from somewhere in the glare of midday sunshine. "You sh-should really be more careful jumping out of thin air like that."

Vic squinted into the light and was able to make out a scrawny girl not much older than herself—she was perhaps twenty—with a fedora tipped back on her fluorescent purple hair. She wore a necklace made out of beer-can pull tabs and a pair of Scrabble-tile earrings; her feet were stuck into Chuck Taylor Converse high-tops, no laces. She looked like Sam Spade, if Sam Spade had been a girl and had a weekend gig fronting a ska band.

"I'm okay. Just scraped myself," Vic said, but the girl had already quit listening. She was staring back at the Shorter Way.

"You know, I've always *wanted* a bridge there," the girl said. "Couldn'ta dropped it in a better s-spot."

Vic raised herself up onto her elbows and looked back at the bridge, which now spanned a wide, noisy rush of brown water. This river was almost as wide as the Merrimack, although the banks were far lower. Stands of birch and century-old oaks massed along the water's edge, which was just a couple feet below the sandy, crumbling embankment.

"Is that what it did? My bridge *dropped*? Like, out of the sky?"

The girl continued to stare at it. She had the sort of unblinking, stuporous stare that Vic associated with pot and a fondness for Phish. "*Mmm*-no. It was more like watching a Polaroid develop. Have you ever s-s-*ssseen* a Polaroid develop?"

Vic nodded, thinking of the way the brown chemical square slowly went pale, details swimming into place, colors brightening steadily, objects taking shape.

"Your bridge faded in where there were a couple old oaks. Goodbye, oaks."

"I think your trees will come back when I go," Vic said—although with a moment to consider it she had to admit to herself she had no idea if this were true. It *felt* true, but she couldn't attest to it as fact. "You don't seem very surprised about my bridge showing up out of nowhere." Remembering Mr. Eugley, how he had trembled and covered his eyes and screamed for her to go away.

"I was watching for you. I didn't know you were going to make *sss*such an ass-kicking entrance, but I also knew you might not sssss—" And without any warning at all, the girl in the hat stopped talking, midsentence. Her lips were parted to say the next word, but no word would come, and a look of strain came across her face, as if she were trying to lift something heavy: a piano or a car. Her eyes protruded. Her cheeks colored. She forced herself to exhale and then just as abruptly continued. "—get here like a normal person. Excuse me, I have a ss-*ss*-ss*stammer*."

"You were *watching* for me?"

The girl nodded but was considering the bridge again. In a slow, dreamy voice, she said, "Your bridge . . . it doesn't go to the other side of the Cedar River, does it?"

"No."

"So where does it go?"

"Haverhill."

"Is that here in Iowa?"

"No. Massachusetts."

"Oh, boy, you've come a long way. You're in the Corn Belt now. You're in the land where everything is flat except the ladies." For a moment Vic was pretty sure she saw the girl leer.

"Excuse me, but . . . can we go back to the part where you said you were *watching* for me?"

"Well, *duh*! I've been expecting you for *months*. I didn't think you'd *ever* sh-show up. You're the Brat, aren't you?"

Vic opened her mouth, but nothing would come.

Her silence was answer enough, and her surprise clearly pleased the other girl, who smiled and tucked some of her fluorescent hair back behind one ear. With her upturned nose and slightly pointed ears, there was something elvish about her. Although that was possibly a side effect of the setting: They were on a grassy hill, in the shade of leafy oaks, between the river and a big building that from the back had the look of a cathedral or a college hall, a fortress of cement and granite with white spires and narrow slots for windows, perfect for shooting arrows through.

"I thought you'd be a boy. I was expecting the kind of kid who won't eat lettuce and picks his nose. How do you feel about lettuce?"

"Not a fan."

She squeezed her little hands into tight fists and shook them over her head. "Knew it!" Then she lowered her fists and frowned. "Big nose picker?"

"Blow it, don't show it," Vic said. "Did you say this is Iowa?"

"Sure did!"

"Where in Iowa?"

"Here," said the girl in the hat.

"Well," Vic started, feeling a flash of annoyance, "I mean, yeah, I know, but, like—here *where*?"

"Here, *Iowa*. That's the name of the town. You're right down the road from beautiful Cedar Rapids, at the Here Public Library. And I know all about why you came. You're confused about your bridge, and you're trying to figure things out. Boy, is *this* your lucky day!" She clapped her hands. "You found yourself a librarian! I can help with the figuring-out thing and point you toward some good poetry while I'm at it. It's what I do."

The Library

THE GIRL THUMBED BACK HER OLD-TIMEY FEDORA AND SAID, "I'M Margaret. Just like *Are You There God? It's Me, Margaret,* only I hate when people call me that."

"Margaret?"

"No. God. I've got a big enough ego as it is." She grinned. "Margaret Leigh. You can just call me Maggie. If we go inside and I get you a Band-Aid and a cup of tea, do you think your bridge will stay?"

"Yes. I think so."

"Okay. Cool. I *hope* your bridge doesn't disappear on you. I'm sure we could get you home without it—we could hold a fund-raiser or s-s-something—but it might be better if you went back the way you came. Just so you don't have to explain to your parents how you wound up in Iowa. I mean, it wouldn't be *too* bad if you had to ss-*ss*-ssstay awhile! I have a bed down in Romantic Poetry. I crash here some nights. But you could bunk there and I could camp out with my uncle in his trailer, at least until we raise your bus fare."

"Romantic Poetry?"

"Shelves 821-point-2 through 821-point-6. I'm not supposed to suh-ss-sleep in the library, but Ms. Howard lets me get away with it if it's only now and then. She pities me, because I'm an orphan and kind of weird. That's okay. I don't mind. People make out like it's a terrible thing to be pitied, but I say, Hey! I get to sleep in a library and read books all night! Without pity, where would I be? I'm a total pity s-s-ss*slut.*"

She took Vic's upper arm and helped her to her feet. She bent and collected the bicycle and leaned it against a bench. "You don't have to lock it up. I don't think anyone in this town is imaginative enough to think of s-s-stealing something."

Vic followed her up the path, through a sliver of wooded park, to the rear of the great stone temple of books. The library was built into the side of the hill, so it was possible to walk through a heavy iron door into what Vic guessed would be a basement. Maggie turned a key hanging from the lock and pushed the door inward, and Vic did not hesitate to enter. It didn't cross her mind to mistrust Maggie, to wonder if this older girl might be leading her into a dark cellar with thick stone walls, where no one would be able to hear her scream. Vic instinctively understood that a girl who wore Scrabble tiles as earrings and called herself a pity slut did not present much in the way of threat. Besides, Vic had wanted to find someone who could tell her if she was crazy, not someone who *was* crazy. There was no reason to be afraid of Maggie, unless Vic thought the Shortaway could willfully lead her wrong, and on some level Vic knew that it couldn't.

The room on the other side of the iron door was ten degrees cooler than the parkland outside. Vic smelled the vast vault filled with books before she saw it, because her eyes required time to adjust to the cavernous dark. She breathed deeply of the scent of decaying fiction, disintegrating history, and forgotten verse, and she observed for the first time that a room full of books smelled like dessert: a sweet snack made of figs, vanilla, glue, and cleverness. The iron door settled shut behind them, the weight of it clanging heavily against the frame.

Maggie said, "If books were girls, and reading was s-ss-ssss—fucking, this would be the biggest whorehouse in the county and I'd be the most ruthless pimp you ever met. Whap the girls on the butts and send them off to their tricks as fast and often as I can."

Vic laughed, then clapped a hand over her mouth, remembering that librarians hated noise.

Maggie led her through the dim labyrinth of the stacks, along narrow corridors with walls of high shelves.

"If you ever have to escape in a hurry," Maggie said, "like, if you were on the run from the cops, just remember: Stay to your right and keep going down the steps. Fastest way out."

"You think I'll have to escape the Here Public Library in a hurry?"

"Not today," Maggie said. "What's your name? People must call you something besides the Brat."

"Victoria. Vic. The only person who ever calls me the Brat is my father. It's just his joke. How come you know my nickname but not my name? And what did you mean, you were *expecting* me? How could you be expecting me? *I* didn't even know I was coming to see you until about ten minutes ago."

"Right. I can help with all that. Let me s-stanch your bleeding first, and then we'll have questions and answers."

"I think answers are more important than my knee," Vic said. She hesitated then, and with a feeling of unaccustomed shyness said, "I scared someone with my bridge. A nice old guy back home. I might've really messed up his life."

Maggie looked across at her, eyes shining brightly in the darkness of the stacks. She gave Vic a careful once-over, then said, "That's not a very bratty thing to s-say. I've got doubts about this nickname of yours." The corners of her mouth moved in the smallest of smiles. "If you upset someone, I doubt you meant it. And I doubt you did any lasting damage. People have pretty rubbery brains. They can take quite a bit of bouncing around. Come on. Band-Aids and tea. And answers. They're all right this way."

They emerged from the stacks into a cool, stone-floored, open area, a sort of shabby office. It was, Vic thought, an office for a private investigator in a black-and-white movie, not a librarian with a punk haircut. It had the five essential props for any PI's home base: a gunmetal gray desk, an out-of-date pinup-girl calendar, a coatrack, a sink with rust stains in it—and a snub-nosed .38 in the center of the desk, holding down some papers. There was also a fish tank, a big one, filling a five-foot-long socket in one wall.

Maggie removed her gray fedora and tossed it at the coatrack. In the soft light from the fish tank, her metallic purple hair glowed, a thousand burning neon filaments. While Maggie filled an electric teakettle, Vic wandered to the desk to inspect the revolver, which turned out to be a bronze paperweight with an inscription on the smooth grip: PROPERTY A. CHEKHOV.

Maggie returned with Band-Aids and motioned for Vic to get up on the edge of the desk. Vic sat where Maggie pointed and put her feet on the worn wooden chair. The act of bending her legs brought the stinging sensation in her knee back to the forefront of her mind. With it came a deep, nasty throb of pain in her left eyeball. It was a feeling like the eye was caught between the steel prongs of some surgical instrument and being squeezed. She rubbed at it with her palm.

Maggie touched a cold, damp washcloth to Vic's knee, cleaning grit out of the scrape. She had lit a cigarette at some point, and the smoke was sweet and agreeable; Maggie worked on Vic's leg with the quiet efficiency of a mechanic checking the oil.

Vic took a long, measuring look at the big fish tank set into the wall. It was the size of a coffin. A lone golden koi, with long whiskers that lent him a wise appearance, hovered listlessly in the tank. Vic had to look twice before her eyes could make visual sense of what was on the bottom of the tank: not a bed of rocks but a tumble of white Scrabble tiles, hundreds of them, but only four letters: F I S H.

Through the wavering, green-tinted distortion of the tank, Vic could see what lay on the other side: a carpeted children's library. About a dozen kids and their mothers were gathered in a loose semicircle around a woman in a neat tweed skirt, who sat in a chair that was too small for her and who was holding up a board book so the little guys could look at the pictures. She was reading to them, although Vic could not hear her through the stone wall, over the bubbling of the air handler in the fish tank.

"You're just in time for story hour," Maggie said. "Ss-story hour is the best hour of the day. It's the only hour I care about."

"I like your fish tank."

"It's a whore to clean," Maggie said, and Vic had to squeeze her lips together to keep from shouting with laughter.

Maggie grinned, and the dimples reappeared. She was, in her chubby-cheeked, bright-eyed way, more or less adorable. Like a punk-rock Keebler elf.

"I'm the one who put the Scrabble tiles in there. I'm kind of nuts for the game. Now twice a month I've got to haul them out and run them in the wash. It's a bigger pain in the ass than rectal cancer. Do you like Scrabble?"

Vic glanced at Maggie's earrings again and noticed for the first time that one was the letter F and the other was the letter U.

"I've never played it. I like your earrings, though," Vic said. "You ever get in trouble for them?"

"Nah. No one looks too closely at a librarian. People are afraid of going blind from the glare of *ssss*-ssso much compressed wisdom. Check it out: I'm twenty years old, and I'm one of the top five SS-Scrabble players in the whole state. I guess that might say more about Iowa than it says about me." She pasted the Band-Aid over Vic's scrape and patted it. "All better."

Maggie crunched out her cigarette in a tin can half filled with sand and slipped away to pour the tea. She returned a moment later with a pair of chipped cups. One said LIBRARIES: WHERE *SHHH* HAPPENS. The other said DO ***NOT*** MAKE ME USE MY LIBRARIAN VOICE. When Vic took her mug, Maggie leaned around her to open the drawer. It was the drawer where a PI would've kept his bottle of hooch. Maggie came up with an old purple faux-velvet bag with the word SCRABBLE stamped into it in fading gold letters.

"You asked me how I knew about you. How I knew you were coming. *SSS-SS-SSS*—" Her cheeks began to color with strain.

"Scrabble? It has something to do with Scrabble?"

Maggie nodded. "Thanks for finishing my sentence for me. A lot of people who *sss*-stammer *hate* that, when people finish their *sss*-sentences. But as we've already established, I enjoy being an object of pity."

Vic felt heat rise into her face, although there was nothing sarcastic in Maggie's tone. Somehow that made it worse. "Sorry."

Maggie appeared not to hear. She planted herself in a straight-backed chair next to the desk.

"You came across the bridge on that bike of yours," Maggie said. "Can you get to the covered bridge *without* it?"

Vic shook her head.

Maggie nodded. "No. You use your bike to daydream the bridge into existence. And then you use your bridge to find things, right? Things you need? Like, no matter how far away they are, the thing you need is always right on the other s-ss-side of the bridge?"

"Yeah. *Yeah.* Only I don't know why I can do it, or *how,* and sometimes I feel like I'm only *imagining* all my trips across the bridge. Sometimes I feel like I'm going crazy."

"You're not crazy. You're creative! You're a *s-ss-ss*-strong creative. Me, too. You've got your bike, and I've got my letter tiles. When I was twelve, I saw an old *SS-Suh*-Scrabble game in a garage sale, going for a dollar. It was on display, the first word already played. When I saw it, I knew I was *s-ss-suh—had* to have it. I needed to have it. I would've paid anything for it, and if it wasn't for sale, I woulda grabbed it and run. Just being *close* to this Scrabble board for the first time threw a kind of shimmy into reality. An electric train turned itself on and ran right off its tracks. A car alarm went off down the road. There was a TV playing inside the garage, and when I saw the SSS-Suh-*Scrabble* set, it went crazy. It started blasting s-ss-suh—"

"Static," Vic said, forgetting the promise she had made to herself only a moment before, not to finish any of Maggie's sentences for her, no matter how badly she stammered.

Maggie didn't seem to mind. "Yes."

"I get something like that," Vic said. "When I'm crossing the bridge, I hear static all around me."

Maggie nodded, as if she found this the least surprising thing in the world. "A few minutes ago, all the lights blinked off in here. The power died in the whole library. That's how I knew you were getting close. Your bridge is a short circuit in reality. Just like my tiles. You *find* things, and my tiles *spell* me things. They told me you'd be coming today and I could find you out back. They told me the Brat would ride across the bridge. They've been chattering about you for months."

"Can you show me?" Vic asked.

"I think I need to. I think that's part of why you're here. Maybe my tiles have a thing they want to spell for *you*."

She undid the drawstring, reached into the sack and took some tiles out, dropped them clattering onto the desk.

Vic twisted around to look at them, but they were just a mess of letters. "Does that say something to you?"

"Not yet." Maggie bent to the letters and began to push them around with her pinkie.

"It *will* say something?"

Maggie nodded.

"Because they're magic?"

"I don't think there's anything magic about them. They wouldn't work for anyone else. The tiles are just my knife. *Suh-s*-something I can use to poke a hole in reality. I think it always has to be a thing you love. I always loved words, and Scrabble gave me a way to play with them. Put me in a Scrabble tournament, someone is going to walk away with their ego all slashed up."

She had by now shuffled the letters around to spell THE BRAT HAD LUNCH TO RIDE F T W T.

"What's F-T-W-T mean?" Vic asked, turning her head to see the tiles upside down.

"Not a damn thing. I haven't figured it out yet," Maggie said, frowning and moving the tiles around some more.

Vic sipped at her tea. It was hot and sweet, but no sooner had she swallowed than she felt a chill sweat prickle on her brow. Those imaginary forceps, clenching her left eyeball, tightened a little.

"Everyone lives in two worlds," Maggie said, speaking in an absentminded sort of way while she studied her letters. "There's the *real* world, with all its annoying facts and rules. In the *real* world, there are things that are true and things that aren't. Mostly the real world s-s-s-suh-*sucks.* But everyone also lives in the world inside their own head. An *inscape,* a world of thought. In a world made of thought—in an inscape—*every* idea is a fact. Emotions are as real as gravity. Dreams are as powerful as history. Creative people, like writers, and Henry Rollins, spend a lot of their time hanging out in their thoughtworld. *S-s-strong* creatives, though, can use a knife to cut the stitches *between* the two worlds, can bring them together. Your bike. My tiles. Those are our knives."

She bent her head once more and shifted the tiles around in a decisive way. Now they read, THE BRAT FOUND HER CHILD A RICH TWIT.

"I don't know any rich twits," Vic said.

"You also look a little young to be with child," Maggie said. "This is a hard one. I wish I had another *essss-s-s.*"

"So my bridge *is* imaginary."

"Not when you're on your bike. Then it's real. It's an inscape pulled into the normal world."

"But your Scrabble bag. That's just a bag. It's not *really* like my bike. It doesn't do anything obviously imposs—"

But as Vic spoke, Maggie took up her bag, unlaced the strings, and shoved her hand in. Tiles scraped, clattered, and clicked, as if she were pushing her hand down into a bucket of them. Her wrist, elbow, and upper arm followed. The bag was perhaps six inches deep, but in a moment Maggie's arm had disappeared into it up to the shoulder, without so much as putting a bulge in the fake velvet. Vic heard her digging deeper and deeper, into what sounded like *thousands* of tiles.

"Aaa!" Vic cried.

On the other side of the fish tank, the librarian reading to the children glanced around.

"Big old hole in reality," Maggie said. It now looked as if her left arm had been removed at the shoulder, and the amputation was, for some reason, capped by a Scrabble bag. "I'm reaching into my inscape to get the tiles I need. Not into a bag. When I say your bike or my tiles are a knife to open a s-s-slit in reality, I'm not being, like, metaphorical."

The nauseating pressure rose in Vic's left eye.

"Can you take your arm out of the bag, please?" Vic asked.

With her free hand, Maggie tugged on the purple velvet sack, and her arm slithered out. She set the bag on the table, and Vic heard tiles clink within it.

"Creepy. I know," Maggie said.

"How can you *do* that?" Vic asked.

Maggie drew a deep breath, almost a sigh. "Why can some people s-s-speak a dozen foreign languages? Why can Pelé do the over-his-head bicycle kick? You get what you get, I reckon. Not one person in a million is good-looking enough, talented enough, and lucky enough to be a movie s-s-star. Not one person in a million knew as much about words as a poet like Gerard Manley Hopkins did. He knew about inscapes! He came up with the term. S-some people are movie stars, some people are soccer stars, and you're a suh-s-strong creative. It's a little weird, but so is being born with mismatched eyes. And we're not the only ones. There are others like us. I've met them. The tiles pointed me toward them." Maggie bent to her letters again and began to push them here and there. "Like, there was a girl I met once who had a wheelchair, a beautiful old thing with whitewall tires. She could use it to make herself disappear. All she had to do was wheel her chair backward, into what she called the Crooked Alley. That was *her* inscape. She could wheel herself into that alley and out of existence, but s-s-ss-*still* see what was happening in our world. There isn't a culture on earth that doesn't have stories about people like you and me, people who use totems to throw a kink into reality. The Navajo . . ." But her voice was sinking in volume, dying away.

Vic saw a look of unhappy understanding cross Maggie's face. She was staring at her tiles. Vic leaned forward and looked down at them. She just had time to read them before Maggie's hand shot out and swept them away.

THE BRAT COULD FIND THE WRAITH

"What's that mean? What's the Wraith?"

Maggie gave Vic a bright-eyed look that seemed one part fright, and one part apology. "Oh, kittens," Maggie said.

"Is that something you lost?"

"No."

"Something you want me to find, though? What is it? I could help you—"

"No. *No.* Vic, I want you to promise me you *aren't* going to go find him."

"It's a guy?"

"It's *trouble.* It's the worst trouble you can imagine. You're, like, what? Twelve?"

"Thirteen."

"Okay. S-s-s-ss-suh-*suh*—" Maggie got stuck there, couldn't go on. She drew a deep, unsteady breath, pulled her lower lip into her mouth, and bit down, sank her teeth into her own lip with a savagery that almost made Vic cry out. Maggie exhaled and went on, without any trace of a stammer at all: "So promise."

"But why would your Scrabble bag want you to know I could find him? Why would it *say* that?"

Maggie shook her head. "That's not how it works. The tiles don't *want* anything, just like a *knife* doesn't want anything. I can use the tiles to get at facts that are out of reach, the way you might use a letter opener to open your mail. And this—*this*—is like getting a letter with a bomb inside. It's a way to blow your own little self up." Maggie sucked on her lower lip, moving her tongue back and forth over it.

"But why shouldn't I find him? You said yourself that maybe I was here so your tiles could tell me something. Why would they bring this Wraith guy up if I'm not supposed to go looking for him?"

But before Maggie could reply, Vic bent forward and pressed a hand to her left eye. The psychic forceps were squeezing so hard the eye felt ready to burst. She couldn't help it, made a soft moan of pain.

"You look terrible. What's wrong?"

"My eye. It gets bad like this when I go across the bridge. Maybe it's because I've been sitting with you for a while. Normally my trips are quick." Between her eye and Maggie's lip, it was turning out to be a damaging conversation for the both of them.

Maggie said, "The girl I told you about? With the wheelchair? When she first began using her wheelchair, she was healthy. It was her grandmother's, and she just liked playing with it. But if she stayed too long in Crooked Alley, her legs went numb. By the time I met her, she was entirely paralyzed from the waist down. These things, they *cost* to use. Keeping the bridge in place could be costing you right now. You oughta only use the bridge s-s-sparingly."

Vic said, "What does using your tiles cost you?"

"I'll let you in on a secret: I didn't always s-s-s-s-suh-suh-suh-*stammer*!" And she smiled again, with her visibly bloodied mouth.

It took Vic a moment to figure out that this time Maggie had been putting her stammer on.

"Come on," Maggie said. "We should get you back. We sit here much longer, your head will explode."

"Better tell me about the Wraith, then, or you're going to get brains all over your desk. I'm not leaving till you do."

Maggie opened the drawer, dropped her Scrabble bag into it, and then slammed it with unnecessary force. When she spoke, for the first time her voice lacked any trace of friendliness.

"Don't be a goddamn—" She hesitated, either at a loss for words or stuck on one.

"Brat?" Vic asked. "Starting to fit my nickname a little better now, huh?"

Maggie exhaled slowly, her nostrils flaring. "I'm not fooling, Vic. The Wraith is s-s-someone you need to stay away from. Not everyone who can do the things we can do is nice. I don't know much about the Wraith except he's an old man with an old car. And the car is *his* knife. Only he uses his knife to cut throats. He takes children for rides in his car, and it *does* something to them. He uses them up—like a vampire—to stay alive. He drives them into his own inscape, a bad place he dreamed up, and he leaves them there. When they get out of the car, they aren't children anymore. They aren't even human. They're creatures that could only live in the cold s-s-space of the Wraith's imagination."

"How do you know this?"

"The tiles. They began telling me about the Wraith a couple years ago, after he grabbed a kid from L.A. He was working out on the West Coast back then, but things changed and he moved his attention east. Did you see the ss-s-story about the little Russian girl who disappeared from Boston? Just a few weeks ago? Vanished with her mother?"

Vic had. In her neck of the woods, it had been the lead news story for several days. Vic's mother watched every report with a kind of horror-struck fascination; the missing girl was Vic's own age, dark-haired, bony, with an awkward but attractive smile. A cute geek. *Do you think she's dead?* Vic's mother had asked Chris McQueen, and Vic's father had replied, *If she's lucky*.

"The Gregorski girl," Vic said.

"Right. A limo driver went to her hotel to pick her up, but someone knocked him out and grabbed Marta Gregorski and her mother. That was *him*. That was the Wraith. He drained the Gregorski girl and then dumped her with all the other children he's used up, in some fantasy world of his own. An inscape no one would ever want to visit. Like your bridge, only bigger. *Much* bigger."

"What about the mother? Did he drain her, too?"

"I don't think he can feed off adults. Only children. He's got s-ss-someone who works with him, like a Renfield, who helps him with the kidnappings and takes the grown-ups off his hands. You know Renfield?"

"Dracula's henchman or something?"

"Close enough. I know that the Wraith is very old and he's had a bunch of Renfields. He tells them lies, fills them up with illusions, maybe persuades them they're *heroes,* not kidnappers. In the end he always s-suh-*sacrifices* them. That's how they're of the most use to him. When his crimes are uncovered, he can shift the blame onto one of his handpicked dumb-asses. He's been taking children for a long time, and he's good at hiding in the shadows. I've put together all kinds of details about the Wraith, but I haven't been able to learn anything about him that would really help me identify him."

"Why can't you just ask the tiles what his name is?"

Maggie blinked and then, in a tone that seemed to mix sadness with a certain bemusement, said, "It's the rules. No proper names allowed in S-S-Scrabble. That's why my tiles told me to expect the Brat instead of Vic."

"If I found him, found out his name or what he looked like," Vic said, "could we stop him then?"

Maggie slapped one palm down on the desktop, so hard that the teacups jumped. Her eyes were furious—and scared.

"Oh, gee, Vic! Aren't you even *listening* to me? If you found him, you could get *dead,* and then it would be my fault! You think I want that on my conscience?"

"But what about all the kids he'll take if we *don't* do anything? Isn't that also sending children to their . . ." Vic let her voice trail off at the look on Maggie's face.

Maggie's features were pained and sick. But she reached out, got a tissue from a box of Kleenex, and offered it to Vic.

"Your left eye," she said, and held up the dampened cloth. "You're crying, Vic. Come on. We need to get you back. *Now.*"

Vic did not argue when Maggie took her hand and guided her out of the library, and down the path, under the shade of the oaks.

A hummingbird drank nectar from glass bulbs hanging in one of the trees, its wings whirring like small motors. Dragonflies rose on the thermal currents, their wings shining like gold in the mid-western sun.

The Raleigh was where they had left it, leaned against a bench. Beyond was a single-lane asphalt road that circled around the back of the library, and then the grassy margin above the river. And the bridge.

Vic reached for her handlebars, but before she could take them, Maggie squeezed her wrist.

"Is it safe for you to go in there? Feeling like you do?"

"Nothing bad has ever happened before," Vic said.

"That's not a very reassuring way to ph-ph-phrase things. Do we have an agreement about the Wraith? You're too young to go looking for him."

"Okay," Vic said, righting her bike, putting a leg over. "I'm too young."

But even as she said it, she was thinking about the Raleigh, re-membering the first time she'd seen it. The dealer had said it was too big for her, and her father agreed, told her maybe when she was older. Then, three weeks later, on her birthday, there it was in the driveway. *Well,* her father had said. *You're older now, ain'tcha?*

"How will I know you made it across the bridge?" Maggie said.

"I always make it," Vic said. The sunlight was a steel pin, pushing back into Vic's left eyeball. The world blurred. Maggie Leigh split into twins for a moment; when she came back together again, she was offering Vic a sheet of paper, folded into quarters.

"Here," Maggie said. "Anything I didn't cover about inscapes and why you can do what you can do is explained here, by an expert on the subject."

Vic nodded and put it in her pocket.

"Oh!" Maggie called. She tugged at one earlobe, then the other, and then pushed something into Vic's hand.

"What are these?" Vic asked, looking into her palm at the Scrabble-tile earrings.

"Armor," Maggie said. "Also a concise *s-s-stuh-*stammerer's guide for dealing with the world. The next time someone disappoints you, put these on. You'll feel tougher. That's the Maggie Leigh guarantee."

"Thank you, Maggie. For everything."

"'S what I'm here for. Fount of knowledge—that's me. Come back to be s-s-sprinkled with my wisdom anytime."

Vic nodded again, didn't feel she could bear to say anything else. The sound of her own voice threatened to bust her head open, like a lightbulb under a high heel. So instead she reached out and squeezed Maggie's hand. Maggie squeezed back.

Vic leaned forward, bearing down on the pedals, and rode into darkness and the annihilating roar of static.

Haverhill, Massachusetts

The next thing she was clear on was walking up the hill, through the Pittman Street Woods, her insides feeling bruised and her face fevery hot. Vic weaved, unsteady on her legs, coming up out of the trees and into her yard.

She could not see out of her left eye. It felt as if it had been removed with a spoon. The side of her face was sticky; for all she knew, the eye had popped like a grape and was running down her cheek.

Vic walked into one of her swings, knocking it out of her way with a rattle of rusty chains.

Her father had his Harley out in the driveway, was wiping it down with a chamois. When he heard the clatter of the swings, he glanced up—and dropped the chamois, his mouth opening as if to cry out in shock.

"Holy fuck," he said. "Vic, are you all right? What *happened*?"

"I was on my Raleigh," she said. She felt this explained all.

"Where is your bike?" he asked, and looked past her, down the road, as if it might be lying in the yard.

It was the first Vic realized she wasn't pushing it. She didn't know what had happened to it. She remembered hitting the bridge wall, halfway across, and falling off the bike, remembered the bats going *shree-shree* in the dark and flying into her, striking her with soft, felty impacts. She began to shiver uncontrollably.

"I was knocked off," she said.

"Knocked off? Did someone hit you with their car?" Chris McQueen took her in his arms. "Jesus Christ, Vic, you've got blood all over you. *Lin!*"

Then it was like the other times, her father lifting her and carrying her to her bedroom, her mother rushing to them, then hurrying away to get water and Tylenol.

Only it was not like the other times, because Vic was delirious for twenty-four hours, with a temperature that climbed to 102. David Hasselhoff kept coming into her bedroom, pennies where his eyes belonged and his hands in black leather gloves, and he would grab her by a leg and ankle and try to drag her out of the house, out to his car, which was not K.I.T.T. at all. She fought him, screamed and fought and struck at him, and David Hasselhoff spoke in her father's voice and said it was all right, try to sleep, try not to worry, that he loved her—but his face was blank with hate, and the car's engine was running, and she knew it was the Wraith.

Other times she was aware that she was shouting for her Raleigh. "Where's my bike?" she shouted, while someone held her shoulders. "Where is it? I need it, I *need* it! I can't *find* without my bike!" And someone was kissing her face and shushing her. Someone was crying. It sounded awfully like her mother.

She wet the bed. Several times.

On her second day home, she wandered into the front yard naked and was out there for five minutes, wandering around, looking for her bike, until Mr. de Zoet, the old man across the street, spotted her, and ran to her with a blanket. He wrapped her up and carried her to her house. It had been a long time since she had gone across the street to help Mr. de Zoet paint his tin soldiers and listen to his old records, and in the intervening years she had come to think of him as a cranky old

Nazi busybody who once called the cops on her parents, when Chris and Linda were having a loud argument. Now, though, she remembered that she liked him, liked his smell of fresh coffee and his funny Austrian accent. He had told her she was good at painting once. He had told her she could be an artist.

"The bats are stirred up now," Vic told Mr. de Zoet in a confidential tone of voice as he handed her to her mother. "Poor little things. I think some of them flew out of the bridge and can't find their way home."

She slept during the day, then lay awake half the night, her heartbeat too fast, afraid of things that made no sense. If a car drove by the house and its headlights swept the ceiling, she would sometimes have to cram her knuckles into her mouth to keep from screaming. The sound of a car door slamming in the street was as terrible as a gunshot.

On her third night in bed, she came out of a drifting fugue state to the sound of her parents talking in the next room.

"When I tell her I couldn't find it, she's going to be fuckin' heartbroken. She loved that bike," her father said.

"I'm glad she's done with it," said her mother. "The best thing to come out of this is that she'll never ride it again."

Her father uttered a burst of harsh laughter. "That's tender."

"Did you hear some of the things she was saying about her bike the day she came home? About riding it to find death? That's what I think she was doing in her mind, when she was really sick. Riding her bike away from us and off into . . . whatever. Heaven. The afterlife. She scared the shit out of me with all that talk, Chris. I never want to see the goddamned thing again."

Her father was silent for a moment, then said, "I still think we should've reported a hit-and-run."

"You don't get a fever like that from a hit-and-run."

"So she was already sick. You said she went to bed early the night before. That she looked pale. Hell, maybe that was part of it. Maybe she had a touch of fever and pedaled into traffic. I'll never forget what she looked like coming into the driveway, blood leaking from one eye like she was weeping . . ." His voice trailed off. When he spoke again, his tone was different, challenging and not entirely kind. *"What?"*

"I just . . . don't know why she already had a Band-Aid on her left knee." The TV babbled for a while. Then her mother said, "We'll get her a ten-speed. Time for a new bike anyway."

"It'll be pink," Vic whispered to herself. "Any money says she'll buy something pink."

On some level Vic knew that the loss of the Tuff Burner was the end of something wonderful, that she had pushed too hard and lost the best thing in her life. It was her knife, and a part of her already understood that another bike would, in all likelihood, not be able to cut a hole through reality and back to the Shorter Way Bridge.

Vic slid her hand down between the mattress and the wall, and reached beneath her bed, and found the earrings and the folded piece of paper. She had possessed the presence of mind to hide them the afternoon she came home, and they had been under the bed ever since.

In a flash of psychological insight, uncommon for a girl of thirteen, Vic saw that soon enough she would recall all of her trips across the bridge as the fantasies of a very imaginative child and nothing more. Things that had been real—Maggie Leigh, Pete at Terry's Primo Subs, finding Mr. Pentack at Fenway Bowling—would eventually feel like nothing more than daydreams. Without her bike to take her on occasional trips across the Shorter Way, it would be impossible to maintain her belief in a covered bridge that flicked in and out of existence. Without the Raleigh, the last and only proof of her finding trips were the earrings cupped in her palm and a folded photocopied poem by Gerard Manley Hopkins.

F U, the earrings said. Five points.

"Why can't you come up to the lake with us?" Vic's mother was saying through the wall—the sound of a whine creeping into her voice. Linda and Chris had moved on to the subject of getting out of town for the summer, something Vic's mother wanted more than ever, in the aftermath of Vic's illness. "What could you have to do down here?"

"My job. You want me to spend three weeks up on Lake Winnipesaukee, get ready to stay in a tent. The goddamn place you have to have is eighteen hundred bucks a month."

"Is three weeks with Vic all by myself supposed to be a *vacation*? Three weeks of solo parenting, while you stay here to work three days a week and do whatever else you do when I call the job and the guys tell me you're out with the surveyor. You and him must've surveyed every inch of New England by now."

Her father said something else, in a low, ugly tone that Vic couldn't catch, and then he turned the volume up on the TV, cranking it loud enough that Mr. de Zoet across the street could probably hear it. A door slammed hard enough to make glasses rattle in the kitchen.

Vic put on her new earrings and unfolded the poem, a sonnet that she did not understand at all and already loved. She read it by the light of the partially open door, whispering the lines to herself, reciting it as if it were a kind of prayer—it *was* a kind of prayer—and soon her thoughts had left her unhappy parents far behind.

As kingfishers catch fire, dragonflies dráw fláme

As kingfishers catch fire, dragonflies dráw fláme;
As tumbled over rim in roundy wells
Stones ring; like each tucked string tells, each hung bell's
Bow swung finds tongue to fling out broad its name;
Each mortal thing does one thing and the same:
Deals out that being indoors each one dwells;
Selves—goes itself; myself *it speaks and spells,*
Crying Whát I do is me: for that I came.

Í say móre: the just man justices;
Kéeps gráce: thát keeps all his goings graces;
Acts in God's eye what in God's eye he is—
Christ—for Christ plays in ten thousand places,
Lovely in limbs, and lovely in eyes not his
To the Father through the features of men's faces.

—Gerard Manley Hopkins

DISAPPEARANCES 1991–1996

Various Locales

The Russian girl whom Maggie Leigh had mentioned was named Marta Gregorski, and in Vic's neck of the woods her abduction was indeed big news for several weeks. This was partly because Marta was a minor celebrity in the world of chess, mentored by Kasparov and ranked a grandmaster by the age of twelve. Also, though, in those first days after the fall of the USSR, the world was still adjusting to the new Russian freedoms, and there was a feeling that the disappearance of Marta Gregorski and her mother should've been the stuff of an international incident, an excuse for another Cold War showdown. It took a while to realize that the former Soviet republic was too busy disintegrating to even take notice. Boris Yeltsin was riding around on tanks, shouting until he was red in the face. Former KGB agents were scrambling to find good-paying jobs with the Russian mafia. It was weeks before anyone thought to denounce the decadent, crime-ridden West, and the denouncing wasn't very enthusiastic at that.

A clerk working the front desk of the Hilton DoubleTree on the Charles River had seen Marta and her mother exit through the revolving door a little before six on a warm, drizzly evening. The Gregorskis were expected at Harvard for a dinner and were meeting their car. Through the rain-smeared window, the clerk saw Marta and then her mother climb into a black vehicle. She thought the car had running boards because she saw the little Russian girl take a step up before sliding into the back. But it was dark out and the clerk was on the phone with a guest who was pissed he couldn't open his mini-fridge, and she hadn't noticed more.

Only one thing was certain: The Gregorski women had not climbed into the *right* car, the town car that had been rented for them. Their driver, a sixty-two-year-old named Roger Sillman, was parked on the far side of the turnaround, in no condition to pick them up. He was out cold and would remain parked there, sleeping behind the wheel, until he came to at nearly midnight. He felt sick and hungover but assumed he had simply (and uncharacteristically) nodded off and that the girls had caught a cab. He did not begin to wonder if something more had happened until the next morning and did not contact the police until he was unable to reach the Gregorskis at their hotel.

Sillman was interviewed by the FBI ten times in ten weeks, but his story never changed and he was never able to provide any information of value. He said he had been listening to sports radio, with time to kill—he was forty minutes early on his pickup—when a knuckle rapped on his window. Someone squat, in a black coat, standing in the rain. Sillman had rolled down the glass and then—

Nothing. Just: nothing. The night melted away, like a snowflake on the tip of his tongue.

Sillman had daughters of his own—and granddaughters—and it ate him alive to imagine Marta and her mother in the hands of some sick Ted Bundy–Charles Manson fuck who would screw them till they were both dead. He couldn't sleep, had bad dreams about the little girl playing chess with her mother's severed fingers. He strained and strained with all his will to remember something, anything. But only one other detail would come.

"Gingerbread," he sighed to a pock-scarred federal investigator who was named Peace but looked more like War.

"Gingerbread?"

Sillman looked at his interrogator with hopeless eyes. "I think while I was passed out, I dreamed about my mom's gingerbread cookies. Maybe the guy who knocked on the glass was eatin' one."

"Mm," said Peace-not-War. "Well. That's helpful. We'll put an APB out on the Gingerbread Man. I'm not hopeful it'll do us much good, though. Word on the street is you can't catch him."

In November 1991, a fourteen-year-old boy named Rory McCombers, a freshman at the Gilman School in Baltimore, met a Rolls-Royce in his dorm's parking lot. He was on his way to the airport, was joining his family in Key West for Thanksgiving break, and believed that the car had been sent for him by his father.

In fact, the driver that Rory's father had sent for him was passed out in his limo, half a mile away. Hank Tulowitzki had stopped at a Night Owl to gas up and use the bathroom, but he could remember nothing at all after topping off his tank. He woke up at one in the morning in the trunk of his own car, which was parked a few hundred feet down the road from the Night Owl in a public lot. He'd been kicking and screaming for most of five hours before an early-morning jogger heard him and summoned the police.

A Baltimore pedophile later confessed to the crime and described in pornographic detail the way he had molested Rory before strangling him to death. But he claimed not to remember where he had buried the body, and the rest of the evidence didn't fit; not only did he not have access to a Rolls-Royce, he didn't have a valid driver's license. By the time the cops decided the kiddie fiddler was a dead end—just a perv who got off on describing the sexual assault of a minor, someone who confessed to things out of boredom—there were new abductions to work on and the ground on the McCombers investigation was very cold.

Neither Rory's driver, Tulowitzki, or the Gregorskis' driver, Sillman, had his blood tested until more than a day after the abductions took place, and any lingering presence of sevoflurane in their bodies went undetected.

For all they had in common, the disappearance of Marta Gregorski and the kidnapping of Rory McCombers were never connected.

One other thing the two cases had in common: Neither child was seen again.

Haverhill

CHRIS McQUEEN TOOK OFF THE AUTUMN VIC BEGAN HIGH SCHOOL.

Her freshman year was already off to a rocky start. She was pulling straight C's, except for art. Her art teacher had put a comment on her quarterly summary, six hastily scrawled words—*"Victoria is gifted, needs to concentrate"*—and given her a B.

Vic drew her way through every study hall. She tattooed herself in Sharpie, to irritate her mother and impress boys. She had done a book report in comic-strip form, to the amusement of all the other kids who sat in the back of the class with her. Vic was getting an A-plus in entertaining the other burnouts. The Raleigh had been replaced by a Schwinn with silver-and-pink tassels on the handlebars. She didn't give a fuck about the Schwinn, never rode it. It embarrassed her.

When Vic walked in, home from an after-school detention, she found her mother on the ottoman in the living room, hunched over, her elbows on her knees, and her head in her hands. She had been crying . . . still was, water leaking from the corners of her bloodshot eyes. She was an ugly old woman when she wept.

"Mom? What happened?"

"Your father called. He isn't going to come home tonight."

"Mom?" Vic said, letting her backpack slide off her shoulder and fall to the floor. "What's that mean? Where's he going to be?"

"I don't know. I don't know where, and I don't know why."

Vic stared at her, incredulous. "What do you mean you don't know why?" Vic asked her. "He isn't coming home because of *you,* Mom. Because he can't stand *you.* Because all you ever do is *bitch* at him, stand there and *bitch* when he's tired and wants to be left alone."

"I've tried so hard. You don't know how hard I've tried to accommodate him. I can keep beer in the fridge and dinner warm when he gets home late. But I can't be twenty-four anymore, and that's what he really doesn't like about me. That's how old the last one was, you know." There was no anger in her voice. She sounded weary, that was all.

"What do you mean, 'the *last* one'?"

"The last girl he was sleeping with," Linda said. "I don't know who he's with now, though, or why he'd decide to take off with her. It's not as if I've ever put him in a position where he had to choose between home and the girl on the side. I don't know why this time is different. She must be some nice little piece."

When Vic spoke again, her voice was hushed and trembling. "You lie so bad. I hate you. I hate you, and if he's leaving, I'm going with him."

"But, *Vicki,*" said her mother in that strange, drifting tone of exhaustion. "He doesn't want you with him. He didn't just leave *me,* you know. He left *us.*"

Vic turned and fled, slamming the door shut behind her. She ran into the early-October afternoon. The light came at a low slant through the oaks across the street, gold and green, and how she loved that light. There was no light in the world like you saw in New England in early fall.

She was up and on her embarrassing pink bike, she was riding, crying but hardly aware of it, her breath coming in gasps, she was around the house and under the trees, she was riding downhill, the wind whining in her ears. The ten-speed was no Raleigh Tuff Burner, and she felt every rock and root under its slim tires.

Vic told herself she was going to find him, she would go to him now, he loved her and if she wanted to stay with him, her father would find a place for her, and she would never come home, never have to listen to her mother bitch at her about wearing black jeans, dressing like a boy, hanging with burnouts, she just had to ride down the hill and the bridge would be there.

But it wasn't. The old dirt road ended at the guardrail overlooking the Merrimack River. Upriver, the water was as black and smooth as smoked glass. Below, it was in torment, shattering against boulders in a white froth. All that remained of the Shorter Way were three stained concrete pylons rising from the water, crumbling at the top to show the rebar.

She rode hard at the guardrail, willing the bridge to appear. But just before she hit the rail, she dumped her bike on purpose, skidded across the dirt in her jeans. She did not wait to see if she had hurt herself but leaped up, gripped the bike in both hands, and flung it over the side. It hit the long slope of the embankment, bounced, and crashed into the shallows, where it got stuck. One wheel protruded from the water, revolving madly.

Bats dived in the gathering dusk.

Vic limped north, following the river, with no clear destination in mind.

Finally, on an embankment by the river, under 495, she dropped into bristly grass, among litter. There was a stitch in her side. Cars whined and hummed above her, producing a vast, shivery harmonic on the massive bridge spanning the Merrimack. She could *feel* their passage, a steady, curiously soothing vibration in the earth beneath her.

She didn't mean to go to sleep there, but for a while—twenty minutes or so—Vic dozed, carried into a state of dreamy semiconsciousness by the thunderous roar of motorcycles, blasting past in twos and threes, a whole gang of riders out in the last warm night of the fall, going wherever their wheels took them.

Various Locales

It was raining hard in Chesapeake, Virginia, on the evening of May 9, 1993, when Jeff Haddon took his springer spaniel for the usual after-dinner walk. Neither of them wanted to be out, not Haddon, not his dog, Garbo. The rain was coming down so hard on Battlefield Boulevard that it was bouncing off the concrete sidewalks and the cobblestone driveways. The air smelled fragrantly of sage and holly. Jeff wore a big yellow poncho, and the wind snatched at it and rattled it furiously. Garbo spread her back legs and squatted miserably to pee, her curly fur hanging in wet tangles.

Haddon and Garbo's walk took them past the sprawling Tudor home of Nancy Lee Martin, a wealthy widow with a nine-year-old daughter. Later he told the investigators with Chesapeake PD that he glanced up her driveway because he heard Christmas music, but that wasn't quite the truth. He didn't hear Christmas music then, not over the pounding roar of the rain on the road, but he always walked past her house and always looked up her driveway, because Haddon had a bit of a crush on Nancy Lee Martin. At forty-two she was ten years older than him but still looked much like the Virginia Tech cheerleader she had once been.

He peered up the lane just in time to see Nancy coming out the front door, with her daughter, Amy, racing ahead of her. A tall man in a black overcoat held an umbrella for her; the girls had on slinky dresses and silk scarves, and Jeff Haddon remembered his wife saying that Nancy Lee was going to a fund-raiser for George Allen, who had just announced he was running for governor.

Haddon, who owned a Mercedes dealership and who had an eye for cars, recognized her ride as an early Rolls-Royce, the Phantom or the Wraith, something from the thirties.

He called out and lifted a hand in greeting. Nancy Lee Martin might've waved back, he wasn't sure. As her driver opened the door, music flooded out, and Haddon could've sworn he heard the strains of "Little Drummer Boy," sung by a choir. That was an odd thing to hear in the spring. Maybe even Nancy Lee thought it odd—she seemed to hesitate before climbing in. But it was raining hard, and she didn't hesitate long.

Haddon walked on, and when he returned, the car was gone. Nancy Lee Martin and her daughter, Amy, never arrived at the George Allen fund-raiser.

The driver who had been scheduled to pick her up, Malcolm Ackroyd, vanished as well. His car was found off Bainbridge Boulevard, down by the water, the driver's-side door open. His hat was found in the weeds, saturated with blood.

In late May of 1994, it was Jake Christensen of Buffalo, New York, ten years old and traveling alone, flying in from Philadelphia, where he attended boarding school. A driver had been sent to meet him, but this man, Bill Black, suffered a fatal heart attack in the parking garage and was found dead behind the wheel of his stretch limo. Who met Jake at the airport—who drove him away—was never determined.

The autopsy revealed that Bill Black's heart had failed after absorbing near-lethal doses of a gas called sevoflurane; it was a favorite of dentists. A faceful would switch off a person's awareness of pain and make him highly suggestible—a zombie, in other words. Sevoflurane wasn't so easy to get—you needed a license to practice medicine or dentistry to obtain it—and it seemed a promising lead, but statewide interviews with oral surgeons and the people they employed went exactly nowhere.

In 1995 it was Steve Conlon and his twelve-year-old daughter, Charlie (Charlene, actually, but Charlie to her friends), on their way to a father-daughter dance in Plattsburgh, New York. They ordered a stretch limo, but it was a Rolls-Royce that turned up in their driveway instead. Charlie's mother, Agatha, kissed her daughter on the forehead before she left, told her to have fun, and never laid eyes on her again.

She saw her husband, though. His body was found, bullet through the left eye, behind some bushes, in a rest area off Interstate 87. Agatha had no trouble identifying the body, in spite of the damage to his face.

Months later, in the fall, the phone rang in the Conlon house, a little after two-thirty in the morning, and Agatha, only half awake, answered. She heard a hiss and crackle, as of a long-distance connection being made, and then several children began to sing "The First Noel," their high, sweet voices quivering with laughter. Agatha believed she heard her daughter's voice among them and began to scream her name: "Charlie, Charlie, where are you?" But her daughter did not reply, and in another moment the children hung up on her.

The phone company, however, said no call had been made to her house at that time, and the police wrote it off as the late-night fantasy of a distraught woman.

Around fifty-eight thousand nonfamily child abductions occur each year in America, and in the early nineties the disappearances of Marta Gregorski, Rory McCombers, Amy Martin, Jake Christensen, Charlene Conlon, and the adults who vanished with them—with few witnesses, in different states, under various conditions—were not connected until much later. Not until well after what happened to Vic McQueen at the hands of Charles Talent Manx III.

Haverhill

IN LATE MARCH OF VIC'S SENIOR YEAR, HER MOTHER WALKED IN ON her and Craig Harrison in Vic's bedroom at one in the morning. It wasn't like Linda caught them screwing, or even kissing, but Craig had a bottle of Bacardi and Vic was pretty drunk.

Craig left with a shrug and a smile—*G'night, Mrs. McQueen, sorry we woke you*—and the next morning Vic took off for her Saturday shift at Taco Bell without speaking to her mother. She wasn't looking forward to getting home and certainly wasn't ready for what was waiting when she did.

Linda sat on Vic's bed, which was neatly made up with fresh linens and a plumped-up pillow, just like a bed in a hotel. The only thing missing was the mint.

Everything else was gone: Vic's sketchbook, Vic's books, Vic's computer. There were a couple of things on the desk, but Vic didn't immediately register them. The sight of her cleaned-out room made her short of breath.

"What did you do?"

"You can earn your things back," Linda said, "as long as you stick to my new rules and my new curfew. I'll be driving you to school from now on, and work, and anywhere else you need to go."

"You had . . . you had no right . . ."

"I found some things in one of your drawers," her mother continued, as if Vic had not spoken. "I'd like to hear your explanation for them."

Linda nodded at the other side of the room. Vic turned her head, this time really taking in what was sitting on her desktop: a pack of cigarettes, an Altoids tin containing what looked like red and orange Valentine's Day candies, some sampler bottles of gin, and two banana-scented condoms in purple packages. One of the condom wrappers was torn open and empty.

Vic had bought the condoms from a vending machine at the Howard Johnson's and had torn one open to make a balloon character out of it, inflating the rubber and drawing a face on the side. She had dubbed this character Dickface and had amused the kids in third-period study hall with him, walking him across her desk while the teacher was out of the room. When Mr. Jaffey returned from the men's, the room smelled so strongly of bananas that he asked who had brought pie, which caused everyone to bust up.

Craig had left the cigarettes one night when he was over, and Vic had held on to them. She didn't smoke (yet), but she liked to tap a cigarette out of the packet and lie in bed smelling the sweet tobacco: Craig's smell.

The Ecstasy tablets were what Vic took to make it through the nights when she couldn't sleep, when her thoughts whirled shrieking through her head like a flock of crazed bats. Some nights she would close her eyes and would see the Shorter Way Bridge, a lopsided rectangle opening into darkness. She would *smell* it, the ammonia stink of bat piss, the odor of mildewed wood. A pair of headlamps would blink on in the dark, at the far end of the bridge: two circles of pale light set close together. Those headlights were bright and terrible, and sometimes she could still see them glowing before her, even when she opened her eyes. Those headlights made her feel like screaming.

A little X always smoothed things out. A little X made her feel like she was gliding, a breeze in her face. It put the world into a state of smooth, subtle motion, as if she were on the back of her father's motorcycle, banking into a turn. She didn't need to sleep when she was on Ecstasy, was too in love with the world to sleep. She would call her friends instead and tell them she loved them. She would stay up late and sketch tattoo designs to help her across the gap between girl next door and fuck-you-dead stripper. She wanted to get a motorcycle engine above her breasts, let the boys know what a great ride she was, and never mind that at seventeen she was, pathetically, almost the last virgin in her class.

The little gin samplers were nothing. The gin was just something she kept on hand to swallow Ecstasy.

"Think what you want," Vic said. "I don't give a fuck."

"I suppose I should be grateful you're at least using protection. You have a child out of wedlock, don't expect me to help you. I won't have anything to do with it. Or you."

What Vic wanted to tell her was that that was a pretty good argument for getting pregnant as soon as possible, but what came out was "I didn't sleep with him."

"Now you're lying. September fourth. I thought you slept over at Willa's. In your diary it says—"

"You looked in my fucking diary?"

"—you slept with Craig all night long for the first time ever. You think I don't know what that means?"

What it meant was that they had slept together—with their clothes on, under a comforter, on Willa's basement floor, with six other kids. But when she woke, he was spooned against her, one arm over her waist, breathing against the back of her neck, and she had thought, *Please don't wake up,* and had for a few moments been so happy she could hardly stand it.

"Yeah. It means we screwed, Mom," Vic said softly. "Because I was tired of sucking his cock. Nothing in it for me."

What little color was left in her mother's face drained out of it.

"I'm keeping your personal items locked up," she said. "I don't care if you are almost eighteen, you live under my roof, and you'll live by my rules. If you can follow the new program, then in a few months . . ."

"Is that what you did when Dad disappointed you? Locked up your pussy for a few months to see if he'd get with the program?"

"Believe me, if I had a chastity belt somewhere in the house, I'd have *you* wearing it," her mother said. "You dirty-mouthed little hooker."

Vic laughed, a wild, agonized sound.

"What an ugly person you are inside," she said, the most vicious thing she could think to say. "I'm out of here."

"If you leave, you'll find the door locked when you come back," her mother said, but Vic wasn't listening, was already on her way out the bedroom door.

Out in the Cold

SHE WALKED.

The rain was a fine sleet that soaked through her army-navy jacket and made her hair crunchy with ice.

Her father and his girlfriend lived in Durham, New Hampshire, and there was some way to get to them by using the MBTA—take the T to the North Station, then switch to Amtrak—but it was all a lot of money Vic didn't have.

She went to the T station anyway and hung around for a while, because it was out of the rain. She tried to think who she could call for train fare. Then she thought fuck it, she would just call her father and ask him to drive down and get her. She was honestly not sure why she hadn't thought of it before.

She had only been to see him once in the last year, and it had gone badly. Vic got into a fight with the girlfriend and threw the remote control at her, which by some wild chance had given her a black eye. Her father sent her back that evening, wasn't even interested in her side of the story. Vic had not talked to him since.

Chris McQueen answered on the second ring and said he'd accept the charges. He didn't sound happy about it, though. His voice rasped. The last time she'd seen him, there had been a lot of silver in his hair that hadn't been there a year ago. She had heard that men took younger lovers to stay young themselves. It wasn't working.

"Well," Vic said, and was suddenly struggling not to cry again. "Mom threw me out, just like she threw you out."

That wasn't how it happened, of course, but it felt like the right way to begin the conversation.

"Hey, Brat," he said. "Where are you? You okay? Your mom called and told me you left."

"I'm at this train station. I don't have any money. Can you come get me, Dad?"

"I can call you a cab. Mom will pay the fare when you get home."

"I can't go home."

"Vic. It would take me an hour to get there, and it's midnight. I have work tomorrow at five A.M. I'd be in bed already, but instead I've been sittin' by the phone worrying about you."

Vic heard a voice in the background, her father's girlfriend, Tiffany: "She's not coming here, Chrissy!"

"You need to work this out with your mother now," he said. "I can't go choosing sides, Vic. You know that."

"She is *not* coming here," Tiffany said again, her voice strident, angry.

"Will you tell that cunt to shut her fucking mouth?" Vic cried, almost screamed.

When her father spoke again, his voice was harder. "I will not. And considering you beat her up the last time you were here—"

"The fuck!"

"—and never apologized—"

"I never touched that brainless bitch."

"—okay. I'm going. This conversation is finished. You'n spend the fucking night in the rain as far as I'm concerned."

"You chose her over me," Vic said. "You *chose her.* Fuck you, Dad. Get your rest so you're ready to blow things up tomorrow. It's what you do best."

She hung up.

Vic wondered if she could sleep on a bench in the train station but by two in the morning knew she couldn't. It was too cold. She considered calling her mother collect, asking her to send a cab, but the thought of asking for her help was unbearable, so she walked

Home

SHE DID NOT EVEN TRY THE FRONT DOOR, BELIEVING THAT IT WOULD be bolted shut. Her own bedroom window was ten feet off the ground, not to mention locked. The windows out back were locked, too, as was the sliding glass door. But there was a basement window that wouldn't lock, wouldn't even close all the way. It had been open a quarter of an inch for six years.

Vic found a pair of rusting hedge shears and used them to slice away the screen, then pushed the window back and wiggled in through the long, wide slot.

The basement was a large, unfinished room with pipes running across the ceiling. The washer and dryer were at one end of the room, by the stairs, and the boiler was at the other end. The rest was a mess of boxes, garbage bags stuffed full of Vic's old clothes, and a tartan easy chair with a crappy framed watercolor of a covered bridge propped up on the seat. Vic vaguely remembered painting it back in junior high. It was ugly as fuck. No sense of perspective. She amused herself by using a Sharpie to draw a flock of flying pricks in the sky, then chucked it and pushed down the back of the easy chair so it almost made a bed. She found a change of clothes in the dryer. She wanted to dry her sneakers but knew that the *clunk-te-clunk* would bring her mother, so she just set them on the bottom step.

She found some puffy winter coats in a garbage bag, curled up in the chair, and pulled them over her. The chair wouldn't flatten all the way, and she didn't imagine she could sleep, kinked up like she was, but at some point she closed her eyes for a moment, and when she opened them, the sky was a slice of brilliant blue outside the long slot of the window.

What woke her was the sound of feet thumping overhead and her mother's agitated voice. She was on the phone in the kitchen. Vic could tell from the way she was pacing.

"I *did* call the police, Chris," she said. "They told me she'll come home when she's ready." And then she said, "No! No, they *won't,* because she's not a missing child. She's seventeen fucking years old, Chris. They won't even call her a runaway at seventeen."

Vic was about to climb out of her seat and go upstairs—and then she thought, *Fuck her. Fuck the both of them.* And eased back into the chair.

In the moment of decision, she knew it was the wrong thing to do, a terrible thing to do, to hide down here while her mother went out of her head with panic upstairs. But then it was a terrible thing to search your daughter's room, read her diary, take things she had paid for herself. And if Vic did a little Ecstasy now and then, that was her parents' fault, too, for getting divorced. It was her father's fault for hitting her mother. She knew now that he had done that. She had not forgotten seeing him rinsing his knuckles in the sink. Even if the mouthy, judgmental bitch did have it coming. Vic wished she had some X now. There was a tab of it in her backpack, zipped into her pencil case, but that was upstairs. She wondered if her mother would go out looking for her.

"But *you're* not raising her, Chris! *I* am! I'm doing it *all by myself*!" Linda almost screamed, and Vic heard tears in her voice and did, for a moment, almost reconsider. And again held back. It was as if the sleet of the night before had been absorbed through her skin, into her blood, and made her somehow colder. She longed for that, for a coldness inside, a perfect, icy stillness—a chill that would numb all the bad feelings, flash-freeze all the bad thoughts.

You wanted me to get lost, and so I did, Vic thought.

Her mother slammed the phone down, picked it up, slammed it again.

Vic curled under the jackets and snuggled up.

In five minutes she was asleep again.

The Basement

NEXT SHE WOKE, IT WAS MIDAFTERNOON AND THE HOUSE WAS empty. She knew the moment she opened her eyes, knew by the quality of the stillness. Her mother could not bear a perfectly silent house. When Linda slept, she ran a fan. When Linda was awake, she ran the TV or her mouth.

Vic peeled herself from the chair, crossed the room, and stood on a box to look out the window that faced the front of the house. Her mother's rusty shitbox Datsun wasn't there. Vic felt a nasty pulse of excitement, hoped Linda was driving frantically around Haverhill, looking for her, at the mall, down side streets, at the houses of her friends.

I could be dead, she thought in a hollow, portentous voice. *Raped and left for dead down by the river, and it would be all your fault, you domineering bitch.* Vic had a headful of words like "domineering" and "portentous." She might only be pulling C's in school, but she read Gerard Manley Hopkins and W. H. Auden and was light-years smarter than both her parents, and she knew it.

Vic put her still-damp sneakers in the dryer to bang around and went upstairs to have a bowl of Lucky Charms in front of the TV. She dug her emergency tablet of Ecstasy out of her pencil case. In twenty minutes she was feeling smooth and easy. When she closed her eyes, she felt a luxuriant sensation of moving, of gliding, like a paper airplane on an updraft. She watched the Travel Channel, and every time she saw an airplane, she held her arms out like wings and pretended to soar. Ecstasy was motion in pill form, as good as flying through the dark in an open-top convertible, only you didn't have to get off the couch to go for a ride.

She washed out her bowl and the spoon in the sink and dried them and put them back where they belonged. She turned off the TV. The hour was getting late, she could tell by the slant of the light through the trees.

Vic went back into the basement to check her shoes, but they were still wet. She didn't know what to do with herself. Under the stairs she found her old tennis racket and a can of balls. She thought she might hit against the wall for a while, but she needed to clear a stretch first, so she started moving boxes—which was when she found it.

The Raleigh leaned against the concrete, hidden behind a stack of boxes marked for the Salvation Army. It baffled Vic, seeing her old Tuff Burner there. She had been in some kind of accident and lost it. Vic recalled her parents talking about it when they didn't know she could hear.

Except. Except maybe she hadn't heard what she *thought* she'd heard. She remembered her father saying she would be heartbroken when he told her the Tuff Burner was gone. For some reason she had thought it was lost, that he couldn't find it. Her mother had said something about being glad the Tuff Burner was out of the picture, because Vic was so fixated on it.

And she *had* been fixated on it, that was true. Vic had a whole framework of fantasies that involved riding the Tuff Burner across an imaginary bridge to faraway places and fantastic lands. She had ridden it to a terrorist hideout and rescued her mother's missing bracelet and had taken it on a ride to a book-filled crypt where she'd met an elf who made her tea and warned her about a vampire.

Vic moved a finger across the handlebars, collected a thick gray pad of dust on her fingertip. All this time it had been down here gathering dust because her parents hadn't wanted her to have it. Vic had loved the bike, and it had given her a thousand stories, and so naturally her parents took it away.

She missed her stories about the bridge, missed the girl she had been then. She'd been a better person then and knew it.

Vic continued to stare at the bike as she put her sneakers on (they were now both toasty and stinky).

The spring was in almost perfect balance, felt like July in the direct sunshine and like January in the shade. Vic didn't want to walk along the road and risk having her mother spot her on the way back, so she steered the Raleigh around to the rear of the house and the path into the woods. It was the most natural thing in the world to put her leg over it and start riding.

Vic laughed when she climbed onto it. It was too small for her, almost comically so. She imagined a clown squeezed into a tiny, tiny clown car. Her knees rapped the handlebars, and her butt hung over the seat. But when she stood on the pedals, it still felt right.

She took it downhill, into shade that was ten degrees colder than out in the sun, winter breathing her in the face. She struck a root, grabbed air. She didn't actually expect to come off the ground, and she screamed, a thin, happy scream of surprise, and for a moment there was no difference between who she was and who she had been. It still felt good, two wheels spinning below and the wind grabbing her hair.

She did not take it straight to the river but instead followed a narrow trail that cut sidelong across the face of the hill. Vic burst through some brush and came out among a pack of boys standing around a fire in a trash can. They were passing a joint.

"Gimme a toke!" she shouted as she rode by and mock-snatched at the little reefer.

The kid with the joint, a scrawny doof in an Ozzy Osbourne T-shirt, was so startled he choked on the lungful of smoke he was holding. Vic was grinning as she rode away, until the kid with the joint cleared his throat and yelled, “Maybe if you come suck us, you fuckin’ hoor!”

She continued on and away through the chill. A parliament of crows, roosting in the branches of a thick-trunked birch tree, discussed her in the gravest of terms as she rode beneath them.

Maybe if you come suck us, she thought, and for one cold moment the seventeen-year-old girl on the child’s bike imagined turning around and going back to them and getting off and saying, *All right. Who’s first?* Her mother already thought she was a whore. Vic hated to disappoint her.

She had felt good for a few moments, racing across the face of the hill on her old bike, but the happy feeling had burned itself out and left behind a thin, cold rage. She was no longer entirely sure who she was angry with, though. Her anger didn’t have a fixed point. It was a soft whir of emotion to match the soft whir of the spokes.

She thought about riding to the mall, but the idea of having to put on a grin for the other girls at the food court irritated her. Vic wasn’t in the mood to see people she knew, and she didn’t want anyone giving her good advice. She didn’t know where to go, just that she was in the mood to find some trouble. She was sure that if she rode around long enough, she would come across some.

For all her mother knew, Vic had already found trouble, was lying naked and dead somewhere. Vic was glad to have put such an idea in her head. She was sorry that by this evening the fun would be over and her mother would know she was still alive. She half wished there were a way to keep Linda from *ever* finding out what had happened to her, for Vic to vanish from her own life, to go and never come back, and how fine that would be, to leave both of her parents wondering if their daughter was alive or dead.

She relished the thought of all the days and weeks they would spend missing her, tormented by dreadful fantasies about what had happened to her. They would picture her out in the sleet, shivering and miserable, gratefully climbing into the back of the first car that pulled over for her. She might still be alive somewhere in the trunk of this old car (Vic was not aware that it had, in her mind, become an old car of some indeterminate make and model). And they would never know how long the old man kept her (Vic had just decided he must be old, because his car was), or what he did with her, or where he put the body. It would be worse than dying themselves, never knowing what dreadful person Vic had come across, what lonely place he had taken her to, what ending she had found for herself.

By then Vic was on the wide dirt road that led to the Merrimack. Acorns popped beneath her tires. She heard the rush of the river ahead, pouring through its trough of rocks. It was one of the best sounds in the world, and she lifted her head to enjoy the view, but the Shorter Way Bridge blocked her line of sight.

Vic squeezed the brake, let the Raleigh gently roll to a stop.

It was even more dilapidated than she remembered, the whole structure canting to the right so it looked as if a strong wind could topple it into the Merrimack. The lopsided entrance was framed in tangles of ivy. She smelled bats. At the far end, she saw a faint smudge of light.

She shivered in the cold—and also with something like pleasure. She knew, with quiet certainty, that something was wrong in her head. In all the times she'd popped Ecstasy, she had never hallucinated. She supposed there was a first time for everything.

The bridge waited for her to ride out across it. When she did, she knew she would drop into nothing. She would forever be remembered as the stoned chick who rode her bike right off a cliff and broke her neck. The prospect didn't frighten her. It would be the next-best thing to being kidnapped by some awful old man *(the Wraith)* and never heard from again.

At the same time, even though she knew that the bridge wasn't there, a part of her wanted to know what was on the other side of it now. Vic stood on the pedals and rode closer, right to the edge, where the wooden frame rested upon the dirt.

Two words were written on the inside wall, to her left, in green spray paint.

SLEIGH HOUSE
1996

Haverhill

VIC BENT, GRABBED A PIECE OF SHALE, AND FLUNG IT UNDERHANDED out onto the bridge. It hit the wood with a bang, skipped and bounced. There was a faint rustle of movement from above. The bats.

It seemed a sturdy enough hallucination. Although maybe she had also hallucinated the piece of shale.

There were two ways to test the bridge. She could roll forward another twelve inches, put the front tire on it. If it was imaginary, she might be able to throw herself back in time to keep from falling.

Or she could just ride. She could shut her eyes and let the Raleigh carry her forward toward whatever waited.

She was seventeen and unafraid and liked the sound of the wind rustling the ivy around the entrance of the bridge. She put her feet on the pedals and rode. She heard the tires bumpety-thump up onto the wood, heard the planks knocking beneath her. There was no sensation of drop, no ten-story plunge into the arctic cold of the Merrimack River. There was a building roar of white noise. There was a twinge of pain in her left eye.

She glided through the old familiar darkness, the flicker of the static blizzard showing in the gaps between boards. She was already a third of the way across and at the far end could see a dingy white house with an attached garage. The Sleigh House, whatever that was.

The name held no meaning for her and didn't need to. She knew, in an abstract sense, *what* she was riding toward, even if she didn't know the specific *where*.

She had wanted to find some trouble, and the Shorter Way Bridge had never steered her wrong.

The Other End of the Bridge

INSECTS MADE A SAWING NOISE OFF IN THE HIGH BRUSH. IN NEW Hampshire, spring had been a cold, mucky slog, but here—wherever *here* was—the air was warm and breezy. At the edge of her vision, Vic saw flashes of light, glimmers of brightness out in the trees, but in those first few moments she didn't give it any thought.

Vic slipped off the bridge and onto firmly packed dirt. She braked to a stop, put her foot down. She turned her head to look back into the bridge.

The Shorter Way had settled among trees, to one side of the house. It stretched back and away through the hardwoods. When she peered through it, she saw Haverhill on the other end, green and shadowy in the last light of afternoon.

The house, a white Cape Cod, stood alone at the end of a long dirt lane. The grass grew waist-high in the yard. Sumac had invaded from the trees, growing in bunches as tall as Vic herself.

The shades were drawn behind the windows, and the screens were rusted and bellied out, and there was no car in the drive and no reason to think anyone was home, but Vic was immediately afraid of the place and did not believe that it was empty. It was an awful place, and her first thought was that when the police searched it, they would find bodies buried in the backyard.

When she had entered the bridge, she had felt like she was soaring, as effortlessly as a hawk carried on an updraft. She had felt she was gliding and that no harm could come to her. Even now, standing still, she felt like she was moving, sailing forward, but the sensation was no longer pleasant. Now it felt like she was being pulled toward something she didn't want to see, to know about.

From somewhere came the faint sound of a TV or a radio.

Vic looked back again at the bridge. It was only a couple feet away. She exhaled deeply, told herself she was safe. If she was seen, she could wheel the bike around, get back into the bridge, and be gone, before anyone had time to so much as shout.

She got off the bike and began to walk it forward. With each soft crunching footfall, she felt more sure that her surroundings were real, not a delusion engineered by Ecstasy. The radio sounds grew in volume by subtle degrees as she approached the cottage.

Looking out into the trees, Vic saw those glimmering lights again, slivers of brightness hung in the surrounding pines. It took a moment to make sense of what she was seeing, and when she did, she held up and stared. The firs around the house were hung with Christmas ornaments, hundreds of them, dangling from dozens of trees. Great silver and gold spheres, dusted with glitter, swayed in the drifting pine branches. Tin angels held silent trumpets to their lips. Fat Santas put chubby fingers to their mouths, advising Vic to proceed quietly.

As she stood there looking about, that radio sound resolved into the bluff baritone of Burl Ives, encouraging all the world to have a holly jolly Christmas, and never mind it was the third week of March. The voice was coming from the attached garage, a dingy building with a single roll-up door and four square windows looking into it, milky with filth.

She took one baby step, then a second, creeping toward the garage in the same way she might creep out onto a high ledge. On the third step, she looked back to make sure the bridge was still there and that she could get into it in a hurry if she had to. She could.

Another step, and a fifth, and then she was close enough to see through one of the grimy windows. Vic leaned her Raleigh against the wall, to one side of the big garage door.

She pressed her face up to the glass. The garage contained an old black car with a small rear window. It was a Rolls-Royce, the kind of car Winston Churchill was always getting out of in photographs and old films. She could see the license plate: NOS4A2.

That's it. That's all you need. The police can track him down with that, Vic thought. *You have to go now. You have to* ***run.***

But as she was about to step away from the garage, she saw movement through the rear window of the old car. Someone sitting in the backseat shifted slightly, wiggling to find a more comfortable spot. Vic could dimly see the outline of a small head through the foggy glass.

A child. There was a child in the car—a boy, she thought. The kid had a boy's haircut.

Vic's heart was by now beating so hard her shoulders shook. He had a child in his car, and if Vic rode back across the Shorter Way, maybe the law would catch up to the man who owned this old ride, but they would not find the kid with him, because by then he would already be under a foot of dirt somewhere.

Vic didn't know why the child didn't scream or let himself out of the car and run. Maybe he was drugged or tied up, Vic couldn't tell. Whatever the reason, he wasn't getting out unless Vic went in there and got him out.

She drew back from the glass and took another look over her shoulder. The bridge waited amid the trees. It suddenly seemed a long way off. How had it gotten so far away?

Vic left the Raleigh, went around to the side of the garage. She expected the side door to be locked, but when she turned the handle, it popped open. Quavering, high-pitched, helium-stoked voices spilled out: Alvin and the Chipmunks singing their infernal Christmas song.

Her heart quailed at the thought of going in there. She put one foot over the threshold, tentatively, as if stepping onto the ice of a pond that might not yet be safely frozen over. The old car, obsidian and sleek, filled almost all the available space in the garage. What little room was left was jammed with clutter: paint cans, rakes, ladders, boxes.

The Rolls had a roomy rear compartment, the back couch done in flesh-toned kidskin. A boy slept upon it. He wore a rawhide jacket with buttons of bone. He had dark hair and a round, fleshy face, his cheeks touched with a rose bloom of health. He looked as if he were dreaming sweet dreams; visions of sugarplums, perhaps. He wasn't tied up in any way and didn't look unhappy, and Vic had a thought that made no sense: *He's fine. You should go. He's probably here with his father and he fell asleep and his father is letting him rest, and you should just go away.*

Vic flinched from the thought, the way she might've flinched from a horsefly. There was something wrong with that thought. It had no business in her head, and she didn't know how it had got there.

The Shorter Way Bridge had brought her here to find the Wraith, a bad man who hurt people. She had gone looking for trouble, and the bridge never pointed her wrong. In the last few minutes, things she had suppressed for years had come surging back. Maggie Leigh had been real, not a daydream. Vic really *had* gone out on her bike and retrieved her mother's bracelet from Terry's Primo Subs; that had not been *imagined* but *accomplished.*

She tapped on the glass. The child did not stir. He was younger than her, twelve or thereabouts. There was a faint, dusky wisp of hair on his upper lip.

"Hey," she called to him in a low voice. "Hey, kid."

He shifted, but only to roll onto his side so his face was turned away from her.

Vic tried the door. It was locked from the inside.

The steering wheel was on the right side of the car, the side she was already on. The driver's-side window was rolled most of the way down. Vic shuffled toward it. There wasn't much space between the car and the clutter piled against the wall.

The keys were in it, the car running off the battery. The face of the radio was lit a radioactive shade of green. Vic didn't know who was singing now, some old Vegas dude, but it was another one about Christmas. Christmas was almost three months in the rearview mirror, and there was something awful about Christmas music when it was nearly summer. It was like a clown in the rain, with his makeup running.

"Hey, kid," she hissed. "Hey, kid, wake up."

The boy moved slightly, and then he sat up and turned around to face her. Vic saw his face and had to bite back a cry.

It wasn't anything like the face she had seen through the rear window. The boy in the car looked close to death—or beyond death. His face was lunar in its paleness, except for the hollows of his eyes, which were bruise-colored. Black, poisoned veins crawled beneath his skin, as if his arteries were filled with ink, not blood, and erupted in sick branches at the corners of his mouth and eyes and in his temples. His hair was the color of frost on a windowpane.

He blinked. His eyes were shiny and curious, the one part of him that seemed fully alive.

He exhaled: white smoke. As if he stood in a freezer.

"Who are you?" he asked. Each word was a new puff of white vapor. "You shouldn't be here."

"Why are you so cold?"

"I'm not," he said. "You should go. It isn't safe here."

His breath, steaming.

"Oh, God, kid," she said. "Let's get you out of here. Come on. Come with me."

"I can't unlock my door."

"So climb into the front seat," she said.

"I can't," he said again. He spoke like one sedated, and it came to Vic that he had to be drugged. Could a drug lower your body temperature enough to make your breath steam? She didn't think so. "I can't leave the backseat. You really shouldn't be here. He'll come back soon." White, frozen air trickled from his nostrils.

Vic heard him clearly enough but didn't understand much of it, except for the last bit. *He'll come back soon* made perfect sense. Of course *he* was coming back—whoever *he* was (the Wraith). He wouldn't have left the car running off the battery if he weren't going to be back soon, and she had to be gone by the time he returned. They both did.

She wanted more than anything to take off, to bolt for the door, tell the kid she would come back with police. But she could not go. If she ran, she would not just be leaving a sick and abducted child behind. She would be abandoning her own best self, too.

She reached through the window and unlocked the front door and swung it open.

"Come on," she said. "Take my hand."

She reached over the back of the driver's seat, into the rear compartment.

He looked into her palm for a moment, his gaze thoughtful, as if he were attempting to read her future, or as if she had offered him a chocolate and he was trying to decide whether he wanted it. That was the wrong way for a kidnapped child to react, and she knew it, but she still didn't pull her hand back in time.

He gripped her wrist, and she screamed at his touch. His hand, blazing against her skin, was as bad as pressing her wrist to a hot frying pan. It took her an instant to register the sensation not as heat but as *cold*.

The horn sounded with a great blast. In the confined space of the garage, the noise was almost too much to bear. Vic didn't know why it went off. She hadn't touched the steering wheel.

"Let go! You're hurting me," she said.

"I know," he said.

When he smiled, she saw that his mouth was full of little hooks, rows of them, each as small and delicate as a sewing needle. The rows of them seemed to go all the way down his throat. The horn sounded again.

The boy raised his voice and shouted, *"Mr. Manx! Mr. Manx, I caught a girl! Mr. Manx, come see!"*

Vic braced a foot against the driver's seat and threw herself backward, thrusting hard with her leg. The boy was yanked forward. She didn't think he was going to let go—his hand felt as if it were fused to her wrist, his skin *frozen* to hers. But when she drew her hand back across the rear divider, into the front seat, he released her. She fell back into the steering wheel, and the horn went off again. Her fault this time.

The boy hopped up and down on the rear seat in excitement. *"Mr. Manx! Mr. Manx, come see the pretty girl!"* Vapor extruded from his nostrils and mouth.

Vic dropped out of the open driver's-side door and onto the concrete. Her shoulder hit a mess of stacked rakes and snow shovels, and they fell over on top of her with a crash.

The horn went off again and again, in a series of deafening blasts.

Vic shoved the lawn tools off her. When she was on her knees, she looked at her wrist. It was hideous, a black burn in the rough shape of a child's hand.

She slammed the driver's-side door, took one last glance at the boy in the backseat. His face was eager, glistening with excitement. A black tongue lolled out of his mouth and rolled around his lips.

"Mr. Manx, she's running away!" he screamed. His breath frosted over the window glass. *"Come see, come see!"*

She picked herself up and took one clumsy, off-balance step back toward the side door to the yard.

The motor that ran the electric garage door roared to life, the chain overhead pulling it up with a grinding clatter. Vic caught herself, then began going back, fast as she could. The big garage door rose and rose, revealing black boots, silver-gray trousers, and she thought, *The Wraith, it's the Wraith!*

Vic lurched around the front of the car. Two steps led up to a door that she knew would open into the house itself.

The knob turned. The door eased back onto darkness.

Vic stepped through and pushed the door shut behind her and began to move across

A Mudroom

WHERE DIRT-SCUFFED LINOLEUM WAS PEELING UP IN ONE CORNER.

Her legs had never felt so weak, and her ears were ringing from a scream that was stuck in her head, because she knew that if she screamed for real, the Wraith would find her and kill her. About this there was no doubt in her mind—he would kill her and bury her in the backyard, and no one would ever know what had become of her.

She went through a second inner door and into

A Hallway

THAT RAN ALMOST THE ENTIRE LENGTH OF THE HOUSE AND WAS CARpeted in green wall-to-wall shag.

The hall smelled like a turkey dinner.

She ran, not bothering with the doors on either side of her, knowing they would only open into bathrooms and bedrooms. She clutched her right wrist, breathing through the pain.

In ten paces the hall arrived at a little foyer. The door to the front yard was on the left, just beyond a narrow staircase climbing to the second floor. Hunting prints hung on the walls. Grinning, ruddy-faced men held up bunches of dead geese, displaying them to noble-looking golden retrievers. A pair of swinging batwing doors opened into a kitchen on Vic's right. The smell of turkey dinner was stronger here. It was warmer, too, feverishly warm.

She saw her chance, saw it clear in her mind. The man called the Wraith was entering through the garage. He would follow her through the side door and into the house. If she bolted now, rushed across the front yard, she could reach the Shorter Way on foot.

Vic lunged across the foyer, banging her hip on a side table. A lamp with a bead-trimmed shade wobbled, almost fell.

She grabbed the doorknob, turned it, and was about to pull it open when she saw the view through the side window.

He stood in the yard, one of the tallest men she had ever seen, six and a half feet at least. He was bald, and there was something obscene about his pale skull, crawling with blue veins. He wore a coat from another era, a thing with tails and a double line of brass buttons down the front. He looked like a soldier, a colonel in the service of some foreign nation where an army was not called an army but a legion.

He was turned slightly away from the house and toward the bridge, so she saw him in profile. He stood before the Shorter Way, one hand on the handlebars of her bike.

Vic couldn't move. It was as if she had been injected with a paralytic. She could not even force her lungs to pull air.

The Wraith cocked his head to one side, the body language of an inquisitive dog. In spite of his large skull, his features were weasel-like and crowded close together in the center of his face. He had a sunken chin and an overbite, which gave him a very dim, almost feeble look. He looked like the sort of rube who would say every syllable in the word "ho-moh-sex-shu-al."

He considered her bridge, the vast length of it reaching back into the trees. Then he looked toward the house, and Vic pulled her face from the window, pressed her back flat against the door.

"Good afternoon, whoever you are!" he cried. "Come on out and say how do! I will not bite!"

Vic remembered to breathe. It was an effort, as if there were restricting bands strapped around her chest.

The Wraith shouted, "You dropped your bicycle in my yard! Wouldn't you like it back?" After a moment he added, "You dropped your covered bridge in my yard as well! You can have that back, too!"

He laughed. It was a pony's whinny, *heeeeee-eee!* It crossed Vic's mind again that the man might be feeble.

She shut her eyes and held herself rigidly against the door. Then it came to her he hadn't said anything for a few moments and that he might be approaching the front of the house. She turned the bolt, put the chain on. It took three tries to get the chain in place. Her hands were slippery with sweat, and she kept losing her grip on it.

But no sooner had she locked the door than he spoke again, and she could tell by his voice that he was still standing out in the middle of the overgrown yard.

"I think I know about this bridge. Most people would be upset to find a covered bridge sitting in their front yard, but not Mr. Charles Talent Manx the Third. Mr. Charlie Manx is a man who knows a thing or two about bridges and roads turning up where they do not belong. I myself have driven some highways that don't belong. I have been driving for a long time. You would be surprised if you knew how long, I bet! I know about one road I can only get to in my Wraith. It isn't on any map, but it is there when I need it. It is there when I have a passenger who is ready to go to Christmasland. Where does *your* bridge go? You should come out! We sure do have a lot in common! I bet we will be fast friends!"

Vic decided then. Every moment she stood there listening to him was one less moment she had to save herself. She moved, pushed off from the door, raced down the foyer, batted through the batwing doors and into

The Kitchen

IT WAS A SMALL, DINGY SPACE WITH A YELLOW FORMICA-TOPPED TABLE in it and an ugly black phone on the wall, under a sun-faded child's drawing.

Dusty yellow polka-dot streamers dangled from the ceiling, hanging perfectly motionless in the still air, as if someone had thrown a birthday party here, years ago, and had never entirely cleaned up. To Vic's right was a metal door, open to reveal a pantry containing a washer and dryer, a few shelves of dry goods, and a stainless-steel cabinet built into the wall. Beside the pantry door was a big Frigidaire with sloopy bathtub styling.

The room was warm, the air close and stale. A TV dinner baked in the oven. She could envision the slices of turkey in one compartment, mashed potatoes in another, tinfoil covering the dessert. Two bottles of orange pop stood on the counter. There was a door to the backyard. In three steps Vic was there.

The dead boy watched the rear of the house. She knew he was dead now, or worse than dead. That he was a child of the man Charlie Manx.

He stood perfectly still in his rawhide coat and jeans and bare feet. His hood was pushed back to show his pale hair and the black branches of veins in his temples. His mouth was open to show his rows of needle teeth. He saw her and grinned but did not move as she cried out and turned the bolt. He had left a trail of white footprints behind him, where the grass had frozen at the touch of his feet. His face had the glassy smoothness of enamel. His eyes were faintly clouded with frost.

"Come out," he said, his breath smoking. "Come on out here and stop being so silly. We will all go to Christmasland together."

She backed away from the door. Her hip bumped the oven. She turned and began pulling open drawers, looking for a knife. The first one she opened was full of kitchen rags. The second held whisks, spatulas, dead flies. She went back to the first drawer, grabbed bunches of hand towels, opened the oven, and threw them in on top of the turkey dinner. She left the oven door parted a crack.

There was a frying pan on the stove. She grabbed it by the handle. It felt good to have something to swing.

"Mr. Manx! Mr. Manx, I saw her! She's being *a goof*!" the boy shouted. Then he yelled, "This is fun!"

Vic turned and plunged through the batwing doors and back to the front of the house. She peered through the window by the door again.

Manx had walked her bicycle closer to the bridge. He stood before the opening, considering the darkness, head cocked to one side: listening to it, perhaps. Finally he seemed to decide something. He bent and gave the bicycle a strong, smooth shove out onto the bridge.

Her Raleigh rolled across the threshold and into the darkness.

An invisible needle slid into her left eye and back into her brain. She sobbed—couldn't help herself—and doubled over. The needle withdrew, then slid in again. She wanted her head to explode, wanted to die.

She heard a pop, like her ears depressurizing, and the house shuddered. It was as if a jet had screamed by overhead, breaking the sound barrier.

The front hall began to smell of smoke.

Vic lifted her head and squinted out through the window.

The Shorter Way was gone.

She had known it would be, the moment she heard that hard, piercing *pop!* The bridge had collapsed into itself, like a dying sun going nova.

Charlie Manx walked toward the house, the tails of his coat flapping. There was no humor in his pinched, ugly face now. He looked instead like a stupid man, set upon doing something barbaric.

She glanced at the stairs but knew if she went up there, she would have no way back down. That left the kitchen.

When she stepped through the batwing doors, the boy was at the rear door, his face up against the glass of the window set into it. He grinned to show his mouthful of delicate hooks, those fine rows of curving bones. His breath spread feathers of silvery frost across the pane.

The phone rang. Vic yelped as if someone had grabbed her, looked around at it. Her face batted against the yellow polka-dot streamers hanging from the ceiling.

Only they weren't streamers at all. They were strips of flypaper, with dozens of withered, dead fly husks stuck to them. There was bile in the back of Vic's throat. It tasted sour-sweet, like a frappe from Terry's gone bad.

The phone rang again. She grabbed the receiver, but before she picked it up, her gaze fixed on the child's drawing taped directly above the phone. The paper was dry and brown and brittle with age, the tape gone yellow. It showed a forest of crayon Christmas trees and the man called Charlie Manx in a Santa hat, with two little girls, grinning to show a mouthful of fangs. The children in the picture were very like the thing in the backyard that had once been a child.

Vic put the phone to her ear.

"Help me!" she cried. "Help me, please!"

"Where are you, ma'am?" said someone with a childlike voice.

"I don't know, I don't know! I'm lost!"

"We already have a car there. It's in the garage. Go get in the backseat, and our driver will take you to Christmasland." Whoever was on the other end of the line giggled. "We'll take care of you when you get here. We'll hang your eyeballs from our big Christmas tree."

Vic hung up.

She heard a crunch behind her, whirled, and saw that the little boy had slammed his forehead into the window. A spiderweb of shattered glass filled the pane. The boy himself seemed uninjured.

Back in the foyer, she heard Manx force the front door open, heard it catch against the chain.

The child pulled his head back, then snapped it forward, and his forehead hit the window with another hard crunch. Splinters of glass fell. The boy laughed.

The first yellow flames licked out of the half-open oven. They made a sound like a pigeon beating its wings. The wallpaper to the right of the oven was blackening, curling. Vic no longer remembered why she had wanted to start a fire. Something about escaping in a confusion of smoke.

The child reached through the shattered windowpane, his hand feeling for the bolt. Jagged glass points scraped his wrist, peeled up shavings of skin, drew black blood. It didn't seem to bother him.

Vic swung the frying pan at his hand. She threw herself into her swing with her whole weight, and the force of the blow carried her straight into the door. She recoiled, stumbled backward, and sat down on the floor. The boy jerked his hand outside, and she saw that three of his fingers had been smashed out of true, grotesquely bent the wrong way.

"You're funny!" he shouted, and laughed.

Vic kicked her heels, sliding backward on her ass across the cream-colored tiles. The boy stuck his face through the broken windowpane and waggled his black tongue at her.

Red flame belched out of the oven, and for a moment her hair was burning on the right side of her head, the fine hairs crinkling and charring and shriveling up. She swatted at herself. Sparks flew.

Manx hit the front door. The chain snapped with a tinny, clinking sound; the bolt tore free with a loud crack. She heard the door smash into the wall with a house-shaking bang.

The boy reached through the broken window again and unlocked the back door.

Burning strips of flypaper fell around her.

Vic shoved herself up off her ass and turned, and Manx was on the other side of the batwing doors, about to step into the kitchen. He looked at her with a wide-eyed and avid fascination on his ugly face.

"When I saw your bike, I thought you would be younger," Manx said. "But you are all grown. That is too bad for you. Christmasland is not such a good place for girls who are all grown."

The door behind her opened . . . and when it did, there was a feeling of all the hot air being sucked out of the room, as if the world outside were inhaling. A red cyclone of flame whirled from the open oven, and a thousand hot sparks whirled with it. Black smoke gushed.

When Manx swatted through the batwing doors, coming for her, Vic shied away from him, squirming out of reach and ducking behind the big bulky Frigidaire, stepping toward the only place that remained to her, into

The Pantry

SHE GRABBED THE METAL HANDLE OF THE DOOR AND SLAMMED IT shut behind her.

It was a heavy door, and it squalled as she dragged it across the floor. She had never moved such a heavy door in all her life.

It had no lock of any kind. The handle was an iron U, bolted to the metal surface. Vic grabbed it and set her heels apart, her feet planted on the doorframe. A moment later Manx yanked. She buckled, was jerked forward, but locked her knees and held it shut.

He eased off, then suddenly pulled again, a second time, trying to catch her napping. He had at least seventy pounds on her, and those gangly orangutan arms of his, but with her feet braced against the doorframe her arms would come out of their sockets before her legs gave.

Manx stopped pulling. Vic had an instant to look around and saw a mop with a long blue metal handle. It was just to her right, within arm's reach. She pushed it through the U-shaped door latch, so the mop handle was braced across the doorframe.

Vic let go and stepped back, and her legs wobbled, and she almost sat down. She had to lean against the washing machine to keep her feet.

Manx pulled the door again, and the mop handle bashed against the frame.

He paused. When he pulled at the door the next time, he did so gently, in an almost experimental way.

Vic heard him cough. She thought she heard childlike whispering. Her legs shook. They shook so forcefully that she knew if she let go of the washing machine, she'd fall over.

"You have got yourself in a tight spot now, you little firebug!" Manx called through the door.

"Go away!" she screamed.

"It takes a lot of brass to break into a man's house and then tell him to git!" he said. But he said it with good humor. "You are scared to come out, I suppose. If you had any sense, you would be more scared to stay where you are!"

"Go away!" she screamed again. It was all she could think to say.

He coughed once more. A frantic red firelight glimmered at the bottom of the door, broken by two shadows that marked where Charlie Manx had placed his feet. There was another moment of whispering.

"Child," he said to her, "I will let this house burn without a second thought. I have other places to go, and this hidey-hole has been burned for me now, one way or another. Come out. Come out or you will smother to death in there and no one will ever identify your burnt remains. Open the door. I will not hurt you."

She leaned back against the washing machine, gripping the edge with both hands, her legs wobbling furiously, almost comically.

"Pity," he said. "I would've liked to know a girl who had a vehicle of her own, one that can travel the roads of thought. Our kind is rare. We should learn from one another. Well. You will learn from me now, although I think you will not much care for the lesson. I would stay and talk longer, but it is getting a trifle warm in here! I am a man who prefers cooler climes, to be honest. I am so fond of winter I am practically one of Santa's elves!" And he laughed again, that whinnying shit-kicker laugh: *Heeeeee!*

Something turned over in the kitchen. It fell with such an enormous crash that she screamed and almost leaped up onto the washing machine. The impact shook the whole house and sent a hideous vibration through the tiles beneath her. For a moment she thought the floor might be in danger of caving in.

She knew from the sound, from the weight, from the force of it, what he had done. He had gripped that big old fridge, with the sloopy bathtub styling, and overturned it in front of the door.

VIC STOOD A LONG TIME AGAINST THE WASHING MACHINE, WAITING for her legs to stop shaking.

She did not, at first, really believe that Manx was gone. She felt he was waiting for her to throw herself against the door, hammering against it and pleading to be let out.

She could hear the fire. She heard things popping and cracking in the heat. The wallpaper sizzled with a crispy fizzling sound, like someone pitching handfuls of pine needles into a campfire.

Vic put her ear to the door, to better hear the other room. But at the first touch of skin to metal, she jerked her head back with a cry. The iron door was as hot as a skillet left on high heat.

A dirty brown smoke began to trickle in along the left-hand edge of the door.

Vic yanked the steel mop handle free, chucked it aside. She grabbed the handle, meant to give it a shove, see how far she could push it against the weight on the other side—but then she let go, jumped back. The curved metal handle was as hot as the surface of the door. Vic shook her hand in the air to soothe the burned feeling in her fingertips.

She caught her first mouthful of smoke. It stank of melted plastic. It was so filthy-smelling she choked on it, bent over coughing so hard she thought she might vomit.

She turned in a circle. There was hardly space in the pantry to do more than that.

Shelves. Rice-A-Roni. A bucket. A bottle of ammonia. A bottle of bleach. A stainless-steel cabinet or drawer set into the wall. The washing machine and the dryer. There were no windows. There was no other door.

Something glass exploded in the next room. Vic was aware of a gathering filminess in the air, as if she stood in a sauna.

She glanced up and saw that the white plaster ceiling was blackening, directly above the doorframe.

She opened the dryer and found an old white fitted sheet. She tugged it out. Vic pulled it over her head and shoulders, wrapped some fabric around one hand, and tried the door.

She could only barely grip the metal handle, even with the sheet, and could not press her shoulder to the door for long. But Vic flung herself hard against it, once, and again. It shuddered and banged in the frame and opened maybe a quarter of an inch—enough to let in a gush of vile brown smoke. There was too much smoke on the other side of the door to allow her to see anything of the room, to even see flames.

Vic drew back and pitched herself at the door a third time. She hit so hard she bounced, and her ankles caught in the bedsheet, and she fell sprawling. She shouted in frustration, threw off the sheet. The pantry was dirty with smoke.

She reached up, gripped the washing machine with one hand and the handle of the stainless-steel cabinet with the other. But as she pulled herself to her feet, the door to the cabinet fell open, hinges whining, and she crashed back down, her knees giving out.

She rested before trying again, turned her face so her brow was pressed to the cool metal of the washing machine. When she shut her eyes, she felt her mother pressing one cool hand to her fevered forehead.

Vic reclaimed her feet, unsteady now. She let go of the handle of the metal cabinet, and it clapped shut on a spring. The poisonous air stung her eyes.

She opened the cabinet again. It looked into a laundry chute, a dark, narrow metal shaft.

Vic put her head through the opening and looked up. She saw, dimly, another small door, ten or twelve feet up.

He's waiting up there, she knew.

But it didn't matter. Remaining in the pantry wasn't an option.

She sat on the open steel door, which swung down from the wall on a pair of taut springs. Vic squirmed her upper body through the opening, pulled her legs after her, and slid into

The Laundry Chute

VIC WAS, AT SEVENTEEN, ONLY FORTY POUNDS HEAVIER AND THREE inches taller than she had been at twelve, a skinny girl who was all leg. But it was tight inside the chute just the same. She braced herself, back to the wall, knees in her face, feet pressing to the opposite side of the shaft.

Vic began to work her way up the shaft, pushing herself with the balls of her feet, six inches at a time. Brown smoke wafted around her and stung her eyes.

Her hamstrings began to twitch and burn. She slid her back up another six inches, *walking* up the shaft in a hunched, bent, grotesque sort of way. The muscles in the small of her back throbbed.

She was halfway to the second floor when her left foot slipped, squirting out beneath her, and her ass dropped. She felt a tearing in her right thigh, and she screamed. For one moment she was able to hold herself in place, folded over with her right knee in her face and her left leg hanging straight down. But the weight on her right leg was too much. The pain was too much. She let her right foot slide free and fell all the way back to the bottom.

It was a painful, ungraceful fall. She clouted into the aluminum floor of the shaft, spiked her right knee into her own face. Her other foot banged through the stainless-steel hatch and shot back into the pantry.

Vic was, for a moment, dangerously close to panic. She began to cry, and when she stood up in the laundry chute, she did not try to climb again but began to *jump*, and never mind that the top was well out of reach and there was nothing in the smooth aluminum shaft to grab. She screamed. She screamed for help. The shaft was full of smoke, and it blurred her vision, and midscream she began to cough, a harsh, dry, painful cough. She coughed on and on, did not think she would ever stop. She coughed with such force she almost threw up and in the end spit a long stream of saliva that tasted of bile.

It was not the smoke that terrified her, or the pain in the back of her right thigh, where she had definitely yanked a muscle. It was her certain, desperate aloneness. What had her mother screamed at her father? *But* you're *not raising her, Chris!* I *am! I'm doing it* all by myself*!* It was awful to find yourself in a hole, all by yourself. She could not remember the last time she had held her mother: her frightened, short-tempered, unhappy mother, who had stood by her and put her cool hand to Vic's brow in her times of fever. It was awful to think of dying here, having left things as they were.

Then she was making her way up the shaft again, back to one wall, feet to the other. Her eyes gushed. The smoke was thick in the chute now, a brownish, billowing stream all around her. Something was terribly wrong in the back of her right leg. Every time she pushed upward with her feet, it felt as if the muscle were tearing all over again.

She blinked and coughed and pushed and wormed her way steadily up the laundry chute. The metal against her back was uncomfortably warm. She thought that in a very short time she would be leaving skin on the walls, that the chute would burn to the touch. Except it wasn't a chute anymore. It was a chimney, with a smoky fire at the bottom, and she was Santa Claus, scrambling up for the reindeer. She had that idiot Christmas song in her head, have a holly jolly fucking Christmas, going around and around on endless loop. She didn't want to roast to death with Christmas music in her head.

By the time she was close to the top of the chute, it was hard to see anything through all the smoke. She wept continuously and held her breath. The big muscle in her right thigh shook helplessly.

She saw an inverted U of dim light, somewhere just above her feet: the hatch that opened on the second floor. Her lungs burned. She gasped, couldn't stop herself, drew a chestful of smoke, began to cough. It hurt to cough. She could feel soft tissues behind her ribs rupturing and tearing. Her right leg gave, without warning. She lunged as she fell, shoving her arms at the closed hatch. As she did, she thought, *It won't open. He pushed something in front of it, and it won't open.*

Her arms banged through the hatch, out into beautifully cool air. She held on, caught the edge of the opening under her armpits. Her legs dropped down into the chute, and her knees clubbed the steel wall.

With the hatch open, the laundry chute drew air, and she felt a hot, stinking breeze lifting around her. Smoke gushed out around her head. She couldn't stop coughing and blinking, coughing so hard her whole body shook. She tasted blood, felt blood on her lips, wondered if she was coughing up anything important.

For a long moment, she hung where she was, too weak to pull herself out. Then she began to kick, digging her toes against the wall. Her feet clanged and banged. She could not grab much purchase, but she did not need much. Her head and arms were already through the hatch, and getting out of the chute was less a matter of climbing, more a thing of simply leaning forward.

She tipped herself out and onto the shag carpet of a second-floor hallway. The air tasted good. She lay there and gasped like a fish. What a blessed if painful thing, this business of being alive.

She had to lean against the wall to get to her feet. She expected the entire house to be filled with smoke and roaring fire, but it was not. It was hazy in the upstairs hallway, but not as bad as it had been in the chute. Vic saw sunshine to her right and limped across the bushy 1970s-era carpet, to the landing at the top of the stairs. She descended the steps in a stumbling, controlled fall, splashing through smoke.

The front door was half open. The chain hung from the doorframe, with the lock plate and a long splinter of wood dangling from it. The air that came in was watery-cool, and she wanted to pitch herself out into it, but she did not.

She could not see into the kitchen. It was all smoke and flickering light. An open doorway looked into a sitting room. The wallpaper on the far side of the sitting room was burning away to show the plaster underneath. The rug smoldered. A vase contained a bouquet of flame. Streams of orange fire crawled up cheap white nylon curtains. She thought the whole back of the house might be in flame, but here in the front, in the foyer, the hallway was only filled with smoke.

Vic looked out the window to one side of the door. The drive leading up to the house was a long, narrow dirt lane, leading away through the trees. She saw no car, but from this angle she could not see into the garage. He might be sitting there waiting to see if Vic would come out. He might be down at the end of the lane watching to see if she would run up it.

Behind her, something creaked painfully and fell with a great crash. Smoke erupted around her. A hot spark touched her arm and stung. And it came to her that there was nothing left to think about. He was waiting there or he wasn't, but either way there was no place left for her to go except

Out

THE YARD WAS SO OVERGROWN IT WAS LIKE RUNNING THROUGH A tangle of wire. The grass made snares to catch her ankles. There was really no yard to speak of, only an expanse of wild brush and weeds, and forest beyond.

She did not so much as glance at the garage or back at the house, and she did not run for the driveway. She didn't dare test that long straight road, for fear he might be parked along it, spying for her. Instead she ran for the trees. She did not see that there was an embankment until she was going over it, a three-foot drop to the forest floor.

She hit hard on her toes, felt the back of her right thigh *grab* with a painful force. She crashed into a drift of dry branches, struggled free of them, and dropped onto her back.

The pines towered above her. They swayed in the wind. The ornaments that hung in them twinkled and blinked and made flashing rainbows, so it was as if she had been lightly concussed.

When she had her breath back, she rolled over, got on her knees, looked across the yard.

The big garage door was open, but the Rolls-Royce was gone.

She was surprised—almost disappointed—at how little smoke there was. She could see a steady gray film rising from the rear of the house. Smoke spilled from the open mouth of the front door. But she could not hear anything burning from here and could not see any flame. She had expected the house to be a bonfire.

Then Vic was up and moving again. She could not run, but she could hurry in a limping jog. Her lungs felt baked, and every other step there was a fresh ripping sensation in the back of her right thigh. She was less aware of her innumerable other hurts and aches: the cold burn on her right wrist, the steady stabbing pain in her left eyeball.

She stayed parallel to the drive, keeping it fifty feet off on her left, ready to duck behind brush or a tree trunk if she saw the Rolls. But the dirt lane led straight and true away from the little white house, with no sign of the old car, or the man Charles Manx, or the dead boy who traveled with him.

She followed the narrow dirt road for an uncertain period. She had lost her usual sense of time passing, did not have any idea, then or later, how long she made her way through the woods. Each moment was the longest single moment of her life until the next. It seemed to her later that her staggering escape through the trees was as long as all the rest of her childhood. By the time she saw the highway, she had left her childhood well behind her. It smoldered and burnt to nothing, along with the rest of the Sleigh House.

The embankment leading up to the highway was higher than the one she had fallen down, and she had to climb on her hands and knees, grabbing clumps of grass to hoist herself up. As she reached the top of the slope, she heard a rat-a-tat buzzing sound, the whine and blast of an approaching motorcycle. It was coming from her right, but by the time she found her feet, it was already past, big guy in black on a Harley.

The highway ran on a straight line through forest, beneath a confusion of stormy clouds. To her left were lots of high blue hills, and for the first time Vic had a sense of being somewhere high up herself; in Haverhill, Massachusetts, she rarely gave a second thought to altitude, but now she understood that it wasn't the clouds that were low but herself that was high.

She reeled out onto the blacktop, chasing the Harley, shouting, and waving her arms. *He won't hear,* she thought; there was no way, not over the rowdy tear of his own engine. But the big man looked back over his shoulder, and the front wheel of his Harley wobbled, before he straightened out and swerved to the side of the highway.

He didn't have a helmet on and was a fat man with beard on both of his chins, his brown hair curled at the nape of his neck in a luxuriant mullet. Vic ran toward him, the pain stabbing her in the back of the right leg with each step. When she reached the motorcycle, she did not hesitate or explain herself but threw one leg over the seat, getting her arms around his waist.

His eyes were amazed and a little frightened. He had black leather gloves with the fingers snipped off and a black leather jacket, but the coat was unzipped to show a Weird Al T-shirt, and from this close she could see he was not the grown-up she had first taken him for. His skin was smooth and pink beneath the beard, and his emotions were almost childishly plain. He might've been no older than her.

"Dude!" he said. "Are you all right? You been in an accident?"

"I need the police. There's a man. He wanted to kill me. He trapped me in a room and set fire to his house. He's got a little boy. There was a little boy, and I almost didn't get out, and he took the boy with him. We need to go. He might come back." She was not sure any of this made sense. It was the right information, but it seemed to her she had arranged it poorly.

The bearded fat man goggled at her, as if she were speaking to him frantically in a foreign tongue—Tagalog, perhaps, or Klingon. Although as it turned out, if she had addressed him in Klingon, Louis Carmody probably would've been able to translate.

"Fire!" she shouted. "Fire!" She stabbed a finger back in the direction of the dirt lane.

She could not see the house from the highway, and the faint wisp of smoke that rose over the trees might've been from someone's chimney or a pile of burning leaves. But it was enough to break him out of his trance and get him moving.

"Hold the fuck on!" he cried, his voice cracking, going high-pitched, and he gave his bike so much throttle that Vic thought he was going to pop a wheelie.

Her stomach plunged, and she squeezed her arms around his gut, so the tips of her fingers could almost-but-not-quite touch. She thought he was going to dump it; the bike weaved dangerously, the front end going one way, the back end going the other.

But he straightened it out, and the center white line began to flick by in machine-gun staccato; so did the pines to either side of the road.

Vic dared one look back. She expected to see the old black car lurching up out of the dirt road, but the highway was empty. She turned her head and pressed it into the fat kid's back, and they left the old man's house behind, riding toward the blue hills, and they were away and they were safe and it was over.

Above Gunbarrel, Colorado

THEN HE BEGAN TO SLOW DOWN.

"What are you doing?" she cried.

They had traveled less than half a mile down the highway. She looked back over her shoulder. She could still see the dirt road leading up to that awful house.

"Dude," the kid said. "We, like, need to get us some help. They'll have a phone right in here."

They were approaching a pitted and cracked blacktop lane, leading off to the right, and at the corner of the intersection was a country store with a couple pumps out front. The kid ran the bike right up to the porch.

It died all of a sudden, the instant he flipped the kickstand down; he had not bothered to put it in neutral. She wanted to tell him no, not here, this was too close to the guy's house, but the fat boy was already off and giving her his hand to help her down.

She stumbled on the first step going up to the porch and almost fell. He caught her in his arms. She turned and looked at him, blinking at tears. Why was she crying? She didn't know, only knew that she was—helplessly, sipping at the air in short, choked breaths.

Curiously, the fat boy, Louis Carmody, just twenty, a kid with a record of stupid crimes—vandalism, shoplifting, smoking underage—looked like he might start crying himself. She didn't learn his name until later.

"Hey," he said. "*Hey.* I won't let anything bad happen to you. You're all right now. I've got your back."

She wanted to believe him. Already, though, she understood the difference between being a child and being an adult. The difference is that when someone says he can keep the bad things away, a child *believes* him. She wanted to believe him, but she couldn't, so she decided to kiss him instead. Not now, but later—later she would kiss him the best kiss ever. He was chubby and had bad hair, and she suspected he had never been kissed by a pretty girl before. Vic was never going to be modeling in an underwear catalog, but she was pretty enough. She knew he thought so, too, from the reluctant way he let go of her waist.

"Let's go in there and bring a whole mess of law down here," he said. "How about that?"

"And fire trucks," she said.

"That, too," he said.

Lou walked her into a pine-floored country grocery. Pickled eggs floated like cow eyeballs in a jar of yellowing fluid on the counter.

A small line of customers led to the lone cash register. The man behind the counter had a corncob pipe in the corner of his mouth. With his pipe, squinty eyes, and bulging chin, he bore more than a passing resemblance to Popeye the Sailor Man.

A young man in military fatigues stood at the head of the line, holding a few bills in his hand. His wife waited beside him, baby in arms. His wife was, at most, only five years older than Vic herself, her blond hair held back in a ponytail by an elastic loop. The tow-headed infant in her arms wore a Batman onesie with tomato-sauce stains down the front, evidence of a nutritious lunch by way of Chef Boyardee.

"Excuse me," Lou said, raising his thin, piping voice.

No one so much as looked around.

"Didn't you have a milk cow once, Sam?" said the young man in fatigues.

"It's true," said the guy who looked like Popeye, punching some keys on the register. "But you don't want to hear about my ex-wife again."

The old boys gathered around the counter erupted into laughter. The blonde with the baby smiled indulgently and looked around, and her gaze settled on Lou and Vic. Her brow furrowed with concern.

"Everyone listen to me!" Lou screamed, and this time they all heard and turned to stare. "We need to use your phone."

"Hey, honey," said the blonde with the infant, speaking directly to Vic. The way she said it, Vic knew she was a waitress and called everyone honey, or hon, or darling, or doll. "You okay? What happened? You have an accident?"

"She's lucky to be alive," Lou said. "There's a man down the road had her locked up in his house. He tried to burn her to death. The house is still on fire. She only just got out of there. The fucker still has some little kid with him."

Vic shook her head. No—no, that was not exactly right. The little kid was not being held against his will. The little kid wasn't even a little kid anymore. He was something else, something so cold it hurt to touch him. But she couldn't figure out how to correct Lou, and so she said nothing.

The blonde looked at Lou Carmody while he was speaking, then back, and when her gaze returned to Vic, it was subtly altered. It was a look of calm, intense appraisal—a look Vic knew well from her own mother's face. It was the way Linda sized up an injury, judging it on a scale of severity, settling on the appropriate treatment.

"What's your name, darling?" the blonde asked.

"Victoria," Vic said, something she never did, refer to herself by her whole first name.

"You're okay now, Victoria," said the blonde, and her voice was so kind that Vic began to sob.

The blonde took quiet command of the room and everyone in it then, all without raising her voice or ever setting down her toddler. Later, when Vic thought about what she liked best in women, she always thought of the soldier's wife, of her certainty and her quiet decency. She thought of mothering, which was really another word for being present and caring what happened to someone. She wished for that certainty herself, that grounded awareness, that she saw in the soldier's wife, and thought she would like to be a woman such as this: a mother, with the steady, sure, feminine awareness of what to do in a crisis. In some ways Vic's own son, Bruce, was really conceived in that moment, although she would not be pregnant with him for another three years.

Vic sat on some boxes, to one side of the counter. The man who reminded her of Popeye was already on the phone, asking for an operator to give him the police. His voice was calm. No one was overreacting, because the blonde didn't overreact, the others taking their emotional cues from her.

"Are you from around here?" the soldier's wife asked.

"I'm from Haverhill."

"Is that in Colorado?" asked the soldier, whose name was Tom Priest. He was on two weeks' leave and was due to head back to Saudi Arabia by way of Fort Hood that evening.

Vic shook her head. "Massachusetts. I need to call my mom. She hasn't seen me in days."

From that moment on, Vic was never able to work her way back to anything like the truth. She had been missing from Massachusetts for two days. Now she was in Colorado and had escaped a man who had her locked up in his house, who'd tried to burn her to death. Without ever saying she had been kidnapped, it became clear to everyone that this was the case.

That became the new truth, even for Vic herself, in the same way she was able to persuade herself she had found her mother's bracelet in the family station wagon and not at Terry's Primo Subs in Hampton Beach. The lies were easy to tell because they never felt like lies at all. When she was asked about her trip to Colorado, she said she had no memory of being in Charlie Manx's car, and police officers traded sad, sympathetic looks. When they pressed her, she said it was all dark. Dark like she had been locked in the trunk? Yes, maybe. Someone else wrote her statement. She signed it without ever bothering to read it.

The soldier said, "Where'd you get away from him?"

"Right down the road," Louis Carmody said, answering for Vic, who could not find her voice. "Half a mile away. I could lead you back there. It's out in the woods. Dude, they don't get the fire trucks there pretty quick, half the hill will be on fire."

"That's the Father Christmas place," said Popeye, moving his mouth away from the phone.

"Father Christmas?" the soldier said.

A gourd-shaped man in a red-and-white-checked shirt said, "I know it. I been by there hunting. It's weird. The trees outside are decorated for Christmas all year-round. I've never seen anyone there, though."

"This guy set fire to his own house and drove off?" the soldier asked.

"And he's still got a kid with him," Lou said.

"What kind of car is he in?"

Vic opened her mouth to reply, and then she saw movement, outside, through the window in the door, and looked past the soldier, and it was the Wraith, pulling up to the pumps, arriving as if summoned by this very question. Even from a distance, through a closed door, she could hear Christmas music.

Sam's Gas & Sundries

VIC COULDN'T CRY OUT, COULDN'T SPEAK, BUT SHE DIDN'T NEED TO. The soldier saw her face and where she was looking and turned his head to see what had stopped at the pumps.

The driver climbed from the front seat and walked around the car to gas up.

"That guy?" the soldier asked. "The limo driver?"

Vic nodded.

"I don't see a kid with him," Lou said, craning his neck to look out the front picture window.

This was met by a moment of sickened silence, everyone in the store taking stock of what it might mean.

"Does he have a gun?" the soldier said.

"I don't know," Vic said. "I didn't see one."

The soldier turned and started toward the door.

His wife gave him a sharp look. "What do you think *you're* doing?"

The soldier said, "What do you think?"

"You let the police handle it, Tom Priest."

"I will. When they get here. But he's not driving away before they do."

"I'll come with you, Tommy," said the hefty man in the red-and-white-checked shirt. "I ought to be with you anyway. I'm the only man in this room got a badge in his pocket."

Popeye lowered the mouthpiece of the phone, covered it with one hand, and said, "Alan, your badge says 'Game Warden,' and it looks like it came out of a Cracker Jack box."

"It did *not* come out of a Cracker Jack box," said Alan Warner, adjusting an invisible tie and raising his bushy silver eyebrows in an expression of mock rage. "I had to send away to a very respectable establishment for it. Got myself a squirt gun and a real pirate eye patch from the same place."

"If you insist on going out there," said Popeye, reaching under the counter, "take this with you." And he set a big black .45 automatic next to the register, pushed it with one hand toward the game warden.

Alan Warner frowned at it and gave his head a little shake. "I better not. I don't know how many deer I've put down, but I wouldn't like to point a gun at no man. Tommy?"

The soldier named Tom Priest hesitated, then crossed the floor and hefted the .45. He turned it to check the safety.

"Thomas," said the soldier's wife. She jiggled their baby in her arms. "You have an eighteen-month-old child here. What are you going to do if that man pulls a pistol of his own?"

"Shoot him," Tom said.

"Goddamn it," she said, in a voice just louder than a whisper. "*Goddamn* it."

He smiled . . . and when he did, he looked like a ten-year-old boy about to blow out his birthday candles.

"*Cady*. I have to go do this. I'm on active duty with the U.S. Army, and I'm authorized to enforce federal law. We just heard that this guy transported a minor across state lines, against her will. That's kidnapping. I am obligated to put his ass on the ground and hold him for the civilian authorities. Now, that's enough talk about it."

"Why don't we just wait for him to walk on in here and pay for his gas?" asked Popeye.

But Tom and the game warden, Alan, were moving together toward the door.

Alan glanced back. "We don't know he won't just drive away without paying. Stop your fretting. This is going to be fun. I haven't had to tackle nobody since senior year."

Lou Carmody swallowed thickly and said, "I'll back your play," and started after the two men.

The pretty blonde, Cady, caught his arm before he could make three steps. She probably saved Louis Carmody's life.

"You've done enough. I want you to stay right here. You might have to get on the phone in a minute and tell your side of the story to the police," she told him, in a voice that brooked no argument.

Lou sighed, in a shaky sort of way, and his shoulders went slack. He looked relieved, looked like he wanted to lie down. Vic thought she understood—heroism was exhausting business.

"Ladies," Alan Warner said, nodding to Cady and Vic as he went by.

Tom Priest led the other man out the door and pulled it shut behind them, the little brass bell tinkling. Vic watched the whole thing from the front windows. They all did.

She saw Priest and Warner cross the asphalt, the soldier in the lead, carrying the .45 down by his right leg. The Rolls was on the far side of the pumps, and the driver had his back to the two men. He didn't look around as they approached, continued filling the tank.

Tom Priest didn't wait or attempt to explain himself. He put his hand in the center of Manx's back and shoved him into the side of the car. He planted the barrel of the .45 against his back. Alan stood a safe distance away, behind Tom, between the two pumps, letting the soldier do the talking.

Charlie Manx tried to straighten up, but Priest shoved him into the car again, slamming him into the Wraith. The Rolls, built in Bristol in 1938 by a company that would soon be engineering tanks for the Royal Marines, did not so much as rock on its springs. Tom Priest's sunburned face was a rigid, unfriendly mask. There was no hint of the child's smile now; he looked like a vicious son of a bitch in jackboots and dog tags. He gave an order in a low voice, and slowly, *slowly,* Manx lifted his hands and set them on the roof of the Rolls-Royce.

Tom dipped his free left hand into the pocket of Manx's black coat and removed some coins, a brass lighter, and a silver wallet. He set *them* on the roof of the car.

At that point there was a bang, or a thump, at the back end of the Rolls. It was forceful enough to shake the whole vehicle on its frame. Tom Priest glanced at Alan Warner.

"Alan," Tom said—his voice was loud enough now that they could hear him inside. "Go around and get the keys out of the ignition. Let's see what's in the trunk."

Alan nodded and started around the front of the car, pulling his hankie out to squeeze his nose. He made it to the driver's-side door, where the window was open about eight inches, and reached in for the keys, and that was when things began to go wrong.

The window went up. No one was sitting in the car; there was no one to turn the crank. But the glass rose smoothly, all at once, slicing into Alan Warner's arm, trapping it in place. Alan screamed, throwing his head back and shutting his eyes, rising up on his toes in pain.

Tom Priest glanced away from Charlie Manx for a moment—only one—and the passenger door flew open. It caught the soldier in the right side, knocked him into the pump, and turned him halfway around. The gun clattered across the blacktop. The car door seemed to have opened itself. From where Vic stood, it appeared no one had laid a hand on it. She thought, automatically, of *Knight Rider,* a show she had not watched in ten years, and the way Michael Knight's slick

Trans Am could drive itself, think for itself, eject people it didn't like, open its doors for people it did.

Manx dropped his left hand and came up holding the gas hose. He cracked the metal nozzle into Tom's head, banging him across the bridge of the nose and squeezing the trigger at the same time, so gasoline gushed into the soldier's face, down the front of his fatigues.

Tom Priest issued a strangled cry and put his hands over his eyes. Manx hit him again, slamming the nozzle of the hose into the center of his head, as if trying to trepan him with it. Bright, clear gasoline flew, bubbled over Priest's head.

Alan screamed and screamed again. The car began to creep forward, dragging him by the arm.

Priest tried to throw himself at Manx, but the tall man was already stepping back and out of the way, and Tom fell to all fours on the blacktop. Manx poured gasoline all down his back, soaking him as a man might water his lawn with a garden hose.

The objects on top of the car—the coins, the lighter—slid off as the car continued to roll gently forward. Manx reached and caught the bright brass lighter as effortlessly as a first baseman reaching for a lazy infield fly.

Someone shoved Vic from the left—Lou Carmody—and she staggered into the blonde named Cady. Cady was screaming her husband's name, bent over almost double from the force of her own yells. The toddler in her arms was yelling too: *Waddy, Waddy!* The door flew open. Men spilled onto the porch. Vic's view was momentarily obscured by people rushing past her.

When she could see the blacktop again, Manx had stepped back and flicked his lighter. He dropped it onto the soldier's back, and Tom Priest ignited in a great blast of blue fire, which threw a burst of heat with enough force to rattle the windows of the store.

The Wraith was rolling steadily now, dragging the game warden named Alan Warner helplessly along with it. The fat man bellowed, punching his free hand against the door, as if he could pound it into letting him go. Some gasoline had splashed up the side of the car. The rear passenger-side tire was a churning hoop of flame.

Charlie Manx took another step back from the burning, writhing soldier and was hit from behind by one of the other customers, a skinny old man in suspenders. The two of them went down together. Lou Carmody leaped over them both, pulling off his jacket to throw it on Tom Priest's flaming body.

The driver's-side window abruptly went down, releasing Alan Warner, who dropped to the blacktop, half under the car. The Rolls thumped as it passed over him.

Sam Cleary, the store owner who looked like Popeye, rushed past Vic, holding a fire extinguisher.

Lou Carmody was hollering something, swinging his jacket into Tom Priest, beating at him. It was like he was swatting a stack of burning newspaper; big black flakes of ash drifted through the air. It was only later that Vic understood those were flakes of charbroiled skin.

The toddler in Cady's arms slapped a chubby hand against the storefront window. "*Hot!* Hot Waddy!" Cady seemed to suddenly realize that her child could see everything and turned on her heel and carried him across the room, away from the window, sobbing as she fled.

The Rolls trundled another twenty feet before coming to a stop with the bumper against a telephone pole. Flames painted the whole back end, and if there was a child in the trunk, he would've been suffocated or burned to death, but there was no child in the trunk. There was a purse belonging to a woman named Cynthia McCauley, who had disappeared three days before from JFK Airport, along with her son Brad, but neither Brad nor Cynthia was ever seen again. No one could explain the thumping noise that had seemed to come from the rear of the car—like the window rolling up or the door flying open and smashing into Tom Priest, it seemed almost that the car had acted with a mind of its own.

Sam Cleary reached the two old men fighting on the ground and used the fire extinguisher for the first time, bringing it down two-handed to hit Charlie Manx in the face. He would use it for the second time on Tom Priest, not thirty seconds later, by which time Tom was well dead.

Not to mention well done.

INTERLUDE:
THE SPIRIT OF ECSTASY
2000–2012

Gunbarrel, Colorado

THE FIRST TIME VIC MCQUEEN TOOK A LONG-DISTANCE CALL FROM Christmasland, she was an unwed mother, living with her boyfriend in a double-wide, and it was snowing in Colorado.

She had lived in New England her whole life, and she thought she knew about snow, but it was different in the Rockies. The storms were different. She thought of the blizzards in the Rockies as *blue* weather. The snow came down fast and hard and steady, and there was something *blue* about the light, so it was as if she were trapped in a secret world under a glacier: a winterplace where it was eternally Christmas Eve.

Vic would walk outside in her moccasins and one of Lou's enormous T-shirts (which she could wear like nightgowns) to stand in the blue dimness and listen to the snow fall. It hissed in the branches of the pines like static, like white noise. She would stand there breathing in the sweet smell of woodsmoke and pines, trying to figure out how in the hell she had wound up with sore tits and no job, two thousand miles from home.

The best she could work out, she was there on a mission of vengeance. She had returned to Colorado, after graduating from Haverhill High, to attend art school. She wanted to go to art school because her mother was dead set against it and her father refused to pay for it. Other choices her mother couldn't bear and her father didn't want to know about: Vic smoking pot, skipping class to go skiing, making out with girls, shacking up with the fat delinquent who had rescued her from Charlie Manx, getting pregnant without bothering to get married. Linda had always said she wouldn't have anything to do with a baby born out of wedlock, so Vic had not invited her after the birth, and when Linda offered to come, Vic said she'd rather that she didn't. She had not even bothered to send her father a picture of the baby.

She still remembered how good it felt to look into Lou Carmody's face, over coffees in a yuppie café in Boulder, and to say, bluntly and pleasantly, "So I guess I should fuck you for saving my life, huh? Least I can do. Do you want to finish your coffee, or should we just split now?"

After their first time, Lou admitted he had never slept with a girl before, his face glowing dark red, from both his exertions and his embarrassment. Still a virgin in his early twenties: Who said there was no wonder left in the world?

Sometimes she resented Louis, for not being satisfied with sex alone. He had to love her, too. He wanted talk as much as he wanted sex, maybe more; he wanted to do things for her, buy her things, get tattoos together, go on trips. Sometimes she resented herself, for letting him corner her into being his friend. It seemed to her she had planned to be stronger: to simply fuck him a time or two—to show him she was a girl who knew how to appreciate a guy—then drop him and get herself an alternative girlfriend, someone with a pink streak in her hair and a few beads in her tongue. The problem with that plan was, she liked guys better than girls, and she liked Lou better than most guys; he smelled good and he moved slow and he was roughly as difficult to anger as a character from the Hundred Acre Wood. Soft as a character from the Hundred Acre Wood, too. It irritated her that she liked to touch him and lean against him. Her body was constantly working against her, toward its own unhelpful ends.

Lou worked out of a garage he had opened with some cash given to him by his parents, and they lived in the trailer in back, two miles outside of Gunbarrel, a thousand miles from anything. Vic didn't have a car and probably spent a hundred and sixty hours a week at home. The house smelled of piss-soaked diapers and engine parts, and the sink was always full.

In retrospect Vic was only surprised she didn't go crazy sooner. She was surprised that more young mothers didn't lose it. When your tits had become canteens and the soundtrack of your life was hysterical tears and mad laughter, how could anyone expect you to remain sane?

She had a single occasional escape hatch. Whenever it snowed, she left Wayne with Lou, borrowed the tow truck, and said she was going into town for an espresso and a magazine. It was something to tell them. Vic didn't want to let them in on the truth. What she was actually going to do felt like a curiously private, possibly even shameful, personal matter.

So it happened one day, all of them trapped inside together: Wayne was banging on a toy xylophone with a spoon, Lou was burning pancakes, the TV was blaring *Dora the* fucking *Explorer.* Vic let herself into the yard for a smoke. It was blue outside, and the snow fell hissing in the trees, and by the time she had smoked her American Spirit down far enough to burn her fingers, she knew she needed a ride in the tow.

She borrowed the keys from Lou, put on a Colorado Avalanche hoodie, and crossed to the garage, locked up on that frozen blue Sunday morning. Inside, it smelled of metal and spilled oil, an odor very like blood. Wayne had that smell on him, all the time, and she hated it. The boy, Bruce Wayne Carmody—Bruce to his paternal grandparents, Wayne to Vic, and The Bat to Lou—spent most of the day cooing to himself in the safe enclosure of a tire meant for a monster truck. It was what they had instead of a playpen. Her baby's father was a man who owned only two pairs of underwear and had a tattoo of the Joker on his hip. It was something, going over all the things that had led her to this place of high rock, endless snows, and hopelessness. She could not quite work out how she had found her way here. She used to be so good at finding the place she wanted to go.

In the garage she paused, one foot on the running board of the truck. Lou had picked up a job, painting a motorcycle for a pal. He had just finished putting a coat of dull black primer on the gas tank. The gas tank looked like a weapon now, like a bomb.

On the floor, beside the bike, was a sheet of transfer paper with a flaming skull on it and the words HARD CORE written below. Vic took one glance at what Lou had painted on the transfer paper and knew he was going to fuck up the job. And it was a curious thing: Something about the crudity of his illustration, its obvious failings, made her feel almost ill with love for him. Ill—and guilty. Even then some part of her already knew she was going to leave him someday. Even then some part of her felt that Lou—Lou and Wayne both—deserved better than Vic McQueen.

The highway switchbacked for two miles down to Gunbarrel, where there were coffeehouses, candle shops, and a spa that did cream-cheese facials. But Vic got less than halfway there before turning off the highway onto a dirt side road that dropped through the pines into deep lumber country.

She flicked on the headlights and buried the gas pedal. It felt like plunging off a cliff. It felt like suicide.

The big Ford crashed through brush, banged through ruts, tipped over ledges. She drove at unsafe speeds, slewing around corners and throwing snow and rocks.

She was looking for something. Vic stared intently into the headlights, which cut a hole in the falling snow, a white passageway. The snow flurried past, as if she were driving through a tunnel of static.

Vic felt that it was close, the Shorter Way Bridge, waiting just beyond the farthest reach of the headlights. She felt it was a matter of speed. If she could just go fast enough, she could force it back into existence, leap off the rutted logging road and onto the old boards of the bridge. But she never dared push the truck beyond the speed at which she could control it, and she never reached the Shorter Way.

Maybe if she had her bike back. Maybe if it were summer.

Maybe if she were not stupid enough to have had a baby. She hated that she'd had the baby. Now she was fucked. She loved Wayne too much to press the pedal to the floor and go flying into the darkness.

She'd thought love had something to do with happiness, but it turned out they were not even vaguely related. Love was closer to a need, no different from the need to eat, to breathe. When Wayne fell asleep, his hot cheek against her naked breast, his lips smelling sweetly of the milk from her own body, she felt as if *she* was the one who had been fed.

Maybe she could not bring forth the bridge because there was nothing left to find. Maybe she had found everything the world had to offer her: a notion very like despair.

It was no good being a mother. She wanted to start a website, a public-awareness campaign, a newsletter, to get the word out that if you were a woman and you had a child, you lost everything, you would be held hostage by love: a terrorist who would only be satisfied when you surrendered your entire future.

The lumber road dead-ended at a gravel pit, which was where she turned back. As was often the case, she drove back toward the highway with a headache.

No. Not a headache. It wasn't a pain in her head. It was a pain in her left eye. A slow, soft throb.

She drove back to the garage, singing along to Kurt Cobain. Kurt Cobain understood what it tasted like to lose your magic bridge, the transport to the things you needed. It tasted like a gunbarrel—like Gunbarrel, Colorado, perhaps.

She parked in the garage and sat behind the wheel in the cold, watching her breath smoke. She might've sat there forever if the phone hadn't rung.

It was on the wall, right outside the door to the office Lou never used. It was old enough to have a rotary dial—like the phone in Charlie Manx's Sleigh House. Its ring was harsh and brassy.

Vic frowned.

The phone was on a separate line from the one in the house. It was comically referred to as "the business line." No one ever called them on it.

She dropped from the front seat, a good four feet to the concrete floor. She caught the phone on the third ring.

"Carmody's Car Carma," she said.

The phone was painfully cold. Her palm, clutching the receiver, made a pale frost halo on the plastic.

There was a hiss, as if the call were coming from a great distance. In the background Vic heard carolers, the sounds of sweet children's voices. It was a little early for that—mid-November.

A boy said, "Um."

"Hello? Can I help you?"

"Um. Yes," the boy said. "I'm Brad. Brad McCauley. I'm calling from Christmasland."

She recognized the boy's name but at first she couldn't place it.

"Brad," she said. "Can I help you? Where did you say you're calling from?"

"From Christmasland, *silly*. You know who I am. I was in the car," he said. "At Mr. Manx's house. You remember. We had *fun*."

Her chest was icy. It was hard to breathe.

"Oh, fuck you, kid," she said. "Fuck you and your sick motherfucking joke."

"The reason I'm calling," he said, "we're all getting hungry. There hasn't been anything to eat for*ever*, and what's the point of having all these teeth if you can't use them on something?"

"Call back and I'll put the cops on you, you deranged fuck," she said, and banged the phone down in the cradle.

Vic put a hand over her mouth and made a sound somewhere

between a sob and a cry of rage. She bent double and shook in the freezing garage.

When she had recovered herself, she straightened, lifted the phone, and calmly called the operator.

"Can you give me the number that just rang this line?" Vic asked. "We were cut off. I want to be reconnected."

"The line you're on?"

"Yes. I was cut off just a moment ago."

"I'm sorry. I have a phone call from Friday afternoon for an 800 number. Do you want me to connect you?"

"A call came in just a moment ago. I want to know who it was."

There was a silence before the operator replied, a caesura in which Vic could make out the sounds of other operator voices speaking in the background.

"I'm sorry. I don't have any calls to this line since Friday."

"Thank you," Vic said, and hung up.

She was sitting on the floor, beneath the phone, with her arms wrapped around her, when Lou found her.

"You been, like, sitting out here for a while," he said. "Do you want me to bring you a blanket or a dead tauntaun or something?"

"What's a tauntaun?"

"Something like a camel. Or maybe a big goat. I don't think it matters."

"What's Wayne doing?"

"He snoozed off. He's cool. What are you doin' out here?"

He looked around the dimness, as if he thought there was a chance she might not be alone.

She needed to tell him something, make up some explanation for why she was sitting on the floor in a cold, dark garage, so she nodded at the motorcycle he had primed.

"Thinking about the bike you're working on."

He considered her through narrowed eyes. She could tell he didn't believe her.

But then he looked at the motorcycle and the transfer paper on the floor beside it and said, "I'm worried I'm going to fuck it up. You think it'll come out okay?"

"No. I don't. Sorry."

He shot her a startled look. "For real?"

She smiled weakly and nodded.

He heaved a great sigh. "Can you tell me what I did wrong?"

"'Hardcore' is one word, not two. And your *e* looks like the number *8*. But also, you have to write in reverse. When you stick the transfer paper on and make the copy, 'hardcore' is going to be backward."

"Oh. Oh, shit. *Dude.* I'm such an idiot." Lou cast her another hopeful glance. "At least you liked my skull, right?"

"Honestly?"

Lou stared at his feet. "Christ. I was hoping Tony B. would throw me fifty bucks or something for doing a good paint job. If you didn't stop me, I'd probably have to pay *him* fifty for ruining his bike. Why am I not *good* at anything?"

"You're a good dad."

"It ain't rocket science."

No, Vic thought. It was harder.

"Do you want me to fix it?" she asked.

"You ever painted a bike before?"

"No."

He nodded. "Well. Okay. If you fuck it up, we'll just say I did it. No one will be surprised. But if you kick its ass, we should tell people who really painted it. Might pull in some more jobs." He gave her another long look, sizing her up. "You sure you're all right? You aren't out here pondering dark female thoughts are you?"

"No."

"You ever think, like, you shouldn't have quit on therapy? You've been through some shit, dude. Maybe you ought to talk about it. About *him*."

I just did, she thought. *I had a nice little chat with the last kid Charlie Manx kidnapped. He's some kind of cold vampire now, and he's in Christmasland, and he wants something to eat.*

"I think the talking is done," she said, and took Lou's hand when he offered it. "Maybe I'll just paint instead."

Sugarcreek, Pennsylvania

EARLY IN THE SUMMER OF 2001, THE NEWS REACHED BING PARtridge that Charlie Manx was bad sick. Bing was fifty-three by then and had not put his gasmask on in five years.

Bing found out from an article on AOL, which he accessed using the big black Dell computer he had received from NorChemPharm for thirty years of service. He looked at AOL every day for news out of Colorado about Mr. Manx, but there had been nothing for ages until this: Charles Talent Manx III, age unknown, convicted murderer, suspect in dozens of child abductions, had been moved to the hospital wing of FCI Englewood when it proved impossible to wake him up.

> Manx was examined by prominent Denver neurosurgeon Marc Sopher, who described his condition as one for the medical books.
>
> "The patient appears to suffer from adult progeria or a rare form of Werner syndrome," Sopher said. "In the simplest terms, he has begun to age very rapidly. A month is more like a year for him. A year is close to a decade. And this guy was no spring chicken to begin with."

> The doctor said there was no way to tell if Manx's condition could partially explain the aberrant behavior that led to his brutal slaying of PFC Thomas Priest in 1996. He also declined to describe Charlie Manx's current state as a coma.
>
> "He doesn't meet the strict definition [of coma]. His brain function is high—as if he's dreaming. He just can't wake up anymore. His body is too tired. He doesn't have any gas left in the tank."

Bing had often thought of writing Mr. Manx, to tell him he was still faithful, still loved him, would always love him, would be there to serve him until the day he died. But while Bing was maybe not the shiniest bulb on the Christmas tree—ha, ha—he was smart enough to know that Mr. Manx would be furious with him for writing, and correct to be. A letter from Bing would for sure lead to men in suits knocking on the door, men in sunglasses with guns in armpit holsters. *Hello, Mr. Partridge, would you mind answering a few questions? How would you feel about us planting a shovel in your basement, digging around for a bit?* So he had never written, and now it was too late, and the thought made him feel sick.

Mr. Manx *had* passed a message to Bing once, although by what means Bing didn't know. A package had been dropped on the doorstep with no return address on it, two days after Mr. Manx was sentenced to life in Englewood. Inside were a pair of license plates—NOS4A2/KANSAS—and a little card on ivory laid stock, with a Christmas angel stamped into the front.

HOLD THESE.
I MIGHT BE A WHILE
9

Bing had the license plates in the root cellar, where all the rest of his life with Charlie Manx was buried: the empty stolen tanks of sevoflurane, his daddy's .45, and the remains of the women, the mothers that Bing had brought home with him after many a mission of salvation with Mr. Manx . . . *nine* missions in all.

Brad McCauley had been the ninth child they had saved for Christmasland, and his mother, Cynthia, the last whore Bing had dealt with in the quiet room downstairs. In a way she had been saved as well, before she died: Bing had taught her about love.

Bing and Mr. Manx had planned to save one more child in the summer of 1997, and that time Bing would go all the way to Christmasland with Mr. Manx, to live where no one grew old and unhappiness was against the law, where he could ride all the rides and drink all the cocoa and open Christmas gifts every morning. When he thought about the cosmic unfairness of it—of Mr. Manx being ripped away right before he could swing wide the gates of Christmasland to Bing at last—he felt smashed inside, as if hope were a vase that had been dropped from a height, *crunch*.

The worst of it, though, was not losing Mr. Manx or losing Christmasland. It was losing love. It was losing the mommies.

His last, Mrs. McCauley, had been the best. They had long talks in the basement together, Mrs. McCauley naked and tanned and fit, clasped against Bing's side. She was forty but stringy with muscle that she had built up coaching girls' volleyball. Her skin radiated heat and health. She stroked the graying hair on Bing's chest and told him she loved him better than her mother or father, better than Jesus, better than her own son, better than kittens, better than sunshine. It felt good to hear her say it: "I love you, Bing Partridge. I love you so much it's burning me. I'm all kindling inside. It's burning me alive." Her breath had been sweet with the smell of the gingerbread smoke; she was so fit, and so healthy, he had to dose her with his flavored sevoflurane mix once every three hours. She loved him so much she cut her own wrists when he told her they couldn't live together. They made love one last time while she bled out—while she bled all over him.

"Does it hurt?" he asked.

"Oh, Bing, Bing, you silly thing," she said. "I've been burning with love for days. A couple little cuts like these, they don't hurt at all."

She was so pretty—had such perfect mommy tits—he couldn't bear to pour the lye on her until she began to smell. Even with flies in her hair, she was pretty; *extra* pretty, really. The bluebottles glittered like gems.

Bing had visited the Graveyard of What Might Be with Mr. Manx and knew that if Cynthia McCauley had been left to her own devices, she would've killed her son in a steroid-fueled rage. But down in his quiet room, Bing had taught her kindness and love and how to suck cock, so at least she ended her life on a good note.

That was what it was all about: taking something awful and making something good of it. Mr. Manx saved the children, and Bing saved the mommies. Now, though, the mommies were over and done. Mr. Manx was locked-up gone, and Bing's gasmask hung on a hook behind the back door, where it had been since 1996. He read the story in the news about Mr. Manx falling asleep—into a deep, endless sleep, a brave soldier under a wicked enchantment—and then printed it and folded it and decided to pray on it some.

In his fifty-third year, Bing Partridge had become a churchgoing man once again, had returned to the New American Faith Tabernacle in the hopes that God would offer some comfort for one of his loneliest children. Bing prayed that one day he would hear "White Christmas" playing in the driveway and would push back the linen curtain and see Mr. Manx behind the wheel of the Wraith, the window rolled down and the Good Man gazing out at him. *Come on, Bing! Let's go for a ride! Number ten is waiting for us! Let's go grab one more kid and take you to Christmasland! Heaven knows you've earned it!*

He climbed the steep hill, in the smothering heat of a July afternoon. The foil flowers in his front yard—twenty-nine of them—were perfectly still and silent. He hated them. He hated the blue sky, too, and the maddening harmonic of the cicadas throbbing in the trees. Bing trudged up the hill with the news story in one hand ("Rare Condition Befalls Convicted Murderer") and Mr. Manx's final note in the other *("I might be a while. 9.")* to speak to God about these things.

The church stood in a hectare of buckled blacktop, shoots of pale grass as high as Bing's knees sticking up through the cracks. A loop of heavy-duty chain and a Yale lock held the front doors shut. No one except for Bing himself had prayed there for going on fifteen years. The tabernacle had belonged to the Lord once, but now it was property of the moneylenders; a sun-faded sheet of paper in a clear plastic envelope tacked to one of the doors said so.

The cicadas buzzed in Bing's head, like madness.

Out at one end of the lot was a big sign like they'd have out in front of a Dairy Queen or a used-car lot, telling people which hymn they'd be singing that day. ONLY IN GOD and HE'S ALIVE AGAIN and THE LORD NEVER SLEEPS. DEVOTIONS were promised for 1:00 P.M. The sign had been promising those same hymns since Reagan's second term.

Some of the stained-glass windows had holes where kids had chucked rocks at them, but Bing didn't climb in that way. There was a shed out to one side of the church, half hidden back in the dusty poplars and sumac. A rotting cord doormat lay in front of the shed's door. A bright brass key was hidden beneath it.

The key opened the padlock on the sloped cellar doors at the back of the building. Bing let himself below. He crossed a cool subterranean room, wading through the smell of old creosote and mildewed books, and came up into the big open theater of the church.

Bing had always liked church, back in the days when he still went with his mother. He had liked the way the sun came through the twenty-foot-high stained-glass windows, filling the room with warmth and color, and he had liked the way the mommies dressed, in white lace and heels and milky-white stockings. Bing loved white stockings and loved to hear a woman sing. All the mommies who stayed with him in the House of Sleep sang before they took their last rest.

But after the pastor ran away with the whole treasury and the bank locked the church up, Bing found that the place troubled him. He did not like the way the shadow of the steeple seemed to reach for his house in the late of day. Bing found after he started taking mommies back to his home—a place Mr. Manx had christened the House of Sleep—he could hardly stand to look at the top of the hill anymore. The church *loomed,* the shadow of the steeple an accusing finger that stretched down the slope and pointed at his front yard: *HERE IS A DEADLY KILLER! NINE DEAD WOMEN IN HIS BASEMENT!*

Bing tried to tell himself he was being foolish. He and Mr. Manx were heroes, really; they did Christian work. If someone wrote a book about them, you would have to mark them down as the good guys. It did not matter that many of the mothers, when dosed with sevoflurane, would still not admit to their plans to whore their daughters or beat their sons and that several contended they had never taken drugs, did not drink to excess, and did not have criminal records. Those things were in the future, a wretched future that Bing and Mr. Manx worked hard to prevent. If he was ever arrested—because of course no lawman would ever understand the importance and basic goodness of their vocation—Bing felt he could talk about his work with pride. There was no shame in him about *any* of the things he had done with Mr. Manx.

Still, he occasionally had trouble looking up at the church.

He told himself, as he climbed the steps from the basement, that he was being a ninny, that all men were welcome in God's house and Mr. Manx needed Bing's prayers—now more than ever. For himself, Bing had never felt so alone or forlorn. A few weeks earlier, Mr. Paladin had asked Bing what he was going to do with himself after he retired. Bing was shocked and asked why he would retire. He liked his job. Mr. Paladin blinked and said after forty years they would *make* him retire. You didn't get a choice in the matter. Bing had never thought about it. He had assumed that by now he would be drinking cocoa in Christmasland, opening presents in the morning, singing carols in the night.

The vast empty sanctuary did not put his mind at ease that afternoon. Just the opposite, in fact. All the pews were still there, although they were no longer lined up in neat rows but had been shoved this way and that, were as crooked as Mr. Manx's teeth. The floor was littered with broken glass and chunks of plaster, which crunched underfoot. The room smelled rankly of ammonia, of bird piss. Someone had been in here drinking. The bottles and beer cans left behind littered the pews.

He went on, pacing the length of the room. His passage disturbed the swallows in the rafters. The sound of their beating wings echoed, a noise like a magician spraying playing cards into the air.

The light that slanted in through the windows was cold and blue, and motes of dust turned within the bars of sunshine, as if the church were the interior of a snow globe just beginning to settle.

Someone—teenagers, homeless—had made an altar in one of the deep-set window frames. Deformed red candles stood in hardened puddles of wax, and set behind the candles were several photographs of Michael Stipe from R.E.M., a scrawny queer with pale hair and pale eyes. Someone had written *"LOSING MY RELIGION"* on one of the photographs in cherry lipstick. Bing himself felt there had not been a single thing worth listening to in rock music since *Abbey Road*.

Bing set the card from Mr. Manx and the printout from the *Denver Post* in the center of this homemade altar and lit a couple candles for the Good Man. He cleared some space on the floor, kicking aside chunks of broken plaster and a dirty pair of panties—little hearts on them, looked like they'd fit a ten-year-old—and got on his knees.

He cleared his throat. In the vast echoing space of the church, it sounded as loud as a gunshot.

A swallow rattled its wings, gliding from one rafter to another.

He could see a line of pigeons leaning forward to stare down at him with their bright, rabies-red eyes. They watched him with fascination.

He shut his eyes and put his hands together and spoke with God.

"Hey, there, God," Bing said. "It's Bing, that old dumb thing. Oh, God. Oh, God God *God.* Please help Mr. Manx. Mr. Manx has the sleepies, *bad,* and I don't know what to do, and if he doesn't get better and come back to me, I'll never have my trip to Christmasland. I tried my best to do something good with my life. I tried my best to save children and make sure they'd have cocoa and rides and things. It wasn't easy. No one *wanted* us to save them. But even when the mommies screamed and called us awful names, even when their children cried and wet themselves, I loved them. I loved those kids, and I loved their mommies, even if they were *bad* women. And I loved Mr. Manx most of all. Everything he does, he does so other people can be *happy.* Isn't that the kindest thing a person can do—spread a little happiness around? Please, God, if we did any good at all, please, help me, give me a sign, tell me what to do. Please, *pl*ease, please, *pl*—"

His face was tipped back and his mouth was open when something hot hit his cheek, and he tasted something salty and bitter on his lips. He flinched; it was like someone had cum on him. He swiped at his mouth and looked at his fingers, now coated with a whitish green crud, a sloppy liquid mash. It took a moment to identify it as pigeon shit.

Bing groaned: once, then again. His mouth was full of the salt-crème taste of bird shit. The stuff cupped in his palm looked like diseased phlegm. His moaning rose to a scream and he pitched himself backward, kicking plaster and glass, and put his other hand down on something damp and sticky, with the soft texture of Saran Wrap. He glanced down and discovered he had planted his hand on a soiled condom crawling with ants.

He lifted his hand in horror, in revulsion, and the condom stuck to his fingers, and he flicked his hand once, twice, and it flipped up and landed in his hair. He shrieked. Birds exploded from the rafters.

"*What?*" he screamed to the church. "*What?* I came here on my *knees*! I CAME ON MY KNEES! And you do *what*? **WHAT?**"

He grabbed the rubber and yanked, tearing out a fistful of his own wispy gray hair at the same time (when had it all turned gray?). Dust swirled in the light.

Bing Partridge went down the hill in a shambling jog, feeling defiled and ill . . . defiled, ill, and *outraged.* He reeled like a drunk past the foil flowers in his front yard and banged the door shut behind him.

It was the Gasmask Man who stepped out twenty minutes later, a bottle of lighter fluid in each hand.

Before he lit the place up, he boarded over the holes in the windows so the birds couldn't get out. He drizzled most of one bottle over the pews and the heaps of broken wood and plaster on the floor: perfect little premade bonfires. The other bottle he emptied on the figure of Jesus, mounted on his cross up in the apse. He looked cold in his little loincloth, so Bing flicked a match and dressed him in a robe of flame. Mary gazed sadly down at this latest indignity inflicted upon her son from a mural above him. Bing tapped two fingers to the mouthpiece of his mask, blew her a kiss.

Give him a chance to grab child number ten with Mr. Manx, Bing thought, and he didn't care if he had to gas and kill Christ's own mama to get the little bastard.

Besides. There wasn't anything the Holy Ghost had done in Mother Mary's pussy that Bing couldn't have done better, if he had three days alone with her in the House of Sleep.

Gunbarrel, Colorado

THE CHILDREN NEVER CALLED WHEN SHE WAS PAINTING.

It was months before Vic understood this consciously, but on some level of her mind that existed beneath reason, she got it almost right away. When she wasn't painting, when she didn't have creative work to occupy her, she became aware of a growing physical apprehension, like she was standing beneath a crane that was holding a piano aloft; at any moment she felt that the cables could snap and all that weight could fall upon her with a fatal crash.

So she lined up every job she could get and spent seventy hours a week in the garage listening to Foreigner and airbrushing motorcycles for men with criminal records and offensive racial notions.

Vic painted flames and guns and naked chicks and grenades and Dixie flags and Nazi flags and Jesus Christ and white tigers and rotting ghouls and more naked chicks. She didn't think of herself as an artist. Painting kept Christmasland from calling and paid for Pampers. All other considerations were of little importance.

Sometimes, though, the jobs dried up. Sometimes it seemed she had painted every motorcycle in the Rockies and there would never be another gig. When that happened—when she had more than a week or two without painting—she found herself grimly waiting. Readying herself.

Then one day the phone would ring.

It happened in September, on a Tuesday morning, five years after Manx went to jail. Lou had gone out before the sun came up to tow someone out of a ditch, left her with Wayne, who wanted hot dogs for breakfast. All those years smelled of steaming hot dogs and steaming baby shit.

Wayne was parked in front of the tube, and Vic was squirting ketchup into cheap hot-dog rolls when the phone rang.

She stared at the receiver. It was too early for the phone to be ringing, and she already knew who it was, because she had not painted anything in almost a month.

Vic touched the receiver. It was *cold.*

"Wayne," she said.

The boy looked up, finger in his mouth, drool down the front of his X-Men T-shirt.

"Do you hear the phone ringing, Wayne?" she asked.

He stared at her blankly, uncomprehendingly for a moment, then shook his head.

It rang again.

"There," she said. "There, did you hear it? Don't you hear it ringing?"

"No, Em," he said, and wagged his head heavily from side to side.

He turned his attention back to the television.

Vic picked up the receiver.

A child—not Brad McCauley, a different child, a girl this time—said, "*When* is Daddy coming back to Christmasland? What did you *do* with Daddy?"

"You aren't real," Vic said.

In the background she could hear the children caroling.

"Yes I am," the girl said. A white breath of frozen air seethed through the small holes in the earpiece of the receiver. "We're just as real as what's happening in New York this morning. You should see what's happening in New York. It's exciting! People are jumping into the sky! It's *exciting,* and it's *fun*. It's *almost* as fun as Christmasland."

"You aren't real," Vic whispered again.

"You told *lies* about Daddy," she said. "That was *bad*. You're a *bad mother.* Wayne should be with *us.* He could play with us all day. We could teach him how to play scissors-for-the-drifter."

Vic slammed the phone into the cradle. She picked it up and slammed it down once more. Wayne glanced around at her, his eyes wide and alarmed.

She waved a hand at him—*never mind*—and turned away, struggling not to cry, breath hitching.

The hot dogs boiled over, water jumping out of the pot and spattering into the blue flame of the gas burner. She ignored them, sank down onto the kitchen floor, and covered her eyes. It was an act of will to contain her sobs; she didn't want to scare Wayne.

"Em!" her boy called, and she looked up, blinking. "Sumfin' happened to Oscar!"

"Oscar" was his word for *Sesame Street.* "Sumfin' happened, an' Oscar went bye-bye."

Vic wiped at her streaming eyes, took a shuddering breath, turned off the gas. She walked unsteadily to the television. *Sesame Street* had gone to a news break. A big jet had hit one of the World Trade Towers in New York City. Black smoke churned into blue, blue sky.

A few weeks later, Vic made space in the closet-size second bedroom, tidied and swept. She moved an easel in there and mounted bristol board on it.

"Whatchu doing?" Lou asked, pushing his head through the door the day after she set herself up.

"Thought I'd draw a picture book," Vic said. She had the first page sketched in blue pencil, was almost ready to start inking.

Lou peered over her shoulder. "Are you drawing a motorcycle factory?" he asked.

"Close. A robot factory," she said. "The hero is a robot named Search Engine. On each page he has to work his way through a maze and find some items of importance. Power cells and secret plans and stuff."

"I think I'm popping a boner for your picture book. Awesome thing to do for Wayne. He's going to shit."

Vic nodded. She was happy to let Lou think she was doing it for the kid. She had no illusions, though. She was doing it for herself.

The picture book was better than painting Harleys. It was steady work, and it was there every day.

After she started drawing *Search Engine,* the phone never rang unless a credit agency was calling.

And after she sold the book, the credit agencies quit calling, too.

Brandenburg, Kentucky

Michelle Demeter was twelve the first time her father let her drive it. A twelve-year-old girl driving a 1938 Rolls-Royce Wraith through the high grass in the first days of summer with the windows rolled down and Christmas music playing on the radio. Michelle sang along in a big, happy, braying voice—off-key and off-time. When she did not know the lyrics, she made them up.

Come! All ye faithful! Jiggy and triii-umphant!
Come all ye faithful, sing yay for the Lord!

The car swam through the grass, a black shark slicing through a rippling ocean of yellows and greens. Birds scattered before it, darting into a lemon sky. The wheels banged and thudded in unseen ruts.

Her father, crocked and getting crockeder, sat in the passenger seat fiddling with the tuner, a warm Coors between his legs. Only the tuner didn't do anything. The radio jumped from band to band, but everything was white noise. The only station that came in at all was distant, crackling, and awash with background hiss and playing that goddamn holiday music.

"Who is playing this shit in the middle of May?" he asked, and burped, enormously and grotesquely.

Michelle giggled in appreciation.

There was no way to turn the radio off or even down. The volume dial spun uselessly, adjusting nothing.

"This car is like your old man," Nathan said, pulling another Coors out of the six-pack at his feet, popping another top. "A wreck of its former self."

That was just more of his silly talk. Her father wasn't doing so bad. He had invented some kind of valve for Boeing, and it had paid for three hundred acres above the Ohio River. They were driving around it now.

The car, on the other hand, really *had* left its best days behind it. The carpet was gone, and where it belonged was bare, humming metal. There were holes under the pedals, and through them Michelle could see grass whipping by below. The leather on the dash was peeling. One of the back doors didn't match the others, was unpainted and caked with rust. There was no rear window at all, just a round open hole. No backseat either, and a char mark in the rear compartment, where it looked as if someone had tried to light a campfire once.

The girl worked the clutch and the gas and the brake expertly with her right foot, just as her father had taught her. The front seat was cranked all the way forward, and still she had to sit on a pillow so she could see over the high dash and out the window.

"One of these days I'm going to get around to working on this beast. Roll my sleeves up and bring the old lady all the way back to life. Be a hell of a thing to have it completely restored so you could take it to the prom," her father said. "When you're old enough for proms."

"Yah. Good call. Plenty of room in the backseat to make out," she said, twisting her neck to look over her shoulder into the rear.

"It'd also be a nice ride to take you to the nunnery in. You keep your eyes on the road, why don'tcha?" Gesturing with his beer can at the rise and fall of the land and the tangles of grass and brush and goldenrod, no road in sight in any direction, the only sign of human existence the distant barn in the rearview mirror and the jet contrails overhead.

She pumped the pedals. They wheezed and gasped.

The only thing Michelle didn't like about the car was the hood ornament, a creepy silver lady with blind eyes and a flowing gown. She leaned out into the lashing weeds and grinned manically as she was flagellated. That silver lady should've been magical and pretty, but the smile on her face ruined it. She had the demented grin of a madwoman who has just pushed a loved one off a ledge and is about to follow him into eternity.

"She's awful," Michelle said, lifting her chin in the direction of the hood. "Like a vampire lady."

"The bloofer lady," her father said, remembering something he had read once.

"The who? She is *not* called the bloofer lady."

"No," Nathan said. "She's called the Spirit of Ecstasy. She's classic. She's a classic part of a classic car."

"Ecstasy? Like the drug?" Michelle asked. "Wow. Trippy. They were into that back then?"

"No. Not like the drug. Like fun. She's a symbol of never-ending fun. I think she's pretty," he said, although in fact he thought she looked like one of the Joker's victims, a rich lady who had died laughing.

"I been driving out to Christmasland, all the livelong day," Michelle sang softly. For the moment the radio was just a roar of static and whine, and she could sing without competition. *"I been driving out to Christmasland, just to ride in Santa's sleigh!"*

"What's that one? I don't know it," her dad said.

"That's where we're going," she said. "To Christmasland. I just decided."

The sky was trying on a variety of citrus hues. Michelle felt perfectly at peace. She felt she could drive forever.

Her tone was soft with excitement and delight, and when her

father glanced at her, there was a dew of sweat on her forehead and her eyes had a faraway look.

"It's out there, Daddy," she said. "It's out there in the mountains. If we kept going, we could be in Christmasland by tonight."

Nathan Demeter narrowed his eyes and peered out through the dusty window. A vast, pale mountain range towered in the west, with snow-touched peaks higher than the Rockies, a mountain range that had not been there this morning, or even when they set out on this drive, twenty minutes ago.

He looked quickly away, blinking to clear his vision, then looked back—and the mountain range resolved into a looming mass of thunderheads, crowding the western horizon. His heart continued to run a three-legged race in his chest for a few moments longer.

"Too bad you have homework. No Christmasland for you," he said. Even though it was Saturday and no dad anywhere made his twelve-year-old do algebra on a Saturday. "Time to turn us around, sweetheart. Daddy has things to do."

He slouched back in his seat and had a sip of beer, but he didn't want it anymore. He felt the first dull edge of tomorrow's hangover in his left temple. Judy Garland was tragically wishing everyone a merry little Christmas, and what the fuck was the deejay smoking, playing "Have Yourself a Merry Little Christmas" in May?

But the music only lasted until they reached the weedy edge of their property and Michelle laboriously turned the Wraith around to point them back toward home. As the Rolls wheeled in a semicircle, the radio lost what little reception it had and once more became a low roar of white noise, of mad static.

It was 2006 and Nathan Demeter had himself an old junker to fix up, bought in a federal auction, something to play with in his spare time. One of these days he was going to get around to really working on it. One of these days he was going to make the old lady shine.

New York (and Everywhere Else)

HERE IS WHAT THEY SAID ABOUT THE SECOND *SEARCH ENGINE* BOOK in the *New York Times Book Review,* Children's Book section, Sunday, July 8, 2007—the only time any of Vic McQueen's books were reviewed there.

Search Engine's Second Gear

By Vic McQueen.
22 pages. HarperCollins Children's Books. $16.95. (Puzzle/Picture Book; ages 6 to 12)

If M. C. Escher were hired to reimagine Where's Waldo?, *it might look something like Ms. McQueen's fascinating and deservedly popular Search Engine series. The eponymous hero, Search Engine—a cheerful and childlike robot who resembles a cross between C-3PO and a Harley-Davidson—pursues Mad Möbius Stripp across a series of dizzying impossible constructions and surreal mazes. One confounding puzzle cannot be solved without placing a mirror against the edge of the book; another mind bender requires the children to roll the page up into a tube to make a magical covered bridge; a third must be torn out and folded into an origami motorcycle so Search Engine can continue his pursuit at full throttle. Young readers who complete* Search Engine's Second Gear *will find themselves faced with the most terrible puzzle of them all: How long until the next one?!*

FCI Englewood, Colorado

NURSE THORNTON DROPPED INTO THE LONG-TERM-CARE WARD A little before eight with a hot bag of blood for Charlie Manx.

Denver, Colorado

The first Saturday in October 2009, Lou told Victoria McQueen he was taking the kid and going to his mother's for a while. For some reason he told her this in a whisper, with the door shut, so Wayne, out in the living room, couldn't hear them talking. Lou's round face shone with nervous sweat. He licked his lips a lot while he spoke.

They were in the bedroom together. Lou sat on the edge of the bed, causing the mattress to creak and sag halfway to the floor. It was hard for Vic to get comfortable in the bedroom. She kept looking at the phone on the night table, waiting for it to ring. She had tried to get rid of it a few days ago, had unplugged it and shoved it into a bottom drawer, but at some point Lou had discovered it there and plugged it back in.

Lou said some other stuff, about how worried he was, about how everyone was worried. She didn't catch all of it. Her whole mind was bent toward the phone, watching it, waiting for it to ring. She knew it would. Waiting for it was awful. It angered her that Lou had brought her inside, that they couldn't have this conversation out on the deck. It shook her faith in him. It was impossible to have a conversation in a room with a phone. It was like having a conversation in a room with a bat hanging from the ceiling. Even if the bat was asleep, how were you supposed to think about anything else or look at anything else?

If the phone rang, she would yank it out of the wall and get it out to the deck and throw it over the side. She was tempted not to wait, to just do it now.

She was surprised when Lou said maybe she should go see her mother, too. Vic's mother was all the way hell and gone back in Massachusetts, and Lou knew they didn't get on. The only thing that would've been more ridiculous was suggesting that Vic go see her father, whom she had not spoken to in years.

"I'd rather go to jail than stay with my mom. Jesus, Lou. Do you know how many phones my mother has in her house?" Vic asked.

Lou gave her a look that was somehow both distraught and weary. It was a look, Vic thought, of surrender.

"If you want to talk—like, about *anything*—I've got my cell on me," Lou said.

Vic just laughed at that, didn't bother to tell him she had pulled his cell phone apart and shoved it in the garbage the day before.

He took her in his arms, held her in his bearish embrace. He was a big man, glum about being overweight, but he smelled better than any guy she had ever met. His chest smelled of cedar and motor oil and the outdoors. He smelled like responsibility. For a moment, being held by him, she remembered what it had been like to be happy.

"Got to go," he said at last. "Got a lot of driving to do."

"Go where?" she asked, startled.

He blinked, then said, "Like, Vic . . . dude . . . were you listening?"

"Closely," Vic said, and it was true. She *had* been listening. Just not to him. She had been listening for the phone. She had been waiting for it to ring.

After Louis and the kid were gone, she walked through the rooms of the brick town house on Garfield Street that she had paid for with the money she made drawing *Search Engine,* back when she still drew, back before the children in Christmasland started calling again, every day. She brought a pair of scissors with her, and she cut the lines leading into each of the phones.

Vic collected the phones and brought them to the kitchen. She put them in the oven, on the top rack, and turned the dial to BROIL. Hey, it had worked the last time she needed to fight Charlie Manx, hadn't it?

As the oven began to warm, she shoved open the windows, switched on the fan.

After that, Vic sat in the living room and watched TV in her panties and nothing else. First she watched Headline News. But there were too many ringing phones in the CNN studio, and the sound unnerved her. She switched over to SpongeBob. When the phone in the Krusty Krab rang, she changed the channel again. She found a sports-fishing program. That seemed safe enough—no phones in this kind of show—and the setting was Lake Winnipesaukee, where she had spent her childhood summers. She had always liked the way the lake looked just after dawn, a smooth black mirror wrapped in the white silk of early-morning fog.

At first she drank whiskey on the rocks. Then she had to drink it straight, because it smelled too bad in the kitchen to go in there and get ice. The whole town house stank of burning plastic, despite the fan and the open windows.

Vic McQueen was watching one of the fishermen struggle with a trout when a phone began to chirp, somewhere near her feet. She looked down at the scatter of toys on the floor, a collection of Wayne's robots: an R2-D2, a Dalek, and of course a couple of Search Engine figures. One of the robots was a Transformers thing, black with a bulky torso and a red lens for a head. It visibly shivered as it chirped once more.

She picked it up and began to fold the arms and legs inward. She pushed the head down into the body. She snapped the two halves of its torso together and suddenly was looking at a plastic, nonfunctional, toy cell phone.

The plastic, nonfunctional, toy cell phone rang again. She pressed the ANSWER button and held it up to her ear.

"You're a big fat liar—" said Millicent Manx. "And Daddy is going to be mad at you when he gets out. He's going to stick a fork in your eyes and pop them out, just like corks."

Vic carried the toy into the kitchen and opened the oven. Poisonous black smoke gushed out. The cooked phones had charred like marshmallows dropped in a campfire. She threw the Transformer in on top of the melted brown slag and slammed the oven shut again.

The stink was so bad she had to leave the house. She put on Lou's motorcycle jacket and her boots and got her purse and went out. She grabbed the whiskey bottle and pulled the door shut behind her, just as she heard the smoke detector begin to blat.

She was down the street and around the corner when she realized she hadn't put anything on besides the jacket and her boots. She was tramping around greater Denver at two in the morning in her faded pink panties. At least she had remembered the whiskey.

She meant to go home and pull on a pair of jeans, but she got lost trying to find her way back, something that had never happened before, and wound up walking on a pretty street of three-story brick buildings. The night was aromatic with the smell of autumn and the steely fragrance of freshly dampened blacktop. How she loved the smell of road: asphalt baking and soft in high July, dirt roads with their dust-and-pollen perfume in June, country lanes spicy with the odor of crushed leaves in sober October, the sand-and-salt smell of the highway, so like an estuary, in February.

At that time of the night, she had the street almost to herself, although at one point three men on Harleys rolled by. They slowed as they went past to check her out. They weren't bikers, though. They were yuppies, who were probably creeping home to wifey after a boys' night out at an upscale strip club. She knew from their Italian leather jackets and Gap blue jeans and showroom-quality bikes that they were more used to Pizzeria Unos than to living brutal on the road. Still. They took their time looking her over. She raised her bottle of whiskey to them and wolf-whistled with her free hand,

and they grabbed their throttles and took off, tailpipes between their legs.

She wound up at a bookstore. Closed, of course. It was a little indie, with a big display of her books in one window. She had given a talk here a year ago. She had been wearing pants then.

She squinted into the darkened store, leaning close to see which one of her books they were peddling. Book four. The fourth book was out already? It seemed to Vic she was still working on it. She overbalanced and wound up with her face smooshed to the glass and her ass sticking out.

She was glad book four was out. There had been moments when she didn't think she would finish it.

When Vic had started drawing the books, the phone never rang with calls from Christmasland. That was why she had started *Search Engine* in the first place, because when she was drawing, the phones were silent. But then, midway through the third book, radio stations she liked started playing Christmas songs in the middle of the summer and the calls began again. She had tried to make a protective moat around herself, a moat filled with Maker's Mark, but the only thing she had drowned in it was the work itself.

Vic was about to push away from the window when the phone in the bookstore rang.

She could see it lighting up over at the desk, on the far side of the shop. In the gusting, warm silence of the night, she could hear it quite clearly, and she knew it was them. Millie Manx and Brad McCauley and Manx's other children.

"I'm sorry," she said to the store. "I'm not available to take your call. If you'd like to leave a message, you're shit out of luck."

She shoved away from the window, a little too hard, and reeled across the sidewalk. Then the sidewalk ended and her foot plunged over the edge of the curb, and she fell, sat down hard on her ass on the wet blacktop.

It hurt, but not as much as it probably should've. She wasn't sure if the whiskey had muted the pain or if she had been on the Lou Carmody diet for too long and was now carrying a bit of extra padding back there. She worried she had dropped the bottle and broken it, but no, it was right there in her hand, safe and sound. She took a swallow. It tasted of the oak cask and sweet annihilation.

She struggled back to her feet, and another phone rang, in another shop, a darkened coffeehouse. The phone in the bookstore was still ringing, too. Then another went off, somewhere on the second floor of a building over to her right. And a fourth and a fifth. In the apartments above her. Both sides of the street, up and down the lane.

The night filled with a choir of phones. It was like frogs in the spring, an alien harmony of croaks and chirrups and whistles. It was like bells ringing on Christmas morning.

"Go the fuck away!" she screamed, and threw the bottle at her own reflection in a store window across the street.

The plate glass exploded. All the phones stopped ringing at the same time, revelers shocked into quiet by a gunshot.

A half beat later, a security alarm went off inside the store, an electronic wang-dang-doodle and a flashing silver light. The silver light silhouetted the wares on display in the window: bicycles.

The night caught and held in place for one lush, gentle moment.

The bicycle in the window was (of course) a Raleigh, white and simple. Vic swayed. The sensation of being threatened shut itself off as quickly as if someone had flipped a switch.

She crossed the road to the bike shop, and by the time she was crunching across the broken glass, she had her plan worked out. She would steal the bicycle and ride it out of town. She would ride it out to Dakota Ridge, into the pines and the night, would ride until she found the Shortaway.

The Shorter Way Bridge would take her right over the walls of the Supermax prison and on into the hospital ward that held Charlie Manx. That would be a hell of a sight, a thirty-one-year-old in her underwear, gliding along on a ten-speed through the long-term-care ward of a maximum-security lockup at two in the morning. She pictured herself sailing through the dark, between convicts sleeping in their beds. She'd ride right up to Manx, put the kickstand down, yank the pillow out from under his head, and suffocate the filthy man-burner. That would end the calls from Christmasland forever. She knew it would.

Vic reached through the broken glass and picked the Raleigh up and carried it out to the road. She heard the first distant wail of a siren, a yearning, agonized sound that carried a long way in the warm, damp night.

She was surprised. The alarm had only gone off half a minute ago. She didn't think the cops would respond so quickly.

But the siren she heard wasn't cops. It was a fire truck, heading toward her town house, although by the time it arrived, there was not much left to save.

The cop cars showed up a few minutes later.

Brandenburg, Kentucky

He saved the hardest part for last: In May 2012, Nathan Demeter hauled the engine out of the Wraith with a chain fall and spent two days rebuilding it, cleaning pushrods, and replacing the head bolts with parts ordered from a specialty shop in England. The engine was a big 4,257-cc straight-six, and sitting on his worktable it looked like some vast mechanical heart—which was what it was, he supposed. So many of man's inventions—the syringe, the sword, the pen, the gun—were metaphorical cocks, but the internal combustion engine had to have been dreamt up by a man who had looked upon the human heart.

"Be cheaper to rent a limo," Michelle said. "And you wouldn't get your hands dirty."

"If you think I've got a problem with getting my hands dirty," he said, "then you weren't paying much attention the last eighteen years."

"Something to do with your nervous energy, I guess," she said.

"Who's nervous?" he asked, but she just smiled and kissed him.

Sometimes, after he had been working on the car for a few hours, he would find himself stretched across the front seat, one leg hanging out the open door and a beer in hand, playing it back in his head: the afternoons when they went low-riding in the west field, his daughter behind the wheel and the weeds slapping the sides of the Wraith.

She had passed her driver's test on her first try, just sixteen years old. Eighteen now, and she had her own car, a sporty little Jetta, was planning to drive it all the way to Dartmouth after she graduated. The thought of her out on the road by herself—checking into shabby motels and being checked out by the man behind the cash register, by the truckers in the hotel bar—made him antsy, revved him up with nervous energy.

Michelle liked to do the wash, and he liked to let her, because when he came across her underwear in the dryer, colorful lace from Victoria's Secret, he began to worry about things like unwanted pregnancy and venereal disease. He had known how to talk to her about cars. He had liked watching her figure out how to work the clutch, how to steer true. He had felt like Gregory Peck in *To Kill a Mockingbird* then. He didn't know how to talk to her about men or sex and was unsettled by his sense that she didn't need his advice on these matters anyway.

"Who's nervous?" he asked the empty garage one night, and toasted his shadow.

Six days before the big dance, he put the engine back in the Wraith and closed the hood and stood back to consider his work, a sculptor studying the nude that had once been a block of marble. A cold season of banged knuckles and oil under his fingernails and rust flakes falling in his eyes: sacred time, important to him in the way transcribing a holy text was important to a monk in a monastery. He had cared to get it right and it showed.

The ebony body gleamed like a torpedo, like a polished slab of volcanic glass. The rear side door, which had been rusty and mismatched, had been replaced by an original, sent to him by a collector in one of the former Soviet republics. He had reupholstered the interior in kidskin leather, replaced the foldout trays and drawers in the rear of the limo with new walnut components, handmade by a carpenter in Nova Scotia. It was all original, even the vacuum-tube radio, although he had toyed with the idea of installing a CD player, bolting a Bose subwoofer into the trunk. In the end he had decided against it. When you had a *Mona Lisa,* you didn't spray-paint a baseball cap on her.

He had promised his daughter on some long-ago, hot, thunderstormy, summer afternoon that he would fix the Rolls up for her prom, and here it was, finished at last, with just under a week to spare. After prom he could sell it; fully restored, the Wraith was good for quarter of a million dollars on the collectors' market. Not bad for a car that cost just five thousand dollars American when it was released. Not bad at all, when you considered he had paid just twice that to buy it in an FBI auction, ten years earlier.

"Who do you think owned it before you?" Michelle asked one time, after he mentioned where he got it.

"Drug dealer, I imagine," he said.

"Boy," she told him, "I hope no one was murdered in it."

It looked good—but looking good wasn't enough. He didn't think Michelle belonged in it, out on the road, until he had clocked a dozen miles on it himself, seen how it handled when it was all the way up to speed.

"Come on, you beautiful bitch," he said to the car. "Let's wake you up and see what you can do."

Demeter got behind the wheel, banged the door shut behind him, and turned the key.

The engine slammed roughly to life—a ragged, almost savagely triumphant blast of noise—but then immediately settled down to a low, luxuriant rumble. The creamy leather front seat was more comfortable than the Tempur-Pedic bed he slept in. Back in the days when the Wraith had been assembled, things were built like tanks, built to last. This car, he felt sure, would outlive him.

He was right.

He had left his cell phone on his worktable, and he wanted it before he took the car out, didn't want to wind up stranded somewhere if the Wraith decided to throw a rod or some such shit. He reached for the latch, which was when he got his first surprise of the afternoon. The lock slammed down, the sound of it loud enough that he almost cried out.

Demeter was so startled—so unprepared—that he wasn't sure he had really seen it happen. But then the other locks went down, one after another—*bang, bang, bang*—just like someone firing a gun, and he couldn't tell himself he was imagining all that.

"What the *fuck*?"

He pulled at the lock on the driver's-side door, but it stayed down as if welded in place.

The car shuddered from the idling force of the engine, exhaust piling up around the sideboards.

Demeter leaned forward to switch the ignition off, which was when he received his second surprise of the day. The key wouldn't turn. He wiggled it forward and back, then put his wrist into it, but the key was locked into place, fully engaged, couldn't be yanked out.

The radio popped on, playing "Jingle Bell Rock" at top volume—so loud it hurt his ears—a song that had no business playing in the spring. At the sound of it, Demeter's whole body went rough and cold with chickenflesh. He poked the OFF switch, but his capacity for surprise was running thin, and he felt no special amazement when it wouldn't turn off. He punched buttons to change the station, but no matter where the tuner leaped, it was "Jingle Bell Rock" on every channel.

He could see exhaust fogging the air now. He could *taste* it, the dizzying reek, making him light-headed. Bobby Helms assured him that Jingle Bell time was a swell time to haul around in a one-horse sleigh. He had to shut that shit up, had to have some quiet, but when he spun the volume dial, it didn't go down, didn't do anything.

Fog churned around the headlights. His next breath was a mouthful of poison and set off a coughing fit so strenuous it felt as if it were tearing away the inner lining of his throat. Thoughts flashed by like horses on an accelerating carousel. Michelle wouldn't be back home for another hour and a half. The closest neighbors were three-quarters of a mile away—no one around to hear him screaming. The car wouldn't turn off, the locks wouldn't cooperate, it was like something in a fucking spy movie—he imagined a hired killer with a name like Blow Job operating the Rolls-Royce by remote control—but that was crazy. He himself had torn the Wraith down and put it back together, and he knew there was nothing wired into it that would give someone power over the engine, the locks, the radio.

Even as these notions occurred to him, he was fumbling on the dash for the automatic garage-door opener. If he didn't get some air in the garage, he would pass out in another moment or two. For a panicky instant, he felt nothing and thought, *Not there, it's not there*—but then his fingers found it behind the raised hump of the housing for the steering wheel. He closed his hand around it, then pointed it at the garage door and pressed the button.

The door rattled up toward the ceiling. The gearshift banged itself into the reverse position, and the Wraith jumped back at the door, tires shrilling.

Nathan Demeter screamed, grabbed the steering wheel—not to control the car but just to have something to hold on to. The slender whitewalls grabbed at the pebble drive, throwing rocks against the undercarriage. The Wraith fell straight back like a kart on some mad backward rollercoaster, plunging three hundred feet down the steep grade of the drive toward the lane below. It seemed to Nathan that he screamed the whole way, although in fact he stopped well before the car was halfway down the hill. The scream he heard was trapped in his own head.

The Wraith didn't slow as it approached the road but sped up, and if anything was coming from either direction, he would be T-boned at close to forty miles an hour. Of course, even if nothing was coming, the Wraith would shoot across the road, into the trees on the other side, and Nathan assumed he would be launched through the windshield on the recoil. The Wraith, like all the cars of its period, had no safety belts, not even lap belts.

The road was empty, and when the rear tires hit the blacktop, the wheel spun in Nathan's hands, whirring so fast it burned his palms and he had to let go. The Wraith snapped around, ninety degrees to the right, and Nathan Demeter was flipped across the front seat and into the left-hand door, bashed headfirst into the iron frame.

For a time he didn't know how badly he was hurt. He sprawled on the front seat, blinking at the ceiling. Through the passenger-side window, he could see the late-afternoon sky, a profoundly deep blue, with a feathering of cirrus clouds in the upper atmosphere. He touched a tender spot on his forehead, and when his hand came away he was looking at blood on his fingertips, as a flute began to play the opening bars of "The Twelve Days of Christmas."

The car was moving, had clunked down through the gears to fifth all on its own. He knew the roads around his house, felt they were moving east along Route 1638 to the Dixie Highway. Another minute and they would reach the intersection and—and what? Blow right through it, maybe catch a truck coming north and be torn apart? The thought crossed his mind as a possibility, but he couldn't feel any urgency attached to it, didn't think the car was on a kamikaze mission now. He had in some dazed way accepted that the Wraith was operating of its own agency. It had business and meant to do it. It had no use for him, was maybe not even really aware of him, any more than a dog might be aware of the tick stuck in its fur.

He climbed up onto one elbow, swayed, sat up the rest of the way, and looked at himself in the rearview mirror.

He wore a red mask of blood. When he touched his forehead again, he could feel a six-inch gash traversing the upper curve of his scalp. He probed it lightly with his fingers and felt the bone beneath.

The Wraith began to slow for the stop sign at the intersection with the Dixie Highway. He watched, mesmerized, as the gearshift dropped from fourth to third, clunked down into second. He began to scream again.

There was a station wagon ahead of him, waiting at the stop. Three towheaded, chubby-faced, dimple-cheeked children were crammed into the backseat. They twisted around to look at the Wraith.

He slapped his hands on the windshield, smearing rusty red prints on the glass.

"HELP!" he screamed, while warm blood leaked down his brow into his face. "HELP **HELP** HELP ME *HELP ME* ***HELP!***"

The children inexplicably grinned as if he were being quite silly and waved furiously. He began to scream incoherently—the sound of a cow in the abattoir, slipping in the steaming blood of those who went before.

The station wagon turned right at the first break in traffic. The Wraith turned left, accelerating so quickly that Nathan Demeter felt as if an invisible hand were pressing him back into his seat.

Even with the windows up, he could smell the clean, late-spring odors of mown grass, could smell smoke from backyard barbecues and the green fragrance of new-budding trees.

The sky reddened, as if it, too, were bleeding. The clouds were like tatters of gold foil stamped into it.

Absentmindedly, Nathan Demeter noted that the Wraith was handling like a dream. The engine had never sounded so good. So strong. He thought it was safe to say the beautiful bitch was fully restored.

HE WAS SURE HE DOZED, SITTING UP BEHIND THE WHEEL, BUT HE DID not remember nodding off. He only knew that at some point before it was fully dark, he closed his eyes, and when he opened them, the Wraith was racing through a tunnel of whirling snow, a tunnel of December night. The front windows were blurred with his own bloody handprints, but through them he could see snow devils unspooling across the black asphalt of a two-lane highway that he didn't recognize. Skeins of snow moving like living silk, like ghosts.

He tried to think if they could've gone far enough north while he slept to catch a freak spring snowstorm. He discarded the idea as idiotic. He weighed the cold night and the unfamiliar road and told himself he was dreaming, but he did not believe it. His own moment-by-moment tally of tactile experiences—throbbing head, face tight and sticky with blood, back stiff from sitting too long behind the wheel—was too convincing in its depiction of wakefulness. The car held the road like a panzer, never slipping, never wobbling, never slowing below sixty.

The songs played on: "All I Want for Christmas Is You," "Silver Bells," "Joy to the World," "It Came Upon a Midnight Clear." Sometimes Demeter was aware of the music. Sometimes he wasn't. No ads, no news, just holy choirs giving thanks to the Lord and Eartha Kitt promising she could be a very good girl if Santa checked off her Christmas list.

When he shut his eyes, he could picture his cell phone, sitting on the worktable in the garage. Would Michelle have looked for him there yet? Sure—as soon as she got home and found the garage door standing open and the garage itself empty. She would be, by now, out of her mind with worry, and he wished he had his phone, not to call for help—he believed he was well beyond help—but only because he would feel better if he could hear her voice. He wanted to call and tell her that he still wanted her to go to her prom, to try to have fun. He wanted to tell her he wasn't scared of her being a woman—if he had any true anxiety, it had been about himself getting old and being lonely without her, but he didn't think he was going to have to worry about that now. He wanted to tell her she had been the best thing in his life. He had not said that to her lately and had never said it enough.

After six hours in the car, he felt no panic, only a kind of numb wonder. On some level he had come to view his situation as almost natural. Sooner or later a black car came for everyone. It came and took you away from your loved ones, and you never got to go back.

Perry Como warned Nathan in a chipper tone of voice that it was beginning to look a lot like Christmas.

"No shit, Perry," Nathan said, and then, in a hoarse, cracking voice, he began to sing as he thumped on the driver's-side door. He sang Bob Seger; sang about the old-time rock 'n' roll, the type believed to soothe the soul. He belted it out as loud as he could, one verse and another, and when he fell quiet, he found the radio had shut itself off.

Well. That was a Christmas gift right there. *Last one he'd ever get*, he thought.

NEXT TIME HE OPENED HIS EYES, HIS FACE WAS PRESSED TO THE STEERING wheel and the car was idling, and there was so much light it hurt his eyes.

He squinted, the world a bright blue blur. Not at any time in the night had his head hurt as bad as it hurt now. The ache in his skull was so intense he thought he might vomit. It was behind his eyes, a somehow *yellow* glare of pain. All that sunlight was unfair.

He blinked at tears, and the world sharpened, began to come into focus.

A fat man in a gasmask and fatigues stared through the driver's-side window at him, peering in past the smeared bloody handprints on the glass. It was an old gasmask, WWII era or thereabouts, a kind of mustardy green.

"Who the fuck are you?" Nathan asked.

The fat man seemed to be jiggling up and down. Nathan was unable to see the guy's face but thought he was bouncing on his toes with excitement.

The lock on the driver's-side door shot up with a loud, steely bang.

The fat man had something in one hand, a cylinder—it looked like an aerosol can. GINGERSNAP SPICE AIR FRESHENER, it said on the side and showed an old-fashioned painting of a cheerful mommy type pulling a pan of gingerbread men out of the oven.

"Where am I?" Nathan Demeter asked. "Where the hell is this?"

The Gasmask Man twisted the latch and opened the door onto the fragrant spring morning.

"This is where you get out," he said.

St. Luke's Medical Center, Denver

When someone interesting was dead, Hicks always took a picture with them.

There had been a local news anchor, a pretty thirty-two-year-old with splendid white-blond hair and pale blue eyes, who got wasted and choked to death on her own puke. Hicks had slipped into the morgue at 1:00 A.M., pulled her out of her drawer, and sat her up. He got an arm around her and bent down to lap at her nipple, while holding out his cell phone to take a shot. He didn't actually lick her, though. That would've been gross.

There was a rock star, too—a minor rock star anyway. He was the one in that band that had the hit from the Stallone movie. The rock star wasted out from cancer and in death looked like a withered old woman, with his feathery brown hair and long eyelashes and wide, somehow feminine lips. Hicks got him out of the drawer and bent his hand into devil's horns, then leaned in and threw the horns himself, snapped a shot of them hanging out together. The rock star's eyelids sagged, so he looked sleepy and cool.

Hicks's girlfriend, Sasha, was the one who told him there was a famous serial killer down in the morgue. Sasha was a nurse in Pediatrics, eight floors up. She loved his photos with famous dead people; she was always the first person he e-mailed them to. Sasha thought

Hicks was hilarious. She said he ought to be on *The Daily Show.* Hicks was fond of Sasha, too. She had a key to the pharmacy locker, and Saturday nights she'd filch them something good, a little oxy or some medical-grade coke, and on breaks they'd find an empty delivery room and she'd shimmy out of the bottoms of her loose nurse jammies and climb up into the stirrups.

Hicks had never heard of the guy, so Sasha used the computer in the nurses' station to pull up a news story about him. The mug shot was bad enough, a bald guy with a narrow face and a mouthful of sharp, crooked teeth. His eyes were bright and round and stupid in their hollow sockets. The caption identified him as Charles Talent Manx, sent to the federal pen more than a decade before for burning some sorry motherfucker to death in front of a dozen witnesses.

"He's not any big deal," Hicks said. "He just killed one dude."

"Un-*uh.* He's worse than John Wayne Stacy. He killed, like, all kinds of kids. *All* kinds. He had a house where he did it. He hung little angels in the trees, one for ever' one he cut up. It's awesome. It's like creepy symbolism. Little Christmas angels. They called the place the Sleigh House. Get it? Do you get it, Hicks?"

"No."

"Like he slayed 'em there? But also like Santa's sleigh? Do you get it now?" she said.

"No." He didn't see what Santa had to do with a guy like Manx.

"The house got burnt down, but the ornaments are still there, hanging in the trees, like a memorial." She tugged at the drawstring of her scrubs. "Serial killers get me hot. All I can think about is all the nasty shit I'd do to keep 'em from killing me. You go take a pic with him and e-mail it to me. And, like, tell me what you're going to do if I don't get naked for you."

He didn't see any reason to argue with that kind of logic, and he had to make his rounds anyway. Besides, if the guy had killed lots of people, it might be worth taking a pic, to add to his collection. Hicks had already done several funny photographs, but he felt it would be good to have a snap with a serial killer, to demonstrate his darker, more serious side.

In the elevator, alone, Hicks drew his gun on his own reflection and said, "Either this is going in your mouth, or my *big* cock is." Practicing his lines for Sasha.

It was all good till his walkie-talkie went off and his uncle said, "Hey, dumb-ass, keep playing with that gun, maybe you'll shoot yourself and we can hire someone who can actually do this fuckin' job."

He had forgotten there was a camera in the elevator. Fortunately, there was no hidden microphone. Hicks pushed his .38 back into the holster and lowered his head, hoping the brim of his hat hid his face. He took ten seconds, fighting with his anger and embarrassment, then pressed the TALK button on his walkie, meaning to snap off something *really fucking harsh,* shut the old turd up for once. But instead all he managed was "Copy that," in a pinched little squeak that he hated.

His Uncle Jim had gotten him the security job, glossing over Hicks's early departure from high school and the arrest for public drunkenness. Hicks had been at the hospital for only two months and had been cited twice already, once for tardiness, once for not responding to his walkie (at the time it had been his turn in the stirrups). His Uncle Jim had already said if there was a third citation, before he had a full year under his belt, they'd have to let him go.

His Uncle Jim had a spotless record, probably because all he had to do was sit in the security office for six hours a day and watch the monitors with one eye while perusing Skinemax with the other. Thirty years of watching TV, for fourteen dollars an hour and full benefits. That was what Hicks was angling for, but if he lost the security job—if he got cited again—he might have to go back to McDonald's. That would be bad. When he had signed on at the hospital, he had given up the glamour job at the drive-thru window, and he loathed the idea of starting from the bottom rung again. Even worse, it would probably be the end of Sasha, and Sasha's key to the pharmacy locker, and all the fun they had taking turns in the stirrups. Sasha liked Hicks's uniform; he didn't think she'd feel the same way about a McDonald's getup.

Hicks reached basement level one and slouched out. When the elevator doors were closed, he turned back, grabbed his crotch, and blew a wet kiss at them.

"Suck my balls, you homosexual *fat-ass,*" he said. "I bet you'd *like* that!"

There wasn't a lot of action in the basement at eleven-thirty at night. Most of the lights were off, except for one bank of overhead fluorescents every fifty feet, one of the hospital's new austerity measures. The only foot traffic was the occasional person wandering in from the parking lot across the street by way of an underground tunnel.

Hicks's prized possession was parked over there, a black Trans Am with zebra upholstery and blue neon lights set in the undercarriage, so when it roared down the road, it looked like a UFO right out of *E.T.* Something else he'd have to give up if he lost this job. No way could he make the payments flipping burgers. Sasha loved to fuck him in the Trans Am. She was crazy for animals, and the faux-zebra seat covers brought out her wild side.

Hicks thought the serial killer would be in the morgue, but it turned out he was already in the autopsy theater. One of the docs had started in on him, then abandoned him there to finish tomorrow. Hicks flipped on the lights over the tables but left the rest of the room in darkness. He pulled the curtain across the window in the door. There was no bolt, but he pushed the chock in under the door as far as it would go, to make it impossible for anyone to wander in casually.

Whoever had been working on Charlie Manx had covered him with a sheet before going. He was the only body in the theater tonight, his gurney parked under a plaque that said HIC LOCUS EST

UBI MORS GAUDET SUCCURRERE VITAE. Someday Hicks was going to Google that one, find out what the hell it meant.

He snapped the sheet down to Manx's ankles, had himself a look. The chest had been sawed open, then stitched back together with coarse black thread. It was a Y-shaped cut and extended all the way down to the pelvic bone. Charlie Manx's wang was as long and skinny as a Hebrew National. He had a ghastly overbite, so his crooked brown teeth stuck out into his lower lip. His eyes were open, and he seemed to be staring at Hicks with a kind of blank fascination.

Hicks didn't like that much. He had seen his share of deaders, but they usually had their eyes closed. And if their eyes weren't closed, there was a kind of milky look to them, as if something in them had curdled—life itself, perhaps. But these eyes seemed bright and alert, the eyes of the living, not the dead. They had in them an avid, bird-like curiosity. No; Hicks didn't care for that at all.

For the most part, however, Hicks had no anxieties about the dead. He wasn't scared of the dark either. He was a little scared of his Uncle Jim, he worried about Sasha poking a finger up his ass (something she insisted he would like), and he had recurring nightmares about finding himself at work with no pants on, wandering the halls with his cock slapping between his thighs, people turning to stare. That was about it for fears and phobias.

He wasn't sure why they hadn't put Manx back in his drawer, because it looked like they were done with the chest cavity. But when Hicks got him sat up—he propped him against the wall, with his long, skinny hands in his lap—he saw a dotted line curving around the back of his skull, drawn in Sharpie. Right. Hicks had seen in Sasha's newspaper article that Manx had been in and out of a coma for more than a decade, so naturally the docs would want to poke around in his head. Besides, who didn't want to peek at a serial killer's brain? There was probably a medical paper in that.

The autopsy tools—the saw, the forceps, the rib cutters, the bone mallet—were on a wheeled steel tray by the corpse. At first Hicks thought he'd give Manx the scalpel, which looked pretty serial-killerish. But it was too small. He could tell just by looking at it, it wouldn't show up good in the picture he snapped with his shitty camera phone.

The bone mallet was a different story. It was a big silver hammer, with a head shaped like a brick but pointed at one end, the back edge as sharp as a meat cleaver. At the other end of the handle was a hook, what they used to dig under the edge of the skull and pull it off, like a cap from a bottle. The bone mallet was *hardcore.*

Hicks took a minute to fit it into Manx's hand. He pulled a face at the sight of Manx's nasty-long fingernails, split at the ends and as yellow as the guy's fuckin' teeth. He looked like that actor from the *Alien* movie, Lance Henriksen, if someone had shaved Henriksen's head, then smashed him a couple times with the ugly stick. Manx also had thin, pinkish white, saggy tits that reminded Hicks, horribly, of what his own mother had under her bra.

Hicks picked out the bone saw for himself and stuck an arm around Manx's shoulders. Manx sagged, his big bald head resting against Hicks's chest. That was all right. Now they looked like drinking buddies who'd had a few. Hicks dug his cell phone from its holster and held it out from his body. He narrowed his eyes, struck a menacing grimace, and took the shot.

He lowered the corpse and glanced at the phone. It wasn't a great picture. Hicks had wanted to look dangerous, but the pained expression on his face suggested that Sasha had finally wiggled her pinkie up his ass after all. He was thinking about reshooting when he heard loud voices, right outside the autopsy room's door. For one terrible moment, he thought the first voice belonged to his Uncle Jim:

"Oh, that little bastard is in for it. He has no idea—"

Hicks flung a sheet over the body, his heart going off like someone speed-shooting a Glock. Those voices had hitched up right beyond the door, and he was sure they were about to start pushing to come in. He walked halfway to the door to pull out the chock when he realized he was still holding the bone saw. He set it on the tool cart with a shaking hand.

He was already recovering by the time he paced back to the door. A second man was laughing, and the first was speaking again:

"—have all four molars yanked. They'll gas him out with the sevoflurane, and when they smash the teeth, he won't feel a thing. But when he wakes up, he's gonna feel like he got fucked in the mouth with a shovel—"

Hicks didn't know who was having his teeth removed, but once he heard a little more of the voice, he could tell that it wasn't his Uncle Jim out in the hall, just some old bastard with a creaky old-bastard voice. He waited until he heard the two men walk away before he bent to pull the chock free. He counted to five, then slipped out. Hicks needed a drink of water and to wash his hands. He still felt a little trembly.

He took a long, soothing stroll, breathing deeply. When he finally reached the men's room, he didn't just need a drink, he needed to unload his bowels. Hicks took the handicapped stall for the extra leg room. While he was parked there dropping bombs, he e-mailed Sasha the photo of him and Manx together and wrote, *"Bend over & drop youre pants daddee is cumming w/teh saw if u dont do what i say u crazee bitch. Wait 4 me in the room of punishmint."*

But by the time he was leaning over the sink, slurping noisily at the water, Hicks had begun to have worrisome thoughts. He had been so rattled by the sound of voices in the hallway that he could not remember if he had left the body the way he'd found it. Worse: He had a terrible idea he had left the bone mallet in Charlie Manx's hand. If it was found there in the morning, some smart-ass doc would probably want to know why, and it was a safe bet that Uncle Jim would grill the entire staff. Hicks didn't know if he could handle that kind of pressure.

He decided to wander back to the autopsy theater and make sure he had cleaned up properly.

He paused outside the door to peek through the window, only to discover he had left the curtains drawn. That was one thing to fix right there. Hicks eased the door in and frowned. In his haste to get out of the autopsy theater, he had switched all the lights off—not just the lights over the gurneys but also the safety lights that were always on, in the corners of the room and over the desk. The room smelled of iodine and benzaldehyde. Hicks let the door sigh shut behind him and stood isolate in the darkness.

He was running his hand across the tiled wall, feeling for the light switches, when he heard the squeak of a wheel in the dark and the gentle clink of metal on metal.

Hicks caught himself and listened and in the next moment felt someone rushing across the room at him. It was not a sound or anything he could see. It was something he felt on his skin and a sense in his eardrums, like a change in pressure. His stomach went watery and sick. He had reached out with his right hand for the light switch. Now he dropped the hand, feeling for the .38. He had it partway out when he heard something whistling at him in the darkness, and he was struck in the stomach with what felt like an aluminum baseball bat. He doubled over with a woofing sound. The gun sank back into the holster.

The club went away and came back. It caught Hicks in the left side of the head, above his ear, spun him on his heel, and dropped him. He fell straight back, out a plane and down through frozen night sky, falling and falling, and try as hard as he could to scream, he made not a sound, all the air in his lungs pounded right out of him.

WHEN ERNEST HICKS OPENED HIS EYES, THERE WAS A MAN BENT OVER him, smiling shyly. Hicks opened his mouth to ask what had happened, and then the pain flooded into his head and he turned his face and puked all over the guy's black loafers. His stomach pumped up his dinner—General Tso's chicken—in a pungent gush.

"I am *so* sorry, man," Hicks said when he was done heaving.

"It's okay, son," the doc said. "Don't try to stand. We're going to take you up to the ER. You've suffered a concussion. I want to make sure you don't have a skull fracture."

But it was coming back to Hicks, what had happened, the man in the dark hitting him with a metal bludgeon.

"What the fuck?" he cried. "What the *fuck*? Is my gun . . . ? Anyone see my gun?"

The doc—his tag said SOPHER—put a hand on Hicks's chest to prevent him from sitting up.

"I think that one's gone, son," said Sopher.

"Don't try and get up, Ernie," said Sasha, standing three feet away and staring at him with a look of something approximating horror on her face. There were a couple of other nurses standing with her, all of them looking pale and strained.

"Oh, God. Oh, my God. They stole my .38. Did they grab anything else?"

"Just your pants," said Sopher.

"Just my— What? Fucking *what*?"

Hicks twisted his head to look and saw he was bare naked from the waist down, his cock out for the doc and Sasha and the other nurses to look at. Hicks thought he might vomit again. It was like the bad dream he got sometimes, the one about showing up at work with no pants on, everyone staring at him. He had the sudden, wrenching idea that the sick fuck who had ripped his pants off had maybe poked a finger up his asshole, like Sasha was always threatening to do.

"Did he touch me? Did he fucking touch me?"

"We don't know," the doctor said. "Probably not. He probably just didn't want you to get up and chase him and figured you wouldn't run after him if you were naked. It's very possible he only took your gun because it was in your holster, on your belt."

Although the guy hadn't taken his shirt. He had grabbed Hicks's windbreaker, but not his shirt.

Hicks began to cry. He farted: a wet, whistling *blat.* He had never felt so miserable.

"Oh, my God. *Oh, my God.* What the fuck is *wrong* with people?" Hicks cried.

Dr. Sopher shook his head. "Who knows what the guy was thinking? Maybe he was hopped up on something. Maybe he's just some sick creep who wanted a one-of-a-kind trophy. Let the cops worry about that. I just want to focus on you."

"Trophy?" Hicks cried, imagining his pants hung up on a wall in a picture frame.

"Yeah, I guess," Doc Sopher said, glancing over his shoulder, across the room. "Only reason I can think why someone would want to come in here and steal the body of a famous serial killer."

Hicks turned his head—a gong went off in his brain and filled his skull with dark reverberations—and saw that the gurney had been rolled halfway across the room and that someone had yanked the dead body right off it. He moaned again and shut his eyes.

He heard the rapid clip-clop of boot heels coming down the hallway and thought he recognized the goose-stepping gait of his Uncle Jim on the march, out from behind his desk and not happy about it. There was no logical reason to fear the man. Hicks was the victim here; he had been *assaulted,* for chrissake. But alone and miserable in his only refuge—the dark behind his eyelids—he felt that logic didn't enter into it. His Uncle Jim was coming, and a third citation was coming with him, was about to fall like a silver hammer. Hicks had literally been caught with his pants down, and he saw already that at least in one sense he was never going to be stepping into those security pants again.

It was all lost, had been taken away in a moment, in the shadows of the autopsy room: the good job, the good days of Sasha and stirrups and treats from the pharmacy locker and funny photos with dead bodies. Even his Trans Am with the zebra upholstery was gone, although no one would know it for hours; the sick fuck who'd clubbed him senseless had helped himself to the keys and driven away in it.

Gone. Everything. All of it.

Gone off with dead old Charlie Manx and never coming back.

BAD MOTHER
DECEMBER 16, 2011–
JULY 6, 2012

Lamar Rehabilitation Center, Massachusetts

LOU BROUGHT THE BOY TO VISIT FOR AN EARLY CHRISTMAS, WHILE Vic McQueen was in rehab, doing her twenty-eight days. The tree in the rec room was made of wire and tinsel, and the three of them ate powdered doughnuts from the supermarket.

"They all crazy in here?" Wayne asked, no shyness in him, never had been any.

"They're all drunks," Vic said. "The crazies were in the last place."

"So is this an improvement?"

"Upward mobility," Lou Carmody told him. "We're all about the upward mobility in this family."

Haverhill

VIC WAS RELEASED A WEEK LATER, DRY FOR THE FIRST TIME IN HER adult life, and she went home to watch her mother die, to witness Linda McQueen's heroic attempts to finish herself off.

Vic helped, bought her mom cartons of the Virginia Slims she liked and smoked them with her. Linda went on smoking even when she had only one lung left. A battered green oxygen tank stood next to the bed, the words HIGHLY FLAMMABLE printed on the side above a graphic of red flames. Linda would hold the mask to her face for a hit of air, then lower the mask and take a drag off her cigarette.

"It's okay, innit? You aren't worried—" Linda jerked a thumb meaningfully at the oxygen tank.

"What? That you'll blow up my life?" Vic asked. "Too late, Mom. Beat you to it."

Vic had not spent a day in the same house with her mother since leaving the place for good the summer she turned eighteen. She had not realized, as a child, how dark it was inside her childhood home. It stood in the shade of tall pines and received almost no natural light at all, so that even at noon you had to switch lights on to see where the hell you were going. Now it stank of cigarettes and incontinence. By the end of January, she was desperate to escape. The darkness and lack of air made her think of the laundry chute in Charlie Manx's Sleigh House.

"We should go someplace for the summer. We could rent a place up on The Lake, like we used to." She didn't need to say Lake Winnipesaukee. It had always just been The Lake, as if there were no other body of water worth mentioning, in the same way The Town had always meant Boston. "I've got money."

Not so much, actually. She had managed to drink up a fair portion of her earnings. Much of what she hadn't swallowed had been devoured by legal fees or paid out to various institutions. There was still enough, though, to leave her in a better financial position than the average recovering alcoholic with tattoos and a criminal record. There would be more, too, if she could finish the next Search Engine book. Sometimes she thought she had gotten sane and sober to finish the next book, God help her. It should've been for her son, but it wasn't.

Linda smiled in a sly, drowsy way that said they both knew she wasn't going to make it to June, that she would be vacationing that summer three blocks away, in the cemetery, where her older sisters and her parents were buried. But she said, "Sure. Get your boy offa Lou, bring him along. I'd like to spend some time with that kid—if you don't think it would ruin him."

Vic let that one go. She was working on the eighth step of her program and was here in Haverhill to make amends. For years she had not wanted Linda to know Wayne, to be a part of his life. She took pleasure in limiting her mother's contact with the boy, felt it was her job to protect Wayne from Linda. She wished now there had been someone to protect Wayne from herself. She had amends to make to him, too.

"You could introduce your father to his grandson while you're at it," Linda said. "He's there, you know. In Dover. Not far from The Lake. Still making things go boom. I know he'd love to meet the boy."

Vic let that one go, too. Did she need to make amends to Christopher McQueen as well? Sometimes she thought so—and then she remembered him rinsing his raw knuckles under cold water and dismissed the notion.

It rained all spring, cornering Vic inside the Haverhill house with the dying woman. Sometimes the rain fell so hard it was like being trapped inside a drum. Linda coughed fat blobs of red-specked phlegm into a rubber trough and watched the Food Network with the volume turned up too loud. Getting away—getting out—began to seem a desperate thing, a matter of survival. When Vic shut her eyes, she saw a flat reach of lake at sunset, dragonflies the size of swallows gliding over the surface of the water.

But she didn't decide to rent a place until Lou called one night from Colorado to suggest Wayne and Vic spend the summer together.

"Kid needs his mom," Lou said. "Don't you think it's time?"

"I'd like that," she said, struggling to keep her voice level. It hurt to breathe. It had been a good three years since she and Lou had hung it up. She couldn't stomach being loved so completely by him and doing so poorly by him in return. Had to deal herself out.

It was one thing to quit on Lou, though, and another to quit on the boy. Lou said the kid needed his mother, but Vic thought she needed Wayne more. The prospect of spending the summer with him—of starting again, taking another shot at being the mother Wayne deserved—gave Vic flashes of panic. Also flashes of brilliant, shimmering hope. She didn't like to feel things so intensely. It reminded her of being crazy.

"You'd be okay with that? Trusting him with me? After all the shit I pulled?"

"Aw, dude," he said. "If you're ready to get back in the ring, he's ready to climb in there with you."

Vic didn't mention to Lou that when people climbed into the ring together, it was usually to clobber the shit out of each other. Maybe it wasn't such a bad metaphor. God knew Wayne had plenty of valid reasons for wanting to throw a few roundhouses her way. If Wayne needed a punching bag, Vic was ready to take the hits. It would be a way of making amends.

How she loved that word. She liked that it almost sounded like "amen."

She began to hunt, feverishly, for a place to spend the summer, somewhere that would match the picture in her head. If she'd still possessed her Raleigh, she could have found her way to the perfect spot in a matter of minutes, one quick trip across the Shortaway and back. Of course, she knew now that there had never been any trips across the Shorter Way Bridge. She had learned the truth about her finding expeditions while she was in a Colorado mental hospital. Her sanity was a fragile thing, a butterfly cupped in her hands, that she carried with her everywhere, afraid of what would happen if she let it go—or got careless and crushed it.

Without the Shorter Way, Vic had to rely on Google, same as everyone else. It took her until late April to find what she wanted, a spinster's cottage with a hundred feet of frontage, its own dock, float, and carriage house. It was all on one floor, so Linda wouldn't have to climb any stairs. By then a part of Vic really believed that her mother was coming with them, that *amends* would be made. There was even a ramp around the back of the house, for Linda's wheelchair.

The real-estate agent sent a half dozen full-page glossies, and Vic climbed up onto her mother's bed to look at them with her.

"See the carriage house? I'll clean it out and make an artist's studio. I bet it smells great in there," Vic said. "Bet it smells like hay. Like horses. I wonder why I never went through a horse phase. I thought that was mandatory for spoiled little girls."

"Chris and me never exactly killed ourselves spoiling you, Vicki. I was afraid to. Now I don't even think a parent can. Spoil a child, I mean. I didn't figure nothing out until it was too late to do me any good. I never seemed to have much of a feel for parenting. I was so scared of doing the wrong thing I hardly ever did the right thing."

Vic tried out a few different lines in her head. *You and me both* was one. *You did your best—which is more than I can say of myself* was another. *You loved me as hard as you knew how. I'd give anything to go back and love you better* was a third. But she couldn't find her voice—her throat had gone tight—and the moment passed.

"Anyway," Linda said. "You didn't need a horse. You had your bike. Vic McQueen's Fast Machine. Take you farther than any horse ever could. I looked for it, you know. A couple years ago. I thought your father stuck it in the basement, and I had an idea I could give it to Wayne. Always thought it was a bike for a boy. But it was gone. Don't know where it disappeared to." She was quiet, her eyes half closed. Vic eased off the bed. But before she could get to the door, Linda said, "*You* don't know what happened to it, do you, Vic? Your Fast Machine?"

There was something sly and dangerous in her voice.

"It's gone," Vic said. "That's all I know."

Her mother said, "I like the cottage. Your lake house. You found a good place, Vic. I knew you would. You were always good at that. At finding things."

Vic's arms bristled with gooseflesh.

"Get your rest, Mom," she said, moving to the door. "I'm glad you like the place. We should go up there sometime soon. It's ours for the summer after I sign the papers. We should break it in. Have a couple days there, just the two of us."

"Sure," her mother said. "We'll stop at Terry's Primo Subs on the way back. Get ourselves milkshakes."

The already dim room seemed to darken briefly, as if a cloud were moving across the sun.

"Frappes," Vic said, in a voice that was rough with emotion. "If you want a milkshake, you have to go somewhere else."

Her mother nodded. "That's right."

"This weekend," Vic said. "We'll go up there this weekend."

"You'll have to check my calendar," her mother said. "I might have plans."

The rain stopped the next morning, and instead of taking her mother to Lake Winnipesaukee that weekend Vic took her to the graveyard and buried her beneath the first hot blue sky of May.

SHE CALLED LOU AT ONE IN THE MORNING EAST COAST TIME, ELEVEN o'clock Mountain time, and said, "What do you think he'll want to do? It's going to be two months. I don't know if I can keep Wayne entertained for two days."

Lou seemed utterly baffled by the question. "He's twelve. He's easy. I'm sure he'll like all the things you like. What do you like?"

"Maker's Mark."

Lou made a humming sound. "You know, I guess I was thinking more like tennis."

She bought tennis rackets, didn't know if Wayne knew how to play. It had been so long for herself that she couldn't even remember how to score. She just knew that even when you had nothing, you still had love.

She bought swimsuits, flip-flops, sunglasses, Frisbees. She bought suntan lotion, hoping he wouldn't want to spend a lot of time in the sun. In between her stints in the crazy house and rehab, Vic had finished getting her arms and legs fully sleeved in tattoos, and too much sun was poison on the ink.

She had assumed that Lou would fly to the East Coast with him and was surprised when Lou gave her Wayne's flight number and asked her to call when he got in.

"Has he ever flown alone?"

Lou said, "He's never flown at all, but I wouldn't worry about it. *Dude.* The kid is pretty solid at taking care of himself. He's been doing it for a while. He's, like, twelve going on fifty. I think he's more excited about the flight than he is about getting there." This was followed by an awkward, embarrassed silence. "Sorry. That totally came out more douchey than I meant it to."

"It's okay, Lou," she said.

It didn't bother her. There was nothing Lou or Wayne could say that would bother her. She had every bit of it coming. All those years of hating her own mother, Vic had never imagined she would do worse.

"Besides. He isn't really traveling alone. He's coming with Hooper."

"Right," she said. "What's *he* eat anyway?"

"Usually whatever is on the floor. The remote control. Your underwear. The rug. He's like the tiger shark in *Jaws.* The one Dreyfuss cuts open in the fisherman's basement. That's why we named him Hooper. You remember the tiger shark? He had a license plate in his stomach?"

"I never saw *Jaws.* I caught one of the sequels on TV in rehab. The one with Michael Caine."

Another silence followed, this one awestruck and wondering.

"Jesus. No wonder we didn't last," Lou said.

Three days later she was at Logan Airport at 6:00 A.M., standing at the window in the concourse to watch Wayne's 727 taxi across the apron and up to the Jetway. Passengers emerged from the tunnel and streamed by her, hurrying in silent bunches, rolling carry-ons behind them. The crowd was thinning, and she was trying not to feel any anxiety—where the hell was he? Did Lou give her the right flight information? Wayne wasn't even in her custody yet, and she was already fucking up—when the kid strolled out, arms wrapped around his backpack as if it were his favorite teddy bear. He dropped it, and she hugged him, snuffled at his ear, gnawed at his neck until he laugh-shouted for Vic to let him go.

"Did you like flying?" she asked.

"I liked it so much I fell asleep when we took off and missed the whole thing. Ten minutes ago I was in Colorado, and now I'm here. Isn't that insane? Going so far just all of a sudden like that?"

"It is. It's completely insane," she said.

Hooper was in a dog carrier the size of a baby's crib, and it took both of them to wrestle him off the luggage carousel. Drool swung from the big Saint Bernard's mouth. Inside the cage the remains of a phone book lay around his feet.

"What was that?" Vic asked. "Lunch?"

"He likes to chew on things when he's nervous," he said. "Same as you."

They drove back to Linda's house for turkey sandwiches. Hooper snacked on a can of wet food, one of the new pairs of flip-flops, and Vic's tennis racket, still in the plastic wrap. Even with the windows open, the house smelled of cigarette ash, menthol, and blood. Vic couldn't wait to go. She packed the swimsuits, her bristol boards and inks and watercolors, the dog, and the boy she loved but was afraid she didn't know or deserve, and they hauled it north for the summer.

Vic McQueen Tries to Be a Mother, Part II, she thought.

The Triumph was waiting.

Lake Winnipesaukee

THE MORNING WAYNE FOUND THE TRIUMPH, VIC WAS DOWN ON THE dock with a couple of fishing rods she couldn't untangle. She had discovered the rods in a closet in the cottage, rust-flecked relics of the eighties, the monofilament lines bunched up in a fist-size snarl. Vic thought she had seen a tackle box in the carriage house and sent Wayne to look for it.

She sat on the end of the dock, shoes and socks off, feet trailing in the water, to wrestle with the knot. When she was on coke—yeah, she had done that, too—she could've struggled with the knot for a happy hour, enjoying it as much as sex. She would've played that knot like Slash hammering out a guitar solo.

But after five minutes she quit. No point. There would be a knife in the tackle box. You had to know when it made sense to try to untangle something and when to just cut the motherfucker loose.

Besides, the way the sun was flashing on the water hurt her eyes. Especially the left. Her left eye felt *solid* and heavy, as if it were made of lead instead of soft tissue.

Vic stretched out in the heat to wait for Wayne to return. She wanted to doze, but every time she drifted off, she twitched awake all of a sudden, hearing the crazygirl song in her head.

Vic had heard the crazygirl song for the first time when she was in the mental hospital in Denver, which was where she went after she burned the town house down. The crazygirl song had only four lines, but no one—not Bob Dylan, not John Lennon, not Byron or Keats—had ever strung together four lines of such insightful and emotionally direct verse.

No one sleeps a wink when I sing this song!
And I'm going to sing it all night long!
Vic wishes she could ride her fucking bike away!
Might as well wish for a ride in Santa's sleigh!

This song had woken her on her very first evening in the clinic. A woman was singing it somewhere in the lockdown. And she wasn't just singing it to herself; she was serenading Vic directly.

The crazygirl scream-shouted her song three or four times a night, usually just when Vic was drifting off to sleep. Sometimes the crazygirl got to laughing so hard she couldn't carry the tune all the way through to the end.

Vic did some screaming, too. She screamed for someone to shut that cunt up. Other people yelled, the whole ward would get to yelling, everyone screaming to be quiet, to let them sleep, to make it stop. Vic screamed herself hoarse, until the orderlies came in to hold her down and put the needle in her arm.

In the day Vic angrily searched the faces of the other patients, looking for signs of guilt and exhaustion. But *all* of them looked guilty and exhausted. In group-therapy sessions, she listened intently to the others, thinking the midnight singer would give herself away by having a hoarse voice. But they *all* sounded hoarse, from the difficult nights, the bad coffee, the cigarettes.

Eventually the evening came when Vic stopped hearing from the crazygirl with her crazy song. She thought they had moved her to another wing, finally showing some consideration for the other patients. Vic had been out of the hospital for half a year before she finally recognized the voice, knew who the crazygirl had been.

"Do we own the motorcycle in the garage?" Wayne asked. And then, before she had time to process the question, he said, "What are you singing?"

She hadn't realized she was whispering it to herself until that very moment. It sounded much better in a soft voice than it did when Vic had been scream-laughing it in the loony bin.

Vic sat up, rubbing her face. "I don't know. Nothing."

Wayne gave her a dark and doubtful look.

He made his way out onto the dock in mincing, effortful steps, Hooper slouching along behind like a tame bear. Wayne carried a big, battered yellow toolbox, clutched the handle in both hands. A third of the way out, he lost his grip, and it dropped with a crash. The dock shook.

"I got the tackle box," Wayne said.

"That's not a tackle box."

"You said look for a brown box."

"That's yellow."

"It's brown in spots."

"It's *rusted* in spots."

"Yeah? So? Rust is brown."

He unbuckled the toolbox, pushed back the lid, frowned at the contents.

"Easy mistake," she said.

"Is this maybe for fishing?" he asked, and pulled out a curious instrument. It looked like the blade of a dull miniature scythe, small enough to fit in his palm. "It's shaped like a hook."

Vic knew what it was, although it had been years since she'd seen one. Then she registered, at last, what Wayne had said when he first walked out onto the dock.

"Let me see that box," Vic said.

She turned it around to stare in at a collection of flat, rusted wrenches, an air-pressure gauge, and an old key with a rectangular head, the word TRIUMPH stamped into it.

"Where'd you find this?"

"It was on the seat of the old motorcycle. Did the motorcycle come with the house?"

"Show me," Vic said.

The Carriage House

VIC HAD ONLY BEEN IN THE CARRIAGE HOUSE ONCE, WHEN SHE FIRST looked at the property. She had talked to her mother about cleaning the place out and using it as an artist's studio. So far, though, her pencils and paints hadn't made it any farther than the bedroom closet, and the carriage house was as cluttered as the day they had moved in.

It was a long, narrow room, so crowded with junk it was impossible for anyone to walk a straight line to the back wall. There were a few stalls where horses had been kept. Vic loved the smell of the place, a perfume of gasoline, dirt, old dry hay, and wood that had baked and aged for eighty summers.

If Vic were Wayne's age, she would've lived in the rafters, among the pigeons and flying squirrels. That didn't seem to be Wayne's thing, though. Wayne didn't interact with nature. He took pictures of it with his iPhone and then bent over the screen and poked at it. His favorite thing about the lake house was that it had Wi-Fi.

It wasn't that he wanted to stay indoors. He wanted to stay inside his phone. It was his bridge away from a world where Mom was a crazy alcoholic and Dad was a three-hundred-pound car mechanic who had dropped out of high school and who wore an Iron Man costume to comic-book conventions.

The motorcycle was in the back of the carriage house, a paint-spattered tarp thrown over it but the shape beneath still discernible. Vic spotted it from just inside the doors and wondered how she could've missed it the last time she'd stuck her head in here.

But she only wondered for a moment. No one knew better than Vic McQueen how easy it was for an important thing to be lost amid a great deal of visual clutter. The whole place was like a scene she might paint for one of the Search Engine books. Find your way to the motorcycle through the labyrinth of junk—without crossing a trip wire—and escape! Not a bad notion for a scene, really, something to file away for further thought. She couldn't afford to ignore a single good idea. Could anyone?

Wayne got one corner of the tarp and she got the other, and they flipped it back.

The bike wore a coat of grime and sawdust a quarter inch thick. The handlebars and gauges were veiled in spiderwebs. The headlight hung loose from the socket by its wires. Under the dust the teardrop-shaped gas tank was cranberry and silver, with the word TRIUMPH embossed on it in chrome.

It looked like a motorcycle out of an old biker movie—not a biker film full of bare tits, washed-out color, and Peter Fonda but one of the older, tamer motorcycle films, something in black and white that involved a lot of racing and talk about the Man. Vic loved it already.

Wayne ran a hand over the seat, looked at the gray fuzz on his palm. "Do we get to keep it?"

As if it were a stray cat.

Of course they didn't get to keep it. It wasn't theirs. It belonged to the old woman who was renting them the house.

And yet.

And yet Vic felt that in some way it already belonged to her.

"I doubt it even runs," she said.

"So?" Wayne asked, with the casual certainty of a twelve-year-old. "Fix it. Dad could tell you how."

"Your dad already told me how."

For eight years she had tried to be Lou's girl. It had not always been good, and it had never been easy, but there had been some happy days in the garage, Lou fixing bikes and Vic airbrushing them, Soundgarden on the radio and cold bottles of beer in the fridge. She would crawl around the bikes with him, holding his light and asking questions. He taught her about fuses, brake lines, manifolds. She had liked being with him then and had almost liked being herself.

"So you think we can keep it?" Wayne asked again.

"It belongs to the old dame renting us the house. I could ask if she'd sell."

"I bet she'll let us have it," he said. He wrote the word *"OURS"* in the dust on the side of the tank. "What kind of old lady is gonna want to haul ass around on a mother like this?"

"The kind standing right next to you," she said, and reached past him and wiped her palm across the word *"OURS."*

Dust fluffed up into a shaft of early-morning sunshine, a flurry of gold flakes.

Below where the word *"OURS"* had been, Vic wrote *"MINE."* Wayne held up his iPhone and took a picture.

Haverhill

EVERY DAY AFTER LUNCH, SIGMUND DE ZOET HAD AN HOUR TO himself to paint his tiny soldiers. It was his favorite hour of the day. He listened to the Berlin Orchestra performing the Frobisher sextet, *Cloud Atlas,* and painted the Hun in their nineteenth-century helmets and coats with tails and gasmasks. He had a miniature landscape on a six-foot-by-six-foot sheet of plywood that was supposed to represent an acre of Verdun-sur-Meuse: an expanse of blood-soaked mud, burned trees, tangled shrubbery, barbed wire, and bodies.

Sig was proud of his careful brushwork. He painted gold braid on epaulets, microscopic brass buttons on coats, spots of rust on helmets. He felt that when his little men were painted well, they possessed a tension, a suggestion that they might, at any moment, begin to move on their own and charge the French line.

He was working on them the day it finally happened, the day when they finally did begin to move.

He was painting a wounded Hun, the little man grabbing at his chest, his mouth open in silent cry. Sig had a daub of red on the end of the brush, meant to put a splash of it around the German soldier's fingers, but when he reached out, the Hun backed away.

Sigmund stared, studying the one-inch soldier under the bright glare of the lamp on its articulated arm. He reached with the tip of the brush again, and again the soldier swayed away.

Sig tried a third time—*Hold still, you little bastard,* he thought—and missed entirely, wasn't even close, painted a crimson slash across the metal lampshade instead.

And it wasn't just that one soldier moving anymore. It was all of them. They lurched toward one another, wavering like candle flames.

Sigmund rubbed his hand across his forehead, felt a hot and slimy sweat there. He inhaled deeply and smelled gingerbread cookies.

A stroke, he thought. *I am having a stroke.* Only he thought it in Dutch, because for the moment English eluded him, and never mind he had spoken English as his first language since he was five.

He reached for the edge of the table, to push himself to his feet—and missed and fell. Sig hit the walnut floor on his right side and felt something snap in his hip. It broke like a dry stick under a German jackboot. The whole house shook with the force of his fall, and he thought—still in Dutch—*That will bring Giselle.*

"Hulp," he called. *"Ik heb een slag. Nr. Nr."* That didn't sound right, but he needed a moment to figure out why. Dutch. She wouldn't understand Dutch. "Giselle! I have fallen down!"

She didn't come, didn't respond in any way. He tried to think what she could be doing that she wouldn't hear him, then wondered if she was outside with the air-conditioning repairman. The repairman, a dumpy little man named Bing something, had turned up in grease-stained overalls to replace a condenser coil as part of a factory recall.

Sig's head seemed a bit clearer, down here on the floor. When he had been up on the stool, the air had started to seem soupy and slow, overheated, and faintly cloying, what with that sudden smell of gingerbread. Down here, though, it was cooler, and the world seemed inclined to behave. He saw a screwdriver he had been missing for months, nestled among some dust bunnies under the worktable.

His hip was broken. He was sure of that, could feel the fracture in it, like a hot wire embedded under the skin. He thought if he could get up, though, he could use his stool as a makeshift walker to get across the room to the door and out into the hall.

Perhaps he could reach the door and shout for the air-conditioning man. Or to Vic McQueen, across the street. Except: no. Vicki was off in New Hampshire somewhere with that boy of hers. No—if he could get as far as the phone in the kitchen, he would just have to call emergency services and hope Giselle found him before the ambulance pulled in to the driveway. He didn't want to shock her more than was necessary.

Sig reached up with one gangly arm, got the stool, and struggled to his feet, keeping his weight off the left leg. It hurt anyway. He heard bone click.

"Giselle!" he screamed again, his voice a throaty roar. "*Gott dam,* Giselle!"

He leaned over the stool, both hands on its edge, and took a long, trembling breath—and smelled the Christmassy odor of gingerbread again. He almost flinched, the fragrance was so strong and clear.

A stroke, he thought again. This was what happened when you were stroking out. The brain misfired, and you smelled things that weren't there, while the world drooped around you, melting like dirty snow in a warm spring rain.

He turned himself to face the door, which was not twelve paces away. The door to his studio hung wide open. He could not imagine how Giselle could fail to hear him shouting, if she was anywhere in the house. She was either outside by the noisy air conditioner or shopping or dead.

He considered this array of possibilities again—outside by the noisy air conditioner, shopping, or dead—and was disquieted to find the third possibility not quite preposterous.

He lifted the stool an inch off the floor, moved it forward, set it down, hobbled forward with it. Now that he was standing, the inside of his head was going light again, his thoughts drifting like goose feathers on a warm breeze.

A song was running around and around in his head, stuck in an idiot loop. *"There was an old lady who swallowed a fly. I don't know why she swallowed the fly— Perhaps she'll die!"* Only the song grew in volume, building and building until it no longer seemed to be inside his head but in the air around him, coming down the hall.

"There was an old lady who swallowed a spider that wriggled and jiggled and tickled inside her," sang the voice. It was high-pitched, off-key, and curiously hollow, like a voice heard at a distance, through a ventilation shaft.

Sig glanced up and saw a man in a gasmask moving past the open door. The man in the gasmask had Giselle by the hair and was dragging her down the hall. Giselle didn't seem to mind. She wore a neat blue linen dress and matching blue heels, but as she was hauled along, one of the shoes pulled loose and fell off her foot. The Gasmask Man had her long chestnut hair, streaked with white, wrapped around one fist. Her eyes were closed, her narrow, gaunt face serene.

The Gasmask Man turned his head, looked in at him. Sig had never seen anything so awful. It was like in that movie with Vincent Price, where the scientist crossed himself with an insect. His head was a rubber bulb with shining lenses for eyes and a grotesque valve for a mouth.

Something was wrong in Sig's brain, something maybe worse than a stroke. Could a stroke make you hallucinate? One of his painted Huns had strolled right off his model of Verdun and into his back hallway, was abducting his wife. Maybe that was why Sig was struggling to stay upright. The Hun were invading Haverhill and had bombed the street with mustard gas. Although it didn't smell like mustard. It smelled like cookies.

The Gasmask Man held up a finger, to indicate he would be back shortly, then continued down the hallway, towing Giselle by the hair. He began to sing again.

"There was an old lady," the Gasmask Man sang, *"who swallowed a goat. Just opened her throat and swallowed a goat. What a greedy bitch!"*

Sig slumped over the stool. His legs—he couldn't feel his legs. He reached to wipe the sweat out of his face and poked himself in the eye.

Boots clomped across the workshop floor.

It took an effort of will for Sig to lift his head. It felt as if there were a great weight balanced on top of it, a twenty-pound stack of iron.

The Gasmask Man stood over the model of Verdun, looking down at the cratered ruin, stitched with barbed wire. His hands on his hips. Sig recognized the man's clothes at last: He wore the oil-stained jumpsuit of the air-conditioner repairman.

"Little men, little men!" the Gasmask Man said. "I love little men! 'Up the airy mountain, down the rushy glen, we daren't go a-hunting, for fear of little men.'" He looked at Sig and said, "Mr. Manx says I'm a rhyming demon. I say I'm just a poet and didn't know it. How old is your wife, mister?"

Sig had no intention of answering. He wanted to ask what the repairman had done with Giselle. But instead he said, "I married her in 1976. My wife is fifty-nine. Fifteen years younger than myself."

"You dog, you! Robbing the cradle. No kids?"

"*Nr.* No. I have ants in my brain."

"That's the sevoflurane," the Gasmask Man said. "I pumped it in through your air conditioner. I can tell that your wife never had kids. Those hard little tits. I gave 'em a squeeze, and I can tell you, women who have had babies don't have tits like that."

"Why are you doing this? Why are you here?" Sig asked.

"You live across the street from Vic McQueen. *And* you have a two-car garage, but only one car," the Gasmask Man told him.

"When Mr. Manx comes back around the corner, he'll have a place to park. *The wheels on the Wraith go round and round, round and round, round and round. The wheels on the Wraith go round and round, all day long.*"

Sig de Zoet became aware of a series of sounds—a hiss, a scratch, and a thump—repeating over and over. He couldn't tell where they were coming from. The noise seemed to be inside his head, in the same way that the Gasmask Man's song had seemed to be inside his head for a while. That hiss, scratch, and thump was what he had now, in place of thoughts.

The Gasmask Man looked down at him. "Now, Victoria McQueen looks like she has a *real* set of mommy titties. You've seen them firsthand. What do *you* think of her tits?"

Sig stared up at him. He understood what the Gasmask Man was asking but could not think how to reply to such a question. Vic McQueen was just eight years old; in Sig's mind she had become a child again, a girl with a boy's bicycle. She came over now and then to paint figurines. It was a pleasure to watch her work—painting little men with quiet devotion, eyes narrowed as if she were squinting down a long tunnel, trying to see what was at the other end.

"That *is* her place across the street, isn't it?" the Gasmask Man said.

Sig intended not to tell him. Not to collaborate. "Collaborate" was the word that came to his mind, not "cooperate."

"Yes," he heard himself say. Then he said, "Why did I tell you that? Why am I answering your questions? I am not a collaborator."

"That's the sevoflurane, too," the Gasmask Man said. "You wouldn't *believe* some of the things people used to tell me after I gave 'em some of the sweet old gingerbread smoke. This one old grandma, like sixty-four years old at least, told me the only time she ever came was when she took it up the pooper. Sixty-four! *Ugh,* right? *'Will you still need me, will you still ream me, when I'm sixty-four?'*" He giggled, the innocent, bubbling laughter of a child.

"It is a truth serum?" Sig said. It took a profound effort to verbalize this question; each word was a bucket of water that had to be laboriously drawn up from a deep well, by hand.

"Not exactly, but it sure relaxes your intuitions. Opens you up to suggestion. You wait till your wife starts to come around. She'll be gobbling my cock just like it's lunch and she missed breakfast. She'll just think it's the thing to do! Don't worry. I won't make you watch. You'll be dead by then. Listen: Where is Vic McQueen? I've been watching the house all day. It doesn't look like there's anyone home. She isn't away for the summer, is she? That'd be a pain. That'd be a pain in the brain!"

But Sigmund de Zoet didn't answer. He was distracted. It had come to him, finally, what he was hearing, what was producing that hiss, that scratch, that thump.

It wasn't inside his head at all. It was the record he had been listening to, the Berlin Orchestra playing the *Cloud Atlas* sextet.

The music was over.

Lake Winnipesaukee

When Wayne went to day camp, Vic went to work on the new book—and the Triumph.

Her editor had suggested maybe it was time for a holiday-themed *Search Engine,* thought a Christmas adventure could be a big seller. The notion, at first, was a whiff of sour milk; Vic flinched from it reflexively, in disgust. But with a few weeks to turn it over in her mind, she could see how brutally commercial such an item would be. She could picture, as well, how cute Search Engine would look in a candy-cane-striped cap and a scarf. It never once occurred to her that a robot modeled on the engine of a Vulcan motorcycle would not have any need for a scarf. It would *look* right. She was a cartoonist, not an engineer; reality could get stuffed.

She cleared a space in a back corner of the carriage house for her easel and made a start. That first day she went for three hours, using her blue nonphotographic pencil to draw a lake of cracking ice. Search Engine and his little friend Bonnie clutched one another on a chunk of floating glacier. Mad Möbius Stripp was under there in a submarine crafted to look like a kraken, tentacles thrusting up around them. At least she *thought* she was drawing tentacles. Vic worked, as always, with the music turned up and her mind switched off. While she was drawing, her face was as smooth and unlined as a child's. As untroubled, too.

She kept at it until her hand cramped, then quit and walked out into the day, stretching her back, arms over her head, listening to her spine crack. She went into the cottage to pour herself a glass of iced tea—Vic didn't bother with lunch, hardly ate when she was working on a book—and returned to the carriage house to think about what belonged on page two. She figured it couldn't hurt to tinker with the Triumph while she mulled it over.

She planned to bang at the motorcycle for an hour or so and then go back to *Search Engine*. Instead she worked *three* hours and was ten minutes late to pick Wayne up from camp.

After that it was the book in the morning and the bike in the afternoon. She learned to set an alarm so she'd always be on time to get Wayne. By the end of June, she had a whole stack of pages roughed out and had stripped the Triumph down to the engine and the bare metal frame.

She sang while she worked, although she was rarely aware of it.

"No one sleeps a wink when I sing this song. I'm gonna sing it all night long," she sang when she worked on the bike.

And when she worked on the book, she sang, *"Dad been driving us to Christmasland, just to ride in Santa's sleigh. Dad been driving us to Christmasland, just to pass the day away."*

But they were the same song.

Haverhill

On the first of July, Vic and Wayne put Lake Winnipesaukee in the rearview mirror and drove back to her mother's house in Massachusetts. Vic's house now. She kept forgetting.

Lou was flying into Boston to spend the Fourth with Wayne and see some big-city fireworks, something he had never done before. Vic was going to spend the weekend going through the dead woman's stuff, and trying not to drink. She had a notion to sell the house in the fall and move back to Colorado. It was something to talk about with Lou. She could work on *Search Engine* anywhere.

Traffic was bad on 495. They were trapped on the road, under a headache sky of low, fuming clouds. Vic felt that no one should have to put up with a sky like that cold sober.

"Do you worry much about ghosts?" Wayne asked while they were idling, waiting for cars in front of them to move.

"Why? You creeped out about staying the night at Grandma's? If her spirit is still there, it wouldn't wish you any harm. She loved you."

"No," Wayne said, his tone indifferent. "I know ghosts used to talk to you, is all."

"Not anymore," she said, and finally traffic loosened up and Vic could ride the breakdown lane to the exit. "Not ever, kid. Your mom was screwed up in the head. That's why I had to go to the hospital."

"They weren't real?"

"Of course not. The dead stay dead. The past is past."

Wayne nodded. "Who's that?" he asked, looking across the front yard as they turned in to the driveway.

Vic had been thinking about ghosts, not paying attention, and hadn't seen the woman sitting on her front step. As Vic put the car into park, the visitor rose to her feet.

Her visitor wore acid-washed jeans, disintegrating to threads at the knees and thighs, and not in a fashionable way either. She had a cigarette in one hand, trailing a pale wisp of smoke. In the other hand was a folder. She had the stringy, twitchy look of a junkie. Vic could not place her but was sure she knew her. She had no idea who the visitor was, but felt in some way she had been expecting this woman for years.

"Someone you know?" Wayne asked.

Vic shook her head. She was temporarily unable to find her voice. She had spent most of the last half year holding tight to both sanity and sobriety, like an old woman clutching a bag of groceries. Staring into the yard, she felt the bottom of the bag beginning to tear and give way.

The junkie girl in the unlaced Chuck Taylor high-tops raised one hand in a nervous, terribly familiar little wave.

Vic opened the car door and got out, came around the front to get between Wayne and the woman.

"Can I help you?" Vic croaked. She needed a glass of water.

"I hope *s-ss-ss-sss*—" She sounded as if she were hung up on a sneeze. Her face darkened, and she forced out, "*So.* He's *f-f-fuh-free.*"

"What are you talking about?"

"The Wraith," Maggie Leigh said. "He's on the road again. I think you sh-sh-should use your bridge and try to *f-f-f-f-find* him, Vic."

SHE HEARD WAYNE CLIMBING OUT OF THE CAR BEHIND HER, HIS DOOR thumping shut. He opened the rear door, and Hooper leaped from the backseat. She wanted to tell him to get back in the car but couldn't without signaling her fear.

The woman smiled at her. There was an innocence and a simple kindness to her face that Vic very much associated with the mad. She had seen it often enough in the mental hospital.

"I'm *s-s-ss*-sorry," the visitor said. "That wasn't how I *mm-mm-muh*—" Now she sounded like she might be gagging. "—mmm*MM*mmeant to begin. I'm *m-mm-mm*—oh, God. *Mmm-mm-mMMM-MAGGIE.* Bad st-stammer. S-s-s-s-suh-suh—apologies. We had tea once. You s-scraped your knee. Long time ago. You weren't much older than your s-s-suh-ss-ss—" She stopped talking, drew a deep breath, tried again. "Kid here. But I think you *really* m-must remember."

It was awful listening to her try to talk—like watching someone with no legs dragging herself along a sidewalk. Vic thought, *She didn't use to be so bad,* while at the same time remaining convinced that the junkie girl was a deranged and possibly dangerous stranger. She found herself able to juggle these two notions without any sense of contradicting herself whatsoever.

The junkie girl put her hand on Vic's for a moment, but her palm was hot and damp, and Vic quickly pulled away. Vic looked at the girl's arms and saw they were a battlefield of pocked, shiny scars: cigarette burns. Lots of them, some livid pink and recent.

Maggie regarded her with a brief look of confusion that bordered on hurt, but before Vic could speak, Hooper barged past to poke his nose into Maggie Leigh's crotch. Maggie laughed and pushed his snout away.

"Oh, gee. You have your own yeti. That's adorbs," she said. She looked beyond the dog to Vic's son. "And you must b-b-be Wayne."

"How do you know his name?" Vic asked in a hoarse voice, thinking a crazy thing: *Her Scrabble tiles can't give her proper names.*

"You dedicated your first s-ss-s—*book* to him," said Maggie. "We used to have them all at the library. I was so suh-suh-sssssss*psyched* for you."

Vic said, "Wayne? Take Hooper into the house."

Wayne whistled and clicked and walked by Maggie, and the dog shambled after. Wayne firmly shut the door behind both of them.

Maggie said, "I always thought you'd write. You said you would. I wondered if I mm-mm-*my-mm-my—might* hear from you after M-M-Muh-*MmmManx* was arrested, but then I thought you wanted to put him behind you. I almost wrote *you* a few times, b-but first I worried your puh-p-puh-*pp-p*—I worried your folks would question you about me, and later I thought muh-mm-*mm*—perhaps you wanted to put m-me behind you as well."

She tried to smile again, and Vic saw she was missing teeth.

"Ms. Leigh. I think you're confused. I don't know you. I can't help you," Vic said.

What frightened Vic most was her feeling that this was exactly backward. Maggie wasn't the one who was confused—her whole face glistened with lunatic certainty. If anyone was confused, it was Vic. She could see it all in her mind's eye: the dark cool of the library, the yellowing Scrabble tiles scattered on the desk, the bronze paperweight that looked like a pistol.

"If you don't know me, how come you know my last name? I didn't mention it," Maggie said, only with more stuttering—it took close on half a minute to get this sentence out.

Vic held up a hand for silence and ignored this statement as the absurd distraction it was. Of *course* Maggie had mentioned her last name. She had said it when she introduced herself, Vic was sure.

"I see *you* know quite a bit about *me,* though," Vic continued. "Understand that my son knows nothing about Charles Manx. I've never talked to him about the man. And I'm not having him find out from . . . from a stranger." She almost said *a crazy person.*

"Of course. I didn't m-muh-mm-mean to alarm you or s-s-suh-s—"

"But you did anyway."

"B-b-buh-b-but, *Vic*."

"Stop calling me that. We don't know each other."

"Would you prefer if I called you the B-B-Buh-Brat?"

"I don't want you to call me anything. I want you to go."

"B-b-but you had to *know* about Mm-Mm-*Mmm*—" In her desperation to get the word out, she seemed to be moaning.

"Manx."

"Thank you. Yes. We have to d-d-d-decide how to d-d-deal with him."

"Deal with *what*? What do you *mean*, Manx is on the road again? He isn't up for parole until 2016, and the last I heard he was in a coma. Even if he woke up and they did set him free, he'd have to be two hundred years old. But they *didn't* cut him loose, because they would've notified me if they had."

"He's not *that* old. Try a hundred and *ffff-ff-f-f*"—she sounded like she was imitating the sound of a burning fuse—"fifteen!"

"Jesus Christ. I don't have to listen to this shit. You've got three minutes to beat it, lady. If you're still on the lawn after that, I'm calling the police on you."

Vic stepped off the path and into the grass, meaning to walk around Maggie to the door.

She didn't make it.

"They didn't notify you they released him 'cause they *didn't* release him. They think he died. Last Mmmm-*Mm*May."

Vic caught in place. "What do you mean, they *think* he died?"

Maggie extended the manila folder.

She had written a phone number on the inside cover. Vic's gaze caught and held on it, because after the area code the first three digits were her own birthday and the next four numbers were not four numbers at all but the letters FUFU, a kind of obscene stammer in and of themselves.

The folder contained perhaps a half dozen printouts from various newspapers, on stationery that said HERE PUBLIC LIBRARY—HERE, IOWA. The stationery was water-stained and shriveled, foxed at the edges.

The first article was from the *Denver Post*.

ALLEGED SERIAL KILLER CHARLES TALENT MANX DIES, LEAVES QUESTIONS

There was a thumbnail photo of his mug shot: that gaunt face with its protruding eyes and pale, almost lipless mouth. Vic tried to read the article, but her vision blurred over.

She remembered the laundry chute, her eyes streaming and her lungs full of smoke. She remembered thoughtless panic, set to the tune of "A Holly Jolly Christmas."

Phrases from the article jumped out at her: *"degenerative Parkinson's-like illness . . . intermittent coma . . . suspected in a dozen kidnappings . . . Thomas Priest . . . stopped breathing at 2:00 A.M."*

"I didn't know," Vic said. "Nobody told me."

She was too off balance to keep her rage focused on Maggie. She kept thinking, simply, *He's dead. He's dead, and now you can let him go. This part of your life is done because he's dead.*

The thought didn't bring any joy with it, but she felt the possibility of something better: relief.

"I don't know why they wouldn't tell me he was gone," Vic said.

"Mmm-mm—I bet 'cause they were embarrassed. Look at the next page."

Vic glanced wearily up at Margaret Leigh, remembering what she had said about Manx being on the road again. She suspected they were getting to it, to Maggie Leigh's own particular madness, the lunacy that had driven her to come all the way from Here, Iowa, to Haverhill, Massachusetts, just so she could hand this folder to Vic.

Vic turned the page.

ALLEGED SERIAL KILLER'S CORPSE VANISHES
FROM MORGUE
SHERIFF'S DEPARTMENT BLAMES
"MORBID VANDALS"

Vic skimmed the first few paragraphs, then closed the folder and offered it back to Maggie.

"Some sicko stole the body," Vic said.

Maggie said, "D-d-d-don't think so." She didn't accept the folder.

Somewhere down the street, a lawn mower roared to life. For the first time, Vic noticed how hot it was here in the front yard. Even through the overcast, the sun was baking her head.

"So you think he faked his death. Well enough to fool two doctors. Somehow. Even though they had already begun an autopsy on the body. *No. Wait.* You think he really died but then, forty-eight hours later, he came back to life. Pulled himself out of his drawer at the morgue, got himself dressed, and walked out."

Maggie's face—her whole body—relaxed in an expression of profound relief. "*Yes.* I've c-come so *f-f-fff*-far to see you, Vic, because I knew, I just *knew* you'd b-b-buh-believe me. Now look at the next article. There's a mm-mm-muh—a guy in Kentucky who disappeared f-f-from his home in an antique Rolls-Royce. Mmm-*Mmuh-Manx's* Rolls-Royce. The article d-d-doesn't say it was the one that belonged to Manx, buh-buh-but if you look at the p-p-p-p-picture—"

"I'm not going to look at shit," Vic said, and threw the folder in Maggie's face. "Get the fuck out of my yard, you crazy bitch."

Maggie's mouth opened and closed, just like the mouth of the big old koi in the fish tank that was a central feature of her little office in the Here Public Library, which Vic could remember perfectly, even though she had never been there.

Vic's rage was boiling over at last, and she wanted to scald Maggie with it. It was not just that Maggie was blocking the way to Vic's door, or that with her mad babble she threatened to undermine Vic's own sense of what was true—to steal from Vic her hard-won sanity. It was that Manx was dead, really dead, but this lunatic couldn't let Vic have that. Charlie Manx, who had kidnapped God knew how many children, who had kidnapped and terrorized and nearly killed Vic herself—Charles Manx was *in the dirt.* Vic had escaped him at last. Only Margaret fucking Leigh wanted to bring him back, dig him up, make Vic afraid of him again.

"Pick that shit up when you go," Vic told her.

She stepped on some of the papers as she proceeded around Maggie to the door. She was careful not to put her foot on the dirty, sun-faded fedora sitting on the edge of the bottom step.

"He's not d-d-done, Vic," Maggie said. "That's why I wanted—was hoping—you could try to f-f-find him. I know I told you n-not to b-b-b-back when we first met. But you were too young then. You weren't ready. Now I think you're the only one who can fff-find him. Who can stop him. If you still know how. Because if you don't, I'm worried he'll try and f-fuh-fuh-find *you.*"

"The only thing I plan to find is a phone to call the police. If I were you, I wouldn't be here when they show up," Vic said. Then, turning back and getting into Maggie Leigh's face, she said, "I DON'T KNOW YOU. Take your crazy somewhere else."

"B-b-b-buh-but, Vic—" Maggie said, and lifted a finger. "Don't you remember? I g-guh-gggave you those earrings."

Vic walked inside and slammed the door.

Wayne, who was standing just three paces away and who had probably heard the whole thing, jumped. Hooper, who was right behind him, cringed and whined softly, turned and trotted off, looking for someplace happier to be.

Vic turned back to the door and leaned her forehead against it and took a deep breath. It was half a minute before she was ready to look through the fish-eye spyhole into the front yard.

Maggie was just straightening up from the front step, carefully placing her filthy fedora on her head with a certain dignity. She gave the front door of Vic's house a last forlorn look, then turned and limped away down the lawn. She didn't have a car and was in for a long, hot, six-block walk to the closest bus station. Vic watched her until she was out of sight—watched and idly stroked the earrings she was wearing, favorites since she was a kid, a pair of Scrabble tiles: **F & U.**

By the Road

WHEN WAYNE WENT OUT HALF AN HOUR LATER, TO WALK Hooper—no, check that, to get away from his mother and her mood of pressurized unhappiness—the folder was sitting on the top step, all the papers neatly shuffled back into it.

He glanced over his shoulder, through the still-open door, but his mother was up in the kitchen, out of sight. Wayne shut the door. He bent and picked up the folder, opened it, and glanced at a thin stack of printouts. "Alleged Serial Killer." "Morbid Vandals." "Boeing Engineer Vanishes."

He folded the sheaf of paper into quarters and put it in the back pocket of his shorts. He shoved the empty folder down behind the hedges planted along the front of the house.

Wayne was not sure he wanted to look at them and, at just twelve years old, was still not self-aware enough to know he had *already* decided to look at them, that he had made his decision the moment he shoved the folder out of sight behind the hedge. He crossed the lawn and sat on the curb. He felt as if he were carrying nitroglycerin in his back pocket.

He stared across the street, at a lawn of wilted, yellowing grass. The old guy who lived over there was really letting his yard go. The guy had a funny name—Sig de Zoet—and a room full of little model soldiers. Wayne had wandered over the day of Gram's funeral, and the old guy had showed them to him, being nice. He had told Wayne that once upon a time his mother, Vic, had painted a few of his figures. "Your mother hoff a fine brush even then," he said, with an accent like a Nazi. Then his nice old wife had made Wayne a glass of frosted iced tea with slices of orange in it that had tasted just about like heaven.

Wayne thought about going over there to look at the old guy's soldiers again. It would be out of the heat, and it would take his mind off the printouts in his back pocket that he probably shouldn't look at.

He even got as far as pushing himself up off the curb and getting ready to cross the street—but then he looked back at his own house and sat down again. His mother wouldn't like it if he wandered off without saying where he was going, and he didn't think he could head back into the house and ask permission yet. So he stayed where he was and looked at the wilting lawn across the street and missed the mountains.

Wayne had seen a landslide once, just last winter. He had been up above Longmont with his father, to tow a Mercedes that had slid off the road and down an embankment. The family that had been in the car were shaken up but unhurt. They were a normal family: a mom, a dad, two kids. The little girl even had blond pigtails. That's how normal they were. Wayne could tell, just looking at them, that the mom had never been in a mental asylum and that the father didn't have storm-trooper armor hanging in his closet. He could tell that the children had normal names, like John and Sue, as opposed to bearing names lifted from a comic book. They had skis on the roof of the Mercedes, and the father asked Lou if he took AmEx. Not American Express. AmEx. Within minutes of meeting them, Wayne loved the whole family with an irrational fierceness.

Lou sent Wayne down the embankment with the hook and the winch line, but as the boy edged toward the car, there came a sound, from high above: a splintering crack, loud as a gunshot. Everyone looked up into the snowy peaks, the sharp-edged Rockies rising above them through the pines.

As they stared, a white sheet of snow, as wide and long as a football field, came loose and began to slide. It was half a mile to the south, so they were in no danger. After the first crack of its letting go, they could barely even hear it. It was no more than a low roll of distant thunder. Although Wayne could *feel* it. It registered as a gentle thrum in the ground beneath him.

That great shelf of snow slid a few hundred yards and hit the tree line and exploded in a white blast, a tidal wave of snow thirty feet high.

The father who had an AmEx lifted his boy up and set him on his shoulders to watch.

"We are in the wild now, little guy," he said, while an acre of mountaintop forest was smothered under six hundred tons of snow.

"Isn't that a goddamn," Lou said, and looked down the embankment at Wayne. His father's face shone with happiness. "Can you imagine being underneath it? Can you imagine all that shit coming down on you?"

Wayne could—and *did*, all the time. He thought it would be the best way to die: wiped out in a brilliant crash of snow and light, the world roaring around you as it slid apart.

Bruce Wayne Carmody had been unhappy for so long that it had stopped being a state he paid attention to. Sometimes Wayne felt that the world had been sliding apart beneath his feet for years. He was still waiting for it to pull him down, to bury him at last.

His mother had been crazy for a while, had believed that the phone was ringing when it wasn't, had conversations with dead children who weren't there. Sometimes he felt she had talked more with dead children than she ever had with him. She had burned down their house. She spent a month in a psychiatric hospital, skipped out on a court appearance, and dropped out of Wayne's life for almost two years. She spent a while on book tour, visiting bookstores in the morning and local bars at night. She hung out in L.A. for six months, working on a cartoon version of *Search Engine* that never got off the ground and a cocaine habit that did. She spent a while drawing covered bridges for a gallery show that no one went to.

Wayne's father got sick of Vic's drinking, Vic's wandering, and Vic's crazy, and he took up with the lady who had done most of his tattoos, a girl named Carol who had big hair and dressed like it was still the eighties. Only Carol had another boyfriend, and they stole Lou's identity and ran off to California, where they racked up a ten-thousand-dollar debt in Lou's name. Lou was still dealing with creditors.

Bruce Wayne Carmody wanted to love and enjoy his parents, and occasionally he did. But they made it hard. Which was why the papers in his back pocket felt like nitroglycerin, a bomb that hadn't exploded yet.

He supposed if there was any chance it might go off later, he ought to have a look, figure out how much damage it could do and how best to shelter himself from the blast. He pulled the papers out of his back pocket, took a last secretive glance at his house, and folded the pages open on his knee.

The first newspaper article featured a photo of Charles Talent Manx, the dead serial killer. Manx's face was so long it looked like it had melted a little. He had protruding eyes and a goofy overbite and a bald, bulging skull that bore a resemblance to a cartoon dinosaur egg.

This man Charles Manx had been arrested above Gunbarrel almost fifteen years ago. He was a kidnapper who'd transported an unnamed minor across state lines, then burned a man to death for trying to stop him.

No one knew how old he was when they locked him up. He didn't thrive in jail. By 2001 he was in a coma in the hospital wing of the Supermax in Denver. He lingered like that for eleven years before passing away last May.

After that the article was mostly bloodthirsty speculation. Manx had a hunting cottage outside Gunbarrel, where the trees were hung with hundreds of Christmas ornaments. The press dubbed the place the "Sleigh House," which managed two puns, neither of them any good. The article implied he had been imprisoning and slaughtering children there for years. It mentioned only in passing that no bodies had ever been discovered on the grounds.

What did any of this have to do with Victoria McQueen, mother of Bruce Wayne Carmody? Nothing, as far as Wayne could see. Maybe if he looked at the other articles, he would figure it out. He went on.

"Alleged Serial Killer's Corpse Vanishes from Morgue" was next. Someone had broken into St. Luke's Medical Center in Denver, slugged a security guard, and made off with dead old Charlie Manx. The body snatcher had swiped a Trans Am from the parking lot across the street, too.

The third piece was a clipping from a paper in Louisville, Kentucky, and didn't have a damn thing to do with Charles Manx.

It was titled "Boeing Engineer Vanishes; Local Mystery Troubles Police, IRS." It was accompanied by a photograph of a tanned and wiry man with a thick black mustache, leaning against an old Rolls-Royce, elbows resting on the hood.

Bruce frowned his way through the story. Nathan Demeter had been reported missing by his teenage daughter, who had returned from school to find the house unlocked, the garage open, a half-eaten lunch on the table, and her father's antique Rolls-Royce gone. The IRS seemed to think Demeter might've skipped out to evade prosecution for income-tax evasion. His daughter didn't believe it, said he was either kidnapped or dead, but there was no way he would've run out on her without telling her why and where he was going.

What any of this had to do with Charles Talent Manx, Wayne couldn't see. He thought maybe he had missed something, wondered if he ought to go back to the start and reread everything. He was just about to flip back to the first of the photocopies when he spotted Hooper, squatting in the yard across the street, dropping turds the size of bananas in the grass. They were the color of bananas, too: green ones.

"Aw, no!" Wayne cried. "Aw, no, big guy!"

He dropped the papers on the sidewalk and started across the street.

His first thought was to haul Hooper out of the yard before anyone saw. But the curtain twitched in one of the front windows of the house across the street. Someone—the nice old guy or his nice old wife—had been watching.

Wayne supposed the best thing he could do was go over there and make a joke out of it, ask if they had a bag he could use to clean up the mess. The old guy, with his Dutch accent, seemed like he could laugh at just about anything.

Hooper rose, unfolding from his hunch. Wayne hissed at him. "Yer bad. Yer so bad." Hooper wagged his tail, pleased to have Wayne's attention.

Wayne was about to climb the steps to the front door of Sigmund de Zoet's house when he noticed shadows flickering along the lower edge of the door. When Wayne glanced at the spyhole, he thought he saw a blur of color and movement. Someone stood three feet away, right on the other side of the door, watching him.

"Hello?" he called from the bottom of the steps. "Mr. de Zoet?"

The shadows shifted at the bottom of the door, but no one acknowledged him. The lack of a response disquieted Wayne. The backs of his arms prickled with chill.

Oh, stop it. You're just being stupid because you read those scary stories about Charlie Manx. Go up there and ring the bell.

Wayne shook off his unease and began climbing the brick steps, extending one hand for the doorbell. He did not observe that the handle of the door was already beginning to turn, the person on the other side preparing to swing it open.

The Other Side of the Door

BING PARTRIDGE STOOD AT THE SPYHOLE. IN HIS LEFT HAND WAS the doorknob. In his right was the gun, the .38 Mr. Manx had brought from Colorado.

"Boy, boy, go away," Bing whispered, his voice thin and strained with need. "Come again some other day."

Bing had a plan, a simple but desperate plan. When the boy reached the top of the steps, he would throw open the door and pull him into the house. Bing had a can of gingerbread smoke in his pocket, and as soon as he had the kid inside, he could gas him out.

And if the kid began screaming? If the kid screamed and struggled to get free?

Someone was having a barbecue down at the end of the block, kids in the front yard chucking a Frisbee, grown-ups drinking too much and laughing too loud and getting sunburned. Bing might not be the sharpest knife in the kitchen, but he was no fool either. Bing thought a man in a gasmask, with a pistol in one hand, might attract some notice wrestling with a screaming child. And there was the dog. What if the dog lunged? It was a Saint Bernard, big as a bear cub. If it got its big bear-cub head in through the door, Bing would never be able to force it back out. It would be like trying to hold the door shut on a herd of cattle.

Mr. Manx would know what to do—but he was asleep. He had been asleep for more than a day now, was resting in Sigmund de Zoet's bedroom. When he was awake, he was his good old self—good old Mr. Manx!—but when he nodded off, it sometimes seemed he would never wake again. He said he would be better when he was on his way to Christmasland, and Bing knew that it was true—but he had never seen Mr. Manx so old, and when he slept, it was like seeing him dead.

And what if Bing forced the boy into the house? Bing was not sure he could wake Mr. Manx when he was like he was. How long could they hide here before Victoria McQueen was out in the street screaming for her child, before the cops were going door-to-door? It was the wrong place and the wrong time. Mr. Manx had made it clear they were only to watch for now, and even Bing, who was not the sharpest pencil in the desk, could see why. This sleepy street was not sleepy enough, and they would only get one pass at the whore with her whore tattoos and her lying whore mouth. Mr. Manx had made no threats, but Bing knew how much this mattered to him and understood what the penalty would be if he fucked it up: Mr. Manx would never take Bing to Christmasland. Never never never never never.

The boy climbed the first step. And the second.

"I wish I may, I wish I might, first star I see tonight," Bing whispered, and shut his eyes and readied himself to act. "Have the wish I wish tonight: Go the fuck away, you little bastard. We're not ready."

He swallowed rubber-tasting air and cocked the hammer on the big pistol.

And then someone was in the street, shouting for the boy, shouting: *"No! Wayne, no!"*

Bing's nerve endings throbbed, and the gun came dangerously close to slipping out of his sweaty hand. A big silver boat of a car rolled down the road, spokes of sunshine flashing off the rims. It pulled to a halt directly in front of Victoria McQueen's house. The window was down, and the driver hung one flabby arm out, waving it at the kid.

"Yo!" he shouted again. "Yo, Wayne!"

"Yo," not "no." Bing was in such a state of nervous tension that he had heard him wrong.

"What's up, dude?" yelled the fat man.

"Dad!" the child yelled. He forgot all about climbing the steps and knocking on the door, turned and ran down the path, his fucking pet bear galloping alongside.

Bing seemed to go boneless; his legs were wobbly with relief. He sank forward, resting his forehead against the door, and shut his eyes.

When he opened them and looked through the spyhole, the child was in his father's arms. The driver was morbidly obese, a big man with a shaved head and telephone-pole legs. That had to be Louis Carmody, the father. Bing had read up about the family online, had a general sense of who was who but had never seen a picture of the man. He was amazed. He could not imagine Carmody and McQueen having sex—the fat beast would split her in two. Bing wasn't exactly buff, but he'd look like a fucking track star next to Carmody.

He wondered what hold the man had on her to have induced her to have sex with him. Perhaps they had come to financial terms. Bing had looked the woman over at length and would not be surprised. All those tattoos. A woman could get any tattoo she liked, but they all said the same thing. They were a sign reading AVAILABLE FOR RENT.

The breeze caught the papers the boy had been looking at, and they drifted under the fat man's car. When Carmody set his child back on the ground, the boy looked around for them and spotted them but didn't get down on all fours to retrieve them. Those papers worried Bing. They meant something. They were important.

A scarred, scrawny, junkie-looking lady had brought those papers and tried to force them on McQueen. Bing had watched the whole thing from behind the curtain in the front room. Victoria McQueen didn't like the junkie lady. She yelled at her and made ugly faces.

She threw the papers back at her. Their voices had carried, not well but well enough for Bing to hear one of them say "Manx." Bing had wanted to wake Mr. Manx up, but you couldn't wake him up when he was like he was.

Because he isn't really asleep, Bing thought, then shoved the unhappy notion aside.

He had been in the bedroom once to look at Mr. Manx, lying on top of the sheets wearing nothing but boxer shorts. A great Y was cut into his chest and held shut with coarse black thread. It was partially healed but seeped pus and pink blood, was a glistening canyon in his flesh. Bing had stood listening for minutes but did not hear him breathe once. Mr. Manx's mouth lolled open, exuding the slightly cloying, slightly chemical odor of formaldehyde. His eyes were open, too, dull, empty, staring at the ceiling. Bing had crept close to touch the old man's hand, and it had been cold and stiff, as cold and stiff as that of any corpse, and Bing had been gripped with the sickening certainty that Mr. Manx was gone, but then Manx's eyes had moved, just slightly, turning to fix on Bing, to stare at him without recognition, and Bing had retreated.

Now that the crisis was past, Bing let his shaky, weak legs carry him back to the living room. He stripped off his gasmask and sat down with Mr. and Mrs. de Zoet to watch TV with them, needed some time to recover himself. He held old Mrs. de Zoet's hand.

He watched game shows and now and then checked the street, keeping an eye on the McQueen place. A little before seven, he heard voices and a door banged shut. He returned to the front door and watched from the spyhole. The sky was a pale shade of nectarine, and the boy and his grotesquely fat father were wandering across the yard to the rent-a-car.

"We're at the hotel if you need us," Carmody called to Victoria McQueen, who stood on the steps of the house.

Bing didn't like the idea of the boy leaving with the father. The boy and the woman belonged *together.* Manx wanted them both—

and so did Bing. The boy was for Manx, but the woman was Bing's treat, someone he could have some fun with in the House of Sleep. Just looking at her thin, bare legs made his mouth dry. One last bit of fun in the House of Sleep, and then it was on to Christmasland with Mr. Manx, on to Christmasland forever and ever.

But no, there was no reason to get in a sweat. Bing had looked at all the mail in Victoria McQueen's mailbox and had found a bill for a day camp in New Hampshire. The kid was registered there through August. It was true, Bing was probably a few clowns short of the full circus, but he didn't think anyone was going to sign their kid up for a camp that cost eight hundred dollars a week and then just decide to blow it off. Tomorrow was the Fourth of July. The father was probably just here to see the child for the holiday.

The father and the son drove away, leaving behind the unholy ghost of Victoria McQueen. The papers under the car—the ones that Bing wanted so badly to see—were grabbed by the Buick's slipstream and tumbled after it.

Victoria McQueen was leaving, too. She went back into the house but left the door open, and three minutes later she came out with her car keys in one hand and sacks for the grocery store in the other.

Bing watched her until she was gone and then watched the street some more and finally let himself out. The sun had gone down, leaving an irradiated orange haze on the horizon. A few stars burned holes through the darkness above.

"*There was a Gasmask Man, and he had a little gun,*" Bing sang to himself softly, what he did when he was nervous. "*And his bullets were made of lead, lead, lead. He went to the brook, and shot Vic McQueen, right through the middle of her head, head, head.*"

He walked up and down along the curb but could find only a single sheet of paper, crumpled and stained.

Whatever he was expecting, it wasn't a photocopy of a news story about the man from Kentucky who had arrived at Bing's house two months ago in the Wraith, two days ahead of Mr. Manx himself. Mr.

Manx had turned up, pale, starved-looking, bright-eyed, and bloody in a Trans Am with zebra-print upholstery and a big silver hammer propped next to him on the passenger seat. By then Bing already had the plates back on the Wraith and NOS4A2 was ready to roll.

The Kentucky man, Nathan Demeter, had spent quite a while in the little basement room in the House of Sleep before going on his way. Bing preferred girls, but Nathan Demeter knew just what to do with his mouth, and by the time Bing was done with him, they'd had many long, meaningful, manly talks of love.

It appalled Bing to see Nathan Demeter again, in a photo accompanying an article titled "Boeing Engineer Vanishes." It made his tummy hurt. He could not for the life of him imagine why the junkie woman had come to Victoria McQueen with such a thing.

"Oh, boy," Bing whispered, rocking. Automatically, he began to recite again: *"There was a Gasmask Man, and he had a little gun. And his bullets were made of lead, lead—"*

"That's not how it goes," said a small, piping voice from behind him.

Bing turned his head and saw a little blond-headed girl on a pink bicycle, with training wheels. She had drifted down from the barbecue at the end of the street. Adult laughter carried in the warm, humid evening.

"My dad read me that one," she said. "There was a little man, and he had a little gun. He shoots a duck, right? Who is the Gasmask Man?"

"Oooh," Bing said to her. "He's nice. Everybody loves him."

"Well, *I* don't love him."

"You would if you got to know him."

She shrugged, turned her bike in a wide circle, and started back down the street. Bing watched her go, then returned to the de Zoets', clutching the article about Demeter, which was printed on stationery from some library in Iowa.

Bing was sitting in front of the TV with the de Zoets an hour later when Mr. Manx came out, fully dressed, in his silk shirt and tails and narrow-toed boots. His starved, cadaverous face had an unhealthy sheen to it in the flickering blue shadows.

"Bing," Manx said, "I thought I told you to put Mr. and Mrs. de Zoet in the spare room!"

"Well," Bing said, "they aren't hurting anyone."

"No. Of course they're not hurting anyone. They're dead! But that's no reason to have them underfoot either! For goodness' sake, why are you sitting out here with them?"

Bing stared for the longest time. Mr. Manx was the smartest, most observant, thinkingest person Bing had ever met, but sometimes he didn't understand the simplest things.

"Better than no company at all," he said.

Boston

Lou and the kid had a room on the top floor of the Logan Airport Hilton—one night cost as much as Lou made in a week, money he didn't have, but fuck it, that was the easiest kind to spend—and they weren't in bed that night until after Letterman. It was going on 1:00 A.M., and Lou thought for sure that Wayne had to be asleep, so he wasn't ready for it when the kid spoke up, voice loud in the darkness. He said just nine words, but it was enough to make Lou's heart jump into his throat and jam there, like a mouthful of food that wouldn't go down.

"This guy, Charlie Manx," Wayne said. "Is he a big deal?"

Lou thumped his fist between his big man boobs, and his heart dropped back where it belonged. Lou and his heart weren't on such great terms. His heart got so *tired* when he had to walk up stairs. He and Wayne had marched all over Harvard Square and the waterfront that evening, and twice he had needed to pause to get his wind back.

He was telling himself that it was because he wasn't used to being at sea level, that his lungs and heart were adapted for the mountain air. But Lou was no dummy. He had not meant to get so fat. It had happened to his father, too. The guy spent the last six years of his life buzzing around the supermarket in one of those little golf carts for people who were too fat to stand. Lou would rather take a chain saw to his layers of fat than climb into one of those fucking supermarket scooters.

"Did Mom say something about him?" Lou asked.

Wayne sighed and was briefly silent: time enough for Lou to realize he had answered the kid's question without meaning to.

"No," Wayne said at last.

"So where did you hear about him?" Lou asked.

"There was a woman at Mom's house today. Maggie someone. She wanted to talk about Charlie Manx, and Mom got really mad. I thought Mom was going to kick her ass."

"Oh," Lou said, wondering who Maggie someone had been and how she had gotten on Vic's case.

"He went to jail for killing a guy, didn't he?"

"This Maggie woman who came to see your mother? Did *she* say Manx killed a guy?"

Wayne sighed again. He rolled over in his bed to look at his father. His eyes glittered like ink spots in the dark.

"If I tell you how I know what Manx did, am I going to get in trouble?" he asked.

"Not with me," Lou said. "Did you Google him or something?"

Wayne's eyes widened, and Lou could see he hadn't even *thought* of Googling Charlie Manx. He would now, though. Lou wanted to slam the heel of his hand into his forehead. Way to go, Carmody. Way to fucking go. Fat *and* stupid.

"The woman left a folder with some newspaper articles in it. I kind of read them. I don't think Mom would've wanted me to. You aren't going to tell her, are you?"

"What articles?"

"About how he died."

Lou nodded, thought he was beginning to get it.

Manx had died not three days after Vic's mother had passed away. Lou had heard about it the day it happened, on the radio. Vic had been out of rehab only five months and had spent the spring watching her mother waste away, and Lou had not wanted to say anything, was afraid that it would kick the legs out from under her. He had meant to tell her, but the opportunity never presented itself, and then, at a certain point, it became impossible to bring it up. He had waited too long.

Maggie someone must've found out that Vic was the girl who got away from Charlie Manx. The only child to escape him. Maybe Maggie someone was a journalist, maybe she was a true-crime author working on a book. She had come by for a comment, and Vic had given her one: something definitely unprintable and probably gynecological.

"Manx isn't worth thinking about. He doesn't have anything to do with us."

"But why would someone want to talk to Mom about him?"

"You have to ask your mom on that one," he said. "I really shouldn't say anything. If I do, like, *I'll* be the one in trouble. You know?"

Because this was the deal, his bargain with Victoria McQueen, the one they had settled on after she knew she was pregnant and decided she wanted to have the baby. She let Lou name the kid; she told Lou she'd live with him; she said she'd take care of the baby and when the baby was sleeping, the two of them could have some fun. She said she would be a wife in all but name. But the boy was to know *nothing* of Charlie Manx, unless *she* decided to tell him.

At the time Lou agreed, it all seemed reasonable enough. But he had not anticipated that this arrangement would prevent his son from knowing the single best thing about his own father. That his father had once reached past his fear for a moment of real Captain America heroism. He had pulled a beautiful girl onto the back of his motorcycle and raced her away from a monster. And when the monster caught up to them and set a man on fire, Lou had been the one to put out the flames—admittedly too late to save a life, but his heart had been in the right place and he had acted without any thought to the risk he was taking.

Lou hated to think what his son knew about him instead: that he was a walking fat joke, that he made a mediocre living towing people out of snowbanks and repairing transmissions, that he had not been able to hold on to Vic.

He wished he had another chance. He wished he could rescue someone else and Wayne could be watching. He would've been glad to use his big fat body to stop a bullet, as long as Wayne was there to bear witness to it. Then he could bleed out in a haze of glory.

Was there any human urge more pitiful—or more intense—than wanting another chance at something?

His son heaved a sigh, tossed himself onto his back.

"So tell me about your summer," Lou asked. "What's the best part so far?"

"No one is in rehab," Wayne said.

Beside the Bay

LOU WAS WAITING FOR SOMETHING TO DETONATE—IT WAS COMING, any moment now—when Vic wandered over with her hands shoved down in that army jacket of hers and said, "This chair for me?"

He glanced over at the woman who had never been his wife but who had, incredibly, given him a child and made his life mean something. The idea that he had ever held her hand, or tasted her mouth, or made love to her, even now seemed as unlikely as being bitten by a radioactive spider.

To be fair, she was certifiable. There was no telling who a schizophrenic would drop her pants for.

Wayne was on the stone wall overlooking the harbor with some other kids. The entire hotel had turned out for the fireworks, and people were crammed onto the old red bricks facing the water and the Boston skyline. Some sat in wrought-iron deck chairs. Others drifted around with champagne in flutes. Kids ran around holding sparklers, drawing red scratches against the darkness.

Vic watched her twelve-year-old with a mix of affection and sad longing. Wayne hadn't noticed her yet, and she didn't go to him, did nothing to let him know she was there.

"You're just in time for everything to go boom," Lou said.

His motorcycle jacket was folded into the empty seat next to him. He grabbed it and put it over his knee, making room for her beside him.

She smiled before she sat—that Vic smile, where only one corner of her mouth turned up, an expression that seemed somehow to suggest regret as much as happiness.

"My father used to do this," she said. "Light the fireworks for Fourth of July. He put on a good show."

"You ever think of making a day trip to Dover with Wayne to see him? That can't be more than an hour away from The Lake."

"I guess I'd get in touch with him if I needed to blow something up," she said. "If I needed some ANFO."

"Info?"

"ANFO. It's an explosive. What my dad uses to take out stumps and boulders and bridges and so on. It's basically a big, slippery bag of horseshit, engineered to destroy things."

"What is? ANFO? Or your dad?"

"Both," she said. "I already know what you want to talk about."

"Maybe I just wanted us to have Fourth of July together as a family," Lou said. "Couldn't it be that?"

"Did Wayne say something about the woman who turned up at the house yesterday?"

"He asked me about Charlie Manx."

"Shit. I sent him inside. I didn't think he could hear us talking."

"Well. He caught a bunch of it."

"How much? Which parts?"

"This and that. Enough to be curious."

"Did you know that Manx was dead?" she asked.

Lou swiped damp palms on his cargo shorts. "Aw, dude. First you were in rehab, then your mom was dying—I didn't want to lay another thing on you. I was going to tell you at some point. Honestly. I don't like to stress you out. You know. No one wants you to go . . ." His voice faltered and trailed off.

She gave him her lopsided smile again. "Batshit crazy?"

He stared off through the dark at their son. Wayne had lit a new pair of sparklers. He waved his arms up and down, flapping his hands, while the sparklers burned and spit. He looked like Icarus just as everything began going wrong.

"I want things to be easy for you. So you can be around for Wayne. Not, like, I'm laying guilt!" he added quickly. "I'm not giving you a hard time about . . . having a hard time. Wayne and me have been doing okay, just the two of us. I make sure he brushes his teeth, gets his homework done. We go out on jobs together, I let him run the winch. He loves that. He's *totally* into winches and stuff. I just think he knows how to talk to you. Or maybe you know how to listen. Or something. It's a mom thing." He paused, then added, "I should've given you a heads-up about Manx dying, though. Just so you knew there might be reporters coming around."

"Reporters?"

"Yeah. This lady who turned up yesterday—wasn't she a reporter?"

They were sitting under a low tree, and there were pink blossoms in it. A few petals dropped, caught in Vic's hair. Lou ached with happiness, and never mind what they were talking about. It was July, and he was with Vic, and there were blossoms in her hair. It was romantic, like a song by Journey, one of the good ones.

"No," Vic said. "She was a crazy person."

"You mean someone from the hospital?" Lou asked.

Vic frowned, seemed to sense the petals in her hair, swiped a hand back and brushed them away. So much for romance. She was, in truth, about as romantic as a box full of spark plugs.

"You and me have never talked about Charlie Manx much," she said. "About how I wound up with him."

This conversation was headed in a direction he didn't like. They didn't talk about how she wound up with Charlie Manx because Lou didn't want to hear about how the old fuck sexually assaulted her and kept her locked in the trunk of his car for two days. Serious conversations always gave Lou the stomach flutters. He preferred casual banter about the Green Lantern.

"I figured if you wanted to talk about it," he said, "you'd bring it up."

"I never talked about it because I don't know what happened."

"You mean you don't remember. Yeah. Yeah, I get that. I'd block that shit out, too."

"No," she said. "I mean *I don't know.* I remember, but *I don't know.*"

"But . . . if you remember, then you know what happened. Aren't remembering and knowing the same thing?"

"Not if you remember it two different ways. In my head there are two stories about what happened to me, *and they both seem true.* Do you want to hear them?"

No. Not at all.

He nodded anyway.

"In one version, the version I told the federal prosecutor, I had a fight with my mom. I ran away. I wound up at a train station, late at night. I called my dad to see if I could stay with him, and he told me I had to go home. When I hung up, I felt a stinging in my backside. As I turned around, my vision blurred and I fell into Manx's arms. Charlie Manx kept me in the trunk of his car all the way across the country. He only took me out to keep me drugged. I was aware, vaguely, that he had another child with him, a little boy, but he mostly kept us apart. When we got to Colorado, he left me in the trunk and went off to do something with the boy. I got out. Forced the trunk open. I set fire to his place to distract him and ran to the highway. I ran through those awful woods with all the Christmas ornaments swinging from the trees. I ran to you, Lou. And you know the rest after that," she said. "That's one way I remember things happening. Do you want to hear the other way?"

He wasn't sure he did but nodded for her to go on.

"So in a different version of my life, I had a bicycle. My father gave it to me when I was a little girl. And I could use this bicycle to find lost things. I would ride it across an imaginary covered bridge, and the bridge would always take me wherever I needed to go. Like once my mother lost a bracelet and I rode my bike across this bridge and came out in New Hampshire, forty miles away from home. And the bracelet was there, in a restaurant called Terry's Primo Subs. With me so far?"

"Imaginary bridge, superpowered bike. Got it."

"Over the years I used my bicycle and the bridge to find all kinds of things. Missing stuffed animals or lost photos. Things like that. I didn't go 'finding' often. Just once or twice a year. And as I got older, even less. It started to scare me, because I knew it was impossible, that the world isn't supposed to work that way. When I was little, it was just pretend. But as I got older, it began to seem crazy. It began to frighten me."

"I'm surprised you didn't use your special power to find someone who could tell you there was nothing wrong with you," Lou said.

Her eyes widened and lit with surprise, and Lou understood that in fact she had done just that.

"How did you—" she began.

"I read a lot of comics. It's the logical next step," Lou said. "Discover magic ring, seek out the Guardians of the Universe. Standard operating procedure. Who was it?"

"The bridge took me to a librarian in Iowa."

"It *would* be a librarian."

"This girl—she wasn't much older than me—had a special power of her own. She could use Scrabble tiles to reveal secrets. Spell messages from the great beyond. That kind of thing."

"An imaginary friend."

She gave him a small, scared, apologetic smile and a brief shake of the head. "It didn't *feel* imaginary. Not ever. It felt real."

"Even the part where you bicycled all the way to Iowa?"

"Across the Shorter Way Bridge."

"And how long did it take to get from Massachusetts to the corn capital of America?"

"I don't know. Thirty seconds? A minute, tops."

"It took you thirty seconds to pedal from Massachusetts to Iowa? And that part didn't feel imaginary?"

"No. I remember it all like it really happened."

"Okay. Got you. Go on."

"So like I said, this girl in Iowa, she had a bag of Scrabble tiles. She could pull letters out and line them up into messages. Her Scrabble letters helped her unlock secrets, in the same way my bicycle could help me find lost objects. She told me there were other people like us. People who could do impossible things if they had the right vehicle. She told me about Charlie Manx. She warned me about him. She said there was a man, a bad man with a bad car. He used his car to suck the life out of children. He was a kind of vampire—a *road* vampire."

"You're saying you knew about Charlie Manx *before* he ever kidnapped you?"

"No, I'm not. Because in *this version* of my life, he didn't kidnap me at all. In *this version* of my life, I had a dumb fight with my mom, and then after, I used my bicycle to go *looking* for him. I wanted to find some trouble, and I did. I crossed the Shorter Way Bridge and came out at Charlie Manx's Sleigh House. He did his best to kill me, but I got away from him and ran and met you. And the story I told the police, all that stuff about being locked in his trunk and being assaulted—that was just something I made up, because I knew no one would believe the truth. I could tell any story I wanted about Charlie Manx, because I knew that stuff he had really done was worse than any lie I could make up. Remember: In this version of my life, he's not a dirty old kidnapper, he's a fucking vampire."

She was not crying, but her eyes were wet and shiny, luminous in a way that made Fourth of July sparklers look chintzy and dull.

"So he sucked the life out of little kids," Lou said. "And then what? What happened to them?"

"They went to a place called Christmasland. I don't know where that is—I'm not sure it's even in our world—but they get great phone service, because the kids there used to call me all the time." She looked out at the children standing on the stone wall, Wayne among them, and whispered, "They were ruined by the time Manx drained the life out of them. Nothing left in them but hate and teeth."

Lou shuddered. "Jesus."

A small knot of men and women erupted into laughter nearby, and Lou glared at them. It didn't feel as if any people in their general vicinity had any right to be enjoying themselves at this particular moment.

He looked at her and said, "So to recap: There's one version of your life where Charlie Manx, a dirty ol' fuckin' child murderer, kidnapped you from a train station. And you only barely got away from him. That's the *official* memory. But then there's this other version where you crossed an imaginary bridge on a psychically powered bicycle and tracked him down in Colorado all on your own. And that's the *unofficial* memory. The VH1 *Behind the Music* story."

"Yes."

"And both of these memories feel true to you."

"Yes."

"But you know," Lou said, eyeing her intently, "that the story about the Shorter Way Bridge is bullshit. Deep down you *know* it's a story you told yourself, so you don't have to think about what *really* happened to you. So you don't have to think about . . . being kidnapped and all the rest of it."

"That's right," Vic said. "That's what I figured out in the mental hospital. My story about the magic bridge is a classic empowerment fantasy. I couldn't bear the thought of being a victim, so I invented this vast delusion to make me the hero of the story, complete with a whole set of memories of things that never happened."

He sat back in his chair, his motorcycle jacket folded over one knee, and relaxed, breathed deep. Well. That wasn't so bad. He understood now what she was saying to him: that she had been through something awful and it made her a crazy person for a while. She had retreated into fantasy for a time—anyone would!—but now she was ready to put the fantasy away, to deal with things as they were.

"Oh," Lou added, almost as an afterthought. "Shit. This kind of got away from what we were talking about. What does all this have to do with the woman who came to your house yesterday?"

"That's Maggie Leigh," Vic said.

"Maggie Leigh? Who the hell is that?"

"The librarian. The girl I met in Iowa, when I was thirteen. She tracked me down in Haverhill to tell me that Charlie Manx is back from the dead and coming after me."

LOU'S BIG, ROUND, BRISTLY FACE WAS ALMOST COMICALLY EASY TO read. His eyes didn't just widen when Vic told him she'd met a woman from her own imagination. They *popped*, making him resemble a character in a comic strip who has just had a swig from a bottle marked XXX. If there had been smoke jetting from his ears, the picture would've been complete.

Vic had always liked to touch his face and could only barely resist doing it now. It was as inviting as a rubber ball is to a child.

She had been a child the first time she kissed him. They both had been, really.

"*Dude*. What the *fuck*? I thought you said the librarian was *make-believe*. Like your covered bridge of the mind."

"Yep. That's what I decided in the hospital. That all those memories were imagined. An elaborate story I'd invented to protect myself from the truth."

"But . . . she *can't* be imaginary. She was at the house. Wayne *saw* her. She left a folder behind. That's where Wayne read about Charlie Manx," Lou said. Then his big, expressive face came alive with a look of dismay. "Ah, *dude.* I wasn't supposed to *tell* you that. About the folder."

"Wayne looked in it? Shit. I told her to take it with her. I didn't want Wayne to see."

"You can't let him know I told you." Lou made a fist and rapped it on one of his elephantine knees. "I am so *shitty* at keeping secrets."

"You're guileless, Lou. That's one of the reasons I love you."

He lifted his head and gave her a wondering stare.

"I *do,* you know," she said. "It's not your fault I made such a rotten mess of everything. It's not your fault I'm such a colossal fuckup."

Lou bowed his head and considered this.

"Aren't you going to tell me I'm not so bad?" she asked.

"Mmm-no. I was thinking how every man loves a hot girl with a history of making mistakes. Because it's always possible she'll make one with you."

She smiled, reached across the space between them, put her hand on his. "I have a long history of making mistakes, Louis Carmody, but you weren't one of them. Oh, Lou. I get so fucking tired of being in my own head. The screwups are bad, and the excuses are worse. That's what both versions of my life have in common, you know. The *one* thing. In the first version of my life, I'm a walking disaster because Mommy didn't hug me enough and Daddy didn't teach me how to fly kites or something. In the other version, I'm permitted to be a crazy fucking mess—"

"Shhh. Stop."

"—and ruin your life and Wayne's life—"

"Stop kicking yourself."

"—because all those trips through the Shorter Way Bridge messed me up somehow. Because it was an unsafe structure to begin with, and every time I went across it, it took a little more wear. Because it's a bridge, but it's also the inside of my own head. I don't expect that to make sense. I hardly understand it myself. It's pretty Freudian in there."

"Freudian or not, you talk about it like it's real," Lou said. He looked out into the night. He took a slow, deep, steadying breath. "So is it?"

Yes, Vic thought with a wrenching urgency.

"No," she said. "It can't be. I need it *not* to be. Lou, do you remember that guy who shot the congresswoman in Arizona? Loughner? He thought the government was trying to enslave humanity by controlling grammar. To him there was no question it was happening. The proof was all around him. When he looked out the window and saw someone walking the dog, he was *sure* it was a spy, someone the CIA had sent to monitor him. Schizos invent memories all the time: meeting famous people, abductions, heroic triumphs. That's the nature of delusion. Your chemistry fouls up your whole sense of reality. That night I stuck all our phones in the oven and burned our house down? I was *sure* dead children were calling from Christmasland. I heard the phones ringing even though no one else did. I heard voices no one else heard."

"But, *Vic.* Maggie Leigh was at your *house.* The librarian. You didn't *imagine* that. Wayne saw her, too."

Vic struggled for a smile she didn't really feel. "Okay. I'll try and explain how it's possible. It's simpler than you think. There's nothing magic about it. So I have these memories of the Shorter Way Bridge and the bike that took me finding. Only they aren't memories, they're delusions, right? And in the hospital we had group sessions where we'd sit and talk about our crazy ideas. *Lots* of patients in that hospital heard my story about Charlie Manx and the Shorter Way Bridge. I think Maggie Leigh is one of them—one of the other crazies. She latched onto my fantasy and made it her own."

"What do you mean you *think* she was one of the other patients? Was she in your group sessions or not?"

"I have no memory of her in those sessions. What I remember

is meeting Maggie in a small-town library in Iowa. But that's how delusion works. I'm always 'remembering' things." Vic lifted her fingers and made imaginary quotation marks in the air, to indicate the essentially untrustworthy nature of such recollections. "These memories just come to me, all at once, perfect little chapters in this crazy story I wrote in my imagination. But of course there's nothing true about them. They're invented on the spot. My imagination provides them, and some part of me decides to accept them as fact the instant they come to me. Maggie Leigh told me I met her when I was a child, and my delusion instantly provided a story to back her up. *Lou.* I can even remember the fish tank in her office. It had one big koi in it, and instead of rocks it had Scrabble tiles on the floor. Think about how crazy that sounds."

"I thought you were on medicine. I thought you were okay now."

"The pills I take are a paperweight. All they do is pin the fantasies down. But they're still there, and any strong wind that comes along, I can feel them rattling around, trying to slip free." She met his gaze and said, "Lou. You can trust me. I'm going to take care of myself. Not just for me. For Wayne. I'm all right." She did not say she had run out of Abilify a week earlier, had to spread the last few pills out so she didn't come down with withdrawal. She didn't want to worry him any more than necessary, and besides, she planned to refill her prescription first thing next morning. "I'll tell you something else. I don't remember meeting Maggie Leigh in the hospital, but I easily could've. They had me pumped so full of drugs in there I could've met Barack Obama and I wouldn't remember it. And Maggie Leigh, God bless her, is a *lunatic.* I knew it the moment I saw her. She smelled like homeless shelters, and her arms were scarred from where she's been shooting junk or burning herself with cigarettes or both. Probably both."

Lou sat next to her, head lowered, frowning in thought. "What if she comes back? Wayne was pretty freaked."

"We're headed to New Hampshire tomorrow. I don't think she's going to find us up there."

"You could come to Colorado. You wouldn't have to stay with me. We wouldn't have to stay together. I'm not asking for anything. But we could find you a place where you could work on *Search Engine*. The kid could spend the days with me and the nights with you. We got trees and water in Colorado, too, you know."

She sat back in her chair. The sky was low and smoky, the clouds reflecting the lights of the city so that they glowed a dull, dirty shade of pink. In the mountains above Gunbarrel, where Wayne had been conceived, the sky was filled to its depths with stars at night, more stars than you could ever hope to see from sea level. Other worlds were up in those mountains. Other roads.

"I think I'd like that, Lou," she said. "He'll go back to Colorado in September, to go to school. And I'll come with him—if it's all right."

"Of course it's all right. Are you out of your mind?"

For a single instant, long enough for another blossom to fall into her hair, neither of them spoke. Then, at a shared glance, they burst into laughter. Vic laughed so hard, so freely, she had to gasp to get enough air into her lungs.

"Sorry," Lou said. "Probably not the best choice of words."

Wayne, twenty feet away, turned on the stone wall to peer back at them. He held a single dead sparkler in one hand. A ribbon of black smoke drifted from it. He waved.

"You go back to Colorado and find me a place," Vic said to Lou. She waved back at Wayne. "And at the end of August, Wayne will fly back, and I'll be with him. I'd come right now, but we've got the cottage on the lake until the end of August, and he's still got three more weeks of day camp paid for."

"And you've got to finish working on the motorcycle," Lou said.

"Wayne told you about that?"

"Didn't just tell me. He sent me pictures from his phone. Here." Lou tossed her his jacket.

The motorcycle jacket was a big, heavy thing, made of some kind of black nylonlike synthetic and with bony plates sewn into it, Teflon armor. She had thought it was the coolest jacket in the world from the first time she put her arms around it, sixteen years before. The front flaps were covered in faded, frayed patches: ROUTE 66, SOUL, a Captain America shield. It smelled like Lou, like home. Trees and sweat and grease and the clean, sweet winds that whistled through the mountain passes.

"Maybe this will keep you from getting killed," Lou said. "Wear it."

And at that moment the sky above the harbor pulsed with a deep red flash. A rocket detonated in an eardrum-stunning clap. The skies opened and rained white sparks.

The barrage began.

I-95

Twenty-four hours later, Vic drove Wayne and Hooper back to Lake Winnipesaukee. It rained the whole way, a hard summer downpour that rattled on the road and forced her to keep to under fifty miles an hour.

She was across the border and into New Hampshire when she realized she had forgotten to refill her prescription for Abilify.

It required all her concentration to see the road in front of her and stay in her lane. But even if she had been checking the rearview mirror, she would not have noticed the car following at a distance of two hundred yards. At night one set of headlights looks much like any other.

Lake Winnipesaukee

WAYNE WOKE IN HIS MOTHER'S BED BEFORE HE WAS READY. SOMEthing had jolted him out of sleep, but he didn't know what until it came again—a soft *thump, thump, thump* at the bedroom door.

His eyes were open, but he didn't feel awake, a state of mind that would persist throughout the day, so that the things he saw and heard had the talismanic quality of things seen and heard in a dream. Everything that happened seemed hyperreal and freighted with secret meaning.

He did not remember going to sleep in his mother's bed but was not surprised to find himself there. She often moved him to her own bed after he nodded off. He accepted that his company was sometimes necessary, like an extra blanket on a cold night. She was not in bed with him now. She almost always rose before him.

"Hello?" he said, knuckling his eyes.

The knocking stopped—then started again, in a halting, almost questioning way: *Thud? Thud? Thud?*

"Who is that?" Wayne asked.

The knocking stopped. The bedroom door creaked open a few inches. A shadow rose upon the wall, the profile of a man. Wayne could see the big bent crag of a nose and the high, smooth, Sherlock Holmes curve of Charlie Manx's forehead.

He tried to scream. He tried to shout his mother's name. But the only sound he was able to produce was a funny wheeze, a kind of rattle, like a broken sprocket spinning uselessly in some tired machine.

In the mug shot, Charles Manx had been staring straight into the camera, his eyes bulging, his crooked upper teeth pressed into his lower lip to give him a look of dim-witted bafflement. Wayne couldn't know him by his profile, and yet he recognized his shadow in a glance.

The door inched inward. The *thump, thump, thump* came again. Wayne struggled to breathe. He wanted to say something—*Please! Help!*—but the sight of that shadow held him silent, like a hand clamped over his mouth.

Wayne shut his eyes, snatched a desperate breath of air, and shouted, "Go away!"

He heard the door ease inward, whining on its hinges. A hand pressed heavily on the edge of the bed, right by his knee. Wayne forced out a thin, whinnying cry, almost inaudible. He opened his eyes and looked—and it was Hooper.

The big, pale dog stared urgently into Wayne's face, forepaws on the bed. His damp gaze was unhappy, even stricken.

Wayne looked past him at the partly open door, but the Manx shadow wasn't there anymore. On some level Wayne understood it had *never* been there, that his imagination had stitched together a Manx shape out of meaningless shadow. Another part of him was sure he had seen it, a profile so clear it might've been inked on the wall. The door was open wide enough so Wayne could see into the corridor that ran the length of the house. No one was there.

Yet he was sure he had heard a knock, could not have imagined that. And as he stared down the hall, it came again, *thump, thump,* and he looked around and saw Hooper beating his short, thick tail against the floor.

"Hey, boy," Wayne said, digging into the soft down behind Hooper's ears. "You scared me, you know. What brings you?"

Hooper continued to gaze up at him. If someone had asked Wayne to describe the expression on Hooper's big, ugly face, Wayne would've said it looked like he was trying to say he was sorry. But he was probably hungry.

"I'll get you something to eat. Is that what you want?"

Hooper made a noise, a wheezy, gasping sound of refusal, the sound of a toothless gear spinning uselessly, unable to engage.

Only—no. Wayne had heard that sound before, a few moments ago. He had thought he himself was making it. But the sound wasn't coming from him, and it wasn't coming from Hooper. It was outside, somewhere in the early-morning dark.

And still Hooper stared into Wayne's face, his eyes pleading and miserable. *So sorry,* Hooper told him with his eyes. *I wanted to be a good dog. I wanted to be* your *good dog.* Wayne heard this thought in his head, as if Hooper were saying it to him, like a talking dog in a comic strip.

Wayne pushed Hooper aside, got up, and looked out the window into the front yard. It was so dark he could at first see nothing except his own faint reflection on the glass.

And then the Cyclops opened one dim eye, right on the other side of the window, six feet away.

The blood surged to Wayne's heart, and for the second time in the space of three minutes he felt a yell rise into his throat.

The eye opened, slow and wide, as if the Cyclops were just rousing itself. It glowed a dirty hue located somewhere between orange Tang and urine. Then, before Wayne could produce a cry, it began to fade, until there was only a burning copper iris glimmering in the darkness. A moment later it went out completely.

Wayne exhaled unsteadily. A headlight. It was the headlight on the front of the motorcycle.

His mother rose from beside the bike and swiped her hair back from her face. Seen through the old, rippled glass, she didn't seem to really be there, was a ghost of herself. She wore a white halter top and old cotton shorts and her tattoos. It was impossible to make out the details of those tattoos in the dark. It looked as if the night itself were adhering to her skin. But then Wayne had always known that his mother was bound to some private darkness.

Hooper was out there with her, whisking around her legs, water dripping off his fur. He had obviously just come from the lake. It took Wayne a moment to register that Hooper was beside her, which didn't make sense, because Hooper was standing beside *him*. Except that when Wayne looked around, he saw he was alone.

He didn't think about it long. He was still too tired. Maybe he'd been awoken by a dream dog. Maybe he was going crazy like his mother.

Wayne pulled on a pair of cutoffs and went out into the predawn cool. His mother worked on the bike, rag in one hand and a funny tool in the other, that special wrench that looked more like a hook or a curved dagger.

"How'd I get in your bed?" he asked.

"Bad dream," she said.

"I don't remember having a bad dream."

"You weren't the one having it," she said.

Dark birds dashed through the mist that crawled across the surface of the lake.

"You find the busted sprocket?" Wayne asked.

"How do you know it's got a busted sprocket?"

"I don't know. Just from how it sounded when you tried to turn it over."

"You been spending time out in the garage? Working with your dad?"

"Sometimes. He says I'm useful because I have little hands. I can reach in and unscrew things he can't get to. I'm great at taking stuff apart. Not so good at putting stuff together."

"Join the club," she said.

They worked on the bike. Wayne was not sure how long they

were at it, only that by the time they quit, it was hot and the sun was well up above the tree line. They hardly spoke in all the time they worked. That was okay. There was no reason to ruin the greasy, knuckle-scraping effort of fixing the bike with a lot of talk about feelings or Dad or girls.

At some point Wayne sat back on his heels and looked at his mother. She had grease up to her elbows and on her nose, was bleeding from scrapes on her right hand. Wayne was running steel wool over the rust-flecked tailpipe, and he paused to look at himself. He was as filthy as she was.

"I don't know how we're going to get this crap off us," he said.

"We got a lake," she said, tossing her hair and gesturing toward it with her head. "Tell you what. If you beat me to the float, we can have breakfast at Greenbough Diner."

"What do you get if *you* beat *me*?"

"The pleasure of proving that the old woman can still thrash a little piker."

"What's a piker?"

"It's a—"

But he was off and running, grabbing his shirt, snapping it off over his head, flinging it in Hooper's face. Wayne's legs and arms pumped fast and smooth, bare feet slashing through the burning-bright dew in the high grass.

Then she was sailing past him, sticking her tongue out as she reached his side. They hit the dock at the same time. Their bare feet smacked on the boards.

Halfway to the end, she reached out and put her hand on Wayne's shoulder and shoved, and he heard her laughing at him as he lurched drunkenly off balance, his arms pedaling in the air. He hit the water and sank into murky green. He heard the low, deep *bloosh* of her diving off the end of the dock a moment later.

He flailed, came up spitting and hauling ass for the float, twenty feet offshore. It was a big platform of splintery gray boards floating on rusty oil drums; the thing looked like an environmental hazard. Hooper woofed furiously from the dock behind them. Hooper disapproved of merrymaking in general, unless he was the one making it.

Wayne was most of the way to the float when he realized he was alone in the lake. The water was a black sheet of glass. His mother was nowhere to be seen, anywhere, in any direction.

"Mom?" he called. Not afraid. "Mom?"

"You lose," she said, her voice deep, hollow, echoing.

He dived, held his breath, paddled underwater, came up under the float.

She was there, in the darkness, her face glistening with water, her hair shining. She grinned at him when he came up beside her.

"Look," she said. "Lost treasure."

She pointed at a trembling spiderweb, at least two feet wide, decorated with a thousand gleaming beads of silver and opal and diamond.

"Can we still go to breakfast?"

"Yeah," she said. "Got to. Victory over a piker is a lot of things, but it isn't very filling."

Gravel Driveway

HIS MOTHER WORKED ON THE BIKE ALL AFTERNOON.

The sky was the color of a migraine. Thunder sounded once. It was a boom-and-bang, like a heavy truck going over an iron bridge. Wayne waited for rain.

None came.

"Do you ever wish you had adopted a Harley-Davidson instead of having a kid?" he asked her.

"Would've been cheaper to feed," she said. "Hand me that rag."

He handed it to her.

She wiped her hands and fitted the leather seat over a brand-new battery and threw her leg over the saddle. In her cutoff jeans and oversize black motorcycle boots, tattoos scrawled on her arms and legs, she looked like no one anyone would call "Mom."

She turned the key and hit the run switch. The Cyclops opened its eye.

She put one heel on the kickstart, lifted herself up, slammed her weight down. The bike wheezed.

"Gesundheit," Wayne said.

Vic rose and came down hard again. The engine exhaled, blew dust and leaves out the pipes. Wayne didn't like the way she threw all her weight down on the kickstart. He was afraid something would shatter. Not necessarily the bike.

"Come on," she said in a low voice. "We both know why the kid found you, so let's get on with it."

She hit the kickstart again, and then again, and her hair fell into her face. The starter rattled, and the engine produced a faint, brief, rumbling fart.

"It's okay if it doesn't work," Wayne said. Suddenly he didn't like any of this. Suddenly it seemed like crazy business—the sort of crazy business he had not seen from his mom since he was a small boy. "Get it later, right?"

She ignored him. She raised herself up and set her boot squarely on the kickstart.

"Let's go *find,* you bitch," she said, and stomped. "Talk to me."

The engine ba-boomed. Dirty blue smoke shot from the pipes. Wayne almost fell off the fence post he was sitting on. Hooper ducked, then barked in fright.

His mother gave it throttle, and the engine roared. It was frightening, the noise of it. Exciting, too.

"IT RUNS!" he hollered.

She nodded.

"WHAT'S IT SAYING?" he yelled.

She frowned at him.

"YOU TOLD IT TO TALK TO YOU. WHAT'S IT SAYING? I DON'T SPEAK MOTORCYCLE LANGUAGE."

"OH," she said. "HI-YO, SILVER."

"LET ME GET MY HELMET!" WAYNE YELLED.

"YOU'RE NOT COMING."

Each of them screaming to be heard over the sound of the engine battering the air.

"WHY NOT?"

"IT'S NOT SAFE YET. I'M NOT GOING FAR. BE BACK IN FIVE MINUTES."

"WAIT!" Wayne shouted, and held up one finger, then turned and ran for the house.

The sun was a cold white point, shining through the low piles of clouds.

She wanted to move. The need to be on the road was a kind of maddening itch, as hard to leave alone as a mosquito bite. She wanted to get on the highway, see what she could make the bike do. What she could find.

The front door slapped shut. Her son came charging back, carrying a helmet and Lou's jacket.

"COME BACK ALIVE, RIGHT?" he called.

"THAT'S THE PLAN," she said. And then, as she was putting the jacket on, she said, "I WILL BE *RIGHT* BACK. *DON'T WORRY.*"

He nodded.

The world vibrated around her from the force of the engine: the trees, the road, the sky, the house, all of it shuddering furiously, in danger of shattering. She had already turned the bike to face the road.

She punched the helmet down onto her head. She wore the jacket open.

Right before she let the handbrake out, her son bent down in front of the bike and snatched something out of the dirt.

"WHAT?" she asked.

He handed it to her—that wrench that looked like a curved knife, the word TRIUMPH stamped into it. She nodded thanks and pushed it down into the pocket of her shorts.

"COME BACK," he said.

"BE HERE WHEN I DO," she said.

Then she put her feet up, dropped it into first, and she was gliding.

The moment she started moving, everything stopped shaking. The split-tie fence slid away on her right. She leaned as she turned onto the road, and it felt like an airplane banking. It didn't feel as if she were touching the blacktop at all.

She shifted into second. The house dropped away behind her. She cast a last glance over her shoulder. Wayne stood in the driveway, waving. Hooper was out in the street, gazing after her with a curiously hopeless stare.

Vic gave it throttle and shifted into third, and the Triumph *lunged*, and she had to squeeze the handlebars to keep from falling off. A thought flashed through her mind, the memory of a biker T-shirt she had owned for a while: IF YOU CAN READ THIS, THE BITCH FELL OFF.

Her jacket was unzipped, and it scooped up the air and ballooned around her. She rushed on into low fog.

She did not see a pair of close-set headlights come on down the road behind her, glowing dimly in the mist.

Neither did Wayne.

Route 3

TREES AND HOUSES AND YARDS FLASHED BY, DARK, BLURRED SHAPES only dimly apprehended in the mist.

There was no thought in her. The bike rushed her away from thought. She had known that it would, had known the first moment she saw it in the carriage house that it was fast enough and powerful enough to race her away from the worst part of herself, the part that tried to make sense of things.

She triggered the gearshift with her foot again, and then again, and the Triumph jumped forward each time, swallowing the road beneath it.

The fog thickened against her, blowing into her face. It was pearly, evanescent, the sunlight striking through from somewhere up and to the left, causing the whole world to glow around her as if irradiated. Vic felt that a person could not hope for more beauty in this world.

The damp road hissed like static under the tires.

A gentle, almost delicate ache caressed her left eyeball.

She saw a barn in the shifting mist, a long, tall, tilted, narrow structure. A trick of the billowing vapor made it appear to be sitting in the middle of the road, not a hundred yards away, although she knew that the highway would hook off to the left in another moment and swing her past it. She half smiled at how much it looked like her old imaginary bridge.

Vic lowered her head and listened to the susurration of the tires on wet asphalt, that sound that was so like white noise on the radio. What were you listening to when you tuned to static? she wondered. She thought she had read somewhere that it was the background radiation in which the entire universe bathed.

She waited for the road to hook left and bring her around the barn, but it kept on straight. That tall, dark, angular shape rose before her until she was in its shadow. And it wasn't a barn at all, and she only realized that the road ran straight into it when it was too late to turn aside. The mist darkened and went cold, as cold as a dip in the lake.

Boards slammed under the tires, a rapid-fire knocking sound.

The mist was snatched away as the bike carried her up and out of it and into the bridge. She sucked at the air and smelled the stink of bats.

She drove her heel down on the brake and shut her eyes. *This isn't real,* she thought, almost whispered to herself.

The foot pedal for the brake went all the way down, held for a moment—and then came completely off. It fell onto the boards with a deep, hollow thud. A nut and a collection of washers went jingling after it.

The cable that carried the brake fluid flapped against her leg, spurting. The heel of her boot touched the worn boards beneath her, and it was like putting her toe into some nineteenth-century threshing machine. A part of her insisted she was hallucinating. Another part felt her boot striking against the bridge and understood that her hallucination would snap her in two if she dumped the bike.

She had time to look down and back, trying to process what was happening. A gasket spun through the air from somewhere, carving a whimsical arc through the shadows. The front tire wobbled. The world slurved around her, the back tire skidding out and around, slamming madly across loose boards.

She lifted herself up from the seat and slung her weight hard to the left, holding the bike up more by will than by strength. It slid sideways, rattling across the boards. The tires grabbed at last, and the bike came to a shuddering stop and immediately almost fell over. She got a foot down first, held it up, although only barely, gritting her teeth and struggling against the sudden weight.

Vic's breathing echoed raggedly in the barnlike interior of the Shorter Way Bridge, unchanged in the sixteen years since she had last seen it.

She shivered, clammy in her bulky motorcycle jacket.

"Not real," she said, and shut her eyes.

She heard the gentle, dry rustling of the bats overhead.

"Not real," she said.

White noise hissed softly, just on the other side of the walls.

Vic concentrated on her own breath, inhaling slowly and steadily, then exhaling again through pursed lips. She stepped off the bike and stood beside it, holding it up by the handlebars.

She opened her eyes but kept her gaze pointed at her feet. She saw the boards, old, grayish brown, worn. She saw flickering static between the planks.

"Not real," she said for a third time.

She closed her eyes again. She wheeled the bike around, to face back the way she had come. Vic began to walk. She felt the boards sink under her feet, under the weight of the little Triumph Bonneville. Her lungs were tight, and it was hard to draw a full breath, and she felt sick. She was going to have to go back to the mental hospital. She was not going to get to be Wayne's mother after all. At this thought she felt her throat constrict with grief.

"This is *not real.* There is no bridge. I am off my meds and seeing things. That's all."

She took one step and another step and another and then opened her eyes again and was standing with her broken motorcycle in the road.

When she turned her head and looked back over her shoulder, she saw only highway.

The Lake House

THE LATE-AFTERNOON FOG WAS A CAPE THAT FLAPPED OPEN TO ADMIT Vic McQueen and her mean machine, then flapped shut behind her, swallowing even the sound of the engine.

"Come on, Hooper," Wayne said. "Let's go in."

Hooper stood on the margin of the road, staring at him uncomprehendingly.

Wayne called again when he was in the house. He held the door open, waiting for his dog to come to him. Instead Hooper turned his big, shaggy head and peered back along the road—not in the direction Wayne's mother had ridden but the other way.

Wayne couldn't tell what he was looking at. Who knew what dogs saw? What the shapes in the mist meant to them? What odd, superstitious notions they might hold? Wayne was certain dogs were as superstitious as humans. More, maybe.

"Suit yourself," Wayne said, and shut the door.

He sat in front of the TV with his iPhone in one hand and texted with his dad for a few minutes:

Are u at the airport yet?

Yep. They pushed my flight back to 3 so I'm going

to be sitting here awhile.

That sux. What r u gonna do?

Gonna hit the food court. Gonna hit it so hard it CRIES.

Mom got the bike going. She's out riding around.

She wearing her helmet?

Yes. I made her. Coat too.

Good for you. That coat adds +5 to all armor rolls.

LOL. I love u. Have a safe flight.

If I die in a plane crash remember to always bag and board your comics. Love you too.

Then there was nothing more to say. Wayne reached for the remote control, switched on the TV, found SpongeBob. His official stance was that he had grown out of SpongeBob, but with his mother gone he could dispense with the official stance and do what he liked.

Hooper barked.

Wayne got up and went to the picture window, but he couldn't see Hooper anymore. The big dog had vanished into the watery white vapor.

He listened intently, wondering if the bike was coming back. It felt as if his mother had been gone longer than five minutes.

His eyes refocused, and he saw the TV reflected in the picture window. SpongeBob was wearing a scarf and talking to Santa Claus. Santa stuck a steel hook through SpongeBob's brains and threw him into his bag of toys.

Wayne jerked his head around, but SpongeBob was talking to Patrick and there wasn't any Santa Claus.

He was on his way back to the couch when he heard Hooper at the front door at last, his tail going *thump, thump, thump,* just as it had that morning.

"Coming," he said. "Hold your horses."

But when he opened the door, it wasn't Hooper at all. It was a short, hairy, fat man in a tracksuit, gray with gold stripes, the sleeves pushed back to show his forearms. His head was a patchy bristle, as if he had mange. His eyes protruded from above his broad, flattened nose.

"Hello," he said. "Can I use your phone? We've had a terrible accident. We've just hit a dog with our car." He spoke haltingly, like a man reading his lines from a cue card but having trouble making out the words.

"What?" Wayne asked. "What did you say?"

The ugly man gave him a worried look and said, "Hello? Can I use your phone. We've had a terrible accident? We've just hit a dog. With our car!" They were all the same words, but with emphasis in different places, as if he were not sure which sentences were questions and which were declarations.

Wayne looked past the ugly little man. Back down the road, he saw what looked like a dirty roll of white carpet lying in front of a car. In the pale, drifting smoke, it was hard to see either the car or the white mound clearly. Only it wasn't a roll of carpet, of course. Wayne knew exactly what it was.

"We didn't see it, and it was right in the road. We hit it with our car," the little man said, gesturing over his shoulder.

A tall man stood in the mist, next to the right front tire. He was bent over, his hands on his knees, considering the dog in a speculative sort of way, as if he half expected Hooper to get back up.

The little man looked down at his palm for a moment, then back up, and said, "It was a terrible accident." He smiled hopefully. "Can I use your phone?"

"What?" Wayne said again, although he had heard the man perfectly well, even through the ringing in his ears. And besides, he had said the same thing, three times now, with almost no variation at all. "Hooper? Hooper!"

He pushed past the little man. He did not run but went at a fast walk, his gait jerky and stiff.

Hooper looked as if he had dropped onto his side and gone to sleep in the road in front of the car. His legs stuck out straight from his body. His left eye was open, staring up at the sky, filmy and dull, but as Wayne approached, it moved to track him. Still alive.

"Oh, God, boy," Wayne said. He sank to his knees. "Hooper."

In the glare of the headlights, the mist was revealed as a thousand fine grains of water trembling in the air. Too light to fall, they blew around instead, a rain that wouldn't rain.

Hooper pushed creamy drool out of his mouth with his thick tongue. His belly moved in rapid, panting breaths. Wayne couldn't see any blood.

"My Lord," said the man who stood looking down at the dog. "That is what you call bad luck! I am so sorry. The poor thing. You can bet he does not know what happened to him, though. You can take some consolation from that!"

Wayne looked past the dog at the man standing by the front of the car. The man wore black boots that came almost to his knees and a tailcoat with rows of brass buttons on either side of the placket. As Wayne lifted his gaze, he took in the car as well. It was an antique—an oldie but a goodie, his father would say.

The tall man held a silver hammer in his right hand, a hammer the size of a croquet mallet. The shirt beneath his coat was watered white silk, as smooth and shiny as fresh-poured milk.

Wayne lifted his gaze the rest of the way. Charlie Manx stared down at him with large, fascinated eyes.

"God bless dogs and children," he said. "This world is too hard a place for them. The world is a thief, and it steals your childhood from you and all the best dogs, too. But believe this. He is on his way to a better place now!"

Charlie Manx still looked like his mug shot, although he was older—old going on ancient. A few silver hairs were combed across his spotted, bare skull. His scant lips were parted to show a horribly colorless tongue, as white as dead skin. He was as tall as Lincoln and just as dead. Wayne could smell the death on him, the stink of decay.

"Don't touch me," Wayne said.

He got up on unsteady legs and took a single step backward before he thumped into the ugly little man standing behind him. The little man gripped him by the shoulders, forcing him to remain facing Manx.

Wayne twisted his head to look back. If he had the air, he would've screamed. The man behind him had a new face. He wore a rubber gasmask with a grotesque valve where his mouth belonged and glossy plastic windows for eyes. If eyes were windows to the soul, then the Gasmask Man's offered a view of profound emptiness.

"Help!" Wayne screamed. "Help me!"

"That is my aim exactly," said Charlie Manx.

"**Help!**" Wayne screamed again.

"I scream, you scream, we all scream for ice cream," the Gasmask Man said. "Keep shouting. See if that's what you get. Big hint, bucko—no ice cream for screamers!"

"***HELP!***" Wayne shouted.

Charlie Manx put his gaunt fingers over his ears and made a pained face. "That is a lot of filthy noise."

"Boys who make filthy noise don't get any toys," the Gasmask Man said. "Boys who yelp get no help."

Wayne wanted to vomit. He opened his mouth to scream again, and Manx reached out and pressed a finger to his lips. *Shhh.* Wayne almost flinched at the smell of it, an odor of formaldehyde and blood.

"I am not going to hurt you. I would not hurt a child. There is no need for a lot of caterwauling. My business is with your mother. I am sure you are a fine boy. All children are—for a while. But your mother is a lying scallywag who has given false witness against me. That is not the end of it either. I have children of my own, and she kept me from them for years and years. For a decade I could not see their sweetly smiling faces, although I heard their voices often enough in dreams. I heard them calling for me, and I know they went hungry. You cannot think what it is like, to know your children are in need and that you cannot help them. It will drive a normal man to madness. Of course, some would say I did not have far to drive!"

At this both men laughed.

"Please," Wayne said. "Let me go."

"Do you want me to gas him out, Mr. Manx? Is it time for some gingerbread smoke?"

Manx folded his hands at his waist and frowned. "A short nap might be the best thing. It is hard to reason with a child who is so overwrought."

The Gasmask Man began to force-march Wayne around the front of the car. Wayne saw now that it was a Rolls-Royce, and he flashed to one of Maggie Leigh's newspaper articles, something about a man disappearing in Kentucky along with a 1938 Rolls.

"Hooper!" Wayne screamed.

He was being propelled past the dog. Hooper twisted his head, as if snapping at a fly, moving with more life than Wayne would've guessed possible. He bit, shutting his teeth on the Gasmask Man's left ankle.

The Gasmask Man squealed and stumbled. Wayne thought, for an instant, that he might leap free, but the little man had long, powerful arms, like a baboon's, and he got his forearm around Wayne's throat.

"Oh, Mr. Manx," the Gasmask Man said. "He's biting! The dog is biting! He's got his *teeth* in me!"

Manx raised the silver hammer and dropped it on Hooper's head, like a man at a fair, using a sledgehammer to test his strength, hitting the target to see if he could ring a bell. Hooper's skull crunched like a lightbulb under a boot heel. Manx hit him a second time to be sure. The Gasmask Man tore his foot free and turned sideways and kicked Hooper for good measure.

"You dirty dog!" the Gasmask Man cried. "I hope that hurt! I hope that hurt a *lot*!"

When Manx straightened up, there was fresh, wet blood glistening on his shirt in a rough Y shape. It seeped through the silk, trickling from some wound on the old man's chest.

"Hooper," Wayne said. He meant to scream it, but it came out as a whisper, barely audible even to himself.

Hooper's white fur was stained all red now. It was like blood on snow. Wayne couldn't look at what had been done to his head.

Manx bent over the dog, catching his breath. "Well. This pup has chased his last flock of pigeons."

"You killed Hooper," Wayne said.

Charlie Manx said, "Yes. It looks like I have. The poor thing. That is too bad. I have always tried to be a friend to dogs and children. I will try to make it up to you, young man. Consider that I owe you one. Put him in the car, Bing, and give him something to take his mind off his cares."

The Gasmask Man shoved Wayne ahead of him, hopping along, keeping his weight off his right ankle.

The back door of the Rolls-Royce popped and swung wide. No one was sitting in the car. No one had touched the latch. Wayne was baffled—amazed, even—but did not linger on it. Things were moving quickly now, and he couldn't afford to give it thought.

Wayne understood that if he climbed into the backseat, he would never climb out again. It would be like climbing into his own grave. Hooper, though, had tried to show him what to do. Hooper had tried to show him that even when you seemed completely overpowered, you could still show your teeth.

Wayne turned his head and sank his teeth into the fat man's forearm. He locked his jaw and bit down until he tasted blood.

The Gasmask Man shrieked. "It hurts! He's hurting me!"

His hand opened and shut. Wayne saw, in close focus, words written in black marker on the Gasmask Man's palm:

PHONE
ACCIDENT
CAR

"Bing!" hissed Mr. Manx. "*Shhh!* Put him in the car and hush yourself!"

Bing—the Gasmask Man—grabbed a handful of Wayne's hair and *pulled.* Wayne felt as if his scalp were being ripped up like old carpet. Still, he put one foot up, bracing it against the side of the car. The Gasmask Man moaned and punched Wayne in the side of the head.

It was like a flashbulb going off. Only instead of a flash of white light, it was a flash of blackness, behind his eyes. Wayne dropped the foot braced against the side of the car. As his vision cleared, he was pushed through the open door and fell onto all fours on the carpet.

"Bing!" Manx cried. "Close that door! Someone is coming! That dreadful woman is coming!"

"Your ass is grass," the Gasmask Man said to Wayne. "Your ass is *so much* grass. And I am the lawn mower. I'm going to mow your ass, and then I'm going to fuck it. I'm going to fuck you right in the ass."

"Bing, mind me now!"

"Mom!" screamed Wayne.

"I'm coming!" she shouted back, tiredly, her voice arriving from a great distance and without any particular urgency.

The Gasmask Man slammed the car door.

Wayne rose onto his knees. His left ear throbbed where he had been struck, burned against the side of his face. There was a nasty aftertaste of blood in his mouth.

He looked over the front seats and out the windshield.

A dark shape walked up the road. The mist played fun-house tricks with the optics, distorting and enlarging the shape. It looked like a grotesque hunchback pushing a wheelchair.

"Mom!" Wayne screamed again.

The front passenger-side door—which was on the left, where the steering wheel would've been in an American car—opened. The Gasmask Man climbed in, pulled the door shut behind him, then twisted in his seat and pointed a pistol in Wayne's face.

"You want to shut your mouth," the Gasmask Man said, "or I'll drill you. I'll pump you full of lead. How would you like that? Not too much, I bet!"

The Gasmask Man considered his right arm. There was a misshapen purple bruise where Wayne had bitten him, enclosed in parentheses of bright blood where Wayne's teeth had broken the skin.

Manx slid behind the steering wheel. He put his silver mallet on the leather between him and the Gasmask Man. The car was running, the engine producing a deep, resonant purr that was felt more than heard, a kind of luxurious vibration.

The hunchback with the wheelchair came through the mist, until all at once it resolved into the shape of a woman walking a motorcycle, pushing it laboriously by the handlebars.

Wayne opened his mouth to shout for his mother again. The Gasmask Man shook his head. Wayne stared into the black circle of the barrel. It was not terrifying. It was fascinating—like the view from a high peak at the edge of a straight drop.

"No more laughing," the Gasmask Man said. "No more fun. Quaker Meeting has begun."

Charlie Manx dropped the car into drive with a heavy clunk. Then he glanced over his shoulder once more.

"Do not mind him," Manx said. "He is an old spoilsport. I think we can manage to have some fun. I am all but certain of it. In fact, I am about to have some right now."

Route 3

THE BIKE WOULDN'T START. IT WOULDN'T EVEN MAKE HOPEFUL noises. She jumped up and down on it until her legs were worn out, but not once did it produce the low, deep, throat-clearing sound that suggested the engine was close to turning over. Instead it made a soft puff, like a man blowing a contemptuous sigh through his lips: *ffftt.*

There was nothing to do except walk.

She bent to the handlebars and began to push. She took three effortful steps, then paused and looked over her shoulder again. Still no bridge. There had never been any bridge.

Vic walked and tried to imagine how she would begin the conversation with Wayne.

Hey, kid, bad news: I shook something loose on the motorcycle, and it got broke. Oh, and I shook something loose in my head, and that got broke, too. I'm going to have to go in for service. When I get settled in the psycho ward, I'll send you a postcard.

She laughed. It sounded, to her ears, much like a sob.

Wayne. I want more than anything to be the mom you deserve. But I can't. I can't do it.

The thought of saying such a thing made her want to puke. Even if it were true, that didn't make it feel any less cowardly.

Wayne. I hope you know I love you. I hope you know I tried.

The fog drifted across the road and felt as if it were passing right through her. The day had turned unaccountably chilly for early July.

Another voice, strong, clear, masculine, spoke in her thoughts, her father's voice: *Don't bullshit a bullshitter, kid. You wanted to find the bridge. You went looking for it. That's why you stopped taking your meds. That's why you fixed the bike. What are you really scared of? Scared that you're crazy? Or scared that you* aren't?

Vic often heard her father telling her things she didn't want to know, although she had spoken to him only a handful of times in the last ten years. She wondered at that, why she still needed the voice of a man who had abandoned her without a look back.

She pushed her bike through the damp chill of the mist. Water beaded up on the weird, waxy surface of the motorcycle jacket. Who knew what it was made out of—some mix of canvas, Teflon, and, presumably, dragon hide.

Vic removed her helmet and hung it off the handlebars, but it wouldn't stay there, kept dropping into the street. Finally she jammed it back on her head. She pushed, trudging along the side of the road. It crossed her mind she could just leave the bike, come back for it later, but she never seriously entertained the notion. She had walked away from the other bike once, the Raleigh, and had left the best of herself behind with it. When you had a set of wheels that could take you anywhere, you didn't walk away from it.

Vic wished, for maybe the first time in her life, that she owned a cell phone. Sometimes it seemed as if she were the last person in America not to have one. She pretended it was a way of showing off her freedom from the twenty-first century's technological snares. In truth, though, she could not bear the idea of having a phone on her all the time, wherever she went. Could not be at ease knowing she might get an urgent call from Christmasland, some dead kid on the line: *Hey, Ms. McQueen, did you miss us?!?*

She pushed and walked and pushed and walked. She was singing something under her breath. For a long time, she wasn't even aware she was doing it. She imagined Wayne standing at the window at home, staring out into the rain and fog, shifting nervously from foot to foot.

Vic was conscious of—and tried to quash—a gathering feeling of panic out of proportion to the situation. She felt she was needed at home. She had been gone far too long. She was afraid of Wayne's tears and anger—and at the same time looked forward to them, to seeing him, to knowing that everything was all right. She pushed. She sang.

"Silent night," she sang, *"holy night."*

She heard herself and stopped, but the song continued in her head, plaintive and off-key. *All is calm. All is bright.*

Vic felt feverish in her motorcycle helmet. Her legs were soaked and cold from the fog, her face was hot and sweaty from her exertions. She wanted to sit down—no, lie down—in the grass, on her back, staring up at the low, curdled sky. But she could see the rental house at last, a dark rectangle on her left, almost featureless in the fog.

The day was dim by now, and she was surprised there were no lights on in the cottage, aside from the wan blue glow of the TV. She supposed she was surprised, too, that Wayne wasn't in the window watching for her.

But then she heard him.

"Mom!" he shouted. With her helmet on, his voice was muffled, a long way off.

She hung her head. He was fine.

"I'm coming," she called back wearily.

She had almost reached the foot of the driveway when she heard a car idling. She looked up. Headlights glowed in the fog. The car they belonged to had been pulled over at the side of the road, but the moment she spotted it, it began to move, sliding up onto the blacktop.

Vic stood and watched it, and as the car came forward, shedding the fog, she could not say she was entirely surprised. She had sent him to jail, and she had read his obituary, but some part of her had been waiting to see Charlie Manx and his Rolls-Royce again for her entire adult life.

The Wraith slid out of the mist, a black sleigh tearing through a cloud and dragging tails of December frost behind it. December frost in July. The roiling white smoke boiled away from the license plate, old, dented, rust-shot: NOS4A2.

Vic let go of the bike, and it fell with a great crash. The mirror on the left handlebar exploded in a pretty spray of silver splinters.

She turned and ran.

The split-rail fence was on her left, and she reached it in two steps and jumped onto it. She made the top cross-tie when she heard the car lunging up the embankment behind her, and she jumped and landed on the lawn and took one more step, and then the Wraith went through the fence.

A log helicoptered through the air, *whup-whup-whup*, and nailed her across the shoulders. She was slammed off her feet and over the edge of the world, dropped into a bottomless chasm, fell into cold, roiling smoke without end.

The Lake House

THE WRAITH STRUCK THE FENCE OF SKINNED POLES, AND WAYNE WAS flung off the rear seat and onto the floor. His teeth banged together with a sharp clack.

Logs snapped and flew. One of them made a clobbering sound, drumming against the hood. In Wayne's mind that was the sound of his mother's body hitting the car, and he began to scream.

Manx thumped the car into park and turned on the seat to face the Gasmask Man.

"I do not want him to have to watch any of this," Manx said. "Seeing your dog die in the road is pitiful enough. Will you put him to sleep for me, Bing? Anyone can see he has exhausted himself."

"I ought to help you with the woman."

"Thank you, Bing. That is very thoughtful. No, I have her well in hand."

The car rocked as the men climbed out.

Wayne struggled to his knees, lifted his head to look over the front seat, through the window, and into the yard.

Charlie Manx had that silver mallet in one hand and was coming around the front of the car. Wayne's mother was flat on the grass amid a scattering of logs.

The back left-hand door opened, and the Gasmask Man climbed

in next to Wayne. Wayne lunged to his right, trying to get to the other door, but the Gasmask Man caught his arm and pulled him over beside him.

In one hand he had a little blue aerosol can. It said GINGERSNAP SPICE AIR FRESHENER on the side and showed a woman pulling a pan of gingerbread men out of an oven.

"I'll tell you about this stuff right here," the Gasmask Man said. "It may say Gingersnap Spice, but what it really smells like is bedtime. You get a mouthful of this, it'll knock you into next Wednesday."

"No!" Wayne cried. "Don't!"

He flapped, like a bird with one wing nailed to a wooden board. He wasn't flying anywhere.

"Oh, I won't," the Gasmask Man said. "You bit me, you little shit. How do you know I don't have AIDS? *You* could have it. You could have a big, dirty mouthful of my AIDS now."

Wayne looked over the front seat, through the windshield, into the yard. Manx was pacing around behind Wayne's mother, who still hadn't moved.

"I ought to bite you back, you know," the Gasmask Man said. "I ought to bite you *twice,* once for what you did and once more for your dirty dog. I could bite you in your pretty little face. You have a face like a pretty little girl, but it wouldn't be so pretty if I bit your cheek out and spit it on the floor. But we're just going to sit here instead. We're just going to sit here and watch the show. You watch and see what Mr. Manx does with dirty whores who tell dirty lies. And after he's done with her . . . after he's done, it'll be *my* turn. And I'm not half so nice as Mr. Manx."

His mother moved her right hand, opening and closing her fingers, making a loose fist. Wayne felt something unclench inside him. It was as if someone had been standing on his chest and had just stepped off, giving him his first chance in who knew how long to inhale fully. Not dead. Not dead. She was *not dead.*

She swept the hand back and forth, gently, as if feeling in the grass for something she had dropped. She moved her right leg, bending it at the knee. It looked like she wanted to try to get up.

Manx bent over her with that enormous silver hammer of his, lifted it, and brought it down. Wayne had never heard bones break before. Manx struck her in the left shoulder, and Wayne heard it *pop,* like a knothole exploding in a campfire. The force of the blow drove her back down onto her belly.

He screamed for her. He screamed with all the air in his lungs and shut his eyes and lowered his head—

And the Gasmask Man grabbed him by his hair and yanked his head back. Something metal smashed Wayne in the mouth. The Gasmask Man had clubbed him in the face with the can of Gingersnap Spice.

"You open your eyes and watch," the Gasmask Man said.

Wayne's mother moved her right hand, trying to lift herself up, crawl away, and Manx hit her again. Her spine shattered with a sound like someone jumping on a stack of china plates.

"Pay attention," the Gasmask Man said. He was breathing so hard it was steaming up the inside of his mask. "We're just getting to the good part."

Under

VIC SWAM.

She was underwater, she was in the lake. She had plunged almost all the way to the bottom, where the world was dark and slow. Vic felt no need for air, was not conscious of holding her breath. She had always liked going deep, into the still, silent, shadowed provinces of fish.

Vic could've stayed under forever, was ready to be a trout, but Wayne was calling her from the surface world. His voice was a long way off, yet she still heard the urgency in it, heard that he was not yelling but screaming. It took an effort to kick for the surface. Her arms and legs didn't want to move. She tried to focus on just one hand, sweeping it at the water. She opened her fingers. She closed her fingers. She opened them again.

She opened her hand in the grass. Vic was in the dirt, on her stomach, although the sluggish underwater feeling persisted. She could not fathom—ha, ha, fathom, get it?—how she had wound up sprawled in her yard. She could not remember what had hit her. *Something* had hit her. It was hard to lift her head.

"Are you with me, Mrs. Smarty-Pants Victoria McQueen?" someone said.

She heard him but couldn't register what he was saying. It was irrelevant. Wayne was the thing. She had heard Wayne screaming for her, she was sure of it. She had felt him screaming in her bones. She had to get up and see that he was all right.

Vic made an effort to push herself onto all fours, and Manx brought his bright silver hammer down on her shoulder. She heard the bone crack, and the arm caved beneath her. She collapsed, bashed the ground with her chin.

"I did not say you could get up. I asked if you were listening. You will want to listen to me."

Manx. Manx was here, not dead. Manx and his Rolls-Royce, and Wayne was in the Rolls-Royce. She knew this last fact as certainly as she knew her own name, although she had not laid eyes on Wayne in half an hour or more. Wayne was in that car, and she had to get him out.

She began to push herself up once more, and Charlie Manx came down with his silver hammer again and hit her in the back, and she heard her spine break with a sound like someone stepping on a cheap toy: a brittle, plasticky crunch. The blunt force drove the wind out of her and slammed her back to her stomach.

Wayne was screaming again, wordlessly now.

Vic wished she could look around for him, get her bearings, but it was almost impossible to pick her head up. Her head felt heavy and strange, unsupportable, too much for her slender neck to bear. The helmet, she thought. She was still wearing her helmet and Lou's jacket.

Lou's jacket.

Vic had moved one leg, had drawn the knee up, the first part of her plan to get back on her feet. She could feel the dirt under her knee, could feel the muscle in the back of her thigh trembling. Vic had heard Manx pulverize her spine with his second swing, and she was not sure why she could still feel her legs. She was not sure why she wasn't in more pain. Her hamstrings ached more than anything else, bunched tight from pushing the bike half a mile. Everything hurt, but nothing was broken. Not even the shoulder she had heard pop. She drew a great shuddering breath, and her ribs expanded effortlessly, although she had heard them crack like branches in a windstorm.

Except it had never been her bones breaking. She had heard the snapping of those Kevlar plates fitted into the back and shoulders of Lou's bulky motorcycle jacket. Lou had said you could catch a telephone pole at twenty miles an hour wearing his coat and still have a chance at getting back up.

The next time Manx hit her, in the side, she shouted—more in surprise than pain—and heard another loud snap.

"You will want to answer me when I am speaking to you," Manx said.

Her side throbbed—she had felt that one. But the snap had only been another plate going. Her head was almost clear, and she thought if she made a great effort, she could heave herself to her feet.

No you don't, said her father, so close he might've been whispering in her ear. *You stay down and let him have his fun. This is* not *the time, Brat.*

She had given up on her father. Had no use for him and kept their few conversations as short as possible. Did not want to hear from him. But now he was here, and he spoke to her in the same calm, measured tone of voice he'd used when he was explaining how to field a grounder or why Hank Williams mattered.

He thinks he's busted you up real good, kiddo. He thinks you're beat. You try and get up now, he'll know you aren't as bad as he thinks you are, and then he will *get you. Wait. Wait for the right time. You'll know it when it comes.*

Her father's voice, her lover's jacket. For a moment she was aware of both the men in her life looking after her. She had thought they were both better off without her and that she was better off without them, but now here, in the dirt, it came to her that she had never really gone anywhere without them.

"Do you hear me? Can you hear my voice?" Manx asked.

She didn't reply. She was perfectly still.

"P'hraps you do and p'hraps you don't," he said after a moment of thought. She had not heard his voice in more than a decade, but it was still the dumb-ass drawl of a country rube. "What a whore you look, crawling in the dirt in your skimpy little denim shorts. I remember a time, not so long ago, when even a whore would have been ashamed to appear in public dressed like you and to spread her legs to ride a motorbike in lewd parody of the carnal act." He paused again, then said, "You were on a bike the last time, too. I have not forgotten. I have not forgotten the bridge either. Is this a special bike like that other one? I know about special rides, Victoria McQueen, and secret roads. I hope you gallivanted to your heart's content. You will not be gallivanting anymore."

He slammed the hammer into the small of her back, and it was like catching a baseball bat in the kidneys, and she screamed through clenched teeth. Her insides felt smashed, jellied.

No armor there. None of the other times had been like that. Another blow like that one and she would need crutches to get to her feet. Another blow like that one and she would be pissing blood.

"You will not be riding your bike to the bar either, or to the pharmacy to get the medicine you take for your crazy head. Oh, I know all about you, Victoria McQueen, Miss Liar Liar, Pants on Fire. I know what a sorry drunk you are and what an unfit mother and that you have been to the laughing house. I know you had your son out of wedlock, which of course is quite usual for whores such as yourself. To think we live in a world where one such as you is allowed to have a child. Well! Your boy is with *me* now. You stole my children away from me with your lies, and now I claim yours from you."

Vic's insides knotted. It was as bad as being struck again. She was afraid she might throw up in her helmet. Her right hand was pressed hard against her side, into the sick, bunched feeling in her abdomen. Her fingers traced the outline of something in her coat pocket. A crescent-sickle shape.

Manx bent over her. When he spoke again, his voice was gentle.

"Your son is with me, and you will *never* have him back. I don't expect you to believe this, Victoria, but he is better off with me. I will bring him more happiness than you ever could. In Christmasland, I promise you, he will never be unhappy again. If you had a single grateful bone in your body, you would thank me." He prodded her with the hammer and leaned closer. "Come now, Victoria. Say it. Say thank you."

She pushed her right hand into her pocket. Her fingers closed around the wrench that was shaped like a knife. Her thumb felt the ridges of the stamp that said TRIUMPH.

Now. Now is the moment. Make it count, her father told her.

Lou kissed her on the temple, his lips brushing her softly.

Vic shoved herself up. Her back spasmed, a sick flexing in the muscle, almost intense enough to cause her to stagger, but she did not even allow herself to grunt in pain.

She saw him in a blur. He was tall in a way she associated with fun-house mirrors: rail-thin legs and arms that went on forever. He had great, fixed, staring eyes, and for the second time in the space of minutes she thought of fish. He looked like a mounted fish. All his upper teeth bit down into his lower lip, giving him an expression of comic, ignorant bafflement. It was incomprehensible that her entire life had been a carousel of unhappiness, drinking, failed promises, and loneliness, all turning around and around a single afternoon encounter with this man.

She jerked the wrench out of her pocket. It snagged on fabric, and for one terrible instant it almost dropped out of her fingers. She held on, pulled it loose, and slashed it at his eyes. The blow went a little high. The sharp tip of the wrench caught him above the left temple and tore open a four-inch flap of his curiously soggy, loose skin. She felt it grinding raggedly across bone.

"Thank you," she said.

Manx clapped one gaunt hand to his forehead. His expression suggested a man who has been struck by a sudden, dismaying thought. He staggered back from her. One heel slipped in the grass. She stabbed at his throat with the wrench, but he was already out of reach, falling across the hood of his Wraith.

"Mom, oh, *Mom*!" Wayne screamed from somewhere.

Vic's legs were loose and unstable beneath her. She didn't think about it. She went after him. Now that she was up and on her feet, she could see he was an old, old man. He looked like he belonged in a nursing home, a blanket over his knees, a Metamucil shake in one hand. She could take him. Pin him to the hood and stab him in the fucking eyes with her pointy little wrench.

She was almost on top of him when he came up with the silver hammer in his right hand. He gave it a big, swooping swing—she heard it whistle musically in the air—and caught her in the side of her helmet, hard enough to snap her around a hundred eighty degrees and drop her to one knee. She heard cymbals clash in her skull, just like a cartoon sound effect. He looked eighty going on a thousand, but there was a limber, easy strength in his swing that suggested the power of a gangly teenager. Glassy chips of motorcycle helmet fell into the grass. If she had not been wearing it, her skull would've been sticking out of her brain in a mess of red splinters.

"Oh!" Charlie Manx was screaming. "Oh, my Lord, I have been sliced open like a side of beef! Bang! Bang!"

Vic got up too quickly. The late afternoon darkened around her as the blood rushed from her head. She heard a car door slam.

She reeled around, holding her head—the helmet—between her hands, trying to stop the dreadful reverberations resounding within it. The world was jittering just a little, as if she sat on her idling motorcycle again.

Manx was still collapsed across the hood of the car. His harrowed, stupid face shone with blood. But there was another man now, standing at the back end of the car. Or at least it had the shape of a man. It had the head, though, of a giant insect from some 1950s black-and-white movie, a rubbery monster-movie head with a grotesque bristling mouth and glassy blank eyes.

The insect man had a gun. Vic watched it float up and stared into the black barrel, a surprisingly tiny hole, not much bigger than a human iris.

"Bang, bang," the insect man said.

The Yard

When Bing saw Mr. Manx sprawl across the hood of the car, he felt it as a kind of physical jolt, a sensation of recoil. He had felt much the same thing travel up his arm the day he had fired the nail gun into his father's temple, only this was a slam of recoil into the very center of his being. Mr. Manx, the Good Man, was stabbed in the face, and the bitch was coming at him. The bitch meant to kill him, a thought as unimaginable, as horrible, as the sun itself blinking out. The bitch was coming, and Mr. Manx needed him.

Bing gripped the can of Gingersnap Spice, pointed it in the boy's face, and blasted a hissing stream of pale smoke into his mouth and eyes—what he should've done minutes ago, what he *would've* done if he hadn't been so awful mad, if he hadn't decided to make the boy *watch.* The kid flinched, tried to turn his face, but Bing held him by the hair and kept spraying. Wayne Carmody shut his eyes and clamped his lips shut.

"Bing! Bing!" Manx screamed.

Bing screamed himself, desperate to be out of the car and moving, and aware at the same time that he had not dosed the boy well. It didn't matter. There was no time, and the boy was in the car now, couldn't leave. Bing let go of him and dropped the can of Gingersnap Spice into one pocket of his tracksuit jacket. His right hand was pawing for the pistol in the other pocket.

He was out then, slamming the door behind him and pulling out the big oiled revolver. She had on a black motorcycle helmet that showed only her eyes, wide now, seeing the gun in his hand, seeing the last thing she was ever going to see. Three steps away at most, right in his kill zone.

"Bing Bing," he said, "time to do my thing!"

He had already begun to apply pressure on the trigger when Mr. Manx pushed himself up off the hood, putting himself right in the way. The gun went off, and Manx's left ear exploded in a spray of skin and blood.

Manx screamed, clapped his hand to the side of his head where raggedy pieces of ear now hung from the side of his face.

Bing screamed, too, and fired again, into the mist. The sound of the gun going off a second time, when he wasn't prepared for it, startled him so badly that he farted, a high squeak in his pants.

"Mr. Manx! Oh, my God! Mr. Manx, are you all right?"

Mr. Manx dropped against the side of the car, twisting his head around to look at him.

"Well, what do you think? I have been stabbed in the face and my ear is shot to pieces! I am lucky my brains are not running down the front of my shirt, you dumbbell!"

"Oh, my God! I am such an asshole! I didn't mean it! Mr. Manx, I would rather die than hurt you! What do I do? Oh, God! I should just shoot myself!"

"You should shoot *her* is what you should do!" Manx yelled at him, dropping his hand from the side of his head. Red strings of ear dangled and swung. "Do it! Shoot her already! Put her down! Put her down in the dirt and have done with it!"

Bing wrenched his gaze away from the Good Man, his heart slugging in his chest, *ka-bam-bam-bam* like a piano pushed down a flight of stairs in a great crash of discordant sound and slamming wood. His gaze swept the yard and found McQueen, already on the run, loping away from him on her long brown legs. His ears were ringing so loudly he could hardly hear his own gun as it went off again, flame shredding through the ghost-silk of the fog.

Logan Airport

Lou Carmody cleared security and still had an hour to kill, so he hit Mickey D's in the food court. He told himself he would get the grilled chicken salad and a water, but the air was full of the hungry-making odor of french fries, and when he got to the cash register, he heard himself telling the pimply kid he wanted two Big Macs, large fries, and an extra-large vanilla milkshake—the same thing he'd been ordering since he was thirteen.

While he was waiting, he looked to his right and saw a little boy, no more than eight, with dark eyes just like Wayne's, standing with his mother at the next register. The boy stared up at Lou—at Lou's two chins and man tits—not with disgust but with a strange sorrow. Lou's father had been so fat when he died that they had to pay for a special-order coffin, a fucking double-wide that looked like a dinner table with the lid shut.

"Just make it a small milkshake," Lou told his server. He found himself unable to look at the boy again, was afraid to see him staring.

What shamed him was not that he was, as his doctor said, morbidly obese (what a qualifier, "morbidly," as if at a certain point, being overweight were morally similar to necrophilia). What he hated, what made him feel squirmy and ill inside, was his own inability to change his habits. He genuinely could not say the things he needed to say, could not order the salad when he smelled french fries. The last year he had been with Vic, he knew she needed help—that she was drinking in secret, that she was answering imaginary phone calls—but he could not draw the line with her, could not make demands or issue ultimatums. And if she was blasted and wanted to screw him, he could not say he was worried about her; all he could do was clap his hands to her ass and bury his face in her naked breasts. He had been her accomplice right until the day she filled the oven with telephones and burned their house to the ground. He had done everything but light the match himself.

He settled at a table designed for an anorexic dwarf, in a chair only suitable for the ass of a ten-year-old—didn't McDonald's understand their clientele? what were they thinking, providing chairs like this for men like him?—pulled out his laptop, and got on the free Wi-Fi.

He checked his e-mail and looked at cosplay honeys in Power Girl outfits. He dropped in on the Millarworld message boards; some friends were debating which color Hulk should be next. Comic dorks embarrassed him, the dumb shit they argued about. It was obviously gray or green. The other colors were stupid.

Lou was wondering if he could look at SuicideGirls without anyone walking by and noticing when his phone began to hum in the pocket of his cargo shorts. He lifted his rear end and began to dig for it.

He had his hand on it when he tuned in on the music playing over the airport sound system. It was, improbably, that old Johnny Mathis song "Sleigh Ride." Improbable because Boston was roughly as temperate as Venus on that particular afternoon in July; it made Lou sweat just *looking* outside. Not only that—the airport sound system had been rocking something else right up until the moment the phone rang. Lady Gaga or Amanda Palmer or something. Some cute lunatic with a piano.

Lou had his phone out but paused to look at the woman at the next table, a MILF who bore a scant resemblance to Sarah Palin.

"Dude," Lou said, "you hear that?" Pointing at the ceiling. "They're playing Christmas music! It's the middle of the summer!"

She froze with a forkful of coleslaw halfway to her bee-stung lips and stared at him with a mixture of confusion and unease.

"The song," Lou said. "You hear that song?"

Her brow furrowed. She regarded him the way she might've regarded a puddle of vomit—something to avoid.

Lou glanced at his phone, saw Wayne on the caller ID. That was curious; they had just been texting a few minutes ago. Maybe Vic was back from her ride on the Triumph and wanted to talk to him about how it was running.

"Never mind," Lou said to Almost Sarah Palin, and waved a hand in the air, dismissing the subject.

He answered.

"What up, dawg?" Lou said.

"Dad," Wayne said, his voice a harsh whisper. He was struggling not to cry. "Dad. I'm in the back of a car. I can't get out."

Lou felt a low, almost gentle ache, behind his breastbone, in his neck, and, curiously, behind his left ear.

"What do you mean? What car?"

"They're going to kill Mom. The two men. There's two men, and they put me in a car, and I can't get out of the backseat. It's Charlie Manx, Dad. And someone in a gasmask. Someone—" He screamed.

In the background Lou heard a string of popping sounds. His first thought was firecrackers. But it wasn't firecrackers.

Wayne cried, "They're shooting, Dad! They're shooting at Mom!"

"Get out of the car," Lou heard himself say, his voice strange, thin, too high. He was hardly aware he had come to his feet. "Just unlock the door and run."

"I can't. *I can't.* It won't unlock, and when I try and get in the front seat, I just wind up in the back again." Wayne choked on a sob.

Lou's head was a hot-air balloon, filled with buoyant gases, lifting him up off the floor toward the ceiling. He was in danger of sailing right out of the real world.

"The door *has* to unlock. Look around, Wayne."

"I have to go. They're coming back. I'll call when I can. Don't call me, they might hear it. They might hear even if I turn it to mute."

"Wayne! Wayne!" Lou screamed. There was a strange ringing in his ears.

The phone went dead.

Everyone in the food court was staring at him. No one was saying anything. A pair of security cops were approaching, one of them with his hand resting on the molded plastic grip of his .45.

Lou thought, *Call the state police. Call the New Hampshire State Police. Do it right now.* But when he lowered the phone from his face to dial 911, it slipped from his hand. And when he bent to reach for it, he found himself grabbing at his chest, the pain there suddenly doubling, jabbing at him with sharp edges. It was as if someone had fired a staple gun into one tit. He put his hand on the little table to steady himself, but then his elbow folded and he went down, chin-first. He caught the edge of the table, and his teeth clacked together, and he grunted and collapsed onto the floor. His shake went with him. The wax cup exploded, and he sprawled into a cold, sweet puddle of vanilla ice cream.

He was only thirty-six. Way too young for a heart attack, even with his family history. He had known he would pay for not getting the salad.

Lake Winnipesaukee

When the Gasmask Man appeared with his gun, Vic tried to backpedal but couldn't seem to get a signal to her legs. The barrel of the gun held her in place, was as captivating as a mesmerist's pocketwatch. She might as well have been buried in the ground up to her hips.

Then Manx stood up between her and the gunman and the .38 went off and Manx's left ear tore apart in a red flash.

Manx screamed—a wretched cry, not of pain but of fury. The gun went off a second time. Vic saw the agitated mist swirl to her right, a very straight line of cleared air running through it to mark the passage of the bullet.

If you stand here one moment longer, he will shoot you to death in front of Wayne, her father told her, his hand in the small of her back. *Don't stand here and let Wayne see that.*

She darted a look at the car, through the windshield, and her son was there, in the backseat. His face was flushed and rigid, and he was furiously swiping one hand in the air at her: *Go, go! Get away!*

Vic didn't want him to see her running either, leaving him behind. All the other times she had failed him before were nothing to this final, unforgivable failure.

A thought lanced through her, like a bullet tunneling through mist: *If you die here, no one can find Manx.*

"Wayne!" she shouted. "I'll come! Wherever you go, I'll find you!"

She didn't know if he heard her. She could hardly hear herself. Her ears whined, shocked into something close to deafness by the roar of the Gasmask Man's .38. She could barely hear Manx yelling to *Shoot her, shoot her already!*

Her heel squeaked in the wet grass as she turned. She was moving at last. She lowered her head, grabbing at her helmet, wanting it off before she got where she was going. She felt comically slow, feet spinning furiously beneath her, going nowhere, while the grass bunched up under her in rolls, like carpet. There was no sound in the world but for the heavy drumming of her feet on the ground and her breath, amplified by the inside of the helmet.

The Gasmask Man was going to shoot her in the back, bullet in the spine, and she hoped it killed her, because she did not want to lie there sprawled in the dirt, paralyzed, waiting for him to shoot her again. *In the back,* she thought, *in the back, in the back,* the only three words her mind could seem to string together. Her entire vocabulary had been reduced to these three words.

She was halfway down the hill.

She yanked the helmet off at last, threw it aside.

The gun boomed.

Something skipped off the water to her right, as if a child had flung a flat stone across the lake.

Vic's feet were on the boards of the dock. The dock heaved and slammed beneath her. She took three bounding steps and dived at the water.

She struck the surface—thought of the bullet slicing through the fog again—and then she was in the lake, she was underwater.

She plunged almost all the way to the bottom, where the world was dark and slow.

It seemed to Vic that she had, only moments before, been in the dim green drowned world of the lake, that she was returning to the quiet, restful state of unconsciousness.

The woman sailed through the cold stillness.

A bullet struck the lake, to her left, less than half a foot from her, punching a tunnel in the water, corkscrewing into the darkness, slowing rapidly. Vic recoiled and lashed out blindly, as if it could be slapped away. Her hand closed on something hot. She opened her palm, stared at what looked like a lead weight for a fishing line. The disturbed currents rolled it out of her hand, and it sank into the lake and only after it was gone did she understand she had grabbed a bullet.

She twisted, scissored her legs, gazing up now, lungs beginning to hurt. She saw the surface of the lake, a bright silver sheet high over her head. The float was another ten, fifteen feet away.

Vic surged through the water.

Her chest was a throbbing vault, filled with fire.

She kicked and kicked. Then she was under it, under the black rectangle of the float.

She clawed for the surface. She thought of her father, the stuff he used to blast rock, the slippery white plastic packs of ANFO. Her chest was packed full with ANFO, ready to explode.

Her head burst up out of the water, and she gasped, filling her lungs with air.

Vic was in deep shadow, under the boards of the float, between the ranks of rusting iron drums. It smelled of creosote and rot.

Vic fought to breathe quietly. Every exhalation echoed in the small, low space.

"I know where you are!" screamed the Gasmask Man. "You can't hide from me!"

His voice was piping and raggedy and childish. He was a child, Vic understood then. He might be thirty or forty or fifty, but he was still just another of Manx's poisoned children.

And yes, he probably did know where she was.

Come and get me you little fuck, she thought, and wiped her face.

She heard another voice then: Manx. Manx was calling to her. Crooning almost.

"Victoria, Victoria, Victoria McQueen!"

There was a gap between two of the metal barrels, a space of perhaps an inch. She swam to it and looked through. Across a distance of thirty feet, she saw Manx standing on the end of the dock and the Gasmask Man behind him. Manx's face was painted with blood, as if he had gone bobbing for apples in a bucket full of the stuff.

"My, oh, my! You cut me very well, Victoria McQueen. You have made a hash out of my face, and my companion here has managed to shoot off my ear. With friends like these! Well. I am blood all over. I will be the last boy picked at the dance from here on out, you see if I am not!" He laughed, then continued, "It is true what they say. Life really does move in very small circles. Here we are again. You are as hard to keep ahold of as a fish. The lake is a fine place for you." He paused once more. When he began to speak again, there was almost a note of humor in his voice. "Maybe it is just as well. You did not kill me. You only took me away from my children. Fair is fair. I can drive off and leave you as you are. But understand that your son is with me now and you will never have him back. Although I expect he will call sometimes from Christmasland. He will be happy there. I will never hurt him. However you feel now, when you hear his voice again, you will see how it is. You will see it is better that he is with me than with you."

The dock creaked on the water. The engine of the Rolls-Royce idled. She struggled out of the soggy, heavy weight of Lou's motorcycle jacket. She thought it would sink straightaway, but it floated, looking like a black, toxic mess.

"Of course, maybe you will be inclined to come and find us," Manx said. His voice was sly. "As you found me before. I have had years and years to think on the bridge in the woods. Your impossible bridge. I know all about bridges like that one. I know all about roads that can only be found with the mind. One of them is how I find my way to Christmasland. There is the Night Road, and the train tracks to Orphanhenge, and the doors to Mid-World, and the old trail to the Tree House of the Mind, and then there is Victoria's wonderful covered bridge. Do you still know how to get there? Come find me if you can, Vic. I will be waiting for you at the House of Sleep. I will be making a stop there before I arrive in Christmasland. Come find me, and we will talk some more."

He turned and began to clump back up the dock.

The Gasmask Man heaved a great unhappy sigh and lifted the .38, and the gun burped flame.

One of the pine boards above her head snapped and threw splinters. A second bullet zipped across the water to her right, stitching a line in the surface of the lake. Vic flung herself backward, splashing away from the narrow crack through which she had been spying. A third bullet dinged off the rusted stainless-steel ladder. The last made a soft, unremarkable plop right in front of the float.

She paddled, treading water.

Car doors slammed.

She heard the tires crunching as the car backed down across the yard, heard them thud over fallen fence rails.

Vic thought it might be a trick, one of them in the car, the other one, the Gasmask Man, remaining behind, out of sight, with the pistol. She shut her eyes. She listened intently.

When she opened her eyes, she was staring at a great, hairy spider suspended in what was left of her web. Most of it hung in gray shreds. Something—a bullet, all the commotion—had torn it apart. Like Vic, it had nothing left of the world it had spun for itself.

SEARCH ENGINE
JULY 6–7

The Lake

AS SOON AS WAYNE FOUND HIMSELF ALONE IN THE BACKSEAT OF THE Wraith, he did the only sensible thing: He tried to get the fuck out.

His mother had flown down the hill—it seemed more like flying than running—and the Gasmask Man lurched after her in a kind of drunken, straggling lope. Then even Manx himself started toward the lake, hand clutched to the side of his head.

The sight of Manx making his way down the hill held Wayne for an instant. The day had turned to watery blue murk, the world become liquid. Lake-colored fog hung thickly in the trees. The fog-colored lake waited down the hill. From the back of the car, Wayne could only barely see the float out on the water.

Against this background of drifting vapor, Manx was an apparition from a circus: the human skeleton crossed with the stilt walker, an impossibly tall and gaunt and ravaged figure in an archaic tailcoat. His misshapen bald head and beaky nose brought to mind vultures. The mist played tricks with his shadow, so it seemed he was walking downhill through a series of dark, Manx-shaped doorways, each bigger than the last.

It was the hardest thing in the world to look away from him. *Gingerbread smoke,* Wayne thought. He had breathed some of the stuff the Gasmask Man had sprayed at him, and it was making him slow. He scrubbed his face with both hands, trying to shake himself to full wakefulness, and then he began to move.

He had already tried to open the doors in the rear compartment, but the locks wouldn't unlock no matter how hard he pulled at them, and the windows wouldn't crank down. The front seat, though—that was a different story. Not only was the driver's-side door visibly unlocked, the window was lowered about halfway. Far enough for Wayne to wriggle out, if the door refused to cooperate.

He forced himself off the couch and made the long, wearying journey across the rear compartment, crossing the vast distance of about a yard. Wayne grabbed the back of the front seat and heaved himself over and—

Toppled down onto the floor in the back of the car.

The rapid leaping motion made his head spinny and strange. He remained on all fours for several seconds, breathing deeply, trying to still the roiling disquiet in his stomach. Trying as well to determine what had just happened to him.

The gas that had gone up his snoot had disoriented him so that he hardly knew down from up. He had lost his bearings and collapsed into the backseat again; that was it.

He rose to try once more. The world lurched unsteadily around him, but he waited, and at last it was still. He drew a deep breath (more gingerbread taste) and heaved himself over the divider and rolled and sat up on the floor of the backseat once again.

His stomach upended itself, and for a moment his breakfast was back in his mouth. He swallowed it down. It had tasted better the first time.

Down the hill, Manx was speaking, addressing the lake, his voice calm and unhurried.

Wayne considered the rear compartment, trying to establish to himself how he had managed to wind up here *again*. It was as if the backseat went on forever. It was like there was nothing *but* backseat. He felt as dizzy as if he had just climbed off the Gravitron at the county fair, that ride that spun you faster and faster until centrifugal force stuck you to the wall.

Get up. Don't quit. He saw these words in his mind as clearly as black letters painted on the boards of a white fence.

This time Wayne ducked his head and got a running start and jumped over the divider and out of the rear compartment and . . . back into the rear compartment, where he crashed to the carpeted floor. His iPhone leaped out of the pocket of his shorts.

He got up on all fours but had to grab the shag carpet to keep from falling over, was that dizzy and light-headed. He felt as if the car were moving, spinning across black ice, revolving in a great swooping, nauseating circle. The sense of sideways motion was almost overpowering, and he had to briefly shut his eyes to block it out.

When he dared to lift his head and look around, the first thing he saw was his phone, resting on the carpet just a few feet away.

He reached for it, in the slow-motion way of an astronaut reaching for a floating candy bar.

He called his father, the only number he had stored under FAVORITES, one touch. He felt that one touch was almost all he could manage.

"What up, dawg?" Louis Carmody said, his voice so warm and friendly and unworried, Wayne felt a sob rise into his own throat at the sound of it.

Until that moment he had not realized how close he was to tears. His throat constricted dangerously. He was not sure he would be able to breathe, let alone speak. He shut his eyes and had a brief, nearly crippling tactile memory of his cheek pressing to his father's bristly face, his father's rough, three-day growth of spiky brown bear fur.

"Dad," he said. "Dad. I'm in the back of a car. I can't get out."

He tried to explain, but it was hard. It was hard to get all the air he needed to speak, hard to speak through his tears. His eyes burned. His vision blurred. It was hard to explain about the Gasmask Man and Charlie Manx and Hooper and gingerbread smoke and how the backseat went on forever. He wasn't sure what he said. Something about Manx. Something about the car.

Then the Gasmask Man was shooting again. The gun went off over and over as he fired at the float. His pistol jumped in his hand, flashing in the dark. When had it gotten so dark?

"They're shooting, Dad!" Wayne said in a hoarse, strained tone of voice he hardly recognized. "They're shooting at Mom!"

Wayne peered out through the windshield, into the gloom, but couldn't tell if any of the bullets had hit his mother or not. He couldn't see her. She was part of the lake, the darkness. How she took to darkness. How easily she slipped away from him.

Manx did not stay to watch the Gasmask Man shoot the water. He was already halfway up the hill. He clutched the side of his head like a man listening to an earpiece, receiving a message from his superiors. Although it was impossible to conceive of anyone who might be superior to Manx.

The Gasmask Man emptied his gun and turned away from the water himself. He swayed as he began to mount the hill, walking like one supporting a great burden on his shoulders. They would reach the car soon. Wayne did not know what would happen then but still had his wits about him well enough to know that if they saw his phone, they would take it away.

"I have to go," Wayne told his father. "They're coming back. I'll call when I can. Don't call me, they might hear it. They might hear even if I turn it to mute."

His father was shouting his name, but there wasn't time to say more. Wayne hit END CALL and flicked the phone over to mute.

He looked for a place to stick the phone, thinking he would shove it down between the seats. But then he saw there were walnut drawers with polished silver knobs set beneath the front seats. He slid one open, flipped the phone in, and kicked it shut as Manx opened the driver's-side door.

Manx slung the silver hammer onto the front seat and climbed halfway in. He held a silk handkerchief to the side of his face, but he lowered it when he saw Wayne kneeling on the carpeted floor. Wayne made a small, shrill sound of horror at the sight of Manx's face. Two distinct strings of ear dangled from the side of his head. His long, gaunt face wore a dull red wash of blood. A flap of skin hung from his forehead, some of his eyebrow sticking to it. Bone glistened beneath.

"I suppose I look quite a fright," Manx said, and grinned to show pink-stained teeth. He pointed to the side of his head. "Ear today, gone tomorrow."

Wayne felt faint. The back of the car seemed unaccountably dark, as if Manx had brought the night in with him when he opened the door.

The tall man dropped behind the wheel. The door *slammed itself* shut—and then the window cranked itself up. It wasn't Manx, couldn't be Manx doing it. He was clutching one hand to his ear again, and the other was gently pressed to that loose flap of skin across his brow.

The Gasmask Man had reached the passenger-side door and pulled on the handle—but as he did, the lock slammed down.

The gearshift wiggled and clunked into reverse. The car lunged a few feet backward, rocks spitting from under the tires.

"No!" the Gasmask Man screamed. He was holding the latch when the car moved and was almost dragged off balance. He stumbled after the car, trying to keep one hand on the hood, as if he could hold the Rolls-Royce in place. "No! Mr. Manx! Don't go! I'm *sorry*! I didn't mean it! It was a mistake!"

His voice was ragged with horror and grief. He ran to the passenger door and grabbed the latch and pulled again.

Manx leaned toward him. Through the window he said, "You are on my naughty list now, Bing Partridge. You have big ideas if you think I ought to take you to Christmasland after the mess you have made. I am afraid to let you in. How do I know, if I allow you to ride with us, that you will not riddle the car with bullets?"

"I swear, I'll be nice! I'll be nice, I will, I'll be nice as sugar and spice! Don't leave! I'm sorry. I'm so *sawwwwwwwreee*!" The inside of his gasmask was steamed over, and he spoke between sobs. "I wish I'd shot myself! I do! I wish it was *my* ear! Oh, Bing Bing, you stupid thing!"

"That is plenty of your ridiculous noise. My head hurts enough as it is."

The lock banged back up. The Gasmask Man yanked the door open and fell into the car. "I didn't mean it! I swear I didn't mean it. I will do anything! Anything!" His eyes widened in a flash of inspiration. "I could cut *my* ear off! My own ear! I don't care! I don't need it, I have two! Do you want me to cut off my own ear?"

"I want you to shut up. If you feel like cutting something off, you could start with your tongue. Then at least we would have some peace."

The car accelerated in reverse, thudding down onto blacktop, undercarriage crunching. As it hit the road, it slopped around to the right, to face back in the direction of the highway. The gearshift wiggled again and jumped into drive.

In all this time, Manx did not touch the steering wheel or the stick but remained clutching his ear and turned in his seat to look at the Gasmask Man.

The gingerbread smoke, Wayne thought with a kind of dull-edged wonder. It was making him see things. Cars didn't drive themselves. Backseats didn't go on forever.

The Gasmask Man rocked back and forth, making piteous noises and shaking his head.

"Stupid," the Gasmask Man whispered. "I am *so* stupid." He banged his head on the dash, forcefully. Twice.

"You will quit right this instant or I am leaving you by the side of the road. There is no reason for you to take out your failures on the handsome interior of my car," Manx said.

The car jolted forward and began to rush away from the cottage. Manx's hands never left his face. The steering wheel moved minutely from side to side, guiding the Rolls along the road. Wayne narrowed his eyes, fixed his stare upon it. He pinched his cheek, very hard, twisting the flesh, but the pain did nothing to clear his vision. The car went on driving itself, so either the gingerbread smoke was causing him to hallucinate or— But there wasn't an "or" in this line of reasoning. He didn't want to start thinking "or."

He turned his head and looked out the rear window. He had a last glimpse of the lake, under its low blanket of fog. The water was as smooth as a plate of new-minted steel, as smooth as the blade of a knife. If his mother was there, he saw no sign of her.

"Bing. Have a look in the glove compartment and I believe you will find a pair of scissors and some tape."

"Do you want me to cut out my own tongue?" the Gasmask Man asked hopefully.

"No. I want you to bandage my head. Unless you would rather sit there and watch me bleed to death. I suppose that would be an entertaining spectacle."

"No!" the Gasmask Man screamed.

"Well then. You will have to do what you can for my ear and my head. And take off that mask. It is impossible to talk to you while you have that thing on."

The Gasmask Man's head made a popping sound as it came out of the mask, much like a cork popping from a bottle of wine. The face beneath was flushed and reddened, and there were tears streaked all down his flabby, quivering cheeks. He rummaged through the glove compartment and came up with a roll of surgical tape and a pair of little silver scissors. He unzipped his tracksuit to reveal a stained white muscle shirt and shoulders so furry they brought to mind silverback gorillas. He stripped off the undershirt and zipped the jacket up.

The blinker clicked on. The car slowed for a stop sign, then turned onto the highway.

Bing scissored several long strips of undershirt. He folded one neatly and put it against Manx's ear.

"Hold that there," Bing said, and hiccupped in a miserable sort of way.

"I would like to know what she cut me with," Manx said. He glanced into the backseat again, met Wayne's gaze. "I have had a history of poor dealings with your mother, you know. It is like fighting with a bag of cats."

Bing said, "I wish maggots were eating her. I wish maggots were eating her eyes."

"That is a vile image."

Bing looped another long strip of undershirt around Manx's head, binding the pad to his ear and covering the slash across his forehead. He began to fix the undershirt in place with crosswise strips of surgical tape.

Manx was still looking at Wayne. "You are a quiet one. Do you have anything to say for yourself?"

"Let me go," Wayne said.

"I will," Manx said.

They blew past the Greenbough Diner, where Wayne and his mother had eaten breakfast sandwiches that morning. Thinking back on the morning was like thinking back on a half-remembered dream. Had he seen Charlie Manx's shadow when he first woke up? It seemed he had.

"I knew you were coming," Wayne said. He was surprised to hear himself saying such a thing. "I knew all day."

"It is hard to keep a child from thinking about presents on the night before Christmas," Manx said. He winced as Bing pressed another strip of tape in place.

The steering wheel rocked gently from side to side, and the car hugged the curves.

"Is this car driving itself?" Wayne asked. "Or am I just seeing that because he sprayed stuff in my face?"

"You don't need to talk!" the Gasmask Man screamed at him. "Quaker Meeting has begun! No more laughing, no more fun, or we cut out your stupid tongue!"

"Will you stop talking about cutting out tongues?" Manx said. "I am beginning to think you have a fixation. I am speaking to the boy. I do not need you to referee."

Abashed, the Gasmask Man returned to snipping strips of tape.

"You are not seeing things, and it is *not* driving itself," Manx said. "*I* am driving it. I am the car, and the car is me. It is an authentic Rolls-Royce Wraith, assembled in Bristol in 1937, shipped to America in 1938, one of fewer than five hundred on these shores. But it is also an extension of my thoughts and can take me to roads that can exist only in the imagination."

"There," Bing said. "All fixed."

Manx laughed. "For me to be all fixed, we would have to go back and search that woman's lawn for the rest of my ear."

Bing's face shriveled; his eyes narrowed to squints; his shoulders hitched and jerked with silent sobs.

"But he *did* spray something in my face," Wayne said. "Something that smelled like gingerbread."

"Just something to put your mind at ease. If Bing had used his spray properly, you would be resting peaceably already." Manx cast a cool, disgusted look at his traveling companion.

Wayne considered this. Thinking a thing through was like moving a heavy crate across a room—a lot of straining effort.

"How come it isn't making *you two* rest peaceably?" Wayne asked finally.

"Hm?" Manx said. He was looking down at his white silk shirt, now stained crimson with blood. "Oh. You are in your own pocket universe back there. I don't let anything come up front." He sighed heavily. "There is no saving this shirt! I feel we should all have a moment of silence for it. This shirt is a silk Riddle-McIntyre, the finest shirtmaker in the West for a hundred years. Gerald Ford wore nothing but Riddle-McIntyres. I might as well use it to clean engine parts now. Blood will never come out of silk."

"Blood will never come out of silk," Wayne whispered. This statement had an epigrammatic quality to it, felt like an important fact.

Manx considered him calmly from the front seat. Wayne stared back through pulses of bright and dark, as if clouds were fleeting across the sun. But there was no sun today, and that throbbing brightness was in his head, behind his eyes. He was out on the extreme edge of shock, a place where time was different, moving in spurts, catching in place, then jumping forward again.

Wayne heard a sound, a long way off, an angry, urgent wail. For a moment he thought it was someone screaming, and he remembered Manx hitting his mother with his silver mallet, and he thought he might be sick. But as the sound approached them and intensified, he identified it as a police siren.

"She is right up and at them," Manx said. "I have to give your mother credit. She does not delay when it comes to making trouble for me."

"What will you do when the police see us?" Wayne asked.

"I do not think they will bother us. They are going to your mother's."

Cars ahead of them began to pull to either side of the road. A blue-silver strobe appeared at the top of a low hill ahead of them, dropped over the slope, and rushed toward them. The Wraith eased itself to the margin of the road and slowed down considerably but didn't stop.

The police cruiser punched past them doing nearly sixty. Wayne turned his head to watch it go. The driver did not even glance at them. Manx drove on. Or, really, the car drove on. Manx still hadn't touched the wheel. He had folded down the sun visor and was inspecting himself in the mirror.

The bright-dark flashes were coming more slowly now, like a roulette wheel winding down, the ball soon to settle on red or black. Wayne still felt no real terror, had left that behind in the yard with his mother. He picked himself up off the floor and settled on the couch.

"You should see a doctor," Wayne said. "If you dropped me off somewhere in the woods, you could go to a doctor and get your ear and head fixed before I walked back to town or anyone found me."

"Thank you for your concern, but I would prefer not to receive medical treatment in handcuffs," Manx said. "The road will make me better. The road always does."

"Where are we going?" Wayne asked. His voice seemed to come from a distance.

"Christmasland."

"Christmasland," Wayne repeated. "What's that?"

"A special place. A special place for special children."

"Really?" Wayne pondered this for a time, then said, "I don't believe you. That's just something to tell me so I won't be scared." He paused again, then decided to brave one more question. "Are you going to kill me?"

"I am surprised you even need to ask. It would have been easy to kill you back at your mother's house. No. And Christmasland is real enough. It is not so easy to find. You cannot get to it by any road in this world, but there are other roads than the ones you will find on a map. It is outside of our world, and at the same time it is only a few miles from Denver. And then again it is right here in my head"—he tapped his right temple with one finger—"and I take it with me everywhere I go. There are other children there, and not one of them is held against his or her will. They would not leave for anything. They are eager to meet you, Wayne Carmody. They are eager to be your friend. You will see them soon enough—and when you finally do, it will feel like coming home."

The blacktop thumped and hummed under the tires.

"The last hour has seen a lot of excitement," Manx said. "Put your head down, child. If anything interesting happens, I will be sure to wake you."

There was no reason to do a thing Charlie Manx told him, but before long, Wayne found he was on his side, his head resting on the plump leather seat. If there was any more peaceful sound in all the world than the road murmuring under tires, Wayne didn't know what it was.

The roulette wheel clicked and clicked and stopped at last. The ball settled into black.

The Lake

VIC BREASTSTROKED INTO THE SHALLOWS, THEN CRAWLED THE LAST few feet up onto the beach. There she rolled onto her back, legs still in the lake. She shook furiously, in fierce, almost crippling spasms, and made sounds too angry to be sobs. She might've been crying. She wasn't sure. Her insides hurt badly, as if she had spent a day and a night vomiting.

In a kidnapping nothing is more important than what happens in the first thirty minutes, Vic thought, her mind replaying something she had once heard on TV.

Vic did not think what she did in the next thirty minutes mattered at all, did not think any cop anywhere had the power to find Charlie Manx and the Wraith. Still, she shoved herself to her feet, because she needed to do what she could, whether it made a difference or not.

She walked like a drunk in a hard crosswind, swaying, following a wandering path to the back door, which is where she fell again. She went up the steps on hands and knees, used the railing to get to her feet. The phone began to ring. Vic forced herself onward, through another burst of lancing pain, sharp enough to drive the breath out of her.

She reeled through the kitchen, reached the phone, caught it on the third ring, just before it could go to voice mail.

"I need help," Vic said. "Who is this? You have to help me. Someone took my son."

"Aw, it's okay, Ms. McQueen," said the little girl on the other end of the line. "Daddy will drive safe and make sure Wayne has a real good time. He'll be here with us soon. He'll be here in Christmasland, and we'll show him all our games. Isn't that fine?"

Vic hit END CALL, then dialed 911.

A woman told her she had reached emergency services. Her voice was calm and detached. "What's your name and the nature of your emergency?"

"Victoria McQueen. I've been attacked. A man has kidnapped my son. I can describe the car. They only just drove away. Please send someone."

The dispatcher tried to keep the same tone of steady calm but couldn't quite manage it. Adrenaline changed everything.

"How badly are you hurt?"

"Forget that. Let's talk about the kidnapper. His name is Charles Talent Manx. He's . . . I don't know, *old.*" *Dead,* Vic thought but didn't say. "In his seventies. He's over six feet tall, balding, about two hundred pounds. There's another man with him, someone younger. I didn't see him too well." *Because he was wearing a fucking gasmask for some reason.* But she didn't say that either. "They're in a Rolls-Royce Wraith, a classic, 1930s. My son is in the backseat. My son is twelve. His name is Bruce, but he doesn't like that name." And Vic began to cry, couldn't help it. "He has black hair and is five feet tall and was wearing a white T-shirt with nothing on it."

"Victoria, the police are en route. Was either of these men armed?"

"Yes. The younger one has a gun. And Manx has some kind of hammer. He hit me with it a couple times."

"I'm dispatching an ambulance to see to your injuries. Did you happen to get the license plate?"

"It's a fucking Rolls-Royce from the thirties with my little boy in the back. How many of those do you think are driving around?" Her voice snagged on a sob. She coughed it up and coughed up the license-plate tag as well: "En-oh-es-four-ar-two. It's a vanity plate. Spells a German word. Nosferatu."

"What's it mean?"

"What's it matter? Look it the fuck up."

"I'm sorry. I understand you're upset. We're sending out an alert now. We're going to do everything we can to get your son back. I know you're scared. Be calm. Please try to be calm." Vic had a sense that the dispatcher was half talking to herself. There was a wavering tone in her voice, like the woman was struggling not to cry. "Help is on the way. Victoria—"

"Just Vic. Thank you. I'm sorry I swore at you."

"It's all right. Don't worry about it. Vic, if they're in a distinctive car like a Rolls-Royce, that's good. That will stand out. They aren't going to get far in a vehicle like that. If they're *any*where on the road, someone will see them."

But no one did.

WHEN THE EMTS TRIED TO ESCORT HER TO THE AMBULANCE, VIC ELbowed free from them, told them to keep their fucking hands off.

A police officer, a small, portly Indian woman, inserted herself between Vic and the men.

"You can examine her here," she said, leading Vic back to the couch. Her voice carried the lightest of accents, a lilt that made every statement sound both vaguely musical and like a question. "It is better if she doesn't go. What if the kidnapper calls?"

Vic huddled on the couch in her wet cutoffs, wrapped in a throw. An EMT wearing blue gloves planted himself next to her and asked her to drop the blanket and remove her shirt. That got the attention of the cops in the room, who cast surreptitious glances Vic's way, but Vic complied wordlessly, without a second thought. She slopped her wet shirt on the floor. She wasn't wearing a bra, and she covered her breasts with one arm, hunching forward to let the EMT look at her back.

The EMT inhaled sharply.

The Indian police officer—her name tag read CHITRA—stood on Vic's other side, looking down the curve of Vic's back. She made a sound herself, a soft cry of sympathy.

"I thought you said he *tried* to run you over," Chitra said. "You did not say he succeeded."

"She's going to have to sign a form," said the EMT. "A thing that says she refused to get in the ambulance. I need to cover my ass here. She could have cracked ribs or a popped spleen and I could miss it. I want it on record that I don't believe treating her here is in her best medical interest."

"Maybe it's not in my best medical interest," Vic said, "but it *is* in yours."

Vic heard a sound go around the room—not quite laughter but close to it, a low male ripple of mirth. There were by now six or seven of them in the room, standing around pretending not to look at her chest, the tattoo of a V-6 engine set above her breasts.

A cop sat on the other side of her, the first cop she had seen who wasn't in uniform. He wore a blue blazer that was too short at the wrists, a red tie with a coffee stain on it, and a face that would've won an ugly contest walking away: bushy white eyebrows turning yellow at the tips, nicotine-stained teeth, a comically gourdlike nose, a jutting cleft chin.

He dug in one pocket, then another, then lifted his wide, flat rear and found a reporter's notebook in his back pocket. He opened it, then stared at the pad with a look of utter bafflement, as if he had been asked to write a five-hundred-word essay on impressionist painting.

It was that blank look, more than anything else, that let Vic know he wasn't The Guy. He was a placeholder. The person who would matter—the one who would be handling the search for her son, who would coordinate resources and compile information—wasn't here yet.

She answered his questions anyway. He started in the right place, with Wayne: age, height, weight, what he'd been wearing, if she had a recent photo. At some point Chitra walked away, then returned with an oversize hoodie that said NH STATE POLICE on the front. Vic tugged it on. It came to her knees.

"The father?" asked the ugly man, whose name was Daltry.

"Lives in Colorado."

"Divorced?"

"Never married."

"How's he feel about you having custody of the kid?"

"I don't have custody. Wayne is just— We're on good terms about our son. It's not an issue."

"Got a number where we can reach him?"

"Yes, but he's on a plane right now. He visited for the Fourth. He's headed back this evening."

"You sure about that? How do you know he boarded the plane?"

"I'm sure he had nothing to do with this, if that's what you're asking. We're *not* fighting over our son. My ex is the most harmless and easygoing man you've ever met."

"Oh, I don't know. I've met some pretty easygoing fellas. I know a guy up in Maine who leads a Buddhist-themed therapy group, teaches people about managing their temper and addictions through Transcendental Meditation. The only time this guy ever lost his composure was the day his wife served him with a restraining order. First he lost his Zen, then he lost two bullets in the back of her head. But that Buddhist-themed therapy group he runs sure is popular on his cell block in Shawshank. Lotta guys with anger-management issues in there."

"Lou didn't have anything to do with this. I told you, I *know* who took my son."

"Okay, okay. I have to ask this stuff. Tell me about the guy who worked on your back. No. Wait. Tell me about his car first."

She told him.

Daltry shook his head and made a sound that could've been a laugh, if it expressed any humor. Mostly what it expressed was incredulity.

"Your man ain't too bright. If he's on the road, I give him less than half an hour."

"Before what?"

"Before he's facedown in the fecking dirt with some state cop's boot on his neck. You don't grab a kid in an antique car and drive away. That's about as smart as driving an ice-cream truck. Kind of stands out. People look. Everyone is going to notice a period Rolls-Royce."

"It isn't going to stand out."

"What do you mean?" he asked.

She didn't know what she meant, so she didn't say anything.

Daltry said, "And you recognized one of your assailants. This would be . . . Charles . . . Manx." Looking at something he had scribbled in his notepad. "How would you know him?"

"He kidnapped *me* when I was seventeen years old. And held me for two days."

That quieted the room.

"Look it up," she said. "It's in his file. Charles Talent Manx. And he's pretty good at not getting caught. I have to change out of these wet shorts and into some sweats. I'd like to do that in my bedroom, if you don't mind. I feel like Mom has flashed enough skin for one day."

VIC HELD IN HER MIND HER ONE LAST GLIMPSE OF WAYNE, TRAPPED IN the backseat of the Rolls. She saw him swatting a hand at the air—

Go on, get away—almost as if he were angry with her. He had already looked as pale as any corpse.

She saw Wayne in flashes, and it was like the hammer thudding into her again, walloping her in the chest instead of the back. Here he was sitting naked in a sandbox, behind their town house in Denver, a chubby three-year-old with a thatch of black hair, using a plastic shovel to bury a plastic telephone. Here he was on Christmas Day in rehab, sitting on the cracked and crinkly plastic surface of a couch, plucking at a wrapped gift, then tearing the wrapping away to show the white-boxed iPhone. Here he was walking out onto the dock with a toolbox that was too heavy for him.

Bang, each vision of him hit her, and her bruised insides clenched up again. Bang, he was a baby, sleeping naked on her naked breast. Bang, he was kneeling in the gravel next to her, arms greasy to the elbows, helping her to thread the motorcycle chain back onto its sprockets. Sometimes the pain was so intense, so pure, the room darkened at the edges of her vision and she felt faint.

At some point she had to move, couldn't stay on the couch anymore.

"If anyone is hungry, I can make something to eat," she said. It was almost nine-thirty in the evening by then. "I've got a full fridge."

"We'll send out for something," Daltry said. "Don't trouble yourself."

They had the TV on, turned to NECN, New England Cable News. They had gone up with the alert about Wayne an hour before. Vic had seen it twice and knew she couldn't watch it again.

First they would show the photo she had given them of Wayne in an Aerosmith T-shirt and an Avalanche wool cap, squinting into bright spring sunlight. She already regretted it, didn't like how the cap hid his black hair and made his ears stick out.

This would be followed by a photograph of Vic herself, the one from the *Search Engine* website. She assumed they were showing that one to get a pretty girl on the screen—she was wearing makeup and a black skirt and cowboy boots and had her head tipped back to laugh, a jarring image, considering the situation.

They didn't show Manx. They didn't even say his name. They described the kidnappers only as two white males in an antique black Rolls-Royce.

"Why don't they tell people who they're looking for?" Vic asked the first time she saw the report.

Daltry shrugged, said he would find out, got off the couch and wandered into the yard to talk to some other men. When he came back in, though, he didn't offer any new information, and when the report ran the second time, they were still looking for two white males, out of the approximately 14 million white males to be found in New England.

If she saw the report a third time and there wasn't a picture of Charlie Manx—if they didn't say his name—she thought she might put a chair through the TV.

"Please," Vic said now. "I've got some slaw and cold ham. A whole loaf of bread. I could lay out sandwiches."

Daltry shifted in his seat and looked uncertainly at some of the other policemen in the room, torn between hunger and decency.

Officer Chitra said, "I think you should. Of course. I'll come with you."

It was a relief to get out of the living room, which was too crowded with bodies, cops coming and going, walkie-talkies squawking continuously. She stopped to take in the view of the lawn through the open front door. In the glare of the spotlights, it was brighter in the yard at night than it had been in the midday fog. She saw the toppled fence rails and a man in rubber gloves measuring the tire treads imprinted in the soft loam.

The cop cars were flashing their strobes as if at the scene of an emergency, and never mind that the emergency had driven away hours before. Wayne strobed in her mind just like that, and for a moment she felt dangerously light-headed.

Chitra saw her sag and took her elbow, helped her the rest of the way into the kitchen. It was better in there. They had the room to themselves.

The kitchen windows looked out on the dock and the lake. The dock was lit up by more of those big tripod-mounted spotlights. A cop with a flashlight had waded into the water up to his thighs, but she couldn't tell to what purpose. A plainclothesman watched from the end of the dock, pointing and giving directions.

A boat floated forty feet offshore. A boy stood in the front end, next to a dog, staring at the cops, the lights, the house. When Vic saw the dog, she remembered Hooper. She had not thought of him once since seeing the headlights of the Wraith in the mist.

"Someone needs to . . . go look for the dog," Vic said. "He must be . . . outside somewhere." She had to stop every few words to catch her breath.

Chitra looked at her with great sensitivity. "Do not worry about the dog now, Ms. McQueen. Have you had any water? It is important to hydrate yourself."

"I'm surprised he isn't . . . isn't barking his . . . his head off," Vic said. "With all this commotion."

Chitra ran a hand down Vic's arm, once, and again, then squeezed Vic's elbow. Vic looked at the policewoman in sudden understanding.

"You had so much else to worry about," Chitra said.

"Oh, God," Vic said, and began to cry again, her whole body shaking.

"No one wanted to upset you even more."

She rocked, holding herself, crying in a way she hadn't since those first days after her father left her and her mother. Vic had to lean on the counter for a while, wasn't sure her legs had the strength to continue to support her. Chitra reached over and, tentatively, rubbed her back.

"Shhh," said Vic's mother, dead for two months. "Just breathe, Vicki. Just breathe for me." She said it in a light Indian accent, but

Vic recognized her mother's voice all the same. Recognized the feel of her mother's hand on her back. Everyone you lost was still there with you, and so maybe no one was ever lost at all.

Unless they went with Charlie Manx.

In a while Vic sat down and drank a glass of water. She drained the whole thing in five swallows, without stopping for air, was desperate for it. It was lukewarm and sweet and good and tasted of the lake.

Chitra opened cupboards, looking for paper plates. Vic got up and over the other woman's objections began to help with sandwiches. She made a row of paper plates and put two pieces of white bread on each, tears dripping off her nose and falling on the bread.

She hoped Wayne didn't know that Hooper was dead. She thought sometimes that Wayne was closer to Hooper than he was to either her or Lou.

Vic found the ham, coleslaw, and a bag of Doritos and began to make up the plates.

"There's a secret to cop sandwiches," said a woman who had come in behind her.

Vic took one look and knew this was The Guy she had been waiting for, even if The Guy wasn't a guy. This woman had frizzy brown hair and a little snub nose. She was plain at first glance, devastatingly pretty on the second. She wore a tweed coat with corduroy patches on the elbows and blue jeans and could've passed for a grad student at a liberal-arts college, if not for the nine-millimeter strapped under her left arm.

"What's the secret?" Vic asked.

"Show you," she said, and eased herself in, took the spoon, and dumped coleslaw into one of the sandwiches, on top of the ham. She built a roof of Doritos over the coleslaw, squirted Dijon mustard on the chips, buttered a slice of bread, and squished it all together. "The butter is the important part."

"Works like glue, right?"

"Yes. And cops are, by nature, cholesterol magnets."

"I thought the FBI only came in on kidnappings in cases where the kid has been hauled across state lines," Vic said.

The frizzy-haired woman frowned, then glanced down at the laminated card clipped to the breast of her jacket, the one that said

FBI
PSYCH EVAL
Tabitha K. Hutter

over an unsmiling photograph of her face.

"Technically, we're not in it yet," Hutter said. "But you're forty minutes from three state borders and less than two hours from Canada. Your assailants have had your son for almost—"

"My *assailants*?" Vic said. She felt a flush of heat in her cheeks. "Why do people keep talking about my *assailants,* like we don't know anything about them? It's starting to piss me off. *Charlie Manx is the man*. Charlie Manx and someone else are driving around with my kid."

"Charles Manx is dead, Ms. McQueen. He's been dead since May."

"Got a body?"

That gave Hutter pause. She pursed her lips, said, "He has a death certificate. There were photos of him in the morgue. He was autopsied. His chest was split open. The coroner took his heart out and weighed it. Those are convincing reasons to believe he didn't attack you."

"And I've got half a dozen reasons to believe he did," Vic said. "They're all up and down my back. You want me to take my shirt off and show you the bruises? Every other cop in this joint has had a good look."

Hutter stared at her without reply. Her gaze held the simple curiosity of a small child. It rattled Vic, to be *observed* so intently. So few adults gave themselves permission to stare that way.

At last Hutter shifted her eyes, turned her gaze toward the kitchen table. "Will you sit with me?"

Without waiting for an answer, she picked up a leather satchel she'd brought with her and settled at the kitchen table. She peered up expectantly, waiting for Vic to sit with her.

Vic looked to Chitra, as if for advice, remembering how the woman had, for a moment, comforted her and whispered to her like her mother. But the policewoman was finishing the sandwiches and bustling them out.

Vic sat.

Hutter removed an iPad from her briefcase, and the screen glowed. More than ever, she looked like a grad student, one preparing a dissertation on the Brontë sisters, perhaps. She passed her finger over the glass, swiping through some sort of digital file, then looked up.

"At his last medical exam, Charlie Manx was listed at approximately eighty-five years old."

"You think he's too old to have done what he did?" Vic asked.

"I think he's too dead. But tell me what happened, and I'll try to get my head around it."

Vic did not complain that she had already told the story three times, start to finish. The other times didn't count, because this was the first cop who mattered. If any cop mattered. Vic was not sure one did. Charlie Manx had been claiming lives for a long time and had never been caught, passed through the nets that law enforcement threw at him like silver smoke. How many children had climbed into his car and never been seen again?

Hundreds, came the answer, a whisper of a thought.

Vic told her story—the parts of it she felt she *could* tell. She left out Maggie Leigh. She did not mention she had ridden her motorcycle onto an impossible covered bridge of the imagination, shortly before Manx tried to run her down. She did not discuss the psychotropic medication she did not take anymore.

When Vic got to the part about Manx hitting her with the hammer, Hutter frowned. She asked Vic to describe the hammer in detail, tapping the keyboard on her iPad's screen. She stopped Vic again when Vic told her about how she had gotten up off the ground and gone after Manx with the tappet key.

"Tapper what?"

"Tappet key," Vic said. "Triumph made them special just for their bikes. It's a spanner. Kind of wrench. I was working on the motorcycle and had it in my pocket."

"Where is it now?"

"I don't know. I had it in my hand when I had to run. I was probably still holding it when I went in the lake."

"This is when the other man started shooting at you. Tell me about that."

She told.

"He shot Manx in the face?" Hutter said.

"It wasn't like that. He clipped him in the ear."

"Vic. I want you to help me think this through. This man, Charlie Manx, we agree he was probably eighty-five years old at the time of his last medical exam. He spent ten years in a coma. Most coma patients require months of rehabilitation before they can walk again. You are telling me you cut him with this tapper key—"

"Tappet."

"—and then he was shot but still had the strength to drive away."

What Vic could not say was that Manx wasn't like other men. She had felt it when he swung the hammer, a coiled strength that belied his advanced age and gaunt frame. Hutter insisted that Manx had been opened up, that his heart had been removed during the autopsy, and Vic didn't doubt it. For a man who'd had his heart taken out and put back in, a nick in the ear wasn't that big a deal.

Instead she said, "Maybe the other guy drove. You want me to explain it? I can't. I can only tell you what happened. What is your point? Manx has got my twelve-year-old in his car, and he's going to kill him to get even with me, but for some reason we're discussing the limits of your FBI imagination. Why is that?" She looked in Hutter's face, into Hutter's bland, calm eyes, and understood. "Jesus. You don't believe a fucking word, do you?"

Hutter deliberated for a time, and when she spoke, Vic had a sense that she was choosing words carefully. "I believe that your boy is missing, and I believe you've been hurt. I believe that you're in hell right now. Other than that, I'm keeping my mind open. I hope you'll see that as an asset and work with me. We both want the same thing. We want your boy back safe. If I thought it would help, I'd be out there driving around, looking for him. But that's not how I find the bad guys. I find them by collecting information and sorting out what's useful from what isn't. Really, it's not so different from your books. The Search Engine stories."

"You know them? How young *are* you?"

Hutter smiled slightly. "Not that young. It's in your file. Also, an instructor at Quantico uses pictures from *Search Engine* in his lectures, to show us how hard it is to pick out relevant details in a clutter of visual information."

"What *else* is in my file?"

Hutter's smile faltered slightly. Her gaze did not. "That you were found guilty of arson in Colorado in 2009. That you spent a month in a Colorado mental hospital, where you were diagnosed with severe PTSD and schizophrenia. You take antipsychotics and have a history of alcohol—"

"Jesus. You think I *hallucinated* getting the shit kicked out of me?" Vic said, her stomach clenching. "You think I *hallucinated* getting shot at?"

"We have yet to confirm a shooting took place."

Vic pushed back her chair. "He fired at me. He fired six bullets. Emptied his gun." Thinking now. Her back had been to the lake. It was possible every single bullet, even the one that had gone through Manx's ear, had wound up in the water.

"We're still looking for slugs."

"My bruises," Vic said.

"I don't doubt someone fought you," said the FBI agent. "I don't think *anyone* doubts that."

There was something about this statement—some dangerous implication—that Vic couldn't figure out. Who would've fought her if not Manx? But Vic was too exhausted, too emotionally spent, to try to make sense out of it. She didn't have it in her to work out whatever Hutter was stepping around.

Vic looked at Hutter's laminated badge again. PSYCH EVAL. "Wait a minute. Wait a *fucking*—you're not a detective. You're a *doctor*."

"Why don't we look at some pictures?" Hutter said.

"No," Vic said. "That's a complete waste of time. I don't need to look at mug shots. I told you. One of them was wearing a gasmask. The other was Charlie Manx. I know what Charlie Manx looks like. Jesus, why the fuck am I talking to a doctor? I want to talk to a *detective*."

"I wasn't going to ask you to look at pictures of criminals," Hutter said. "I was going to ask you to look at pictures of *hammers*."

It was such a baffling, unexpected thing to hear that Vic just sat there, mouth open, unable to make a sound.

Before anything came to her, there was a commotion in the other room. Chitra's voice rose, wavering and querulous, and Daltry said something, and then there was a third voice, midwestern and emotional. Vic recognized the third voice at once but couldn't work out what it was doing in her house when it ought to be on a plane, if not in Denver by now. Her confusion delayed her reaction time, so that she was not all the way out of her chair when Lou came into the room, trailing an entourage of cops.

He hardly looked like himself. His face was ashy, and his eyes stood out in his big, round face. He looked like he had lost ten pounds since Vic had last seen him, two days earlier. She rose and reached for him, and in the same moment he enfolded her in his arms.

"What are we going to do?" Lou asked her. "What the hell are we going to do now, Vic?"

The Kitchen

When they sat back down at the table, Vic took Lou's hand, the most natural thing in the world. She was surprised to feel the heat in his chubby fingers, and she looked again at his washed-out, sweat-slick face. She recognized that he looked seriously ill but took it for fear.

There were five of them in the kitchen now. Lou and Vic and Hutter sat at the table. Daltry leaned against the kitchen counter, squeezing his alcoholic's nose in a hankie. Officer Chitra stood in the doorway, had hustled the other cops out at Hutter's command.

"You're Louis Carmody," Hutter said. She spoke like the director of the school play, letting Lou know who he would be playing in the spring performance. "You're the father."

"Guilty," Lou said.

"Say again?" Hutter asked.

"Guilty as charged," Lou said. "I'm the dad. Who are you? Are you, like, a social worker?"

"I'm an FBI agent. My name is Tabitha Hutter. A lot of the guys in the office call me Tabby the Hutt." She smiled slightly.

"That's funny. A lot of the guys in the place I work call me *Jabba* the Hutt. Only they do it because I'm a fat shit."

"I thought you were in Denver," Hutter said.

"Missed my flight."

"No shit," said Daltry. "Something come up?"

Hutter said, "Detective Daltry, I'll conduct the Q and A, thank you."

Daltry reached into the pocket of his coat. "Does anyone mind if I smoke?"

"Yes," Hutter said.

Daltry held the pack for a moment, staring at her, then put it back in his pocket. There was a bland, unfocused quality to his eyes that reminded Vic of the membrane that slid across a shark's eyes right before he chomped into a seal.

"Why did you miss your plane, Mr. Carmody?" Hutter asked.

"Because I heard from Wayne."

"You *heard* from him?"

"He called me from the car on his iPhone. He said they were trying to shoot Vic. Manx and the other guy. We only talked for a minute. He had to hang up, 'cause Manx and the other fellow were walking back to the car. He was scared, really scared, but holding it together. He's a little man, you know. He's always been a little man." Lou bunched his fists up on the table and lowered his head. He grimaced, as if he felt a sharp twinge of pain somewhere in his abdomen, and blinked, and tears dripped onto the table. It came over him all of a sudden, without warning. "He has to be a grown-up, 'cause Vic and me did such a shitty job of being grown-ups ourselves." Vic put her hands over his.

Hutter and Daltry exchanged a look, hardly seemed to notice Lou dissolving into tears.

"Do you think your son turned the phone *off* after he talked to you?" Hutter asked.

"I thought if it had a SIM card in it, it didn't matter if it was on or off," Daltry said. "I thought you federal people had a workaround."

"You can use his phone to find him," Vic said, her pulse quickening.

Hutter ignored her, said to Daltry, "We can have that done. It would take a while. I'd have to call Boston. But if it's an iPhone and it's turned on, we can use the Find My iPhone function to locate him right now, right here." She lifted her iPad slightly.

"Right," Lou said. "That's right. I set up Find My iPhone the day we bought it for him, because I didn't want him to lose the thing."

He came around the table to look over Hutter's shoulder at her screen. His complexion was not improved by the unnatural glow of the monitor.

"What's his e-mail address and password?" Hutter asked, turning her head to look up at Lou.

He reached out with one hand to type it himself, but before he could, the FBI agent took ahold of his wrist. She pressed two fingers into his skin, as if taking his pulse. Even from where she sat, Vic could see a spot where the skin gleamed and seemed to have a splash of dried paste on it.

Hutter shifted her gaze to Lou's face. "You had an EKG this evening?"

"I fainted. I got upset. It was, like, a panic attack, dude. Some crazy son of a bitch has my kid. This shit happens to fat guys."

Until now Vic had been too focused on Wayne to give much thought to Lou: how gray he looked, how exhausted. But at this, Vic felt struck through with sudden, sick apprehension.

"Oh, Lou. What do you mean, you *fainted*?"

"It was after Wayne hung up on me. I kind of went down for a minute. I was fine, but airport security made me sit on the floor and get an EKG, make sure I wasn't going to vapor-lock on them."

"Did you tell them your kid had been kidnapped?" Daltry asked.

Hutter flashed him a warning look that Daltry pretended not to see.

"I'm not sure what I said to them. I was sort of confused at first. Like, *dizzy.* I know I told them my kid needed me. I know I told them that. All I could think was I had to get to my car. At some point they said they were going to put me in an ambulance, and I told 'em to go . . . ah . . . have fun with themselves. So I got up and walked away. It's possible a guy grabbed my arm and I dragged him a few feet. I was in a hurry."

"So you didn't talk to the police at the airport about what had happened to your son?" Daltry asked. "Didn't you think you could get here faster if you had a police escort?"

"It didn't even cross my mind. I wanted to talk to Vic first," Lou said, and Vic saw Daltry and Hutter trade another glance.

"Why did you want to talk to Victoria first?" Hutter asked.

"What does it matter?" Vic cried. "Can we just think about Wayne?"

"Yes," Hutter said, blinking, looking back down at her iPad. "That's right. Let's keep the focus on Wayne. How about that password?"

Vic pushed back her chair as Lou poked at the touchscreen with one thick finger. She rose, came around the corner of the table to look. Her breathing was fast and short. She felt her anticipation so keenly it was like being cut.

Hutter's screen loaded the Find My iPhone page, which showed a map of the globe, pale blue continents against a background of dark blue ocean. In the upper right corner, a window announced:

Wayne's iPhone
Locating
Locating
Locating
Locating
Located

A featureless field of gray blanked out the image of the globe. A glassy blue dot appeared in the silver smoothness. Squares of landscape began to appear, the map redrawing itself to show the location of the iPhone in close-up. Vic saw the blue dot traveling on a road identified as THE ST. NICK PARKWAY.

Everyone was leaning in, Daltry so close to Vic she could feel him pressing against her rear, feel his breath tickling her neck. He smelled of coffee and nicotine.

"Zoom out," Daltry said.

Hutter tapped the screen once, and again, and again.

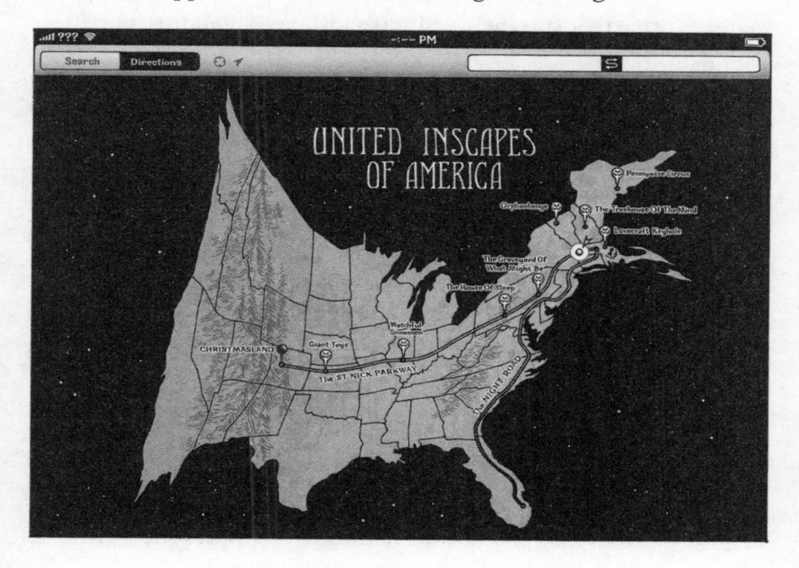

The map depicted a continent that somewhat resembled America. It was as if someone had made a version of the United States out of bread dough and then punched it in the center. In this new version of the nation, Cape Cod was almost half the size of Florida and the Rocky Mountains looked more like the Andes, a thousand miles of grotesquely tortured earth, great splinters of stone heaved up against one another. The country as a whole, however, had substantially shriveled, collapsing toward the center.

Most of the great cities were gone, but other points of interest had appeared in their places. In Vermont there was a dense forest, built up around a place called ORPHANHENGE; in New Hampshire there was a spot marked THE TREE HOUSE OF THE MIND. A little north of Boston, there was something called LOVECRAFT KEYHOLE; it was a crater in the rough shape of a padlock. In Maine, around the Lewiston/Auburn/Derry area, there was a place called PENNYWISE CIRCUS. A narrow highway titled THE NIGHT ROAD led south, reddening the farther it went, until it was a line of blood trickling into Florida.

The St. Nick Parkway was particularly littered with stopping points. In Illinois, WATCHFUL SNOWMEN. In Kansas, GIANT TOYS. In Pennsylvania, THE HOUSE OF SLEEP and THE GRAVEYARD OF WHAT MIGHT BE.

And in the mountains of Colorado, high in the peaks, the point at which the St. Nick Parkway dead-ended: CHRISTMASLAND.

The continent itself drifted in a sea of black, star-littered wastes; the map was captioned not UNITED STATES OF AMERICA but UNITED INSCAPES OF AMERICA.

The blue dot twitched, moving through what should've been western Massachusetts toward Christmasland. But UNITED INSCAPES didn't correspond exactly to America itself. It was probably a hundred fifty miles from Laconia, New Hampshire, to Springfield, Massachusetts, but on this map it looked barely half that.

They all stared.

Daltry took his hankie from his pocket, gave his nose a thoughtful squeeze. "Any of you see Candy Land down there?" He made a harsh, throat-clearing sound that was not quite a cough, not quite a laugh.

Vic felt the kitchen going away. The world at the edges of her vision was a distorted blur. The iPad and the table remained in crisp focus but were curiously distant.

She needed something to anchor her. She felt in danger of coming unmoored from the kitchen floor . . . a balloon slipping out of a child's hand. She took Lou's wrist, something to hold on to. He had always been there when she needed something to hold on to.

When she looked at him, though, she saw a reflection of her own ringing shock. His pupils were pinpricks. His breath was short and labored.

In a surprisingly normal tone of voice, Hutter said, "I don't know what I'm looking at here. Does this mean anything to either of you two? This curious map? Christmasland? The St. Nick Parkway?"

"Does it?" Lou asked, staring helplessly at Vic.

What he was really asking, Vic understood, was *DO we tell her about Christmasland? About the things you believed when you were crazy?*

"No," Vic breathed, answering all questions—spoken and unspoken—at the same time.

The Bedroom

VIC SAID SHE NEEDED TO REST, ASKED IF SHE COULD LIE DOWN FOR A while, and Hutter said of course and that she wasn't going to do anyone any good by driving herself to collapse.

In the bedroom, though, Lou was the one who flung himself down on the bed. Vic couldn't relax. She went to the blinds, picked them apart, looked out at the carnival in her front yard. The night was full of the chatter of radios, the murmur of male voices. Someone out there laughed softly. It was a wonder, to think that less than a hundred paces from the house it was possible for happiness to exist.

If any of the policemen in the street noticed her looking, they probably imagined she was gazing blankly up the road, hoping, pitifully, for a cruiser to come roaring down it, lights flashing, sirens splitting the air, her son in the backseat. Safe. Coming home. His lips sticky and pink with the ice cream the cops had bought him.

But she wasn't looking at the road, hoping with all her heart that someone was going to bring Wayne back to her. If anyone was going to bring him back, it was her. Vic was staring at the Triumph, lying right where she had dropped it.

Lou was heaved on the bed like a beached manatee. When he spoke, he addressed the ceiling.

"Will you come stretch out with me for a while? Just . . . be here with me?"

She dropped the blinds and went to the bed. She put her leg over his legs and clasped herself to his side, as she had not done in years.

"You know that guy who looks like Mickey Rooney's mean twin brother? Daltry? He said you were hurt."

And she realized he hadn't heard the story. No one had told him what had happened to her.

She told it again. At first she was only repeating what she told Hutter and the other detectives. Already the story had the quality of lines learned for a part in a play; she could recite them without thinking.

But then she told him about taking the Triumph for a short run and realized she didn't have to leave out the part about the bridge. She could and should tell him about discovering the Shorter Way in the mist, because it had happened. *Really* happened.

"I saw the bridge," she said quietly, lifting herself up to look into his face. "I rode onto it, Lou. I went looking for it, and there it was. Do you believe me?"

"I believed you the first time you told me about it."

"You fucking liar," she said, but she couldn't help smiling at him.

He reached out and put his hand on the swell of her left breast. "Why wouldn't I believe you? It explained you better than anything. And I'm like that poster on the wall, in *The X-Files:* 'I want to believe.' Story of my life, lady. Go on. You rode across the bridge. Then what?"

"I *didn't* ride across it. I got scared. Really scared, Lou. I thought it was a hallucination. That I was off my nut again. I slammed on the brake so hard that pieces came flying off the bike."

She told him about turning the Triumph around and walking it off the bridge, her eyes shut and her legs shaking. She described how it had sounded in the Shorter Way, the shush and roar, as if she stood behind a waterfall. She said she knew it was gone when she couldn't hear that sound anymore, and then it was a long walk back home.

Vic went on, telling how Manx and the other man were waiting for her, how Manx had come for her with his hammer. Lou was not a stoic. He flinched and twitched and cursed. When she told him about using the tappet key on Manx's face, he said, "I wish't you skullfucked him with the thing." She assured him she had tried her best. He thumped a fist into his own leg when she got to the part about the Gasmask Man shooting Manx in the ear. Lou listened with his whole body, a kind of quivering tautness in him, like a bow pulled to its limit, the arrow ready to fly.

He did not interrupt her, though, until she got to the part where she was running downhill for the lake, to escape them.

"That's what you were doing when Wayne called," he said.

"What happened to you at the airport? *Really.*"

"What I said. I got faint." He rolled his head, as if to loosen his neck, then said, "The map. With the road to Christmasland. What is that place?"

"I don't know."

"It's not in our world, though. Right?"

"I don't know. I kind of think . . . I kind of think it *is* our world. A version of it anyway. The version of it that Charlie Manx carries around in his head. Everyone lives in two worlds, right? There's the physical world . . . but there's also our own private inner worlds, the world of our thoughts. A world made of *ideas* instead of *stuff.* It's just as real as our world, but it's *inside.* It's an *inscape.* Everyone has an inscape, and they all connect, too, in the same way New Hampshire connects to Vermont. And maybe some people can ride into that thought world if they have the right vehicle. A key. A car. A bike. Whatever."

"How can your thought world connect to mine?"

"I don't know. But . . . but, like, if Keith Richards dreams up a song and then you hear it on the radio, you've got his thoughts in your head. My ideas can get in your head just as easily as a bird can fly across the state line."

Lou frowned and said, "So, like, somehow Manx drives kids out of the world of stuff and into his own private world of ideas. Okay. I can go with that. It's weird, but I can go with it. So get back to your story. The guy wearing the gasmask had a gun."

Vic told him about diving into the water, and the Gasmask Man shooting, and then Manx talking to her while she hid under the float. When she was done, she shut her eyes, nestled her face into Lou's neck. She was exhausted—beyond exhausted, really, had traveled to some new precinct of weariness. The gravity was lighter in this new world. If she had not been tethered to Lou, she would've floated away.

"He *wants* you to come looking," Lou said.

"I can find him," she said. "I can find this House of Sleep. I told you. I rode to the bridge before I fucked up the bike."

"Probably threw the chain. You're lucky you kept it shiny side up."

She opened her eyes and said, "You have to fix it, Lou. You have to fix it tonight. As fast as you can. Tell Hutter and the police you can't sleep. Tell them you need to do something to take your mind off things. People react to stress in strange ways, and you're a mechanic. They won't question you."

"Manx tells you to come find him. What do you think he's going to do to you when you do?"

"He ought to be thinking about what *I'm* going to do to *him*."

"And what if he's not at this House of Sleep? Will the bike take you to him wherever he is? Even if he's moving?"

"I don't know," Vic said, but she thought, *No.* She was not sure where this certainty came from, how she could know such a thing, but she did. She recalled, distantly, that she had gone looking for a lost cat once—*Taylor,* she thought—and was sure she had found him only because he was dead. If he had been alive and on the prowl, the bridge wouldn't have had an anchor point to settle on. It could cross the distance between lost and found, but only if what was lost stayed put. Lou saw the doubt in her face, and she went on. "It doesn't matter anyway. Manx has to stop sometime, doesn't he? To sleep? To eat?" In truth, she wasn't sure he needed either food or rest. He had died, been autopsied, had his heart removed . . . then got up and walked away whistling. Who knew what such a man required? Perhaps thinking of him as a man at all was operating from the wrong assumptions. And yet: He bled. He could be hurt. She had seen him pale and staggered. She thought at the very least he would need to recover himself, settle and slumber for a while, same as any wounded creature. His license plate was a joke or boast, *nosferatu*, German word for vampire—an acknowledgment, at some level, of what he was. But in the stories, even vampires crawled back to their coffins and shut the lid now and then. She pushed these ideas aside and finished: "Sooner or later he'll have to stop for something, and when he does, I can get to him."

"You asked me if I thought you were crazy, with all your stuff about the bridge. And I said no. But *this*? This part of it is pretty crazy. Using the bike to find your way to him so he can polish you off. Finish the job he started this morning."

"It's all we've got." She glanced toward the door. "And, Lou, this is the only way we might—*will*—get Wayne back. These people can't find him. *I* can. Are you going to fix it?"

He sighed—a great, unsteady exhalation of air—and said, "I'll try, Vic. I'll try. On one condition."

"What's that?"

"When I get it fixed," Lou said, "you take me with you."

The St. Nicholas Parkway

WAYNE SLEPT FOR A LONG TIME—AN ENDLESS TIME OF QUIET AND peace—and when he opened his eyes, he knew that everything was all right.

NOS4A2 sped through the dark, a torpedo churning through the fathomless depths. They were rising through low hills, the Wraith hugging the curves as if it were on rails. Wayne was rising toward something wonderful and fine.

Snow fell in gentle, goose-feather flakes. The wipers went *swop, swop,* striking them down.

They passed a lone streetlamp in the night, a twelve-foot candy cane topped with a gumdrop, casting a cherry light, turning those falling flakes to feathers of flame.

The Wraith swept along a high curve that afforded a view of the vast tableland below, silver and smooth and flat, and at the far end of it the mountains! Wayne had never seen mountains like them—they made the Rockies look like homely foothills. The smallest of them had the proportions of Everest. They were a great range of stone teeth, a crooked row of fangs, sharp enough, large enough, to devour the sky. Rocks forty thousand feet high pierced the night, held up the darkness, pushed into the stars.

Above it all drifted a silvery scythe blade of moon. Wayne looked up at it, and away, and then looked again. The moon had a hooked nose, a thoughtfully frowning mouth, and a single eye closed in sleep. When it exhaled, a wind rippled across the plains and silvery beds of cloud raced through the night. Wayne almost clapped his hands in delight to look upon it.

It was impossible, though, to look away from the mountains for long. The pitiless, cyclopean peaks drew Wayne's gaze as a magnet will draw iron shavings. For there, in a notch two-thirds of the way up the largest of the mountains, was a bright jewel, pinned to the side of the rock face. It shone, brighter than the moon, brighter than any star. It burned in the night like a torch.

Christmasland.

"You should roll down the window and try to grab one of those sugarflakes!" advised Mr. Manx from the front seat.

For a moment Wayne had forgotten who was driving the car. He had stopped worrying about it. It wasn't important. Getting there was the thing. He felt a throb of eagerness to be there already, rolling in between the candy-cane gates.

"Sugarflake? Don't you mean snowflake?"

"If I meant snowflake, I would've *said* snowflake! Those are flakes of pure cane sugar, and if we were in a plane, we'd be shredding cotton-candy clouds! Go on! Roll down a window! Catch one and see if I am a liar!"

"Won't it be cold?" Wayne asked.

Mr. Manx looked at him in the rearview mirror, the laugh lines crinkling at the corners of his eyes.

He wasn't scary anymore. He was young, and if he was not handsome, he at least looked spiffy, in his black leather gloves and black overcoat. His hair was black now, too, slicked back under his leather-brimmed cap, to show the high, bare expanse of his forehead.

The Gasmask Man was asleep next to him, a sweet smile on his fat, bristly face. He wore a white marine uniform, with a breastful of gold medals upon it. A second glance, though, showed that these medals were in fact chocolate coins in gold-foil wrap. He had nine of them.

Wayne understood now that getting to go to Christmasland was better than going to Hogwarts Academy, or Willy Wonka's Chocolate Factory, or the Cloud City in *Star Wars,* or Rivendell in *Lord of the Rings.* Not one child in a million was allowed into Christmasland, only kids who truly *needed.* It was impossible to be unhappy there, in that place where every morning was Christmas morning and every evening was Christmas Eve, where tears were against the law and children flew like angels. Or floated. Wayne was unclear on the difference.

He knew something else: His mother *hated* Mr. Manx because he wouldn't take *her* to Christmasland. And if she couldn't go, she didn't want Wayne to go either. The reason his mother drank so much was because getting smashed was the closest a person could ever get to feeling the way you felt when you were in Christmasland—even though a bottle of gin was as different from Christmasland as a dog biscuit was from filet mignon.

His mother had always known that someday Wayne would get to go to Christmasland. That was why she couldn't stand to be around him. That was why she ran away from him for all those years.

He didn't want to think about it. He would call her as soon as he got to Christmasland. He would tell her he loved her and that everything was all right. He would call her every day if he had to. It was true she sometimes hated him, that she hated being a mother, but he was determined to love her anyway, to share his happiness with her.

"Cold?" Manx cried, snapping Wayne's thoughts back to the here and now. "You worry like my Aunt Mathilda! Go on. Roll the window down. Besides. I know you, Bruce Wayne Carmody. You are thinking serious thoughts, aren't you? You are a serious little fellow! We need to cure you of that! And we will! Dr. Manx prescribes a mug of peppermint cocoa and a ride on the Arctic Express with the other kids. If you are still feeling in a glum mood after that, then there is no hope for you. Come on and roll down the window! Let the night air in to blow away the gloomies! Don't be an old lady! It is like I am driving somebody's grandmother instead of a little boy!"

Wayne turned to roll down the window, but when he did, he got a nasty surprise. His grandmother, Linda, sat next to him. He had not seen her for months. It was hard to visit with relatives when they were dead.

She was still dead now. She sat in a hospital johnny, untied so he could see her skeletal bare back when she leaned forward. She was sitting on the good beige leather seats with her bare ass. Her legs were scrawny and terrible, very white in the darkness, crawling with old black varicose veins. Her eyes were hidden behind a pair of shiny, silver, newly minted half-dollars.

Wayne opened his mouth to scream, but Grammy Lindy lifted her finger to her lips. *Shhh.*

".down it slow can you ,reverse in think you If .Wayne ,truth the from away you driving He's," she warned him gravely.

Manx cocked his head, as if listening for a noise he didn't like under the hood. Lindy had spoken clearly enough for Manx to hear her, but he didn't look all the way around, and his expression suggested he *thought* he had heard something but wasn't sure.

The sight of her was bad enough, but the nonsense she spoke—nonsense that hovered maddeningly on the edge of meaning—sent a shock of fright through Wayne. The coins over her eyes flashed.

"Go away," he whispered.

".himself for youth your keep and behind soul your leave He'll .snap you until ,band rubber a like out you stretch He'll .soul own your from away you drive He'll," Grammy Lindy explained, pressing a cold finger into his breastbone every now and then for emphasis.

He made a thin whining sound in the back of his throat, recoiling from her touch. At the same time, he found himself struggling to make sense out of her gravely recited gibberish. *He'll snap you*—he got that. *Band rubber?* No, that had to be *rubber band.* There it was.

She was saying things backward, and on some level Wayne understood that this was why Mr. Manx could not quite hear her in the front seat. He could not hear her because he was going forward and she was running in reverse. He tried to remember what else she had said, to see if he could untangle her dead-woman syntax, but it was already fading away from him.

Mr. Manx said, “Roll down the window, little boy! Do it!” His voice suddenly hard, not as friendly as it had been before. “I want you to grab some of that sweetness for yourself! Hurry now! We are almost to a tunnel!”

But Wayne couldn’t roll down the window. To do so would have required him to reach past Lindy, and he was afraid. He was as afraid of her as he had ever been of Manx. He wanted to cover his eyes so he wouldn’t have to see her. He took short little gasping breaths, a runner on the last lap—and his exhalations smoked, as if it were cold in the back of the car, although it didn’t feel cold.

He peered into the front seat for help, but Mr. Manx had changed. He was missing his left ear—it was tatters of flesh, little crimson strings swinging against his cheek. His hat was missing, and the head it had covered was now bald and lumpy and spotted, with just a few silver threads combed across it. A great flap of loose red skin hung from his brow. His eyes were gone, and where they had been were buzzing red holes—not bloody sockets but craters containing live coals.

Beside him the Gasmask Man slept on in his crisp uniform, smiling like a man with a full belly and warm feet.

Through the windshield Wayne could see they were approaching a tunnel bored into a wall of rock, a black pipe leading into the side of the hill.

“Who is back there with you?” Manx asked, his voice humming and terrible. It was not the voice of a man. It was the voice of a thousand flies droning in unison.

Wayne looked around for Lindy, but she was gone, had left him.

The tunnel swallowed the Wraith. In the darkness there were only those red holes where Manx's eyes belonged, staring back at him.

"I don't want to go to Christmasland," Wayne said.

"Everyone wants to go to Christmasland," said the thing in the front seat that used to be a man but was not anymore, and maybe had not been for a hundred years.

They were fast approaching a bright circle of sunlight at the end of the tunnel. It had been night when they entered the hole in the mountain, but they were rushing toward a summery glare, and even when they were still a hundred feet away, the brightness hurt Wayne's eyes.

He put his hands over his face, moaning in distress. The light burned through his fingers, growing ever more intense, until it shone right through his hands and he could see the black sticks of his own bones buried in softly glowing tissue. He felt that at any moment all that sunlight might cause him to ignite.

"I don't like it! I don't *like* it!" he shouted.

The car jolted and banged over pitted road, with enough force to dislodge his hands from his face. He blinked into morning sunlight.

Bing Partridge, the Gasmask Man, sat up and turned in his seat to look back at Wayne. His uniform was gone, and he wore the same stained tracksuit he'd been dressed in the day before.

"No," he said, digging a finger in his ear. "I'm not much of a morning person either."

Sugarcreek, Pennsylvania

"Sun, sun, go away," the Gasmask Man said, and yawned. "Come again some other day." The Gasmask Man was silent for a moment and then said shyly, "I had a nice dream. I dreamed about Christmasland."

"I hope you liked it," Manx said. "The mess you have made of things, dreaming about Christmasland is all you will do!"

The Gasmask Man shrank down in his seat and put his hands over his ears.

They were in a place of hills and high grasses, beneath blue summer sky. A finger lake shone below them to the left, a long splinter of mirror dropped amid hundred-foot pines. The valleys caught patches of morning mist, but they would burn off soon enough.

Wayne rubbed his hands hard into his eye sockets, his brain still half asleep. His forehead and cheeks felt fevery. He sighed—and was surprised to see pale vapor issue from his nostrils, just like in his dream. He had not realized it was so cold in the backseat.

"I'm freezing," Wayne said, although if anything he felt warm, not cold.

"These mornings can be very raw," Manx said. "You will feel better soon."

"Where are we?" Wayne asked.

Manx glanced back at him. "Pennsylvania. We have been driving all night, and you have been sleeping like a baby."

Wayne blinked at him, perturbed and disoriented, although it took him a moment to figure out why. The pad of white gauze was still taped over the ruin of Manx's left ear, but he had stripped off the bandage wrapped around his forehead. The six-inch slash across his forehead was black and rancid-looking, a Frankenstein scar—and yet it looked as if it had been healing for twelve days, not twelve hours. Manx's color was better, his eyes sharper, bright with humor and goodwill toward men.

"Your face is better," Wayne said.

"It is a little easier on the eyes, I guess, but I will not be entering a beauty contest anytime soon!"

"How come you're better?" Wayne asked.

Manx thought about that for a bit, then said, "The car takes care of me. It is going to take care of you, too."

"It's because we're on the road to Christmasland," said the Gasmask Man, looking over his shoulder and smiling. "It takes your frown and turns it upside down, isn't that right, Mr. Manx?"

"I am in no frame of mind for your rhyming idiocies, Bing," Manx said. "Play Quaker Meeting, why don't you?"

NOS4A2 drove south, and no one spoke for a while. In the silence Wayne took stock.

In his whole life, he had never been as scared as he had been the afternoon before. His throat was still hoarse from all the screaming he had done. Now, though, it was as if he were a jug, and every last drop of bad feeling had been poured out of him. The interior of the Rolls-Royce brimmed with golden sunlight. Motes of dust burned in a ray of brilliance, and Wayne raised a hand to swipe at them and watch them roil around, like sand whirling through water—

His mother had dived into the water to get away from the Gasmask Man, he remembered, and he twitched. For a moment he felt a jolt of yesterday's fear, as fresh and raw as if he had touched a stripped copper line and been zapped. What frightened him was not the thought that he was a prisoner of Charlie Manx but that for a moment he had *forgotten* he was a prisoner. For a moment he had been admiring the light and feeling almost happy.

He shifted his gaze to the walnut drawer set below the seat in front of him, where he had hidden his phone. Then he glanced up and discovered Manx watching him in the rearview mirror, smiling just slightly. Wayne shrank back into his seat.

"You said you owed me one," Wayne said.

"I did and I do," Manx said.

"I want to call my mother. I want to tell her I'm all right."

Manx nodded, eyes on the road, hand on the wheel. Had the car been driving itself yesterday? Wayne had a memory of the steering wheel turning on its own, while Manx moaned and the Gasmask Man wiped blood from his face—but this recollection had the shiny, hyperreal quality of the sort of dreams that come to people while they are incapacitated with a particularly bad flu. Now, in the bright, clear sunshine of morning, Wayne was not sure it had really happened. Also, the day was warming; he couldn't see his own breath anymore.

"It is very right that you should want to call her and tell her you are well. I expect, when we get where we are going, that you will want to call her every day! That is just being considerate! And of course she will want to know how you are doing. We will have to ring her up as soon as possible. I can hardly count that as the favor I owe you! What sort of beast would not let a child call his mother? Unfortunately, there is no easy place to stop and let you call, and neither of us thought to bring a phone with us," Manx said. He turned his head and looked over the divider at Wayne again. "I don't suppose *you* thought to bring one, did you?" And smiled.

He knows, Wayne thought. He felt something shrivel inside him, and for a moment he was dangerously close to tears.

"No," he said, in a voice that sounded almost normal. He had to fight to keep from looking at the wooden drawer at his feet.

Manx returned his gaze to the road. "Oh, well. It is too early to call her anyway. It is not even six in the morning, and after the day she had yesterday, we had better let her sleep in!" He sighed and added, "Your mother has more tattoos than a sailor."

"'There was once a young lady from Yale,'" said the Gasmask Man. "'Who had verses tattooed on her tail. And on her behind, for the sake of the blind, a duplicate version in braille.'"

"You rhyme too much," Wayne said.

Manx laughed—a big, unrefined *hee-haw* of a laugh—and slapped the wheel. "That is for sure! Good old Bing Partridge is a rhyming demon! If you look to your Bible, you will see that those are the lowest sort of demon, but not without their uses."

Bing rested his forehead against the window, looking out at rolling countryside. Sheep grazed.

"Baa, baa, black sheep," Bing crooned softly to himself. *"Have you any wool?"*

Manx said, "All those tattoos on your mother."

"Yes?" Wayne said, thinking that if he looked in the drawer, the phone would probably not be there. He thought there was an excellent chance they had removed it while he slept.

"Maybe I am old-fashioned, but I view that as an invitation to men of poor character to stare. Do you think she likes that sort of attention?"

"'There once was a whore from Peru,'" whispered the Gasmask Man, and he giggled softly to himself.

"They're pretty," Wayne said.

"Is that why your father divorced her? Because he did not like her to go out that way, with her legs bare and painted, to distract men?"

"He didn't divorce her. They never got married."

Manx laughed again. "There is a big surprise."

They had left the highway and had slipped out of the hills and into a sleepy downtown. It was a sorry, abandoned-looking place. Storefront windows were soaped over, signs in them saying For Rent.

Plywood sheeting had been nailed up inside the doors of the movie theater, and the marquee read MER Y XMAS SUGAR EEK PA! Christmas lights hung from it, although it was July.

Wayne couldn't stand not knowing about his phone. He could just reach the drawer with his foot. He inched his toe under the handle.

"She has a sturdy athletic look to her, I will give you that," Manx said, although Wayne was hardly listening. "I suppose she has a boyfriend."

Wayne said, "I'm her boyfriend, she says."

"Ha, ha. Every mother says that to her son. Your father is older than your mother?"

"I don't know. I guess. A little."

Wayne caught the drawer with his toe and slid it back an inch. The phone was still there. He nudged it shut. Later. If he went for it now, they would just take it away.

"Do you think she is inclined to look favorably upon older men?" Manx asked.

It bewildered Wayne that Manx was going on and on about his mother and her tattoos and what she thought about older men. He could not have been more confused if Manx had begun to ask him questions about sea lions or sports cars. He couldn't even remember how they had gotten on this particular subject, and he struggled to think it out, to run the conversation in reverse.

If you think in reverse, Wayne thought. *Reverse. In. Think. You. If.* Dead Grandma Lindy had been in his dream, and everything she said came out backward. Most of what she had said to him was gone now—forgotten—but that part of it came back to him with perfect clarity, like a message in invisible ink darkening and appearing on paper held above a flame. If you think in reverse, what? He didn't know.

The car stopped at an intersection. A middle-aged woman stood on the curb, eight feet away. She was in shorts and a headband, jogging in place. She was waiting for her walk light, even though there was no cross traffic.

Wayne acted without thought. He flung himself at the door and banged his hands on the glass.

"Help!" he screamed. "Help me!"

The jogging woman frowned and looked around. She stared at the Rolls-Royce.

"Please help!" Wayne screamed, slapping the window.

She smiled and waved.

The light changed. Manx rolled sedately through the intersection.

To the left, on the other side of the street, Wayne saw a man in a uniform coming out of a doughnut shop. He wore what looked like a policeman's cap and a blue windbreaker.

Wayne pitched himself across the car and banged his fists on the other window. As he did and the man came into focus, Wayne could see it was a postman, not a policeman. A podgy man in his mid-fifties.

"Help me! I'm being kidnapped! *Help, help, help!*" Wayne screamed, his voice cracking.

"He can't hear you," Manx said. "Or, rather, he does not hear what you want him to hear."

The postman looked at the Rolls going by. He smiled and raised two fingers to the brim of his cap in a little salute. Manx drove on.

"Are you done making such a racket?" he said.

"Why don't they hear me?" Wayne asked.

"It is like what they are always saying about Las Vegas: What happens in the Wraith stays in the Wraith."

They were rolling out the other end of the little downtown, beginning to accelerate, leaving behind the four-block stretch of brick buildings and dusty storefronts.

"Don't worry," Manx said. "If you are tired of the road, we will be off it soon enough. I know I am ready for a break from all this highway. We are very close to where we are going."

"Christmasland?" Wayne asked.

Manx pursed his lips in a thoughtful moue. "No. That is still a ways off."

"The House of Sleep," the Gasmask Man told him.

The Lake

Vic closed her eyes for a moment, and when she opened them she was staring at the clock on the night table—5:59. Then the celluloid flaps flipped over to 6:00 A.M. and the phone rang.

The two things happened so closely together that Vic thought at first the alarm was going off, and she couldn't figure out why she had set it for so early in the morning. The phone rang again, and the bedroom door clicked open. Tabitha Hutter peered in on her, eyes bright behind her round spectacles.

"It's a 603 number," she said. "A demolition company in Dover. You better answer. It's probably not him, but—"

"It's not him," Vic said, and fumbled for the phone.

"I didn't hear until late," said her father. "And it took me a while to come up with your number. I waited as long as I could, in case you were trying to sleep. How are you, kid?"

Vic removed the phone from her mouth and said, "It's my dad."

Tabitha Hutter said, "Tell him he's being recorded. All the calls to this number will be recorded for the foreseeable future."

"Did you hear that, Chris?"

"I did. It's okay. Anything they need to do. Christ, it's good to hear your voice, kiddo."

"What do you want?"

"I want to know how you're doing. I want you to know I'm here if you need me."

"First time for everything, huh?"

He exhaled, a thin, frustrated breath. "I understand what you're going through. I went through it, too, once upon a time, you know. I love you, girl. Tell me if I can do anything."

"You can't," she said. "There's nothing for you to blow up right now. It's all blown up. Don't call anymore, Dad. I'm in enough pain already. You just make it worse."

She hung up. Tabitha Hutter watched her from the doorway.

"Did you get your cell-phone experts to try and locate Wayne's phone? Was it any different from when you tried Find My iPhone? It can't have been. If you had any new information, you wouldn't have let me sleep."

"They couldn't locate his phone."

"They couldn't locate it? Or they traced him to the St. Nick Parkway, somewhere east of Christmasland?"

"Does that *mean* something to you? Charlie Manx had a house in Colorado. The trees around the house were hung with Christmas ornaments. The press gave it a name, called it the Sleigh House. Is *that* Christmasland?"

No, Vic thought automatically. *Because the Sleigh House is in* our *world. Christmasland is in Manx's inscape. The Manxscape.*

Hutter had a hell of a poker face, watching Vic with an expression of studious calm. Vic thought if she told this woman that Christmasland was a place in the fourth dimension, where dead children sang carols and made long-distance phone calls, that Hutter's expression wouldn't change at all. She would continue to give Vic that cool, clinical look while police held Vic down and a doctor sedated her.

"I don't know where Christmasland is or *what* it is," Vic said, which was largely true. "I don't understand why that's coming up when you search for Wayne's phone. Do you want to look at hammers?"

The house was still full of people, although they looked less like cops now, more like the Geek Squad from Best Buy. Three young men had set up laptops on the coffee table in the living room: a gangly Asian with tribal tattoos, a skinny kid with a red Jewfro and roughly a billion freckles, and a black man in a black turtleneck that looked like it had been snatched from Steve Jobs's closet. The house smelled of coffee. There was a fresh pot brewing in the kitchen. Hutter poured Vic some and added cream and a spoonful of sugar, just the way Vic took it.

"Is that in my file?" Vic asked. "How I take my coffee?"

"The cream was in the fridge. You must use it for something. And a coffee spoon was sitting in the sugar jar."

"Elementary, my dear Watson," Vic said.

"I used to go dressed as Holmes for Halloween," Hutter said. "Had the pipe and the deerstalker cap and all the rest. What about you? What did you wear for trick-or-treat?"

"A straitjacket," Vic said. "I'd go as an escaped mental patient. It was good practice for the rest of my life."

Hutter's smile flattened and went away.

She sat at the table with Vic and handed her the iPad. She explained how to swipe through the gallery to look at the different pictures of hammers.

"Why does it matter what he hit me with?" Vic asked.

"You don't know what matters until after you've seen it. So you try to see everything."

Vic swiped past sledgehammers, hardware-store hammers, croquet mallets.

"What the hell is this? A database dedicated to hammer murderers?"

"Yes."

Vic glanced at her. Hutter's face had returned to its usual bland state of impassivity.

Vic swiped through some more pictures, then paused. "This. It was this one."

Hutter looked at the screen. On it was a picture of a foot-long hammer with a rectangular stainless-steel head, a crosshatched handle, and a sharp hook curving from the end.

"Are you sure?"

"Yeah. Because of the hook. That's the one. What the hell kind of hammer is that?"

Hutter pulled her lower lip into her mouth, then pushed back her chair and stood up. "Not one you buy at the hardware store. I have to make a call."

She hesitated, one hand on the back of Vic's chair.

"Do you think you'd be up for making a statement to the press this afternoon? We've had good play on the cable news channels. It has a lot of angles. Everyone knows the Search Engine stories, so there's that. I'm sorry to say that a lot of them are talking about this as a real life-and-death game of Search Engine. A personal appeal for help will keep the story active. And awareness is our best weapon."

"Has the press figured out that Manx also kidnapped me when I was a teenager?" Vic asked.

Hutter's brow furrowed, as in thought. "Mm. No, they haven't worked that out yet. And I don't think you should mention it in your statement. It's important to keep the media focused on the information that matters. We need people on the lookout for your son and the car. That's what we talk about. Everything else is insignificant at best, a distraction at worst."

"The car, my son, and Manx," Vic said. "We want everyone on the lookout for Manx."

"Yes. Of course." She took two steps toward the door, then turned back and said, "You've been wonderful, Victoria. You've been very strong in a scary time. You've done so much I hate to ask for more. But when you're ready, we'll need to sit down today and I have to get the whole story in your words. I need to know more about what Manx did to you. It could greatly enhance our chances of finding your son."

"I already *told* you what he did to me. I gave you the whole story yesterday. Bashed me with a hammer, chased me to the lake, drove off with the kid."

"I'm sorry. I'm not making myself clear. I'm not talking about what Manx did to you *yesterday*. I'm talking about 1996. I'm talking about when he kidnapped *you*."

HUTTER, VIC FELT, WAS A THOROUGH WOMAN. PATIENT AND SENSIBLE. She was, in her patient, sensible, thorough way, working toward the conclusion that Vic was deluded about Charlie Manx. But if she didn't believe that Wayne had been taken by Manx, then what did she think *had* happened?

Vic had an awareness of threat she couldn't quite isolate. It was like driving and suddenly knowing there was black ice under the tires and that any sudden movement might send the car spinning out of control.

I don't doubt someone fought you, Hutter had said. *I don't think* anyone *doubts that.*

And: *You spent a month in a Colorado mental hospital, where you were diagnosed with severe PTSD and schizophrenia.*

Sitting at the table with her coffee, in a state of relative quiet and stillness, Vic put it together at last. When it came to her, she felt a cool, dry sensation on the nape of her neck, a prickling across her scalp, the physical indicators of both wonder and horror; she was conscious of feeling both in equal measure. She swallowed some warm coffee to drive away the sick chill and its corresponding sensation of alarm. She made an effort to remain perfectly composed, going over it in her mind.

So. Hutter thought Vic had killed Wayne *herself,* in a psychotic fit. Killed the dog and then drowned Wayne in the lake. They only had her word that someone had fired a gun; no one had found so much as a single bullet, not a single casing. The lead had gone into the water, and the brass had stayed in the gun. The fence was smashed and the yard torn up, the only part of her story they couldn't figure out yet. Sooner or later, though, they'd come up with an explanation for that, too. They'd invent something and force it to fit with the other facts.

They had her pegged as a Susan Smith, the woman from South Carolina who drowned her children, then told a whopping lie about how they'd been kidnapped by a black man, kept the nation whipped up in a frenzy of racial hysteria for about a week. That was why the networks weren't talking about Manx. The police didn't believe in him. They didn't even believe that a kidnapping had occurred at all but were going along with that part of it for now, probably to cover themselves legally.

Vic swallowed the last of her coffee, put the cup in the sink, and stepped out the back door.

She had the backyard to herself. She walked through the dew-cool grass to the carriage house and looked through the window.

Lou was asleep on the floor, beside the motorcycle. The bike was in pieces, side covers off, chain hanging loose. Lou had a canvas tarp folded under his head as a makeshift pillow. His hands were covered in grease. There were black fingerprints on his cheek where he had touched his face in sleep.

"He's been working in there all night," said a voice from behind her.

Daltry had followed her out onto the lawn. His mouth was open in a grin to show a gold tooth. He had a cigarette in one hand.

"I've seen 'at. Plenty of times. 'S how people react when they feel helpless. You wouldn't believe how many women will knit while they're waiting in the emergency room to see if their kid is going to make it through lifesaving surgery. When you feel helpless, you'll do just about any old thing to shut off your head."

"Yeah," Vic said. "That's right. He's a mechanic. It's what he's got instead of knitting. Can I have a cigarette?"

She thought it might steady her, smooth out her nerves.

"I didn't see any ashtrays in the house," he said. He pawed a package of Marlboros from his crummy coat, shook one out for her.

"I quit for my son," she said.

He nodded, didn't reply to that. He came up with a lighter, a big brass Zippo, with a cartoon of some kind stamped on the side. He flicked the starter, and it made crunchy noises and spit sparks.

"Almost out of fuel," he said.

She took it from him and gave it a flick, and a little yellow flame wavered from the tip. She lit her smoke and shut her eyes and inhaled. It was like sliding into a warm bath. She looked up, sighing, and considered the cartoon on the side of the lighter. Popeye threw a punch. KABLOOEY, it said, in a burst of yellow shockwaves.

"You know what surprises me?" he asked while she pulled another long drag off the cigarette and filled her lungs with sweet smoke. "That no one has seen your big old Rolls-Royce. How does a car like that escape notice, is what I wonder. Ain't you surprised no one has seen it?"

He watched her with bright, almost happy eyes.

"No," she said, and it was the truth.

"No," Daltry repeated. "You aren't. Why is that, you think?"

"Because Manx is good at not being seen."

Daltry turned his head and gazed out at the water. "It's something. Two men in a 1938 Rolls-Royce Wraith. I checked an online database. You know there are fewer than four hundred Rolls-Royce Wraiths left in the entire world? There's fewer than a hundred in the whole country. That's a rare goddamn car. And the only person to see him is you. You must feel like you're going crazy."

"I'm not crazy," Vic said. "I'm scared. There's a difference."

"I guess you'd know," Daltry said. He dropped his cigarette in the grass and ground it out with his toe.

He had disappeared back inside the house before Vic realized she was still holding his lighter.

The House of Sleep

Bing's yard was full of tinfoil flowers, brightly colored and spinning in the morning sunlight.

The house was a little pink cake of a place, with white trim and nodding lilies. It was a place where a kindly old woman would invite a child in for gingerbread cookies, lock him in a cage, fatten him for weeks, and finally stick him in the oven. It was the House of Sleep. Wayne felt sleepy just watching the foil flowers spin.

Up the hill from Bing Partridge's house was a church that had nearly burned to the ground. Almost nothing of it remained except for the front façade, with its high pointed steeple, tall white doors, and sooty stained-glass windows. The back side of the church was a caved-in debris field of charred rafters and blackened concrete. There was a sign out front, one of those boards with movable letters, so the pastor could let people know the service schedule. Someone had been fooling with the letters, though, had written a message that probably did not accurately represent the views of the congregation. It read:

THE NEW AMERICAN
FAITH TABERNACLE
GOD BURNED ALIVE
ONLY DEVILS NOW

The wind rose in the huge old oaks, framing the parking lot around the scorched ruin of the church. Wayne could smell char, even with the windows rolled up.

NOS4A2 turned and eased up the driveway, toward a detached garage. Bing squirmed, digging in his pocket, and produced a remote control. The door rolled up, and the car rolled in.

The garage was a hollowed-out block of cement, cool and shady inside, with a smell of oil and iron. The metal odor came from the tanks. There were half a dozen green tanks in the garage—tall, rust-flecked cylinders with red stenciling on the side: FLAMMABLE and CONTENTS UNDER PRESSURE and SEVOFLURANE. They were lined up like soldiers of some alien robot army awaiting inspection. Beyond the rows was a narrow staircase climbing to a second-floor loft.

"Oh, boy, time for breakfast," Bing said. He looked at Charlie Manx. "I will make you the best breakfast you ever ate. Cross my heart and hope to die. The *best*. Just say what you want."

"I want some time alone, Bing," Manx said. "I want some time to rest my head. If I am not very hungry, it is probably because I am full up with all your prattle. Now, *there* are a lot of empty calories."

Bing shrank. His hands crept toward his ears.

"Do not cover your ears and pretend you cannot hear me. You have been an utter disaster."

Bing's face wrinkled. His eyes shut. He began, hideously, to cry. "I could just shoot myself!" he cried.

"Oh, that is a lot of foolishness," Manx said. "Anyway, you would most likely miss and put the bullet in me."

Wayne laughed.

He surprised all of them, including himself. It had been like sneezing, a completely involuntary reaction. Manx and Bing looked into the backseat at him. Bing's eyes streamed, his fat, ugly face distorted with misery. Manx, though—Manx watched Wayne with a kind of wondering amusement.

"You shut up!" Bing screamed. "Don't you *laugh* at me! I'll cut your face off! I'll get my scissors and cut you all to pieces!"

Manx had the silver hammer in his hand, and he thumped it into Bing's chest, pushing him back at his door.

"Hush," Manx said. "Any child will laugh at the antics of a clown. It is perfectly natural."

For a moment it flashed into Wayne's mind how funny it would be if Manx had poked the hammer into Bing's face and busted his nose. In his mind Bing's nose popped like a water balloon filled with red Kool-Aid, an image so hilarious he almost laughed again.

A part of Wayne, a very distant, quiet part, wondered how he could find *anything* funny. Maybe he was still muddled up from the gas that Bing Partridge had sprayed at him. He had slept all night but did not feel rested. He felt ill and drained and warm. Warm most of all: He was boiling in his own skin, wished for a cool shower, a cool dip in the lake, a cool mouthful of snow.

Manx glanced sidelong at Wayne one more time and winked. Wayne flinched, his stomach doing a slow cartwheel.

This man is poison, he thought, and then said it to himself again, only in reverse. *Poison is man this.* And, having composed this odd, stilted, backward phrase, Wayne felt oddly, curiously better about himself, although he couldn't have said exactly why.

"If you are feeling domestic, you could make a rasher of bacon for the growing young man. I am sure he would like that."

Bing lowered his head and wept.

"Go on," Manx said. "Go and be the crybaby in your kitchen where I don't have to listen to it. I will deal with you soon enough."

Bing let himself out and closed the door and walked past the car toward the driveway. As he went by the rear windows, he cast a hating look at Wayne. Wayne had never seen anyone look at him that way, like they genuinely wished to kill him, to strangle him to death. It was funny. Wayne almost burst out laughing again.

Wayne exhaled, slowly, unsteadily, did not want to be thinking any of the things he was thinking. Someone had unscrewed a jar of black moths, and they were fluttering around wildly inside his head now, a whirl of ideas: *fun* ideas. Fun like a broken nose or a man shooting himself in the head.

"I prefer to drive at night," Charlie Manx said. "I am a night person at heart. Everything that is good in the day is even better in the night. A merry-go-round, a Ferris wheel, a kiss from a girl. Everything. Besides. When I turned eighty-five, the sunlight began to bother my eyes. Do you need to go winkie-wee?"

"You mean . . . go pee?"

"Or make chocolate cake?" Manx asked.

Wayne laughed again—a sharp, loud bark—then clapped a hand over his mouth as if he could swallow it back.

Manx watched him with bright, fascinated, unblinking eyes. Wayne did not think he had seen him blink once in all the time they had been together.

"What are you doing to me?" Wayne asked.

"I am driving you away from all the things that ever made you unhappy," Manx said. "And when we get where we are going, you will have left your sadness behind. Come. There's a bathroom here in the garage."

He got out from behind the wheel, and in the same moment the door on Wayne's right unlocked itself, the lock popping up with such a loud bang that Wayne flinched.

Wayne had been planning to run as soon as he had his feet under him, but the air was damp and hot and burdensome. It stuck to him, or maybe he was stuck to it, like a fly caught on flypaper. He got just one step, and then Manx had a hand on the back of his neck. His grip was not painful or rough, but it was *firm*. He effortlessly turned Wayne around, away from the open garage door.

Wayne's gaze caught and held on the rows of battered green tanks, and he frowned. SEVOFLURANE.

Manx followed Wayne's stare, and one corner of his mouth lifted in a knowing smile. "Mr. Partridge has a job with the custodial staff of a chemical plant three miles from here. Sevoflurane is a narcotic and anesthetic, much in demand by dentists. In my day the dentist would anesthetize his patients—even children—with brandy, but sevoflurane is considered far more humane and effective. Sometimes tanks are reported damaged, and Bing takes them out of commission. Sometimes they are not as damaged as they appear."

Manx steered Wayne toward a flight of stairs that led to the second floor of the garage. Beneath the steps was a partly open door.

"Can I bend your ear for a moment, Wayne?" Manx asked.

Wayne pictured Manx grabbing his left ear and wrenching it until Wayne screamed and fell to his knees. Some awful, submerged part of himself also found *this* funny; at the same time, the skin on the back of his neck beneath Manx's gaunt hand went crawly and strange.

Before he could reply, Manx went on. "I am puzzled about some things. I am hoping you can clear up a mystery for me."

With his other hand, he reached beneath his greatcoat and produced a folded sheet of paper, dirty and stained. He unfolded it and held it in front of Wayne's face.

BOEING ENGINEER VANISHES

"A woman with absurdly colored hair turned up at your mother's house the other day. I am sure you remember her. She had a folder full of stories about me. Your mother and this lady made quite a scene in your mother's yard. Bing told me all about it. You will be surprised to know that Bing saw the whole thing from the house across the street."

Wayne frowned, wondered how Bing had been able to watch from across the street. The de Zoets lived over there. An answer suggested itself. It wasn't funny in the slightest.

They reached the door under the stairs. Manx pulled the knob and opened it to reveal a little half bathroom under a slanted roof.

Manx reached for a chain hanging from a bare lightbulb and pulled it, but the room remained dark.

"Bing is letting this place go to the dogs. I will leave the door open to allow you a little light."

He nudged Wayne into the dim bathroom. The door remained ajar about half a foot, but the old man stepped aside to give Wayne his privacy.

"How does your mother happen to know this peculiar lady, and why would they be talking about *me*?"

"I don't know. I never saw her before."

"You read the news stories she brought, though. Stories about me, most of them. I would like to tell you, the news reports about my case are full of the most outrageous libels. I have never killed a single child. Not one. And I am no kiddie fiddler either. The fires of hell are not hot enough for such people. Your mother's visitor did not seem to think I was dead. That is a remarkable notion to have, considering that the papers widely reported upon not only my demise but also my autopsy. Why do you think she had so much faith in my continued survival?"

"I don't know that either." Wayne stood there holding his prick, unable to pee. "My mother said she was a crazy person."

"You are not 'having me on' are you, Wayne?"

"No, sir."

"What did this woman with the curious hair say about me?"

"My mother sent me inside the house. I didn't hear any of it."

"Oh, you are telling me a tall one now, Bruce Wayne Carmody." But he didn't say it like he was angry about it. "Are you having difficulties with your fiddlestick?"

"My what?"

"Your winkie. Your peepee?"

"Oh. Maybe a little."

"It is because we are talking. It is never easy to tinkle when someone is listening to you. I will move three steps away."

Wayne heard Manx's heels rapping on the concrete as he moved off. Almost immediately Wayne's bladder let go, and the urine rained down.

As he peed, he let out a long sigh of relief and tipped back his head.

There was a poster above the toilet. It showed a naked woman on her knees, with her hands tied behind her. Her head was stuffed into a gasmask. A man in a Nazi uniform stood over her, holding a leash, the collar around her neck.

Wayne shut his eyes, pushed his fiddlestick—no, penis, "fiddlestick" was a grotesque word—back into his shorts, and turned away. He washed his hands in a sink with a cockroach clinging to the side. As he did, he was relieved to discover he had not found anything funny about that awful poster.

It's the car. It's being in the car that makes everything seem funny, even when it's awful.

As soon as he had this thought, he knew it was true.

He stepped out of the bathroom, and Manx was there, holding the door open to the backseat of the Wraith. In his other hand was the silver mallet. He grinned to show his stained teeth. Wayne thought he might be able to run as far as the driveway before Manx smashed his head in.

"Tell you what," Manx said. "I would really like to know more about your mother's confidante. I am sure if you put your mind to it, you will remember some details you have forgotten. Why don't you sit in the car and turn it over in your mind? I will go and get your breakfast. By the time I come back, perhaps something will have occurred to you. What do you say to that?"

Wayne shrugged, but his heart surged at the thought of being alone in the car. The phone. He only needed a minute alone to call his father and tell him everything: Sugarcreek, Pennsylvania; pink house, right down the hill from a burned church. The cops would be here before Manx got back with his bacon and eggs. He climbed into the car willingly, without hesitation.

Manx shut the door and knocked on the glass. "I will be back in a jiffy! Don't run away!" And he laughed as the lock banged down.

Wayne knelt on the seat to watch through the rear window as Manx left. When the old man had disappeared into the back of the house, Wayne turned, dropped to the floor, grabbed the walnut drawer beneath the driver's seat, and yanked it open to get his phone.

Gone.

Bing's Garage

SOMEWHERE A DOG BARKED AND A LAWN MOWER STARTED AND THE world went on, but here in the Rolls-Royce the world had caught in place, because the phone was gone.

Wayne pulled the drawer all the way out and put his hand in it, patting down the baize interior, as if the phone might be hiding under the drawer lining somehow. He knew he was not mistaken and that this was the drawer he had put it in, but he closed it and looked in the other drawer, beneath the passenger seat. It was just as empty.

"Where *are* you?" Wayne cried, although he already knew. While he had been washing his hands, Manx had climbed into the backseat and collected the phone himself. He was probably walking around with it in the pocket of his greatcoat right this instant. Wayne felt like crying. He had built a delicate cathedral of hope, deep inside him, and Manx had stepped on it, then lit it on fire. GOD BURNED ALIVE, ONLY DEVILS NOW.

It was stupid—pointless—but Wayne went back and opened the first drawer again, for another look.

There were Christmas ornaments in it.

They had not been there a moment ago. A moment before, the drawer had been absolutely empty. Now, though, the drawer contained an enamel angel with tragic drooping eyes, a great silver snowflake dusted in glitter, and a sleeping blue moon in a Santa Claus cap.

"What is this?" Wayne said, hardly aware he was speaking aloud.

He lifted each out in turn.

The angel hung from a golden loop, turning gently, blowing her horn.

The snowflake looked deadly, a weapon, a ninja's throwing star.

The moon smiled at his own private musings.

Wayne returned the ornaments to the drawer where he had discovered them and gently pushed the drawer shut.

Then: opened it again.

Empty once more.

He exhaled a frustrated, fuming breath and slammed the drawer, whispering furiously, "I want my phone back."

Something *clicked* in the front seat. Wayne looked up in time to see the glove compartment fall open.

His phone sat on a stack of road maps.

Wayne stood in the backseat. He had to hunch, with the back of his head pressed to the ceiling, but it could be done. He felt as if he had just seen a bit of sleight of hand; a magician had passed a palm over a bouquet of flowers and transformed them into his iPhone. Mingled with his sense of surprise—astonishment, even—was an ill tickle of dismay.

The Wraith was teasing him.

The Wraith or Manx—Wayne had a notion that they were the same thing, that the one was an extension of the other. The Wraith was a part of Manx like Wayne's right hand was a part of him.

Wayne stared at his phone, already knowing he had to try to get it, already knowing that the car had some way of keeping it from him.

But never mind the phone; the driver's-side door was unlocked, nothing stopping him from getting out of the car and making a run for it. Nothing except that the last three times he had tried to climb into the front seat, he had somehow wound up in the back again.

He had been drugged then, though. The Gasmask Man had sprayed him with gingerbread smoke, and it had blurred his thoughts. He could hardly pick himself up off the floor. No wonder he kept falling into the backseat. The real wonder was that he had hung on to consciousness as long as he had.

Wayne lifted his right hand, preparing to reach across the divider, and noticed at that moment that he was still holding the Christmas ornament in the shape of the moon. He had, in fact, been rubbing his thumb along its smooth, sickle-shaped curve for a full minute now: a thoughtless gesture that he found curiously soothing. He blinked at it, briefly befuddled—he could've sworn he'd put all three ornaments back in their drawer.

That moon, Wayne noticed now, with its plump cheeks and big nose and long eyelashes, somewhat resembled his own father. He put it in his pocket, then lifted his hand once more and reached over the divider, in the direction of the glove compartment.

As his fingers crossed into the front seat, they *dwindled.* His fingertips became fleshy nubs that ended at the first knuckle. When he saw it happening, his shoulders jumped in a nervous reflex, but he did not pull back his hand. It was grotesque but also somehow fascinating.

He could still *feel* the ends of his fingers. He could rub his fingertips together, feel the leathery pad of his thumb stroking the end of his index finger. He just couldn't *see* them.

Wayne reached farther over the divider, pushed his whole hand across the invisible barrier. His arm dwindled to a smooth pink stump, a painless amputation. He opened and closed a fist he couldn't see. It was *there;* he could feel his hand was *there.* He just wasn't sure where *there* was.

He reached a little farther, in the general direction of the glove compartment and his phone.

Something poked him in the back. At the same moment, the fingers of his invisible right hand struck something solid.

Wayne turned his head to look behind him.

An arm—*his* arm—stretched out of the seat behind him. It didn't look as if it had torn through the seat but as if it had *grown* from it. The hand at the end of the arm was skin. So was the wrist. But close to the seat, the flesh darkened and roughened and became worn old beige leather, stretching out from the seat itself, putting visible strain on the fabric around it.

The natural thing to do would've been to scream, but Wayne was all screamed out. He made a fist with his right hand. The hand growing from the backseat clenched its fingers. It made his stomach go all funny, controlling a disembodied arm that had sprouted from a seat cushion.

"You should try thumb wrestling with yourself," Manx said.

Wayne jumped, and in his alarm he pulled his right arm back. The disembodied limb protruding from the seat went away, was *inhaled* back into the leather, and in the next instant was attached to his shoulder again, where it belonged. Wayne clasped the hand against his chest. His heart rapped swiftly beneath it.

Manx was bent to peer in through the rear driver's-side window. He grinned to show his crooked, protruding upper teeth.

"There is plenty of fun to be had in the back of this old car! You could not find more fun on four wheels!"

He had a plate in one hand, scrambled eggs and bacon and toast. In the other was a glass of orange juice.

"You will be glad to know there is nothing whatsoever healthy about this meal! It is all butter and salt and cholesterol. Even the orange juice is bad for you. It is actually something called 'orange drink.' I have never taken a vitamin in my life, though, and I have lived to a very advanced age. Happiness will do more for you than any wonder drug the apothecaries can invent!"

Wayne sat down on the rear couch. Manx opened the door,

leaned in, and offered him the plate and the juice. Wayne noticed he had not been provided with a fork. Manx might carry on as if they were best friends, but he was not about to provide his passenger with a stabby weapon . . . a simple, perfectly clear reminder that Wayne was not a pal but a prisoner. Wayne took the plate—and then Manx climbed into the backseat to sit beside him.

Manx had said that hell was not too hot for the sort of men who fiddled with children, but Wayne readied himself, expected to be touched now. Manx would reach between Wayne's legs, ask him if he ever played with his fiddlestick.

When Manx made his move, Wayne was ready to fight, and lose, and be molested. He would throw his breakfast at the guy. He would bite.

It wouldn't matter. If Manx wanted to pull Wayne's pants down and do . . . do *whatever*—he would do it. He was bigger. It was that simple. Wayne would do his best to live through it. He would pretend his body belonged to someone else and would think about the avalanche he had seen with his father. He would imagine being buried in snow with a kind of quiet relief. Someday he *would* be buried somewhere (sooner rather than later, he thought), and it wouldn't matter anymore what Manx had done to him. He just hoped his mother never found out. She was so unhappy already, had fought so hard not to be crazy, not to be drunk, he couldn't stand to imagine he would be the source of any more pain for her.

But Manx did not touch him. He sighed and stretched out his legs.

"I see you have already picked an ornament to hang up when we arrive at Christmasland," Manx said. "To mark your passage into that world."

Wayne glanced at his right hand and was surprised to see he was holding that sleepy moon again, running his thumb over the curve of it. He had no memory of taking it from his pocket.

"My daughters brought little angels to mark the end of *their* journey," Manx said in a distant, musing voice. "Take care of it, Wayne. Guard it as if it were your own life!"

He clapped Wayne on the back and nodded toward the front of the car. Wayne followed his gaze . . . and saw that he was looking at the open glove compartment. At the phone.

"Did you really think you were going to hide something from me?" Manx asked. "Here in this car?"

It didn't seem like the kind of question that required an answer.

Manx crossed his arms tightly over his chest, almost as if giving himself a hug. He was smiling to himself. He didn't look angry at all.

"Hiding something in this car is as bad as putting it in the pocket of my coat. I am bound to notice. Not that I can blame you for trying! Any boy would try. You should eat those eggs. They will get cold."

Wayne found himself struggling not to cry. He threw his moon on the floor.

"Here! Here! Do not be sad! I can't stand for any child to be unhappy! Would it make you feel better to talk to your mother?"

Wayne blinked. A single tear splatted on a greasy piece of bacon. The thought of hearing his mother's voice set off a small explosion inside Wayne's body, a throb of need.

He nodded.

"Do you know what would make *me* feel better? If you told me about this woman who brought all the news stories to your mother. If you will scratch my back, I will scratch yours!"

"I don't believe you," Wayne whispered. "You won't call her. No matter what I do."

Manx looked over the divider, into the front seat.

The glove compartment snapped shut with a loud *clack!* It was so surprising that Wayne almost dumped his plate of eggs.

The drawer beneath the front driver's seat slid open all by itself, almost without sound.

The phone rested in it.

Wayne stared at it, his breathing shallow, effortful.

"I have not told you a lie yet," Manx said. "But I understand that you would be reluctant to trust me. Here is the thing: You know I will not give you the phone if you don't tell me about your mother's visitor. I will put it on the floor of this garage and back my car over it. That will be fun! To be honest, I think cell phones were invented by the devil. Now, think if you *did* tell me what I want to know. One way or another, you will have learned something important. If I do not let you call your mother, you will have learned I am a big fat liar and you will never have to trust me again about anything. But if I *do* let you call her, then you will know I am as good as my word."

Wayne said, "But I don't know *any*thing about Maggie Leigh that *you* don't know."

"Well, now you have told me her name. See! The learning process has already begun."

Wayne cringed, feeling he had just committed an unforgivable betrayal.

"Ms. Leigh said something that frightened your mother. What was it? Tell me and I will let you call your mother right this instant!"

Wayne opened his mouth, not sure what he was going to say, but Manx stopped him. He grabbed his shoulder then and gave it a gentle squeeze.

"Do not go making up stories, Wayne! Our deal is off if you are not straight with me from the get-go! Twist the truth even a little and you will regret it!"

Manx reached down and plucked a piece of bacon off the plate. One of Wayne's teardrops glistened on it, a bright, oily gem. Manx bit off half and began to chew, teardrop and all.

"Well?" Manx asked.

"She said you were on the move," Wayne said. "That you were out of jail and that Mom had to watch out. And I guess that's what frightened my mother."

Manx frowned, chewing slowly, his jaw moving in an exaggerated way.

"I didn't hear anything else. Really."

"How did your mother and this woman know each other?"

Wayne shrugged. "Maggie Leigh said she met my mother when she was a kid, but my mom said she had never met her before."

"And which of them do you think was telling the truth?" Manx asked.

That one caught Wayne off guard, and he was slow to reply. "My . . . mother."

Manx swallowed his bite of bacon and beamed. "See. That was easy. Well. I am sure your mother will be glad to hear from you." He began to lean forward to reach for the phone—then sank back into his seat. "Oh! There is one more thing. Did this Maggie Leigh say anything about a *bridge*?"

Wayne's whole body seemed to pulse in reaction to this question; a kind of tingling throb surged through him, and he thought, *Don't tell him that.*

"No," he said, before he had time to think. His voice went thick and choked, as if his lie were a piece of toast that had momentarily jammed in his throat.

Manx turned a sly, sleepy smile upon him. His eyelids sank to half-mast. He began to move, putting one foot out the open door, rising to go. At the same time, the drawer with the phone in it came to life, slamming shut with a loud bang.

"I mean *yes*!" Wayne cried, grabbing him by the arm. The sudden movement upset the plate in his lap, turning it over, dumping eggs and toast on the floor. "Yes, *all right*! She said she had to find you again! She asked if she could still use the bridge to find you!"

Manx paused, half in, half out of the car, Wayne's grip still on his forearm. He stared down at Wayne's hand with that look of dreamy amusement.

"I thought we agreed you were going to tell the truth from the get-go."

"I did! I just forgot for a moment! Please!"

"You forgot, all right. You forgot to tell me the truth!"

"I'm sorry!"

Manx didn't seem upset at all. He said, "Well. It was a momentary lapse. Maybe I can still allow a phone call. But I am going to ask you one more question, and I want you to *think* before you answer. And when you *do* answer, I want you to tell me the *truth,* so help you God. Did Maggie Leigh say anything about how your mother would *get* to this bridge? What did she say about the bike?"

"She . . . she didn't say anything about the bike! No, I swear!" Because Manx had started to pull his arm free. "I don't think she knew anything about the Triumph!"

Manx hesitated. "The Triumph?"

"Mom's motorcycle. You remember. The one she was pushing up the road. She's been fixing it for weeks. She works on it all the time, even when she should be sleeping. Is that the bike you mean?"

Manx's eyes had assumed a cool, remote quality. His face softened. He bit his lower lip with his little teeth. It was an expression that made him look feebleminded.

"Huh! Your mother is trying to build a new ride. So she can do it again. So she can *find* me. You know, I wondered if she might be getting up to her old tricks as soon as I saw her pushing that motorcycle! And this Maggie Leigh—I imagine she has a ride of her own. Or she at least knows about those who *travel* on the other roads. Well. I have some more questions, but I am better off putting them to Ms. Leigh directly." Manx's hand slipped into the pocket of his greatcoat, drew out the photocopied news story about Nathan Demeter, and turned the sheet of paper so Wayne could look at it. Manx tapped the header on the old stationery:

HERE PUBLIC LIBRARY
HERE, IOWA

"And *Here* is where to look for her!" Manx said. "It is a good thing it is on the way!"

Wayne was breathing rapidly, as if he had just run a very long distance. "I want to call my mom."

"No," Manx said, and jerked his arm free. "We had a deal. The truth, the whole truth, and nothing but the truth. My ears are still stinging from that whopper you tried to slip by me! That was too bad. You will learn soon enough that it is pretty hard to pull the wool over my eyes!"

"No!" Wayne screamed. "I told you everything you wanted to know! You promised! You said I'd have one more chance."

"I said *maybe* I would allow a phone call if you told me the truth about your mother's bike. But you didn't know anything, and anyway, I did not say I would allow this phone call *today*. I think we will have to wait until tomorrow. I think if you have to wait until tomorrow, you will learn a very valuable lesson: No one likes a big fibber, Wayne!"

He shut the door. The lock banged down.

"No!" Wayne screamed again, but Manx had already turned away, was walking across the garage, weaving between the tall green gas tanks toward the stairs to the loft. "No! It's not fair!"

Wayne dropped off the seat, onto the floor. He grabbed the brass handle of the drawer with his phone in it and pulled, but it didn't budge, might as well have been nailed shut. He put one foot on the back of the divider between the front and the rear compartment and threw all his weight backward. His sweat-slippery hands came right off the handle, and he fell back into the seat.

"Please!" Wayne screamed. "Please!"

At the bottom of the stairs, Manx looked back at the car. There was an expression of weary tragedy on his face. His eyes were damp with sympathy. He shook his head, although whether in refusal or simply as a gesture of disappointment, it was impossible to tell.

He pressed a button on the wall. The automatic garage door rumbled down. He flipped a switch and turned out the lights before going upstairs and left Wayne alone in the Wraith.

The Lake

By the time Hutter was done with her that afternoon, Vic felt wrung out, as if she were recovering from a bout of stomach flu. Her joints were sore, and her back throbbed. She was desperately hungry but when presented with a turkey sandwich was almost overcome with an urge to vomit. She couldn't even choke down a whole piece of toast.

She told Hutter all the old lies about Manx: how he had injected her with something and put her in his car, how she had escaped him in Colorado at the Sleigh House. They sat in the kitchen, Hutter asking the questions and Vic answering them as best she could, while cops came in and out.

After Vic had told the story of her kidnapping, Hutter wanted to hear about the years after. She wanted to know about the derangement that had led Vic to spend time in a mental hospital. She wanted to know about the time Vic burned her own house down.

"I didn't mean to burn the house down," Vic said. "I was just trying to get rid of the phones. I stuck them all in the oven. It seemed like the simplest way to stop the phone calls."

"The phone calls from dead people?"

"From dead kids. Yes."

"Is that the predominant theme of your delusions? Does it always revolve around dead children?"

"Did. Was. Past tense," Vic said.

Hutter stared at Vic with all the affection of a snake handler approaching a venomous cobra. Vic thought, *Just ask me already. Ask me if I killed my little boy. Get it out in the open.* She met Hutter's gaze without blinking or flinching. Vic had been hammered, shot at, nearly run over, institutionalized, addicted, had come close to being burned alive and had run for her life on several occasions. An unfriendly stare was nothing.

Hutter said, "You might want to rest and freshen up. I've scheduled your statement for five-twenty. That should get us the maximum prime-time coverage."

Vic said, "I wish I thought there was something I knew—something I could tell you—that would help you find him."

"You've been very helpful," Hutter said. "Thank you. I have a lot of good information here."

Hutter looked away, and Vic imagined that the interview was over. But as she rose to go, Hutter reached for something leaning against the wall: some sheets of bristol board.

"Vic," Hutter said, "there is one other thing."

Vic stood still, a hand on the back of her chair.

Hutter put the stack of bristol board on the table, turned so Vic could look at the illustrations. *Her* illustrations, the pages from the new book, *Search Engine's Fifth Gear,* the holiday story. What she had been working on when she wasn't assembling the Triumph. Hutter began to shuffle the big card-stock pages, giving Vic a moment to take in each picture, rendered in nonphotographic blue pencil, inked, then finished in watercolors. The paper rasped in a way that made Vic think of a fortune-teller shuffling a tarot deck, preparing to deal a very bad outlook.

Hutter said, "I told you, they use the Search Engine puzzles at Quantico to teach students about careful observation. When I saw that you had part of a new book out in the carriage house, I couldn't help myself. I'm stunned by what you've got on the page here. You really do give Escher a run for his money. Then I looked close and started wondering. This is for a Christmas book, isn't it?"

The urge to get away from the pile of bristol board—to shrink from her own drawings, as if they were photographs of skinned animals—surged inside her and then was smothered in a moment. She wanted to say she had never seen any of these pictures before, wanted to scream she didn't know where they had come from. Both of these statements would've been fundamentally true, but she clamped down on them, and when she spoke, her voice was weary and disinterested.

"Yeah. My publisher's idea."

"Well," Hutter said, "do you think—I mean, is it possible—that *this* is Christmasland? That the person who grabbed your son is aware of what you've been working on and that there's some kind of connection between your new book and what we saw when we tried to track your son's iPhone?"

Vic stared at the first illustration. It showed Search Engine and little Bonnie, clasping each other on a shattered plate of ice, somewhere in the Arctic Ocean. Vic remembered drawing a mechanical squid, piloted by Mad Möbius Stripp, coming up through the ice beneath them. But this drawing showed dead-eyed children under the ice, reaching up through the cracks with bony white claws. They grinned to show mouths filled with delicate hooked fangs.

On another page Search Engine hunted for a way through a maze of towering candy canes. Vic remembered drawing that—drawing in a sweet, lazy trance, swaying to the Black Keys. She did not remember drawing the children who hid in corners and side alleys, holding scissors. She did not remember drawing little Bonnie staggering about blind, her hands clapped over her eyes. *They're playing scissors-for-the-drifter,* she thought randomly.

"I don't see how," Vic said. "No one has seen these pages."

Hutter raced her thumb down one edge of the stack of paper and said, "It struck me as a bit surprising that you'd be drawing Christmas scenes in the middle of the summer. Try to think. Is there any chance what you've been working on could tie in to—"

"In to Charlie Manx's decision to pay me back for sending him to jail?" Vic asked. "I don't think so. I think it's pretty straightforward. I crossed him, and now it's get-even time. If we're all done, I'd like to lie down."

"Yes. You must be tired. And who knows? Maybe if you have a chance to rest, something else will come to you."

Hutter's tone was calm enough, but Vic thought she heard an insinuation in this last statement, the suggestion that they both understood that Vic had more to tell.

Vic didn't know her own house. There were magnetic whiteboards leaning against the couches in her living room. One of them had a map showing the Northeast; another had a timeline written in red marker. Folders crammed full of printouts were stacked on every available surface. Hutter's geek squad was squeezed together on the couch like college students in front of an Xbox; one of them was talking into a Bluetooth earpiece while the others worked on laptops. No one looked at her. She didn't matter.

Lou was in the bedroom, in the rocking chair in the corner. She eased the door shut behind her and crept to him through the dark. The curtains were drawn, the room gloomy and airless.

His shirt was smeared with black fingerprints. He smelled of the bike and the carriage house—a not-unpleasant cologne. There was a sheet of brown paper taped to his chest. His round, heavy face was gray in the dim light, and with that note hanging off him he looked like a daguerreotype of a dead gunslinger: THIS IS WHAT WE DO TO OUTLAWS.

Vic looked at him, at first with concern, then alarm. She was reaching for his chubby forearm, to see if she could find his pulse—she was *sure* he wasn't breathing—when he inhaled suddenly, one nostril whistling. Just asleep. He had dropped off to sleep in his boots.

She drew her hand back. She had never seen him look so fatigued or so sick. There was gray in his stubble. It seemed somehow wrong that Lou, who loved comics, and his son, and boobies, and beer, and birthday parties, should ever get old.

She squinted at the note, which read:

"Bike still isn't right. Needs parts that will take weeks to order. Wake me up when you want to talk about it."

Reading those four words—"bike still isn't right"—was nearly as bad as reading "Wayne found dead." She felt they were dangerously close to the same thing.

Not for the first time in her life, she wished that Lou had never picked her up on his motorcycle that day, wished that she had slipped and dropped to the bottom of the laundry chute and smothered to death there, sparing her the trouble of dragging her ass through the rest of her sorry life. She would not have lost Wayne to Manx, because there would be no Wayne. Choking to death on smoke was easier than feeling what she felt now, a kind of tearing inside that never stopped. She was a bedsheet, being ripped this way and that, and soon enough would be nothing but rags.

She sat on the edge of the bed, staring vacantly into the darkness and seeing her own drawings, the pages Tabitha Hutter had shown her from the new *Search Engine.* She did not know how anyone could look at such work and suspect her of innocence: all those drowned children, all those drifts of snow, all those candy canes, all that hopelessness. They were going to lock her up soon, and then it would be too late to do anything for Wayne. They were going to lock her up, and she couldn't blame them in the slightest; she suspected Tabitha Hutter of weakness for not putting her in handcuffs already.

Her weight creased the mattress. Lou had dumped his money and his cell phone in the center of the quilt, and now they slid toward her, came to rest against her hip. She wished there were someone to call, to tell her what to do, to tell her that everything would be all right. Then it came to her that there was.

She took Lou's phone and slipped into the bathroom and shut the door. There was another door at the opposite end of the bathroom that looked into Wayne's bedroom. Vic moved toward this door to close it, then hesitated.

He was *there:* Wayne was there, in his room, under his bed, staring out at her, his face pale and frightened. She felt as if she'd been kicked in the chest by a mule, her heart galumphing hard behind her breastbone, and she looked again, and it was just a stuffed monkey, lying on its side. Its brown eyes were glassy and despairing. She clicked the door to his room shut, then stood with her forehead resting against it, waiting to get her breath back.

With her eyes closed, she could see Maggie's phone number: the Iowa 319 area code, followed by Vic's own birthday, and the letters FUFU. Maggie had paid good money for that number, Vic felt sure— because she knew that Vic would remember it. Maybe she knew that Vic would *need* to remember it. Maybe she knew that Vic would turn her away when they first met. All kinds of maybes, but only one that Vic cared about: Was her son maybe alive?

The phone rang and rang, and Vic thought if it kicked her to voice mail, she would not be able to leave a message, would not be able to force a sound up through her constricting throat. On the fourth ring, when she had decided that Maggie wasn't going to answer, Maggie answered.

"*V-V-V-Vic!*" Maggie said, before Vic could manage a word. Maggie's caller ID had to be telling her she'd just received a call from Carmody's Car Carma—she couldn't *know* it was Vic on the line, but she did know, and Vic was not surprised. "I wanted to call as suh-s-ss-ssss-*soon* as I heard, but I wasn't sure it was a good idea. How are you? It ss-suh-says on the news you were assaulted."

"Forget that. I need to know if Wayne is all right. I know you can find out."

"I *already* know. He hasn't been hurt."

Vic's legs began trembling, and she had to put a hand on the counter to steady herself.

"Vic? V-V-Vic?"

She could not answer immediately. It took all her concentration to keep from crying.

"Yes," Vic said finally. "I'm here. How much time do I have? How much time does *Wayne* have?"

"I don't know how that p-p-puh-part of it works. I just don't know. What have you told the p-p-p-puh-puh-police?"

"What I had to. Nothing about you. I did my best to make it sound believable, but I don't think they're buying it."

"Vic. Puh-p-please. I want to help. Tell me how I can help."

"You just did," Vic said, and hung up.

Not dead. And there was still time. She thought it over again, a kind of chant, a song of praise: *Not dead, not dead, not dead.*

She wanted to go back into the bedroom and shake Lou awake and tell him the bike had to run, he had to fix it, but she doubted he'd been sleeping for more than a few hours, and she didn't like his gray pallor. Tugging at the back of her mind was an awareness that he had not been entirely straight with anyone about what had dropped him in Logan Airport.

Maybe she would look at the bike herself. She didn't understand what could be so wrong with it that he couldn't fix it. It had run only yesterday.

She stepped out of the bathroom and tossed the phone at the bed. It slid across the bedspread and fell with a clatter and crack to the floor. Lou's shoulders twitched at the sound, and Vic caught her breath, but he didn't wake.

She opened the bedroom door and twitched in surprise herself. Tabitha Hutter was on the other side of it. Vic had caught her in the act of raising one fist, about to knock.

The two women stared at each other, and Vic thought, *Something is wrong.* Her second thought was, of course, that they had found Wayne—in a ditch somewhere, drained of blood, throat slit ear to ear.

But Maggie said he was alive, and Maggie *knew,* so that wasn't it. It was something else.

Vic looked past Hutter, down the hall, and saw Detective Daltry and a state trooper waiting a few yards back.

"Victoria," Tabitha said, in a neutral tone. "We need to talk."

Vic stepped into the hall and eased the bedroom door shut behind her.

"What's up?"

"Is there a place we can have a private conversation?"

Vic looked again at Daltry and the uniformed cop. The cop was six feet tall and sunburned, and his neck was as thick as his head. Daltry's arms were crossed, hands stuck under his armpits, his mouth a thin white line. He had a can of something in one big leathery hand—pepper spray, probably.

Vic nodded at the door to Wayne's bedroom. "We won't bother anyone in here."

She followed the small woman into the little room that had been Wayne's for only a few weeks before he was taken away. His bedsheets—they had *Treasure Island* scenes printed on them—were folded back as if waiting for him to slip into them. Vic sat on the edge of the mattress.

Come back, she said to Wayne, with all her heart. She wanted to ball his sheets up in her hands and smell them, fill her nose with the scent of her boy. *Come back to me, Wayne.*

Hutter leaned against the dresser, and her coat fell open to show the Glock under her arm. Vic looked up and saw that the younger woman had on a pair of earrings this afternoon: gold pentagons with the Superman insignia enameled on them.

"Don't let Lou see you in those earrings," Vic said. "He might be overcome with an uncontrollable desire to hug you. Geeks are his kryptonite."

"You have to come clean with me," Hutter said.

Vic bent forward, reached under the bed, found the plush monkey, pulled it out. It had gray fur and gangly arms and wore a leather jacket and a motorcycle helmet. GREASE MONKEY, said the patch on its left breast. Vic had no memory of buying the thing.

"About what?" she asked, not looking at Hutter. She laid the monkey on the bed, head on the pillow, where Wayne belonged.

"You haven't been straight with me. Not once. I don't know why. Maybe there are things you're scared to talk about. Possibly there are things you're ashamed to talk about, in front of a roomful of men. Or it could be you think you're protecting your son in some way. Maybe you're protecting someone else. I don't know what it is, but here's where you tell me."

"I haven't lied to you about anything."

"Stop fucking with me," Tabitha Hutter said in her quiet, passionless voice. "Who is Margaret Leigh? What is her relationship to you? How does she know that your son hasn't been hurt?"

"You're tapping Lou's cell phone?" Feeling a little stupid even as she said it.

"Of *course* we are. For all we know, he had a part in this. For all we know, *you* did. You told Margaret Leigh that you tried to make your story believable but that we weren't buying it. You're right. I don't buy it. I never did."

Vic wondered if she could throw herself at Tabitha Hutter, slam her back over the dresser, get the Glock away from her. But the smart-aleck bitch probably knew special FBI kung fu, and anyway, what good would it do? What would Vic do then?

"Last chance, Vic. I want you to understand. I am going to have to arrest you on suspicion of involvement—"

"In what? An assault on myself?"

"We don't know *who* bruised you up. For all we know, it was your son, trying to fight you off."

So. There it was. Vic was interested to find she felt no surprise at all. But then maybe the real surprise was only that they had not reached this point sooner.

"I do not want to believe that you played a role in your son's disappearance. But you know someone who can provide you with information about his well-being. You've withheld facts. Your explanation of events sounds like a textbook paranoid delusion. This is your last opportunity to clear things up, if you can. Think before you speak. Because after I'm done with you, I'm going to start on Lou. He's been withholding evidence as well, I am sure of it. No dad spends ten hours straight trying to fix a motorcycle the day after his son has been kidnapped. I ask him questions he doesn't want to answer, he starts the engine to drown me out. Like a teenager turning up the music so he doesn't have to listen when Mom says it's time to clean his room."

"What do you mean . . . he started the engine?" Vic asked. "He started the Triumph?"

Hutter produced a long, slow, weary exhalation. Her head sank; her shoulders sagged. There was, finally, something besides professional calm in her face. There was, at last, a look of exhaustion and maybe, also, defeat.

"Okay," Hutter breathed. "Vic. I'm sorry. I am. I hoped we could—"

"Can I ask you something?"

Hutter looked at her.

"The hammer. You had me look at fifty different hammers. You seemed surprised by the one I picked, the one I said Manx used on me. Why?"

Vic saw something in Hutter's eyes—the briefest flicker of uncertainty.

"It's called a bone mallet," Hutter said. "They're used in autopsies."

"Was one missing from the morgue in Colorado where they were holding Charlie Manx's body?"

Hutter didn't reply to that one, but her tongue darted out and touched her upper lip, glossing it—the closest thing to a nervous gesture Vic had ever seen out of her. In and of itself, that was a kind of answer.

"Every word I have told you is true," Vic said. "If I left anything out, then it was only because I knew you wouldn't accept those parts of the story. You would write them off as delusional, and no one would blame you."

"We have to go now, Vic. I'll have to handcuff you. If you want, though, we can put a sweater over your lap and you can hide your hands beneath them. No one has to see. You'll sit up front in my car with me. No one will think it's a big deal when we go."

"What about Lou?"

"I'm afraid I can't allow you to speak with him right now. He'll be in a car behind us."

"Can't you let him sleep? He isn't well, and he was up for twenty-four hours straight."

"I'm sorry. It's not my job to worry about Lou's well-being. It's my job to worry about your son's well-being. Stand up, please." She pushed back the right flap of her tweed jacket, and Vic saw she wore handcuffs on her belt.

The door to the right of the dresser swung back, and Lou stumbled out of the bathroom, tugging on his fly. His eyes were bloodshot with exhaustion.

"I'm awake. What's up? What's the story, Vic?"

"Officer!" Hutter called as Lou took a step forward.

His mass occupied a third of the room, and when he moved into the center of it, he was between Vic and Hutter. Vic came to her feet and stepped around him, to the open bathroom door.

"I have to go," Vic said.

"So go," Lou said, and planted himself between her and Tabitha Hutter.

"Officer!" Hutter shouted again.

Vic crossed through the bathroom and into her bedroom. She shut the door behind her. There was no lock, so she grabbed the armoire and dragged it squealing across the pine boards to block the bathroom door. She turned the bolt on the door to the hall. Two more steps carried her to the window that looked into the backyard.

She pulled the shade, unlocked the window.

Men shouted in the hall.

She heard Lou raising his voice, his tone indignant.

"Dude, what's your beef? Let's all settle the hell down, why don't we?" Lou said.

"Officer!" Hutter shouted for a third time, but now she added, "Holster your firearm!"

Vic raised the window, put her foot against the screen, and pushed. The whole screen popped out of the frame and flopped into the yard. She followed it, sitting on the windowsill with her legs hanging out, then dropping five feet onto the grass.

She had on the same cutoffs she'd been wearing yesterday, a Bruce Springsteen T-shirt from The Rising Tour, had no helmet, no jacket. She didn't even know if the keys were in the bike or if they were sitting amid Lou's change on the bed.

Back in the bedroom, she heard someone crash into a door.

"Be cool!" Lou shouted. "Dude, like, *seriously*!"

The lake was a flat silver sheet, reflecting the sky. It looked like melted chrome. The air was swollen with a sullen, liquid weight.

She had the backyard to herself. Two sunburned men in shorts and straw hats were fishing in an aluminum boat about a hundred yards offshore. One of them lifted a hand in a wave, as if he found the sight of a woman exiting her house by way of a back window a perfectly common sight.

Vic let herself into the carriage house through the side door.

The Triumph leaned on its kickstand. The key was in it.

The barn-style doors of the carriage house were open, and Vic could see down the driveway to where the media had assembled to record the statement she was never going to make. A small copse of cameras had been planted at the bottom of the drive, pointed toward an array of microphones at the corner of the yard. Bundles of cable snaked back in the direction of the news vans, parked to the left.

There was no easy way to turn left and weave through those vans, but the road remained open to the right, heading north.

In the carriage house, she could not hear the commotion back in the cottage. The room contained the smothered quiet of a too-hot afternoon in high summer. It was the time of day of naps, stillness, dogs sleeping under porches. It was too hot even for flies.

Vic put her leg over the saddle, turned the key to the ON position. The headlight flicked to life, a good sign.

Bike still isn't right, she remembered. It wasn't going to start. She knew that. When Tabitha Hutter came into the carriage house, Vic would be frantically jumping up and down on the kickstart, dry-humping the saddle. Hutter already thought Vic was crazy; that pretty picture would confirm her suspicions.

She rose up and came down on the starter with all her weight, and the Triumph blammed to life with a roar that blew leaves and grit across the floor and shook the glass in the windows.

Vic put it into first and released the clutch, and the Triumph slipped out of the carriage house.

As she rolled out into the day, she glanced to the right, had a brief view of the backyard. Tabitha Hutter stood halfway to the carriage house, flushed, a strand of curly hair pasted to her cheek. She had not drawn her gun, and she did not draw it now. She did not even call out, just stood there and watched Vic go. Vic nodded to her, as if they had struck an agreement, and Vic was grateful to Hutter for holding up her end. In another moment Vic had left her behind.

There was two feet of space between the edge of the yard and that bristling islet of cameras, and Vic aimed herself at it. But as she neared the road, a man stepped into the gap, pointing his camera at her. He held it at waist level, was staring at a monitor that folded out from the side. He kept his gaze on his little viewscreen, even though it had to be showing him a life-threatening visual: four hundred pounds of rolling iron, piloted by a madwoman, coming right down the hill at him. He wasn't going to move—not in time.

Vic planted her foot on the brake. It sighed and did nothing.

Bike still isn't right.

Something flapped against the inside of her left thigh, and she looked down and saw a length of black plastic tubing hanging free. It was the line for the rear brake. It wasn't attached to anything.

There was no room to get past the yahoo with the camera, not without leaving the driveway. She gave the Triumph throttle, banged it into second gear, speeding up.

An invisible hand made of hot air pressed back against her chest. It was like accelerating into an open oven.

Her front tire went up onto the grass. The rest of the bike followed. The cameraman seemed to hear the Triumph at last, the earth-shaking growl of the engine, and jerked his head up just in time to see her buzz by him, close enough to slap his face. He reared back so rapidly he threw himself off balance, began to topple over.

Vic blasted past. Her slipstream spun him like a top, and he fell into the road, helplessly tossing his camera as he went down. It made an expensive-sounding crunch hitting the blacktop.

As she came off the lawn and into the road, the back tire tore off the top layer of grass, just exactly the way she used to peel dried Elmer's glue off her palms in third-grade arts and crafts. The Triumph lurched to one side, and she felt she was about to drop it, smashing her leg beneath it.

But her right hand remembered what to do, and she gave the bike more throttle still, and the engine thundered, and it popped out of the turn like a cork that has been pushed underwater and released. The rubber found the road, and the Triumph leaped away from the cameras, the microphones, Tabitha Hutter, Lou, her cottage, sanity.

The House of Sleep

WAYNE COULD NOT SLEEP AND HAD NOTHING WITH WHICH TO DIStract his mind. He wanted to throw up, but his stomach was empty. He wanted out of the car but could see no way to manage it.

He had an idea to pull out one of the wooden drawers and beat it against a window, hoping to smash it. But of course the drawers wouldn't open when he tugged on them. He made a fist and threw all his weight into a tremendous haymaker, hit one of the windows with as much force as he could muster. A shivery, stinging jolt of pain shot up his knuckles and into his wrist.

The pain did not deter him; if anything, it made him all the more desperate and reckless. He pulled back his head and drove his skull into the glass. It felt as if someone had set a three-inch iron railway spike against his brow and pounded it in with Charlie Manx's silver hammer. Wayne was snapped back into blackness. It was as terrible as falling down a long flight of stairs, a sudden stomach-turning plunge into the dark.

His vision returned to him momentarily. At least he thought it was momentarily—maybe it was an hour later. Maybe it was three hours. However long it had been, when his sight and thoughts had cleared, he found that his sense of calm had been restored as well. The inside of his head was filled with a reverberating emptiness, as if someone had played a great crashing chord on a piano some minutes ago and the last echoes of it were only now fading away.

A dazed lassitude—not entirely unpleasant—stole over him. He felt no desire to move, to shout, to plan, to cry, to worry about what was next. His tongue gently probed at one of his lower front teeth, which felt loose and tasted of blood. Wayne wondered if he had struck his head so hard he'd managed to partially jar the tooth out of its socket. The roof of his mouth prickled against his tongue, felt abrasive, sandpapery. It didn't concern him much, was just something he noticed.

When he did finally move, it was only to stretch an arm out and pluck his moon ornament off the floor. It was as smooth as a shark's tooth, and its shape reminded him a bit of the special wrench his mother had used on the motorcycle, the tappet key. It was a kind of key, he thought. His moon was a key to the gates of Christmasland, and he could not help it—the notion delighted him. There was no such thing as arguing with delight. Like seeing a pretty girl with the sunlight in her hair, like pancakes and hot chocolate in front of a crackling fire. Delight was one of the fundamental forces of being, like gravity.

A great bronze butterfly crawled on the outside of the window, its furred body as thick as Wayne's finger. It was soothing to watch it clamber about, occasionally waving its wings. If the window was open, even a crack, the butterfly might join him in the backseat, and then he'd have a pet.

Wayne stroked his lucky moon, thumb moving back and forth, a simple, thoughtless, basically masturbatory gesture. His mother had her bike, and Mr. Manx had his Wraith, but Wayne had a whole moon to himself.

He daydreamed about what he'd do with his new pet butterfly. He liked the idea of teaching it to land on his finger, like a trained falcon. He could see it in his mind, resting on the tip of his index finger, fanning its wings in a slow, peaceful sort of way. Good old butterfly. Wayne would name it Sunny.

In the distance a dog barked, soundtrack of an indolent summer day. Wayne picked the loose tooth out of his gums and put it in the pocket of his shorts. He wiped the blood on his shirt. When he went back to rubbing his moon, his fingers spread the blood all over it.

What did butterflies eat? he wondered. He was pretty sure they dined on pollen. He wondered what else he could train it to do: if he could teach it to fly through burning hoops or walk across a miniature tightrope. He saw himself as a street performer, in a top hat, with a funny black stick-on mustache: Captain Bruce Carmody's Bizarre Butterfly Circus! In his mind he wore his moon ornament like a general's badge, right on his lapel.

He wondered if he could teach the butterfly to do wild loop-de-loops, like an airplane in a stunt show. The thought crossed his mind that he could rip off a wing and then it would fly in loop-de-loops for sure. He imagined that a wing would tear off like a piece of sticky paper, a slight resistance at first, then a satisfying little peeling sound.

The window rolled itself down an inch, the handle squeaking softly. Wayne did not rise. The butterfly reached the top of the glass, beat its wings once, and sailed in to land on his knee.

"Hey, Sunny," Wayne said. He reached out to pet it with his finger, and it tried to fly away, which was no fun. Wayne sat up and caught it with one hand.

For a while he tried to teach it to do tricks, but it wasn't long before the butterfly tired out. Wayne set it on the floor and stretched back on the couch to rest, a bit tired himself. Tired but feeling all right. He had milked a couple of good loop-de-loops out of the butterfly before it stopped moving.

He shut his eyes. His tongue restlessly probed the prickly roof of his mouth. His gum was still leaking, but that was okay. His own blood tasted good. Even as he dozed, his thumb went on stroking his little moon, the glossy-smooth curve of it.

Wayne did not open his eyes again until he heard the garage door rumbling into the ceiling. He sat up with some effort, the pleasant lethargy settled deep into his muscles.

Manx slowed as he approached the side of the car. He bent and tilted his head to one side—a querulous, doglike movement—and stared in through the window at Wayne.

"What happened to the butterfly?" he asked.

Wayne glanced at the floor. The butterfly was in a pile, both wings and all its legs torn off. He frowned, confused. It had been all right when they'd started playing.

Manx clucked his tongue. "Well, we have tarried here long enough. We had best be on our way. Do you need to go winkie-wee?"

Wayne shook his head. He looked at the butterfly again, with a creeping sense of unease, maybe even shame. He had a memory of tearing off at least one wing, but at the time it had seemed . . . *exciting.* Like peeling the tape off a perfectly wrapped Christmas present.

You murdered Sunny, Wayne thought. He unconsciously squeezed his moon ornament in one fist. *Mutilated it.*

He did not want to remember pulling its legs off. Picking them off one at a time while it kicked frantically. He scooped Sunny's remains up in one hand. There were little ashtrays, set into the doors, with walnut lids. Wayne opened one, stuffed the butterfly into it, let it fall shut. There. That was better.

The key turned itself in the ignition, the car jolting to life. The radio snapped on. Elvis Presley promised he would be home for Christmas. Manx eased in behind the steering wheel.

"You have snored the day away," he said. "And after all of yesterday's excitement, I am not surprised! I am afraid you slept through lunch. I would've woken you, but I reckoned you needed your sleep more."

"I'm not hungry," Wayne said. The sight of Sunny, all torn to pieces, had upset his stomach, and the thought of food—for some reason he had a visual image of sausages sweating grease—nauseated him.

"Well. We will be in Indiana this evening. I hope you have recovered your appetite by then! I used to know a diner on I-80 where you could get a basket of sweet-potato fries caked in cinnamon and sugar. *There* is a one-of-a-kind taste sensation for you! You cannot quit eating until they are all gone and you are licking the paper." He sighed. "I *do* like my sweets. Why, it is a miracle my teeth have not rotted out of my head!" He turned and grinned at Wayne over his shoulder, displaying a mouthful of brown mottled fangs, pointing this way and that. Wayne had seen elderly dogs with cleaner, healthier-looking teeth.

Manx clutched a sheaf of papers in one hand, held together by a big yellow paper clip, and he sat in the driver's seat, thumbing through them in a cursory sort of way. The pages looked like they had already been handled some, and Manx considered them for only half a minute before leaning over and shutting them in the glove compartment.

"Bing has been busy on his computer," Manx said. "I remember an era when you could get your nose sliced off for sticking it too far into another man's business. Now you can find out anything about anyone with the click of a button. There is no privacy and no consideration, and everyone is prying into things that aren't their affair. You can probably check on the intertube and find out what color underwear I have on today. Still, the technology of this shameless new era does offer some conveniences! You would not believe all the information Bing has dug up on this Margaret Leigh. I am sorry to say your mother's good friend is a drug addict and a woman of low character. I cannot say I am stunned. With your mother's tattoos and unfeminine mode of speech, that is exactly the crowd I would expect her to run with. You are welcome to read all about Ms. Leigh yourself if you like. I would not want you to be bored while we are on the road."

The drawer under the driver's seat slid open. The papers about Maggie Leigh were in them. Wayne had seen this trick a few times now and should've been used to it but wasn't.

He leaned forward and pulled out the sheaf of papers—and then the drawer banged shut, slamming closed so quickly and so loudly that Wayne cried out and dropped the whole mess on the floor. Charlie Manx laughed, the big, hoarse *hee-haw* of a country shithead who has just heard a joke involving a kike, a nigger, and a feminist.

"You did not lose a finger, did you? Nowadays cars come with all sorts of options nobody needs. They have radio beamed in from satellites, seat warmers, and GPS for people who are too busy to pay attention to where they are going—which is usually nowhere fast! But this Rolls has an accessory you will not find in many modern vehicles: a sense of humor! You'd better stay on your toes while you're in the Wraith, Wayne! The old lady almost caught you napping!"

And what a hoot that would've been. Wayne thought if he'd been a little slower, there was a good chance the drawer could've broken his fingers. He left the papers on the floor.

Manx put his arm on the divider and turned his head to look through the rear window as he backed out of the garage. The scar across his forehead was livid and pink and looked two months old. He had removed the bandage from his ear. The ear was still gone, but the chewed ruin had healed over, leaving a ragged nub that was slightly more palatable to the eyes.

NOS4A2 rolled halfway down the driveway, and then Manx pulled to a stop. Bing Partridge, the Gasmask Man, was walking across the yard, holding a plaid-patterned suitcase in one hand. He had put on a stained, dirty FDNY baseball cap to go with a stained, dirty FDNY T-shirt and grotesquely girlish pink sunglasses.

"Ah," Manx murmured. "It would've been just as well if you had slept through this part of the day also. I am afraid the next few minutes may be disagreeable, young Master Wayne. It is never pleasant for a child when the grown-ups fight."

Bing walked in a swift-legged way to the trunk of the car, bent, and tried to open it. Except the trunk remained shut. Bing frowned, struggling with it. Manx was twisted around in his seat to watch him through the rear window. For all his talk about how things were soon to become disagreeable, there was the hint of a smile playing at the corners of his lips.

"Mr. Manx!" Bing called. "I can't get the trunk open!"

Manx didn't answer.

Bing limped to the passenger-side door, trying to keep his weight off the ankle that Hooper had gnawed on. His suitcase banged against his leg as he walked.

As he put his hand on the latch for the passenger door, the lock banged down of its own accord.

Bing frowned, tugged on the handle. "Mr. Manx?" he said.

"I can't help you, Bing," Manx said. "The car doesn't want you."

The Wraith began to roll backward.

Bing wouldn't let go of the handle and was pulled alongside. He jerked at the latch again. His jowls wobbled.

"Mr. Manx! Don't go! Mr. Manx, wait for me! You said I could come!"

"That was before you let her get away, Bing. You let us down. *I* might forgive you. You know I have always thought of you as a son. But I have no say in this. You let her get away, and now the Wraith is letting *you* get away. The Wraith is like a woman, you know! You cannot argue with a woman! They are not like men. They do not operate by reason! I can feel that she is spitting mad at you for being so careless with your gun."

"No! Mr. Manx! Give me another chance. Please! I want another chance!"

He stumbled and banged his suitcase against his leg once again. It spilled open, dumping undershirts and underwear and socks down the length of the driveway.

"Bing," Manx said. "Bing, Bing. Go away. I'll come and play some other day."

"I can do better! I'll do whatever you want! Please, oh, please, Mr. Manx! *I want a second chance!*" Screaming now.

"Don't we all," Manx said. "But the only person who has been granted a second chance is Victoria McQueen. And that's just no good, Bing."

As the car backed up, it began to swing around, to face the road. Bing was pulled right off his feet and collapsed on the blacktop. The Wraith dragged him for several feet, squalling and yanking at the handle.

"Anything! *Any*thing! Mr. Manx! *Anything for you! My life! For you!*"

"My poor boy," Manx said. "My poor, sweet boy. Do not make me sad. You are making me feel awful! Let go of the door, please! This is hard enough!"

Bing let go, although Wayne could not say if he was doing as he was told or if his strength simply gave out. He flopped in the road, on his stomach, sobbing.

The Wraith began to accelerate away from Bing's house, away from the burned wreck of the church up the hill. Bing scrambled back to his feet and jogged after them for perhaps ten yards, although he was quickly outdistanced. Then he stopped in the middle of the road and began to beat his head with his fists, punching himself in the ears. His pink sunglasses hung askew, one lens smashed in. His wide, ugly face was a bright, poisonous shade of red.

"I would do *anything*!" Bing screamed. *"Anything! Just! Give! Me! One! More! Chance!"*

The Wraith paused at a stop sign, then turned the corner, and Bing was gone.

Wayne turned to face forward.

Manx glanced at him in the rearview mirror.

"I'm sorry you had to see all of that, Wayne," Manx said. "Terrible to see someone so upset, especially a goodhearted fellow like Bing. Just terrible. But also . . . also a bit silly, don't you think? Did you see how he wouldn't let go of the door? I thought we were going to drag him all the way to Colorado!" Manx laughed again, quite heartily.

Wayne touched his lips and realized, with a sick pang in his stomach, that he was smiling.

Route 3, New Hampshire

THE ROAD HAD A CLEAN SMELL, OF EVERGREENS, OF WATER, OF WOODS.

Vic thought there would be sirens, but when she looked in the left-hand mirror, she saw only a half mile of empty asphalt, and there was no sound at all but the controlled roar of the Triumph.

A passenger jet slid through the sky twenty-four thousand feet above her: a brilliant spoke of light, headed west.

At the next turn, she left the lake road and swung into the green hills mounded over Winnipesaukee, headed west herself.

She didn't know how to get to the next part, didn't know how to make it work, and thought she had very little time to figure it out. She had found her way to the bridge the day before, but that seemed a fantastically long time ago, almost as long ago as childhood.

Now it seemed too sunny and bright for something impossible to happen. The clarity of the day insisted on a world that made sense, that operated by known laws. Around every bend there was only more road, the blacktop looking fresh and rich in the sunshine.

Vic followed the switchbacks, climbing steadily into the hills, away from the lake. Her hands were slippery on the handlebars, and her foot hurt from pushing the sticky shift through the gears. She went faster and then faster still, as if she could tear that hole in the world by speed alone.

She blew through a town that was little more than a yellow caution light hanging over a four-way intersection. Vic meant to run the bike until it was out of gas, and then she might drop it, leave the Triumph in the dust, and start running, right down the center of the road, running until the fucking Shorter Way Bridge appeared for her or her legs gave out.

Only it wasn't going to appear, because there was no bridge. The only place the Shortaway existed was in her mind. With every mile this fact became clearer to her.

It was what her psychiatrist had always insisted it was: an escape hatch she leaped through when she couldn't handle reality, the comforting empowerment fantasy of a violently depressed woman with a history of trauma.

She went faster, taking the curves at almost sixty.

She was going so fast it was possible to pretend the water streaming from her eyes was a reaction to the wind blowing in her face.

The Triumph began to climb again, hugging the inside of a hill. On a curve, near the crest, a police cruiser blasted past, going the other way. She was close to the double line and felt the slipstream snatch at her, giving her a brief, dangerous moment of wobble. For an instant the driver was just an arm's length away. His window was down, his elbow hanging out, a dude with two chins and a toothpick in the corner of his mouth. She was so close she could've snatched the toothpick from between his lips.

In the next moment, he was gone and she was over the hill. He had probably been gunning it for that four-way intersection with the yellow caution light, looking to cut her off there. He would have to follow the winding road he was on all the way into town before he could turn and come back after her. She had maybe a full minute on him.

The bike swung through a high, tight curve, and she had a glimpse of Paugus Bay below, dark blue and cold. She wondered where she would be locked up, when she would next see the water. She had spent so much of her adult life in institutions, eating institutional food, living by institutional rules. Lights-out at eight-thirty. Pills in a paper cup. Water that tasted like rust, like old pipes. Stainless-steel toilet seats, and the only time you saw blue water was when you flushed.

The road rose and dropped in a little dip, and in the hollow there was a country store on the left. It was a two-story place made out of peeled logs, with a white plastic sign over the door that said NORTH COUNTRY VIDEO. Stores still rented videos out here—not just DVDs but videotapes, too. Vic was almost past the place when she decided to swing into the dirt lot and hide. The parking area extended around back, and it was dark there beneath the pines.

She stood on the rear brake, already going into her turn, when she remembered there *was* no rear brake. She grabbed the front brake. For the first time, it occurred to her that *it* might not be working either.

It was. The front brake grabbed hard, and she almost went over the handlebars. The rear tire whined shrilly across the blacktop, painting a black rubber streak. She was still sliding when she hit the dirt lot. The tires tore at the earth, raised clouds of brown smoke.

The Triumph jackhammered another twelve feet, past North Country Video, crunching to a stop at last in the back of the lot.

A nighttime darkness waited beneath the evergreens. Behind the building, a loop of sagging chain barred access to a footpath, a dusty trench carved through weeds and ferns. A dirt-bike run, maybe, or out-of-use hiking trail. She had not spied it from the road; no one would, set back as it was in the shadows.

She didn't hear the cop car until it was very close, her ears full of the sound of her own ragged breath and overworked heart. The cruiser shrieked past, the undercarriage crashing as it skipped over the frost heaves.

She saw a flicker of movement at the edge of her vision. She looked up at a plate-glass window, half pasted over with posters advertising the Powerball. A fat girl with a nose ring was staring out at her, her eyes wide with alarm. She had a phone to her ear, and her mouth was opening and closing.

Vic looked at the footpath on the other side of that chain. The narrow rut was drifted with pine needles. It pointed steeply downhill. She tried to think what was down there. Route 11, most likely. If the path didn't lead to the highway, she could at least follow it until it petered out, then park the bike in the pines. It would be peaceful among the trees, a good place to sit and wait for the police.

She shifted into neutral and walked it around the chain. Then she put her feet on the pegs and let gravity do the rest.

Vic rode through a felty darkness that smelled sweetly of firs, of Christmas—a thought that made her shiver. It reminded her of Haverhill, of the town woods, and of the slope behind the house where she had grown up. The tires bumped over roots and rocks, and the bike shimmied across the uncertain ground. It took great concentration to guide the motorcycle along the narrow rut. She stood on the pegs to watch the front tire. She had to stop thinking, had to go empty, couldn't spare any room inside her head for the police, or Lou, or Manx, or even Wayne. She could not try to work things out now; she had to focus instead on staying balanced.

It was, anyway, difficult to remain frantic in the piney gloom, with the light slanting down through the boughs and an atlas of white cloud inscribed on the sky above. The small of her back was stiff and tight, but the pain was sweet, made her aware of her own body working in concert with the bike.

A wind rushed in the tops of the pines with a gentle roar, like a river in flood.

She wished she had had a chance to take Wayne on the motorcycle. If she'd been able to show him this, these woods, with their sprawling carpet of rusty pine needles, beneath the sky lit up with the first best light of July, she thought it would've been a memory for both of them to hold on to for the rest of their lives. What a thing it would be, to ride through the scented shadows with Wayne clutching her tight, to follow a dirt path until they found a peaceful place to stop, to share out a homemade lunch and some bottles of soda, to doze off together by the bike, in this ancient house of sleep, with its floor of mossy earth and its high ceiling of crisscrossing boughs. When she closed her eyes, she could almost feel Wayne's arms around her waist.

But she only dared close her eyes a moment. She breathed out and looked up—and in that moment the motorcycle arrived at the bottom of the slope and crossed twenty feet of flat ground to the covered bridge.

Shorter Way

VIC TAPPED THE REAR BRAKE WITH HER FOOT, AN AUTOMATIC GESture that did nothing. The motorcycle kept on, rolling almost to the entrance of the Shorter Way Bridge before she remembered the front brake and eased herself to a stop.

It was ridiculous, a three-hundred-foot-long covered bridge sitting right on the ground in the middle of the woods, bridging nothing. Beyond the ivy-tangled entrance was an appalling darkness.

"Yeah," Vic said. "Okay. You're pretty Freudian."

Except it wasn't. It wasn't Mommy's coochie; it wasn't the birth canal; the bike wasn't her symbolic cock or a metaphor for the sexual act. It was a bridge spanning the distance between lost and found, a bridge over what was possible.

Something made a fluttering sound in among the rafters. Vic inhaled deeply and smelled bats: a musty animal smell, wild and pungent.

All those times she had crossed the bridge, not once had it been the fantasy of an emotionally disturbed woman. That was a confusion of cause and effect. She had been, at moments in her life, an emotionally disturbed woman because of all those times she had crossed the bridge. The bridge was not a symbol, maybe, but it was an expression of thought, *her* thoughts, and all the times she had crossed it had stirred up the life within. Floorboards had snapped. Litter had been disturbed. Bats had woken and flown wildly about.

Just inside the entrance, written in green spray paint, were the words THE HOUSE OF SLEEP →.

She put the bike into first and bumped the front tire up onto the bridge. She did not ask herself if the Shorter Way was really there, did not wonder if she was easing into a delusion. The issue was settled. Here it was.

The ceiling above was carpeted in bats, their wings closed around them to hide their faces, those faces that were her own face. They squirmed restlessly.

The boards went *ka-bang-bang-bang* under the tires of the bike. They were loose and irregular, missing in places. The whole structure shook from the force and weight of the bike. Dust fell from the beams above in a trickling rain. The bridge had not been in such disrepair when she last rode through. Now it was *crooked,* the walls visibly tilting to the right, like a corridor in a fun house.

She passed a gap in the wall, where a board was missing. A flurry of luminous particles snowed past the narrow slot. Vic eased almost to a stop, wanted a closer look. But then a board under the front tire cracked with a sound as loud as a gun firing, and she felt the wheel drop two inches. She grabbed the throttle, and the bike jumped forward. She heard another board snap under the back tire as she lunged ahead.

The weight of the bike was almost too much for the old wood. If she stopped, the rotted boards might give way beneath her and drop her into that . . . that . . . whatever that was. The chasm between thought and reality, between imagining and having, perhaps.

She couldn't see what the tunnel opened onto. Beyond the exit she saw only glare, a brightness that hurt her eyes. She turned her face away and spied her old blue-and-yellow bicycle, its handlebars and spokes hung with cobwebs. It was dumped against the wall.

The front tire of her motorcycle thumped over the wooden lip and dropped her out onto asphalt.

Vic glided to a stop and put her foot down. She shaded her eyes with one hand and peered about.

She had arrived at a ruin. She was behind a church that had been destroyed by fire. Only its front face remained, giving it the look of a movie set, a single wall falsely suggesting a whole building behind it. There were a few blackened pews and a field of smoked and shattered glass, strewn with rusting beer cans. Nothing beside remained. A sun-faded parking lot, boundless and bare, stretched away, lone and level, as far as she could see.

She banged the Triumph into first and took a ride around to the front of what she assumed was the House of Sleep. There she halted once more, the engine rumbling erratically, hitching now and then.

There was a sign out front, the sort with letters on clear plastic cards, that could be shifted around to spell different messages; it seemed more like the kind of sign that belonged in front of a Dairy Queen than in front of a church. Vic read what was written there, and her body crawled with chill.

THE NEW AMERICAN
FAITH TABERNACLE
GOD BURNED ALIVE
ONLY DEVILS NOW

Beyond was a suburban street, slumbering in the stuporous heat of late day. She wondered where she was. It might still be New Hampshire—but no, the light was wrong for New Hampshire. It had been clear and blue and bright there. It was hotter here, with oppressive clouds mounded in the sky, dimming the day. It felt like thunderstorm weather, and in fact, as she stood there straddling the bike, she heard the first rumbling detonation of thunder in the distance. She thought that in another minute or two it might begin to pour.

She scanned the church again. There were a pair of angled doors set against the concrete foundation. Basement doors. They were locked with a heavy chain and a bright brass lock.

Beyond, set back in the trees, was a sort of shed or barn, white with a blue-shingled roof. The shingles were fuzzed with moss, and there were even some weeds and dandelions growing right from the roof. There was a large barn door at the front, big enough to admit a car, and a side door with just one window. A sheet of paper was taped up inside the glass.

There, she thought, and when she swallowed, her throat clicked. *He's in there.*

It was Colorado all over again. The Wraith was parked inside the shed, and Wayne and Manx were sitting in it, waiting out the day.

The wind lifted, hot, roaring in the leaves. There was another sound as well, somewhere behind Vic, a kind of frantic, mechanical whirring, a steely rustle. She looked down the road. The closest house was a well-kept little ranch, painted strawberry pink with white trim so it resembled a Hostess snack cake, the ones with coconut on them. Sno Balls, Vic thought they were called. The lawn was filled with those spinning tinfoil flowers that people stuck in their yards to catch the wind. They were going crazy now.

A stubby, ugly retiree was out in his driveway, holding a pair of garden shears, squinting up at her. Probably a neighborhood-watch type, which meant if she wasn't dealing with a thunderstorm in five minutes, she would be dealing with the cops.

She rode the bike to the edge of the lot, then switched it off, left the keys in it. She wanted to be ready to go in a hurry. She looked again at the shed, standing to one side of the ruin. She noticed, almost as an afterthought, that she had no spit. Her mouth was as dry as the leaves rustling in the wind.

She felt pressure building behind her left eye, a sensation she remembered from childhood.

Vic left the bike, began walking toward the shed on her suddenly unsteady legs. Halfway there she bent and picked up a broken chunk of asphalt, the size of a dinner plate. The air vibrated with another distant concussive roll of thunder.

She knew it would be a mistake to call her son's name but found her lips shaping the word anyway: *Wayne, Wayne.*

Her pulse hammered behind her eyeballs, so the world seemed to twitch unsteadily around her. The overheated wind smelled of steel shavings.

When she was within five steps of the side door, she could read the hand-lettered sign taped up on the inside of the glass:

NO ADMITTANCE
TOWN PERSONNEL ONLY!

The chunk of asphalt went through the window with a pretty smash, tore the sign free. Vic wasn't thinking anymore, just moving. She had lived this scene already and knew how it went.

She might have to carry Wayne if there was something wrong with him, as there had been something wrong with Brad McCauley. If he was like McCauley—half ghoul, some kind of frozen vampire—she would fix him. She would get him the best doctors. She would fix him like she had fixed the bike. She had made him in her body. Manx could not simply unmake him with his car.

She shoved her hand through the shattered window to grab the inner doorknob. She fumbled for the bolt, even though she could see that the Wraith wasn't in there. There was room for a car, but no car was present. Bags of fertilizer were stacked against the walls.

"Hey! What are you doing?" called a thin, piping voice from somewhere behind her. "I can call the cops! I can call them right now!"

Vic turned the bolt, threw the door open, stood gasping, looking into the small, cool, dark space of the empty shed.

"I should've called the police already! I can have the whole *bunch* of you arrested for breaking and entering!" screamed whoever it was.

She was hardly listening. But even if she had been paying close attention she might not have recognized his voice. It was hoarse and strained, as if he had recently been crying or was about to start. There on the hill it did not once cross her mind that she had heard it before.

She turned on her heel, taking in a squat, ugly man in an FDNY T-shirt, the retiree who had been out in his yard with hedge clippers. He still held them. His eyes bulged behind glasses with thick black plastic frames. His hair was short and bristly and patchy, black mottled with silver.

Vic ignored him. She scanned the ground, found a chunk of blue rock, grabbed it, and stalked across to the slanted doors that led to the basement of the burned church. She dropped to one knee and began to strike at the big brassy Yale lock that kept those doors shut. If Wayne and Manx weren't in the shed, then this was the only place that was left. She didn't know where Manx had stashed the car, and if she found him asleep down there, she had no plans to ask him about it before using this stone on his head.

"Come on," she said to herself. "Come on and open the fuck up."

She banged the stone down into the lock. Sparks flew.

"That's private property!" cried the ugly man. "You and your friends have no right to go in there! That's it! I'm calling the police!"

It caught her notice then, what he was yelping. Not the part about the police. The other part.

She threw the stone aside, swiped at the sweat on her face, and shoved herself to her heels. When she rounded on him, he took two frightened steps back and nearly tripped over his own feet. He held the garden shears up between them.

"Don't! Don't hurt me!"

Vic supposed she looked like a criminal and a lunatic. If that was what he saw, she couldn't blame him. She had been both at different times in her life.

She held her hands out, patting the air in a calming gesture.

"I'm not going to hurt you. I don't want anything from you.

I'm just looking for someone. I thought there might be someone in there," she said, gesturing with her head back toward the cellar doors. "What did you say about 'my friends'? What friends?"

The ugly little gnome swallowed thickly. "They aren't here. The people you're looking for. They left. Drove away a little while ago. A half an hour or so. Maybe less."

"*Who?* Please. *Help me. Who* left? Was it someone in an—"

"An old car," the little man said. "Like an antique. He had it parked there in the shed . . . and I think he spent the night in there!" Pointing at the slanted basement doors. "I thought about calling the police. It isn't the first time there's been people in there doing drugs. But they're gone! They aren't here anymore. He drove away a while ago. A half an hour—"

"You said that," she told him. She wanted to grab him by his fat neck and shake him. "Was there a boy with him? A boy in the back of the car?"

"Why, I don't know!" the man said, and put his fingers to his lips and stared into the sky, an almost comic look of wonder on his face. "I *thought* there was someone with him. In the back. Yes. Yes, I bet there *was* a kid in the car!" He glanced at her again. "Are you all right? You look awful. Do you want to use my phone? You should have something to drink."

"No. Yes. I—thank you. All right."

She swayed, as if she had stood up too quickly. He had been here. Wayne had been here and gone. Half an hour ago.

Her bridge had steered her wrong. Her bridge, which always led her across the distance between lost and found, had not set her down in the right place at all. Maybe this was the House of Sleep, this derelict church, this litter of charred beams and broken glass, and she had *wanted* to find this place, had wanted it with all her heart, but only because Wayne was supposed to be here. Wayne was supposed to be *here*—not out on the road with Charlie Manx.

That was it, she supposed, in a weary sort of way. Just as Maggie

Leigh's Scrabble tiles could not give proper names—Vic remembered that now, was remembering a lot this morning—Vic's bridge needed to anchor either end on solid earth. If Manx was on an interstate somewhere, her bridge couldn't connect. It would be like trying to poke a bullet out of the air with a stick. (Vic flashed to a memory of a lead slug tunneling through the lake, remembered slapping at it, then finding it in her hand.) The Shortaway didn't know how to carry her to something that wouldn't stand still, so it had done the next-best thing. Instead of leading her to where Wayne was, it had brought her to where Wayne had last been.

Lurid red flowers grew along the foundation of the strawberry pink house. It was set up the street and away from other houses, a place nearly as lonely as a witch's cottage in a fairy tale—and in its own way as fantastical as a house made of gingerbread. The grass was neatly kept. The ugly little man led her around back, to a screen door that opened into a kitchen.

"I wish I could have a second chance," he said.

"At what?"

He seemed to need a moment to think about it. "A chance to do things over. I could've stopped them from going. The man and your son."

"How could you have known?" she asked.

He shrugged. "Did you come a long way?" he asked in his thin, off-key voice.

"Yes. Sort of," she said. "Not really."

"Oh. I see now," he said, without the slightest trace of sarcasm.

He held the door open for her, and she preceded him into the kitchen. The air-conditioning was a relief, almost as good as a glass of cold water with a sprig of mint in it.

It was a kitchen for an old woman who knew how to make homemade biscuits and gingerbread men. The house even smelled a little like gingerbread men. The walls were hung with cutesy kitchen plaques, rhyming ones.

I PRAY TO GOD ON MY KNEES
DON'T LET MOMMY FEED ME PEAS.

Vic saw a battered green metal tank propped in a chair. It reminded her of the oxygen tanks that had been delivered weekly to her mother's house in the last few months of Linda's life. She assumed that the man had a wife somewhere who was unwell.

"My phone is your phone," he said in his loud, off-key voice.

Thunder cannonaded outside, hard enough to shake the floor.

She passed the kitchen table on her way to an old black phone, bolted to the wall next to the open basement door. Her gaze shifted. There was a suitcase on the table, unzipped to show a mad tangle of underwear and T-shirts, also a winter hat and mittens. Mail had been pushed off the table onto the floor, but she didn't see it until it was crunching underfoot. She stepped quickly off of it.

"Sorry," she said.

"Don't worry!" he said. "It's my mess. It's my mess, and I'll clean it up." He bent and scooped up the envelopes in his big, knuckly hands. "Bing, Bing, you ding-a-ling. You made a mess of everything!"

It was a bad little song, and she wished he hadn't sung it. It seemed like something someone would do in a dream beginning to go rotten around the edges.

She turned to the phone, a big, bulky thing with a rotary dial. Vic meant to pick up the receiver but then rested her head against the wall and shut her eyes instead. She was so tired, and her left eye hurt so fucking much. Besides. Now that she was here, she didn't know who to call. She wanted Tabitha Hutter to know about the church at the top of the hill, the torched house of God (GOD BURNED ALIVE ONLY DEVILS NOW) where Manx and her son had spent the night. She wanted Tabitha Hutter to come here and talk to the old man who had seen them, the old man named Bing (Bing?). But she didn't even know where *here* was yet and wasn't sure it was in her interest to call the police until she did.

Bing. The name disconcerted her in some way.

"What did you say your name is?" she asked, wondering if she could've heard him wrong.

"Bing."

"Like the search engine?" she asked.

"That's right. But I use Google."

She laughed—a sound that expressed exhaustion more than humor—and cast a sidelong glance toward him. He had turned his back to her, was tugging something off a hook next to the door. It looked like a shapeless black hat. She had another glance at that old, dented green tank and saw that it wasn't oxygen after all. The stenciling on the side said SEVOFLURANE, FLAMMABLE.

She turned away from him, back to the phone. She lifted the receiver but still didn't know who she wanted to call.

"That's funny," she said. "I have a search engine of my own. Can I ask you a weird question, Bing?"

"Sure," he said.

She glided her finger around the rotary dial without turning it.

Bing. Bing. Less like a name, more like the sound a little silver hammer would make hitting a glass bell.

"I'm a bit overtaxed, and the name of this town is slipping my mind," she said. "Can you tell me where the hell I am?"

Manx had a silver hammer, and the man with him had a gun. *Bang,* he'd said. *Bang.* Right before he shot her. Only he said it in a funny, singsongy way, so it was less like a threat, more like a jump-rope rhyme.

"You bet," Bing said from behind her, his voice muffled, as if he had a hankie over his nose.

She recognized his voice then. It had been muffled the last time she'd heard it and her ears had been ringing from gunfire but she recognized his voice at last.

Vic pivoted on her heel, already knowing what she would see.

Bing wore his old-fashioned WWII gasmask again. He still held the garden shears in his right hand.

"You're in the House of Sleep," he said. "This is the end of the line for you, bitch."

And he hit her in the face with the garden shears and broke her nose.

The House of Sleep

VIC TOOK THREE SMALL, STAGGERING STEPS BACKWARD, AND HER heels struck a doorsill. The only open door was the one into the basement. She had time to recall this before the next thing happened. Her legs gave way, and she fell straight back, as if to sit down, but there was no chair there. There was no floor either. She dropped and kept dropping.

This is going to hurt, she thought. There was no alarm in the idea; it was the simple acceptance of fact.

She experienced a brief feeling of suspension, her insides going elastic and strange. The wind swished past her ears. She glimpsed a bare lightbulb overhead and plywood sheeting between exposed beams.

Vic hit a stair, ass-first, with a bony crunch, and was flipped, as casually as someone might toss a pillow in the air. She thought of her father pitching a cigarette out the window of a moving car, the way it would hit the asphalt and sparks would fly on impact.

The next step she hit on her right shoulder, and she was thrown again. Her left knee clubbed something. Her left cheek struck something else—it felt like getting booted in the face.

Vic assumed when she hit bottom that she would smash like a vase. Instead she landed on a lumpy mound of plastic-wrapped softness. She slammed into it face-first, but the lower part of her body continued traveling, her feet pedaling madly in the air. *Look, Mom, I'm doing a handstand!* Vic remembered screaming one Fourth of July, staring at a world where the sky had become grass and the ground had become stars. She thudded to a stop at last, lying on her back on the plastic-wrapped mass, the staircase now behind her.

Vic stared back up the steep flight of steps, seeing them upside down. She could not feel her right arm. There was a pressure in her left knee that she believed would soon turn to excruciating pain.

The Gasmask Man came down the steps, holding the green metal tank in one hand, carrying it by the valve. He had left the pruning shears behind. It was terrible, the way the gasmask took his face away, replacing his mouth with a grotesque, alien knob and his eyes with clear plastic windows. A part of her wanted to scream, but she was too stunned to make any noise.

He came off the bottom step and stood with her head between his boots. It occurred to her too late that he was going to hurt her again. He lifted the tank in both hands and brought it down into her stomach, pounded the air out of her. Vic coughed explosively and rolled onto her side. When she got her breath back, she thought she would throw up.

The tank clanged as he set it down. The Gasmask Man collected a handful of her hair and yanked. The tearing pain forced a weak cry out of her, in spite of her decision to remain silent. He wanted her on all fours, and she obliged him because it was the only way to make the pain stop. His free hand slipped under her and groped her breast, squeezing it the way someone might test a grapefruit for firmness. He tittered.

Then he dragged. She crawled while she could, because it hurt less, but it didn't matter to him whether it hurt or not, and when her arms gave out, he kept dragging, pulling her along by her hair. She was horrified to hear herself scream the word *"Please!"*

Vic had only confused impressions of the basement, which seemed less a room than a single long corridor. She glimpsed a washer and dryer; a naked female mannequin wearing a gasmask; a grinning bust of Jesus, pulling his robe open to show an anatomically correct heart, the side of his face browned and blistered as if he had been held in a fire. She heard a metallic, droning chime coming from somewhere. It went on and on without cessation.

The Gasmask Man stopped at the end of the hall, and she heard a steely clunk, and he slid aside a heavy iron door on a track. Her perceptions couldn't keep up with the pace of events. A part of her was still back down the hallway, just catching a glimpse of that burned Jesus. Another part of her was in the kitchen, seeing the battered green tank leaning in the chair, SEVOFLURANE, FLAMMABLE. A part of her was up at the torched wreckage of the New American Faith Tabernacle, holding a rock in both hands and banging it down into a shiny brass lock, hard enough to throw copper sparks. A part of her was in New Hampshire, bumming a smoke off Detective Daltry, palming his brass lighter, the one with Popeye on it.

The Gasmask Man forced her to walk on her knees across the track, still yanking her by the hair. In his other hand, he dragged the green tank, SEVOFLURANE. That was what was making the chiming sound—the base of the tank rang softly and continuously as it was pulled across the concrete. It droned like a Tibetan prayer bowl, a monk rolling the hammer around and around the holy dish.

When she was over the track, he jerked her forward, hard, and she found herself on all fours once again. He planted his foot in her ass and shoved, and her arms gave out.

She went down on her chin. Her teeth banged together, and a blackness leaped up from every object in the room—the lamp in the corner, the cot, the sink—as if each piece of furniture had a secret shadow self that could be jolted awake, startled into flight like a flock of sparrows.

For a moment that flock of shadows threatened to descend upon her. She chased it back with a cry. The room smelled like old pipes, concrete, unwashed linens, and rape.

Vic wanted to get up, but it was hard enough remaining conscious. She could feel that trembling, living darkness, ready to come uncoiled and spring up all around her. If she passed out now, she would at least not feel him raping her. She would not feel him killing her either.

The door rattled and banged shut with a silvery clash that reverberated in the air. The Gasmask Man gripped her shoulder, pushed her onto her back. Her head rolled loosely on her neck, and her skull rapped the pitted concrete. He knelt over her with a clear plastic mask in one hand, contoured to fit over her mouth and nose. The Gasmask Man took her by the hair and pulled her head up to snap the mask over her face. Then he put his hand on it and held it there. Clear plastic tubing ran back to the tank.

She swatted at the hand clamping the mask to her face, tried to scratch his wrist, but he now wore a pair of heavy canvas gardening gloves. She couldn't get at any vulnerable meat.

"Breathe deep," he said. "You'll feel better. Just relax. Day is done, gone the sun. God burned to death, and I shot him with my gun."

He kept the one hand over the mask. With the other he reached back and twisted a valve on the tank. She heard a hiss and felt something cool blowing against her mouth, then gasped at a saccharine blast of something that smelled like gingerbread.

She grabbed at the tubing and wound it around one hand and yanked. It came out of the valve with a tinny pop. The tank hissed a visible stream of white vapor. The Gasmask Man glanced back at the green metal tank but did not seem perturbed.

"About half of them does that," he said. "I don't like it because it wastes the tank, but if you want to do things hard, we can do them hard."

He ripped the plastic mask off her face, tossed it into the corner.

She started to push her way up onto her elbows, and he drove his fist into her stomach. She doubled over, wrapping her arms around the hurt, holding it tightly, like a loved one. She took a big whooping breath, and the room was filled with the woozy-making fragrance of gingerbread-scented gas.

The Gasmask Man was short—half a foot shorter than Vic—and dumpy, but despite that he moved with the agility of a street performer, a guy who could play the banjo while strolling around on stilts. He picked up the tank in both hands and walked it toward her, pointing the open valve at her. The gas was a white spray as it came from the end of the valve but soon dispersed, became invisible. She gulped another mouthful of air that tasted like dessert. Vic crab-walked backward, pushing herself across the floor on hands and feet, sliding on her butt. She wanted to hold her breath but couldn't do it. Her trembling muscles were starved for oxygen.

"Where are you going?" he asked through his gasmask. He walked after her with the tank. "It's airtight in here. Anywhere you go, you still gotta breathe. I got three hundred liters in this tank. I could knock out a tent fulla elephants with three hundred liters, honey."

He kicked one of her feet, knocking her legs askew, then pushed the toe of his left sneaker into her crotch. She choked on a cry of revulsion. Vic had a fleeting but intense sensation of violation. For one moment she wished the gas had already put her out, didn't want to feel his foot there, didn't want to know what was going to happen next.

"Bitch, bitch, go to sleep," the Gasmask Man said, "Take a nap while I fuck you deep." He tittered again.

Vic pushed herself back into a corner, thumped her head on the plastered wall. He was still walking at her, holding the tank, fogging the room. The sevoflurane was a white mist that made every object soft and diffuse at the edges. There had been one cot on the other side of the room, but now there were three, tightly overlapping one another, and they were half hidden behind the smoke. In the gathering haze, the Gasmask Man himself split in two, then came back together.

The floor was slowly tipping beneath her, turning into a slide, and at any moment she'd go whisking down it, away from reality and into unconsciousness. She kicked her heels, fighting to hold on, to hold fast in the corner of the room. Vic held her breath, but her lungs were filled not with air but with pain, and her heart was slamming like the engine of the Triumph.

"You're here, and it's all better!" the Gasmask Man shrieked, his voice delirious with excitement. "You're my second chance! You're here, and now Mr. Manx will come back and I'll get to go to Christmasland! You're here, and I'm *finally* going to get what's coming to me!"

Images flickered rapidly through her mind, like playing cards shuffled by a magician. She was in the backyard again, Daltry thumbing his lighter, getting no flame, so she took it from him, and blue fire leaped from the starter on her first try. She had paused to look at the picture on the side of the lighter, Popeye throwing a roundhouse, and a sound effect, she couldn't remember what. Then she visualized the warning on the side of the tank of sevoflurane: FLAMMABLE. This was followed by a simple thought, not an image but a decision. *Take him with me. Kill this little turd.*

The lighter—she *thought*—was in her right-hand pocket. She went to dig it out, but it was like reaching into Maggie's bottomless Scrabble bag; it went on forever and forever and forever.

The Gasmask Man stood at her feet, pointing the valve down at her, holding the tank in both arms. She could hear the tank whispering to her, a long, deadly command to be silent: *Shhh.*

Her fingers touched a slab of metal, closed around it. She yanked her hand out of her pocket and held the lighter up between her and the Gasmask Man, as if it were a cross to ward off a vampire.

"Don't make me," she gasped, and tasted another mouthful of poison gingerbread smoke.

"Don't make you what?" he said.

She flipped back the top of the lighter. The Gasmask Man heard it click, saw it for the first time, drew back a step.

"Hey," he said, a note of warning in his voice. He took another step back, cradling the tank in his arms like a child. "Don't! That isn't safe! Are you *crazy*?"

Vic thumbed the steel gear. It made a harsh, scraping noise and spit a burst of white sparks, and for one miraculous moment it lit a ribbon of blue fire in the air. The flame unwound like a snake, the air burning, racing straight back at the tank. That faint white vapor, spraying from the valve, became a savage tongue of fire.

The sevoflurane tank was, briefly, a flamethrower with a short range, spraying flame from side to side as the Gasmask Man reeled away from Vic. He stumbled backward three more steps—inadvertently saving her life in the process. In the flaring light, Vic could read what it said on the side of the lighter:

KABLOOEY.

It was as if the Gasmask Man were pointing a rocket launcher at his chest and triggered it at point-blank range. It exploded through the bottom, a cannonade of white burning gas and shrapnel that lifted him off his feet and punched him back into the door. Three hundred liters of pressurized sevoflurane exploded all at once, turning the tank into a jumbo stick of TNT. Vic had no frame of reference for the sound it made, a great slam that felt like sewing needles stabbed into her eardrums.

The Gasmask Man struck the iron door almost hard enough to tear it off its track. Vic saw him crash into it through a blast of what seemed like pure light, the air glowing with a gassy brilliance that made half the room disappear for an instant in a blinding white flash. She instinctively lifted her hands to protect her face and saw the fine gold hairs on her bare arms crinkling and shriveling from the heat.

In the aftermath of the explosion, the world was changed. The room beat like a heart. Objects throbbed in time to the slamming of her pulse. The air was filled with a whirling golden smoke.

When she had entered the room, she'd seen shadows leaping up from behind the furniture. Now they were casting flashes of brightness. Like the tank of gas, they seemed to be trying to swell and erupt.

She felt a wet trickling on her cheek and thought it was tears, but when she touched her face, her fingertips came away red.

Vic decided she ought to go. She got up and took a step, and the room slewed violently to the left, and she fell back down.

She took a knee, just like they told you to do in Little League when someone was hurt. Burning scraps fell through the air. The room lurched to the right, and she lurched with it, onto her side.

The brightness jumped up from the cot, the sink, flashed around the edges of the doorway. She had not known that every object in the world could contain a secret core of both darkness and light, needing only a violent shock to reveal one or the other. With each thump of her heart, the brightness brightened. She could not hear any sound except the ragged working of her lungs.

She breathed deeply the perfume of burned gingerbread. The world was a bright bubble of light, doubling in size before her, swelling, straining, filling her vision, growing toward the inevitable—

Pop.

CHRISTMASLAND
JULY 7–9

The St. Nicholas Parkway

NORTH OF COLUMBUS, WAYNE CLOSED HIS EYES FOR A MOMENT, and when he opened them, the Christmas moon was sleeping in the night above and either side of the highway was crowded with snowmen who turned their heads to watch the Wraith pass.

The mountains rose before them, a monstrous wall of black stone at the edge of the world. The peaks were so high it looked as if the moon itself might get snagged among them.

In a fold a little below the highest part of the highest mountain was a basket of lights. It shone in the darkness, visible from hundreds of miles away, a great glowing Christmas ornament. The sight of it was so exciting that Wayne could hardly remain in his seat. It was a cup of fire, a scoop of hot coals. It throbbed, and Wayne throbbed with it.

Mr. Manx had one hand loose on the wheel. The road was so straight it could've been drawn with a ruler. The radio was on, and a boys' choir sang "O Come All Ye Faithful." In Wayne's heart was an answer to their sacred invitation: *We are on our way. We are coming as fast as we can. Save a little Christmas for us.*

The snowmen stood in bunches, in families, and the breeze generated by the car snatched at their striped scarves. Snowmen fathers and snowgirl mothers with their snowchildren and snowpuppies.

Top hats were in abundance, as were corncob pipes and carrot noses. They waved the crooked sticks of their arms, saluting Mr. Manx, Wayne, and NOS4A2 as they went by. The black coals of their eyes gleamed, darker than the night, brighter than the stars. One snowdog had a bone in his mouth. One snowdaddy held a mistletoe over his own head, while a snowmommy was frozen in the act of kissing his round white cheek. One snowchild stood between decapitated parents, holding a hatchet. Wayne laughed and clapped; the living snowmen were the most delightful thing he had ever seen. What foolishness they got up to!

"What do you want to do first when we get there?" Mr. Manx asked from the gloom of the front seat. "When we get to Christmasland?"

The possibilities were so exciting it was hard to put them in order. "I'm going in the rock-candy cave to see the Abominable Snowman. No! I'm going to ride in Santa's Sleigh and save him from the cloud pirates!"

"There is a plan!" Manx said. "Rides first! Games after!"

"What games?"

"The kids have a game called scissors-for-the-drifter, which is the best time you've ever had! And then there is stick-the-blind. Son, you have not had fun until you have played stick-the-blind with someone really spry. Look! Over on the right! There is a snow lion biting the head off a snow sheep!"

Wayne turned his whole body to look out the right-hand window, but when he did, his grandmother was in his way.

She was just as he had seen her last. She was brighter than anything in the backseat, as bright as snow in the moonlight. Her eyes were hidden behind silver half-dollars that flashed and gleamed. She had sent him half-dollars for his birthdays but had never come herself, said she didn't like to fly.

".sky false a is That," said Linda McQueen. ".same the not are fun and Love .reverse in go to trying aren't You .fight to trying aren't You."

"What do you mean, the sky is false?" Wayne asked.

She pointed out the window, and Wayne craned his neck and looked up. A moment ago the sky had been whirling with snow. Now, though, it was filled with static—a million billion fine flecks of black and gray and white, buzzing furiously over the mountains. The nerve endings behind Wayne's eyeballs pulsed at the sight of it. It wasn't painfully bright—it was actually quite dim—but there was something about the furious motion of it that made it hard to watch. He flinched, shut his eyes, drew back. His grandmother faced him, eyes hidden behind those coins.

"If you wanted to play games with me, you should've come to visit me in Colorado," Wayne said. "We could've talked backward as much as you wanted. We didn't even talk forward when you were alive. I don't understand why you want to talk now."

"Who are you speaking with, Wayne?" Manx asked.

"Nobody," Wayne said, and reached past Linda McQueen, opened the door, and shoved her out.

She weighed nothing. It was easy, like pushing away a bag of sticks. She flipped out of the car and hit the blacktop with a dry thud and shattered with a pretty musical smashing sound, and at that moment Wayne jumped awake in

Indiana

AND TURNED HIS HEAD AND LOOKED OUT THE REAR WINDOW. A bottle had smashed in the road. Powdered glass cobwebbed the asphalt, shards tinkling and rolling. Manx had tossed a bottle of something. Wayne had seen him do this once or twice already. Charlie Manx didn't seem like the sort of guy inclined to recycle.

When Wayne sat up—digging his knuckles into his eyes—the snowmen were gone. So were the sleeping moon and the mountains and the burning gem of Christmasland in the distance.

He saw high green corn and a honky-tonk with a lurid neon sign depicting a thirty-foot-tall blonde in a short skirt and cowboy boots. When the sign blinked, she kicked a foot, tipped her head back, closed her eyes, and kissed the darkness.

Manx looked at him in the rearview mirror. Wayne felt flushed and muddleheaded from sleeping heavily, and perhaps for that reason it did not startle him to see how young and healthy Manx looked.

His hat was off, and he was as bald as ever, but his scalp was smooth and pink, not white and splotchy. It had, only yesterday, looked like a globe, displaying a map of continents no one in his right mind would ever want to visit: the Isle of Sarcoma, North Liver Spot. Manx's eyes peered out from beneath sharp, arched eyebrows, the color of hoarfrost. Wayne did not think he had seen him blink once in the days they'd been together. For all he knew, the man had no eyelids.

Yesterday morning he had looked like a walking corpse. Now he looked like he was in his mid-sixties, vital and healthy. But there was a kind of avid stupidity in his eyes—the greedy stupidity of a bird looking at carrion in the road and wondering if it could get some tasty bits without being run down.

"Are you eating me?" Wayne asked.

Manx laughed, a harsh caw. He even sounded like a crow.

"If I have not taken a bite out of you yet, I am not likely to," Manx said. "I am not sure you would make much of a meal. There is not a lot of meat on you, and what *is* there is starting to smell a bit gamy. I am holding out for an order of those sweet-potato fries."

Something was wrong with Wayne. He could feel it. He could not put his finger on what it was. He was achy and sore and feverish, but that might've just been from sleeping in the car, and this was something more. The best he could manage was a sense that his reactions to Manx were off. He had almost been surprised into laughter when Manx said the word "gamy." He had never heard a word like that dropped into conversation before, and it struck him as hilarious. A normal person, though, wouldn't laugh at his kidnapper's choice of words.

"But you're a vampire," Wayne said. "You're taking something out of me and putting it into you."

Manx considered him briefly in the rearview mirror. "The car is making both of us better. It is like one of these vehicles they have now that they call hybrids. Do you know about the hybrids? They run half on gasoline, half on good intentions. But this is the *original* hybrid! This car runs on gasoline and *bad* intentions! Thoughts and feelings are just another kind of energy, same as oil. This vintage Rolls-Royce is getting fine mileage out of all your bad feelings and all the things that ever hurt and scared you. I am not speaking poetically. Do you have any scars?"

Wayne said, "I slipped with a putty knife, and it gave me a scar right here." He held up his right hand, but when he looked at it, he could not find the hairline scar that had always been on the ball of his thumb. It mystified him what could've happened to it.

"The road to Christmasland removes all sorrows, eases all pain, and erases all scars. It takes away all the parts of you that weren't doing you any good, and what it leaves behind is made clean and pure. By the time we arrive at our destination, you will be innocent not only of pain but also of the *memory* of pain. All your unhappiness is like grime on a window. When the car is done with you, it will be cleared away and you will shine clear. And so will I."

"Oh," Wayne said. "What if I wasn't in the car with you? What if you went to Christmasland alone? Would the car still make you . . . younger? Would it still make you shine?"

"My, you have a lot of questions! I bet you are a straight-A student! No. I cannot get to Christmasland alone. I cannot find the road by myself. Without a passenger the car is just a car. That is the best thing about it! I can be made happy and well only by making *others* happy and well. The healing road to Christmasland is just for the innocent. The car will not let me hog it all for myself. I have to do good for others if I want good to be done to me. If only the rest of the world worked that way!"

"Is this the healing road to Christmasland?" Wayne asked, peering out the window. "It looks more like I-80."

"It *is* Interstate 80 . . . now that you are awake. But just a minute ago, you were dreaming sweet dreams and we were on the St. Nick Parkway, under old Mr. Moon. Don't you remember? The snowmen and the mountains in the distance?"

Wayne would not have been more jolted if they had hit a deep pothole. He did not like to think that Manx had been in his dream with him. He flashed back, briefly, to a memory of that deranged sky filled with static. *Sky false a is that.* Wayne knew that Grandma Lindy was trying to tell him something—trying to give him a way to protect himself from what Manx and his car were doing to him—but he didn't understand her, and it seemed like it would be too much effort to figure it out. Besides, it was a little late for her to start giving him advice. She had not exactly strained herself to tell him anything of use when she was alive, and he suspected her of disliking his father just because Lou was fat.

"When you drift off, we will find it again," Manx said. "The sooner we get there, the sooner you can ride the Sleighcoaster and play stick-the-blind with my daughters and their friends."

They were in a trench slicing through a forest of corn. Machines stood over the rows, black girders that arced in the sky like the proscenium above a stage. The thought occurred to Wayne that those machines were sprayers, full of poison. They would drench the corn in a lethal rain to keep it from being eaten by invasive species. Those exact words—"invasive species"—rang through his brain. Later the corn would be lightly washed and people would eat it.

"Does anyone ever leave Christmasland?" Wayne asked.

"Once you get there, you will not want to leave. Everything you could ever want will be right there. There are all the best games. There are all the best rides. There is more cotton candy than you could eat in a hundred years."

"But *could* I leave Christmasland? If I wanted to?"

Manx gave him an almost hostile glance in the mirror. "Then again, maybe some teachers felt you were badgering them with all your questions. What were your grades like?"

"Not very good."

"Well. You will be glad to know there is no school in Christmasland. I hated school myself. I would rather make history than read about it. They like to tell you that learning is an adventure. But that is a lot of hooey. Learning is learning. *Adventure* is adventure. I think once you know how to add and subtract and can read suitably well, anything else is likely to lead to big ideas and trouble."

Wayne took this to mean that he would not be able to leave Christmasland. "Do I get some last requests?"

"Look here. You act like you have been sentenced to death. You are not on death row. You will arrive at Christmasland better than ever!"

"But if I'm not coming back, if I have to be in Christmasland forever . . . there are some things I want to do before I get there. Can I have a last meal?"

"What do you mean? Do you think you will not be fed in Christmasland?"

"What if there's food I want that I can't get there? Can you get whatever you want to eat in Christmasland?"

"There is cotton candy and cocoa and hot dogs and the candy on a stick that always hurts my teeth. There is everything a child could want."

"I'd like an ear of corn. A buttered ear of corn," Wayne said. "And a beer."

"I am sure it would be no trouble to get you some corn and—What did you say? Root beer? There is good root beer out here in the Midwest. Even better is sarsaparilla."

"Not root beer. A *real* beer. I want a Coors Silver Bullet."

"Why would you want a beer?"

"My dad said I'd get to have one with him on the porch when I was twenty-one. He said I could have one on the Fourth of July and watch the fireworks. I was looking forward to it. I guess that isn't going to happen now. Also, you said it's Christmas every day in Christmasland. I guess that means no July Fourth. They aren't very patriotic in Christmasland. I'd like some sparklers, too. I had sparklers in Boston."

They went over a long, low bridge. The grooved metal hummed soulfully under the tires. Manx did not speak again until they reached the other side.

"You are full of talk tonight. We have gone a thousand miles, and this is the most I have heard out of you. Let's see if I have this right. You would like me to buy you a tallboy, an ear of sweet corn, and enough fireworks for your own private Fourth of July. Are you sure there is not anything else you might want? Were you planning to have goose-liver pâté and caviar with your mother when you graduated from high school?"

"I don't want my own private Fourth of July. I just want some sparklers. And maybe a couple rockets." He paused, then said, "You told me you owed me one. For killing my dog."

There followed a period of grim silence.

"I did," Manx admitted at last. "I had put that out of my mind. I am not proud of it. Would you consider us square if I got you a beer and an ear of corn and some fireworks?"

"No. But I won't ask for anything else." He looked out the window and spied the moon. It was a chipped sliver of bone, faceless and remote. Not as good as the Christmasland moon. Everything was better in Christmasland, Wayne supposed. "How did you find *out* about Christmasland?"

Manx said, "I drove my daughters there. And my first wife." He paused, then added, "My first wife was a difficult woman. Hard to satisfy. Most redheads are. She had a long list of complaints that she held against me, and she made my own children mistrust me. We had two daughters. Her father gave me money to set me up in business, and I spent it on a car. This car. I thought Cassie—that was my first wife—would be happy when I came home with it. Instead she was impertinent and difficult as always. She said I had wasted the money. I said I was going to be a chauffeur. She said I was going to be a pauper and so were they. She was a scornful woman and abused me in front of the children, which is a thing no man should stand." Manx flexed his hands on the wheel, his knuckles whitening. "Once my wife threw an oil lamp at my back, and my best coat caught fire. Do you think she ever apologized? Well! Think again. She would make fun of me at Thanksgiving and family get-togethers, pretending she was me and that she had just been set aflame. She would run around gobbling like a turkey and waving her arms, screaming, 'Put me out, put me out!' Her sisters always had a good laugh at that. Let me tell you something. The blood of a redheaded woman is three degrees cooler than the blood of a normal woman. This has been established by medical studies." He gave Wayne a wry look in the rearview. "Of course, the very thing that makes them impossible to live with is what makes it hard for a man to stay away, if you catch my meaning."

Wayne didn't but nodded anyway.

Manx said, "Well. All right then. I think we have reached an understanding. I know a place where we can buy fireworks so loud and bright you will be deaf and blind by the time we are done shooting them off! We should get to the Here Library just after dark tomorrow. We can shoot them off there. By the time we are done launching rockets and throwing cherry bombs, people will think the Third World War is under way." He paused, then added in a sly tone, "Perhaps Ms. Margaret Leigh will join us for the festivities. I wouldn't mind lighting a fuse under her, just to teach her a thing or two about minding her own beeswax."

"Why does she matter?" Wayne asked. "Why don't we just leave her alone?"

A large green moth hit the windshield with a soft, dry smack, made an emerald smear on the glass.

"You are a clever young man, Wayne Carmody," Manx said. "You read all the stories about her. I am sure if you put your mind to it, you will see why she is of concern to me."

Back when it was still light, Wayne had flicked through the collection of papers Manx had brought to the car, items Bing had found online that concerned Margaret Leigh. There were a dozen stories in all, telling a single larger story about abandonment, addiction, loneliness . . . and odd, unsettling miracles.

The first piece dated back to the early nineties and had run in the

Cedar Rapids Gazette: "Psychic or Lucky Guesser? Local Librarian's 'Wild Hunch' Saves Kids." It told the story of a man named Hayes Archer who lived in Sacramento. Archer had packed his two sons into his brand-new Cessna and lifted off with them for a moonlight flight along the California coast. His plane wasn't the only thing that was new. So was his pilot's license. Forty minutes after heading out, Archer's single-engine Cessna made several erratic maneuvers, then disappeared from the radar. It was feared he had lost sight of land in a gathering fog and crashed into the sea while trying to find the horizon. The story got some play in the national news, Archer being worth a small fortune.

Margaret Leigh had called the police in California to tell them Archer and his children weren't dead, hadn't crashed into the sea. They had made land and gone down in a gorge. She couldn't give the exact location but felt that the police should search the coast for some point at which it was possible to find salt.

The Cessna was discovered forty feet off the ground, upside down in a redwood tree, in—wait for it—Salt Point State Park. The boys were unharmed. The father had a broken back but was expected to survive. Maggie said her unlikely insight had come to her in a flash while playing Scrabble. The article ran alongside a photograph of the upside-down plane and another of Maggie herself, bent over a Scrabble board at a tournament. The caption below this second photo said, *"With Her Lucky Hunches, It's Too Bad Maggie's Game of Choice Is Scrabble and Not the Lottery!"*

There had been other insights over the years: a child found in a well, information about a man lost at sea while attempting to sail around the world. But they came less and less often, further and further apart. The last, a little article about Maggie helping to locate a runaway, had appeared in 2000. Then there was nothing until 2008, and the articles that followed were not about miracles but something like the opposite.

First there had been a flood in Here, Iowa, a lot of damage, a drowned library. Maggie had nearly drowned herself, trying to rescue books, and been treated for hypothermia. Fund-raisers failed to collect enough money to keep the library open, and the place was shuttered.

In 2009 Maggie had been charged with public endangerment for starting a fire in an abandoned building. She had drug paraphernalia in her possession at the time.

In 2010 she had been arrested and charged with squatting and possession of heroin.

In 2011 she was arrested for solicitation. Maybe Maggie Leigh could predict the future, but her psychic gift had not warned her to stay clear of the undercover cop in the lobby of a Cedar Rapids motel. She got thirty days for it. Later that same year, she was picked up again, but this time her destination was the hospital, not jail; she was suffering from exposure. In that article her "plight" was described as "all too frequent among Iowa's homeless," which was how Wayne found out she was living on the street.

"You want to see her because she knew you were coming and she told my mom," Wayne said finally.

"I *need* to see her because she knew I was on the road and wanted to make *trouble* for me," Manx said. "And if I do not have words with her, I cannot be sure she will not make trouble for me again. This is not the first time I have had to deal with someone of her ilk. I try whenever possible to avoid people like her. They are always nettlesome."

"People like her . . . You mean other librarians?"

Manx snorted. "You are being coy with me. I am glad to see you recovering your sense of humor. I mean to say there are other people besides me who can access the secret shared worlds of thought." He reached up and tapped his temple, to show where that world resided. "I have my Wraith, and when I am behind the wheel of this car, I can find my way onto the secret roads that lead to Christmasland. I have known others who could use totems of their own to turn reality inside out. To reshape it like the soft clay it is. There was Craddock McDermott, who claimed that his spirit existed in a favorite suit of his. There is the Walking Backwards Man, who has an awful watch that runs in reverse. You do not want to meet the Walking Backwards Man in a dark alley, child! Or anywhere else! There is the True Knot, who live on the road and are in much the same line of work as myself. I leave them be and they are glad to return the favor. And our Maggie Leigh will have a totem of her own, which she uses to pry and spy. Probably these Scrabble tiles she mentions. Well. She seems to have taken quite an interest in me. I guess if we are driving by, it would only be polite to pay a visit. I would like to meet her and see if I can't cure her of her curiosity!"

He shook his head and then laughed. That husky-hoarse caw of his was an old man's laugh. The road to Christmasland could make his body young, but it couldn't do anything about the way he laughed.

He drove. The dotted yellow line stammered past on the left.

Finally Manx sighed and went on. "I don't mind telling you, Wayne, almost all of the trouble I've ever known started with one woman or another. Margaret Leigh and your mother and my first wife were all cut from the same cloth, and Lord knows there have been plenty more where they came from. Do you know what? All the happiest times in my life were times when I was free of the feminine influence! When I didn't have to make accommodations. Men spend most of their lives being passed from woman to woman and being pressed into service for them. You cannot imagine the life I have saved you from! Men cannot stop thinking about women. They get thinking about a lady and it is like a hungry man thinking about a rare steak. When you are hungry and you smell a steak on the grill, you get distracted by that tight feeling in your throat and you quit thinking. Women are aware of this. They take advantage of it. They set terms, same as your mother sets terms before you come to dinner. If you don't clean your room, change your shirt, and wash your hands, you aren't allowed to sit at the dinner table. Most men figure they are worth something if they can meet the terms a woman sets for them. It provides them with their whole sense of value. But when you take a woman out of the picture, a man can get a little quiet inside. When there's no one to bargain with, except for yourself and other men, you can figure yourself out. That always feels good."

"Why didn't you divorce your first wife?" Wayne asked. "If you didn't like her?"

"No one did back then. It never even crossed my mind. It crossed my mind to leave. I even did leave a time or two. But I came back."

"Why?"

"I got hungry for steak."

Wayne asked, "How long ago was it—when you were first married?"

"Are you asking how old I am?"

"Yes."

Manx smiled. "I will tell you this: On our first date, Cassie and I went to see a silent movie! It was that long ago!"

"What movie?"

"It was a horror picture from Germany, although the title cards were in English. During the scary parts, Cassie would hide her face against me. We attended the show with her father, and if he had not been there, I believe she would've crawled into my lap. She was only sixteen at the time, just a nub of a thing, graceful and considerate and shy. This is the way with many women. In youth they are precious gems of possibility. They shudder with feverish life and desire. When they turn spiteful, it is like a chick molting, shedding the fuzz of youth for darker feathers! Women often give up their early tenderness as a child gives up his baby teeth."

Wayne nodded and thoughtfully tugged one of his upper teeth out of his mouth. He poked his tongue at the hole where it had been, the blood oozing in a warm trickle. He could feel a new tooth, beginning to protrude where the old one had been, although it felt less like a tooth, more like a small fishing hook.

He put the lost tooth in the pocket of his shorts, with the others. He had lost five teeth in the thirty-six hours he had been in the Wraith. He wasn't worried about it. He could feel rows and rows of small new teeth coming in.

"Later, you know, my wife accused me of being a vampire, just like you," Manx said. "She said I was like the fiend in that first movie we saw together, the German picture. She said I was draining the life out of our two daughters, feeding off them. But here it is, so many years later, and my daughters are still going strong, happy and young and full of fun! If I were trying to drain the life out of them, I guess I did a poor job of it. For a few years there, my wife made me so unhappy I was about ready to kill her and me and the children, too, just to be done with it. But now I can look back and laugh. Have a peek at my license plate sometime. I took my wife's horrid ideas about me and made a joke out of them. That is the way to survive! You have to learn to laugh, Wayne. You have to keep finding ways to have fun! Do you think you can remember that?"

"I think so," Wayne said.

"This is all right," Manx told him. "Two guys driving together at night! This is just fine. I don't mind saying you are better company than that Bing Partridge. At least you do not feel the need to make a foolish song out of everything." In a shrill, piping voice, Manx sang, *"I love you, I love me, I love playing with my winkie-wee!"* He shook his head. "I have had a number of long trips with Bing, and each was longer than the last. You cannot imagine what a relief it is to be with someone who is not always singing foolish songs or asking foolish questions."

"Can we get something to eat soon?" Wayne asked.

Manx slapped the wheel and laughed. "I guess I spoke too quickly—because if that is not a foolish question, it is close to it, young Master Wayne! You were promised some sweet-potato fries, and by God I mean for you to have them. I have brought over a hundred children to Christmasland in the last century, and I have not starved one to death yet."

The diner of the fabled sweet-potato fries was another twenty minutes west, an installation of chrome and glass set in a parking lot the size of a football field. Sodium-vapor lights on thirty-foot-high steel poles lit the blacktop as bright as day. The lot was crowded with eighteen-wheelers, and through the front windows Wayne could see that every stool along the bar was occupied, as if it were twelve noon and not twelve at night.

The whole country was on the watch for an old man and a child in an antique Rolls-Royce Wraith, but not one person in the diner looked outside and took note of them, and Wayne was not surprised. He had by now accepted that the car could be *seen* but not *noticed.* It was like a channel on TV that was broadcasting static—everyone skipped right over it. Manx parked up front, nose-in to the side of the building, and it did not once occur to Wayne to try jumping or screaming or banging on the glass.

"Don't go anywhere," Manx said, and winked at Wayne before he climbed out of the car and made his way inside.

Wayne could see through the windscreen and into the diner, and he watched Manx weave through the crowd bunched around the front counter. The TVs above the bar showed cars zooming around a racetrack; then the president behind a podium, waving his finger; then an icy blonde speaking into a microphone while she stood in front of a lake.

Wayne frowned. The lake looked familiar. The picture cut, and suddenly Wayne was looking at the rental house on Winnipesaukee, cop cars parked along the road out front. There in the diner, Manx was watching the TV, too, his head tilted back to see.

The picture cut again, and Wayne saw his mother coming out of the carriage house on the Triumph. She wasn't wearing a helmet, and her hair whipped behind her, and she rode straight at the camera. The cameraman couldn't get out of the way in time. His mother side-swiped him as she sped past. The falling camera offered a whirling view of sky, grass, and gravel before hitting the ground.

Charlie Manx walked briskly out of the diner, got behind the wheel, and NOS4A2 glided back onto the road.

His eyes were filmed over, and the corners of his mouth were pinched in a hard, disagreeable frown.

"I guess we're not going to have those sweet-potato fries," Wayne said.

But if Charlie Manx heard him, he gave no sign.

The House of Sleep

SHE DID NOT FEEL HURT; SHE WAS NOT IN PAIN. PAIN WOULD COME later.

Nor did it seem to her that she woke up, that there was ever a single moment of rising to awareness. Instead the parts of her began, reluctantly, to fit themselves back together. It was long, slow work, as long and slow as fixing the Triumph had been.

She remembered the Triumph before she even remembered her own name.

Somewhere a phone rang. She heard it clearly, the brash, old-fashioned rattle of a hammer on a bell, once, twice, three times, four. The sound called her back to the world but was gone by the time she knew she was awake.

The side of her face was wet and cool. Vic was on her stomach, on the floor, head turned to the side, cheek in a puddle. Her lips were dry and cracked, and she could not remember ever being so thirsty. She lapped at the water and tasted grit and cement, but the puddle was cool and good. She licked her lips to moisten them.

There was a boot near her face. She could see the black rubber waffling on the sole and a dangling shoelace. She had been seeing this boot off and on for an hour now, registering it for a moment, then forgetting about it as soon as she closed her eyes again.

Vic could not say where she was. She supposed she should get up and find out. She thought there was a good chance that the carefully fitted-together fragments of herself would collapse once more into glittering powder when she tried, but she didn't see any way around it. She sensed that no one would be coming to check on her anytime soon.

She had been in an accident. On the motorcycle? No. She was in a basement. She could see the stained concrete walls, the surface flaking away to show stone behind. She could make out a faint basement odor as well, partly obscured by other smells: a strong reek of seared metal and a whiff of fecal matter, like an open latrine.

She got her hands under her and pushed herself up to her knees.

It didn't hurt as bad as she thought it would. She felt aches in her joints, in the small of her back, in her ass, but they were like the aches caused by flu, not like the aches of shattered bones.

When she saw him, it came back to her, all of it, in a single piece. Her escape from Lake Winnipesaukee, the bridge, the ruined church, the man named Bing who had tried to gas her and rape her.

The Gasmask Man was in two pieces, connected by a single fatty string of gut. The top half of him was out in the hall. His legs were just inside the door, his boots close to where Vic had been sprawled.

The metal tank of sevoflurane had shattered, but he still held the pressure regulator that had been attached to the top, and some of the tank was attached to that—a helmet-shaped dome of twisted metal spikes. He was the thing that smelled like the ruptured septic tank, probably because his internal septic tank had in fact ruptured. She could smell his bowels.

The room looked skewed, knocked crooked. Vic felt dizzy taking it all in, as if she had sat up too quickly. The bed had been flipped over, so she could see the underside of it, the springs and legs. The sink had come away from the wall, hung at a forty-five-degree angle above the floor, supported only by a pair of pipes, which had come loose from their braces. Water bubbled from a cracked joint, pooling upon the floor. Vic thought if she had dozed a while longer, there was an excellent chance she could've drowned.

It took some doing to get to her feet. Her left leg didn't want to unbend, and when it did, she felt a stab of pain intense enough to cause her to draw a sharp breath through clenched teeth. The kneecap was bruised in shades of green and blue. She didn't dare put much weight on it, suspected it would fold under any real pressure.

Vic took a last look around the room, a visitor to a grubby exhibit in some museum of suffering. No, nothing else to see here. Let's move along, folks. We have some fabulous pieces to examine in the next room.

She stepped between the Gasmask Man's legs and then over him, being careful not to snag a foot on that low gut-string trip wire. The sight of it was so unreal she couldn't feel ill.

Vic maneuvered around the top half of his body. She didn't want to look at his face and kept her eyes averted while she moved past him. But before she had gone two steps back the way she'd come, she couldn't help herself and glanced over her shoulder.

His head was turned to the side. The clear eyewindows showed staring, shocked eyes. The respirator had been punched backward to fill his open mouth, a gag made of melted black plastic and charred fiber.

She made her way down the hall. It was like crossing the deck of a boat beginning to capsize. She kept drifting to her right and putting a hand against the wall to steady herself. Only there was nothing wrong with the hallway. Vic herself was the boat in danger of rolling over, sinking back down into a churning darkness. She forgot to go easy once and let her weight settle on the left leg. The knee immediately folded, and she threw out an arm, grabbing for something to support her. Her hand closed on the bust of Jesus Christ, his face charred and bubbled on one side. The bust sat atop a bookshelf crammed with pornography. Jesus grinned at her lewdly, and when she drew her hand away, it was streaked with ash. GOD BURNED ALIVE ONLY DEVILS NOW.

She would not forget about the left leg again. A thought occurred to her, random, not even entirely intelligible: *Thank God it's a British bike.*

At the base of the stairs, her feet caught on a mound of garbage bags, a plastic-wrapped weight, and she tipped forward and fell into it—for the second time. She'd landed on this same mass of garbage bags when the Gasmask Man had knocked her down the stairs; they had cushioned her fall and quite likely saved her from shattering her neck or skull.

It was cold and heavy but not entirely stiff. Vic knew what was under the plastic, knew by the sharp raised edge of hip and the flat plane of chest. She did not want to see or know, but her hands tore at the plastic anyhow. The corpse wore a Glad-bag shroud, held tightly shut by duct tape.

The smell that gushed out was not the odor of decay but worse in some ways: the cloying fragrance of gingerbread. The man beneath was slim and had probably been handsome once. He hadn't decomposed so much as mummified, his skin shriveling and yellowing, the eyes sinking back into his sockets. His lips were parted as if he had died in the middle of uttering a cry, although that might've been an effect of his flesh tightening and drawing back from his teeth.

Vic exhaled; it sounded curiously like a sob. She put her hand on the man's cold face.

"I'm sorry," Vic said to the dead man.

She couldn't fight it, had to cry. She had never been what anyone would call a crying woman, but in some moments tears were the only reasonable response. To weep was a kind of luxury; the dead felt no loss, wept for no one and nothing.

Vic stroked the man's cheek again and touched a thumb to his lips, and that was when she saw the sheet of paper, mashed up and shoved into his mouth.

The dead man looked at her pleadingly.

Vic said, "Okay, friend," and plucked the paper out of the dead man's mouth. She did it without any disgust. The dead man had faced a bad end here, had faced it alone, had been used, and hurt, and discarded. Whatever the dead man had wanted to say, Vic wanted to listen, even if she was too late for it to do any good.

The note was written in smudged pencil, with a shaky hand. The scrap of paper was a torn shred of Christmas wrapping.

> My head is clear enuff to write. Only time in days. The essentials:
>
> - I am Nathan Demeter of Brandenburg, KY
> - Was held by Bing Partridge
> - Works for a man named Manks
> - I have a daughter, Michelle, who is beautiful and kind.
>
> Thank God the car took me, not her. Make sure she reads the following:
>
> I love you girl. He can't hurt me too bad because when I close my eyes I see you.
>
> It is all right to cry but don't give up on laughter.
>
> Don't give up on happiness.
>
> You need both. I had both.
>
> Love you kid—your father

Vic read it while sitting against the dead man and was careful not to cry on it.

After a time she swiped at her face with the backs of her hands. She looked up the stairs. The thought of how she had come down them produced a brief but intense sensation of dizziness. It amazed her that she had gone down them and lived. She had come down a lot quicker than she was going to go up. The left knee was throbbing furiously now, stabs of white pain shooting from it in rhythm with her pulse.

She thought she had all the time in the world to make it up the stairs, but halfway to the top the phone began to ring again. Vic hesitated, listening to the brash clang of hammer on bell. Then she began to hop, clutching the handrail and hardly touching her left foot to the floor. *I'm a little Dutch girl, dressed in blue. Here are the things I like to do,* sang a piping little-girl voice in her mind, chanting a hopscotch song that Vic had not thought of in decades.

She reached the top step and went through the door into blinding, overpowering sunlight. The world was so bright it made her woozy. The phone rang again, going off for the third or fourth time. Pretty soon whoever was calling would quit.

Vic grabbed for the black phone, hanging from the wall just to the right of the basement door. She held the doorframe in her left hand, realized only absently that she was still holding the note from Nathan Demeter. She put the receiver to her ear.

"My Lord, Bing," said Charlie Manx. "Where have you been? I have been calling and calling. I was beginning to worry you had done something rash. It is not the end of the world, you know, that you are not coming with me. There may be another time, and meanwhile there are many things you can do for me. For starters you can fill me in on the latest news about our good friend Ms. McQueen. I heard a news report a while ago that she rode away from her little cottage in New Hampshire and vanished. Has there been any word of her since? What do you think she's been up to?"

Vic swallowed air, exhaled slowly.

"Oh, she's been all kinds of busy," Vic said. "Most recently she's been helping Bing redecorate his basement. I felt like it needed some color down there, so I painted the walls with the motherfucker."

Manx was silent just long enough for Vic to wonder if he had hung up. She was about to say his name, find out if he was still there, when he spoke again.

"Good gravy," he said again. "Do you mean to tell me poor Bing is dead? I am sorry to hear it. We parted on unhappy terms. I feel bad about that now. He was, in many ways, a child. He did some awful things, I suppose, but you cannot blame him! He did not know any better!"

"Shut up about him. You listen to me. I want my son back, and I'm coming to get him, Manx. I'm coming, and you don't want to be with him when I find him. Pull over. Wherever you are, pull over. Let my boy out at the side of the road, unhurt. Tell him to wait for me and that Mom will be there before he knows it. Do that and you don't have to worry about me looking for you. I'll let you slide. We'll call it even." She didn't know if she meant it, but it sounded good.

"How did you get to Bing Partridge's, Victoria? That is what I want to know. Was it like in Colorado that time? Did you go there on your bridge?"

"Is Wayne hurt? Is he all right? I want to talk to him. Put him on."

"People in hell want ice water. You answer my questions and we'll see if I answer yours. Tell me how you got to Bing's and I will see what I can do."

Vic trembled furiously, the beginnings of shock settling in. "You tell me first if he's alive. God help you if he isn't. If he isn't, Manx, if he *isn't,* what I did to Bing is nothing compared to what I'll do to you."

"He is well. He is a perfect little ray of sunshine! You get that, and that's all you get for now. Tell me how you arrived at Bing's. Was it on your motorbike? It was a bicycle in Colorado. But I suppose you have a new ride now. And did your new ride take you to your bridge? Answer me and I'll let you speak to him."

She tried to decide what to say, but no lie would come to mind, and she wasn't sure it would change a damn thing if he knew. "Yeah. I crossed the bridge, and it took me here."

"So," Manx said. "You've got yourself a mean set of wheels. You've got a bike with an extra gear, is that it? But it didn't take you to *me*. It took you to the House of Sleep. Now, I think there is a reason for that. I've got a ride with a few extra gears in it myself, and I know something about how they work. These things do have their quirks." He paused, then said, "You told me to pull over and leave your son by the side of the road. You said you would be there before he knows it. The bridge can only take you to a fixed point, is that it? That would make sense. It's a *bridge,* after all. The two ends have to rest on something, even if it is just resting on two fixed ideas."

"My son," she said. "My son. I want to hear his voice. You promised."

"Fair is fair," Charlie Manx said. "Here he is, Vic. Here is the little man himself."

Shoot the Moon Fireworks, Illinois

IN THE DUSTY BRIGHT OF EARLY AFTERNOON, MR. MANX SWUNG THE Wraith off the road and into the dooryard of a fireworks warehouse. The place advertised itself with a sign that showed an engorged and furious moon with a rocket jammed in one eye, bleeding fire. Wayne laughed just to see it, laughed and squeezed his moon ornament.

The shop was a single long building with a wooden hitching post out front for horses. It came to Wayne then that they were back out west, where he had lived most of his life. Places up north had hitching posts out front sometimes, if they wanted to look rustic, but when you got out west, you sometimes saw piles of dry horseshit not far from posts like that; that was how you knew you were back in cowboy country. Although a lot of cowboys rode ATVs and listened to Eminem these days.

"Are there horses in Christmasland?" Wayne asked.

"Reindeer," Manx said. "Tame white reindeer."

"You can ride them?"

"You can feed them right out of your hand!"

"What do they eat?"

"Whatever you offer them. Hay. Sugar. Apples. They are not fussy eaters."

"And they're all white?"

"Yes. You do not see them very often, because they are so hard to pick out against the snow. There is always snow in Christmasland."

"We could paint them!" Wayne exclaimed, excited by the thought. "Then they would be easier to see." He had been having a lot of exciting thoughts lately.

"Yes," Manx said. "That sounds like fun."

"Paint them red. Red reindeer. As red as fire trucks."

"That would be festive."

Wayne smiled at the thought of it, of a tame reindeer patiently standing in place while he ran a paint roller over it, coloring him a bright candy-apple red. He ran his tongue over his prickly new teeth, mulling the possibilities. He thought when he got to Christmasland, he would drill a hole in his old teeth, put a string through them, and wear them as a necklace.

Manx leaned to the glove compartment and opened it and removed Wayne's phone. He had been using it off and on all morning. He was, Wayne knew, calling Bing Partridge and not getting an answer. Mr. Manx never left a message.

Wayne looked out the window. A man was coming out of the fireworks place with a bag in one arm. He held the hand of a blond-haired little girl skipping along beside him. It would be funny to paint a little girl bright red. To take her clothes off and hold her down and paint her wriggling, tight little body. To paint all of her. To paint her right, you would want to shave off all that hair of hers. Wayne wondered what a person could do with a bag full of blond hair. There had to be something fun you could do with it.

"My Lord, Bing," Mr. Manx said. "Where have you been?" Opening his door and climbing out of the car to stand in the lot.

The girl and her father climbed into his pickup, and the truck backed out across the gravel. Wayne waved. The little girl saw him and waved back. Wow, she had great hair. You could make a rope four feet long out of all that smooth, golden hair. You could make a silky golden noose and hang her with it. That was a wild idea! Wayne wondered if anyone had ever been hanged with their own hair.

Manx was on the phone for a while in the parking lot. He paced, and his boots raised chalk clouds in the white dust.

The lock popped up on the door behind the driver's seat. Manx opened it and leaned in.

"Wayne? Do you remember yesterday I said if you were good, you could talk to your mother? I would hate for you to think Charlie Manx doesn't know how to keep his word! Here she is. She would like to hear how you are doing."

Wayne took the phone.

"Mom?" he said. "Mom, it's me. How are you?"

There was hiss and crackle, and then he heard his mother's voice, choked with emotion. "Wayne."

"I'm here. Can you hear me?"

"Wayne," she said again. "*Wayne.* Are you okay?"

"Yeah!" he said. "We stopped for fireworks. Mr. Manx is buying me some sparklers and maybe a bottle rocket. Are you all right? You sound like you're crying."

"I miss you. Mama needs you back, Wayne. I need you back, and I'm coming to get you."

"Oh. Okay," he said. "I lost a tooth. A *few* teeth, actually! Mom, I love you! Everything is okay. I'm okay. We're having fun!"

"Wayne. You're *not* okay. He's doing something to you. He's getting in your head. You have to stop him. You have to fight him. He's not a good man."

Wayne felt a nervous flutter in his stomach. He moved his tongue over his new, bristling, hooklike teeth. "He's buying me fireworks," he said sullenly. He had been thinking about fireworks all morning, about punching holes in the night with rockets, setting the sky on fire. He wished it were possible to light clouds on fire. That would be a sight! Burning rafts of clouds falling from the sky, gushing black smoke as they went down.

"He killed Hooper, Wayne," she said, and it was like being slapped in the face. Wayne flinched. "Hooper died fighting for you. *You* have to fight."

Hooper. It felt as if he had not thought of Hooper in years. He remembered him now, though, his great sad, searching eyes staring out of his grizzled yeti face. Wayne remembered bad breath, warm silky fur, stupid cheer . . . and how he had died. He had chomped the Gasmask Man in the ankle, and then Mr. Manx—then Mr. Manx—

"Mom," he said suddenly. "I think I'm sick, Mom. I think I'm all poisoned inside."

"Oh, baby," she said. She was crying again. "Oh, baby, you hold on. Hold on *to yourself.* I am coming."

Wayne's eyes stung, and for a moment the world blurred and doubled. It surprised him, to feel close to tears. He did not really feel sad after all; it was more like the memory of sadness.

Tell her something she can use, he thought. Then he thought it again, but slowly this time, and backward: *Use. Something.* ***Tell.***

"I saw Gran'ma Lindy," he blurted suddenly. "In a dream. She talked all scrambled up, but she was trying to say something about fighting him. Only it's hard. It's like trying to lift a boulder with a spoon."

"Whatever she said, just do it," his mother said. "Try."

"Yeah. Yeah, I will. Mom. Mom, something else," he said, his voice quickening with a sudden urgency. "He's taking us to see—"

But Manx reached into the back of the car and snapped the phone out of Wayne's hand. His long, scrawny face was flushed, and Wayne thought there was a vexed look in his eyes, as if he had lost a hand of cards he'd expected to win.

"Well, that is enough chitchat," Mr. Manx said, in a cheery voice that did not match the glare in his eyes, and he slammed the door in Wayne's face.

As soon as the door was closed, it was as if an electrical current had been cut. Wayne slumped back into the leather cushions, feeling tired, his neck stiff and his temples throbbing. He was upset, he realized. His mother's voice, the sound of her crying, the memory of Hooper biting and dying, worried him and gave him a nervous tummy.

I am poisoned, he thought. *Poisoned am I.* He touched his front pocket, feeling the lump made by all the teeth he had lost, and he thought of radiation poisoning. *I am being irradiated,* he thought next. "Irradiated" was a fun word, a word that brought to mind giant ants in black-and-white movies, the kinds of films he used to watch with his father.

He wondered what would happen to ants in a microwave. He supposed they would just fry; it didn't seem likely they would grow. But you couldn't know without trying it! He stroked his little moon ornament, imagining ants popping like corn. There had been a vague notion in the back of his mind—something about trying to *think* in reverse—but he couldn't hold on to it. It wasn't *fun.*

By the time Manx got back into the car, Wayne was smiling again. He wasn't sure how long it had been, but Manx had finished his phone call and gone into Shoot the Moon Fireworks. He had a slender brown paper bag, and poking out of the top of the bag was a long green tube in a single cellophane package. The labels on the side of the tube identified it as an AVALANCHE OF STARS—THE PERFECT ENDING TO THE PERFECT NIGHT!

Manx looked over the front seat at Wayne, his eyes protruding a little from his head, his lips stretched in a disappointed grimace.

"I have bought you sparklers and a rocket," Manx said. "Whether we will use either of them is another question. I am sure you were about to tell your mother we are on our way to see Miss Maggie Leigh. That would've been spoiling my fun. I am not sure why I should go out of my way to provide you with a good time when you seem set on denying me *my* small pleasures."

Wayne said, “I have a terrible headache.”

Manx shook his head furiously and slammed the door and tore out of the dusty lot, throwing a cloud of brown smoke. He was in a sulk for two or three miles, but not far from the Iowa border a fat hedgehog tried to waddle across the road, and the Wraith struck it with a loud thud. The sound was so noisy and unexpected that Wayne couldn’t help himself and yelped with laughter. Manx looked back and gave him a warm, begrudging smile, then put on the radio, and the two of them sang along to “O Little Town of Bethlehem,” and everything was better.

The House of Sleep

"Mom, something else. He's taking us to see—" Wayne said, but then there was a clatter, a thunk, and the loud thud of a slamming door.

"Well, that is enough chitchat," Manx said, in his sunny, carnival barker's voice. "The good little man has been through a lot lately. I wouldn't like him to become overwrought!"

Vic wept. She put a fist against the kitchen counter and swayed, crying into the phone.

The child she had heard on the other end of the line spoke in Wayne's voice . . . but was not Wayne. Not exactly. There had been a dreamy, spacey disconnect—not only from the situation but from the serious, self-contained child he had always been. He had only finally sounded like himself at the very end, after she reminded him about Hooper. Then, for a moment, he seemed confused and afraid, but himself. He sounded drugged, too, like a person just resurfacing from deep anesthesia.

The car was *anesthetizing* him in some way. Anesthetizing him while it drained him of his essential Wayneness, leaving behind only a happy, thoughtless *thing*. A vampire, she guessed, like Brad McCauley, the cold little boy who had tried to kill her at the cottage above Gunbarrel all those years ago. There was a line of reasoning there that she could not bear to follow, that she had to turn away from or she might start to scream.

"Are you all right, Victoria? Should I call back another time?"

"You're killing him," she said. "He's dying."

"He's never been more alive! He's a fine boy. We get along like Butch and Sundance! You can trust me to treat him well. You have my promise, in fact, that I will not hurt him. I have never hurt any child. Not that anyone would know it after all the lies you told about me. I have lived my entire life in the service of children, but you were happy to tell everyone what a great kiddie fiddler I am. I would be within my rights, you know, to do terrible things to your son. I would only be living up to the tall tales you told about me. I hate to fall short of the myth. But I don't have it in me to be vicious to children." He paused, then added, "Adults, however, are a different story."

"Let him go. Please let him go. This isn't about him. You know it isn't about him. You want to get even with me. I understand. Park somewhere. Just park and wait. I'll use my bridge. I'll find you. We can trade. You can let him out of the car, and I'll get in, and you can do whatever you like to me."

"You would have a lot of making up to do. You told the whole world that I sexually assaulted you. I feel bad that I stand accused of something I never had the pleasure to try."

"You want that? Would that make you happy?"

"If I raped you? Goodness no! I am just being spleeny. I do not understand such depravity. I am aware that many women enjoy a brisk whack on the backside during the sexual act and to be called degrading names, but that is merely a bit of sport. To take a woman against her wishes? I don't think so! You may not believe it, but I have daughters of my own. I will tell you, though, sometimes I think that you and I got off on the wrong foot! I am sorry about that. We never had a chance to get to know each other. I bet you would have liked me if we had met under other circumstances!"

"Holy shit," she said.

"It is not so unbelievable! I have been married twice and have rarely been without female companionship. Someone found *something* to like."

"What are you saying? You want to fucking *date*?"

He whistled. "Your mouth! You could make a stevedore blush! Considering how your first date with Bing Partridge went, I suppose it would be better for my long-term health if we just settle for talking. Come to think of it, our first couple of encounters weren't terribly romantic. You wear a man down, Victoria." He laughed again. "You've cut me, lied about me, and sent me to jail. You're worse than my first wife. Still . . . you've got something that keeps a man coming back for more! You do keep a boy thinking!"

"I'll give you something to think about. Think about this: You can't drive forever. Sooner or later you'll have to pull over. Sooner or later you're going to stop somewhere to close your eyes for a while. And when you open them, I'll be there. Your friend Bing got off easy, Charlie. I am one mean, degenerate cunt, and I will fucking burn you to death in your car and take my son back."

"I am sure you will *try*, Victoria," he said. "But have you stopped to think what you will do if you finally catch up to us and he doesn't *want* to go with you?"

The phone went dead.

AFTER MANX HUNG UP, VIC BENT OVER, GASPING, AS IF SHE HAD JUST finished a long and furious run. Her weeping was an angry thing, as physical and exhausting as vomiting. It was in her heart to take the receiver and begin smashing it into the wall, but a colder part of her stayed her hand.

If you're going to be mad, she heard her father say, *then use it, and don't be used* by *it*.

Had he ever actually said such a thing? She didn't know, only that she heard his voice in her head.

When she was done crying, her eyes were sore and her face burned. She started to walk to the sink, felt something tug at her hand, and realized she was still holding the receiver, which was attached to the wall phone by a long black coiled line.

Vic walked it back to its cradle, then stood looking at the rotary dial. She felt empty and sore, yet now that her crying jag was past, she also felt, for the first time in days, a kind of peace, much like the calm she felt when she was sketching one of her Search Engine illustrations.

There were people to call. There were choices to make.

In a Search Engine puzzle, there was always a lot of distracting visual information, a lot of *noise.* The first book had culminated inside an alien spaceship. Search Engine had to find his way through a cross section of the craft, flipping various self-destruct switches as he went and arriving finally at the escape pod. Between him and freedom, there were lasers, locked doors, radiation-filled compartments, and angry extraterrestrials that looked like big cubes of coconut jelly. Adults had a harder time with it than children did, and Vic had gradually realized that this was because grown-ups were always trying to see their way through to the end, and they couldn't do it because there was too much information. There was too much to look at, too much to think about. Children, though, didn't stand back from the puzzle and look at the whole thing. They pretended they *were* Search Engine, the hero of the story, down inside the puzzle itself, and they looked at only the little bit *he* could see, each step of the way. The difference between childhood and adulthood, Vic had come to believe, was the difference between imagination and resignation. You traded one for the other and lost your way.

Vic saw—already—that she didn't *really* need to find Manx at all. It was as hopeless as trying to hit one flying arrow with another.

He thought—she had *let* him think—that she was going to try to use the bridge to *catch up* to him. But she didn't need to do that. She knew where he was going. Where he *had* to go. She could head there anytime she liked.

But that was jumping ahead of herself. Christmasland was down the road a ways, both figuratively and actually.

She had to be ready to fight when she saw Manx again. She thought it would come to killing him, and she needed to know how to do it. More than that: There was the question of Wayne. She had to know if Wayne would still be himself by the time he got to Christmasland, if what was happening to him was reversible.

Vic knew someone who could tell her about Wayne, and she knew someone else who could tell her how to fight. Someone who could even get her the weapons she'd need to threaten the only thing Manx obviously cared about. But both of those people were down the road, too. She would see each of them in turn. Soon.

First, though. There was a girl named Michelle Demeter who had lost her father and who needed to know what had happened to him. She had been wondering long enough.

Vic cast a measuring glance at the angle of the light out the kitchen window, judged it to be late afternoon. The sky was a deep blue dome; the storm that had been rolling in when she'd arrived must have blown through. If anyone had heard the tank of sevoflurane exploding and tearing Bing Partridge in two, they had likely thought it just a roll of thunder. She supposed she'd been unconscious for three, maybe four hours. She had a look at the stack of envelopes on the kitchen counter. The Gasmask Man's mail was addressed to:

BING PARTRIDGE
25 BLOCH LANE
SUGARCREEK, PENNSYLVANIA 16323

That was going to be a hard one to explain. Four hours was not enough time to get to Pennsylvania from New Hampshire, not even with the hammer down all the way. Then it occurred to her that she didn't *need* to explain it. Other people could worry about explanations.

She dialed. She knew the number by heart.

"Yes?" Lou said.

She had not been sure that Lou would answer—she had expected Hutter. Or possibly the other one, the ugly cop with the bushy white eyebrows, Daltry. She could tell him where to find his lighter.

The sound of Lou's voice made her feel a little weak, robbed her momentarily of her certainty. She felt she had never loved him the way he deserved—and that he had always loved her more than *she* deserved.

"It's me," she said. "Are they listening?"

"Ah, shit, Vic," Lou said. "What do you think?"

Tabitha Hutter said, "I'm here, Vic." Jumping onto the line and into the conversation. "You've got a lot of people here pretty upset. Do you want to talk about why you ran away?"

"I went to go get my kid."

"I know there are things you haven't told me. Maybe things you were *afraid* to tell me. But I need to hear them, Vic. Whatever you've been doing for the last twenty-four hours, I'm sure you think you *had* to do it. I'm sure you thought it was right—"

"Twenty-four hours? What do you mean . . . twenty-four hours?"

"That's how long we've been looking for you. You pulled one heck of a disappearing act. We'll have to talk about how you did that sometime. Why don't you tell me where—"

"It's been *twenty-four hours*?" Vic cried again. The idea that she had lost a whole day seemed, in its own way, as incredible as a car that ran on human souls instead of unleaded.

Hutter said, quietly, patiently, "Vic, I want you to stay where you are."

"I can't do that."

"You have to—"

"No. Shut up. Just listen. You need to locate a girl named Michelle Demeter. She lives in Brandenburg, Kentucky. Her father has been missing for a while. She's probably out of her mind with worry. He's here. Downstairs. In the basement. He's dead. Been dead for a few days, I think. Do you have that?"

"Yes, I—"

"You treat him well, goddamn it. Don't just stick him in a drawer in some fucking morgue. Get someone to sit with him until his daughter shows up. He's been alone long enough."

"What happened to him?"

"He was killed by a man named Bing Partridge. Bing was the guy in the gasmask who shot at me. The man you didn't think existed. He was working with Manx. I think they have a long history together."

"Vic. Charlie Manx is dead."

"No. He isn't. I saw him, and so did Nathan Demeter. Demeter will back up my story."

"Vic," Tabitha said. "You just told me Nathan Demeter is dead. How is he going to back up your story? I want you to slow down. You've been through a lot. I think you've had a—"

"I have not had a fucking break with reality. I have not been having imaginary conversations with a dead man. Demeter left a note, all right? A note naming Manx. Lou! Lou, are you still on the line?"

"Yeah, Vic. I'm here. Are you okay?"

"I talked to Wayne this morning, Lou. He's alive. He's still alive, and I'm going to get him back."

"Oh, Jesus," he said, and his voice went rough with emotion, and she knew he was trying not to cry. "Oh, Jesus. What did he say?"

"He hasn't been hurt," she said.

"Victoria," Tabitha Hutter said. "When did you—"

"Hang on!" Lou cried. "Vic, dude. You can't do this alone. You can't cross this bridge alone."

Vic readied herself, as if she were aiming a rifle on a distant target, and said, as calmly and clearly as she could manage, "Listen to me, Lou. I have to make one stop, and then I'm going to see a man who can get some ANFO for me. With the right ANFO, I can blow Manx's world right off the map."

"What info?" Tabitha Hutter said. "Victoria, Lou is right. You can't deal with this on your own. Come in. Come in and talk to us. What man are you going to see? What is this information you need?"

Lou's voice was slow and ragged with emotion. "Get out of there, Vic. We can horseshit around some other time. They're coming for you. Get out of there and go do what you have to do."

"Mr. Carmody?" Tabitha said. There was a sudden note of tension underlying her voice. *"Mr. Carmody?"*

"I'm gone, Lou. I love you."

"Back atcha," he said. He sounded choked with emotion, barely hanging on.

She set the phone gently in its cradle.

She thought he understood what she was telling him. He had said, *We can horseshit around some other time,* a sentence that almost made sense in context. Almost but not quite. There was a second meaning there, but no one besides Vic would have been able to detect it. Horseshit: a principal component of ANFO, the substance her father had been using to blow up shelf rock for decades.

She limped on her bad left leg to the sink and ran some cool water, splashed it onto her face and hands. Blood and grime circled the drain in pretty pink swirls. Vic had bits of Gasmask Man all over her, drops of liquefied Bing dripping down her shirt, splattered up her arms, probably in her hair. In the distance she heard the wail of a police siren. The thought crossed her mind that she should've had a shower before calling Lou. Or searched the house for a gun. She probably needed a gun more than she needed a shampoo.

She pushed open the screen door and went carefully down the back steps, keeping the weight off her left knee. She would have to keep it extended while she rode. She had a bad moment, wondering how she would shift gears with the left foot—then remembered it was a British bike. Right. The gearshift was on the right side of the bike, a configuration that hadn't been legal in the United States since before she was born.

Vic walked up the hill, face turned to the sun. She closed her eyes, to concentrate her senses on the good warmth against her skin. The sound of the siren grew louder and louder behind her, the Doppler effect causing the shriek to rise and fall, swell and collapse. Tabitha Hutter would lop off heads when she found out they had approached the house with their sirens blaring, giving Vic plenty of advance notice they were coming.

At the top of the hill, as she lurched into the parking lot of the New American Faith Tabernacle, she looked back and saw a police car swerving onto Bloch Lane, sliding to a stop in front of Bing's house. The cop didn't even swing into the driveway, just slewed to a halt with the car at an angle, blocking half the road. The cop behind the wheel flung himself out so quickly his head bumped the doorframe and his hat was knocked into the road. He was so young. Vic couldn't imagine dating him, let alone being arrested by him.

She continued on and in three more steps could no longer see the house below. She had a moment to wonder what she would do if her bike wasn't there, if some kids had discovered it with the keys in the ignition and taken it for a ride. But the Triumph was right where she had left it, tilted over on its rusted kickstand.

It wasn't easy to stand it up. Vic made a small sobbing sound of pain, pushing with her left leg to straighten it.

She turned the key over, flipped the switch to RUN, and stomped on the gas.

The bike had been rained on and sat out all night, and it would've been no surprise to her if it didn't want to start, but the Triumph boomed right away, seemed almost impatient to go.

"I'm glad one of us is ready," she said.

She turned it in a circle and rolled it out of the shadows. She took it around the ruin of the church, and as she glided along, it began to rain. Water fell glittering and brilliant from the sunlit sky, raindrops as cold as October. It felt good on her skin, in her dry, bloody, dirty hair.

"Rain, rain," she said softly. "Come again and wash this mess away."

The Triumph and the woman upon it inscribed a great hoop around the charred sticks that had once been a house of worship.

When she had returned to the place where she started, the bridge was there, set back in the woods, just as it had been the day before. Only it had turned itself around, so as she drove onto it, she entered from what she thought of as the eastern side. There was green spray paint on the wall to her left.

HERE → it said.

She rolled onto the old rotten boards. Planks rattled beneath her tires. As the sound of the engine faded in the distance, a crow landed at the entrance to the bridge and stared into its dark mouth.

When the bridge disappeared two minutes later, it went all at once, popped out of existence like a balloon pricked by a pin. It even banged like a balloon and emitted a clear, shimmering shockwave that hit the crow like a speeding car, blew off half its feathers, and threw it twenty feet. It was dead by the time it hit the ground—just another piece of roadkill.

Laconia, New Hampshire

HUTTER SAW IT BEFORE ANYONE ELSE DID, EVEN THOUGH IT WAS HAPpening right in front of all of them. Lou Carmody began to go down. His right knee buckled, and he put a hand against the big oval table in the conference room.

"Mr. Carmody," she said.

He sank into one of the rolling office chairs, fell into it with a soft crash. His color had changed, his big grizzled face taking on a milky pallor, a sweat shining greasily on his forehead. He put one wrist to his brow as if feeling for a fever.

"Mr. Carmody," Hutter said again, calling down the table and across the room to him.

There were men all around him; Hutter didn't understand how they could stand there and not see that the guy was having a heart attack.

"I'm gone, Lou," Vic McQueen said, her voice coming through the Bluetooth headset in Hutter's ear. "I love you."

"Back atcha," Carmody said. He wore a headpiece identical to Tabitha Hutter's own; almost everyone in the room was wearing one, the whole team listening in on the conversation.

They were in a conference room at the state police headquarters outside Laconia. It could've been the conference room at a Hilton or a Courtyard Marriott: a big, bland space with a long, oval central table and windows looking out on an expanse of parking lot.

McQueen hung up. Hutter tore out her earpiece.

Cundy, her lead tech, was on his laptop, looking at Google Maps. It was zoomed in on Sugarcreek, Pennsylvania, to show Bloch Lane. Cundy rolled his eyes up to look at Hutter. "We'll have cars there in three minutes. Maybe less. I just spoke with the locals, and they're on the way with sirens blasting."

Hutter opened her mouth, meant to say, *Tell them to turn their fucking sirens off.* You didn't warn a federal fugitive that the cops were closing in. That was fundamental.

But then Lou Carmody leaned all the way forward, so his face was resting on the table, his nose squashed to the wood. He grunted softly and clutched at the tabletop as if he were at sea and clinging to a great chunk of driftwood.

And so what Hutter said instead was, "Ambulance. Now."

"You want . . . an ambulance to go to Bloch Lane?" Cundy asked.

"No. I want an ambulance to come here," she said, moving swiftly away from him and around the table. She raised her voice, "Gentlemen, give Mr. Carmody some air, please. Step back. Step back, please."

Lou Carmody's office chair had been slowly rolling backward, and at that exact moment it slid out from beneath him and Carmody went straight down, as if dropped through a trapdoor.

Daltry was the closest to him, standing just behind the chair with a mug that said WORLD'S BEST GRANDDAD. He leaped aside and slopped black coffee down his pink shirt.

"The fuck hit him?" Daltry asked.

Hutter went down on one knee next to Carmody, who was half under the table. She put her hands on one big sloping shoulder and pushed. It was like trying to flip a mattress. He slumped onto his back, his right hand grabbing his Iron Man T-shirt, twisting it into a knot between his man tits. His cheeks were loose, and his lips were gray. He let out a long, ragged gasp. His gaze darted here and there, as if he were trying to get his bearings.

"Stay with us, Lou," she said. "Help will be here soon."

She snapped her fingers, and his gaze found her at last. He blinked and smiled uncertainly. "I like your earrings. Supergirl. I would've never figured you for Supergirl."

"No? Who would you have figured me for?" she asked, just trying to keep him talking. Her fingers closed on his wrist. There was nothing for a long moment, and then his pulse whapped, a single big kick, and then another stillness, and then a flurry of rapid beats.

"Velma," he said. "You know? From *Scooby-Doo*."

"Why? Because we're both dumpy?" Hutter asked.

"No," he said. "Because you're both smart. I'm scared. Will you hold my hand?"

She took his hand in hers. He gently moved his thumb back and forth over her knuckles.

"I know you don't believe anything Vic told you about Manx," he said to her in a sudden, fierce whisper. "I know you think she's out of her mind. You can't let facts get in the way of the truth."

"Jinkies," she said. "What's the difference?"

He surprised her by laughing—a rapid, helpless, panting sound.

She had to ride to the hospital with him in the ambulance. He wouldn't let go of her hand.

Here, Iowa

By the time Vic came out of the other end of the bridge, she had slowed to almost nothing and the bike was in neutral. She remembered acutely her last visit to the Here Public Library, how she had rushed headlong into a curb and been flung for a knee-scraping slide across a concrete path. She didn't think she could take a crash in the state she was in now. The bike didn't care for neutral, though, and as it thumped down onto the asphalt road that ran behind the library, the engine died with a thin, dispirited wheeze.

When Vic had last been Here, the strip of park behind the library had been raked and clean and shady, a place to throw down a blanket and read a book. Now it was half an acre of mud, gouged with tread marks from loaders and dump trucks. The century-old oaks and birch had been plucked from the ground and bulldozed into a twelve-foot-high mound of dead wood, off to one side.

A single park bench remained. Once it had been dark green, with wrought-iron arms and legs, but the paint had peeled and the wood beneath was splintery, sun-baked almost to colorlessness. Maggie dozed upright, chin on chest, in one corner of the bench, in the direct, unforgiving light of day. She held a carton of lemonade in one hand, a fly buzzing around its mouth. Her sleeveless T-shirt exposed scrawny, withered arms, spotted with the scars from dozens of cigarette burns. She had at some point blasted her hair with fluorescent orange dye, but the brown and gray roots were showing. Vic's own mother had not looked so old when she died.

The sight of Maggie—so worn, so emaciated, so ill used, and so alone—hurt Vic more sharply than the ache in her left knee. She forced herself to remember, in careful detail, how in a moment of anger and panic she had thrown papers in this woman's face, had threatened her with police. Her sense of shame was exquisite, but she did not allow herself to shove it aside. She let it burn, the tip of a cigarette held firmly against skin.

The front brake shrilled as Vic settled to a stop. Maggie lifted her head, pushed some of her brittle-looking sherbet hair back from her eyes, and smiled sleepily. Vic put the kickstand down.

Maggie's smile vanished as quickly as it had come. She rose unsteadily to her feet.

"Oh, V-V-Vic. What did you *do* to yourself? You've got blood all over you."

"If it makes you feel better, most of it isn't mine."

"It doesn't. Makes me f-f-f-feel ffff-*ffaint.* Didn't I have to put Band-Aids on you *last* time you were here?"

"Yeah. I guess you did," Vic said. She looked past Maggie at the library. The first-floor windows were covered over with plywood sheeting. The iron door at the rear was crisscrossed with yellow police tape. "What happened to your library, Maggie?"

"S-s-seen better days. Like muh*muh*muh-**mmm**-mm*me,*" Maggie said, and grinned to show her missing teeth.

"Oh, Maggie," Vic said, and for an instant she felt very close to crying again. It was Maggie's uneven grape-soda-colored lipstick. It was the dead trees in a pile. It was the sun, too hot and too bright. Maggie deserved some shade to sit in. "I don't know which one of us needs a doctor more."

"Oh, gosh, I'm okay! Just m-muh-my s-stuh-stammer is worse."

"And your arms."

Maggie looked down at them, squinting in puzzlement at the constellation of burns, then looked back up. "It helps me talk normal. Helps me with other s-s-st-st-stuff, too."

"What helps you?"

"P-p-p-puh-puh-pain. C'mon. Let's go in. Mama Maggie will ffffff*fix* you up."

"I need something besides fixing, Maggie. I have questions for your tiles."

"M-m-*muh*-might not have answers," Maggie said, turning up the path. "They don't work s-ss-so well anymore. They st-st-st-stammer, too, now. But I'll try. After we get you cleaned up and I muh-muh-mother you some."

"I don't know if I have time for mothering."

"Sure you do," Maggie said. "He hasn't muh-muh-muh-made it to Christmasland yet. We both know you can't catch him before then. Be like trying to grab a handful of fffff-*fffog*."

Vic gingerly descended from the bike. She was almost hopping to keep the weight off her left leg. Maggie put an arm around her waist. Vic wanted to tell her she didn't need a crutch, but the truth was she *did*—she doubted she could make it to the back of the library without help—and her arm went automatically over Maggie's shoulders. They walked a step or two, and then Maggie paused, twisting her head to look back at the Shorter Way, which once again spanned the Cedar River. The river seemed wider than Vic remembered, the water boiling right up to the edge of the narrow road that looped behind the library. The thicket-covered embankment that had once lined the water had been washed away.

"What's on the other end of the bridge this time?"

"Couple of dead people."

"Will anyone ff-f-ffuh-ffollow you through?"

"I don't think so. There are police looking for me back there, but the bridge will pop out of existence before they find it."

"There were p-p-puh-police *here*."

"Looking for me?"

"I don't know! Muh-mm-*mmmm*maybe! I was coming back from the drugstore and s-s-saw 'em parked out f-f-f-front. So I took off. I stuh-st-stay here s-s-s-sometimes, s-s-sometimes other puh-p-places."

"Where? I think the first time we met, you said something about living with relatives—an uncle or something?"

Maggie shook her head. "He's gone. Whole trailer p-puh-park is gone. Washed away."

The two women limped toward the back door.

"They're probably looking for you because I called you. They might be tracking your cell phone," Vic said.

"Thought of that. Dumped it after you called. I knew you wouldn't need to call again to f-find m-m-mm*me*. No worries!"

The yellow tape across the rusting iron door read DANGER. A sheet of paper, slipped inside a clear plastic envelope and stuck to the door, identified the structure as unsound. The door was not locked but held ajar by a chunk of concrete. Maggie ducked the tape and pushed it inward. Vic followed her into darkness and ruin.

The stacks had once been a vast, cavernous vault that smelled fragrantly of ten thousand books, aging gently in the shadows. The shelves were still there, although banks of them had been toppled like twelve-foot-tall iron dominoes. Most of the books were gone, although some remained in rotting heaps scattered here and there, stinking of mildew and decay.

"The big f-f-flood was in 2008, and the walls are *st-st-still* wet."

Vic brushed one hand against the cold, moist concrete and found that it was true.

Maggie held her as they picked their way carefully through the debris. Vic kicked a pile of beer cans. As her eyes adjusted to the gloom, she saw that the walls had been tagged with graffiti, the usual assortment of six-foot cocks and dinner-plate-proportioned tits. But there was also a grand message, scrawled in dripping red paint:

PLEEZ BE QUITE IN THE LIBERY PEPLER TRYING TO GET HI!

"I'm sorry, Maggie," Vic said. "I know you loved this place. Is anyone doing anything to help out? Were the books moved to a new location?"

"You bet," Maggie said.

"Nearby?"

"P-p-pretty close. The town dump is just a m-m-mm-mile downriver."

"Couldn't someone do something for the old place?" Vic said. "What is it? A hundred years old? It *must* be a historical site."

"You got that right," Maggie said, and for an instant there was no trace of a stammer in her voice at all. "It's history, baby."

Vic caught a glimpse of her expression in the shadows. It was true: Pain really did help Maggie with her stammer.

The Library

MAGGIE LEIGH'S OFFICE BEHIND THE FISH TANK WAS STILL there—in a manner of speaking. The tank was empty, with filthy Scrabble tiles heaped in the bottom, the cloudy glass walls giving a view of what had once been the children's library. Maggie's gunmetal desk remained, although the surface had been gouged and scratched and someone had spray-painted a gaping red vulva on one side. An unlit candle bent over a pool of violet wax. Maggie's paperweight—Chekhov's gun, and yes, Vic got the joke now—held her place in the hardcover she was reading, *Ficciones* by Borges. There was a tweed couch that Vic didn't remember. It was a yard-sale number, some rents in it patched with duct tape and some holes not patched at all, but at least it wasn't damp, didn't stink of mildew.

"What happened to your koi?" Vic asked.

"I'm not sure. I think s-s-someone ate it," Maggie said. "I hope it m-m-made *sss*-someone a good meal. No one sh-sh-should go hungry."

There were syringes and rubber tubing on the floor. Vic was careful not to step on any needles as she made her way to the couch and lowered herself upon it.

"Those aren't m-m-m-mine," Maggie said, nodding to the syringes, and she went for the broom that was leaning in a corner where once there had been a coatrack. The broom itself doubled as the coatrack now; Maggie's filthy old fedora hung upon it. "I haven't sh-sh-shot up ss-ss-since last year. Too *expensive.* I don't know how *anyone* can afford to get high in *this* economy."

Maggie set her hat on her sherbet-colored hair with the dignity and care of a drunk dandy about to sway out of the absinthe hall and into the rainy Paris night. She took up her broom and swept. The syringes clattered in a glassy sort of way across the cement.

"I can wrap your leg and give you some Oxy," Maggie said. "*Way* cheaper than heroin."

She bent to her desk, found a key, unlocked the bottom drawer. She reached in and removed an orange pill bottle, a carton of cigarettes, and a rotting purple Scrabble bag.

"Sobriety is even cheaper than OxyContin," Vic said.

Maggie shrugged and said, "I only take as needed." She poked a cigarette into the corner of her mouth, lit a match with her thumbnail: a good trick.

"When is it needed?"

"It's a painkiller. I take it to kill pain." She drew smoke, put the lighter down. "That's all. What happened to you, Vuh-V-V-Vic?"

Vic settled back into the couch, head on the armrest. She could not bend her left knee all the way or unbend it, could hardly bear to move it. She could hardly bear to *look* at it; it was twice the size of the other knee, a purple-and-brown map of bruises.

She began to talk, telling about the last two days as best as she could remember, getting things out of order, providing explanations that seemed more confusing than the things they were meant to explain. Maggie did not interrupt or ask for clarification. A faucet ran for half a minute, then stopped. Vic let out a sharp, pained breath when Maggie put a cold, damp washcloth against her left knee and gently held it there.

Maggie opened her medicine bottle and shook out a little white pill. Fragrant blue smoke unspooled from her cigarette, draped her like the ghost of a scarf.

"I can't take that," Vic said.

"Sh-sh-sure you can. You don't have to d-d-dry-swallow 'em. I've got lemonade. It's a little warm but pretty tasty!"

"No, I mean, it'll put me to sleep. I've slept too much already."

"On a concrete f-f-f-floor? After you were gassed? That isn't s-suh-sleep." She gave Vic the tablet of OxyContin. "That's unconsciousness."

"Maybe after we talk."

"If I try to help you ff-ff-find out what you want to know, do you pruh-p-promise you won't r-ride off till you rest?"

Vic reached for the other woman's hand and squeezed it. "I do." Maggie smiled and patted Vic's knuckles, but Vic did not let go of her. She said, "Thank you, Maggie. For everything. For trying to warn me. For helping me. I'd give anything to take back the way I acted when I saw you in Haverhill. I was scared of you. That's not an excuse. There isn't any excuse. There's a lot of things I wish I could redo. You can't imagine. I wish there was something I could do to show you how sorry I am. Something I could give you besides words."

Maggie's whole face lit up: a child seeing a kite lift into the blue, blue sky.

"Oh, darn, V-V-V-Vic. You're gonna muh-m-make me cry! What's better in the whole world than words? Besides, you're *already* doing s-s-something," Maggie said. "You're *here.* It's so nice to have someone to talk to! Not that it's m-m-m-much fun to talk to m-muh-mm*me*!"

"Shhh. You shush with that. Your stammer doesn't bother me half as much as it bothers you," Vic said. "The first time we met, you told me that your Scrabble tiles and my bike were both knives for cutting through the stitches between reality and thought. You had that right. That's not the only thing they can cut. They wound up cutting both of us good. I know that my bridge—the Shorter Way—damaged me. In here." She reached up and tapped her left temple. "I traveled across it a few times too many, and it put my mind out of joint. I've never been right. I burned down my home. I burned down my life. I ran away from both of the boys I love because I was scared of damaging them or not being enough for them. That's what my knife did to me. And you've got this thing with your speech—"

"'S like I mmm-mm-managed to cut out my own tongue with my knife."

"Seems like the only one who never winds up bleeding from using his psychic knife is Manx."

"Oh, no! Oh, no, V-V-V-*Vic*! Muh-Muh-Manx has had it worst! He's been bled completely dry!" Maggie lowered her eyelids, drawing a deep, luxurious lungful of smoke. The tip of her cigarette throbbed in the darkness. She removed the cigarette from her mouth, looked at it thoughtfully for a moment, and then stabbed it into her own bare thigh, through one of the tears in her jeans.

"Jesus!" Vic shouted. She sat up so quickly that the room lurched hard in one direction and her stomach lurched hard in the other. She fell back against the armrest, overcome by dizziness.

"For the best," Maggie said through clenched teeth. "I want to be able to *talk* to you. Not just sp-spray you with spit." The breath spurted out of her in short, pained exhalations. "'S only way I can get my tiles to say anything anyhow, and sometimes even that isn't enough. Was necessary. What were we saying?"

"Oh, Maggie," Vic said.

"Don't make a big deal. Let's get to it, or I'll have to do that again. And the m-m-more I do it, the less well it works."

"You said Manx is bled dry."

"That's right. The Wraith makes him young and strong. It p-preserves him. But it's cost him his ability to feel regret or empathy. That's what his knife cut out of him: his humanity."

"Yeah. Except it's going to cut the same thing out of my son, too. The car changes the children Manx takes with him on his trips to Christmasland. It turns 'em into fuckin' vampires or something. Doesn't it?"

"Close enough," Maggie said. She rocked back and forth, eyes shut against the pain in her leg. "Christmasland is an inscape, right? A place Manx invented out of thought."

"A make-believe place."

"Oh, it's a real place. Ideas are as real as rocks. Your bridge is real, too, you know. It isn't *actually* a covered bridge, of course. The rafters, the roof, the boards under your tires—they're stage dressing for s-s-something more basic. When you left the Gasmask Man's house and came here, you didn't cross a bridge. You crossed an *idea* that *looked like* a bridge. And when M-Muh-Manx gets to Christmasland, he'll be arriving at an idea of happiness that looks like . . . I don't know . . . Santa Claus's workshop?"

"I think it's an amusement park."

"Amusement p-park. That sounds about right. Manx doesn't have happiness anymore. Only amusement. It's an idea of endless fun, endless youth, dressed up in a form his dumb little mind can understand. His vehicle is the instrument that opens the way. S-s-suffering and unhappiness provide the energy to run the car and open his p-passage to that puh-p-place. This is also why he has to take the kids with him. The car needs something he no longer has. He drains unhappiness from the children just like a B-movie v-v-vampire sucking blood."

"And when he uses them up, they're monsters."

"They're still children, I think. They're just children who can't understand anything *except* fun. They've been remade into Manx's idea of childhood perfection. He wants kids to be f-f-*ffforever* innocent. Innocence ain't all it's cracked up to be, you know. Innocent little kids rip the wings off flies, because they don't know any better. *That's* innocence. The car takes what Manx needs and changes his passengers so they can live in his world of thought. It sharpens their teeth and robs them of their need for warmth. A world of pure thought would be pretty cold, I bet. Now, take your pill, Vic. You need to rest and get your strength back before you ride out of here to f-f-face him again." She held out her palm with the tablet in it.

"Maybe I *could* use something. Not just for my knee. For my head," Vic told her, and then winced at a fresh stab of pain in her left eyeball. "I wonder why I always feel it behind my left eye, whenever I use my bridge. Been like that since childhood." She laughed shakily. "I wept blood once, you know."

Maggie said, "Creative ideas form in the right side of the brain. But did you know the right side of your brain sees out from your left eye? And it must take a lot of energy to shove a thought out of your head and into the real world. All that energy zapping you right"—she pointed at Vic's left eye—"there."

Vic looked longingly at the pill. Still she hesitated.

"You are going to answer my questions, yes? With your tiles."

"You haven't asked anything I need them for yet."

"I need to know how to *kill* him. He died in prison, but it didn't stick."

"You already know the answer to that one, I think."

Vic took the OxyContin from Maggie's hand and accepted the carton of lemonade when she offered it. The juice was warm and sticky and sweet and good. She knocked the Oxy down on the first swallow. The pill left a faint, bitter aftertaste.

"The car," Vic said. "The Wraith."

"Yeah. When the car fell apart, *he* fell apart. At some point someone probably yanked the engine right out of it, and he dropped dead at last. But then the engine was put back and the car was fixed up, and there you go. As long as the car is roadworthy, so is he."

"So if I destroy the car . . . I destroy him."

Maggie took a long suck on her cigarette. The tip of it was the brightest thing in the dark. "Bet on it."

"Okay," Vic said. It had only been a minute or two, but the pill was already starting to kick in. When she closed her eyes, she felt as if she were gliding soundlessly on her old Tuff Burner, moving through a dim and shady forest . . .

"Vic," Maggie said gently, and Vic pulled her head up off the armrest and blinked rapidly, realized she had been just a moment from dozing off.

"Some pill," she said.

"What do you need to ask my tiles?" Maggie prodded. "You better get to it, while you still can."

"My kid. I'm going to have to go to Christmasland to get him. They'll be there tonight, I think, or early tomorrow morning, and I'm going to be there, too. But by then Wayne will be . . . different. I could hear it in his voice when I talked to him. He's fighting it, but the car is making him into one of those fucking things. Can I fix him? I need to know that. If I get him back, is there some way to cure him?"

"I don't know. No child has ever come back ff-from Christmasland."

"So ask. Your bag of letters can tell you that, can't it?"

Maggie slid off the edge of the couch onto the floor. She gave the moth-eaten sack a gentle shake. The tiles clicked and rattled within.

"Let's see what we can s-suh-see," she said, and plunged a hand inside. She troweled about, came up with a fistful of tiles, and dropped them on the floor.

XOXOOXOXXO

Maggie stared at them with a look of weary dismay.

"This is all I get most days. Hugs and kisses f-f-for the lonely, stammering girl." Maggie swept one hand across the floor, grabbing the letters and jamming them back into the bag.

"Okay. It's okay. It was worth a try. You can't know everything. You can't find out everything."

"No," Maggie said. "When you come to a library to f-f-find something out, you should get what you want."

She dug around in her faux-velvet pouch and came up with another fistful of tiles, threw them at the floor.

PPPPPPPPP

"Don't st-st-stick your tongue out at me," she said to her letters.

She snatched up the tiles, dropped them in the bag, then shoved her hand in the Scrabble purse once again. This time her arm disappeared almost to the elbow, and Vic heard what sounded like hundreds of tiles grinding and clattering around. Maggie came up with another fistful, let them fall.

FUFUFUFU

"Fuck me? Fuck *me*?" Maggie cried. "Throw my earrings back in my face? Fff-f-ff-fuh-fuck *you*."

She plucked her cigarette out of her mouth, but before she could sink it into her own arm, Vic sat up, caught her wrist.

"Don't," Vic said. The room swooped this way and that, as if Vic were sitting in a swing. Still, she held Maggie's arm. Maggie stared up at her, her eyes bright in their sunken hollows . . . bright and frightened and exhausted. "We'll get it another time, Maggie. Maybe I'm not the only one who needs some rest. You were in Massachusetts a week and a half ago. You came back by bus the whole way?"

"I hitched some," Maggie said.

"When's the last time you ate?"

"Yesterday I had a s-s-s-suh-sandwich from s-s-s-s-s—" And like that she went mute. Her face darkened from red to a deep, grotesque shade of violet, as if she were strangling. Spit foamed at the corners of her lips.

"Shhh," Vic said. "Shhh. Okay. So we'll get you something to eat."

Maggie exhaled smoke, glanced around for a place to extinguish her cigarette, and then put it out in the far armrest. It hissed, and a black coil of smoke drifted toward the ceiling.

"After your nap, V-V-Vic."

Vic nodded, slumping backward. She didn't have it in her to wrangle with Maggie.

"I'll nap and you'll nap," Vic said. "And then we'll get you some food. Get you some clothes. Save Wayne. Save the library. Make things better. Do it all. Wonder Twin powers activate. Lie down."

"Okay. You take the couch. I've got a nice old blanket. I can just stretch out on the f-f-fl-fluh—"

"With *me,* Maggie. There's room on the couch for us both." Vic was awake but seemed to have lost the ability to force her eyes open again.

"You wouldn't mind?"

"No, sweetheart," Vic said, as if she were speaking to her son.

Maggie slipped onto the couch beside her and pressed herself to Vic's side, her bony hip against Vic's, her bony elbow across Vic's stomach.

"Will you hold me, Vic?" Maggie asked in a tremulous voice. "It's been a long time s-s-since anyone nice held m-m-muh-me. I m-m-muh-mean, I know you're not into girls, since you have a k-k-kid and all, but—"

Vic put her arm around Maggie's waist and held the thin, shivering woman against her.

"You can shut up now, you know," Vic said.

"Oh," Maggie said. "Oh, okay. That's a relief."

Laconia

THEY WOULDN'T LET LOU WALK ANYWHERE, DIDN'T WANT TO TAKE A chance that the fat man might get dizzy and fall onto his face, so after his examination he sat in a wheelchair and a man-nurse wheeled him to recovery.

The man-nurse was his age and had sleepy eyes with dark circles under them, and a jutting Cro-Magnon forehead. His name tag said, improbably, BILBO. He had a spaceship tattooed on one hairy forearm: *Serenity* from the TV show *Firefly*.

"'I am a leaf on the wind,'" Lou said, and the man-nurse said, "Dude, don't say that. I don't want to start crying on the job."

The detective followed, carrying Lou's clothes in a paper bag. Lou didn't like the way the guy smelled of nicotine and menthol, but mostly of nicotine, and he didn't like the way the guy seemed too small for his clothes so everything sagged: his shirt, his clam-colored trousers, his shabby jacket.

Daltry asked, "What are you two talking about?"

"*Firefly*," the man-nurse said, without looking back. "We're Browncoats."

"What's that mean? You two gonna gay-marry?" Daltry asked, and laughed at his own joke.

Bilbo the man-nurse said, "Jesus. Go back to the fifties, dude." But he didn't say it loud enough for Daltry to hear.

Recovery was a single big room containing two rows of beds, each bed parked in its own little compartment defined by pale green curtains. Bilbo wheeled Lou almost to the far end of the room before turning toward an empty bed on the right.

"Your suite, monsieur," Bilbo said.

Lou heaved himself up onto the mattress while Bilbo hung a bright sack of fluid from the stainless-steel rack standing alongside. Lou still had the intravenous cannula taped to his right arm, and Bilbo plugged it into the drip. Lou felt the fluid right away, a strong, icy stream that measurably dropped the whole temperature of his body.

"Should I be afraid?" Lou asked.

"Of an angioplasty? No. On the scale of medical complexity, it's only slightly trickier than having your wisdom teeth removed. Just have the surgery. No fear."

"Uh-uh," Lou said. "I'm not talking about the angioplasty. I mean the stuff you're pumping into me. What is it? Something serious?"

"Oh. This is nothing. You're not going under the knife today, so you don't get the good shit. This is a blood-thinning agent. Also, it'll mellow you out. Got to keep the mellows going."

"It'll put me to sleep?"

"Faster than a marathon of *Dr. Quinn, Medicine Woman.*"

Daltry dropped the paper bag into the chair next to the bed. Lou's clothes were folded up and stacked in a pile, his boxers on top, big as a pillowcase.

"How long has he got to be here?" Daltry asked.

"We'll hold him for observation overnight."

"That's not real good goddamn timing."

"Artery stenosis is famously inconvenient," Bilbo said. "It never calls in advance. Just drops in to party whenever it feels like it."

Daltry slipped his cell phone out of his pocket.

"You can't use that here."

Daltry said, "Where can I use it?"

"You'd have to walk back through the emergency room and go outside."

Daltry nodded, gave Lou a slow, disapproving look. "Don't go anywhere, Mr. Carmody." He turned and started down the length of the room.

"And he paddled away in his douche canoe," Bilbo said.

"What if *I* need to make a call?" Lou said. "Can I make a call before I go beddy-bye? My son, man. Have you heard about my son? I need to call my parents. They're not going to be able to sleep tonight until I let them know what's happening."

A lie. If he got his mother on the phone and started telling her about Wayne, she would have no idea who he was talking about. She was in assisted living and only capable of recognizing Lou himself one day out of three. It would be even more surprising if his father were interested in the latest news. He had been dead for four years.

"I can snag you a phone," Bilbo said. "Something we can plug in next to the bed. Just try and relax. I'll be back in five."

He stepped away from the bed, drew the curtain shut, and walked away.

Lou didn't wait, and he didn't think about it. He was the kid on the motorcycle again, hauling skinny Vic McQueen up onto the seat behind him, feeling her trembling arms around his waist.

He threw his legs over the side of the cot and jerked the cannula out of his arm. A fat BB of blood swelled up from the needle hole.

As soon as he heard Vic's voice over the earpiece, he'd felt the blood rushing to his head, had felt his pulse banging in his temples. His head had started to get heavy, as if his skull were full of liquid metal instead of brain tissue. What was worse, though, was that the room began to *move* in his peripheral vision. That sensation of the world beginning to rotate around him made him motion sick, and he had to stare directly down at the table to block it out. But then his head got so heavy he tilted over and kicked his chair out from under him.

It wasn't a heart attack, was it? he asked the doctor while she listened to his throat with her stethoscope. *Because if it was a heart attack, it wasn't as bad as I thought it would be.*

No. Not a heart attack. But you may have suffered from a transient ischemic attack, she said, a pretty black woman with a smooth, dark, ageless face.

Yeah, Lou told her. *I figured it was either a heart attack or a transient schematic attack. Transient schematic attack was my second choice.*

Ischemic. It's a kind of mini-stroke. I'm hearing a hollow whoosh *in your carotid artery.*

Ah. That's what you were listening to. I was just about to tell you I think my heart is lower.

She smiled. She looked like she wanted to pinch his cheek and give him a cookie. *What I'm hearing is serious plaque buildup.*

Seriously? I brush twice a day.

Different kind of plaque. In your blood. Too much bacon. She patted his belly. *Too much butter on your popcorn. You'll have to have an angioplasty. Possibly a stent. If you don't receive one, you could suffer a major, even fatal stroke.*

I've been ordering salads when I go to McDonald's, he told her, and was surprised to feel tears stinging at the backs of his eyes. He was, nonsensically, relieved that the cute little FBI agent wasn't around to see him crying again.

Now Lou grabbed the brown paper bag in the chair and wiggled into his underwear and jeans, pulling them on under his hospital johnny.

He had passed out after talking to Vic; the world had gone greasy and slick, and he couldn't hold on to it. It squirted right out of his fingers. But up until the moment he passed out, he was listening to her. He understood, just from the pitch of her voice, that she wanted him to do something, that she was trying to *tell* him something. *I have to make one stop, and then I'm going to go see a man who can get some ANFO for me. With the right ANFO, I can blow Manx's world right off the map.*

Tabitha Hutter, and all the other cops who were listening in on the call, heard what Vic *wanted* them to hear: They heard "info" instead of "ANFO." It was like one of Vic's Search Engine pictures, only a picture made of sound instead of color. You didn't notice what was right in front of you because you didn't know how to look—or, in this case, listen. But Lou had always known how to listen to her.

Lou yanked off his johnny, pulled on his shirt.

ANFO. Her father was the man who blew things up—took out ledge rock, tree stumps, and old pilings with ANFO—and who had blown Vic off without a look back. He had not ever even held Wayne, and Vic had talked to him perhaps only a dozen times in a dozen years. Lou had spoken with him more often, had sent him photos and video of Wayne by way of e-mail. He knew from things Vic had told him that the man was a wife beater and a cheat. He knew, too, from things Vic had *not* told him, that she missed him and loved him with an intensity perhaps matched only by what she felt for her son.

Lou had never met the man but knew where he lived, knew his number—and knew that Vic was going to see him. Lou would be waiting when she got there. She wanted him there, or she wouldn't have told him.

He stuck his head out through the curtain, looked down an aisle made by rows of hanging sheets.

He saw a doctor and a nurse—a female nurse, not Bilbo—standing together, running down items on a clipboard, but their backs were turned to him. Lou carried his sneakers in one hand, slipped into the aisle, turned right, and pushed through a pair of swinging doors into a wide white hallway.

He wound his way through the building, moving in a direction that felt like it would take him away from the emergency-room entrance. He tugged his Vans on as he went.

The lobby ceiling was fifty feet high and had big slabs of pink crystal hanging from it, giving it a Fortress of Solitude vibe. Water splashed in a black slate fountain. Voices echoed. The smell of coffee and muffins wafting from a Dunkin' Donuts made his stomach clutch with hunger. The thought of eating a sugared jelly doughnut was like imagining putting the barrel of a loaded gun in his mouth.

I don't need to live forever, he thought. *Just please for however long it takes to get my son back.*

A pair of nuns were getting out of a cab, right out in front of the revolving door. That was damn close to divine intervention as far as Lou was concerned. He held the door for them, then climbed into the backseat. The rear of the cab sank on its springs.

"Where we going?" the cabbie said.

To jail, Lou thought, but what he said was, "Train station."

Bilbo Prince watched the cab lurch away from the curb in a gush of filthy blue exhaust, noted the number and the license plate, then turned and walked away. He drifted down halls, up stairs, down stairs, and exited at last through the ER entrance on the opposite side of the hospital. The old cop, Daltry, waited there, having himself a smoke.

"He took off," Bilbo said. "Like you said he would. Caught a cab outside the lobby."

"You get the cab number?"

"And the license," Bilbo said, and told him both.

Daltry nodded and opened his cell phone. He pressed a single button and put it to his ear, then half turned away from Bilbo.

"Yep. He's moving," he said to whoever was on the other end of the line. "Hutter says just watch him, so we watch him. See where he goes and be ready to step in if the fat bastard starts to vapor-lock again."

Daltry hung up, pitched his smoke, and started moving away, into the parking lot. Bilbo trotted after him and tapped his shoulder. The old guy looked back. His brow furrowed, and his expression suggested he recognized Bilbo but already couldn't quite remember who he was or how they knew each other.

"That it, man?" Bilbo said. "Where's the love?"

"Oh. Oh, right." Daltry dug around in his pocket and came up with a ten-dollar bill and stuck it in Bilbo's hand. "There you go. Live long and prosper. Isn't that what you Trekkers say?"

Bilbo looked from the grimy ten-dollar bill—he'd been expecting at least a twenty—to the tattoo of *Serenity* on his hairy arm. "Yeah. I guess. But I'm not a *Star Trek* fan. My tattoo here? This is *Serenity,* not the *Enterprise.* I'm a Browncoat, man."

"More like turncoat," Daltry said, and laughed. Flecks of spittle hit Bilbo in the face.

Bilbo wanted to throw the ten dollars at his feet and walk away, show the ugly, loudmouthed fuck what he thought of his money, but then he reconsidered and stowed the cash in his pocket. He was saving for a *Buffy* tattoo on the other arm. Ink wasn't cheap.

Here, Iowa

When Maggie came awake, her arm was slung over Vic's waist and Vic's head was resting against her breastbone. She was the most goshdarn pretty woman that Maggie had ever been in bed with, and Maggie wanted to kiss her but wouldn't. What Maggie really wanted to do was comb Vic's snarled, windblown hair, straighten it out, make it shine. She wanted to wash Vic's feet and rub them with oil. Maggie wished they had had more time together and a chance to talk about something besides Charlie Manx. Not that Maggie really wanted to talk. She wanted to listen. Maggie dreaded that moment in any conversation when it was her turn to open her big, dumb m-m-mouth.

Maggie sensed she hadn't been asleep for long and had a pretty good idea she wouldn't be able to sleep again for hours. She untangled herself from Vic, smoothed her hair back from her face, and slipped away. It was time to spell, and now that Vic was asleep, Maggie could do what she needed to do to make the tiles behave.

She lit a smoke. She lit a candle. Arranged her fedora just so. Maggie set her Scrabble bag before her and loosed the golden thread. She considered the darkness within for a time, inhaling deeply on her cigarette. It was late, and she wanted to crush some Oxy and have a snort, and she couldn't do it until she had done this one thing for Vic. She reached up and found the collar of her white muscle shirt and pulled it down, exposing her left breast. She removed her cigarette and shut her eyes and put it out. She held it against the top of her breast for a long time, grinding it into the tender flesh, letting out a thin, whining breath through her clenched teeth. She could smell herself burning.

She flicked the extinguished cigarette away and bent over the desk, wrists pressed against its edge, blinking at tears. The pain in her breast was sharp and intense and wonderful. Sacred.

Now, she thought, *now, now*. She had a brief window in which to use the tiles, to force sense out of gibberish: a minute or two at most. It seemed to her sometimes that this was the only fight that mattered: the struggle to take the world's chaos and make it mean something, to put it to words.

She took a fistful of letters, dumped them before her, and began to sort. She moved tiles here and there. She had played this game for her entire adult life, and soon enough she had it. In a few minutes, the spelling was done, no trouble at all this time.

When she saw she had it, she let out a long, satisfied breath, as if she had just set down a great weight. She didn't have any idea what the message meant. It had an epigrammatic quality about it, seemed less like a fact, more like the closing line of a lullaby. But Maggie was sure she had it right. She always knew when she had it right. It was as sure and simple a thing as a key clicking into a lock and turning a bolt. Maybe Vic could glean some meaning from it. She would ask her when she was awake.

She copied out the message from the Great Scrabble Bag of Fate on a sheet of water-stained Here Public Library stationery. She read it over. It was good. She was conscious of an unfamiliar glow of satisfaction, was unused to being happy with herself.

She collected her letters one at a time and returned them to the velvet bag. Her breast throbbed, nothing transcendent about the pain now. She reached for her cigarettes, not to burn herself again but just for a smoke.

A boy walked through the children's library carrying a sparkler.

She saw him through the clouded glass of the old fish tank, a black figure against the paler darkness of the room beyond. As he walked, he swung his right arm and the sparkler spit a hot copper spray, drew red lines in the gloom. He was there for only a moment and then moved out of sight, carrying his sputtering torch with him.

Maggie leaned toward the fish tank to bang on the glass, scare the shit out of him and run him off, then remembered Vic and caught herself. Kids broke in to throw firecrackers and smoke cigarettes and cover the walls in graffiti, and she hated it. She had once come across a squad of teenagers down in the stacks, passing a jay around a campfire made of old hardcovers, and she had turned into a crazy woman, chasing them out with a busted chair leg, aware that if the peeling wallpaper caught fire, she would lose her last, best home. *Book burners!* she had screamed at them, and for once she had not stuttered at all. *Book burners! I'll cut off your balls and rape your women!* It was five to one, but they had fled before her as if they'd seen a ghost. Sometimes she thought she *was* a ghost, that she had really died in the flood, died with the library and just hadn't realized it yet.

She had a last look at Vic, huddled on the couch, fists balled under her chin. This time Maggie couldn't help herself. The door was over there, close to the couch, and as Maggie went by, she paused, and bent over, and kissed her temple, lightly. In sleep one corner of Vic's mouth turned up in a wry smile.

Maggie went looking for the boy in the shadows. She stepped out into what had once been the children's library and eased the door shut behind her. The carpet had been peeled up into mildewed strips and rolled over against the wall in a series of stinking bundles. The floor beneath was wet concrete. Half of an enormous globe occupied one corner of the room, the northern hemisphere upended and filled with water and pigeon feathers, sides streaked with bird crap. America turned upside down and shit on. She noticed, absentmindedly, that she was still carrying her bag of Scrabble tiles, had forgotten to put them back in the desk. Dumb.

She heard a sound not unlike butter sizzling in a pan, off somewhere to her right. Maggie started around the U-shaped walnut desk, where once she had signed out *Coraline* and *The House with a Clock in Its Walls* and *Harry Potter.* As she approached the stone gallery that led back to the central building, she saw a leaping yellow glare.

The boy stood at the far end of the gallery with his sparkler. A small, stocky black figure, hood pulled up to hide his face. He stood staring, his sparkler pointed down at the floor, pouring sparks and smoke. In the other hand was a long silver can of something. She smelled wet paint.

".myself stop can't I," he said, in a hoarse, strange voice, and laughed.

"What?" she said. "Kid, get out of here with that."

He shook his head and turned and wandered away, this child of shadow, moving like a figure in a dream, lighting a path into some cavern of the unconscious. He swayed drunkenly, almost careening off one wall. He *was* drunk. Maggie could smell the beer from here.

"Hey!" she said.

He disappeared. Somewhere ahead she heard echoing laughter. In the remote gloom of the periodicals room, she saw a new light—the guttering, sullen glare of a fire.

She began to run. She kicked syringes and bottles clattering across the concrete floor, ran past boarded-over windows. Someone, the kid possibly, had spray-painted a message in red on the wall to her right: GOD BURNED ALIVE ONLY DEVILS NOW. The paint was still dripping, bright red, as if the walls were bleeding.

She ran into the periodicals room, a space as big as a modest-size chapel and with ceilings just as high. During the flood it had been a shallow Sargasso, a scum of magazines covering the water, a swollen mass of *National Geographics* and *New Yorkers*. Now it was a big, bare cement chamber with dried, hardened newspapers stuck to floors and walls, rotten piles of magazines drifted in the corners, some sleeping bags spread where bums had camped out—and a wire trash can, boiling with greasy smoke. The drunk little bastard had dropped his sparkler in it on top of a mess of paperbacks and magazines. Green and orange sparks spit from somewhere deep inside the burning nest. Maggie saw a copy of *Fahrenheit 451* shriveling and blackening.

The boy considered her from the far side of the room, from within a dark, high stone archway.

"Hey!" she screamed again. "*Hey*, you little shit!"

".late too it's but ,can I as hard as fighting I'm," he said, rocking from side to side. ".me follow don't ,please ,please ,*Please*"

"Hey!" she said, not listening, *unable* to listen, none of it making any sense anyway.

She looked around for something to smother the flames, snatched up one of the sleeping bags, blue and slippery and smelling faintly of puke. She held her Scrabble sack under one arm while she crammed the sleeping bag in on top of the flames, pressing down hard, choking the fire. She flinched from the heat and the smell, an odor of cooked phosphorous and burned metal and charring nylon.

When she looked up again, the boy was gone.

"Get the fuck out of my library, you little creep! Get the fuck gone before I catch up to you!"

He laughed somewhere. It was hard to tell where he was. His laughter was a breathless, echoing, untraceable sound, like a bird flapping its wings high in the rafters of some abandoned church. She thought, randomly, *God burned alive, only devils now.*

She went on toward the lobby, her legs shaking. If she caught the crazy, drunk little bastard, he would not think God had burned alive. He would think God was a dyke librarian, and he would know the fear of her.

Maggie was halfway across the periodicals room when the rocket went off with a great whistling scream. That sound was a jolt straight to the nerve endings, made her want to scream herself and dive for cover. Instead she ran, ducked low like a soldier under fire, all the breath shooting out of her.

She made it to the vast central room, with the sixty-foot-high ceilings, in time to see the bottle rocket hit the roof, spin, bounce off an arch, and ricochet down toward the dull marble floor: a missile of emerald flame and crackling sparks. A chemical-smelling smoke coiled throughout the room. Embers of fey green light tumbled from above, falling like flakes of some infernal, radioactive snow. Burn the place down—the fucking pint-size lunatic was in here to burn the place *down.* The rocket was still flying, hit the wall to her right, and exploded in a bright, fizzling flash, with a crack like a gunshot, and she shouted and ducked and covered the side of her face. An ember touched the bare skin of her right forearm, and she flinched at the sharp stab of pain.

In the far room, the reading room, the boy laughed breathlessly and ran on.

The rocket was out, but the smoke in the lobby still flickered, glowing an unearthly jade hue.

Maggie charged after him, beyond thought now, rattled and angry and afraid. The boy couldn't escape through the front door—that was locked from the outside with a chain—but there was a fire door in the reading room that the bums kept propped open. Beyond was the eastern parking lot. She could catch him there. She didn't know what she'd do with him when she had her hands on him, and a part of her was scared to find out. As she hit the reading room, she saw the door to the outside already settling shut.

"You shit," she whispered. "You *shit.*"

She slammed through the door and out into the parking lot. Across the paved expanse, a single functioning streetlamp cast a nimbus of light. The center of the lot was brightly lit, but the edges were in darkness. The boy waited beside the lamppost. Little bastard had another sparkler going and was standing not far from a Dumpster filled with books.

"Are you out of your goshdarn mind?" Maggie said.

The boy shouted, "I see you through my magic window!" He

drew a burning hoop in the air, at the level of his face. "Now your head is burning!"

"You st-st-start a fire in there and someone could get killed, you little asshole!" Maggie said. "Like you!"

She was short of breath and trembling, and her extremities prickled strangely. She clutched her Scrabble bag in one sweat-damp hand. She began stalking across the lot. Behind her the fire door clicked shut. Goddamn it. The kid had kicked away the stone that kept it from locking. She'd need to go all the way around the building to get back inside now.

"Look!" the child cried. "Look! I can write in flames!"

He slashed the tip of the sparkler in the air, a white spoke of light so intense it left a glowing afterimage on Maggie's optic nerve, creating the illusion of pulsing letters in the air.

R
U
N

"Who are you?" she asked, swaying a little herself, catching in place halfway across the lot—not sure she had just seen what she thought she'd seen. That he had spelled what she thought he'd spelled.

"Look! I can make a snowflake! I can make Christmas in July!" And he drew a snowflake in the air.

Her arms bristled with gooseflesh.

"Wayne?"

"Yes?"

"Oh, Wayne," she said. "Oh, God."

A pair of headlights snapped on in the shadows beyond the Dumpster, off to her right. A car idled along the curb, an old car with close-set headlamps, so black she had not seen it in the greater darkness around it.

"Hello!" called a voice from somewhere behind those headlights.

He was on the passenger side of the car—no, wait, the driver's side; it was all reversed on a British car. "What a night to go driving! Come on over, Ms. Margaret Leigh! It *is* Margaret Leigh, isn't it? You look just like your photograph in the paper!"

Maggie squinted into the headlights. She was telling herself to move, get out of the middle of the parking lot, but her legs were stuck in place. The fire door was an impossible distance away, twelve steps that might as well have been twelve hundred, and anyway, she had heard it clap shut behind her.

It occurred to her that there was, at best, a minute or so left to her life. She asked herself if she was ready for it. Thoughts darted like sparrows racing in the dusk just when she most desperately wanted her mind to be still.

He doesn't know Vic is here, she thought.

And: *Get the boy. Get the boy and get him away.*

And: *Why doesn't Wayne just run?*

Because he couldn't anymore. Because he didn't know he was supposed to. Or he *knew* but couldn't act on it.

But he had tried to tell *her* to run, had written it in flame, on the darkness. Had maybe even been trying, in his garbled way, to warn her in the library.

"Mr. Manx?" Maggie called, still unable to move her feet.

"You have been looking for me all your life, Ms. Leigh!" he shouted. "Well! Here I am at last! I am sure you have lots of questions for me. I know I have lots of questions for you! Come sit with us. Come have an ear of corn!"

"Let the b-b-b-b—" Maggie began, then choked up, couldn't force it out, her tongue as helpless as her legs. She wanted to say, *Let the boy go,* but her stammer wouldn't let her have that.

"C-c-cat got your t-t-tongue?" Manx shouted.

"Fuck you," she said. There. That came out clean and clear. And *f* had always been one of her toughest letters.

"Get over here, you scrawny bitch," Charlie Manx said. "Get in the car. Either you're riding with us or we're riding *over* you. Last chance."

She breathed deeply and smelled waterlogged books, the perfume of rotting cardboard and paper that had dried beneath the furnace of the July sun. If a single breath could summarize an entire life, she supposed that would do. It was almost time.

It came to her then that she had nothing left to say to Manx. She had said it all. She turned her head and fixed her gaze on Wayne.

"You have to run, Wayne! Run and hide!"

His sparkler had gone out. A grimy smoke trickled away from it.

"Why would I do that?" he said. ".sorry I'm" He coughed. His frail shoulders jumped. "We're going to Christmasland tonight! It's going to be fun! .sorry so I'm" He coughed again, then shrieked, "How about *you* run instead! That would be a *fun* game! !myself to on hold can't I"

Tires whined shrilly on the asphalt. Her paralysis broke. Or maybe she had never been paralyzed. Maybe her muscles and nerves—the meat and wiring—had always understood what the conscious mind didn't want to know, that it was already too late to get out of the way. She bolted across the lot, toward Wayne, some unformed, absurd notion in her head that she could get to him, pull him into the woods, into safety. She crossed in front of the Wraith. An icy light rose around her. The engine roared. She glanced sidelong, thinking, *Please let me be ready,* and the car was there, the grille so close that her heart seemed to fill her mouth. He was not aiming the Rolls at her but instead rushing up alongside and past her. He had one hand on the wheel and was stretching his upper body out the open window. The wind sucked his black hair back from his high, bare brow. His eyes were wide and avid with hilarity, and there was a look of triumphant joy stamped across his face. In his right hand, he held a silver hammer as big as God.

She did not feel the mallet connect with the back of her neck. There was a sound, like she had stepped on a lightbulb, a pop and a crack. She saw a flash, a white, brilliant blink of light. Her fedora whirled away like a tossed Frisbee. Her feet continued racing over the blacktop, but when she looked down they were pedaling in air. She had been lifted right off the ground.

Maggie hit the side of the car as she came down. She spun and struck the asphalt and rolled, arms flying. She went over and over and wound up against the far curb, on her back. Her cheek was pressed to the rough blacktop. *Poor Maggie,* Maggie thought, with genuine if somewhat muted sympathy.

She found she could not lift her head or even turn it. At the periphery of her vision, she could see that her left leg was bent *inward* at the knee, the hinge folding in a direction in which it was never meant to go.

Her velvet sack of letters had hit near her head and vomited tiles across the parking lot. She saw an H, an M, a U, some other letters. You could spell HUM with that. *Do you know you're dying, Ms. Leigh? No, but HUM a few bars and I'll fake it,* she thought, and coughed in a way that might've been laughter. She blew a pink bubble from her lips. When had her mouth got all full of blood?

Wayne stepped down into the parking lot, swinging his arms back and forth. His face had a white, sick gleam to it, but he was smiling to show a mouthful of shiny new teeth. Tears tracked down his face.

"You look funny," he said. "That was funny!" Blinking at tears. He wiped the back of one hand, thoughtlessly, across his face, spreading a bright streak across his downy cheek.

The car idled, ten feet away. The driver's-side door opened. Boots scraped on the blacktop.

"I did not think there was anything funny about her falling into the side of the Wraith!" Manx said. "There is one hell of a dent in the side of my Wraith now. To be fair, there is a bigger dent in this scrawny bitch. Back in the car, Wayne. We have to make some miles if we're going to reach Christmasland before sunup."

Wayne sank to one knee beside her. His tears had left red lines on his pale cheeks.

Your mother loves you, Maggie imagined telling him, but all that came out was a wheeze and blood. She tried to tell him with her eyes instead. *She wants you back.* Maggie reached for his hand, and Wayne took hers and squeezed.

".sorry I'm," he said. ".it help Couldn't"

"'S all right," she whispered, not really saying it, just moving her lips.

Wayne let go of her hand. "You rest," he said to her. "You just rest here. Dream something nice. Dream about Christmasland!"

He hopped to his feet and trotted out of sight. A door opened. A door closed.

Maggie's gaze shifted to Manx's boots. He was almost standing on her scattering of Scrabble tiles. She could see other letters now: a P, an R, a T, an I. Could make TRIP with that. *I think he broke my neck—what a TRIP!* she thought, and smiled again.

"What are you smiling about?" Manx asked, his voice shuddering with hate. "You have nothing to smile about! You are going to be dead, and I am going to be alive. You could've lived, too, you know. For another day anyway. There were things I wanted to know . . . like who else you told about me. I wanted— Don't you look away from me when I am talking to you!"

She had shut her eyes. She didn't want to stare at his upside-down face from here on the ground. It wasn't that he was ugly. It was that he was stupid. It was the way his mouth hung open to show his overbite and his crooked brown teeth. It was the way his eyes bulged from his skull.

He put his boot in her stomach. If there was any justice, she wouldn't have been able to feel it, but there was no justice and never had been, and she screamed. Who knew you could hurt so bad and not pass out from it?

"You listen, now. You did not have to die like this! I am not such

"No," Vic said. "I don't want it. That's not what I came for. That's no good."

Outside, the police siren cut off with a strangled *squonk!*

"*I* think it's good," said Charlie Manx, his hand on the cross-hatched handle. It had been Charlie Manx on the other side of the counter all along, Charlie Manx dressed like a cook, in a blood-stained apron and a cocked white hat, a line of zinc down his bony nose. "And what's good stays good, no matter how many heads you split open with it."

He lifted the hammer, and Vic screamed and threw herself back from him and right out of the dream, into

Real Life

VIC WOKE, AWARE THAT THE HOUR WAS LATE AND THAT SOMETHING was wrong.

She could hear voices, muted by stone and distance, could identify the speakers as male, even if she could not determine what they were saying. She smelled the faintest whiff of burned phosphorous. She had the muddled idea that she'd slept right through a commotion, sealed in the soundproofed sarcophagus fashioned by Maggie's pharmaceuticals.

She rolled herself up to a sitting position, feeling she ought to get dressed and go.

After a few moments, she determined she was already dressed. She had not even removed her sneakers before falling asleep. Her left knee was a poisonous shade of violet and as fat as one of Lou's knees.

A red candle burned in the darkness, reflecting an image of itself in the fish tank's glass. There was a note over on the desk; Maggie had left her a note before going. That was thoughtful of her. Vic could see her .38-caliber paperweight, Chekhov's gun, holding it down. Vic was hoping for instructions, a set of simple steps that would bring Wayne back to her, make her leg better, make her head better, make her life better. Barring that, just a note saying where Maggie had gone would be all right: *"Ran to the Nite Owl for ramen and drugs will be right back xoxo."*

Vic heard the voices again. Someone kicked a beer can, not far away. They were moving toward her, they were close, and if she didn't blow out the candle, they were going to wander into the old children's wing and see the light shining through the fish tank. Even as this thought came to her, she understood that it was already almost too late. She heard glass crunching underfoot, boot heels moving closer.

She sprang up. Her knee collapsed. She dropped onto it, bit down on a scream.

When Vic tried to stand, the leg refused to cooperate. She stretched it out behind her with great care—shutting her eyes and *pushing* through the pain—and then dragged herself across the floor, using her knuckles and her right foot. What it saved in agony, it made up for in humiliation.

Her right hand grabbed the back of the rolling chair. Her left took the edge of the desk. She used the two to hoist herself up and sway forward over the desktop. The men were in the other room, right on the other side of the wall. Their flashlights had not yet swung toward the fish tank, and she thought it possible they had not observed the dim, coppery shine of the candle flame yet, and she bent forward to blow it out, then caught herself staring down at the note written on a sheet of Here Library stationery.

"WHEN THE ANGELS FALL, THE CHILDREN GO HOME."

The paper was spattered with water stains, as if long ago someone had read this message and wept.

Vic heard one of the voices in the next room: *Hank, we got a light.* This was followed, a moment later, by a crackle of voices on a walkie-talkie, a dispatcher passing along a message in numbered code. There was a 10-57 at the public library, six officers responding, victim dead on the scene. Vic had bent to put out the candle, but "victim dead" stopped her. She leaned forward, lips pursed, but had forgotten what she'd intended to do.

The door behind her moved, wood scraping against stone, hitting some loose glass and sending it tinkling.

"Excuse me," came the voice behind her. "Ma'am, could you step over here? Please keep your hands in full sight."

Vic picked up Chekhov's gun and turned around with it and pointed it at his chest. "No."

There were two of them. Neither had his gun out, and she was not surprised. She doubted if most police officers unsnapped their holsters in the line of duty even once in an average year. Chubby white boys, the both of them. The one in front pointed a powerful penlight at her. The other was stuck in the doorway behind him, still half in the children's library.

"Ay!" squeaked the boy with the light. "Gun! Gun!"

"Shut up. Stay where you are," she said. "Keep your hands away from your belts. And drop that flashlight. It's right in my fucking eyes."

The cop dropped it. It shut off the moment it fell from his hand, clattered across the floor.

They stood there, freckled and dumpy and scared, the candlelight rising and falling over their faces. One of them was probably coaching his son's Little League team tomorrow. The other probably liked being a cop because it meant free milkshakes at McDonald's. They reminded her of kids playing dress-up.

"Who's dead?" she said.

"Ma'am, you need to put that gun down. No one wants to get hurt tonight," he said. His voice wavered and cracked like an adolescent boy's.

"Who?" she said, her voice choking up on her, wavering at the edge of a scream. "Your radio said someone is dead. Who? Tell me now."

"Some woman," said the guy in back, stuck in the doorway. The guy in front had raised his hands, palms out. She couldn't see what the other guy was doing with his hands—probably drawing his gun—but he didn't matter yet. He was jammed behind his partner, would have to shoot through him to get her. "No ID."

"What color was her hair?" Vic cried.

The second man said, "Did you know her?"

"What color was her fucking hair?"

"It had orange sprayed into it. Like, orange-soda-colored. You know her?" asked the second cop, the one who probably had his gun out.

It was difficult to work the fact of Maggie's death into her mind. It was like being asked to multiply fractions while suffering from a head cold—too much work, too baffling. Only a moment ago, they had been stretched out on the couch together, Maggie's arm over her waist and her legs against the backs of Vic's thighs. The heat of her had put Vic right to sleep. It amazed Vic that Maggie had slipped off to die someplace while Vic herself slept on. It was bad enough that only a few days before, Vic had yelled at Maggie, had cursed and threatened her. This seemed far worse, graceless and inconsiderate, for Vic to sleep peacefully while Maggie died somewhere out in a street.

"How?" Vic asked.

"Car, maybe. Looks like she got clipped by a car. Jesus. Just put the gun down. Put the gun down and let's talk."

"Let's not," Vic said, and turned her head and blew out the candle, dropping all three of them into

The Dark

VIC DIDN'T TRY TO RUN. MIGHT AS WELL TRY TO FLY.

Instead she stepped rapidly backward, around the desk and against the wall, keeping the cops in front of her. The blackness was absolute, was a geography of blindness. One of the cops shouted, stumbled in the dark. There was a scuffle of boot heels. Vic believed that the one in back had pushed the other out of his way.

She tossed the paperweight. It made a banging, sliding, rattling thud as it skidded away from her across the floor. Something for them to think about, confuse them about where she was. Vic began to move, keeping the left leg stiff, trying not to put much weight on it. She sensed rather than saw an iron bookshelf on her left and slipped behind it. Somewhere in the blind nightworld, a cop knocked over the broom leaning against the wall. It fell with a bang, followed by a yelp of fright.

Her foot found the edge of a step. *If you ever need to get out in a hurry, stay right and keep going down the steps,* Maggie had told her, Vic couldn't remember when. There was a way out of all this darkness, somewhere at the bottom of an unguessable number of stairs. Vic descended.

She moved in a hop, and once her heel came down on a wet, spongy book and she nearly landed on her ass. Vic fell against the wall, steadied herself, and continued. Somewhere behind her she heard shouts, more than two men now. Her breath rasped in her throat, and it occurred to her again that Maggie was dead. Vic wanted to cry for her, but her eyes were so dry they hurt. She wanted Maggie's death to make everything quiet and still—the way it was supposed to be in a library—but instead everything was bellowing cops and whistling breath and the knocking of her own pulse.

She hopped down a last short flight of steps and saw a slash of nighttime darkness standing out against the fuller, more complete darkness of the stacks. The back door stood partly open, held ajar by a chunk of rock.

Vic slowed as she approached it, expecting to peer out and see a festival of cops in the muddy field behind the library, but when she looked, there was no one. They were all on the far, eastern side of the building. Her motorcycle stood alone, close to the bench, where she had left it. The Cedar River bubbled and churned. The Shorter Way was not there, but then she hadn't expected it to be.

She yanked the door open and ducked out under yellow tape, holding the left leg stiff, chugging along in her crooked hop. The sound of police scanners carried on the rich, damp heat of the night. She could not see the cop cars, but one of them had its party lights on, and the strobe flashed against the low, cloudy murk above the library.

Vic climbed onto the Triumph, threw the kickstand up, stomped on the starter.

The Triumph boomed.

The rear door of the library opened. The cop who came through it—tearing down the tape as he spilled outside—had his gun in both hands, pointed at the ground.

Vic turned the Triumph in a slow, tight circle, wanting the bridge to be there, spanning the Cedar River. It wasn't. She was cruising along at less than five miles an hour, and that simply wasn't fast enough. She had never found the Shorter Way going so slowly. It was a matter of speed and emptiness—shutting her head off and riding.

"You! Get off the bike!" the cop yelled. He began to jog toward her, pointing his gun off to one side.

She steered the Triumph up the narrow road that ran behind the library, banged it into second gear, and gunned it up the hill. The wind snatched at her bloody, matted hair.

Vic cycled up the back road and around to the front of the building. The library fronted a wide avenue, crowded with police cruisers, the night twitching with strobes. At the sound of her engine, men in blue turned their heads to look. There was a small crowd as well, held back by yellow sawhorses, dark figures craning their necks, hoping to see a little blood. One of the cruisers was parked right across the narrow road that looped behind the library.

You're boxed in, shithead, she thought.

She wheeled the Triumph around, back the way she had come. The Triumph dropped down the pitch of the road as if it were dropping over a cliff. She threw it into third gear, continuing to accelerate. She rushed past the library, over on her left. She dived down toward that muddy half-acre field where Maggie had been waiting for her. A cop waited there now, next to Maggie's bench.

Vic had the Triumph up to almost forty by now. She pointed it toward the river.

"Just work, you motherfucker," she said. "I don't have time for your bullshit."

She banged it into fourth gear. Her lone headlight rushed across the blacktop, over the dirt, out onto the muddy brown turmoil of the river. She rushed toward the water. Maybe, if she were very lucky, she would drown. Better than getting fished out and locked up and knowing that Wayne was going to Christmasland and she couldn't do a thing about it.

Vic shut her eyes and thought, *Fuck it fuck it fuck it* ***fuck it.*** They were perhaps the only true words of prayer she had ever been able to utter with all her heart. Her ears roared with the sound of her own blood.

The bike slammed up onto the muddy ground, punched across it toward the river, and then she heard wood hammering under the tires and the bike began to slew and slip. She opened her eyes, found herself shuddering through the darkness across the rotting old boards of the Shorter Way Bridge. At the other end was only darkness. The roaring in her ears was not blood at all but static. A storm of white light whirled between the cracks in the walls. The whole lopsided bridge seemed to shudder around her under the weight of the bike.

She rushed past her old, cobwebbed Raleigh and was pitched out into damp, buggy, pine-scented darkness, her back tire clawing at soft earth. Vic planted her foot on the brake that didn't work and grabbed reflexively at the brake that did. The bike turned sideways and slid. The ground was covered in a springy bed of moss, and the Triumph bunched it up under its tires like loose carpet.

Vic was on a slight embankment, out in the piney woods somewhere. Water dripped in the branches, although it was not actually raining. She kept the bike up while it did a sideways judder across the ground, then cut the engine, snapped down the kickstand.

She looked back into the bridge. At the far end, she could see the library and that freckled, whey-faced cop standing at the entrance to the Shorter Way. He rotated his head slowly, looking at the entrance to the bridge. In another moment he would step inside.

Vic squeezed her eyes shut and lowered her head. The left eye hurt, as if it were a metal bolt being screwed into the socket.

"Go away!" she yelled, gritting her teeth.

There was a great clap of sound, as if someone had slammed an enormous door, and a shockwave of hot air—air that smelled like ozone, like a burned metal pan—was flung out at her, almost blew over the bike, and her with it.

She looked up. At first she could not see much through the left eye. Her vision out of that eye was obscured by blurred patches, like splashes of muddy water on a window. But from the other she could see that the bridge had popped out of existence, leaving behind tall pines, the reddish trunks glistening from a recent rain.

And what had happened to the cop at the other end? Vic wondered if he'd put a foot over the threshold—or stuck in his head. What happened if some part of him was over the edge, on the bridge?

She visualized a child poking fingers under a paper cutter and then bringing the long blade down.

"You can't do anything about that now," she said, and shuddered.

Vic turned, taking in her surroundings for the first time. She was behind a single-story log house, light glowing in a kitchen window. Beyond it, on the other side of the cabin, was a long gravel lane leading back to a road. She had never seen the place before, but she thought she knew where she was, and in another moment she was sure. As she stood astraddle her bike, the back door opened and a small, thin man appeared behind the screen, looking up the hill at her. He had a cup of coffee in one hand. She could not see his face but recognized him by shape alone, by the tilt of his head, even though she had not seen him in more than ten years.

She was at her father's house at last. She had given the cops the slip and made it back to Chris McQueen.

Dover, New Hampshire

A LOUD CLAP, LIKE THE WORLD'S BIGGEST DOOR SLAMMING SHUT. An electronic squeal. A deafening roar of static.

Tabitha Hutter shouted and flung her headphones down.

Daltry, sitting on her right, flinched but kept his own headphones on for a moment longer, his face screwed up in pain.

"What just happened?" Hutter asked Cundy.

Five of them were packed in the rear of a panel truck that said KING BOAR DELI on the side—fitting, considering they were jammed in like sausages. The truck was parked next to a CITGO station, across the road and a hundred feet south of the drive that led up to Christopher McQueen's house.

They had teams in the woods, closer in to McQueen's cabin, shooting video and using parabolic microphones to listen in. The footage and sound were being broadcast back to the truck. Until a moment ago, Hutter had been able to see the driveway on a pair of monitors, rendered in the supernatural emerald of night vision. Now, though, they showed only a blizzard of green snow.

The picture had gone out at the same time they lost their sound. One moment Hutter had been listening to Chris McQueen and Louis Carmody speaking in low voices in the kitchen. McQueen had been asking Lou if he wanted coffee. In the next instant, they were gone, replaced by a furious blast of radio hiss.

"Don't know," Cundy said. "Everything just went down." He jabbed at the keyboard of his little laptop, but the screen was a smooth face of black glass. "It's like we got hit with a motherfucking EMP." Cundy was funny when he swore: a dainty little black man with a piping voice and the trace of a British accent, pretending he was street instead of MIT.

Daltry tugged his own headphones off. He peeked down at his watch and laughed: a dry, startled sound that had nothing to do with amusement.

"What?" Hutter asked.

Daltry turned his wrist so she could see the face of his watch. It looked almost as old as he was, a watch with a clock face and a tarnished silver band that had probably been tinted to look like gold once upon a time. The second hand rolled around and around, moving *backward*. The hour and minute hands had both frozen perfectly still.

"It killed my watch," he said. He laughed again, this time looking toward Cundy. "Did all this shit do that? All your electronics? Did all this shit just blow up and wipe out my watch?"

"I don't know what did it," Cundy said. "Maybe we was touched by lightning."

"What fucking lightning? You hear any thunder?"

"I did hear a loud clap," Hutter said. "Just as everything cut out."

Daltry put a hand in the pocket of his coat, tugged out his cigarettes, then seemed to remember that Hutter was sitting beside him and gave her a sidelong glance of wry disappointment. He let the pack slip back into his pocket.

"How long will it take to get video and sound restored?" Hutter asked.

"It could've been a sunspot," Cundy said, as if she hadn't spoken. "I've heard the sun is kicking up with a solar storm."

"Sunspot," Daltry said. He placed his palms together, as in prayer. "You think sunspot, huh? You know, I can just tell you went to six years of college and majored in neuroscience or something, because only a truly gifted mind could talk himself into such utter horseshit. It's dark out, you autistic fuck."

"Cundy," Hutter said, before Cundy could come around in his chair and start some kind of male dick-measuring contest. "How long before we're back online?"

He shrugged. "I don't know. Five minutes? Ten? To reboot the system? Unless there's a nuclear war going on out there. In which case it'll probably take longer."

"I'll go look for a mushroom cloud," Tabitha Hutter said, getting up off the bench and doing a shuffling sideways walk toward the rear doors.

"Yeah," Daltry said. "Me, too. If the missiles are flying, I want a smoke before we get wiped out."

Hutter turned the latch, opened the heavy metal door to the damp night, and jumped down. Mist hung beneath the streetlights. The night throbbed with insect song. Across the street, fireflies lit the ferns and weeds in gassy green flashes.

Daltry lowered himself down beside her. His knees cracked.

"Christ," he said. "I thought for sure I'd be dead of something at this age."

His company did not cheer her but only made her more conscious of her own aloneness. Hutter had believed she would have more friends by now. The last man she'd dated said something to her, shortly before they broke up: "I don't know, maybe I'm boring, but I never really feel like you're there when we're out to dinner. You live in your head. I can't. No room for me in there. I don't know, maybe you'd be more interested in me if I were a book."

She had hated him at the time, and hated herself a little, but later, looking back, Hutter had decided that even if that particular boyfriend *had* been a book, he would've been one from the Business & Finance aisle and she would've passed him by and looked for something in SF & Fantasy.

Hutter and Daltry stood together in the almost empty parking lot. She could see into the CITGO, through the big plate-glass windows. The Pakistani behind the cash register kept flashing them nervous looks. Hutter had told him he wasn't under surveillance, that the federal government thanked him for his cooperation, but he almost certainly believed that his phone was tapped and they were eyeing him as a potential terrorist.

"You think you should've gone to Pennsylvania?" Daltry asked.

"Depending on how this turns out, I might go tomorrow."

"Fuckin' horror show," Daltry said.

Hutter had been getting voice mails and e-mails all night about the house on Bloch Lane in Sugarcreek. They had the place covered in a tent and you had to wear a rubber suit and a gasmask to get through the door. They were treating the joint like it was contaminated with Ebola. A dozen forensics experts were in there, state and federal, pulling the place apart. They had been excavating bones from one wall of a root cellar all afternoon. The guy who had lived there, Bing Partridge, had melted most of the remains with lye; what he couldn't destroy he stored, much the way a bee stores honey, in little cells, lightly mudded over.

He had not gotten around to dissolving his most recent kill, a guy named Nathan Demeter from Kentucky—the corpse that Vic McQueen had mentioned on the phone. He had vanished a little more than two months ago, along with his vintage Rolls-Royce Wraith. Demeter had picked up the car in a federal auction, more than a decade before.

Its prior owner was one Charles Talent Manx, former resident at FCI Englewood in Colorado.

Demeter had mentioned Manx in the note he'd written shortly before his death by strangulation; he had misspelled the name, but it was pretty clear whom he was talking about. Hutter had seen a scan of the note, had read it herself a dozen times.

Tabitha Hutter had learned the Dewey decimal system and then organized the books in her Boston apartment according to it. She had a plastic box filled with carefully handwritten recipes, ordered by region and food type (main course, appetizers, desserts, and one category labeled "p.c.s.," for postcoital snacks). She took private, almost guilty pleasure in defragmenting her hard drive.

She sometimes imagined her own mind as a futuristic apartment with a clear glass floor, clear glass stairs, furniture made out of clear plastic, everything seeming to float: clean, dustless, ordered.

But it wasn't like that now, and when she tried to think about what had happened in the last seventy-two hours, she felt overwhelmed and confused. She wanted to believe that information brought clarity. Not for the first time in her life, however, she had the disconcerting notion that it was often the opposite. Information was a jar of flies, and when you unscrewed the lid, they went everywhere and good luck to you trying to round them all up again.

Hutter inhaled the mossy-smelling night, shut her eyes, and cataloged the flies:

Victoria McQueen had been abducted at age seventeen by Charles Manx, a man who had almost certainly kidnapped others. He was at that time driving a Rolls-Royce Wraith, the 1938 model. Vic got away from him, and Manx was jailed for transporting her across state lines and murdering an active-duty soldier. In another sense Vic had not escaped him at all. Like so many survivors of trauma and probable sexual assault, she was made a prisoner again and again—of her addictions, of madness. She stole things, did drugs, bore a child out of wedlock, and burned through a string of failed relationships. What Charlie Manx had not been able to do she had been trying to do for him ever since.

Manx had spent close to twenty years locked up in the FCI Englewood Supermax. After drifting in and out of a coma for most of a decade, he had died this past spring. The coroner had estimated his age at ninety—no one knew the exact number, and while he was still cogent, Manx had claimed to be a hundred sixteen years old. The body had been snatched from the morgue by vandals, creating a minor scandal, but there was no question of his death. His heart had weighed 10.2 ounces, a bit light for a man of his size. Hutter had seen a photograph of it.

McQueen claimed she'd been assaulted again, just three days ago, by Charlie Manx and a man in a gasmask, and that these men had driven off with her twelve-year-old son in the back of a vintage Rolls-Royce.

It had been reasonable to doubt her story. She'd been badly beaten—but her injuries might've been inflicted by a twelve-year-old struggling for his life. There were tire tracks on the lawn, but they could've been made by her motorcycle as easily as by a car—the soft, wet earth held no usable prints. She claimed she'd been shot at, but forensics had failed to recover a single bullet.

Also, more damningly: McQueen had secretly contacted a woman, Margaret Leigh, a heartland hooker and drug addict who seemed to have information about the missing child. When McQueen was confronted about Leigh, she fled on a motorcycle, taking nothing. And had disappeared as if she'd dropped down a mine shaft.

Ms. Leigh had been impossible to locate. She had drifted through a series of shelters and halfway houses in Iowa and Illinois, had not paid taxes or held a job since 2008. Her life had an unmistakably tragic arc: Once she had been a librarian and a beloved if eccentric local Scrabble competitor. Leigh also once held a reputation as something of an amateur psychic, of occasional use to law enforcement. What did that mean?

Then there was the hammer. The hammer had been on Hutter's mind for days. The more she learned, the heavier that hammer weighed in her thoughts. If Vic were going to make up a story about being attacked, why not say Manx had come at her with a baseball bat, a shovel, a crowbar? Instead McQueen described a weapon that had to be a bone mallet, just like the one that had gone missing with Manx's body—a detail that had never appeared in any news report.

Finally there was Louis Carmody, Vic McQueen's occasional lover, father of their child, the man who had driven her away from Charlie Manx all those years ago. Carmody's stenosis was not a put-on; Hutter had spoken to the doctor who treated him, and she had confirmed he had suffered from one, possibly two, "prestroke" events in the space of a week.

"He should not have left the hospital," the doctor said to Hutter, as if Hutter herself were to blame for his departure. In a sense she was. "Without an angioplasty, any strain on his heart could initiate an ischemic cascade. Do you understand? An avalanche in the brain. A major infarction."

"You're saying he could stroke out," Hutter said.

"At any minute. Every minute he's out there, he's like a guy lying down in the middle of a road. Sooner or later he will be run over."

And still Carmody had walked out of the hospital, grabbed a cab to the train station half a mile away. There he'd bought a ticket for Boston, presumably in some half-assed attempt to throw law enforcement off, but then walked down the street to a CVS where he made a call to Dover, New Hampshire. Forty-five minutes later Christopher McQueen arrived in a pickup, and Carmody got into the passenger seat. And here they were.

"So. What do you think Vic McQueen was into?" Daltry asked.

The tip of his cigarette flared in the dark, casting an infernal light on his seamed, ugly face.

"Into?"

"She made a beeline for this guy Bing Partridge. She hunted him down to get information about her son. Which she did. She said so, didn't she? She was obviously involved with some reprehensible shit-buckets. That's why the kid was grabbed, don't you think? She was being taught a lesson by her business partners."

"I don't know," Hutter said. "I'll ask her when I see her."

Daltry lifted his head, blew smoke into the pale mist. "I bet human trafficking. Or child pornography. Hey, that makes sense, doesn't it?"

"No," Hutter said, and began to walk.

At first she was just stretching her legs out, restless to move. Walking helped her think. She put her hands in the pockets of her FBI windbreaker and took herself around the deli truck, down to the edge of the highway. When she looked across the road, she could see a few lights from Christopher McQueen's house through the pines.

The doctor said that Carmody was lying in the road, waiting to get run down, but that wasn't quite right. It was worse than that. He was strolling up the middle of the street, willfully walking right into oncoming traffic. Because there was something at this house that he needed. No, correction: that *Wayne* needed. It was important enough that all other considerations, including Lou's own continued survival, could be set aside. It was there in that house. It was two hundred feet away.

Daltry caught up to her as she was crossing the road. "So what are we doing now?"

"I want to sit with one of the surveillance crews," Hutter said. "If you're coming, you'll have to put out that cigarette."

Daltry dropped it in the road and stepped on it.

When they were across the highway, they walked along the gravel margin. They were forty feet from the drive to Christopher McQueen's cabin when a voice called.

"Ma'am?" someone said softly.

A small, stout woman in a midnight blue rain jacket stepped from under the boughs of a spruce. It was the Indian woman, Chitra. She held a long stainless-steel flashlight in one hand, but she didn't switch it on.

"It's me. Hutter. Who's here?"

"Myself and Paul Hoover and Gibran Peltier." They were one of two teams positioned in the trees, watching the house. "Something's wrong with the equipment. The bionic dish quit. The camera won't turn on."

"We know," Daltry said.

"What happened?" Chitra asked.

"Sunspot," Daltry said.

Christopher McQueen's House

Vic left the Triumph by the trees, on a slight rise above her father's house. When she stood up from the bike, the world lurched. She had a sensation of being a small figure in a glass snow globe, being tilted this way and that by an insensitive toddler.

She started down the slope and was surprised to find she could not walk in a straight line. If a cop pulled her over, she doubted she could pass a basic sobriety test, never mind that she had not had a drop to drink. Then it occurred to her that if a cop pulled her over, he would probably cuff her and give her a couple of swats with the nightstick while he was at it.

Her father's shape was joined at the back door by that of a big, broad-chested man with an immense stomach and a neck thicker than his shaved head. Lou. She could've picked him out of a crowd from five hundred feet away. Two of the three guys who had loved her in her life, watching her make her unsteady way down the hill; the only one missing was Wayne.

Men, she thought, were one of the world's few sure comforts, like a fire on a cold October night, like cocoa, like broken-in slippers. Their clumsy affections, their bristly faces, and their willingness to do what needed to be done—cook an omelet, change lightbulbs, make with hugging—sometimes almost made being a woman fun.

She wished she were not so aware of the vast gulf between what the men in her life *thought* she was worth and her actual value. She had, it seemed to her, always asked and expected too much and given too little. She seemed almost to have a perverse impulse to make anyone who cared about her regret it, to find the thing that would most appall those people and then do that until they had to run away as a matter of self-preservation.

Her left eye felt like a great screw, slowly turning, twisting tighter and tighter in her eyesocket.

For a dozen steps, her left knee refused to bend. Then, halfway across the backyard, it folded without warning and she dropped down onto it. It felt as if Manx were smashing it with his hammer.

Her father and Lou came spilling out the door, hurrying toward her. She waved a hand in a gesture that seemed to mean, *Don't worry about it, I'm cool.* She found, however, that she could not stand back up. Now that she was down on one knee, the leg would not unfold.

Her father looped one arm around her waist. He pressed his other hand against her cheek.

"You're burning up," he said. "Jesus, woman. Let's get you inside."

He took one arm and Lou took the other, and they hauled her to her feet. She turned her head against Lou for a moment and inhaled deeply. His round, grizzled face was wan, greasy with damp, beads of rainwater all over his bald skull. Not for the first time in her life, she thought he had missed his century and his country: He would've made a fine Little John and would've been perfectly at ease fishing in Sherwood Forest.

I would be so happy for you, she thought, *if you found someone worth loving, Lou Carmody.*

Her father was on her other side, his arm around her waist. In the dark, well away from his little log house, he was the same man he had been when she was a kid—the man who'd joked with her while he put Band-Aids on her scrapes and who took her for rides on the back of his Harley. But as he stepped into the light spilling from the open back door, she saw a man with white hair and a face made gaunt with age. He had a regrettable mustache and leathery skin—the skin of a lifelong smoker—with deep lines etched into his cheeks. His jeans were loose and baggy on his nonexistent ass and pipe-cleaner legs.

"What's that pussy tickler doing on your face, Dad?" she asked.

He shot her a surprised sidelong look, then shook his head. Opened his mouth and closed it. Shook his head again.

Neither Lou nor her father wanted to let go of her, and so they had to turn sideways to shuffle in through the door. Chris went first and helped her over the doorsill.

They paused in a back hallway, a washer and dryer on one side, some pantry shelves on the other. Her father looked at her again.

"Oh, Vic," he said. "What in God's name's been done to you?" And he shocked her by bursting into tears.

It was noisy, choked, unpretty crying that shook his thin shoulders. He cried with his mouth open so she could see his metal fillings in the back of his teeth. She felt a little like crying herself, could not believe she looked any worse than he did. It seemed to her she had last seen him only a while ago—it felt like last week—and he had been fit, limber, and ready, with calm, pale eyes that suggested he wouldn't run from anything. Although he *had* run. And so what? She had not done any better herself. By many measures she had probably done worse.

"You should see the other guy," she said.

Her father made a choked sound halfway between a sob and a laugh.

Lou looked back out through the screen door. The night beyond smelled of mosquitoes—an odor a bit like stripped wire, a bit like rain.

"We heard a noise," Lou said. "Like a bang."

"I thought it was a backfire. Or a gun going off," her father said. Tears streamed down his leathery cheeks, hung gemlike in his bushy, tobacco-stained mustache. All he needed was a gold star on his chest and a pair of Colt revolvers.

"Was that your bridge?" Lou asked. His voice soft and gentle with wonder. "Did you just come across?"

"Yes," she said. "I just came across."

They helped her into the small kitchen. Just one light was on, a smoked-glass dish hanging over the table. The room was as tidy as a show kitchen, the only sign that anyone lived here the smooshed filters in the amber ashtray and the haze of cigarette smoke in the air. And the ANFO.

The ANFO was on the table in an unzipped school backpack, a mass of twenty-kilo sacks. The plastic was slippery and white, covered in warning labels. They were packed tight and smooth. Each was about the size of a loaf of bread. Vic knew without lifting them that they would be heavy, like picking up bags of unmixed concrete.

They eased her into a cherrywood chair. She stretched out her left leg. She was conscious of an oily sweat on her cheeks and forehead that could not be wiped away. The light over the table was too bright. Being near it was like someone gently forcing a sharpened pencil back through her left eye and into her brain.

"Can we turn that off?" she asked.

Lou found the switch, flipped it, and the room was dark. Somewhere down a hall, another lamp was on, casting a brownish glow. She didn't mind that one so much.

Outside, the night throbbed with peepers, a sound that made Vic think of a great electrical generator, humming in pulses.

"I made it go away," she said. "The bridge. So no one could follow me across it. That's . . . that's why I'm warm. I've been across it a few times in the last two days. It makes me a little feverish. It's okay, though. It's nothing."

Lou sank into a chair across from her. The wood creaked. He

looked ridiculous, sitting at the little wooden table, like a bear in a tutu.

Her father leaned against the kitchen counter, his arms crossed over his slender, sunken chest. The darkness, she thought, was a relief to them both. Here they were both shadows, and he could be himself again, the man who sat in her bedroom when she was sick and told her stories about places he had gone on his motorcycle, scrapes he'd been in. She could be the person she was when they shared the same house, a girl she liked very much, missed very much, and with whom she had little in common.

"You used to get like this when you were small," her father said, his thoughts perhaps running along the same course. "You'd come in from riding around town on your bike, usually with something in one hand. A lost doll. A lost bracelet. And you'd be a little warm and telling lies. Your mom and I used to talk about it all the time. About where you went. We thought maybe you had light fingers, that you were . . . ah, borrowing things, then bringing them back when people noticed they were gone."

"*You* didn't think that," she said. "You didn't think I was out stealing."

"No. I guess that one was mostly your mother's theory."

"What was *your* theory?"

"That you were using your bike like a dowsing rod. You know about dowsing rods? Old-timers in these parts would get a piece of yew or hazel and wave it around looking for water. Sounds crazy, but where I grew up, you didn't dig a well without talking to a dowser first."

"You're not too far off. You remember the Shorter Way?"

He lowered his head in thought. In profile he looked almost exactly like the man he had been at thirty.

"Covered bridge," he said. "You and the other kids used to dare each other to cross it. Thing gave me fits. Looked ready to fall into the river. They took it down—1985?"

"'86. Except it never really came down for me. When I needed to find something, I could ride out into the woods and it would reappear, and I could go across it to whatever was missing. As a kid I used my Raleigh. Remember the Tuff Burner you got me for my birthday?"

"It was too big for you," he said.

"I grew into it. Like you said I would." She paused, then nodded back in the direction of the screen door. "Now I've got my Triumph out there. Next time I go across the Shorter Way Bridge, it'll be to meet Charlie Manx. He's the one who has Wayne."

Her father did not reply. His head remained bowed.

"For what it's worth, Mr. McQueen," Lou said, "I believe every crazy-ass word of this."

"You just came across it? Just now?" her father asked. "This bridge of yours?"

"Three minutes ago I was in Iowa. Seeing a woman who knows—*knew*—about Manx."

Lou frowned, heard Vic putting Maggie in past tense, but she went on before he could interrupt and ask a question she couldn't bear to answer.

"You don't have to take it on faith. Once you tell me how to use the ANFO, I'll make the bridge reappear, so I can be on my way. You'll *see* it. It's bigger than your house. Remember Snuffleupagus on *Sesame Street*?"

"Big Bird's imaginary friend?" her father asked, and she could sense him smiling in the dark.

"The bridge isn't like that. It isn't some make-believe thing only I can see. If you absolutely had to see it, I could bring it back right now, but . . . but I'd rather not until it's time to go." She reached, unconsciously, to rub at the cheekbone below her left eye. "It's getting to be like a bomb going off in my head."

"You're not riding off right now anyway," he said. "You just got here. Look at you. You're in no shape. You need rest. A doctor, probably."

"I've had all the rest I need, and if I head to a hospital, any doctor I see is going to prescribe a pair of handcuffs and a trip to the lockup. The feds think— I don't know what they think. That I killed Wayne, maybe. Or that I'm into something illegal and he was snatched to teach me a lesson. They don't believe me about Charlie Manx. I can't blame them. Manx died. A doctor even performed a partial autopsy on him. I sound like a fucking nutjob." She caught herself, eyed him in the dark. "How come *you* believe me?"

"Because you're my girl," he said.

He said it so plainly and gently that she couldn't help hating him, felt a sudden, unexpected sickness rising in her breast. She had to look away. Had to take a deep breath to keep her voice from shuddering with emotion.

"You left me, Dad. You didn't just leave Mom. You left *us.* I was in trouble, and you took off."

He said, "By the time I knew it was a mistake, it was too late to come back. That's usually how it is. I asked your mom to take me back, and she said no, and she was right to."

"You still could've stayed close. I could've come to your place on weekends. We could've spent time together. I wanted you there."

"I was ashamed. I didn't want you to look at the girl I was with. The first time I saw you two together was the first time I realized I didn't belong with her." He waited a moment, then said, "I can't say I was happy with your mother. I can't say I enjoyed almost twenty years of being judged by her and always found wanting."

"Did you let her know that with the back of your hand a couple times, Dad?" she said, her voice curdled with disgust.

"I did," he said. "In my drinking days. I asked her to forgive me before she died, and she did. That's something, although I don't forgive myself for it. I'd tell you I'd give anything to take it all back, but I don't believe that kind of line is worth much."

"*When* did she forgive you?"

"Every time we talked. I talked to her every day in the last six months. She'd call when you went to AA meetings. To joke around. To tell me about how you were doing. What you were drawing. What Wayne was up to. How you and Lou were managing. She'd e-mail me photos of Wayne." He stared at her in the dark for a moment and said, "I don't expect you to forgive me. I made some choices that are unforgivable. The worst things you think about me—they're all true. But I love you and always have, and if I can do anything to help you now, I will."

She put her head down, almost between her knees. She felt winded and light-headed. The darkness around her seemed to swell and recede like a kind of liquid, like the surface of a black lake.

"I won't try and justify my life to you. It can't be justified," he said. "I did a few good things, but I never got carried away with myself."

She couldn't help herself. She laughed. It hurt her sides and felt a little like retching, but when she lifted her head, she found she could look at him.

"Yeah. Me neither," she said. "I did a few good things, but I never got carried away. Mostly I was best at blowing shit up. Just like you."

"Speaking of blowing shit up," Lou said. "What are we doing with this?" He gestured toward the backpack filled with ANFO.

He had a paper tag looped around his exposed wrist. Vic stared at it. He saw her looking, and he blushed and tucked it into the sleeve of his flannel coat.

Lou went on. "This is explosive, right? How safe is it for you to be smoking in here around it?"

Her father inhaled deeply on his cigarette, then leaned in between them and deliberately put the butt out in the ashtray next to the backpack.

"Safe enough, long as you don't drop it into a campfire or something. The detonators are in that bag hanging offa Vic's chair." Vic glanced around and saw a shopping bag strung over one post of the chair back. "Any one of those sacks of ANFO would be ideal for blowing up the federal building of your choice. Which is hopefully not what you're planning on."

"No," Vic said. "Charlie Manx is headed to a place called Christmasland. It's this little kingdom he's got set up for himself where he thinks no one can touch him. I'm going to meet him there and take Wayne back, and I'm going to blast his place into the dirt while I'm at it. Crazy fuck wants every day to be like Christmas, but I'll give him the fucking Fourth of July."

Outside

EVERY TIME TABITHA HUTTER SETTLED AND WENT STILL, THE MOSquitoes returned, whining at one ear or the other. Brushing her cheek, she startled two of them, sweeping them off her and into the night. If Hutter had to work a stakeout, she preferred the car, liked air-conditioning and her iPad.

It was a matter of principle not to complain. She would die of blood loss first, sucked dry by the fracking little vampires. She especially wasn't going to grumble about it in front of Daltry, who squatted down with the others and then sat there like a statue, a smirk on his mouth and his eyelids half closed. When a mosquito settled on his temple, she slapped it and left a bloody smudge on his skin. He jerked but then nodded his appreciation.

"They love you," he said to her. "The mosquitoes. They love all that tender lady flesh, gently marinated in grad school. You probably taste like veal."

There were three others at the surveillance post in the woods, including Chitra, all of them dressed in lightweight black rain shells over tactical body armor. One agent held the sonic dish—a black gun with a mouth like a megaphone and a coiled black telephone cord stretching to the receiver in his ear.

Hutter leaned forward, tapped his shoulder, whispered, "Are you getting anything out of that?"

The man with the listening device shook his head. "I hope they're getting something at the other position. I don't hear anything except white noise. It's been nothing but static ever since that little burst of thunder."

"It wasn't thunder," Daltry said. "It didn't sound anything like thunder."

The guy shrugged.

The house was a one-story log cabin with a pickup parked out front. A single dim lamp was on in a front sitting room. One of the shades was halfway up, and Hutter could see a television (turned off), a couch, a hunting print on the wall. Some girlie white lace curtains hung in another front window, indicating a bedroom. There couldn't be much else in there: a kitchen in back, a bathroom, maybe a second bedroom, although that would be pushing it. So that meant Carmody and Christopher McQueen were in the back of the house.

"Is it possible they're whispering?" Hutter asked. "And your equipment isn't sensitive enough to pick them up?"

"When this is working, it's about sensitive enough to pick up loud thoughts," said the man with the earpiece. "The problem is that it's *too* sensitive. It caught a blast of something it couldn't handle and maybe blew a capacitor."

Chitra rooted in a gym bag and came up with a can of Deep Woods OFF.

"Thank you," Hutter said, taking it from her. She glanced at Daltry. "You want?"

They rose together so she could spray him down.

Standing, she could see a bit of the slope behind the house rising toward the tree line. Two squares of warm, amber-hued light spread out across the grass, light from the windows at the rear of the house.

She squeezed the button, sprayed white mist over Daltry. He shut his eyes.

"You know what I think that big slamming sound was?" he said. "That fat bastard keeling over. Thanks, that's enough." She stopped spraying. He opened his eyes. "You going to be okay if he drops dead?"

"He didn't have to run," she said.

"You didn't have to let him." Daltry grinned when he said it. "You enabled the poor boy."

Hutter felt an urge, clear and simple, to spray OFF into Daltry's eyes.

And there it was, the source of her discomfort, her restlessness. Louis Carmody seemed too trusting, too good-humored, too worried about his boy, too kind to his ex to have had anything to do with Wayne's disappearance. He was, Hutter thought, an innocent, but she had hung him out there anyway, to see where he'd lead her, and never mind he could drop from a stroke at any time. If the big man stroked out, was that on her head? She supposed it was.

"We needed to see what he'd do. Remember. This isn't about *his* well-being. It's about the boy's."

Daltry said, "You know why I like you, Hutter? Really like you? You're a bigger son of a bitch than I am."

Hutter thought, not for the first time, that she hated a lot of cops. Ugly, mean drunks who believed the worst of everyone.

She shut her eyes and misted OFF over her head and face and neck. When she opened her eyes and exhaled, to blow away the poison, she saw that the lights in the back of the house had gone out, had vanished from the lawn. She wouldn't have noticed it if she were crouching down.

Hutter shifted her gaze to the front room. She could see the hall leading to the back of the house, but no one came down it. She glanced at the front bedroom, waited for someone to turn a light on there. No one did.

Daltry hunkered down with the others, but she remained standing. After a minute he craned his head back to look at her.

"Are you pretending to be a tree?"

"Who do we have watching the rear of the house?" she asked.

The second state trooper, a guy who had until now not spoken, looked back at her. His face was pale and freckled, and with his ginger hair he somewhat resembled Conan O'Brien.

"No one. But there's nothing back there. Miles of woods, no trail. Even if they made us, they wouldn't run that—"

Hutter was already stalking away, hands stretched out in front of her to protect her face from branches.

Chitra caught up to her in four steps. She had to hustle to keep up, her handcuffs jangling on her belt.

"You are concerned?" she asked.

Behind her she heard a branch snap, heard shoes crunching in the deadfall. That would be Daltry, following in no particular hurry. He was as bad as the mosquitoes; she needed a spray to repel *him*.

"No," Hutter said. "You had a position. There was no reason not to hold it. If they leave, they'll go out the front door. That's completely reasonable."

"So . . . ?"

"I'm puzzled."

"About . . . ?"

"Why they're sitting in the dark. They shut the lights off back here, but they didn't come into the front of the house. So that means they're sitting in the back of the house with the lights off. Doesn't that seem peculiar?"

On her next step, her foot sank into cold, brackish water, three inches deep. She grabbed the slender trunk of a birch sapling to steady herself. In another yard Hutter was in up to her knees. The water didn't look any different from the ground, a black surface carpeted in leaves and branches.

As Daltry came up along beside them, he plunged into the water up to his thighs, staggered, nearly fell.

"We could use a light," Chitra said.

"Or a snorkel," Daltry said.

"No light," Hutter said. "And you can go back if you don't like getting wet."

"What? And miss all the fun? I'd rather drown."

"Don't get our hopes up," Hutter told him.

Inside

McQueen sat at the table with them in the dark. He had the bag of detonators in his lap and had removed one and held it in his hand. Lou was not reassured to see that the detonator in no way resembled the high-tech devices used to ignite explosives on *24* or in a *Mission: Impossible* film. They were instead little black timers from Home Depot, with curiously familiar-looking brass-ended wires dangling from them.

"Uh, Mr. McQueen? Dude?" Lou asked. "That looks like the kind of timer I use to switch on the Christmas lights when it's getting dark."

"That's all it is," he said. "Best I could do on short notice. The sacks are prepped, which means the compounds inside have been soaked in diesel and wired with a small charge. You just tie in the line, same as you'd tie in your Christmas lights. The black hand tells you what time it is. The red hand tells you when it'll turn on your lights. Or, in this case, go off with about twenty thousand foot-pounds of force. Enough to tear off the front of a three-story building, if the charge is placed right." He paused and looked at Vic. "Don't wire them until you get where you're going. You don't want to be bouncing around on your bike with these wired up."

Lou wasn't sure what frightened him more: the knapsack full of

ANFO or the way the guy looked at his daughter, his watery pale eyes so clear and cool as to have nearly no color at all.

"I kept it simple and real al-Qaeda," McQueen said, and dropped the timer back into the shopping bag. "This wouldn't pass state requirements, but it would do okay in Baghdad. Ten-year-olds strap this stuff to their bodies and blow themselves up without any trouble all the time. Nothing will get you to Allah faster. Guaranteed."

Vic said, "I understand." Reaching for the backpack and pushing up from the table. "Dad, I have to go. It isn't safe for me to be here."

"I'm sure you wouldn't have come if there was any other way," he said.

She leaned toward him and kissed his cheek. "I knew you'd have my back."

"Always," he said.

He held on to her, arm around her waist. His gaze reminded Lou of certain mountain lakes that appeared crystalline and pure because acid rain had killed everything in them.

"Minimum safe distance for an open-air blast—that's a bomb on the surface of the ground—is a hundred feet. Anyone within a hundred feet will have their insides jellied by the shockwave. Have you scoped out this joint? This Christmasland? Do you know where you're going to place your charges? It'll probably take an hour or two to safely wire and set these things."

"I'll have time," she said, but Lou knew from the way she held her father's gaze, from the look of perfect calm on her face, that she was full of it.

"I won't let her kill herself, Mr. McQueen," Lou said, pushing himself up and reaching for the grocery bag full of timers. He plucked it out of Christopher McQueen's lap before the man could move. "You can trust me."

Vic blanched. "What are you talking about?"

"I'm going with you," Lou said. "Wayne's my fuckin' kid, too. Anyway. We had a deal, remember? I fix the bike and you take me along. You don't get to go off and do this thing without me being there to make sure you don't blow the both of you up. Don't worry. I'll ride bitch seat."

"What about me?" Chris McQueen said. "You think I could follow you across the magic rainbow bridge in my truck?"

Vic drew a thin breath. "No. I mean . . . just no. *Neither* of you can come. I know you want to help, but neither of you can go with me. Look. This bridge . . . it's real, you'll both be able to see it. It'll be here, with us, in our world. But at the same time, in some way I don't understand, it also mostly exists in my head. And the structure isn't very safe anymore. Hasn't been safe since I was a teenager. It could collapse under the weight of carrying another mind. Besides. I might have to come back through with Wayne sitting behind me. Probably *will* have to come back through that way. If he's on the bike, Lou, where are you going to sit?"

"Maybe I could just follow you back across on foot. You ever think of that?" Lou asked.

"That's a bad idea," she said. "If you saw it, you'd understand."

"Well," Lou said, "let's go see."

She gave him a look that was pained and pleading. A look like she was fighting the urge to cry.

"I *need* to see," Lou said. "I need to know this is real, and not because I'm worried you're crazy but because I need to believe there's a chance here for Wayne to come home."

Vic gave her head a savage shake, but then she swiveled on her heel and hobbled for the back door.

She got two steps before she began to tilt over. Lou caught her arm.

"Look at you," he said. "*Dude.* You can hardly stay upright."

The heat coming off her sickened him.

"I'm okay," she said. "This will be over soon."

But in her eyes was a dull shine of something worse than fear—

desperation, maybe. Her father had said that any numb-ass ten-year-old could strap himself to ANFO and blow himself to Allah, and it came to Lou now that this was in fact a rough approximation of her plan.

They pushed through the screen door, into the cool of the night. Lou had noticed Vic swiping her hand under her left eye now and then. She was not crying, but water ran from the eye uncontrollably, a faint but continuous trickle. He had seen that before, in the bad days in Colorado, when she answered phones that weren't ringing and talked to people who weren't there.

Except they *had* been there. It was strange how quickly he had acclimated himself to that idea, how little struggle it had been to accept the terms of her madness as fact after all. Perhaps it wasn't so incredible. He had long accepted that everyone had his own world inside, each as real as the communal world shared by all but impossible for others to access. She had said she could bring her bridge into this world but that in some way it also existed only in her mind. It sounded like delusion until you remembered that people made the imaginary real all the time: taking the music they heard in their head and recording it, seeing a house in their imagination and building it. Fantasy was always only a reality waiting to be switched on.

They stepped past the woodpile, out from under the overhang of the roof and into the gentle, trembling mist. He glanced back as the screen door slapped shut again, Christopher McQueen following them out. Vic's dad snapped his lighter and lowered his head to set fire to another cigarette, then looked up and squinted through the smoke at her bike.

"Evel Knievel used to ride Triumphs," he told them, the last thing any of them said before the cops came out of the woods.

"EFF BEE EYE!" shouted a familiar voice from the tree line. "DON'T MOVE. HANDS IN THE AIR, HANDS IN THE AIR, ALL OF YOU!"

A dull throb of pain shot up the left side of Lou's neck, a thing he felt in his jaw, in his *teeth.* It crossed his mind that Vic wasn't the only one in possession of high explosive—he had a grenade ready to go off in his brain.

Of the three of them, only Lou seemed to think "HANDS IN THE AIR" was more than a suggestion. Lou's hands began to drift upward, palms out, although he still held the bag of detonators, the plastic strap looped over one thumb. He could see Chris McQueen at the periphery of his vision, over by the woodpile. The guy was perfectly motionless, still hunched in the act of lighting his cigarette, the tip glowing, his lighter in his other hand.

Vic, though. Vic bolted at the first shout, slipping away from Lou and staggering across the yard, her left leg stiff, refusing to bend. Lou dropped his hands and reached for her, but she was already ten feet away. By the time the woman coming out of the woods shouted "ALL OF YOU!" Vic had thrown one leg over the saddle of the Triumph. The other foot was coming down on the kickstart. The motorcycle roared to life in a shattering blast of noise. It was hard to imagine that a bag of ANFO could be any louder.

"NO, VIC, NO, VIC, *NO*! I *WILL* HAVE TO SHOOT YOU!" cried Tabitha Hutter.

The little woman was coming through the wet grass in a kind of sideways jog, holding an automatic pistol in both hands, just like cops did on TV shows. She was already close—fifteen, twenty feet away, close enough for Lou to see that her spectacles were dappled with raindrops. She had two others with her: the detective, Daltry, and a state trooper Lou recognized, an Indian woman. Daltry's trousers were soaked to the crotch, and he had dead leaves sticking to his pant legs, and he looked bad-tempered about it. He had a gun but was holding it out from his body, pointed away and at the ground. Taking them in, Lou recognized—half consciously—that only one of them was an immediate threat. Daltry's gun was pointing away, and Hutter couldn't see through her glasses. The Indian woman, though, held her gun on Vic, pointing it at Vic's center mass, and her eyes had a tragic look to them—her eyes seemed to say, *Please,* please *do not make me do something I don't want to do.*

"I'm going to get Wayne, Tabitha!" Vic shouted. "If you shoot me, you'll kill him, too. I'm the only way he's coming home."

"Wait!" Lou cried. "Wait! No one shoot anyone!"

"STOP MOVING!" Hutter shouted.

Lou didn't know who the hell she was talking about—Vic was sitting on her bike, and Chris was over at the woodpile, hadn't taken a single step. It was only when she twitched the barrel of the gun to point it at *him* that he realized *he* was the one moving. Without thinking about it, and with his hands up by his head, he had begun to cross the yard, stepping between Vic and the police officers.

By now Hutter was just three long steps away from him. She squinted through her glasses, the barrel of the gun lowered to point at Lou's vast expanse of belly. She might not be able to see him very well, but he supposed it was like shooting at a barn; the challenge would be in missing him.

Daltry had turned toward Christopher McQueen but in a sign of profound indifference did not bother to even cover him with his gun.

Lou said, "Hang on. No one's the bad guy here. The bad guy is Charlie Manx."

"Charlie Manx is dead," Tabitha Hutter said.

"Tell that to Maggie Leigh," Vic said. "Charlie just murdered her in Iowa at the Here Public Library. One hour ago. Check it out. I was there."

"You were—" Hutter started, then shook her head, as if to whisk a mosquito away from her face. "Get off the bike and lie facedown on the ground, Vic."

In the distance Lou heard other voices shouting, heard branches splintering, people charging through the bush. The sounds came from the other side of the house, which meant they probably had as much as twenty seconds before they were encircled.

Vic said, "I have to ride," and clunked the motorcycle into first gear.

"I'm going with her," Lou said.

Hutter continued to approach. The barrel of the gun was almost but not quite close enough to grab.

"Officer Surinam, will you cuff this man?" Hutter said.

Chitra Surinam began to move past and around Hutter. She lowered the barrel of her gun, and her right hand dropped to reach for the cuffs dangling from the side of her utility belt. Lou had always wanted a utility belt, like Batman's, with a grappling-hook gun on it and a few flash-bang bombs. If he had a utility belt and a flash-bang bomb now, he could throw one and blind the cops, and he and Vic could make their getaway. Instead he was holding a bag of Christmas-light timers from Home Depot.

Lou took a step back, so he was next to the bike, close enough to feel the blazing heat of the shuddering pipes.

"Give me the bag, Lou," Vic said.

Lou said, "Ms. Hutter. Ms. Hutter, please, *please,* radio your guys and ask about Maggie Leigh. Ask about what just happened in Iowa. You're getting ready to arrest the only person who can get my kid back. If you want to help our son, you need to let us go."

"No more talk, Lou," Vic said. "I've got to leave."

Hutter squinted, as if she were having trouble seeing through her glasses. No doubt she was.

Chitra Surinam closed in on him. Lou held out one hand, as to ward her off, and he heard a steely cranking sound and found she had thrown one bracelet of the handcuffs on him.

"Whoa!" he said. "Whoa, dude!"

Hutter slipped a cell phone out of her pocket, a silver rectangle the size of a hotel soap. She did not dial a number but depressed a single button. The phone blooped, and a male voice came through static.

"Cundy here. You throw down on the bad guys out there?"

Hutter said, "Cundy. Any word on the hunt for Margaret Leigh?"

The phone hissed.

Chitra said to Lou, "Your other hand, please, Mr. Carmody. Your other hand."

He didn't give it to her. Instead he held his left hand up out of reach, the plastic bag looped over his thumb, as if it were a bag of stolen candy and he was the schoolyard bully who had snatched it and didn't intend to give it back.

Cundy's voice came through the hiss, his tone unhappy. *"Uh, are you feeling especially psychic today? We just got word. Five minutes ago. I was going to tell you when you got back."*

The shouts from the other side of the house were closer.

"Tell me now," Hutter said.

"What the fuck *is* this?" Daltry asked.

Cundy said, *"She's dead. Margaret Leigh was beaten to death. The cops there like McQueen for it. She was spotted leaving the scene on her motorcycle."*

"No," Hutter said. "No, that's . . . that's impossible. Where did this happen?"

"Here, Iowa. A little over an hour ago. Why is it so imposs—"

But Hutter hit the button again, cut him off. She looked past Lou at Vic. Vic was twisted around on the saddle, the bike shuddering beneath her, staring back at her.

"It wasn't me," Vic said. "It was Manx. They're going to find out she was beaten to death with a hammer."

At some point Hutter had lowered her gun entirely. She put her phone in the pocket of her coat, wiped at the water on her face.

"A bone mallet," Hutter said. "The one Manx took with him when he walked out of that morgue in Colorado. I don't—I *can't*—understand this. I'm trying, Vic, but I just can't make sense of it. *How* is he up and walking? How are you here when you were just in Iowa?"

"I don't have time to explain about the rest. But if you want to know how I got here from Iowa, stick around. I'll show you."

Hutter said to Chitra, "Officer, will you please . . . take the cuffs off Mr. Carmody? They won't be necessary. Maybe we should just talk. Maybe all of us should just talk."

"I don't have time to—" Vic started, but none of them heard the rest.

"Oh, what the fuck is this?" Daltry said, turning away from Chris McQueen and bringing up his gun to aim at Vic. "Get off the motorcycle."

"Officer, holster your weapon!" Hutter cried.

"The fuck I will," Daltry said. "You're out of your mind, Hutter. Shut off the bike, McQueen. Shut it off *now*."

"Officer!" Hutter yelled. "I am in charge here, and I said—"

"On the ground!" screamed the first FBI agent around the eastern side of the house. He had an assault rifle. Lou thought it might be an M16. "ON THE FUCKING GROUND!"

It seemed as if everyone was yelling, and Lou felt another dull wallop of pain in his temple and the left side of his neck. Chitra wasn't looking at him, her head twisted around to stare at Hutter with a mix of anxiety and wonder.

Chris McQueen flicked his cigarette into Daltry's face. It hit below his right eye in a spray of red sparks, and Daltry flinched, the barrel of his gun lurching off target. Chris's free hand found a piece of stovewood at the top of the woodpile, and he came around with it and clubbed Daltry across the shoulder hard enough to stagger him.

"Get out of here, Brat!" he yelled.

Daltry took three stumbling steps across the mucky earth, steadied himself, lifted the gun, and put one bullet into McQueen's stomach and another into his throat.

Vic screamed. Lou turned toward her, and as he did, his shoulder bumped Chitra Surinam. This was, unfortunately, a bit like being bumped by a horse. Surinam put one foot back into the soggy earth, bent her ankle wrong, and went straight backward, sitting down in the wet grass.

"Everyone lower your weapons!" Hutter cried. "Goddamn it, HOLD YOUR FIRE!"

Lou reached for Vic. The best way to get his arms around her was to put a leg over the back of the bike.

"Off the motorcycle, off the motorcycle!" hollered one of the men in body armor. There were three of them coming across the grass with their machine guns.

Vic's face was turned to look back at her father, her mouth stretched open in her last cry, her eyes blind with amazement. Lou kissed her fevered cheek.

"We need to go," he said to her. "Now."

He closed his arms around her waist, and in the next instant the Triumph was under way and the night was lit up with the thunderous rattle of machine-gun fire.

Out Back

THE SOUND OF THE GUNS SHOOK THE DARKNESS ITSELF. VIC FELT ALL that noise tearing through her, mistook it for the impact of bullets, and reflexively grabbed the throttle. The back tire smoked and slipped across the wet earth, peeled up a long, soggy strip of grass. Then the Triumph jumped forward, into the darkness.

A part of her was still looking back, watching her father double over, reaching for his own throat, hair falling across his eyes. His mouth open as if he were trying to vomit.

A part of her was catching him before he could sink to his knees, was holding him in her arms.

A part of her was kissing his face. *I'm right here, Dad,* she told him. *I'm right here with you.* She was so close to him she could smell the fresh-poured-copper smell of his blood.

Lou's soft, bristly cheek was pressed to the side of her neck. He was spooned against her, the backpack full of explosives crushed between their bodies.

"Just ride," he said. "Get us where we have to go. Don't look, just ride."

Dirt flew up on her right as she twisted the bike around, pointing it upslope, toward the trees. Her ears registered the sound of bullets smacking into the soil behind them. Through the racket of gunfire, she picked out Tabitha Hutter's voice, wavering with strain:

"STOP SHOOTING, STOP SHOOTING!"

Vic couldn't think and didn't need to. Her hands and feet knew what to do, her right foot kicking up into second gear, then third. The bike scrambled up the wet hill. The pines rose in a dark wall before them. She lowered her head as they cut in between the tree trunks. A branch swatted her across the mouth, stung her lips. They broke through the brush, and the tires found the boards of the Shorter Way Bridge and began to clatter over them.

"What the fuck?" Lou cried.

She hadn't entered straight on, and her head was still down, and her shoulder hit the wall. The arm went dead, and she was shoved back into Lou.

In her mind her father was falling into her arms again.

Vic pulled on the handlebars, veering to the left, getting them away from the wall.

In her mind she was saying, *I'm right here,* while the two of them sank together to the ground.

One of the floorboards cracked under the front tire, and the handlebars were wrenched out of her hands.

She kissed her father's temple. *I'm right here, Dad.*

The Triumph careened into the left-hand wall. Lou's left arm was smashed against it, and he grunted. The force of him striking the wall made the whole bridge shudder.

Vic could smell the scalpy odor of her father's hair. She wanted to ask him how long he had been alone, why there was no woman in the house. She wanted to know how he kept himself, what he did to pass his evenings. She wanted to tell him she was sorry and that she still loved him; for all the bad, she still loved him.

Then Chris McQueen was gone. She had to let him go, let him slide free from her arms. She had to ride on without him.

Bats shrilled in the dark. There was a sound like someone riffling through a deck of cards, only vastly amplified. Lou twisted his head to look up between the rafters. Big, gentle, unshakable Lou did not scream, hardly made a sound at all, but he took a great sharp breath of air and ducked as dozens, perhaps hundreds, of bats, disturbed from their rest, dropped from the ceiling and rained upon them, whirling through the dank space. They were everywhere, brushing against their arms, their legs. One of them whisked by Vic's head, and she felt its wing graze her cheek and caught a glimpse of its face as it flitted past: small, pink, deformed, yet oddly human. She was looking at her own face, of course. It was all that Vic could do to stop herself from shrieking as she struggled to keep the Triumph on course.

The bike was almost to the far end of the bridge now. A few of the bats darted lazily out into the night, and Vic thought, *There goes part of my mind.*

Her old Raleigh Tuff Burner appeared before her. It seemed to race toward her, the headlight rushing over it. She realized, a half instant too late, that she was going to hit it and that the consequences would be brutal. The front tire smacked the Raleigh dead-on.

The Triumph seemed to snag and catch on the rusted, cobwebbed bicycle and was already turning sideways and toppling over as it exited the covered bridge. A dozen bats poured out with them.

The tires tore raggedly at dirt, then grass. Vic saw the ground fall away, saw they were about to tip over an embankment. She had a glimpse of pine trees, decorated with angels and snowflakes.

Then they went over a steep drop. The bike turned, dumping them off the side. It followed them down, crashing onto the both of them in an avalanche of hot iron. The world cracked open, and they fell into darkness.

The Sleigh House

LOU WAS AWAKE FOR CLOSE TO AN HOUR BEFORE HE HEARD A DRY, quiet crackling and saw little white flakes dropping into the dead leaves around him. He tipped his head back and squinted into the night. It had begun to snow.

"Lou?" Vic asked.

His neck was stiffening up, and it hurt to lower his chin. He looked over at Vic, lying on the ground to his right. She had been asleep a moment ago, but now she was with him, eyes open wide.

"Yeah," he said.

"Is my mother still here?"

"Your mother's with the angels, babe," he said.

"The angels," Vic said. "There's angels in the trees." Then: "It's snowing."

"I know. In July. I've lived in the mountains my whole life. I know spots where the snow stays year-round, but I've never seen the snow *fall* this time of year. Not even up here."

"Where?" she asked.

"Right above Gunbarrel. Where it all started."

"It started in Terry's Primo Subs when my mother left her bracelet in the bathroom. Where'd she go?"

"She wasn't here. She's dead, Vic. Remember?"

“She was sitting with us for a while. Over there.” Vic lifted her right arm and pointed at the embankment above them. The tires from the motorcycle had torn deep gouges in the slope, long, muddy trenches. “She said something about Wayne. She said Wayne will still have a little time when he gets to Christmasland, because he’s been running himself backward. Two steps back for every two miles forward. He won’t be one of those things. Not yet.”

She was stretched out on her back, arms at her sides, ankles together. Lou had put his flannel-lined coat over her; it was so big it covered her to her knees, as if it were a child’s blanket. Vic turned her head to look at him. She had a vacuity of expression that scared him.

“Oh, Lou,” she said, almost tonelessly. “Your poor face.”

He touched his right cheek, tender and swollen from the corner of his mouth to the edge of his eye socket. He didn’t remember how he got that one. The back of his left hand was badly burned, a steady throb of pain—when they came to rest, the hand had been caught under the bike, a hot pipe pressed against it. He couldn’t stand to look at it. The skin was black and cracked and glistening. He kept it down by his side, where Vic couldn’t see it either.

It didn’t matter about his hand. He didn’t think he had much time left. That sensation of ache and pressure in his throat and left temple was constant now. His blood felt as heavy as liquid iron. He was walking around with a gun to his head, and he thought at some point, before the night was over, it would go off. He wanted to see Wayne again before that happened.

He had pulled her from the bike as they went over the embankment, managed to roll so she was under him. The bike glanced off his back. If the Triumph had hit Vic—who probably weighed a hundred and five pounds with a brick in each pocket—it probably would’ve snapped her spine like a dry twig.

“You believe this snow?” Lou asked.

She blinked and wiggled her jaw and stared into the night. Flecks of snow dropped onto her face. “It means he’s almost here.”

Lou nodded. That was what he thought it meant.

"Some of the bats got out," she said. "They came out of the bridge with us."

He suppressed a shiver, couldn't suppress the feeling of his skin crawling. He wished she hadn't mentioned the bats. He had caught a glimpse of one, brushing past him, its mouth open in a barely audible shriek. As soon as he looked at it, he wished he had not seen it, wished he could *unsee* it. Its shriveled pink face had been horribly like Vic's own.

"Yeah," he said. "I guess they did."

"Those things are . . . me. The stuff in my head. When I use the bridge, there's always a chance some of them will escape." She rolled her head on her neck to look at him again. "That's the toll. There's always a toll. Maggie had a stutter that got worse and worse the more she used her Scrabble tiles. Manx had a soul once, probably, but his car used it up. Do you understand?"

He nodded. "I think."

"If I say some things that don't make sense," she said, "you have to let me know. If I start to seem confused, you straighten me out. Do you hear me, Lou Carmody? Charlie Manx will be here soon. I need to know you've got my back."

"Always," he said.

She licked her lips, swallowed. "Good. That's good. Good as gold. What's gold stays gold forever, you know? That's why Wayne is going to be okay."

A snowflake caught in one of her eyelashes. The sight of it struck him as almost heartbreaking in its beauty. He doubted he would ever see anything so beautiful again in his life. To be fair, he was not anticipating living beyond the evening.

"The bike," she said, and blinked again. Alarm rose upon her features. She sat up, elbows resting on the ground behind her. "The bike has to be all right."

Lou had pried it out of the dirt and leaned it against the trunk of a red pine. The headlight hung from its socket. The right-hand mirror had been torn off. It was missing both mirrors now.

"Oh," she said. "It's all right."

"Well. I don't know. I haven't tried starting it. We don't know what might've come loose. You want me to—"

"No. It's okay," she said. "It'll start."

The breeze blew the dusting of snow at a slant. The night filled with soft chiming sounds.

Vic lifted her chin, looked into the branches above them, filled with angels, Santas, snowflakes, globes of silver and gold.

"I wonder why they don't smash," Lou said.

"They're horcruxes," Vic said.

Lou shot a look at her, hard, worried. "You mean like in Harry Potter?"

She laughed—a frightening, unhappy sound. "Look at all of them. There is more gold and there are more rubies in these trees than there were in all of Ophir. And it will end the same here as it did there."

"'Oh, fear'?" he asked. "You're not making sense, Vic. Come back to me."

She lowered her head, shook it as if to clear it, then put a hand against her neck, grimaced in pain.

Vic looked up at him from beneath her hair. It shocked him—how suddenly like herself she seemed. She had that Vic smirk on her face and that look of mischief in her eyes that had always turned him on.

She said, "You're a good man, Lou Carmody. I may be one crazy bitch, but I love you. I'm sorry about a lot of things I put you through, and I wish like hell you'd met someone better than me. But I am not sorry we had a kid together. He's got my looks and your heart. I know which one is worth more."

He put his fists on the ground and slid on his butt to be next to her. He reached her side and put his arm around her and hugged her to his chest. Rested his face in her hair.

"Who says there's better than you?" he said. "You say things about yourself I wouldn't let anyone else in the world get away with saying." He kissed her scalp. "We made a good boy. Time to get him back."

She pulled away from him to look up in his face. "What happened to the timers? The explosives?"

He reached for the backpack, a few feet away. It was open.

"I started work on them," he said. "A little while ago. Just something to do with my hands while I waited for you to wake up." He gestured with his hands, as if to show how useless they were when they were empty. Then he put his left mitt down, hoping she hadn't noticed how badly it was burned.

The cuffs dangled from the wrist of his other hand. Vic smiled again, tugged on them.

"We'll do something kinky with these later," she said. Except she said it in a tone of inexpressible weariness, a tone that suggested not erotic anticipation but the distant memory of red wine and lazy kisses.

He blushed; he had always been an easy blusher. She laughed and pecked his cheek.

"Show me what you've got done," she said.

"Well," he told her, "not much. Some of the timers are no good—they got smashed while we were making our great escape. I've got four of them wired up." He reached into the sack and removed one of the slippery white packages of ANFO. The black timer dangled close to the top, connected to a pair of wires—one red and one green—that went down into the tight plastic bag containing the prepared explosive. "The timers are just little alarm clocks, really. One hand shows the hour, the other shows when they're set to switch on. See? And you press here to start them running."

It made his armpits prickle with monkey sweat, just holding one of the slick packs of explosive. A fucking Christmas-light timer was the only thing between the two of them and an explosion that wouldn't leave even fragments.

"There's one thing I don't get," he said. "When are you going to plant them? And where?"

He got to his feet and craned his head, looking either way, like a child about to cross a busy road.

They were in among trees on the sunken floor of the forest. The drive leading up to the Sleigh House was directly behind him, a gravel lane running along the embankment, a road barely wide enough to allow the passage of a single car.

To his left was the highway, where, almost exactly sixteen years before, a stringy teenage girl with coltish legs had come bursting out of the underbrush, her face blackened with soot, and been seen by a fat twenty-year-old on a Harley. At the time Lou had been riding away from a bitter argument with his father. Lou had asked for a little money, wanted to get his GED, then apply to state college and study publishing. When his father asked why, Lou said so he could start his own comic-book company. His father put on a puss and said why not use money as toilet paper, it would come to the same thing. He said if Lou wanted an education, he could do what *he* had done, and join the marines. Maybe lose some of the fat in the process and get a real haircut.

Lou took off on his bike so his mother wouldn't see him crying. It had been in his mind to drive to Denver, enlist, and disappear from his father's life, spend a couple years in the service overseas. He would not return until he was a different man, someone lean and hard and cool, someone who would allow his father to hug him but would not provide a hug in return. He would call his father "sir," sit stiffly at attention in his chair, resist smiling. *How do you like my haircut, sir?* he might ask. *Does it meet your high standards?* He wanted to drive away and come back remade, a man his parents didn't know. As it was, that was very much what happened, although he never got as far as Denver.

To his right was the house where Vic had nearly burned to death.

Not that it was a house anymore, not by any conventional definition. All that remained was a sooty cement platform and a tangle of burned sticks. Amid the ruin was a blistered and blackened old-fashioned Frigidaire on its side, the smoked and warped frame of a bed, part of a staircase. A single wall of what had once been the garage appeared almost untouched. A door set in that wall stood open, implying an invitation to come on in, pull up some burned lumber, have a seat, and stay awhile. Broken glass silted the rubble.

"I mean . . . this isn't, like, Christmasland, right?"

"No," she said. "It's the doorway. He probably doesn't *need* to come here to cross over, but it's easiest for him here."

Angels held trumpets to their lips, drifted and swayed in the flecks of snow.

"*Your* doorway—" he said. "The bridge. It's gone. It was gone by the time we hit the bottom of the slope."

"I can get it back when I need it," she said.

"I wish we could've brought those cops through with us. Led 'em right across. Maybe they could've pointed all those guns at the right guy."

She said, "I think the less weight put on the bridge, the better. It's an avenue of last resort. I didn't even want to bring *you* across."

"Well. I'm here now." He still held a glossy package of ANFO in one hand. He slipped it gently back in with the others and hefted the backpack. "What's the plan now?"

She said, "The first part of the plan is that you give those to me." She took one strap of the backpack. He stared at her for a moment, the pack between them, not sure he ought to allow her to have it, then let go. He had what he wanted; he was here now, and no way she could get rid of him. She hooked it over her shoulder.

"The second part of the plan—" she started, then turned her head and looked toward the highway.

A car slid along through the night, the light of its headlamps stammering through the trunks of the pines, casting absurdly long shadows across the gravel drive. It slowed as it approached the turn-off toward the house. Lou felt a dull throb of pain behind his left ear. The snow fell in fat goose-feather flakes, beginning to collect on the dirt road.

"Jesus," Lou said, and he hardly recognized his own strained voice. "It's him. We aren't ready."

"Get back here," Vic said.

She grabbed him by the sleeve and backpedaled, walking him across the carpet of dry, dead leaves and pine needles. The two of them slipped into a stand of birch trees. For the first time, Lou noticed their breath smoking in the moonlit-silvered night.

The Rolls-Royce Wraith turned onto the long gravel road. A reflection of the bone-colored moon floated on the windshield, caught in a cat's cradle of black branches.

They watched it make its stately approach. Lou felt his thick legs trembling. *I just need to be brave for a little while longer,* he thought. Lou believed with all his heart in God, had believed since he was a kid and saw George Burns in *Oh, God!* on video. He sent up a mental prayer to skinny, wrinkled George Burns now: *Please. I was brave once, let me be brave again. Let me be brave for Wayne and Vic. I'm going to die anyway, so let me die the right way.* It came to him then that he had wanted this, had often daydreamed of it: a final chance to show he could lay aside fear and do the thing that needed to be done. His big chance had come at last.

The Rolls-Royce rolled past them, tires crunching on the gravel. It seemed to slow as it came abreast of them, not fifteen feet off, as if the driver had seen them and was peering out at them. But the car did not stop, merely proceeded on its unhurried way.

"The second part?" Lou breathed, aware of his pulse rapping painfully in his throat. Christ, he hoped he didn't stroke out until it was all over.

"What?" Vic asked, watching the car.

"What was the second part of the plan?" he asked.

"Oh," she said, and took the other bracelet of his handcuffs and locked it around the narrow trunk of a birch tree. "The second part is you stay here."

In the Trees

On Lou's sweet, round, bristly face was the look of a child who has just seen a car back over his favorite toy. Tears sprang to his eyes, the brightest thing in the dark. It distressed her to see him nearly crying, to see his shock and disappointment, but the sound of the handcuff snapping shut—that sharp, clear click, echoing on the frozen air—was the sound of a final decision, a choice made and irreversible.

"Lou," she whispered, and put a hand on his face. "Lou, don't cry. It's all right."

"I don't want you to go alone," he said. "I wanted to be there for you. I said I would be there for you."

"You were," she said. "You still will be. You're with me wherever I go: You're part of my inscape." She kissed his mouth, tasted tears, but did not know if they were his or her own. She pulled back from him and said, "One way or another, Wayne is walking away tonight, and if I'm not with him, he's going to need you."

He blinked rapidly, weeping without shame. He did not struggle at the cuffs. The birch was perhaps eight inches thick and thirty feet high. The bracelet of the cuff barely fit around it. He stared at her with a look of grief and bewilderment. He opened his mouth but couldn't seem to find any words.

The Wraith pulled up to the right of the blasted ruin, alongside the single standing wall. It stopped there, idling. Vic looked toward it. In the distance she could hear Burl Ives.

"I don't understand," he said.

She reached down past the cuff to finger the paper hoop around his wrist; the one they had given him in the hospital, the one she had seen back in her father's house.

"What's this, Lou?" she asked.

"Oh, that?" he asked, and then made a sound that was half laugh, half sob. "I passed out again. It's nothing."

"I don't believe you," she said. "I just lost my father tonight, and I can't lose you, too. If you think I'm going to risk your life any more than it's already been risked, then you're crazier than I am. Wayne needs his dad."

"He needs his mother, too," he said. "So do I."

Vic smiled—her old Vic smile, a little rakish, a little dangerous.

"No promises," she said. "You're the best, Lou Carmody. You're not just a good man. You are a real honest-to-God hero. And I don't mean because you put me on the back of your motorcycle and drove me away from this place. That was the easy part. I mean because you've been there for Wayne every single day. Because you made school lunches and you got him to his dentist appointments and you read to him at night. I love you, mister."

She looked up the road again. Manx had gotten out of the car. He crossed through his own headlights, and she had her first good look at him in four days. He wore his old-fashioned coat with the double line of brass buttons and tails. His hair was black and shiny, slicked back from the enormous bulge of his brow. He looked like a man of thirty. In one hand he held his enormous silver hammer. Something small was cupped in the other hand. He stepped out of the lights and into the trees, disappearing briefly into shadow.

"I have to go," she said. She leaned in and kissed the side of Lou's cheek.

He reached for her, but she slipped away and walked to her Triumph. She looked it up and down. There was a fist-size dent in the teardrop-shaped gas tank, and one of the pipes was hanging loose, looked like it might drag on the ground. But it would start. She could feel it waiting for her.

Manx stepped out of the woods and stood between the taillights at the rear of the Wraith. He seemed to look straight at her, although it didn't seem possible that he could see her in the dark and falling snow.

"Hello!" he called. "Are you with us, Victoria? Are you here with your mean machine?"

"Let him go, Charlie!" she shouted. "Let him go if you want to live!"

Even at a distance of two hundred feet, she could see Manx beaming at her. "I think you know by now I am not so easy to kill! But come along, Victoria! Follow me to Christmasland! Let's go to Christmasland and finish this thing! Your son will be glad to see you!"

Without waiting for a reply, he climbed in behind the wheel of the Wraith. The taillights brightened, dimmed, and the car began to move again.

"Oh, Jesus, Vic," Lou said. "Oh, Jesus. This is a mistake. He's ready for you. There's got to be another way. Don't do it. Don't follow him. Stay with me, and we'll find another way."

"Time to ride, Lou," she said. "Watch for Wayne. He'll be along in a little bit."

She put her leg over the saddle and turned the key in the ignition. The headlight flickered for a moment, dimly, then guttered out. Vic shivered steadily in her cutoffs and sneakers, put her heel on the kickstart, threw her weight down. The bike coughed and muttered. She leaped again, and it made a listless, flatulent sound: *brapp.*

"Come on, honey," she said softly. "Last ride. Let's bring our boy home."

She rose to her full height. Snow caught in the fine hairs on her arms. She came down. The Triumph blasted to life.

"Vic!" Lou called, but she couldn't look at him now. If she looked at him and saw him crying, she would want to hold him and she might lose her nerve. She put the bike in gear. "Vic!" he shouted again.

She left it in first while she gunned it up the steep, short slope of the embankment. The back tire fished this way and that in the snow-slippery grass, and she had to put a foot down on the dirt and *push* to get over the hump.

Vic had lost sight of the Wraith. It had circled the blasted wreck of the old hunting lodge and disappeared through a gap in the trees on the far side. She slammed the bike up into second, then third, accelerating to catch up. Stones flew from under the tires. The bike felt loose and wobbly on the snow, which had now accumulated to a fine dusting on the gravel.

Around the ruin, into high grass, and then to a sort of dirt track through the fir trees, barely wide enough to accommodate the Wraith. It was really just a pair of narrow ditches, with a mass of ferns growing in the space between.

The boughs of the pines leaned in above her, making a close, dark, narrow corridor. The Wraith had slowed to let her catch up, was only about fifty feet ahead of her. NOS4A2 rolled on, and she followed its taillights. The icy air sliced through her thin T-shirt, filled her lungs with raw, frozen breath.

The trees began to fall away on either side of her, opening into a rock-strewn clearing. There was a stone wall ahead, with an old brick tunnel set into it, a tunnel hardly wide enough to admit the Wraith. Vic thought of her bridge. *This is* his *bridge,* she thought. A white metal sign was bolted to the stone, next to the tunnel entrance. PARK IS OPEN EVERY DAY ALL YEAR-ROUND! GET READY TO SCREAM HIP-HIP *SNOW*-RAY, KIDS!

The Wraith slipped into the tunnel. Burl Ives's voice echoed back down the brick-lined hole at her—a passageway Vic doubted had existed even ten minutes before.

Vic entered behind him. The right-hand pipe dragged on the cobbles, throwing sparks. The boom of the engine echoed in the stone-walled space.

The Wraith exited the tunnel ahead of her. She was close behind him, roaring out of the darkness, through the open candy-cane gates, past the nine-foot Nutcrackers standing guard, and into Christmasland at last.

TRIUMPH
ONE ETERNAL CHRISTMAS EVE

Christmasland

The Wraith led her down the main boulevard, Gumdrop Avenue. As the car eased along, Charlie Manx bopped on the horn, three times and then three times again: *da-da-da, da-da-da,* the unmistakable opening bars of "Jingle Bells."

Vic followed, shivering uncontrollably now in the cold, struggling to keep her teeth from banging together. When the breeze rose, it sliced through her shirt as if she wore nothing at all, and fine grains of snow cut across her skin like flecks of broken glass.

The tires felt unsteady on the snow-slick cobbles. Gumdrop Avenue appeared dark and deserted, a road through the center of an abandoned nineteenth-century village: old iron lampposts, narrow buildings with gabled roofs and dark dormer windows, recessed doorways.

Except as the Wraith rolled along, the gaslights sprang to life, blue flames sparking in their frost-rimed casements. Oil lamps lit themselves in the windows of the shops, illuminating elaborate displays. Vic rumbled past a candy store called Le Chocolatier, its front window showing off chocolate sleighs and chocolate reindeer and a large chocolate fly and a chocolate baby with the chocolate head of a goat. She passed a shop called Punch & Judy's, wooden puppets dangling in the window. A girl in a blue Bo-Peep outfit held her wooden hands to her face, her mouth open in a perfect circle of surprise. A boy in Jack-Be-Nimble short pants held an ax smeared luridly with blood. At his feet were a collection of severed wooden heads and arms.

Looming behind and beyond this little town market were the attractions, as lifeless and dark as the main street had been when they entered. She spied the Sleighcoaster, towering in the night like the skeleton of some colossal prehistoric creature. She saw the great black ring of the Ferris wheel. And behind it all rose the mountain face, a nearly vertical sheet of rock frosted in a few thousand tons of snow.

Yet it was the vast expanse above that grabbed and held Vic's attention. A raft of silver clouds filled fully half the night sky, and gentle, fat flakes of snow drifted lazily down. The rest of the sky was open, a harbor of darkness and stars, and hanging pendant in the center of it all . . .

A giant silver crescent moon, with a face.

It had a crooked mouth and a bent nose and an eye as large as Topeka. The moon drowsed, that enormous eye closed to the night. His blue lips quivered, and he issued a snore as loud as a 747 taking off; his exhalation caused the clouds themselves to shudder. In profile the moon over Christmasland looked very much like Charlie Manx himself.

Vic had been mad for many years but in all that time had never dreamed or seen anything like it. If there had been anything in the road, she would've hit it; it took close to ten full seconds to prise her gaze free from it.

What finally caused her to look down was a flicker of motion at the periphery of her vision.

It was a child, standing in a shadowed alley between the Olde Tyme Clock Shoppe and Mr. Manx's Mulled-Cider Shed. The clocks sprang to life as the Wraith passed them, clicking and ticking and tocking and chiming. A moment later a gleaming copper contraption sitting in the window of the Cider Shed began to huff, chuff, and steam.

The child wore a mangy fur coat and had long, unkempt hair, which seemed to indicate femininity, although Vic could not be entirely sure of gender. She—it—had bony fingers tipped with long, yellow fingernails. Its features were smooth and white, with a fine black tracery under the skin, so that its face resembled a crazed enamel mask, devoid of all expression. The child—the thing—watched her pass by, without a word. Its eyes flashed red, as a fox's will, when reflecting the glow of passing headlights.

Vic twisted her head to peer back over her shoulder, wanting another look, and saw three other children emerging out of the alley behind her. One appeared to be holding a scythe; two of them were barefoot. Barefoot in the snow.

This is bad, she thought. *You're already surrounded.*

She faced forward again and saw a rotary directly ahead, which circled the biggest Christmas tree she had ever seen in her life. It had to be well over one hundred twenty feet tall; the base of the trunk was as thick as a small cottage.

Two other roads angled off the great central rotary, while the remaining portion of the circle was lined by a hip-high stone wall that overlooked . . . nothing. It was as if the world ended there, dropping away into endless night. Vic had a good look as she followed the Wraith partway around the circle. The surface of the wall glittered with fresh snow. Beyond was an oil slick of darkness, coagulated with stars: stars rolling in frozen streams and impressionistic swirls. It was a thousand times more vivid, but every bit as false, as any sky Vic had ever drawn in her Search Engine books. The world *did* end there: She was looking out at the cold, fathomless limits of Charlie Manx's imagination.

Without any warning, the great Christmas tree lit all at once, and a thousand electric candles illuminated the children gathered around it.

A few sat in the lowest branches, but most—perhaps as many as thirty—stood beneath the boughs, in nightdresses and furs and ball gowns fifty years out of date and Davy Crockett hats and overalls and policeman uniforms. At first glance they all seemed to be wearing delicate masks of white glass, mouths fixed in dimpled smiles, lips too full and too red. Upon closer inspection the masks resolved into faces. The hairline cracks in these faces were veins, showing through translucent skin; the unnatural smiles displayed mouths filled with tiny, pointed teeth. They reminded Vic of antique china dolls. Manx's children were not children at all but cold dolls with teeth.

One boy sat in a branch and held a serrated bowie knife as long as his forearm.

One little girl dangled a chain with a hook on it.

A third child—boy or girl, Vic could not tell—wielded a meat cleaver and wore a necklace of bloodied thumbs and fingers.

Vic was now close enough to see the ornaments that decorated the tree. The sight forced the air out of her in hard, shocked breath. Heads: leather-skinned, blackened but not spoiled, preserved partially by the cold. Each face had holes where the eyes had once been. Mouths dangled open in silent cries. One decapitated head—a thin-faced man with a blond goatee—wore green-tinted glasses with heart-shaped, rhinestone-studded frames. They were the only adult faces in sight.

The Wraith turned at an angle and stopped, blocking the road. Vic dropped the Triumph into first gear, squeezed the brake, and came to a halt herself, thirty feet away from it.

Children began to spread out from beneath the tree, most of them drifting toward the Wraith but some circling behind her, forming a human barricade. Or inhuman barricade, as the case might be.

"Let him go, Manx!" Vic shouted. It took all her will to keep her legs steady, shaken as she was from a mixture of cold and fear. The sharp chill of the night stung her nostrils, burned her eyes. There was no safe place to look. The tree was hung with every other grown-up unfortunate enough to find his or her way to Christmasland. Surrounding her were Manx's lifeless dolls with their lifeless eyes and lifeless smiles.

The door of the Wraith opened and Charlie Manx stepped out.

He set a hat on his head as he rose to his full height—Maggie's fedora, Vic saw. He adjusted the brim, cocked it just so. Manx was younger than Vic herself now, and almost handsome, with his high cheekbones and sharp chin. He was still missing a piece of his left ear, but the scar tissue was pink and shiny and smooth. His upper teeth protruded, sticking into his lower lip, which gave him a characteristically daffy, dim-witted look. In one hand he held the silver hammer, and he swung it lazily back and forth, the pendulum of a clock ticking away moments in a place where time did not matter.

The moon snored. The ground shook.

He smiled at Vic and doffed Maggie's hat in salute to her but then turned to look upon the children, who came toward him from beneath the branches of their impossible tree. The long tails of his coat swirled around him.

"Hello little ones," he said. "I have missed you and missed you! Let's have some light so I can look at you."

He reached up with his free hand and pulled an imaginary cord dangling in the air.

The Sleighcoaster lit up, a tangled thread of blue lights. The Ferris wheel blazed. Somewhere nearby a merry-go-round began to turn, and music rang out from invisible speakers. Eartha Kitt sang in her dirty-sweet, naughty-nice voice, telling Santa what a good girl she had been in a tone that suggested otherwise.

In the bright carnival lights, Vic could see that the children's clothes were stained with dirt and blood. Vic saw one little girl hurrying toward Charlie Manx with open arms. There were bloody handprints on the front of her tattered white nightgown. She reached Charlie Manx and put her arms around his leg. He cupped the back of her head, squeezed her against him.

"Oh, little Lorrie," Manx said to her. Another, slightly taller girl, with long, straight hair that came to the backs of her knees, ran up and embraced Manx from the other side. "My sweet Millie," he said. The taller girl wore the red-and-blue uniform of a Nutcracker, with crossed bandoliers over her thin chest. The girl had a knife stuck into her gold belt, its bare blade as polished and shiny as a mountain lake.

Charlie Manx straightened up but kept his arms around his girls. He turned to look at Vic, his face tight, shining with something that might've been pride.

"Everything I have done, Victoria, I have done for my children," Charlie said. "This place is beyond sadness, beyond guilt. It's Christmas every day here, forever and ever. Every day is cocoa and presents. Behold what I've given my two daughters—the flesh of my flesh and the blood of my blood!—and all these other happy, perfect children! Can you really give your son better? Have you ever?"

"She's pretty," said a boy behind Vic, a small boy with a small voice. "She's as pretty as my mother."

"I wonder how she'll look without her nose," said another boy, and he laughed breathlessly.

"What can you give Wayne besides unhappiness, Victoria?" Charlie Manx asked. "Can you give him his own stars, his own moon, a rollercoaster that rebuilds itself every day in new hoops and loops, a chocolate shop that never runs out of chocolates? Friends and games and fun and freedom from sickness, freedom from death?"

"I didn't come to bargain, Charlie!" Vic yelled again. It was hard to keep her gaze fixed on him. She kept glancing from side to side and fighting the urge to look over her shoulder. She sensed the children creeping in around her, with their chains and hatchets and knives and necklaces of severed thumbs. "I came to kill you. If you don't give my boy back to me, all this will have to go. You and your children and this whole half-wit fantasy. Last chance."

"She's the prettiest girl ever," said the little boy with the little voice. "She has pretty eyes. Her eyes are like my mom's eyes."

"Okay," said the other boy. "You can have her eyes, and I'll get her nose."

From off in the dark under the trees came a crazed, hysterical, singing voice:

In Christmasland we'll build a Snowgirl!
And make believe that she's a silly clown!
We'll have lots of fun with Missus Snowgirl
Until the other kiddies cut her down!

The little boy tittered.

The other children were silent. Vic had never heard a more terrible silence.

Manx put his pinkie to his lips: a fey gesture of consideration. Then he lowered his hand.

"Don't you think," he said, "we should ask Wayne what *he* wants?" He bent and whispered to the taller of his two girls.

The girl in the Nutcracker uniform—Millie, Vic thought—walked barefoot to the rear of the Wraith.

Vic heard scuffling to her left, snapped her head around, and saw a child, not two yards away. It was a plump little girl in a matted white fur coat, open to show she wore nothing beneath except a filthy pair of Wonder Woman panties. When Vic looked at her, she went perfectly still, as if they were playing some demented game of Red Light, Green Light. She clutched a hatchet. Through her open mouth, Vic saw a socket filled with teeth. Vic believed she could discern three distinct rows of them, going back down her throat.

Vic looked back at the car, as Millie reached for the door and opened it.

For a moment nothing happened. The open door yawned with luxuriant darkness.

She saw Wayne grip the edge of the door with one bare hand,

saw him put his feet out. Then he slid down from the seat and out onto the cobblestones.

He was gape-mouthed with wonder, looking up at the lights, at the night. He was clean and beautiful, his dark hair swept back from his terribly white brow and his red mouth opened in an amazed grin—

And she saw his teeth, blades of bone in sharp, delicate rows. Just like all the others.

"Wayne," she said. Her voice was a strangled sob.

He turned his head and looked at her with pleasure and amazement.

"Mom!" he said. "*Hey!* Hey, Mom, isn't it *incredible*? It's real! It's *really* real!"

He looked over the stone wall, into the sky, at the great low moon with its sleeping silver face. He saw the moon and laughed. Vic could not remember the last time he had laughed so freely, so easily.

"Mom! The moon has a face!"

"Come here, Wayne. Right now. Come to me. We have to go."

He looked at her, a dimple of confusion appearing between his dark eyebrows.

"Why?" he said. "We just got here."

From behind him Millie put an arm around Wayne's waist, spooning against his back like a lover. He twitched, looking around in surprise, but then went still as Millie whispered in his ear. She was terribly beautiful, with her high cheekbones and full lips and sunken temples. He listened intently, eyes wide—then his mouth widened to show even more of his bristling teeth.

"Oh! Oh, you're *kidding*!" He looked at Vic in astonishment. "She says we *can't* go! We can't go anywhere because I have to unwrap my Christmas present!"

The girl leaned in and began to whisper fervently into Wayne's ear.

"Get away from her, Wayne," Vic said.

The fat girl in the fur coat shuffled a few steps closer, was almost close enough to plunge the hatchet into Vic's leg. Vic heard other steps behind her, the kids moving in.

Wayne gave the girl a puzzled, sidelong look and frowned to himself, then said, "Sure you can help unwrap my present! Everyone can help! Where is it? Let's go get it, and you can tear into it right now!"

The girl drew her knife and pointed it at Vic.

Beneath the Great Tree

"WHAT DID YOU JUST SAY, VICTORIA?" MANX ASKED. "LAST CHANCE? I think this is *your* last chance. I would turn that bike around while you still can."

"Wayne," she called, ignoring Manx and meeting her son's gaze directly. "Hey, are you still thinking in reverse like your grammy told you? Tell me you're still thinking in reverse."

He stared at her, blankly, as if she had asked him a question in a foreign language. His mouth hung partly open. Then, slowly, he said, ".Mom ,*hard* it's but ,trying I'm"

Manx was smiling, but his upper lip drew back to show those crooked teeth of his, and Vic thought she saw the flicker of something like irritation pass across his gaunt features. "What is this tomfoolery? Are you playing games, Wayne? Because I am all for games—just so long as I am not left out. What was that you just said?"

"Nothing!" Wayne said—in a tone of voice that suggested he genuinely meant it, was as confused as Manx. "Why? What did it *sound* like I said?"

"He said he's mine, Manx," Vic said. "He said you can't have him."

"But I already have him, Victoria," Manx said. "I have him, and I am not letting him go."

Vic slipped the backpack off her shoulder and into her lap. She unzipped the bag, plunged a hand in, and lifted out one of the tight plastic sacks of ANFO.

"So help me if you do not let him go, then Christmas is over for every fucking one of you. I'll blow this whole place right off this ledge."

Manx thumbed the fedora back on his head. "My, how you cuss! I have never been able to get used to such language out of young women. I have always thought it makes a girl sound like the lowest sort of trash!"

The fat girl in the fur coat took another shuffling half step forward. Her eyes, set back in small piggy folds, flashed red in a way that made Vic think of rabies. Vic gave the bike a smidge of gas, and it jumped forward a few feet. She wanted to put a bit of distance between her and the children closing in on her. She turned the ANFO over, found the timer, set it for what looked like about five minutes, pressed the button to start it running. In that instant she expected a final annihilating flash of white light to wipe away the world, and her insides squeezed tight, preparing for some last, rending burst of pain. Nothing of the sort happened. Nothing happened at all. Vic was not even sure it was running. It didn't make a sound.

She held the plastic pack of ANFO over her head.

"There's a shitty little timer on this thing, Manx. I think it'll go off in three minutes, but I could be wrong a minute or two in either direction. There's a whole bunch more in this sack. Send Wayne to me. Send him now. When he's on the bike, I turn it off."

He said, "What do you have there? It looks like one of those little pillows they give you on an airplane. I flew once, from St. Louis to Baton Rouge. I will never do that again! I was lucky to get off alive. It bounced the whole way, as if it were on a string and God was playing yo-yo with us."

"It's a bag of shit," Vic said. "Like you."

"It's a— What did you say?"

"It's ANFO. An enriched fertilizer. Soak this shit in diesel and it's the most powerful explosive this side of a crate of TNT. Timothy McVeigh destroyed a twelve-story federal building with a couple of these. I can do the same to your entire little world and everything in it."

Even across a distance of thirty feet, Vic could see the calculation in his eyes while he thought it through. Then his smile broadened. "I don't believe you'll do that. Blow yourself up and your son, too. You'd have to be crazy."

"Oh, man," she said. "Are you just figuring that out?"

His grin faded by degrees. His eyelids sank, and the expression in his eyes turned dull and disappointed.

He opened his mouth then and screamed, and when he did, the moon opened its one eye and screamed with him.

The eye of the moon was bloodshot and bulging, a sac of pus with an iris. Its mouth was a jagged tear in the night. Its voice was Manx's voice, so amplified that it was nearly deafening:

> "GET HER! *KILL* HER! SHE CAME HERE TO END CHRISTMAS! KILL HER *NOW*!"

The ledge shook. The branches of that enormous Christmas tree flailed at the darkness. Vic lost her grip on the brake, and the Triumph jerked forward another six inches. The backpack full of ANFO slithered out of her lap and fell onto the cobblestones.

Buildings shuddered beneath the shouting of the moon. Vic had never experienced an earthquake before and could not catch her breath, and her terror was a wordless thing that existed below the level of conscious thought, below the level of language. The moon began to scream—just *scream*—an inarticulate roar of fury that caused the falling snowflakes to whirl and blow about madly.

The fat girl took a step and *threw* the hatchet at Vic, like an Apache in a Western. The heavy, blunt edge clubbed Vic in her bad left knee. The pain was transcendent.

Vic's hand came off the brake again, and the Triumph lunged once more. The backpack was not left behind, however, but was dragged along behind the Triumph. A strap had caught on the rear foot peg, which Lou had put down when he climbed on the bike behind her. Lou Carmody, as always, to the rescue. She still had the ANFO, even if it was out of reach.

ANFO. She was even now holding one package of ANFO, clutched to her chest with her left hand, the timer presumably ticking away. Not that it *actually* ticked, or made any sound whatsoever to suggest that it was working.

Get rid of it, she thought. *Somewhere that will show him how much damage you can do with these things.*

The children surged at her. They rushed from beneath the tree, pouring onto the cobblestones. She heard the soft pattering of feet behind her. She looked around for Wayne and saw the tall girl still holding him. They stood beside the Wraith, the girl behind him with an arm gently encircling his chest. In her other hand was her crescent-shaped knife, which Vic knew she would use—on Wayne—before letting him go.

In the next instant, a child leaped, throwing himself at her. Vic yanked the throttle. The Triumph bolted forward, and the child missed her entirely, crunched into the road on his stomach. The backpack full of ANFO skipped and bounced over the snowy cobbles, hung up on that rear peg.

Vic gunned the bike straight at the Rolls-Royce, as if she meant to drive right into it. Manx grabbed the little girl—Lorrie?—and shrank back toward the open door, the protective gesture of any father. In that gesture Vic understood everything. Whatever the children had become, whatever he had done to them, he had done to make them safe, to keep them from being run down by the world. He believed in his own decency with all his heart. So it was with every true monster, Vic supposed.

She pushed down on the brake, clenching her teeth against the stabbing, ferocious pain in her left knee, and twisted the handlebars, and the bike was slung around, almost a hundred eighty degrees. Behind her was a line of children—a dozen of them, running up the road after her. She gave it gas again, and the Triumph came screaming at them, and almost all of them scattered like dry leaves in a hurricane.

One of them, though, a willowy girl in a pink nightdress, crouched and remained in Vic's path. Vic wanted to blow right through her, run her the fuck down, but at the last moment Vic gave the handlebars a twist, trying to veer around her. She couldn't help herself, couldn't drive into a child.

The bike wobbled dangerously on the slippery rocks and lost speed, and suddenly the girl was on the bike. Her claws—they were, really, the claws of an old crone, with their long, ragged fingernails—grabbed Vic's leg, and the girl hauled herself up onto the seat behind her.

Vic accelerated again, and the bike leaped forward, speeding up as it flung itself around the rotary.

The girl on the bike behind her was making noises, choked, snarling sounds, like a dog. One hand slipped around Vic's waist, and Vic almost shouted at the cold of it, a cold so intense it burned.

The girl gripped a length of chain in the other hand, which she lifted and brought down on Vic's left knee, as if she somehow knew exactly what would hurt most. A firecracker went off behind Vic's kneecap, and she sobbed and shoved her elbow backward. The elbow struck the girl in her white face with its crackling enamel skin.

The girl cried out—a strangled, broken sound—and Vic glanced back and her heart gave a sick lurch in her chest and she promptly lost control of the Triumph.

The girl's pretty little-girl face had deformed, lips stretching wide, becoming like the mouth of a flukeworm, a ragged pink hole encircled with teeth going all the way down her gullet. Her tongue was black, and her breath stank of old meat. She opened her mouth until it was wide enough for someone to put an arm down her throat, then clamped her teeth on Vic's shoulder.

It was like being brushed by a chainsaw. The sleeve of Vic's T-shirt and the skin beneath were torn into a bloody mess.

The bike went down on its right side, hit the ground in a spray of golden sparks, and slid screeching across the cobblestones. Vic did not know if she jumped or was thrown, only that she was already off the bike and tumbling, rolling across the bricks.

> "SHE'S DOWN, SHE'S DOWN, CUT HER, KILL HER!"

the moon screamed, and the ground shook beneath her, as if a convoy of eighteen-wheelers were thundering past.

She was on her back, arms flung out, head on the stones. She stared at the silvered galleons of the clouds above her *(move)*.

Vic tried to decide how badly she was hurt. She could not feel her left leg at all anymore *(move)*.

Her right hip felt abraded and sore. She lifted her head slightly, and the world swooped around her with a nauseating suddenness *(move **move**)*.

She blinked, and for an instant the sky was filled not with clouds but with static, a charged flurry of black and white particles *(MOVE)*.

She sat up on her elbows and looked to her left. The Triumph had carried her halfway around the circle, to one of the roads branching off into the amusement park. She stared across the rotary and saw children—perhaps as many as fifty—streaming toward her through the dark in a silent run. Beyond them was the tree as tall as a ten-story building, and beyond that, somewhere, were the Wraith and Wayne.

The moon glared down at her from in the sky, its horrible, bloodshot eye bulging.

"SCISSORS-FOR-THE-DRIFTER! SCISSORS-FOR-THE-*BITCH*!"

bellowed the moon. But for an instant he flickered out of sight, like a TV caught between channels. The sky was a chaos of white noise. Vic could even hear it hissing.

MOVE, she thought, and then abruptly found herself on her feet, grabbing the motorcycle by the handlebars. She heaved her weight against it, crying out as a fresh jolt of withering pain passed through her left knee and her hip.

The little girl with the flukeworm mouth had been thrown into the door of a shop on the corner: Charlie's Costume Carnival! It—*she*—sat against the door, shaking her head as if to clear it. Vic saw that the white plastic sack of ANFO had, somehow, wound up between the girl's ankles.

ANFO, Vic thought—the word had achieved the quality of a mantra—and she leaned over and grabbed the backpack, still tangled on the rear peg. She slipped it loose, hung it on her shoulder, and put a leg over the bike.

The children running at her should've been screaming, or war-whooping, or something, but they came on in a silent rush, pouring out of the snowy central circle and spilling across the cobblestones. Vic jumped on the kickstart.

The Triumph coughed, did nothing.

She jumped again. One of the pipes, which was now broken loose and dangled over the cobblestones, puffed some watery exhaust, but the engine made only a tired, choked sound and died.

A rock hit the back of her head, and a black flash exploded behind her eyes. When her vision cleared, the sky was full of static again—for a moment—then blurred and re-formed as clouds and darkness. She hit the kick-starter.

She heard sprockets whirring, refusing to engage, going dead.

The first of the children reached her. He did not have a weapon of any kind—perhaps he was the one who had thrown the rock—but his jaw unhinged, opening into an obscene pink cavern filled with row upon row of teeth. He fastened his mouth on her bare leg. Fish-hook teeth punctured meat, caught in muscle.

Vic shouted in pain and kicked out with her right foot, to shake the boy loose. Her heel struck the kick-starter, and the engine erupted into life. She grabbed the throttle, and the bike hurtled forward. The boy was yanked off his feet, flung to the stones, left behind.

She looked over her left shoulder as she raced down the side road toward the Sleighcoaster and the Reindeer-Go-Round.

Twenty, thirty, perhaps forty children sprinted down the road behind her, many of them barefoot, their heels whacking on the stones.

The child who had been tossed into the doors of Charlie's Costume Carnival was sitting up now. She bent forward, reaching out for the white plastic sack of ANFO by her feet.

There was a white flash.

The explosion caused the air to ripple and warp with heat, and Vic believed for a moment that it would lift the bike off the road and fling it into the air.

Every window on the street exploded. The white flash became a giant ball of flame. Charlie's Costume Carnival caved in and slid apart in an avalanche of flaming brickwork and a snowstorm of glittering, pulverized glass. The fire belched out across the street, picked up a dozen children as if they were sticks, and tossed them into the night. Cobblestones erupted from the road and launched themselves into the air.

The moon opened its mouth to cry out in horror, its one great eye bulging in fury—and then the shockwave hit the false sky and the whole thing wobbled, like an image reflected in a fun-house mirror. The moon and stars and clouds dissolved into a field of white electrical snow. The blast carried down the street. Buildings shuddered. Vic inhaled a lungful of burned air, diesel smoke, and powdered brick.

Then the wavering repercussions of the blast faded and the sky flickered back into being.

The moon screamed and screamed, sounds almost as loud and violent as the explosion itself.

She sped past a hall of mirrors, past a waxwork, and on to the brightly lit and rotating carousel, where wooden reindeer pranced in place of horses. There she grabbed the brake and brought the bike to a fishtailing halt. Her hair was frizzled from the heat of the explosion. Her heart slugged in her chest.

She looked back toward the debris field that had been the market square. She needed a moment to register—to accept—what she was seeing. First one child, then another, then a third emerged from the smoke, coming down the road after her. One of them was still smoking, hair charred. Others were sitting up across the street. Vic saw a boy thoughtfully brush glass out of his hair. He should've been dead, had been picked up and thrown into a brick wall, every bone in his body should've been smashed into chips, but there he was, getting to his feet, and Vic found that her weary mind was not entirely surprised by this development. The children caught in the explosion had been dead even before the bomb detonated, of course. They were not any *more* dead now—or any less inclined to stop coming after her.

She swung the backpack off her shoulder and checked its contents. She hadn't lost any. Lou had wired timers into four of the packs of ANFO, one of which was now gone. There were a couple other sacks of the ANFO, down toward the bottom, that had no timers on them at all.

Vic slung the bag back over her shoulder and rode, past the Reindeer-Go-Round and on another few hundred yards to the rear of the park and the great Sleighcoaster.

It was running empty, carts made to look like red sleighs diving and roaring past on the rails, swooping and rising into the night. It was an old-fashioned rollercoaster, of the sort that had been popular in the thirties, made entirely of wood. The entrance was a great glowing face of Santa Claus—you walked in through his mouth.

Vic pulled out a sack of ANFO, set the timer for five minutes, tossed it in between Santa's gaping jaws. She was about to take off when she happened to look up at the rollercoaster and saw the mummified bodies: dozens of crucified men and women, their skin blackened and withered, eyes gone, their clothes filthy, frozen rags. A woman in pink leg warmers that screamed 1984 had been stripped to the waist; Christmas ornaments dangled from her pierced breasts. There was a shriveled man in jeans and a thick coat, with a beard that brought to mind Christ, sporting a holly wreath instead of a crown of thorns on his head.

Vic was still staring up at the corpses when a child came out of the dark and stuck a kitchen knife into the small of her back.

He could not have been older than ten, and his cheeks were dimpled by a sweet, lovely smile. He was barefoot, wore overalls and a checked shirt, and with his golden bangs and serene eyes he was a perfect little Tom Sawyer. The knife was buried to the hilt, sinking into muscle, the springy tissue beneath, and perhaps perforating an intestine. She felt a pain unlike any she had ever experienced, a sharp and blessed twinge in her bowels, and she thought, with real surprise, *He just killed me. I just died.*

Tom Sawyer pulled the knife back out and laughed gaily. Her own son had never laughed with such easy pleasure. She did not know where the boy had come from. He seemed to have simply appeared; the night had thickened and made a child.

"I want to play with you," he said. "Stay and play scissors-for-the-drifter."

She could've hit him, elbowed him, kicked him, anything. Instead she gave the bike throttle and simply roared away from him. He stepped aside and watched her go, still holding the blade, wet and shiny with her blood. He was still smiling, but his eyes were puzzled, brow furrowed with confusion, as if he were wondering, *Did I do something wrong?*

The timers were imprecise. The first sack of ANFO had been set to go off in what she estimated was five minutes but had taken closer to ten. She had set the timer on the Sleighcoaster ANFO just exactly the same and should've had plenty of time to reach safe distance. But when she was less than a hundred yards away, it erupted. The ground buckled beneath her, seemed to roll like a wave. It felt as if the air itself were cooking. She drew a breath that was hot enough to sear her lungs. The bike staggered forward, the baking wind hammering at her shoulders, at her back. She felt a fresh, sharp twinge of pain in her abdomen, as if she were being stabbed all over again.

The Sleighcoaster collapsed in on itself like a shattering, roaring heap of kindling. One of the carts came free of the tracks and blazed through the night, a flaming missile that soared through the darkness and slammed into the Reindeer-Go-Round, smashing the white steeds to flinders. Steel screamed. She looked back just in time to see a rising mushroom cloud of flame and black smoke as the Sleighcoaster toppled.

She looked away, got the bike going again, weaving around the smoking head of a wooden reindeer, a rack of shattered antlers. She cut down another side street, one she believed would lead her back to the rotary. There was a bad taste in her mouth. She spit blood.

I am dying, she thought, with surprising calm.

She hardly slowed at the foot of the grand Ferris wheel. It was a beautiful thing, a thousand blue will-o'-the-wisp lights aligned along its hundred-foot spokes. Cabins roomy enough for a dozen people each, with black-tinted windows and gaslights glowing inside, rotated dreamily.

Vic fished out another sack of ANFO, set the timer for five minutes, more or less, and hooked it upward. It caught in one of the spokes, close to the central hub. Vic thought of her Raleigh Tuff Burner, the way the wheels had whirred and how she loved the autumn light in

New England. She was not going back. She was never going to see that light again. Her mouth kept filling with blood. She was sitting in blood now. The stabbing sensation came in the small of her back again and again. Only it didn't hurt in any conventional sense. She recognized what she was feeling as pain, but it was also, like childbirth, an experience bigger than pain, a feeling that something impossible was being made possible, that she was about to complete some enormous undertaking.

She rode on and soon arrived back at the central rotary.

Charlie's Costume Carnival—a solid cube of flame, barely recognizable as a building—stood on the corner sixty or seventy yards away. On the other side of the great Christmas tree was the parked Rolls-Royce. She could see the glow of its high headlights beneath the branches. She did not slow but rode straight at the tree. Vic slipped the backpack off her left shoulder. She reached into it, her other hand on the throttle, found the last sack of ANFO with a timer, twisted the dial, and pushed the button to start it running.

The front tire skipped over a low stone curb, and she thumped up onto snow-dusted grass. The darkness congealed into shapes, children rising up before her. She was not sure they would move, thought they would hold their ground and force her to plow through them.

Light rose around her, a great flash of reddish brilliance, and for an instant she could see her own shadow, impossibly long, rushing ahead of her. The children were illuminated in a ragged, uneven line, cold dolls in bloodstained pajamas, creatures armed with broken boards, knives, hammers, scissors.

The world filled with a roar and the shriek of tortured metal. Snow whipped around, and children were knocked to the dirt by the shockwave. Behind her the Ferris wheel erupted outward in two jets of flame, and the great circle crashed straight down, dropping from its struts. The impact shook the world and knocked the sky over Christmasland back into an agitation of static. The branches of the immense fir tree clawed at the night with a kind of hysteria, a giant fighting for its life.

Vic sailed beneath the wild and flailing boughs. She flipped the backpack out of her lap, chucked it in against the trunk—her Christmas gift for Charles Talent Manx.

Behind her the Ferris wheel rolled into town with a great reverberating sound of iron grinding against stone. Then, like a penny that has rolled along a table and lost its momentum, it tilted to one side and fell upon a pair of buildings.

Beyond the toppled Ferris wheel, beyond the ruin of the Sleighcoaster, an enormous shelf of snow, loosed from the peaks of the high, dark mountain, began to crash down upon the back of Christmasland. For all the deafening roars of explosions and collapsing buildings, there had been no sound yet like this. It was somehow more than sound, was a vibration felt as deep as bone. A blast of snow hit the towers and quaint shops at the back of the park. They were annihilated. Walls of colored rock blew outward before the oncoming avalanche and were promptly covered over. The rear of the town collapsed into itself and vanished in a roiling surf of snow, a tidal wave deep enough and broad enough to swallow Christmasland whole. The ledge beneath shook so hard that Vic wondered if it might snap off the side of the mountain, drop the whole park into . . . what? The emptiness that waited beyond Charlie Manx's pinched little imaginings. The narrow canyons of the roads filled with a flash flood of snow, high enough to consume everything before it. The avalanche did not fall upon Christmasland so much as *erase* it.

As the Triumph carried her across the rotary, the Wraith came into sight. It stood covered in a fine film of brick dust, engine rumbling and headlights glowing through air filled with fine particulate matter, a billion grains of ash, snow, and rock swirling on the hot, spark-filled wind. Vic glimpsed Charlie Manx's little girl, the one named Lorrie, in the passenger seat of his car, peering out the side window into the sudden darkness. The lights of Christmasland had, in the last few moments, blinked out, all of them, and the only illumination that remained was the hissing white static above.

Wayne was by the open trunk of the car, twisting himself this way and that to be free of the girl, the one named Millie. Millie clutched him from behind, one arm reaching around his chest to hold a fistful of his filthy white T-shirt. In her other hand was that curious hooked knife. She was trying to pull it up to stick it through his throat, but he had her wrist, kept the blade down and his face turned away from its questing edge.

"You need to do what Daddy wants!" she was screaming at him. "You need to get in the trunk! You have fussed long enough!"

And Manx. Manx was moving. He had been at the driver's-side door, shoveling his precious Lorrie into the car, but now he strode across the uneven ground, swinging his silver hammer, looking soldierly in his legionnaire's coat, which was buttoned to the neck. Muscles bunched at the corners of his jaw.

"Leave him, Millie! There isn't time!" Manx hollered at her. "Leave him and let's go!"

Millie sank her flukeworm teeth into Wayne's ear. Wayne screamed and thrashed and snapped his head, and the lobe of his ear parted company with the rest of his face. He ducked and made a funny corkscrewing motion in the same instant and came right out of his T-shirt, leaving Millie holding an empty, blood-streaked rag.

"Oh, Mom! Oh, Mom! Oh—" Wayne shouted, which was the same thing backward as it was forward. He took two running steps, slipped in the snow, went down on all fours in the road.

And dust swirled in the air. And the darkness shook with cannonades, blocks of stone falling into more stone, a hundred fifty thousand tons of snow, all the snow Charlie Manx had ever seen and ever imagined, came crashing toward them, flattening everything before it.

Manx stalked on, six strides from Wayne, already lifting his arm back to drop his silver hammer on Wayne's lowered head. It had been designed for crushing skulls, and Wayne's would be child's play.

"Get out of my way, Charlie!" Vic hollered.

Manx half turned as she blew past him. Her slipstream grabbed and spun him, sent him staggering back on his heels.

Then the last of the ANFO, the backpack of it, exploded beneath the tree and seemed to take the entire world with it.

Gumdrop Lane

HIGH-PITCHED WHINE.

A confusion of dust and drifting motes of flame.

The world slid itself into an envelope of silence, in which the only sound was a soft droning, not unlike the emergency broadcasting signal.

Time softened, ran with the sweet drag of syrup trickling down the side of a bottle.

Vic glided through the atmosphere of ruin and watched a chunk of burning tree the size of a Cadillac bounce in front of her, appearing to move at less than a fifth of its actual speed.

In the silent snowstorm of debris—a whirling pink smoke—Vic lost sight of Charlie Manx and his car. She only dimly apprehended Wayne pushing himself up off all fours, like a runner coming out of the blocks. The girl with the long red hair was behind him with the knife, clutching it in both hands now. The ground shuddered and tipped her off balance, sent her reeling back into the stone wall at the edge of the drop.

Vic weaved around the girl. The child, Millie, turned her head to watch Vic go, her flukeworm mouth open in a sickened look of rage, the rows of teeth churning inside her throat hole. The girl pushed off the wall, and as she did, it gave way and took her along with it. Vic saw her lurch back into nothing and drop into that white storm of light.

Vic's ears whined. She believed she was calling Wayne's name. He ran from her—running blind and deaf—and did not look back.

The Triumph carried her up alongside him. She twisted at the waist and reached and caught him by the back of his shorts and hauled him onto the bike behind her, without slowing. There was plenty of time to manage this. Everything was moving so quietly and slowly, she could have counted each individual ember floating in the air. Her perforated kidney twanged in shock at this abrupt movement from the waist, but Vic, who was dying quickly now, did not let it trouble her.

Fire flurried from the sky.

Somewhere behind her, the snow of a hundred winters smothered Christmasland, a pillow pressed over the face of a terminally ill man.

It had felt good, to be held by Lou Carmody, to smell his odor of pines and of the garage, and even better to have her own son's arms around her again, cinching her waist.

In the droning, apocalyptic darkness, there was at least no Christmas music. How she hated Christmas music. She always had.

Another burning lump of tree fell to her right, hit the cobbles, and exploded, throwing coals the size of dinner plates. A fiery arrow, as long as Vic's forearm, whizzed through the air and sliced her forehead open above her right eyebrow. She did not feel it, although she saw it pass by before her eyes.

She clicked the Triumph effortlessly into fourth gear.

Her son squeezed her tighter. Her kidney twanged again. He was squeezing the life out of her, and it felt good.

She put her left hand over his two hands, knotted together at her navel. She stroked his small white knuckles. He was still hers. She knew because his skin was warm, not frozen and dead, like Charlie Manx's pint-size vampires. He would always be hers. He was gold, and gold didn't come off.

NOS4A2 erupted from the billowing smoke behind her. Through the dead, droning silence, she heard it, heard an inhuman growl, a precision-engineered, perfectly articulated roar of hate. Its tires carried it juddering and crashing over a field of smashed rock. Its headlights made the storm of dust—that blizzard of grit—shine like a flurry of diamonds. Manx was bent to the wheel, and he had his window down.

"I'LL SLAUGHTER YOU, YOU MISERABLE BITCH!" he screamed, and she heard that, too, though distantly, like the hush heard in a seashell. "I'M GOING TO RUN YOU DOWN, THE BOTH OF YOU! YOU KILLED ALL OF MINE, AND I'M GOING TO KILL YOURS!"

The bumper struck her rear tire, gave the Triumph a hard jolt. The handlebars jerked, trying to pull out of her grip. She held on. If she didn't, the front tire would turn sharply to one side or the other, and the bike would dump them, and the Wraith would thud right over them.

The bumper of the Wraith slammed into them again. She was shoved forward, hard, head almost striking the handlebars.

When she lifted her chin and looked up, the Shorter Way Bridge was there, its mouth black in the cotton-candy-colored haze. She exhaled, a long rush of breath, and almost shivered with relief. The bridge was there and would take her out of this place, back to where she needed to go. The shadows that waited within were, in their way, as comforting as her mother's cool hand on her fevered forehead. She missed her mother, and her father, and Lou, and was sorry they had not all had more time together. It seemed to her that all of them, not just Louis, would be waiting for her on the other side of the bridge, waiting for her to climb off the bike and fall into their arms.

The Triumph banged up onto the bridge, over the wooden sill, and began to rattle over the boards. To her left she saw the old familiar green spray paint, three sloppy letters: LOU →.

The Wraith boomed up into the bridge behind her, struck the rusted old Raleigh, and sent it flying through the air. It whistled past Vic on her right. The snow came roaring behind, an obliterating blast of it, choking the far end of the bridge, filling it like a cork jammed into a bottle.

"YOU TATTOOED CUNT!" Charlie Manx screamed, his voice echoing through the vast hollow space. "YOU TATTOOED ***HOOR***!"

The bumper banged into the back of the Triumph. The Triumph careened to the right, and Vic's shoulder slammed into the wall with such force she was almost torn off the saddle. The board shattered to show the furious white static beyond. The Shorter Way rumbled and shuddered.

"Bats, Mama," Wayne said, his voice soft, the voice of a younger, smaller child. "Look at all the bats."

The air filled with bats, shaken loose from the ceiling. They whirled and raced about in a panic, and Vic lowered her head and flew through them. One struck her in the chest, fell to her lap, flapped hysterically, took to the air again. Another brushed the side of her face with a felty wing. It was a soft, secret, feminine warmth.

"Don't be afraid," Vic told him. "They won't hurt you. You're Bruce Wayne! All the bats in here are on *your* side, kiddo."

"Yes," Wayne agreed. "Yes. I'm Bruce Wayne. I remember." As if he had for a while forgotten. Perhaps he had.

Vic glanced back and saw a bat strike the windshield of the Wraith, with enough force to smash a white spiderweb into the glass, directly in front of Charlie Manx's face. A second bat thwacked into the other side of the windshield, in a spray of blood and fur. It remained caught in one of the windshield wipers, frantically beating a shattered wing. A third and a fourth bat smacked into the glass, bouncing off, flying away into the dark.

Manx screamed and screamed, a sound not of fear but of frustration. Vic did not want to hear the other voice in the car, the child's voice—"No, Daddy, too fast, Daddy!"—but she caught it all the same, sounds amplified and carrying in the enclosed space of the bridge.

The Wraith slipped off course, swung to the left, and the front bumper hit the wall and tore away a three-foot section to reveal the hissing white static on the other side, an emptiness beyond thought.

Manx pulled at the wheel, and the Wraith lurched across the bridge, over to the right, hit the other wall. The sound of boards splintering and snapping was like machine-gun fire. Boards burst and shattered beneath the car. A hail of bats drummed into the windscreen, caving it in. More bats followed, whirling in the cockpit, striking Manx and his child about the head. The little girl began to scream. Manx let go of the wheel, flailing at them.

"Get away! Get away from me you god-awful things!" he screamed. Then there were no words, and he was just screaming.

Vic hauled on the throttle, and the bike launched itself forward, rushing the length of the bridge, through the darkness boiling with bats. It raced toward the exit, doing fifty, sixty, seventy, taking off like a rocket.

Behind her the front end of the Wraith crashed through the floor of the bridge. The rear end of the Rolls-Royce lifted into the air. Manx slid forward, into his steering wheel, his mouth opening in a terrified howl.

"No!" Vic thought he screamed. Or maybe . . . maybe it was *Snow!*

The Wraith pitched forward into snow, into white roar, tearing the bridge apart as it went. The Shorter Way Bridge seemed to *fold* in the center, and suddenly Vic was racing uphill. It collapsed in toward the middle, either end rising, as if the bridge were trying to close itself like a book, a novel that had reached its ending, a story that reader and author alike were about to set aside.

NOS4A2 dropped through the decayed and rotting floor of the bridge, fell into the furious white light and buzzing static, plunged a thousand feet and twenty-six years, dropping through time to hit the Merrimack River in 1986, where it was crushed like a beer can as it slammed into the water. The engine block came straight back through the dashboard and buried itself in Manx's chest, an iron heart that weighed four hundred pounds. He died with a mouth full of motor oil. The body of the child that had sat beside him was sucked out in the current and dragged nearly to Boston Harbor. When her corpse was discovered, four days later, she had several dead, drowned bats tangled in her hair.

Vic accelerated—eighty, ninety. Bats gushed out of the bridge around her into the night, all of them, all her thoughts and memories and fantasies and guilt: kissing Lou's big, bare chest the first time she ever took off his shirt; riding her ten-speed in the green shade of an August afternoon; banging her knuckles on the carburetor of the Triumph as she worked to tighten a bolt. It felt good to see them fly, to see them set free, to be set free of them herself, to let go of all thought at last. The Triumph reached the exit and flew with them. She rode the night for a moment, the motorcycle soaring through the frozen dark. Her son held her tight.

The tires hit the ground with great force. Vic was thrown hard against the handlebars, and the twinge in her kidney became an agonized tearing sensation. *Keep it shiny side up,* she thought, slowing fast now, the front tire wobbling and shaking, the whole bike threatening to fling them off and go down with them. The engine screamed as the motorcycle slammed over the rutted ground. Vic had returned to the clearing in the woods where Charlie Manx had led them over into Christmasland. Grass whipped frantically against the sides of the bike.

She slowed and slowed and slowed, and the bike gasped and died.

She coasted. At last the Triumph eased to a stop at the tree line, and she could safely turn her head and look back. Wayne looked with her, his arms still clenching her tightly, as if they were, even now, racing along at close to eighty miles an hour.

Across the field she saw the Shorter Way Bridge and a gusher of bats pouring out of it into the starry night. Then, almost gently, the entrance to the bridge fell backward—there was suddenly nothing behind it—and vanished before it hit the ground with a weak pop. A faint ripple spread out across the high grass.

The boy and his mother sat on the dead bike, staring. Bats shrilled softly in the dark. Vic felt very easy in her mind. She was not sure there was much of anything left in there now, except for love, and that was enough.

She drove her heel into the kick-starter. The Triumph sighed its regrets. She tried again, felt things tearing inside her, spit more blood. A third time. The kick-starter almost refused to go down, and the bike made no sound at all.

"What's wrong with it, Mama?" Wayne asked in his new, soft, little-boy's voice.

She wiggled the bike back and forth between her legs. It creaked gently but otherwise made no other sound. Then she understood, and laughed—a dry, weak laugh, but genuine.

"Out of gas," she said.

COME ALL YE FAITHFUL
OCTOBER

Gunbarrel

WAYNE WOKE ON THE FIRST SUNDAY IN OCTOBER, TO THE CLASH OF church bells pealing down the block. His father was there, sitting on the edge of the bed.

"What were you dreaming?" his new, almost-thin father asked him.

Wayne shook his head.

"I don't know. I don't remember," he lied.

"I thought maybe you were dreaming about Mom," New Lou said. "You were smiling."

"I guess I must've been thinking about *something* fun."

"Something fun? Or something good?" New Lou asked, watching him with his curious New Lou eyes—inquisitive and bright. "Because they aren't always the same."

"I don't remember anymore," Wayne told him.

Better to say that than to say he'd been dreaming about Brad McCauley and Marta Gregorski and the other children in Christmasland. Not that it *was* Christmasland anymore. It was just The White now. It was just the furious white static of a dead channel, and the children ran in it, playing their games. Last night's game had been called bite-the-smallest. Wayne could still taste blood. He moved his tongue around and around inside the sticky socket of his mouth. In his dream he'd had more teeth.

"I'm taking the tow," Lou said. "Got a piece of work needs doing. You want to come with me? You don't have to. Tabitha could stay here with you."

"Is she here? Did she sleep over?"

"No! No," Lou said. He seemed genuinely surprised by the idea. "I just mean I could call her and have her come by." His brow furrowed in concentration, and after a moment he went on, speaking more slowly. "I don't think I'd feel okay about that right now: a sleepover. I think that would be strange . . . for everyone."

Wayne thought the most interesting part of this statement was the "right now" part, implying that his father *might* feel okay about a sleepover with Ms. Tabitha Hutter at some later date, TBD.

Three nights ago they had all come out of a movie—they did that now sometimes, went to movies together—and Wayne had looked back in time to see his father take Tabitha Hutter by the elbow and kiss the corner of her mouth. The way she'd inclined her head and smiled slightly, Wayne understood that it was not their first kiss. It was too casual, too practiced. Then Tabitha had seen Wayne looking and slipped her arm free of Lou's hand.

"It wouldn't bother me!" Wayne said. "I know you like her. I like her, too!"

Lou said, "Wayne. Your mom . . . your mom was— I mean, saying she was my best friend doesn't even *begin* to—"

"But now she's dead. And you should be happy. You should have fun!" Wayne said.

Lou eyed him gravely—with a kind of sorrow, Wayne thought.

"Well," Lou said. "I'm just saying, you can stay here if you want. Tabitha is right down the street. I can have her here in three minutes. You gotta love a babysitter who comes with her own Glock."

"No. I'll keep you company. Where did you say we're going?"

"I didn't," Lou said.

TABITHA HUTTER CAME BY ANYWAY, UNANNOUNCED, BUZZING UP TO the apartment while Wayne was still in his pajamas. She did that on occasion, came by with croissants, which she said she would trade for coffee. She could've bought coffee, too, but she claimed she liked the way Lou made it. Wayne knew an excuse when he heard one. There wasn't anything special about Lou's coffee, unless you liked your brew with an aftertaste of WD-40.

She had transferred to the Denver office to assist in the ongoing McQueen investigation—a case in which no charges had been filed or ever would be filed. She had an apartment in Gunbarrel and usually ate with Lou and Wayne once a day, ostensibly to talk about what Lou knew. Mostly, though, they talked about *Game of Thrones*. Lou had finished reading the first book right before he went in for his angioplasty and his gastric bypass, which were performed at the same time. Tabitha Hutter was there when Lou woke up, the day after the surgery. She said she wanted to make sure he lived to read the rest of the series.

"Hey, kids," Tabitha said. "You sneaking out on me?"

"There's a job needs doing," Lou said.

"On Sunday morning?"

"People fuck up their cars then, too."

She yawned into the back of her hand, a small, frizzy-haired woman in a faded Wonder Woman T-shirt and blue jeans, no jewelry, no accessories whatsoever. Aside from the nine-millimeter strapped to her hip. "Okay. Make me a cup of coffee before we go?"

Lou half smiled at this but said, "You don't *have* to come. This could take a while."

She shrugged. "What else am I going to do with myself? Outlaws like to sleep in. I've been FBI for eight years, and I've never once had cause to shoot anyone before eleven in the morning. Not as long as I get my coffee anyway."

LOU GOT A DARK ROAST BREWING AND WENT TO START THE TRUCK, Tabitha following him out the door. Wayne was alone in the hall, pulling on his sneakers, when the phone rang.

He looked at it sitting in its black plastic cradle on an end table just to his right. It was a few minutes past seven, early for a call—but maybe it was about the job they were getting ready to go off on. Maybe whoever had ditched his car was being helped by someone else. It happened.

Wayne answered.

The phone hissed: loud roar of white noise.

"Wayne," said a breathy girl with a Russian accent. "When are you coming back? When are you coming back to play?"

Wayne couldn't answer, his tongue sealed to the roof of his mouth, his pulse ticking in his throat. It wasn't the first time they had called.

"We need you. You can rebuild Christmasland. You can *think* it all back. All the rides. All the shops. All the games. There's nothing to play with here. You have to help us. With Mr. Manx gone, there's only *you*."

Wayne heard the front door open. He hit END. As Tabitha Hutter stepped into the hallway, he was setting the phone back in its cradle.

"Someone call?" she asked, a kind of calm innocence in her gray-green eyes.

"Wrong number," Wayne said. "I bet the coffee is done."

Wayne wasn't okay, and he knew it. Kids who were okay did not answer phone calls from children who had to be dead. Kids who were okay didn't dream dreams like his. But neither of these things—not the phone calls or the dreams—was the clearest indicator that he was Not Okay. No. What really marked him out as Not Okay was the way he felt when he saw a photo of a plane crash: *charged,* jolted by excitement and guilt, as if he were looking at pornography.

He had been out driving with his father the week before and had seen a chipmunk run in front of a car and get squashed, and he had barked with sudden surprised laughter. His father had snapped his head around and looked at Wayne with hollow-eyed wonder, had pursed his lips to speak but then said nothing—silenced perhaps by the ill look of shock and unhappiness on Wayne's face. Wayne didn't *want* to think it was funny, a little chipmunk zigging when it should've zagged, getting wiped out by someone's Goodyear. That was the kind of thing that made Charlie Manx laugh. He just couldn't help himself.

There was the time he saw a thing about genocide in the Sudan on YouTube and had discovered a smile on his own face.

There was a story about a little girl being kidnapped in Salt Lake City, a pretty twelve-year-old blond girl with a shy smile. Wayne had watched the news report in a state of rapt excitement, *envying* her.

There was his recurring sense that he had three extra sets of teeth, hidden somewhere behind the roof of his mouth. He ran his tongue around and around his mouth and imagined he could *feel* them, a series of little ridges right under the flesh. He knew now that he had only *imagined* losing his ordinary boy teeth, had hallucinated this under the influence of the sevoflurane, just as he had hallucinated Christmasland *(lies!).* But his memory of those other teeth was more real, more vivid, than the stuff of his everyday life: school, trips to the therapist, meals with his dad and Tabitha Hutter.

He felt sometimes that he was a dinner plate that had cracked down the middle and then been glued back together, and the two parts did not *quite* line up. One side—the part of the plate that marked his life before Charlie Manx—was microscopically out of true with the other part of the plate. When he stood back and looked at that crooked plate, he could not imagine why anyone would want to keep it. It was no good now. Wayne did not think this with any despair—and that was part of the problem. It had been a long time since he'd felt anything like despair. At his mother's funeral, he had very much enjoyed the hymns.

The last time he saw his mother alive, they were rolling her on a gurney toward the back of an ambulance. The paramedics were in a hurry. She had lost a great deal of blood. They would eventually pump three liters into her, enough to keep her alive for the night, but they were too slow to deal with the perforated kidney and intestine, not aware that her system was boiling with her body's own poisons.

He had jogged alongside her, holding her hand. They were in the gravel parking lot of a general store, down the road from the ruin of Manx's lodge. Later Wayne would learn that his mother and father had held their very first conversation in that parking lot.

"You're okay, kiddo," Vic said to him. She was smiling, although her face was spattered with blood and filth. There was an oozing wound over her right eyebrow, and she had a breathing tube stuck up her nose. "Gold don't come off. What's good stays good, no matter how much of a beating it takes. You're okay. You'll always be okay."

He knew what she was saying. She was saying he wasn't like the children in Christmasland. She was saying he was still himself.

But Charlie Manx had said something different. Charlie Manx said blood didn't come out of silk.

Tabitha Hutter had a first tentative sip of her coffee and glanced out the window over the kitchen sink. "Your dad has the truck out front. Grab a jacket in case it's cold? We should go."

"Let's ride," Wayne said.

THEY SQUEEZED TOGETHER INTO THE TOW TRUCK, WAYNE SITTING IN the middle. There was a time when all three of them wouldn't have fit, but New Lou didn't take up as much space as the old Lou. New Lou had a Boris Karloff–in–*Frankenstein* look, with gangly hanging arms and a collapsed stomach beneath the big barrel of his chest. He had Frankenstein scars to match, running up from under the collar of his shirt along the length of his neck and behind his left ear, where they had performed the angioplasty. In the wake of that and the gastric bypass, his fat had just melted away, like so much ice cream left in the sun. The most striking thing was his *eyes.* It didn't make sense that losing weight should change his eyes, but Wayne was more aware of them now, more conscious of his father's intense, questing gaze.

Wayne settled into place beside his dad, then sat up, to get away from something digging into his back. A hammer—not an autopsy mallet but just an ordinary carpenter's hammer, the wooden handle worn. Wayne set it next to his father's hip.

The tow truck climbed away from Gunbarrel, following switchbacks through old firs, rising steadily into a spotless blue sky. Down in Gunbarrel it was warm enough in the direct rays of the sun, but up here the tops of the trees swished restlessly in a chill breeze that smelled fragrantly of the turning aspens. The slopes were streaked with gold.

"And gold doesn't come off," Wayne whispered, but just look: Leaves were coming off all the time, whisking out across the road, sailing the breeze.

"What did you say?" Tabitha asked.

He shook his head.

"How about some radio?" Tabitha asked, and reached past him to turn on some music.

Wayne could not say why he preferred silence, why the idea of music made him apprehensive.

Through a thin crackle of static, Bob Seger expressed his fondness for that old-time rock and roll. He averred that if anyone put on disco, he would be ten minutes late for the door.

"Where did this accident happen?" Tabitha Hutter asked, and, Wayne noted distantly, there was a faint tone of suspicion in her voice.

"We're almost there," Lou said.

"Was anyone hurt?"

Lou said, "This accident happened a while ago."

Wayne didn't know where they were going until they passed the country store on the left. It wasn't a store anymore, of course, and hadn't been for a decade. The pumps remained out front, one of them blackened, the paint boiled off where it had caught fire the day Charlie Manx stopped for a fill. The hills above Gunbarrel had their share of abandoned mines and ghost towns, and there was nothing so remarkable about a lodge-style house with smashed windows and nothing inside except shadows and cobwebs.

"What do you have in mind, Mr. Carmody?" Tabitha Hutter asked.

"Something Vic wanted me to do," Lou said.

"Maybe you shouldn't have brought Wayne."

"Actually, I think maybe I shouldn't have brought *you,*" Lou said. "I intend to tamper with evidence."

Tabitha said, "Oh, well. I'm off this morning."

He continued on past the general store. In half a mile, he began to slow. The gravel road to the Sleigh House was on the right. As he turned in, the static rose in volume, all but erasing Bob Seger's grainy, affable voice. No one got good reception around the Sleigh House. Even the ambulance had found it difficult to send a clear message to the hospital below. Something to do with the contours of the shelf rock, perhaps. It was easy in the notches of the Rockies to ride out of sight of the world below—and among the cliffs and the trees and the scouring winds, the twenty-first century was revealed to be only an imaginary construct, a fanciful notion that men had superimposed on the world, of no relevance whatsoever to the rock.

Lou stopped the truck and got out to move aside a blue police sawhorse. Then they went on.

The tow truck rattled across the washboarded dirt road, easing down almost to the dooryard of the ruin. The sumac was reddening in the fall chill. A woodpecker assaulted a pine somewhere. After New Lou put the truck into park, there was nothing coming from the radio but a roar of white noise.

When Wayne shut his eyes, he could picture them, those children of the static, those children lost in the space between reality and thought. They were so close he could almost hear their laughter underneath the radio hiss. He trembled.

His father put a hand on his leg, and Wayne opened his eyes and looked at him. Lou had slid down out of the truck but reached back into the cab to set a big hand on his knee.

"It's okay," his father said. "This is all right, Wayne. You're safe."

Wayne nodded—but his father misunderstood him. He wasn't afraid. If he was trembling, it was with nervous excitement. The other kids were so *close,* waiting for him to come back and dream into existence a new world, a new Christmasland, with rides, and food, and games. It was in him to do this. It was in *everyone.* He needed something, some tool, some instrument of pleasure, of fun, that he could use to tear a hole out of this world and into his own secret inner landscape.

Wayne felt the metal head of the hammer against his hip and looked at it and thought, *Maybe.* Take the hammer and bring it down on the top of his father's head. When Wayne imagined the sound it would make—the deep, hollow knock of steel against bone—he tingled with pleasure. Take it to the center of Tabitha Hutter's pretty, round, smart, smug, bitch-cunt face, smash her glasses, smash the teeth right out of her mouth. That would be fun. The thought of her pretty full lips rimmed with blood gave him a frankly erotic charge. When he was done with them, he could go for a walk in the woods, back to the cliff face, where the brick tunnel to Christmasland had been. Take the hammer and hit the rock, swing the hammer until the stone split, until there was a fissure he could squeeze himself into. Swing that hammer until he cracked the world open, made a space for him to crawl through, back into the world of thought, where the children waited.

But while he was still thinking it over—fantasizing about it—his father removed his hand and took up his hammer.

"Oh, what is this about?" Tabitha Hutter said under her breath, and undid her seat belt and got out on her side.

The wind soughed through the pines. Angels swayed. Silver globes refracted the light in brilliant, polychromatic sprays.

Lou stepped off the road, picking his way down the embankment. He lifted his head—he had just one chin now, and it was a good one—and turned his wise-turtle stare on the ornaments in the branches. After a time he picked one down, a white angel blowing a gold trumpet, set it on a rock, and smashed it with the hammer.

There was a momentary squall of feedback amid the static on the radio.

"Lou?" Tabitha asked, coming around the front of the truck, and Wayne thought if he slid behind the wheel and put it in drive, he could run her down. He imagined the sound of her skull striking the grille and started to smile—the idea was quite amusing—but then she moved on into the trees. He blinked rapidly, to clear aside this awful, lurid, wonderful vision, and jumped down out of the truck himself.

The wind rose, tossed his hair.

Lou found a glitter-spackled silver ornament, a globe as big as a softball, tossed it in the air, and swung the hammer like a baseball bat. The glittery sphere exploded in a pretty spray of opalescent glass and copper wire.

Wayne stood close to the truck, watching. Behind him, through the loud roar of the static, he heard a children's choir singing a Christmas song. They sang about the faithful. Their voices were far away but clear and sweet.

Lou crushed a ceramic Christmas tree and a china plum sprinkled with gold glitter and several tin snowflakes. He began to sweat and removed his flannel coat.

"Lou," Tabitha said again, standing at the top of the embankment. "Why are you doing this?"

"Because one of these is his," Lou said, and nodded at Wayne. "Vic brought most of him back, but I want the rest."

The wind screamed. The trees lunged. It was a little frightening, the way the trees were beginning to pitch back and forth. Pine needles and dead leaves flew.

"What do you want me to do?" Tabitha asked.

"Bare minimum? Don't arrest me."

He turned away from her, found another ornament. It was crushed with a musical tinkling.

Tabitha looked at Wayne. "I've never been one for just doing the bare minimum. You want to help? Looks like fun, doesn't it?"

Wayne had to admit it did.

She used the butt of her gun. Wayne used a rock. In the car the Christmas choir rose and swelled, until even Tabitha noticed it and pointed an uneasy, wondering glance back at the truck. Lou ignored it, though, continued crushing glass holly leaves and wire crowns, and in a few moments the white noise rose again in a roar, burying the song.

Wayne smashed angels with trumpets, angels with harps, angels with hands folded in prayer. He smashed Santa, and all his reindeer, and all his elves. At first he laughed. Then, after a while, it wasn't as funny. After a while his teeth began to ache. His face felt hot, then cold, then so cold it burned, icy-hot. He didn't know why, didn't give it much in the way of conscious thought.

He was raising a blue chunk of shale to smash a ceramic lamb when he saw movement at the upper edge of his vision and lifted his head and spied a girl standing by the ruin of the Sleigh House. She wore a filthy nightgown—it had been white once but now was mostly rust-colored from smears of dried blood—and her hair was in tangles. Her pale pretty face was stricken, and she was crying silently. Her feet were bloody.

"Pomoshch," she whispered. The sound of it was almost lost in the whistling wind. *"Pomoshch."* Wayne had never heard the Russian word for "help" before but understood well enough what she was saying.

Tabitha saw Wayne staring, turned her head, spotted the girl.

"Oh, my God," she said softly. "Lou. Lou!"

Lou Carmody stared across the yard at the girl, Marta Gregorski, missing since 1991. She had been twelve when she disappeared from a hotel in Boston and was twelve now, twenty years later. Lou regarded her with no particular surprise at all. He looked gray and tired, sweat slicking the loose flesh of his cheeks.

"I have to get the rest, Tabby," Lou said. "Can you help her?"

Tabitha turned her head and gave him a frightened, bewildered look. She holstered her gun, turned, and began to walk swiftly through the dead leaves.

A boy came out of the brush behind Marta, a black-haired boy of ten, wearing the dirty blue-and-red uniform of a Beefeater. Brad McCauley's eyes were stricken, wondering, and terrified all at once; he cast a sidelong glance at Marta, and his chest began to hitch with sobs.

Wayne swayed on his heels, staring at the two of them. Brad had been wearing his Beefeater outfit in his dream last night. Wayne felt light-headed, like sitting down, but the next time he rocked back on his heels—he was close to falling over—his father caught him from behind, set one massive hand on Wayne's shoulder. Those hands didn't quite go with his New Lou body, made his large, gawky frame look that much more badly put together.

"Hey, Wayne," Lou said. "Hey. You c'n wipe your face on my shirt if you want."

"What?" Wayne asked.

"You're crying, kiddo," Lou said. He held out his other hand. In it were ceramic shards: pieces of a smashed moon. "You've been crying for a while now. I guess this one was yours, huh?"

Wayne felt his shoulders jerk in a convulsive shrug. He tried to answer but couldn't force any sound from his tight throat. The tears on his cheeks burned in the cold wind, and his self-control gave way, and he buried his face in his father's stomach, missing for a moment the old Lou, with his comforting, bearish mass.

"I'm sorry," he whispered, his voice choked, strange. He moved his tongue around his mouth but could not feel his secret teeth anymore—a thought that set off such an explosion of relief he had to hang on to his father to keep from falling down. "I'm sorry. Dad. Oh, Dad. I'm sorry." His breath coming in short, jolting sobs.

"For what?"

"I don't know. Crying. I got snot on you."

Lou said, "No one has to apologize for tears, dude."

"I feel sick."

"Yeah. Yeah, I know. 'S okay. I think you're suffering from the human condition."

"Can you die from that?" Wayne said.

"Yes," Lou said. "It's pretty much fatal in every case."

Wayne nodded. "Okay. Well. I guess that's good."

Behind them, far away, Wayne could hear Tabitha Hutter's clear, steady, calming voice, asking names, telling children they would be all right, that she was going to take care of them. He had an idea, if he turned around, that he would see maybe a dozen of them now, and the rest were on their way, out of the trees, leaving the static behind.

He could hear some of them sobbing. The human condition: It was contagious, apparently.

"Dad," Wayne said. "If it's all right with you, can we skip Christmas this year?"

Lou said, "If Santa tries to come down our chimney, I'll send him back up with my boot in his ass. It's a promise."

Wayne laughed. It sounded much like a sob. That was all right.

Out on the highway, there was the ferocious roar of an approaching motorcycle. Wayne had an idea—a desperate, awful idea—that it was his mother. The children had all come back from something like death, and perhaps it was her turn. But it was just some dude out on the road, taking his Harley for a spin. It blasted past with a deafening roar, sun glinting off chrome. It was early October, but in the strong, direct light of the morning sun, it was still warm. Fall was here, winter coming right behind it, but for now there was still a little good riding weather left.

Begun the Fourth of July 2009
Completed over the holidays, 2011
Joe Hill, Exeter, New Hampshire

ACKNOWLEDGMENTS

- The Nice List -

If you have enjoyed this book, then much of the thanks goes to my editor, Jennifer Brehl, at William Morrow, who pointed me to the story within the story. If it disappointed you, the fault is mine alone.

Gabriel Rodríguez is one of my brothers. My love and thanks to him for his illustrations and friendship and vision. When I am lost, I can always trust Gabe to draw me a map.

The work on this story began in the summer of 2009, in my friend Ken Schleicher's garage. Ken was fixing up his 1978 Triumph Bonneville and drafted me as an extra pair of hands. Those were some good evenings and made me want to write about bikes. My thanks to the whole Schleicher clan for opening their home and their garage to me.

The work on this story ended after my mother read it and told me she liked it and also that my final chapter wouldn't do. She was right. She usually is. I threw out the last fifteen pages and wrote something better. Tabitha King is a creative thinker of the first order and taught me to love words, to search for their secret meanings, and to stay attuned to their private histories. More important, though, her example as a parent taught me how to be a father: to listen more than

I talk, to make chores into play (or meditation), to see that the kids keep their fingernails clipped.

In between the beginning and the ending of the work, I went for a motorcycle ride with my dad. He rode his Harley; I took my Triumph. He told me he liked my bike, even if the engine did remind him of a sewing machine. That's a Harley snob for you. It was a happy ride, following him along his back roads with the sun on my shoulders. I guess I have been cruising his back roads my whole life. I don't regret it.

This book received the close eye of not one, but *two* copy editors: the gifted Maureen Sugden, who has kept me straight on three novels now, and my pal Liberty Hardy from RiverRun Books, who pounced on my mistakes like a catnip-addled kitten after a ball of yarn. Liana Faughnan came in at the last minute to make sure my timeline was sound. I suspect the book is still riddled with errors, but that just goes to show you can only help a person so much.

Love and thanks to the remarkable team at William Morrow that works so hard to make me look good: Liate Stehlik, Lynn Grady, Tavia Kowalchuk, Jamie Kerner, Lorie Young, Rachel Meyers, Mary Schuck, Ben Bruton, and E. M. Krump. That goes for the crowd at Gollancz, too: Jon Weir, Charlie Panayiotou, and Mark Stay. I am particularly grateful to my UK editor and friend, Gillian Redfearn, who is a one-woman morale booster and spine-straightener.

My agent, Mickey Choate, read this book I don't know how many damn times, and always came back with insight, ideas, and encouragement. He made it a much better book, in every possible way.

You know who is awesome? Kate Mulgrew is awesome, for reading this book on audio. I was charmed and blown away by Kate's reading of my short story "By the Silver Waters of Lake Champlain," and I can't say how much I appreciate her coming back to read this much longer story of childhood, wonder, and loss.

Twitter is a hive buzzing with thought, argument, and geek-passion, and I'm grateful to every single person who has ever traded a tweet with me. As a world of shared ideas, Twitter is a kind of Inscape in and of itself, and a good one.

My thanks to everyone who picked up this book, or downloaded it, or listened to it on audio. I hope like hell you enjoyed it. What a blast—what a gift—to get to do this for a living. I don't ever wanna stop.

Hugs and kisses and buckets of appreciation to Christina Terry, who was a constant sounding board in the final drafts of the book and who made sure I had a life and some fun beyond my work. Thanks for getting my back, lady.

I am also grateful to Andy and Kerri Singh, Shane Leonard and Janice Grant, Israel and Kathryn Skelton, Chris Ryall, Ted Adams, Jason Ciaramella and his boys, Meaghan and Denise MacGlashing, the Bosa clan, Gail Simone, Neil Gaiman, Owen King, Kelly Braffet, Zelda and Naomi. My love and appreciation to Leanora.

I am a lucky guy to be the father of Ethan, Aidan, and Ryan King, the funniest, most imaginative men I know. Your dad loves you.

- The Naughty List -

People who skim or outright skip acknowledgments pages. Please contact the management for your free, all-expenses-paid pass to Christmasland.

A NOTE ON THE TYPE

This book was set in a variant of Caslon, a typeface designed in the eighteenth century by William Caslon I (1692–1766), an English gunmaker and famed printer of the eighteenth century. He is not related in any way to Paul Caslon, who went to Christmasland in 1968, and who escaped into The White with Millie Manx after the terrible Christmas Eve when SugarCandy Mountain fell. After a long timeless time, Millie led him and two more kids—Francine Flynn and Howard Hitchcock—out of the static and into the pines. They watched from back in the trees as the other children (the quitters!) came out of the forest, all of them carrying on, sobbing and *poor-me*-ing, snot and tears all over their faces. Millie did a quiet imitation of the way they were weeping and snotting on themselves and it was such good sport Paul had to bite down with two rows of teeth to keep from laughing.

They would settle with those kids later. Quitters were only good for one thing: being "it" in a game of scissors-for-the-drifter or bite-the-smallest.

But when the first ambulance turned onto the road to Sleigh House, they knew it was time to go. Millie led the other three to the blue spruce where their ornaments were hung together, well back from where Wayne Carmody (King of the Quitters!) was smashing decorations with his father. Each of Charlie's True Children collected his or her own special ornament and together they slipped away down the hill, before they could be discovered. It was sad that Christmasland was gone, but there was no point in crying over spilled milk or cataclysmic avalanches, and besides: now the whole world is their playground!

And it really doesn't matter if they can't live in an eternal Christmas anymore. After all: Christmas is just a state of mind, and as long as you keep a little holiday spirit in your heart, every day is Christmas Day.

THE FIREMAN

Joe Hill

The NUMBER ONE *New York Times* Bestselling Novel

The fireman is coming. Stay cool.

Nobody knew where the virus came from.
FOX News said it had been set loose by ISIS, using spores that had been invented by the Russians in the 1980s. MSNBC said sources indicated it might've been created by engineers at Halliburton and stolen by culty Christian types fixated on the Book of Revelation. CNN reported both sides. While every TV station debated the cause, the world burnt.

Pregnant school nurse, HARPER GRAYSON, had seen lots of people burn on TV, but the first person she saw burn for real was in the playground behind the school. With epic scope and emotional impact, this is one woman's story of survival at the end of the world.

• • •

'A *Lord of the Flies* for the Twitter generation. Clever, gripping and packs a hell of a punch' Joanne Harris

'This book is incredible' Lev Grossman

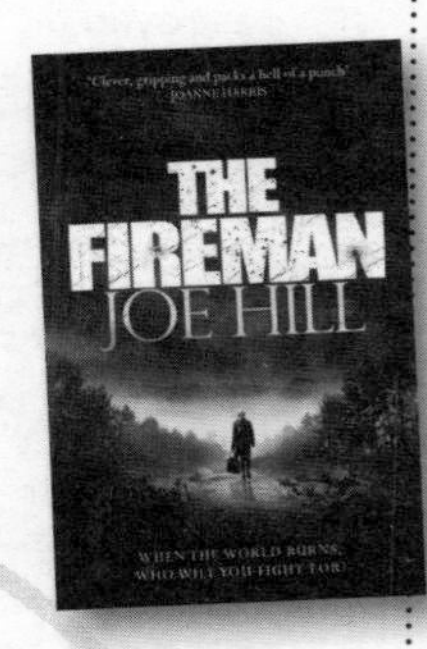

'Joe Hill has always been good, but he's created something incandescent here, soaring and original. He's a master storyteller who writes with fire in his veins' Lauren Beukes

'Ominously superb' Nick Harkaway

'An end of the world tale with a blazing heart of hope at its core. A contender for book of the year' Sarah Pinborough

'Hill's enthralling fourth thriller hits another home run'
Starred Library Journal Review

HORNS

Joe Hill

The novel which spawned the major Hollywood film starring Daniel Radcliffe

Once, Ignatius Perrish lived a life of privilege. Second son of a renowned American musician, and the younger brother of a rising late-night TV star, Ig had security, wealth and a place in his community. He even had the love of Merrin Williams – a love founded on shared daydreams, mutual daring, and unlikely midsummer magic.

Then beautiful, vivacious Merrin is gone. Raped and murdered under inexplicable circumstances, with Ig the only suspect. While he was never tried for the crime, in the court of public opinion Ig was and always will be guilty.

After spending a night drunk and doing terrible things, Ig woke up to one hell of a hangover, a raging headache . . . and a pair of horns growing from his temples.

Now Ig finds he can hear people's deepest, darkest secrets, and he means to use this ability to find whoever killed Merrin and destroyed his life. Being good and praying got him nowhere. It's time the devil had his due.

• • •

'A perfect story that will creep you out and play with your emotions' ***The Book Plank***

'A terrific read which helps to bolster Joe Hill's already high status in my personal pantheon of storytellers' *SFF World*

'Joe Hill digs beneath the surface of civility to expose the brutal and savage sides of human nature. The result is an excellent read, full of dark wit and disturbing revelations' ***Waterstones Books Quarterly***